To Dust

T. Nelson Taylor

CineCapture
Press

CineCapture Press
PO Box 263701
Tampa, FL 33685

Please visit www.tnelsontaylor.com

First Editions: November 2022
(Print and Electronic)

Printed in the USA

The events and characters portrayed in this book are fictitious. Places, names, incidents and events are either used fictitiously or a complete product of the author's imagination. Any similarity to actual events, real persons, living, dead, or both is coincidental and not intended by the author. In other words, this book is a work of fiction... you know... make-believe, fantasy—not real.

United States Copyright Office Data:

Author: Taylor, T. Nelson
Hardback ISBN: 979-8-9866787-5-7
Paperback ISBN: 979-8-9866787-6-4
Electronic ISBN: 979-8-9866787-7-1

Chapters

For Maria

"Oh God, what have I done?"

~Innumerable Unnamed Scientists

Was it a Dream?

Through his dripping-wet binoculars, steamed from northwestern Argentina's intense pre-dawn humidity and his accumulated perspiration, Anund Hammett peered down through the jungle upon the darkened windows of a fortified asylum. Four sizable rectangles of glass were visible from his concealed position, one for each building, and his handlers provided no additional intelligence as to which of those windows might eventually frame his target. The arced layout of the installation could be surveilled without exaggerated movement from his location four hundred meters up a steep, tangled hillside from an unfenced and turbulent stream. It was a hazard that provided cover of sound, yet easily exposed anyone's attempt to navigate across it. Hammett considered three factors regarding that stream: First, that anyone caught in it would be shot without interrogation. Second, that it was likely stocked with underfed red-bellied piranhas. Third, that he must eventually cross it.

I can't wait to cool off!

Hammett was at the end of a six-day hike across the border from Chile. His feet burned and ached. He lacked focus, and his mind strayed across endless tangents. He calculated his probability of success at less than five percent this time. After all, Simon Wiesenthal's ghost hunts had become the fodder of ridicule, albeit lucrative derisions, to most of his field operatives by the end of the 1960s. As well, Hammett's preceding reputation emanated primarily from resourceful covert intelligence, not so much as a field operator, and even less as a tactical marksman. Wiesenthal's choices were nonetheless limited, and as it happened, Hammett's skills with a sniper's rifle were more than sufficient.

It was February 29, 1972, late summer in this saw-toothed Eden near the western border of Tucumán Provence. Leap Day. *How appropriate.* Simon relayed a degree of confidence from his informants that Martin Bormann did not, in fact, perish on the streets of Berlin at the end of World War II as it was widely reported without direct evidence.

"ODESSA regurgitates their baseless conclusions at every mention, repeated ad nauseum. They ratlined him to Buenos Aires the same as Josef Mengele. I know it!"

South American Bormann sightings occurred regularly since the end of the war, and Simon wanted him badly.

"How nice it would be to capture Hitler's vertraute!"

More enticing was the fact that Wiesenthal somehow deduced Mengele might also continue his anthropological malpractice at the very same compound. Argentina's Dirty War produced over 8,000 missing communist revolutionaries, many of whom were whisked away to clandestine prison camps. This particular one was not very far from Paraguay, to which Doctor Mengele evacuated several years prior. The camps were perfect laboratories for Mengele, who correctly assessed that no one cared enough to look for a couple dozen missing comunistas.

Hammett reached into a middle vest pocket, grabbed a small cotton wad, and gently wiped the condensation from the Bausch and Lomb eyepieces. To his right rested a prototype Steyr SSG 69 rifle on an unfolded bipod, and a Zeiss Diavari scope with a modified mount perched atop—front lens capped until the right moment. He marveled at its lightness and stealth. It weighed next to nothing compared with the rest of his 25-kilogram pack, half of which contained armaments mandated by Wiesenthal's quartermaster. Two extra five-round magazines for the Steyr, a Heckler & Koch P9 with four extra clips, an Uzi 9mm with five 32-round clips, and a standard-issue Ka-Bar knife gifted by a U.S. Navy pilot buddy who had retired at the beginning of actions in Vietnam. Hammett kept that knife unsheathed in his left hand at night should a stray jaguar catch his scent; the P9 clutched in his right. The rest of the pack contained the bare necessities for the hike: A week's worth of high-protein supplement bars, four one-liter canteens, maps, matches, a Zippo lighter, flares, extra socks, a camouflaged ripstop nylon sheet, assorted first-aid needs and relevant pharmaceuticals, flashlight with extra batteries, and a radio transmitter.

Movement!

Finally, motion, second window from the left. A light switched on, flooding the room and grounds just outside with brilliant white photons, creating a blacker darkness everywhere else. Hammett squinted in momentary pain, wiped his eyes, and refocused. A woman glided past the window in a lab coat. Asian—Korean or Japanese—but he couldn't determine which at that distance. A nurse, perhaps. It wasn't important. Hammett wasn't there for her, and he wasn't there for the prisoners; he signed on for the objective only, and that objective was bringing a hardcore Nazi to justice. Two, if he should be so fortunate.

More movement. This time it came from an elevated platform on the northernmost building's rooftop. A powerful searchlight methodically blazed through 100 meters of the stream's banks, and in doing so, exposed another sentinel patrolling along the southern fence line. Hammett strained to reckon his strategy. Two outside guarding the east, and at least two additional sentries protecting the west. How many more inside? Only 20-25 prisoners were expected in Mengele's clinic, and they were likely narcotized beyond any will to escape. How many guards were necessary?

Anund knew he had the advantages of surprise and con-cealment, but under pressure—the deadliest of pressures—how well would he perform? Which strategy gave him the best probability of success? He vacillated downing the immediate threat first. The soldado closest to him on the ground moved lethargically and would easily fall, but the guard on the roof would assuredly hit the alarm and begin scanning woods, spraying shots at any movement or reflection. Hammett should be the faster marksman in that race, but why race? Eliminating the search beam on higher ground made more sense, he thought. The guard by the river wouldn't hear the shot, or the impact of it. But then, would Target #2 remain visible if the light shifted away? Even so, he was the lower of two hurdles. The dawn's delayed twilight would soon peek over the hilltop directly in front of his position. It was a major disadvantage should he hesitate. He could not wait until the sun was in his face. Time was running out. Should he simply dispatch his main objective at first opportunity and flee back across the Chilean border? He crossed several streams on the way in; water abounded, but food was in short supply. He could manage that easily if he was lucky. *Luck?* The options were fomenting cerebral discord. Hammett felt around an upper right-hand vest pocket for the Benzedrine inhaler. It was there, just where he placed it before departing Santiago, but he sighed and didn't bother removing it. *I'm sweaty enough as it is! No use for aqueous eyes.*

Twilight had begun, and the sentries returned to their initial positions. If Hammett were to make his move, to take his shots, it might as well be now. He glanced at his watch's luminescent green hands. 6:02. Diligently, he swabbed the binocular lenses one last time before capping, casing and slipping them into his rucksack. He eased over to the Steyr, uncapped the scope, and marked his preferred target zones, practicing a cadence between the two shots. Deep breath, full exhale, tap... tap. Inhale, full release, tap... tap. His right cheek warmed the composite stock it rested upon, and he became comfortable with the scope's feel. Its barely visible #4 reticle pinpointed the unsuspecting bastards' skulls adequately, and there was no windage to consider. *Just like the water gun races at the fair. Wait—elevation!*

A week earlier, his rangemaster warned of basic arc elevation and parallax when firing from an elevated position, and he was definitely shooting downhill. *"...tend to miss low,"* he said. *400 meters at 15 degrees slope, and adjust for perception. Don't overdo it, Harwin... God help me!* Two muted clicks on the elevation adjustment and Anund quickly re-centered his sights on the searchlight operator's forehead. He consciously felt his heart beating with symptomatic anticipation anxiety and began the breathing routine to relax. His finger tightened on the trigger as he slowly inhaled his deepest breath, then exhaled. Tap.

One muted thump from his suppressor and the operator dropped as a freefalling stone, violently swinging the searchlight around and upward, across Hammett's position. The scorching beam blinded him momentarily during the automatic move to his second target. He wouldn't have more than two ticks before a whistle blew, but no sooner did the thought occur than the spots faded and the guard appeared in his scope exactly where expected. An easier shot, in fact, because the man had frozen in his tracks, craning to comprehend what just happened. Tap. Hammett watched the man collapse upon himself without a single utterance or dramatic lunge for help. There would be no further movement from him, so the scope shifted back to the first target and reconciled the same. The searchlight pointed skyward over the southern fence line, an innocuous direction Hammett determined, that is, until someone else ventured outside and happened to notice.

With cautious alacrity, Hammett unpacked the Uzi, unfolded its stock, inserted a magazine, and chambered its first round. He also unholstered the P9, chambered a round, and flipped the safety off before reholstering the weapon. Leaving the rucksack and his rifle behind, Hammett snaked down the hillside to the awaiting stream below. Again, he surveilled the compound for movement, and there was none. No movement through the windows, either. Not knowing the depth of the stream, he carefully waded into it, cradling the Uzi above the water. At first, he felt nothing, but slowly the frigid torrent seeped through his khakis, and moments later, down through his boots. It was chilly, but as he fantasized earlier, it was welcome. Welcome until he was knee-deep and began to feel the faint impacts of probing piranhas high on his calves, just above the boot collars. He knew they wouldn't attack unless he tantalized them with an open wound in the water. A scratched mosquito bite could be hazardous in those circumstances. Hammett gave them no further consideration, quickening his pace across the stream, stumbling over loose stones and twigs on its bottom. Upon reaching the other side, he crept towards the only illuminated window, careful to remain outside the spill of its light.

From the shadows, he peered inside to discover the nurse observed earlier. She was definitely Asian as Hammett guessed. Japanese, and not as attractive as his scope implied. She appeared to be in her upper 50s with a noticeably pained face; a sorrow to her eyes that communicated her complicity in terror—her accessory to evil as she administered an IV to a young sedated soldado. Across the room laid another man, much older and slovenly in appearance due to unkempt dressings and his haggard, gray beard. Along the back wall was an office desk, and seated at that desk with his back turned was a middle-aged, dark-haired man wearing trousers and a white lab coat that must have been pressed by a professional just that morning. *Mengele?* Hammett traipsed across the Andean volcanic wastelands in pursuit of Martin Bormann, who had yet to make an appearance, but Wiesenthal would pay just as much, maybe more, for the infamous Doctor Mengele.

At that moment, a florescent light flickered on from a building to Hammett's immediate left. He instinctively crouched, catching his breath, and then crawled over to it for a look. It was an overcrowded bunk with five men too many, each poorly maintained and groggy. Hammett decided to make his way around to one of three interconnecting corridors' doorways he observed through the binoculars earlier, hoping it was unlocked. Slowly he rotated the doorknob in quiet desperation, but it wouldn't budge. Without delay, he scrambled around to another corridor furthest away from the two illuminated structures and attempted to open that door. This time there was no abrupt stop in rotation; the unlocked door crept open, and before fully committing to entry, he peeked inside to make sure the hallway was empty and unguarded. Not a soul, but entering the narrow passageway meant he must confront anyone who took notice, and given no other places to hide, it was a likely prospect.

Hammett suddenly increased his pace with deliberate action. He decided that, if detected, he must not hesitate in the wielding of death. His grip tightened on the Uzi as he ventured towards the first lit building, and as he rounded the final corner, Hammett came to face his primary objective. The suddenness of the recognition bungled the raising of his Uzi, and Bormann used that opportunity to fling a heavy ceramic coffee cup at him. Hammett ducked and fired a short burst as Bormann turned, one bullet striking his lower-left abdomen, the others embedding themselves in a plaster wall far behind him. Bormann clutched at his wound and lunged in the opposite direction to avoid another volley. An astonished guard lunged from the doorway and inadvertently sacrificed himself. Hammett felt the sting of a syringe on the back of his neck. He let go of the Uzi and swung around to remove it, but it was far too late; the anesthetic had already taken effect. As Hammett collapsed, he heard vignettes of rioting men in the background and the screams of a woman, presumably the Japanese nurse he saw earlier, then nothing.

"You are extremely fortunate, Doctor Hammett," said a man with a decidedly southwestern Bavarian accent.

Anund struggled with the blinding lights and bright institutional walls, the fog of narcosis, the sting of an intravenous needle in his left arm, and the unknown curly-haired man hovering over him. He tried to sit up, but stiffness and exhaustion prevented it.

"Careful, Doctor; you are in no condition yet."

Hammett grasped at the dull pain throbbing at the nape of his neck, feeling at a dime-sized welt. "I suppose I should ask where I am. Never mind, I'm obviously in some sort of medical facility, but where, and what time, I mean... what day is it? Where's Bormann? And, who are you?"

"I must answer your last question first. I am Doctor Edgar Pichler, und before you inquire, we have not previously made acquaintance. We are in an isolated security wing of the Hospital Italiano de Buenos Aires, und you have been here for three days. It is March 5th, und according to a betrieber of mine named Franco, you have been unconscious for a minimum of five days. Franco is an infiltrator who managed two years inside the upper echelons of the Montoneros, an extreme leftist guerilla faction—"

"I know who they are."

"Excuse me, Doctor, but I would be, how do the Englanders put it, derelict not to provide a comprehensive debriefing."

"I don't understand. Where is Martin Bormann?"

"Of course not. It is not expected for you to fully comprehend that which has not been conveyed, Herr Doctor."

Hammett grimaced, "Then, by all means—"

"Ja. Franco reported being in the compound at the time of your incursion, one building south in Barrack Ten. A matter of coincidence that day excluded his particular sample group from the sedation. They arrived one week prior und just completed lab sterilization, delousing, etcetera. Fortunately for you, this man and a few others maintained their wits!"

"And I suppose he somehow rescued me?"

"This is correct, und of course there is more. Franco witnessed a guard's head combust from his window. They watch the windows; always probing for opportunity, you know. He presumed it to be your second execution since the searchlight flipped around beforehand. Excellent marksmanship, by ze way, und may I ask at what distance?"

"You may ask. I don't recall. Busy, you see."

"Disappointing. Ah, well, perhaps I should advance to the relevant information. You breached the laboratory—Josef Mengele's new laboratory—and chaos erupted. You inquire of Martin Bormann. That was the first man you shot in the hallway. The second, the last remaining guard, died soon after. During the chaos, Franco and two others overpowered a nurse and gained control of the main laboratory. Mengele and Bormann escaped. Franco found you unconscious on the hallway floor with two half-emptied syringes adjacent. Four hours later, the camp was liberated by Presidente Lanusse's rangers. We recovered them, Doctor, the two syringes. The first tested positive for anesthetic, a sodium thiopental derivative of some variety, and apparently enough of it injected to induce coma."

"What was in the second," Hammett interrupted.

"That is precisely why I am here, Herr Doctor. We do not know what was in the second syringe. It is an unknown compound. There is a puncture wound on your left buttock that indicates you were injected with it, perhaps after the anesthetic took effect."

Hammett's face became ashen as he stared at a building across the street. "I still don't know who you are... why I'm here, and why you're here, *Pichler*. German, is it? Why should I believe anything you've told me? Too many damned Deutschlanders around here. Are my eyes still brown?"

"Doctor Hammett, yes they are, und it is correct what you say, 'too many'. I am Austrian, actually. You are here because Franco brought you to me. I am here because we share object-ives, but there is a difference in reasoning. You came to arrest or apparently assassinate Bormann and Mengele, unapologetic Nazi resurrectionists, for Simon Wiesenthal, a man I greatly respect. I am here because of Mengele's latest research, that being a continuation of a secret project involving paranormal heritage." Pichler paused for a moment of expected reaction.

Hammett broke his gaze through the window and turned around. "Involving... *what?*"

"When the Red Army liberated Auschwitz, they found several files cached in a discreet compartment below Mengele's desk. To save time, allow me in saying that we acquired duplicates of these files."

"We?"

"In a moment, Doctor. The files detailed experiments conducted as the result of discoveries made during a most repugnant indulgence—recreational surgeries merely to observe the results. The pertinent discovery was one of para-normality, Doctor. An eleven-year-old boy moved a small metal ramekin with his mind while being sewn to his twin brother. Mengele simply wanted to see if he could conjoin twins. They died from gangrene several days afterward—one brother mercifully in a coma, the other kept in perpetual agony during these paranormal experiments. Unadulterated evil, Doctor Hammett, no moral conscience. Torture, pain, murder, und sadism. His methods are truly sickening, und yet I am tasked to capture more of his research before the justice occurs. My field of research is psychology, particularly, a branch of gestaltism. You may know the famous phrase, 'The whole is other than the sum of the parts.' I deal with the 'other'."

"Is something wrong with me? What's going to happen?"

"We do not know, and because we do not know, we must observe your condition and, more importantly, your behavior for the next few months. I can relay that this hospital found nothing at all wrong with you, no detected abnormalities or disease. Your bloodwork was given top priority and the full gamut of tests. Nothing."

Hammett swallowed slowly, discomforted from a stiff, dry throat. "Does anyone else know I'm here?"

"Yes. We informed Wiesenthal upon learning your status. At this moment he is on a 747 from Vienna, due later this afternoon. You will be released to his custody upon arrival, and he will have no further use for your services."

"What? What did you tell him? I can't believe you'd take such liberties with my affairs! How dare you!"

"You must relax, Doctor Hammett. Simon Wiesenthal is already acquainted with us, although not by our true moniker, und under a different pretense. At this very moment, others from his professional pool are zeroing on both Mengele und Bormann just outside Asunción, Paraguay—Limpio. Franco is assisting President Stroessner's marines, und it is extremely unlikely they will avoid capture this time. Stroessner hates Nazis. Their mere mention of them creates hackles and a foamed mouth. He also fears any potential economic reprisals from the United States und England, where he has created friends among their wealthiest chief executives. We, of course, made that possibility vividly apparent. Once they are captured, if alive, they will be vigorously interrogated und then transferred to Israel's Mossad."

"There's that 'we' again."

"Und that, Doctor, is what I need to convey—to negotiate—before Wiesenthal arrives."

"Huh?" Hammett shrugged. "If you think I'll start bending spoons for the TV cameras, you're out of your mind!"

Pichler sighed and took a deep breath. "You will not have heard of us. We are The Brotherhood of Truth, or formally, *La*

Fratellanza di Verità, und we have existed since the Dark Ages. We are not here for the manipulations or propagation of historically temporary governments, popular ideologies, or any particular religious faith. Our autonomous countervailing prevents human catastrophe from the totalitarian-minded echelons—the morally-corrupted organizations that perhaps began with noble intentions and slowly devolved to unchecked malevolence. Over the centuries, we found no entity—no government, no institution, no person, nobody—immune from the evil. With few exceptions, its temptation eventually becomes irresistible, even within our own organization, as we were nearly exposed und exterminated by a malcontent during the Spanish Inquisition; a repugnant chapter in the Brotherhood. I have other examples.

"At risk of nefarious appearances, it might beguile you to know it was actually La Fratellanza who smuggled nuclear secrets to the Soviet Union in 1945 through Klaus Fuchs. He was a brother until 1949 when his psychosis appeared, und he would become my first assignment. Klaus grew unstable, remorseful, und unpredictable, so we revoked further acknowledgement und communication utilizing the usual protocols. After nine years in a British prison und under threat, Brezhnev *enticed* him to East Germany for the remainder of his career, und I should mention, our intelligence indicates he never divulged knowledge of our existence."

Hammett clinched his teeth and turned towards Pichler, who continued, "Before you judge us, Doctor Hammett, consider that America is the only nation to ever detonate nuclear weapons on another country. Who would have stopped their imperialist designs if the playing field was not leveled? Have you not noticed that America now employs a policy of proactive warfare, not reactive, or rather, defensive?"

"Did it ever occur to you, *Doktor Pichler*, that by using those weapons and saving innumerous lives, the horrors of atomic warfare exemplified in Japan serves as the ultimate deterrent?"

"That is not our conclusion. Furthermore, you should be aware that it was La Fratellanza who covertly leaked intelligence to the Allies' Alsos Mission, preventing the Reich from developing its own atomic program. Where the pretext for evil exists, we activate. More importantly, when an entity hoards a technology or other knowledge deemed essential for the common good, we also take action. Vaccines, astronomy, unpublished patents, the supernatural; inclusivity for everyone."

"Then certainly you know everything there is to know about Roswell." Hammett quipped.

"As a matter of fact, yes. It was not an alien saucer, nor was it a weather balloon. It was an experimental hypersonic spy aircraft from the Soviet Union that flew over the Arctic, over Canada, und over most of Colorado before malfunctioning. The United States would never admit such a breach of their airspace. Likewise, the Soviets could not find any useful propaganda by lauding the accomplishment. It failed. This is why the Americans soon after created NORAD. Anything else you would like to know about us, Herr Doctor?"

Hammett laughed, "Nothing immediately comes to mind."

"Perfectly understandable given your condition." Pichler stood up and approached the bedside. "Well then, let me tell you—we want you for a mission, und after that mission, the opportunity to join our group in perpetuity."

"Why do you want me? What do you know about me?"

"Doctor Hammett, La Fratellanza has been surveilling your exploits for many years. With the few understandable exceptions such as, well, this past mission und your mishap at the Berghof—Operation Foxley—your professional records und integrity speak to our needs. We do not request the services of an assassin, however; we want you strictly for your expertise in intelligence gathering und logistics... fields in which we believe you superior in talent."

"I wasn't involved in Foxley."

"Dishonesty is of no use here, *Herr Doktor.* I know you were there, I know the name of your commander, your specific orders, und I know the very rock on which you twisted your left ankle. I know the rifle you carried, und I know the telescope you damaged when you fell on it. Please do not ask me to name it all, Doctor, but the rifle was a Karabiner 98k, und it was fitted with a modified Bausch und Lomb telescope to appear as the standard Mauser issue. It included your favored #4 sight. I possess your Steyr, by ze way."

Hammett's gaze returned to the window. Pichler's information caused systemic discomfort accompanying the squinting under brilliant light, a discomfort that deep breaths and circumspect behavioral strategy couldn't arrest.

"Will Simon know about this *mission* of yours?"

"No, he will not. He cannot know."

"Well, sorry Doctor Pichler, I simply don't know you. I've nothing to vet your identity, background and intentions. Furthermore, you've created a set of circumstances that make a man such as yourself virtually impossible to verify. I thank you for purportedly saving my life, of course, but you must understand that I simply cannot align myself with someone unknown and unqualified to me. Surely, you must have anticipated my refusal under these circumstances."

"I had hoped that Wiesenthal himself would provide enough corroborative endorsement to satiate your concerns, but I should also attack your curiosity. Let me tell you about this mission; see if it changes your mind."

"It appears I have a couple hours to kill."

"Obviously, all correspondence we share is strictly confidential with extremely punitive ramifications should you break our gentleman's agreement."

"Yes, those protocols you mentioned. Seems I'm without options, so what else am I to do but agree?"

Pichler smiled. "What do you know about this year's Olympics?"

"Opening ceremonies slated for August 26 in Munich. Not much else, except a tip the Americans will sweep archery."

"Und a Palestinian terrorist organization named Black September? What do you know about them? Und by that, I mean, what knowledge do you possess that we might not? Remember, Doctor Hammett, we know quite a lot of your operations."

Hammett lifted a finger and pointed it at Pichler. "That gentleman's confidentiality agreement is a two-way contract, mate."

"I have no issues with your conditions, Doctor."

"Excellent, because what I have to say—"

"It may not be relevant to the mission, exactly, although I am curious as to your insights."

"I assume you know Mossad has enlisted two dozen operatives to crush the Black September and bring Fatah to its knees. You might also know that I handpicked a squad of those operatives for Director Zamir. You might *not* know however, that a mission was deferred as a political favor for an Israeli ally, resulting in a 'successful' BSO outcome. Ultimately, their mission executed opposition to more potent enemy. Now, what are you implying, Pichler? That the BSO is targeting Munich? Who? Jordanians? Israelis?"

"The latter, but this situation has been managed by an operator in Beirut, who, at the optimal time, will notify the Bundeskriminalamt."

"The BKA in West Berlin? Pardon the eschewing of scientific vernacular Doctor Pichler, but are you nuts? The BKA is primarily comprised of former SS and party men! You think they'll bother with an investigation?"

"If it potentially interrupts the Games und their image as a credible agency, yes. Otherwise, they risk exposure. We assign operatives in the aspiration of a peaceful sports competition, which should be free of politics. However, Deutschland's Olympics security issues and middle-eastern territorial disputes are not our first concern. We are more interested with the marionettes; the evil that cultivates terror for their own ascension or profit. Another organization, which until now you are completely unaware, is called the Spada Sacra. Our intelligence on them is relatively limited, but we know they are a militarized faction of, but unknown to, the Roman Catholic Church, und we've been battling them since our inception. Any attempts to inform the Vatican have been thwarted by insiders. In fact, the Spada Sacra supplied the impetus for our own creation. We maintain surveillance on their current leader, a bishop named Vasco Tagliabue, whom we believe responsible for manipulating the Bay of Pigs by signaling the Russians, who promptly notified Castro. Spada Sacra are also indirectly responsible for Kennedy's assassination, the Gulf of Tonkin, and the disappearance of Australian Prime Minister Harold Holt five years ago. I should, however, include that they are not always successful. La Fratellanza celebrated numerous successes against the Spada Sacra, but never ascertained enough intelligence to mount a full campaign. This is where your expertise becomes relevant, Doctor Hammett; The Brotherhood asks that you join our mission to pursue Tagliabue und the Spada Sacra. When we have the advantage—the ability to outmaneuver their efforts—we will finally expose them to the Vatican so that they can never return."

Hammett's eyes darted about in perspicacious thought. Several moments passed, his silence became perceived as indecision. So much to consider.

"Doctor Pichler, I lay here in this bed as little more than a mercenary. I endeavor to solicit only virtuous missions—those that fit my morality—and I attempt to make a comfortable living in the process. Thus far, I've been successful. You offer a mission, an objective, and it fits my personal agenda in that regard, but what of the compensation and my lifestyle? What are you offering, *really?*"

"Doctor Hammett, we use the honor system; if you legitimately need something, you shall have it. Our resources are modest in the global scope, but not marginal. There are, of course, intelligence opportunities translatable towards excess if that is your desire. An educated guess is that you will largely find those pursuits impotent unless they create advantage in your work. We are all too busy to spend a fortune, if that is your goal. That is not to say our lifestyle is not occasionally without its rewards. Our work requires a certain degree of levity to remain mentally healthy, Doctor."

"All work and no play—"

"Precisely." Pichler adjusted his frames. "What do you say?"

Hammett peered once more through the window across Buenos Aires' tangled vista. "Tell me more about Tagliabue."

"Okay Doctor." Pichler paused to collect his thoughts. "Bishop Vasco Tagliabue became a priest during World War II at the age of 23, two years earlier than Canon Law typically allows, but granted due to a shortage of available candidates. I should note that this was not uncommon in Italy. Twelve years later, records state Pope Pius XII himself ordained Tagliabue a bishop at Saint Peter's und appointed him to the Eserra Diocese, north of Naples. He served two years und then became somewhat of a transient, appearing under official pretenses at cathedrals around the globe, yet never attached to any one in particular. He is a gifted man, quite intelligent in strategy und heuristic in human problem-solving; a pragmatic thinker, und a most difficult enigma. While Bishop Tagliabue is perhaps our most wanted non-grata, he is not the primary objective of your mission. Our latest intelligence states that

Tagliabue has recruited, or rather, adopted a young boy with, in my professional opinion, a far greater potential for licentious villainy. His name is..."

Narciso

"Perhaps the comprehensive brief is necessary," said Pichler.

Hammett nodded. His return to consciousness included the full sensory reboot: a throbbing narcotic hangover, emptiness of nutrition, the telltale bedpan odor, the dull burn of the IV, and a yearning for a long, hot shower with time to think. Here was this man soliciting a lifetime in service to some mysterious organization that, according to him, had been around virtually forever, and yet somehow, not a soul in his ocean of acquaintances ever hinted of its existence. No mentions or concerns regarding classified clearances or non-disclosure agreements, either, as if they never mattered. An anxiety welled. One he could not define beyond distractive melancholy. So many directions he could take, and yet there seemed only one logical option—the one in front of him.

"Can you manage or is something the matter?" Pichler asked, snapping his fingers to gain Hammett's undivided attention.

"Yes. Well, yes, mostly."

"Is it an irritation?"

"Not sure. I feel nauseous, empty... it's ever so slight. My guess is that it's an accompaniment to resuscitation. If it intensifies, I'll interrupt you, but I should be okay. Please continue. Spada Sacra—"

Pichler paused for a moment. "Yes. They originated as a faction of the Praetorian Guard—the Roman emperors' private security force—the most elite und accomplished infantry und cavalry. The Praetorians came into being several generations before Julius Caesar's rule, protecting generals und other such important figures who quickly realized the importance in having a superior unit encircling them. Yet it was Julius, und in particular Augustus, who used this superior force as reliable protection in the field; a deterrent to coup d'états, und, common to those times, a motivational catalyst in politics. During his rule, Augustus increased the ranks to over 9,000. Nine double-sized legions. Three of which he kept in Rome for his protection, und the other six garrisoned throughout Italy. Each of these garrisons were governed by a prefect, und in time, these prefects became quite influential. It does not take a substantial imagination to calculate the aggregate power derived from such an exceptional assemblage. My guess is that you already know their role in Claudius' insertion after murdering Caligula, so I will not dawdle on impertinent facts. For the next 150 or so years, the Guard mechanically influenced the breadth of Roman politics, brushing away any opposition to its agendas. At one point, their ranks grew to over 15,000, but it became a costly, unsustainable behemoth, und later reduced to a manageable 10,000. In the hundred years that followed, the Guard became increasingly bold in their conspiracies to eliminate undesirable candidates und advance those favored to positions capable of maintaining the Guard's ascendency. This cycle was finally interrupted somewhat by Aurelian in 273AD, who maintained strict ethical standards und dealt extreme punishment to offenders. Naturally, he fell victim to Praetorian swords in short order. A secretary caught in a lie, feared reprisal, forged documents calling for the execution of certain officials known to collaborate with the Guard, etcetera. They killed him without bothering to verify or validate the directive, und thus continued the cycle of manipulations for another hundred years."

Hammett smirked, "Thanks for the history lesson, but—"

"Almost there, Doctor Hammett." Pichler reached for the paper cup of water and looked at his watch before taking two large gulps, slowly swallowing to relax his throat. "Getting to the point, Herr Doctor, although the following emperor, Diocletian, eliminated their direct duty as his personal guards, the Praetorians remained as an elite field legion, und they became highly political und controlling during those next few decades until circumstances brought them in direct contradiction between two quarrelling empires, east and west. The Guard backed an eastern usurper named Maxentius against a more powerful Constantine from the west. Maxentius lost the battle and subsequently drowned while fleeing across the Tiber River. Obviously, a poor swimmer. Immediately, Constantine abolished the Praetorian Guard, scattering its remains across a newly united empire, or so he thought.

"There remained skeletal parts of the Guard's network across the eastern reaches of the empire, und within two generations, they surreptitiously set the demise of Rome through the proliferation of Christianity. It was here that the newborn Spada Sacra realized exponential power and influence utilizing the least effort. No longer was it necessary to maintain tens of thousands, or thousands, or even hundreds in their ranks; they could achieve their objectives with only a few squads. They operate underneath, surgically striking only when conditions allow deniability und impetus towards another; an existing enemy, or entity with motive. The Spada Sacra use their network in detection of leverage points, 'miracles', and other developments deemed useful to their agenda. Their power is the control of power, and no institution since the Roman Empire has ever been allowed to advance beyond its oversight."

Further intrigued, Hammett sat up a little more, adjusting his pillow for extra support, digesting Pichler's narrative. "Okay, my apologies; the effects have almost receded, but the…"

"Now, Doctor, I insist you relax. Overcoming the drugs might not take as long, but five days unconsciousness should..."

"That's what I was going to say." Hammett interrupted. "Please continue. I believe we haven't much time until Simon arrives."

Pichler reached for his cup and gargled another mouthful of water, his tone graveled and scratchy at first.

"Without delving into every campaign sanctioned by the Spada Sacra, let us simplify und postulate that the organization has functioned approximately for fifteen millennia; successfully recruiting, generation after generation. How is this possible without detection? La Fratellanza believe they employ similar und combined methods exercised by the Praetorian Guard and the Holy See—the jurisdiction of the Roman Catholic Church—within whose fabric the Spada Sacra is woven. Potential candidates are preselected when they are very young. Aptitude tests from schools are monitored for excellence, parish familial records sifted for optimal conditions."

"What conditions?"

"The Spada Sacra prefers to source children from disheveled families—broken, angry, dysfunctional, or optimally, orphanages... dystopia. These children eagerly accept their new guardians with albeit misguided, but extremely fierce loyalty. Nobody loves them but the church, und the church is ever-present for them. Psychosocial development occurs there. Spada Sacra boys endure a lifetime of training in the church, ascending the priesthood, but with notable, astonishing, differences. In addition to their ecclesiastical curriculum, they are instructed in tactical defense, beginning with basic martial arts, defensive and offensive, und later accelerating into advanced weapons training und strategy. Additionally, they are provided a curriculum in human relations—the deviant variety—wherein they learn und rehearse nefarious manipulation, practicing on the general population. Widowers persuaded into giving their inheritances to the church, girls provided with outrageous accusations regarding their boyfriends to determine if they quarrel, or husbands tempted and extorted. The list is endless und cruel, und cruelty is a goal of the recruiter. Who can be the *cruelest*, Doctor Hammett, but the person who has experienced it firsthand?"

A fresh anxiety burned Hammett's insides. A sickening, involuntary, retch-like guttural grip took hold, uneasy to control and convulsive, with indefinable causation. Pichler sensed something amiss, observing Hammett's reactions as he spoke, recording mental notes of the phrases that triggered negative reactions, as well as those he deemed benign. As long as Hammett remained in control, he would not make further inquiry; Hammett was sensitive to pride.

"But for the boys of the Spada Sacra, the ultimate cruelty mechanizes from the final selection process. Since it cannot maintain or utilize its entire seminary, only the gilt-edged graduates ascend into their ranks, absorbed where aptitudes dictate. They are ceremoniously whisked away to new assignments—parishes, or rather, prefects controlled by a member. There is at least one in every country of significance.

"Und now the disgusting part. Those not selected are individually separated und 'assigned' as deacons to a faraway diocese, but ultimately never seen or heard from again. This attritive process continues throughout the hierarchy of the Spada Sacra. Only the prefects handpick their own successors, und any challengers are furtively exterminated. Before you inquire, the leader of the Spada Sacra normally carries the ordained title of Cardinal, but Tagliabue succeeded his mentor before the milestone occurred. Unlike the rest of the hierarchy, the leader also handpicks his own inner circle of potential successors, indifferent to the Praetorian system. La Fratellanza believed Tagliabue to be peculiarly ambitious during his time in the cardinal's circle, und cannot disregard the possibility that he murdered them all to achieve preeminence."

Hammett toiled from the unceasing nausea, and although it had plateaued, his breathing became exaggerated.

Pichler lifted the top of his left sleeve, revealing a large-crystaled watch with a brown leather band. "We only have a few minutes. Perhaps I should wait und—"

"No, no; I'll manage. Tell me about the boy."

"If you insist."

Hammett motioned for expediency.

"Narciso Esposito was conceived by two nomadic Gitano—Spanish Romani gypsies—heroin smugglers masquerading as part of a dance troop in Valencia. The mother died four years later from an overdose; the father abandoned him under the lions of Saint Mary's Cathedral. The archdiocese provided foster care during the following months. Its seminary wasted little time before initiating his lessons. A year passed, und an elderly Portuguese priest finally adopted him. If Esposito's demeanor was already piteous, it became exponentially repugnant when the seminary sisters discovered that he had been sexually abused by this priest. The church quietly annulled the adoption und reassigned the priest to mission work in Alexandrovsk, Siberia. The mission lasted three years. During that time, young Esposito excelled in his studies, demonstrating exceptional talent for mathematics und a keen interest, if not curious interest, in papal history. I say curious because he remained interested in the church's leadership: cardinals, bishops, etcetera. By no coincidence, our good friend Vasco Tagliabue, took notice of Esposito and befriended him through regular rotation as a favored altar boy.

"A year passed, und Tagliabue apparently made the decision to indoctrinate Narciso by making an example of the returning pedophilic Portuguese priest. Tagliabue supplied Narciso with a stiletto und together they cornered him in a dark alleyway two streets from the archdiocese. The Portuguese reportedly had over thirty thrust wounds, a severed throat, and pulverized genitals. No evidence to link them to the assassination, of course. Clerical investigations are typically met with great resistance, with a preference for conducting them internally. They escaped detection technically, und by judicial politics. We assume now that Esposito, from that moment, became a protégé of Tagliabue.

"Wait." Hammett interrupted. "How—"

"A deacon overheard two of their conversations. In caution, he waited one year before approaching the Vatican. He was immediately intercepted by the Spada Sacra and vanished. A missive from the same deacon soon after appeared at a parish in Perpignan, Spain—one that happens to maintain relations with one of our brothers. The communique detailed instructtions on where to find a complete written transcription of those conversations."

"Rather lucky," said Hammett.

Pichler sighed. "This is not how I would describe it."

"Sorry. Please continue."

"Psychologically, Esposito contains all the classic examples und exposures requisite for a serial murderer's profile. Once he completes Spada Sacra's training, Esposito will become extremely dangerous, yet there is something else you must understand.

"Remember that for many centuries these people have acquired extraordinary technologies. Some of these technologies we managed to rescue, others became as myth for those witnesses who escaped with their lives, but nothing else. Purportedly, there are wild notions of distance gliding suits since the mid-seventeenth century, used only surgical night strikes. Laser-intersection array television monitors; flat pictures produced by matrix-interlaced projection. Medical technologies, of course, are most relevant to our goals und have the highest acquisition value. There are rumors of rapid healing remedies—deep lacerations undetectable after 36 hours. Another whisper spoke of a chemical for comprehensive blood vessel cleansing without damage or weakening to ze walls, fundamentally resetting your cardio-vascular clock. Other compounds that destroy fat cells, increase lung capacity, und enhance sexual performance, all archived in the proscription of vanity.

"Many more exist, but one particularly alarming device has made two appearances in our encounters, the first in the latter 19th century, and again during a World War II spree, und its cruelty has no equal. It is in the form of an ornate mace sometimes used as walking cane. We call it the Amethylizer. If not in his hand, it is never out of reach of Bishop Tagliabue."

"What's so devastatingly terrible about it?"

"Imagine noninvasive quadriplegia complicated with a loss of immediate memory. That is one of its cruelest functions."

Hammett's undulating nausea persisted without change in intensity. Forced deep breathing kept it at a manageable equilibrium. "And how does it work?"

"Of course, we do not know exactly how it works. La Fratellanza knows only the following facts about it: That it is a cane-like mace composed of bronze und dark esche, er, ash wood. The wood und bronze have exquisite filigree, a most intricate ornamentation, carved und etched in fine detail. An unusually flawless Russian amethyst crystal, estimated at over 150 carats, no less, rests at the top. When the user activates the weapon, a bright violet glow soon after emanates from the crystal. Any contact with that crystal causes permanent nerve damage to the area contacted. A hand, a leg, or when thrust again someone's spinal column, para to quadriplegia occurs within moments of contact. It carries the potential penalty of irreversible damage for the unlucky bastard. Worse, if you can imagine anything worse, if the Amethylizer comes in contact with the base of one's skull, not only nerve damage und paralysis, but complete memory loss. You would not know how you became paralyzed, or even when it occurred—total amnesia. Furthermore, Doctor Hammett, it is possible this device contains more than one level of intensity. Rarely, but in a few instances, regardless of intentions, strategy, or less likely, compassion, some of the Amethylizer's victims completed full recoveries. This is a recorded fact, although the recovery times varied."

Hammett, maintaining his breathing cadence, grinned, "Twist of irony calling it an Amethylizer, Pichler."

"I do not understand."

"Don't you see? Amethyst!"

"You must excuse me, Herr Doctor, I am not a geologist, gemologist, or given to arcane trivia."

"Obviously not privy in Greek mythology either."

Suddenly, Hammett's nausea abated, and his diction afforded greater confidence in a tone bordering sarcastic.

"Amethyst, *Herr Pichler*, is derived from 'amethystos'. Greek for 'not drunken'—sobriety! Dionysus."

"I see. The merrymaker, yes? Quite the opposite effect, this weapon, und you should be advised to keep well away should Tagliabue or any of his guards wield it."

"Goes without saying. So, one question, and I guess it's an important one. How does one shut it off without tagging themselves?"

"Held with both hands, using one to twist the tip in the opposite direction."

"Of course." Hammett smirked.

"Doctor Hammett, in the short time since Tagliabue und Esposito conjugated, the boy has become adroit in collections and disposals. One cannot underestimate the skills of the Spada Sacra; they have maintained their existence longer than any functioning organization on this planet except for two eastern monarchies and the Catholic Church itself. They are effective, ruthless, und resolute in action. Never forget this, Herr Doctor."

Three pronounced knocks preceded the creaked opening of Hammett's room door. A petite brunette in a spotless white nurse's uniform dollied a loaded meal cart to the bedside.

"Ah, the most excellent timing." Pichler smiled, picked up his straw fedora and jacket from his chair, and started for the open doorway. "You have my contact information with your belongings, Herr Doctor. We desire to see you very soon, at least within the next week for a comprehensive examination. I do not suggest a lengthier delay, considering."

My belongings?

Hammett sighed as Pichler slipped past the nurse with a cordial acknowledgement. She smiled and, without a word, removed Hammett's IV and rolled its apparatus away towards a corner of the room. She removed the bandages surrounding the IV next, followed by an antiseptic sponge rinse. A standard bandage finalized her attendances, and on her way to the door, she simply uttered, "Eat, *por favor*" in an encouraging Spanish accent.

As she left the room, Hammett spent several moments recollecting everything said by Pichler. Difficult questions and emotions begat dissonant melodies echoing within the chambers of thought. Reflective waves in a half-life symphony of hypotheses. Albeit with quantifiable success, he in fact failed to accomplish his primary objective as a field operator. Bormann and Mengele remained at large, trapped in Paraguay, but able to create additional destructiveness should the Paraguayan marines and Pichler's Franco also blunder. Perhaps his employability as an operator would become marginalized in the process. Who would hire him now, anyway? He was getting older and already felt the sting of age-discrimination on two previous solicitations. Always, the competitors were younger, and younger meant fearless agility, but to a greater degree of importance, it meant less expensive when experience and guile could be forsaken. He was practically alone in a foreign hospital, no family to speak of, and in several months, he might face the prospect of financial insolvency. He stared at a tepid platter of lifeless institutional vegetables, rice, and a pulverized slab of roast pork.

And what about the Brotherhood?

His penchant for calculative logic embarked on a deductive bender, grinding the benefits and advantages of the Spada Sacra job—if there actually *was* a Spada Sacra. Covert connections. He'd become a fainter ghost within an illaudable organization: working conditions largely unknown, personnel unknown, potential hazards largely unknown, and those that were already conveyed appeared extremely perilous. On one hand, risks, both positive and negative. On the other, equivalence. Right now, the available information funneled towards the obvious conclusion. He must explore La Fratellanza.

Hammett picked up a fork and foraged for a warm carrot slice that managed some color, but he wouldn't have time to consume it. A subtle knock preceded Simon Wiesenthal's entry. The handle dropped, the door slowly creaked open, and Simon's balding head and convalescent countenance protruded, seeking permission to enter without actually requesting it. He glided into the room, donning his best joviality even though he carried the weight of a million monkeys on his back. He didn't wait for Hammett to meet his handshake, grabbing him on the shoulder in an awkward embrace. Hammett managed to hold on to his fork in the meantime.

"Good day to you Anund, or at least I hope it is because you are above ground and apparently out of the danger."

Hammett placed his fork down on the tray, nodding. "I'm okay, I suppose. How was the flight? You look a little pale."

Wiesenthal dragged a hand across his face, as if to wipe the dread sweat of another holocaust. "Unpleasant, being trapped in an oscillating aluminum tube for thirteen hours, but this was not my problem. The cab driver nearly gave me a heart attack on ze way here. Maniac! I continue surviving..."

"Ah." Hammett offered Wiesenthal a chair, and he took it. "You know I have an immediate concern, right? A question, or rather, a validation."

Wiesenthal wiped his face again. Beads of sweat appeared constantly due to the excessive heat generated by his tweed jacket. "Of course, Anund. You must know my feelings about Pichler. Impeccable. I have consulted his practice many times over the years. He was indispensable during Eichmann and Stangl's profiling sessions and later during ze trials. I trusted him implicitly when he said you are needed for an assignment, and that is fine by the way. Your services will not be required in ze foreseeable future, but Anund, I believe this to be a good thing. Unfortunate for your current employment perhaps, but for humanity, a good thing. I am aware of all your efforts—Bormann and Mengele located! At last, we will have them. This is important, Anund, because you caused it to happen." Wiesenthal reached into his jacket and withdrew a thick envelope. "That is why you are due ze entire balance of your fee, Anund. Here it is, all of it, ten thousand dollars U.S., and do not worry about this hospital's bill; we have taken care of it, of course."

"I don't know what to say; I don't feel as though I deserve anything."

"Say nothing! You could have just as easily ended up in the pool of bones Edgar told me about."

"Huh? Pichler never mentioned any pool."

"Oh yes. Said they found one of the guards on the banks of a pool of a stream. His lower half was removed by the fish in that pool, and the bottom of it was full of human bones. Hundreds. I shall not go into further detail, Anund; it appears that I have interrupted your meal."

Stones and twigs, Hammett thought.

Wiesenthal withdrew a handkerchief from his jacket and sponged his face. "Please continue; I must visit the café downstairs for a drink with ice cubes before I melt away! I will return by the time you are finished. You will tell me what happened exactly in Tucumán."

A moment later and Wiesenthal was quietly shutting the squeaky door to Hammett's recovery room on his way down a secured corridor with two sentries located by double doors at the other end. Hammett again picked up his fork, but the food was cold now, and the window beckoned his pondering gaze. The intense anxiety he felt previously had dissipated, and his sense of control slowly returned. The street below bustled.

A Palace of Cards

"BASTARDS!" Monsignor Trovarto raised a tightly clenched fist.

Chris' eyes remained transfixed to the ballroom's projector screen. His knees buckled and he dropped to the floor, numb. Dao Ming attempted to break his fall, but the physics overcame her best effort. Deep gasps echoed from La Fratellanza, then cries for justice and extermination of the Spada Sacra. Matthew's eyes burned at the screen with the dilated pupils of primal fury. His jaws oscillated wildly, and the grinding of teeth could be heard if not for the entire chamber's retching. He looked at the laptop on the podium and focused further at its pinhole camera. Matt then looked at its angle and choked.

He doesn't just see us; he sees all of us!

Immediately, he reached for the adjacent notepad, folded a page and placed it on top of the laptop, covering the lens.

Narciso Esposito turned towards his camera and laughed. "Belated actions, Commander. I may no longer see *you*, but the Brotherhood are completely exposed."

Anund Hammett started to feel a familiar uneasiness descend upon him; the augur of anxiety, the welling of bile, a pretext of proximate evil. He scanned the entire ballroom for traces of an infiltrator, but saw nothing extraordinary. Anastasia sensed it and jumped on stage with a distressed expression as she ran to catch him doubled over in pain. She grasped his hand and felt the shock of intense empathy.

"Oh God!" she panted. "We must escape!"

Patrick also jumped onto the stage and yanked her away. "What's wrong, Annie? Are we in danger?"

"You know this—why this happens, Patrick. I have seen it twice before with him."

Hammett took control of himself by regulating his breathing. "You must evacuate everyone immediately. Use the microphone on the podium. Hurry!"

"Commander? Are you there?" Bishop Esposito's voice resonated once more from the public address system. "They must bring the device to me within five days else young Emily will suffer a most disagreeable chastening. The rendezvous location is now within a file on this device, easily located. Doctor Miller, please confirm."

Hammett limped towards Chris. "No, you mustn't obey him! You cannot give in to the Spada Sacra; he lies! Emily will never be released, and we will lose her, you, Dao, the device—everything for which we worked! I beg you, do not go!"

"FATHER!" Anastasia screamed at the top of her lungs.

An explosion shattered the conference hall from one of its back corners. The compression shockwave sent several proximate members of the Brotherhood to complete oblivion, including one of the sentries. A few others in the immediate blast zone were shredded, bifurcated, suffered amputations, or simply vanished within a ruby red mist. No movement. A gaping breach slowly emerged from the cloud of thick soot and debris. Automatic gunfire erupted, sending those with any remote cognizance to the floor. Many were caught off-guard and never made it, absorbing the fusillade's brunt with their flesh. From the breach poured militants cloaked in black jellabiyas and maroon turbans. They brandished Kalashnikov rifles, rocket-propelled grenades, and extra magazines strapped across their chests. The inside of the conference hall was now darker, creating enough contrast to slow their advance; their eyes struggled to adjust.

The last sentry in the room, alive but bleeding from the shrapnel that tore through his left bicep, rushed to the stage and found Hammett, Chris, Dao, Matt, Trovarto, Patrick, Anastasia and Rocco crouched behind it. Further away was Jet Sun, a leader of Tibet's Gelugpa monastery, who was anxiously assessing any opportunity to escape. Hammett froze at the sight of his longtime friend and mentor, Edgar Pichler, obliterated behind his table. Only his face, reposed in torment, was recognizable.

"Oh, Edgar, no!" Hammett moaned.

"We must leave!" Jet Sun shouted as he peered over the stage.

The militant's sporadic gunfire deafened by compression, dust, fumes, and acrid cordite choked the unveiled.

"Throw it!" Hammett yelled to the guard.

The sentry reached into his jacket and flung a lime-sized metallic ball high into the air towards the middle of the conference room. He turned back to the rear of the stage and yelled, "Do not look at it!" but Matt missed the order.

The ball's outer hull sprung open and unfolded a miniature double propeller system that immediately began to rotate at high velocity. A second later, the rotating ball flashed intense green laser pulses at the eyes of the intruders, temporarily blinding them with painful radiation. The device searched with facial recognition and indiscriminately attacked any it detected. Within moments, all attackers were either incapacitated and screaming, or cowering without a clear view, fearing their own demise.

"What was that?" Chris whispered to Hammett.

"It's called a Medusa Pill. It will hover there until it's either shot down or the battery dies, which will occur in approximately three minutes unless another wave necessitates additional fire. We must escape while they are pinned. The entrance should still be protected by the outer sentries; they have instructions."

Chris paused for a moment and started to stand up. "Okay, but I'm going for the laptop."

"NO! You can always make another!" Hammett lunged on stage towards Chris. A single shot rang out, followed by a flash from the Medusa Pill. Distant screams echoed as Anund Harwin Hammett slumped at Chris' feet.

"My God! Someone HELP!" Chris crouched behind podium, the laptop in one hand, the other applying pressure to the gushing exit wound on Hammett's left upper back. "He's been shot!"

"Papa!" Cried Anastasia, jumping to help. Again, the indiscriminate Medusa flashed, and she felt the heat of its beam on her right cheek as she turned away.

The three were safely behind the wooded podium, so long as no one started shooting at them, which would surely happen if they remained there much longer. Hammett's breathing was considerably labored and irregular. He coughed and convulsed.

"Help me turn him over," said Anastasia.

Jet Sun joined and stood watching over them as Chris pulled Hammett's arm as hard as he could to create the needed inertia. Anastasia pushed his lower torso, and he slowly made the turn, exposing the entry wound near his heart. Blood drained from it in waves, and Anastasia raced to apply pressure. The more pressure she applied, the more her father winced in pain and labored for breath.

"Lightly, Tulip. I need to relay something important to you and Doctor Miller, the others—" Again, he coughed and a small amount of blood accompanied it. Rocco, Patrick, Dao, and Matthew gathered as close as they could to try and hear.

"This is the business of politics. Unfortunately, my languidness is due to my propensity for copiousness." He coughed and tremored in pain. "Perhaps it's meant this way for me. Many could argue. I am one hundred and two years old. Old enough, I think."

Chris glared at him, astonished. "How..."

"It is no longer important as Master Sun knows. Listen! You must enlighten the world of us—all of you. Converse with mutual admiration and respect. Tolerance is the stance of disdain. Preach acceptance; talk to each other. Help them find commonality. Learn to become as one. Promise me!" And with his last breath, he turned to Chris. "You must decide. Let Emily go, help billions, or risk us all. The Spada Sacra will never allow your freedom. No trust, never!"

Chris squeezed his hand gently, "I can't live without her. She's all I have left in this world, Monkey Man, but if it is in my power to do so, you have my promise."

"He's gone!" Patrick shouted.

"No one is truly dead," said Jet Sun gazing upon Hammett's uninhabited eyes. "There is more than a memory that survives."

Hammett's motion ceased. Chris felt something in the palm of his hand as he let go of Hammett's. A tiny silver rectangular ingot. Hammett's final expression was that of intent. Chris remained in shock as the chamber's screams returned. Anastasia started balling uncontrollably in the arms of her brother; his anger rose to the boiling point. He caught Patrick's mutual expression as his eyes darted about, looking for anything to engage. Suddenly, the Medusa Pill plummeted to the floor.

Monsignor Trovarto pulled Chris away. "We must leave. Now!" He pointed towards the ornate double doors in which they previously entered, at least 25 meters away and partially exposed to the militants' line of fire. That is, as soon as the gunmen realized the Medusa's threat had exhausted.

All crouched in low-profile; the group scurried towards the entrance. Bodies over pools of blood littered their path, and the moans of desperate and dying brothers droned in the background. Focus on the doors created tunnel vision, and the group barely noticed the other survivors joining their exodus. Alongside them, several religious representatives from their

36

transatlantic flight bolted for the doors, grabbing anyone with ability to make the run.

Ten meters away, Dr. Amid Harwaziz's hand latched onto Jet Sun's ankle, pulling him down in the process. A bullet cratered into the wall just where Jet Sun would have been.

"Please!" Harwaziz shouted, his own ankle trapped under a fallen table.

Jet Sun kicked it away with a lightning thrust, freeing Harwaziz as another round careened off a nearby chair. Jet Sun helped him to his feet. More shots thundered throughout the convention hall as the dozen or so remaining members of La Fratellanza finally reached the doors. A single militant, wearing a meticulously coifed ducktail beard, rose above the debris, aimed his rifle at the group, and in a brusque directive yelled, "STOP NOW! There is no chance for escape!"

Matthew was the first to reach the gargantuan doors, and it was immediately clear he could not open them alone. Monsignor Trovarto and Patrick slammed their bodies against the right door, creating enough force necessary to pry it open, but it stopped pivoting upon reaching the body of a sentry. Matthew poked his head through and discovered the other sentry crushing the throat of a militant a few feet down the hall. The sentry dropped the limp body and ran to the doorway, grabbing the arms of his fallen comrade and pulled him aside.

"A Medusa; do you have one?" Matt yelled.

The guard nodded affirmatively as he dropped the limbs of the other sentry. He reached into his jacket pocket and withdrew the ball.

"Throw it now!" Matt yelled, pointing behind him into the convention hall.

As soon as he released it, shots blasted mortar from the walls just above their heads.

"Run and do not look back!" Trovarto grabbed Anastasia's left arm and yanked her through the doorway behind him just as the shooting erupted.

The group bolted into the hallway and, as the door closed behind them, sounds of automatic gunfire and screams could be heard from the other side. Two militants with drawn scimitars appeared through a door just off their right side. Jet Sun and Dao Ming leapt forth to confront them. Jet Sun snatched a flagpole and used it as a pike, thrusting it into the nearest swordsman's abdomen, causing him to double over and drop his weapon in agony. The other took a massive chop directly at Dao Ming's abdomen, missing her as she dove aside, launching a foot into the side of her assailant's knee joint. He collapsed mouth wide open in disbelief, his leg twisted into an unnatural angle upon the ground. Jet Sun launched the pole into that open mouth, impacting the back of his throat and penetrating further through the esophagus. He snapped the pole off at the swordsman's teeth and proceeded to smash it upon the head of the other foe, shattering the pole in the process. The man collapsed, knocked cold from the impact. The hallway was clear as far as they could surveil, and a silent rampage to the valet ensued.

"How do we know they haven't already disabled our vehicles?" Patrick asked.

"We do not," replied Trovarto. "But it is-a our only chance to escape these maniacs who shoot first and do not-a ask any questions."

A moment later, the group made it to the valet's stand. The vans were parked close by, but their security detail was missing. It was quiet, and, had the carnage of moments earlier not occurred, anyone would believe it a normal day; business as usual.

"The Medusa must still be active," said Trovarto, breathing heavily from the run. "Get into the vans before it expires; we must return to the airport."

"Why?" Matthew asked. "Can't we go to the Egyptian Police? Wait; strike that."

Matt suddenly realized that the local police and likely the military were already in league with either the militants. W*ho else would boldly attack a major and famous facility in broad daylight?* He also fingered their main tent pole, the U.S. government, which of course would be shadowed by Blue Ops.

"Where do we go, then?"

"We must-a get to our aircraft. Please, board the vans!"

The group halved and threw themselves into the vehicles. Chris, Dao, Matt, Trovarto, Rocco, and Anastasia took the lead van. The hulking sentry jumped into the driver's seat and engaged the ignition. Patrick, Jet Sun, Doctor Harwaziz, and four of the religious representatives, including the shinshoku gon-gūji, two rabbis, and a turbanless Sikh, stampeded into the other.

Trovarto took the front passenger seat and turned to the sentry. "There is-a rear exit to this compound, yes?"

"Yes, a service gate on the northwest side, but—"

"But what?"

"It is a manned gate, always locked."

"You do not-a worry about that; drive through it."

"I always wanted to do that." The guard smiled as he accelerated away from the valet, speeding towards the back gate with the other van following closely behind.

They rounded the final corner before the gate became visible, and just as the guard stated, the heavy steel structure was locked, but no personnel were present. The driver abruptly slammed on the brakes, tossing everyone not seatbelted towards the front. The van behind them barely missed, skidding to a halt just off their left rear corner.

"What are you doing?" Trovarto yelled as the driver jumped out.

"Opening the gate. It is too strong for us to ram without damage."

The large man sprinted, as fast as a 175kg man could, towards the guard shack to actuate the gate's motor. On the way in, the driver noticed a pair of feet protruding from just behind the shack in a thicket of palms. The shack itself was empty. Gunfire and screeching tires echoed from the other side of the conference hall, and the driver knew they were out of time. Any moment a race would begin, and they were contending in passenger vans—loaded passenger vans with diesel-sipping hamsters under the hood. Without additional consideration, he flipped a lever, causing the gate to slide away. He raced back to the van and jumped in, threw the shifter into Drive and stomped the accelerator. There was no resistance on their way around the compound, and sparse traffic in the immediate vicinity of the palace. The vans diligently traced around it making Cairo's Ring Road within a few moments. The driver checked his rearview mirrors; nothing, yet.

Monsignor Trovarto's eyes twitched in furious thought. "Take us through town, not around."

The driver's head whipped abruptly, stunned by the directive. "But why? It will take us two, three times longer to reach the airport that way. The traffic is terrible!"

"Because-a they can catch us on the Ring. Once we enter the traffic, they will be delayed same as-a us, and remain there with enough time for us to board and depart."

Trovarto reached into his cassock, withdrew a phone, and called ahead to his pilot. "Si, red depart. *Ripetere, Partenza Rosso, Courso DR diretto, l'evasione. Ah, oui, bella. Grazie.*"

The vans weaved through an increasing confluence of traffic, keeping a tight formation and maintaining a non-ostentatious speed. Attracting the police would undoubtedly create an undesirable variable, suffice to reconcile the consequences should those officers belong to the militants that massacred La Fratellanza. *The Brotherhood!* Trovarto thought. *Who is-a to lead us now?* There were only a handful remaining. Those poor souls at the conference room; gone without any explanation. Just death.

"Did you recognize the man back at-a the palace? Do you know who attacked us?"

The driver looked ahead, concentrating on the traffic. "Yes. His name is Mukhtar Arwa Lal... Al-Ghaiz. You know of them?"

"Al-Ghaiz, yes, I am afraid I do. Not terrorists, marauders in the name of Islam. They pretend extremism as-a means to plunder. In private, they care nothing for Muhammad, nor do they pray towards Mecca. In fact, they don't-a pray at all unless someone is-a looking."

The driver glanced across. "Mukhtar is no idiot, Monsignor. He might send others to the airport ahead of us if he has not someone already there."

Chris clung tight to Dao, both of them locked in a blind stare. She listened intently at the conversation in front of her—other people testing them perhaps, or just out to destroy La Fratellanza. The information vacuum created silence except for the high-winding diesel, the wind, and the occasional horn blast. For Chris, everything—his entire world—sensory deprived. He didn't hear the first sentence from the van's forward occupants, just a dull mumble and a blur of images. Waves of emotion locked him away in a spiked cell. *Emily is not lost!* It would kill him to prove the concept, and he would sacrifice everything to get his daughter back. Hammett was dead and he couldn't change that outcome. Chris knew nothing about The Brotherhood, except that he would have been liquidated without their intervention. The contorted faces of the Smileys flashed. And all of this for what—a completely incidental contraption? *Why was it so damned important? They destroyed the lab for it. Poor Julie. They might as well have finished poor Jack Kattner for it, too.*

So many bodies thrown into a pit over that laptop. What would happen if I chucked it out of the window, smashing it to miniscule pieces? Emily...

"Dao, how am I going to get her back? I mean, get her back *and* we live. Every scenario, each alternative, I cannot see past the exchange. There must be additional leverage to guarantee our survival, otherwise—"

"Too many variables. This Spada Sacra, if they insist on stealing your reader and capturing us for the sake of what? Hoarding the technology? It intrigues me to understand why they desperately seek us. To know their ultimate purpose will assist our strategy. Their weaknesses become our strengths— our advantage. We must not give them everything they want, *chǒng'ér.*"

Dao looked deeply into his eyes and wiped a bead of sweat from his forehead. His grinding concentration couldn't be broken. He maintained a blank gaze into the sea of traffic and narrowing buildings ahead. Noise, pollution, decaying early twentieth-century French façades, neglected for decades, rehabilitation forsaken; a choking scourge awaiting architectural emancipation. It was easier to lose oneself in such chaos, and Chris became increasingly numb to his surroundings, including Dao Ming.

"The reader!" Matt yelled.

All in the van suddenly turned towards Chris and the laptop he clutched tightly.

"They are tracking us with it!"

Dao reached for the computer and Chris slowly relented. She pried the back cover off, found the GPS transmitting module that Kattner installed adjacent a modified battery, removed it and handed it forward to Trovarto, who immediately tossed it through the window in disgust.

"Sloppy of me," he grumbled.

Dao handed the laptop to Chris. He barely moved to receive it, continuing his blank stare into the abyss.

The vans' pace dwindled to a hectic stop-and-go crawl; pedestrians taking advantage of each momentary gap, increasing the discord and potential for attracting the throngs of street vendors, some of whom might recollect Trovarto's habiliment if interrogated. The second van, driven by Harwaziz, experienced the same conditions and failed to maintain their tight formation. A peddler jumped in front, causing Harwaziz to dive on the brakes. A merging taxi wedged his grill into the gap, blessing his fortune, but Harwaziz was no longer in control. Over the next several blocks, the cab allowed others ahead, and in turn, those drivers practiced the same courtesy. The distance grew until the vans were almost out of sight of each other. Trovarto constantly checked his mirrors and turned completely around when necessary, but the widening gap made it increasingly difficult, and the density ahead appeared to worsen.

"I am losing them!" He yelled, frantically shifting positions.

"There is nothing one can do, Monsignor," replied the sentry, stressed from the tumult. "They must try to reach us."

Several minutes and two blocks passed. Ultimately, Harwaziz fell too far behind for Trovarto's observation.

After a few periodic scans to Trovarto slowly turned forward. "They are in God's hands now."

The sentry glanced over, "As are we."

The traffic worsened in the vicinity of Ramses Railway Station. Multiple seemingly uncontrolled intersections converging in unconventional directions, several lanes wide and infested with commercial transports, all vying for a slot—any slot. Blasting horns, flailing arms and redundant insults shouted in Egyptian Arabic at terrified women attempting to cross insane intersections, and unconcerned men passing wherever and whenever they pleased.

"This is madness!" Trovarto commented.

"This is Cairo," said the sentry.

Doctor Harwaziz frantically stabbed the accelerator but every time he did, another zombified tamarind juice peddler leapt in front from the curb, fully expecting the van's undivided attention. Patrick craned to see around several buses intertwined within the pulsating human matrix ahead, becoming frustrated with their lack of progress.

"We're dropping too far behind, man. They're gone! Can't you get around this?"

Harwaziz shouted in Arabic towards a young mother, "Do not endanger your child!" and then, exasperated, turned toward Patrick. "If we are truly separated, then there is no reason to continue this path. We must circumvent this anarchy and recoup time. I know a, you call it, shortcut to the Salah Salem Road. It is a higher capacity with no pedestrians, and it is the direct route to the airport."

Just past the railway station, Monsignor Trovarto's sentry threaded an eyelet towards an accelerating convoy moving too fast for meddling pedestrians. "*Allahu Akbar,*" he whispered.

Trovarto's expression changed from that of anxiety to relief, adjusting his posture. "Yes. Yes, he is!"

"The airport is but twelve kilometers from here. We will arrive soon."

Trovarto looked back once more to see if somehow the other van also broke free from the melee. A minute later and the highway curved away from the long straight they had just traversed, eliminating any chance of sighting their brothers. With that finality, Trovarto turned back around and resigned any further surveillance.

Traffic thinned over the next few kilometers, and the sentry steadily increased his pace towards the airport. The faster they arrive, the quicker his responsibility shifts, he thought. But then, he remembered his responsibilities were the protection of the Brotherhood at any hardship, and at any cost. He suddenly realized that his life just changed; he was no longer safe or in control within his own homeland; the oath given as a defender of the Brotherhood was no longer recited words. The quickening pace of traffic allowed little room for anxiety to settle in his mind, constant decision-making distracted him. It did not, however, distract the others seated behind him. They became wracked with apprehension, worry, dread, sorrow, and anger. So much had been lost at the Palace Mena, and so much more rested upon their shoulders now. But no more weight could befall Doctor Christopher Miller. His capacity crested with the news of Emily's kidnapping, and ever since, a numbness crept upon him like the heat of morphine methodically coursing one's veins after the injection. Slow, expanding, burning... *rage*. Its vignette shrouded all but the most distant visible route; the traffic disappearing at the horizon's convergence. Dao saw it in his eye's reflection as she held onto him.

"Five minutes, maybe six." The sentry said. "Lal must have anticipated our return to the airport, Monsignor, should something go wrong."

"You overestimate his-a resources, brother. In-a order for organizations such as-a his to remain obscure, they must maintain a small footprint at all times. He cannot predict our every option and dispatch safeguards. Optimism is-a our friend, always, just as it is his enemy today. I believe we will arrive safely, but I do not-a express this without due regard. *Veloce, per favore!*"

"What about the others?"

"I pray for them."

At last, Cairo International's northwestern quadrant came into view, and the tail of their jet remained just where they left it just a few hours earlier—parked on the tarmac in front of Terminal 4. The Kobri Al Matar freeway stretched just three more kilometers before the airport's entrance, then it was back down the adjacent, parallel Airport Road almost another kilometer before reaching the secured gates of their terminal.

"I see them, I think!" Rocco shouted from the rear of the van.

Anastasia and Matthew turned to confirm his sighting, but the sentry exited to the airport's main entrance before the other van came back into view. Within moments, they were advancing the opposite direction towards Terminal 4, but views of the freeway were periodically obscured by dense landscaping. Even so, Matt caught a shuttered glimpse of their colleagues frantically barreling towards the airport's entrance. The momentary shuttered flash provided only half the picture. What Matthew didn't see was a speeding column of two dark Mercedes sedans and an armored SUV—a black, six-wheeled Mercedes G63 AMG—less than a football field's length behind it and closing.

Matt and Rocco kept their eyes focused rearward towards the U-turn they themselves navigated just moments before. Seconds later, it appeared, and just as their van swung into Terminal 4's valet, the enormous G63 broke across the wooded divide, crashing into the driver's side of the other van. Glass and liquids exploded as metal crushed and twisted. The massive Mercedes emerged virtually unblemished, but the van collapsed into itself, spinning airborne into the road's drainage ditch.

"NO!" Rocco yelled, as Matt clenched his teeth in anger.

"Do not stop. Take us directly to the plane." Trovarto directed.

Two gunmen jumped out of the 6X6, taking covered positions with their AKs aimed at the smoldering van. One of the black sedans shuttered to a grinding stop alongside the truck. Three of its passenger doors swung open, and heavily-armed gunmen bailed out.

"Bypass them!" Mukhtar Lal barked from the passenger's seat of the third sedan. "The first van is more important!"

But Mukhtar's rifles could not compel the Terminal 4's coded and reinforced automatic gate, let alone its tire-shredding barrier, for there were no guards to be directly influenced; only cameras and radio-actuated motors. Those cameras rapidly panned and zoomed upon his conveyance and its weaponry protruding from the windows, triggering a general security alarm throughout the entire airport. He might as well have phoned a nuclear bomb threat, as the deafening whine of multiple sirens erupted across the complex.

"Go back!" Matt shouted, pointing backwards as the van pulled alongside their jet.

Trovarto jumped out and sprinted towards the portside airstairs. As instructed, their pilot scrambled, ready for immediate departure; jet fully refueled, preflight checked, decoy flight plan submitted, engines idling.

Just before climbing onboard, Trovarto turned towards Matt and yelled, "We cannot go back, Matthew. Lal will have already contacted conspirators he likely controls within the airport, as well as the Egyptian military. He will have launched his interceptors, if-a he has not already, and have us shot down on sight!"

"He appears to want us alive."

"Yes, and-a if he cannot have us, he will kill us. Now or later. We are all exposed!"

Ushered by the sentry driver, Chris and Dao climbed out of the van and dashed towards the stairs. Rocco and Anastasia were a few steps behind.

"Matthew, we cannot delay! Please!" Trovarto shouted as Matt threw his arms up in disgust. "Please!"

"He is correct, sir," said the sentry, tugging at Matthew.

"Damnit!" Matt cried.

The jet had already begun rolling before the airstairs fully sealed the fuselage, and Matt strapped himself into a recliner opposite Chris and Dao.

Mukhtar Lal instructed his driver to abandon pursuit, realizing he had no chance of catching a jet blasting towards the end of Runway 5L. Instead, he phoned his command center.

"Contact Captain Chigaru's base, 232 Tactical, NOW! There is a prototype light jet departing Cairo at this moment. It will be the only one of its kind in Egypt. Get the flight plan; forward it to Chigaru. Have him blow it out of the sky." He cracked the back of his hand across his driver's shoulder. "Take me back to the other van."

Shifting Sands

Lal climbed out of his Mercedes and onto the debris-strewn access road moments later. Amid Harwaziz's half-ejected corpse, mauled by asphalt and torn metal, dripped from the remains of the van's forward compartment as it smoldered in a stench of antifreeze, molten plastics, and battery acid. Jet Sun suddenly lunged from behind the wreck, only to face the barrel of a Kalashnikov.

"Jet Sun of the Potala gelugs," Mukhtar Lal chided. "Your lion roars no more."

Other survivors slowly emerged behind Jet Sun. Two rabbis patted blood from throbbing facial lacerations and clutched bruised shoulders. The shinshoku limped to their side, his left thigh red and drenched. Finally, the Sikh joined them, somehow unscathed. A thunderous rumble in the distance captured their attention. It was the massive thrust of the Gulfstream as it launched towards the north, just as Lal guessed. His humorless guttural laughter overtook the jet's sonance.

"Do not envy them. In five minutes, they feed the Nile."

Lal felt a sudden, intense burning sensation along his forearms and hands. His astonishment succeeded a building pain, trading metrics with increasing vocalization until it became a grating scream. His rifle dropped to the ground, and his knees along with it.

"The telepath! NOW!" Lal shouted.

A flanking rifleman frantically took aim and launched a dart into Patrick's abdomen, breaking his concentration and releasing his hold on Mukhtar Lal. Within seconds, Patrick collapsed against the van, unconscious.

Lal shook off the effects of Patrick's attack, slowly stood up, and barked more commands. Two men appeared from a black cargo truck parked at the rear of Lal's column. They jogged rapidly towards Patrick, carrying a large duffle. On arrival, they unzipped it and removed a transparent polymer body bag fitted with ventilation hoses attached to a compressor.

Jet Sun lunged forward; the barrel of the Kalashnikov rifle sank deep into his solar plexus. "What are you doing to him?"

Lal turned around. "It is an inflatable capsule with a sterile environment. The machine feeds clean air mixed with a vapor. He will remain unconscious for as long as I please, awakened only when the right buyer pleases. As for you, Master Sun, there is a standing offer I intend to collect which includes a sizeable premium if you are alive and undamaged. But do not mistake my greed in keeping you alive, *lion*; the death bounty is also sufficient."

Lal shifted his gaze towards his comrade that had eased behind the four clergymen. Coldly, methodically, he raised his rifle and, in rapid succession, slaughtered each of them where they knelt. Each headshot echoed through the terminals and hangars, reverberating outward into the faint whine of approaching sirens. At the same time, Jet Sun felt a piercing sting at the nape of his neck; one snowflake amidst an avalanche of emotion.

As he collapsed towards the ground he grunted, "Who?"

Mukhtar Lal kneeled to catch his head, and just as Jet Sun faded, Lal whispered, "Ramelan."

Emily shunned all contact with her captors, most of all those from a man who had displayed cruel behavior, and quite possibly cruel intentions. She sat on a thin cot in the furthest corner of a makeshift holding cell, tucked in a compact ball with arms folded across her knees and her face buried deeply into them, shivering. It had been several hours since Bishop Narciso Esposito destroyed the playful friend she had come to know as Uncle Jack; the big, important man at Amerimem Industries who spoiled her with little company trinkets and occasional passes to lands of merriment. He was always cheerful and never visited empty-handed. Emily struggled to maintain that image in between the flashed horrors of his execution; the reduction to a squealing heap of unnatural contortion, scooped from the floor and carted away to some nondescript chamber within the cathedral's vast network of catacombs.

Esposito hovered in front of her misery for several moments. "You must stand in my presence, child."

Emily continued shivering and said nothing.

Allowing a few more ticks, Esposito continued, "If you lack the energy to stand for me, you must eat then."

"Not hungry." Emily muttered in a barely audible scratch, her throat dry and tight.

"You will need your strength for later. We will talk, and you will learn the truth about your family. Please, eat."

Emily said nothing, tightening further. Her trembling intensified.

Several moments passed as Esposito studied her reaction. "Very well. You will become hungry soon enough; first for food, then for knowledge." In the corner of an eye, he caught the entrance of a young messenger.

"*Perdonami, Eccellenza; c'è una chiamata.*"

Annoyed, Esposito turned to follow him. "Order a comforting meal for our new guest. Something appropriate and irresistible."

The messenger bowed to Esposito as he passed by, and then he glanced in assessment towards Emily, still tightly wound into her quivering ball.

Find them. Bring the scientists to me, and do not lose the device this time.

Esposito entered a cramped operations alcove and acknowledged the video phone. "What is it?"

"Secure your line."

Esposito reached beneath a fold in his robe, just below the left beltline, withdrew a square, black wafer, and adhered it to the microphone.

"Yes." He said blankly.

"Your tone, Narciso; it is not to my satisfaction."

"Eminence, I—"

"We will discuss this later. Cairo takes precedence. I understand there was an attack on the palace."

"Mukhtar Lal, naturally."

"Barbarian. He knows not what he does, only if it profits. What do you know?"

"The offer was conveyed, as you know, Eminence; the connection terminated shortly afterward. The tracking device is active although the location indicates disposal."

"So, you have no idea if they avoided Lal."

"As a matter of fact, due to our contact at the airport, I do, and you should be pleased; he eradicated all but a handful of the *Brotherhood,* including our dearly beloved."

"Hammett?"

"Yes, and Pichler."

"God be praised. And what of the others. Tell me!"

"I suspect they are headed to Tel Aviv, if their trajectory holds."

"You suspect."

Esposito jerked around to face Tagliabue with faint but detectible snarl, which brought a similarly impish grin across the cardinal's complexion.

"Forgive my insightfulness, Eminence, but you test me, you have always tested me, with contemptuous provocation."

"You forget your place, Narciso. Do not speak to me this—"

"During my adolescence, I soon realized your desire for temperament amongst your disciples, and later, after acceptable behavior had been achieved, I often wondered if your prodding became something else."

At once, Tagliabue's and Esposito's expressions interchanged, and the old man's aired an unobjectionable severity for the first time to his protégé.

"Incarcerate your tongue, Narciso. Your insights and intuition serve you well in all spheres except those closest to you— matters of the heart. Emotion. It will get the better of us. Now, it does not matter if you suspect a destination of Tel Aviv, we need to *know*. And you added a suspicious 'if' to that trajectory. This concerns me."

Esposito paused to relieve his inner tension. "Eminence, with regard to Trovarto's aircraft, there are only two possibilities at this moment: Mukhtar Lal is a classically pubescent and vindictive tactician. He will undoubtedly scramble an interceptor from a northern base and shoot them down—for no advantage, naturally. His regular use of the Egyptian Air Force has been delineated in great detail within our archives. There are several variables at issue, but the most interesting one is which aircraft he might choose. An American F-16 could, in fact, intercept their jet before depleting its fuel reserves. A Mirage could do the same, except at low altitude, its top speed is paltry—subsonic—a negligible difference to their civilian jet. This is, Eminence (Esposito's smirk returned), *assuming* that civilian aircraft possesses the advertised engines."

"And the other?"

"Beyond their primary cities, Middle Eastern radar, military and civilian, are less than reliable. Trovarto will undoubtedly reduce altitude at any moment, evade electronic detection, and change course. In other words, the trajectory towards Israel might be a ruse, and their true course unknown."

"We should not allow such intervening risk, Narciso. Simplified, Trovarto and the scientists must escape. To where is not important; all paths ultimately terminate at your feet."

In hearing Tagliabue's words, Esposito's grin grew slightly wider, his eyes focused slightly further. "Our contact at Ismailiyah may be useful."

"I will make sure of it."

"I think it is time, don't you?" Monsignor Trovarto's low voice finally interrupted a taciturn intercom system, one that had been silent with anxiety for only a few minutes, save for one short directive from Cairo's regional controller before Commander Jeanette Montluc deactivated the jet's radios and transponder beacon.

She turned to him with a concerned expression. "*Es-tu sûr?*"

"*Bien sûr,*" he replied with a relaxed, assured tone.

Montluc, a sharp brunette with stark blue eyes, was a French Armée de l'Air Rafale jock stationed in Kandahar. She pressed the cabin's intercom switch and spoke authoritatively. "Secure yourselves immediately; evasive maneuvering begins in one minute."

Chris Miller never blinked or changed position. He continued staring blankly forward. Dao Ming checked his restraining belt, and then her own. Matt did the same while tapping Dao's right shoulder. "Evasive maneuvers?"

She turned around, "It could not be a reactive measure. There would be no warning. This is proactive."

On time, the muted roar of the twin Rolls Royce turbofans went silent, and a dramatic forward weight-shift involuntarily planted their foreheads on their knees. From his view out the window Matt knew the pilot, for all practical purposes, slammed on the brakes, sending the nosecone skyward, allowing it to rapidly descend within a very short distance, and more importantly, time. The jet was halfway to Port Said when Commander Montluc executed her relatively G-tolerant version of Pugachev's Cobra maneuver; a skill-demanding stunt placing great stress on an airframe. Few aircraft were capable of it. Her 'old' Rafale made the cut. Stall warnings blared from Bitchin' Bob, the jet's computerized warning system. Highlighted messages flashed on the screens, and the yoke violently shook. All of which she anticipated and ignored. Montluc's concentration remained unmolested until...

"Father!" She looked right.

Two things happened in rapid succession: Monsignor Trovarto's left inner ear violently pulsated, propelling him into an excruciating seizure. Montluc caught a peripheral glimpse of him compressing it, wincing, but she kept her focus on the instrument screen and the extremely pitched horizon. Bob's terse altitude warnings counted down in the background. "500, 400, 300... Pull Up! Pull Up!"

The other issue occurred simultaneously within the radar towers at both Cairo International Airport and Al Ismailiyah Air Base, both 40 miles away in opposite directions. Minimum Safe Altitude Warnings flashed on the datablocks of their scopes, and startling alarms blared. In disbelief, Cairo's Air Traffic Control (ATC) frantically radioed, expecting an eminent crash. Ismailiyah's controller, on the other hand, anticipated such a maneuver and alerted the single pilot already scrambled towards the ramp.

Bouncing on broken concrete, dust and sand pitting his sunglasses, he peered down onto the screen of his phone as his hands shielded it from the intense rays overhead. Orders to splash a business jet. He cocked a thin grin. It wasn't his first, and if these sorts of missions were publicized, he would have been an "ace" several times over. Chigaru enjoyed the light work; his only *real* opponents existed in a simulator. This would be his largest and fastest target to date; something he savored as a new classification, yet all his contact relayed was "a newer business jet" and he didn't think much else of it. He had destroyed nearly a dozen private jets, mostly opium runners not cooperating with Mukhtar Lal, and a few legitimate executives who simply made an unfortunate business decision. Even so, Chigaru's lacking urgency displayed a certain hubris renowned by his comrades. They envied his position as the most frequently utilized pilot in the force.

Against gravity's tremendous strain, Matt twisted his head around just enough to see the port wingtip flexed backward beyond the window's top, bouncing violently in its own vapor trail. A normal flight attitude slowly returned, and the aircraft rapidly accelerated towards the deck. Trovarto's headache intensified. He struggled to keep an eye on the horizon, attempting to stave off increased motion sickness, but his inner ear betrayed all signals. An intense nausea crept into him.

"Must you fly this low?" He moaned.

"Monsignor, *Oui*. The Nile delta is only eight meters above sea level. There are no mountains or hills to make a radar shadow, so yes, we must descend to the lowest possible altitude. It was my best to simulate a crash for the ATCs. If we are detected again, even the slightest snapshot, our true course will be exposed."

"And which course is that?" She heard from over her right shoulder. Dao Ming stood in the doorway struggling to maintain balance, unfazed by the astonishing cockpit view—the fantastic rush barely four meters below her feet.

"Towards the northwest." Trovarto strained. "Corsica... to rendezvous with our mutual friend."

"Madam Ming, you must return to your seat at once and fasten your belt! Instruct everyone, *s'il vous plaît*. I must make any maneuver necessary for the next fifteen minutes."

Dao shook her head, took another look across the horizon, and vacated flight deck. After relaying Captain Montluc's directive to the others, she turned towards Chris, who was maintaining his vacuous forward gaze.

"We're not going to Israel."

Chris finally broke his stare and looked into her eyes with a certain foreknowledge. "I didn't think so. It's too convenient, too predictable. Besides, the Nile Delta is beneath us. We're headed west, aren't we?"

"Yes. Northwest, to Corsica. Remember the person who requested you to Cairo?"

Chris searched his mind. The man with the French accent. The man that thought it safer to leave Emily in the hands of a complete stranger. He clenched his teeth, and a fist. He was incognizant of his physical reaction—the empty rage. Slowly it eased. He realized, indeed, Emily was in danger, but if she had come to Cairo, he thought; the variables and probabilities overwhelmed him. He took a deep breath. *At least she is alive. It could be worse, much worse.*

"What is he to us?" Chris asked with a slight tinge of sarcasm gracing his tone. "The new leader of the *Brotherhood*?"

Dao grabbed Chris' chin and made him look at her. "I do not know much of this man, but I know this; he is one of its primary financial engines. I believe he owns this aircraft and another similar to it, although—"

A sharp thud on the portside wing shuddered the fuselage. *"Mon Dieu!"* All eyes peered through the windows and were relieved to discover nothing unusual. No apparent damage. Jeanette Montluc feverishly surveyed the wing and her controls. Everything felt normal. That is, normal for a passenger jet travelling at treetop level, 600 knots indicated.

"What was it?" Trovarto asked, shielding his mouth with an open sick bag, expecting the inevitable.

"I do not know. We did not hit anything; I do not see any damage. Too, er, sharp for a bird strike, and there are no remains."

"I was afraid of-a this."

"Forgiveness, *Père*, I do not think it was an attack. We would not exist. The problem is that I cannot activate our radar, else we would become detectable to ATC and other aircraft."

"He is with us; leave it to Him."

Montluc glanced at Trovarto and grimaced. *"Père*, you should not be here in this condition."

"La veritá."

Trovarto unbuckled his harness and retreated rearward. On his way to the aft lavatory, he staggered beside Matthew's seat and grabbed his shoulder. "Go see Captain Montluc. I believe she could-a use your help."

"Christ sake's Father, you don't look so good!"

"It is-a the Ménière's, you know." Trovarto covered his mouth and continued towards the rear.

Matt unbuckled and climbed into the flight deck, to the surprise of Montluc. "Er, can I be of assistance?"

Matt looked through the windshield in amazement. "Looks like your hands are full. Jesus! Haven't seen this in a while!"

"Yes."

"The Monsignor told me to come up here—to help."

"Then have a seat, Commander." Montluc stumbled, occupied with the necessary level of concentration for her maneuvering, and also with Matt's playfulness.

He strapped in and familiarized himself with the controls. "You know if they scramble a fighter, flying this low is pointless, right?"

"That would be incorrect, Commander. You are seated in a classified Gulfstream ERCA Special prototype commissioned by my uncle. Extended range, carbon topsides and graphene reinforced spars, aerobatic-enabled with specified safeguards removed. Her topsides are intentionally coated azure. Engines cruise with an excusable Doppler profile. We must reach the sea for maximum stealth effect. She is also the first such provisionally-approved large jet for a single pilot, although I enjoy the extra set of eyes."

"Just beautiful."

"*Merci.*"

"The plane, I mean." Matt pretended to stumble.

Montluc batted a lash. "Any flight experience, Commander?"

"Zero. Well, I don't think you'd count simulator time."

"Which simulator?"

"Navy friend snuck me in to the Hornet sims at Pensacola several years back. Just a couple hours for fun. Crashed mostly. F-18s, you know."

"I know what they are, Commander. I have time in them. Spanish exchange. Two days. Excellent, of course; not my favorite." She smiled. "Two hours is not enough to be of any flight use to me, ah but your eyes and ears will do nicely."

Matt blushed. "Soo... how did you get into flying these?"

"I learned that flying the big jets was not for me. Slow, always the big city airports. Boring. And for this I fail the interviews. They ask about the flight efficiency systems; I refused to compromise pilot control. Flying for Monsieur Du Rennes is far more interesting for someone with my skills. No?

The commercial program automates the cockpit to save a few Euro. We have seen what happens when a pilot is not in full control at all times. And they call this safety improvements. It is simply a matter of time before we are all passengers in automated drones, flown by a centralized command center subject to cyberattack. Our militaries have been perfecting it for years. *Non merci!*"

"Right." Matthew sighed, knowing he was out of his league with this woman in this setting. "So, what was that bump a few moments ago?"

"I do not know. Something must have hit us, but I see nothing; the aircraft shows no errors and no damage. I felt it on the yoke; a small quiver, the smallest dip to port."

Matt noticed Montluc's firm grip on the controls and the intense concentration she displayed. Her command of the aircraft impressed him. As well, Montluc's dossier on Matthew impressed her. An American SEAL, sitting next to her, admiring her skills. Her father never dreamed...

*   *   *

"Lost?" Captain Chigaru rolled his eyes at the apparent lack of competency displayed by Al Ismailiyah's radar operator. "Then is it a crash, or no?"

A voice hesitantly cackled over the radio's secured link, "Not confirmed."

"Listen you imbecile, I have not the luxury of waiting until a live report from Channel 1. Tell me everything you know."

An uncomfortable pause, eight seconds at the most, was four seconds longer than Chigaru felt reasonable before demanding a response. An additional four seconds passed before the nervous voice returned.

"The trajectory indicates reduction in altitude from Flight Level Two One Zero to Sea Level over a distance of one kilometer, indicating a terminal trajectory, except—" The controller lifted off the key and another unacceptable lapse of time accrued.

"Except what? Over."

Again, four seconds ticked away before the voice returned.

"Two calls have been received by police services requesting information regarding an extremely fast, low-flying aircraft. The first call originated from a farmer located four kilometers southwest of Al Kubra. The second followed in less than two minutes, described the same aircraft, and it came from some *marā'* in Muhallat Misir."

"It does not matter if it came from a woman, fool!"

Chigaru knew every city, every town, and every small village throughout the Nile Basin. Without a moment's thought, he dropped the stick, banking hard towards the west and lit his Falcon's afterburner.

"Listen to me carefully Ismailiyah, what was the time of that last summons?"

"Police records indicate eight minutes elapsed, but—"

Captain Chigaru didn't wait for the rest of the controller's statement—the crucial part suggesting a few minutes' lag between the first moment of the call, the conversation, and the time logged at the police station. He lowered the volume on his headset, concentrating on the western horizon as he accelerated beyond the sound barrier.

A clap of thunder echoed through the Basin, shaking the foundations of every building within a 30-kilometer radius. Emergency telephone lines exploded with frantic calls decreeing every manner of apocalyptic prophecy from Armageddon, to nuclear war, to the return of Set. The unauthorized speed also caught the attention of every air base controller, and ergo, every base commander around the Basin. Without their knowledge, which of course meant without their consent, alerts were also transmitted via hidden proprietary hardware to an undisclosed location in the United States, who preferred immediate tactical knowledge of its arms customers. These alerts were, in fact, quite routine given the planned training exercises of these nations, except the supersonic flight outside a normal training area, let alone over a populated region, triggered a flash seismic advisory to the United States Geological Survey. Moments later, corroborative reports found their way to a small office in the Pentagon, and that office, on relevant occasions, shared its information with an even smaller office located just off Corridor 7, fourth floor, A-Ring.

"What city is that just up ahead?" Matt asked.

"Rasheed, and thirty seconds after it, the Mediterranean, at which point I must descend to three meters."

"In *this* thing? No way!"

"Relax, Commander. This aircraft employs a highly accurate altitude module, capable of maintaining our desired height within one meter, average. Elevator reactions compensate drafts and ground effects within 20 milliseconds detection."

"Please," Matt panted, "Just don't take your hands of the controls to prove it to me."

Montluc smiled.

Chigaru's F-16 thundered across the basin towards the west-northwest on intercept. "My calculation has them within sixty kilometers, yet my radar does not detect them. Why is this? The latest pulse-Doppler is useless!" Captain Chigaru cursed over the radio.

"They were reported at ten meters' altitude. The radar your American friends sold you cannot differentiate certain aircraft at that altitude, Captain."

Montluc checked the panel clock. "In five minutes, we turn west."

"Why?" Matt asked.

"It is likely that someone on the ground saw us and reported to the authorities, in which case an interceptor would be launched. If it is a Mirage, they must fly very high to catch us, otherwise they are not much faster than this aircraft. If they sortie one of your F-16s, they are 50% faster at low altitude, except the range is limited. In either situation, they could have our current heading and plot intercept; therefore I should turn away as soon as there is the least chance of visual detection, 80 kilometers from the coastline over the Alexandria Canyon. We must hope that the fishermen pay us no account."

Matthew Jacobson nervously stared at the bright yellow digital clock in the lower-right corner of the instrument panel as the seconds slowly counted. Five minutes, and barely two had elapsed. He toggled one of the displays to a rear-facing camera. It showed the ongoing shockwave of air shattering the sea, creating a whitewashed wake. He watched it for another minute to see if Montluc noticed.

"Excuse me," he pointed. Won't this make it easier for someone to see us?"

Montluc glanced at the screen and sighed faintly in disappointment. "Yes, but we have no choice. I decrease velocity, they catch us. I increase altitude, they see us electronically, and this includes detection by Egyptian weapons systems."

"Better that their weapons don't see us." Matt said, looking at the clock. "Thirty seconds to go."

The passage of time seemed to slow further in grand contrast to the ferocity of movement against a timeless sea. Montluc's anxiety peaked when it came time to dip the port wing without increasing altitude. As smooth as the fly-by-wire system assisted her efforts, the wingtips flexibility whipped against the turbulent effect of the Mediterranean's endless variations. She let it drop to within a single meter of the whitecaps and remained sharply focused through the window, rapidly adjusting to every slight oscillation returned through the yoke.

"Tell me just before the compass marks bearing Two Seven Zed, *s'il vous plaît*. I cannot turn to look."

The wing crested the spray of an odd wave, and Captain Montluc instinctively reacted by easing the roll a few degrees.

"Almost there..." Matt said with a pensive voice. "Now!"

Montluc leveled the wings and set the autopilot's heading. Due west. "Perfect. Now we must remain on this heading for the next fifteen minutes. Maybe then we have a reasonable chance of escape."

Again, Matthew fixated on the clock, unable to transition to any other occupation. The seconds dripped slowly, annoyingly. Four minutes drained away and a speck of white on the horizon to starboard caught Matt's periphery. He scanned for confirmation, rubbing his eyes and the dance of sunlight sparkles across the horizon's curve.

"Please tell me you did not see a boat." Montluc pined.

"I'm not sure. I thought I saw something, but not anymore."

The fuel warning system had been sounding for five minutes when Captain Chigaru received radio concerning the possible sighting of a low-flying aircraft 50 kilometers west of his position. He ruminated for several moments, weighing the prospects of failure against the source or his mission directive.

"Your fuel is below one thousand kilos; you will not make base even if fortune finds them."

"Fool!" Chigaru shouted. "I have plenty to intercept and cruise to the fishbeds of Matruh!"

The radio remained silent while the Egyptian falcon arced westward at 10,000 feet, scanning the seas for what should be and easy sighting of a commuter jet. Yet, his eyes seemingly could not cooperate. There was no heat or sooty smoke trail, or brilliant reflections in the sunlight, just the vast, timeless, cerulean deep.

Several minutes passed, and Chigaru reassessed his situation. To continue at his present velocity meant risking a return to base, or the shoreline itself. He would definitely be bailing somewhere off the coast, and he knew of two patrol boats stationed in Rommel Bay at Mersa Matruh. Command would not appreciate his efforts no matter his mission's classification. Losing an expensive aircraft was not worth whatever target escaping his homeland. In addition, the tourists were not to be disturbed in the middle of sunbathing hours by a military mission. Captain Chigaru had made up his mind after glancing at the fuel gauge one last time. 500 kilos. He might still make Matruh on that, he thought, and then he saw it. Between Langmuir streaks he had previously discounted, and somehow masked for a few crucial minutes behind the left rear seam of his canopy, a tiny white speck of wake turbulence. He passed them!

"You see that, don't you? Two o'clock high?" Matt pointed.

Captain Montluc immediately tapped the cabin's intercom system. "Alert! Please tighten your belts immediately. Extreme maneuvers in five seconds."

At once, the blissful whine of the engines turned to a noticeable roar. The increase in gravity became more than merely detectible as Montluc jerked the yoke back momentarily, increasing altitude enough to make a sharp roll to starboard without dipping the wing into the drink. It was a hard right break for 90 degrees.

"Back under him and out to sea—perfect." Matt laughed with a hint of dire sarcasm.

Chigaru took a second look and saw the break. He frantically scanned to his starboard rear quarter, expecting the Gulfstream to emerge. His left hand slipped the throttle back.

His thick black mustache twitched, and he dropped the stick to the right. He stared at the heads-up display and could not believe his sidewinders' inability to lock.

"They are there!" He shouted into his mask. "Cannons then." *Just one pass is all I need.*

And then it came—the rain of gunfire dotting the ocean surface in front of and around the Gulfstream. Montluc slung the yoke wildly to the left, not mindful of maximum g-forces, allowing the jet's computers to sort that information. Two more bursts of cannon fire flayed the sea.

"We will not survive this!" She cried.

Another burst, and the aircraft shuttered, absorbing multiple impacts atop the port wing. Jet fuel erupted from several places, aerating in a mist, dangerously streaming to-wards the fuselage's port engine. Captain Chigaru smiled wide at the sight of the fuel cloud, and the small chunks of debris flaking off the wing. He took another glance at his fuel gauges and broke off towards Matruh, reducing the throttle for maximum efficiency.

Bob was more than bitchin'. Warning lights flooded the cockpit as Montluc struggled with her emergency management decisions. The cloud of jet fuel had not ceased streaming from the port wing. The catastrophic danger of explosion was eminent if it saturated the port engine's intake. She was unaware of her assailant's position, but the firing had ceased. *Will he return? What to do?*

The frustrating fury overwhelmed her briefly before she decided that if her attacker were indeed closing for the coup de grace, efforts to save the plane would indeed be futile. She yanked back on the yoke, climbed several hundred feet in an instant and flicked on the radar. To her amazement, the scope indicated a single contact, as expected, yet it was rapidly moving in the opposite direction, already ten kilometers aft.

"He must think we are destroyed!" Montluc cried.

Matt looked at her with a smile before the warnings overrode his relief. "Are we?"

Montluc frantically activated the proper controls to shut down the port engine, and then another few commands to pump what fuel remained in the port wing into the central tanks. She took a long hard look backwards through the port window and assessed the damage.

"The tanks have self-sealing bladders, except they are not made for multiple 20mm hits. The autopilot is activated; I must go back and make a closer inspection."

Unbuckling her harness, Montluc climbed out of the cockpit and hustled to a window. The eyes of all in the cabin went wide. She surveyed the damage: two half-dollar sized holes gushing fuel, with the spray trailing just underneath the turbine's intake, and a cracked and wavering spoiler. *Likely hydraulics issues and other internal destruction.* She could not see the wing's underside, and it would have alarmed her further. One of the flap hinges had been decimated, along with part of the landing gear's door. *Landing will be questionable. Impossible that the fly-by-wire computer was programmed for this scenario*, she thought.

"Catastrophic?" Dao Ming asked.

Montluc turned to her. "Unknown. We have been shot, so yes, there are issues. We are in no immediate danger, thank God."

Chris sat forward, his speech slightly broken and nervous. "W-what about the Monsignor? He pointed towards the aft lavatory. "He—"

Montluc didn't wait for Chris to finish, she ran to the back and rapidly smacked the lavatory's door with an open hand. "*Père?*"

Air to the Throne

Captain Montluc pounded the door with her right hand until she felt it sting sharply under the knuckles. She tugged at the handle. Locked. She reached into a trouser pocket and retrieved a multi-tool, similar to a robust Swiss Army knife, designed specifically for the Gulfstream. Her selected appliance was a thin stainless-steel dowel, and she inserted into a discrete hole just above the lavatory's door handle, unlocking its mechanism. Monsignor Trovarto spilled out of the doorway, unconscious, with traces of regurgitation dripping from his mouth.

"*Mon Dieu!*" Montluc yelped, covering her mouth.

Dao Ming jumped from her seat and raced down the aisle towards the others. On arrival, she helped Montluc drag Trovarto to the nearby sofa and placed him supine upon it, clutching his wrist and checking respiration.

Montluc sighed. "His heart is strong, and he is breathing." She turned to Dao. "Can you monitor him? I need to go, um—" She pointed forward.

"Yes, please, go fly the plane!"

Montluc turned back to face everyone in the cabin. "I need someone to monitor that wing. If it worsens, I need to know about it."

Chris looked up at her. "If it becomes worse than it already is, my guess is you *will* know about it."

Montluc pursed her lips and made haste to the flight deck. Dao, on the other hand, smiled sarcastically.

"Did that make you feel better?" She asked.

Chris cocked his head. "Yes, I suppose it did."

"Good, now please come here and assist with our friend."

Upon Montluc's return, Matthew slipped off one of his headset's earphones. "I appreciate your confidence, but *this...*"

He pointed around the cockpit towards several warning beacons.

"No actual flight experience, wing shot to hell, and we're on one engine out in the middle of the sea. I mean, Jesus!"

She slid over the center console and back into her seat. "The Monsignor has experienced a seizure and is unconscious. I found him in the lavatory. If you wish to pray to Jesus, do so for him; the plane will fly itself all the way to Corsica should I desire. Land itself too."

"Oh—I, uh..."

"Did not know? Of course you did not know; you were here."

Montluc busily set about extinguishing the myriad of yellow and red rectangles blinking on the glass instrument panel. She then concocted a new visual flight plan via satellite. Before submitting it, she reignited the port engine and adjusted the autopilot for Flight Level 105 (10,500 feet) heading 310°, speed 350 knots.

Matt started to inquire, but Montluc anticipated. "Any higher and there is a decompression risk. We do not know the full integrity of the fuselage. Any faster and friction may rip apart the wing. See this?"

She pointed at the distance to destination marker on the navigation screen. "Over one thousand miles, nautical; three hours, estimated. I must fly in Italian airspace in case we incur a problem."

Matt cringed. "A lot can happen in three hours." He checked his wristwatch. *We arrived in Egypt just over four hours ago!*

• • •

Brigadier General Barbara Anne Tomlinson, in her late fifties after almost 40 years continuous service in the United States Air Force, except for two extended "familial" medical leaves, ascended the political ranks in an unwritten, but unsurprising way. A discriminated female officer had two choices, and those options were only granted to candidates displaying exceptional leadership skills and lengthy accomplishment records in the first place. Some took the seemingly less nefarious route of granting sexual favors, and those ascendants were never granted commands of strategic importance or political value. The Pentagon placated them with an exorbitant compensation package upon meeting minimum qualification, and what they craved from infancy—what their parents could not provide in most cases—security; knowing their commands were safe from transfer or mandatory retirement unless previously agreed, or until 30 years' time in service. Historically, these officers transition from well drilling to diamond digging by the age of 40, about the time their desirability reverts to the upcoming mineworkers.

Then there are the other types such as General Tomlinson, whose archetypal elite Philly 500 upbringing underscored the value of achieving and maintaining prominence. The 500 professed as prospectors of leverage, and she became quite adept at it. While her barrack sisters serviced anyone on the promotions board—the licentious types, and there always existed at least one—she was waiting patiently by a window or a cracked doorway snapping photos of the poor bastard. Once she made major, her skills transitioned to increasingly more complex schemes, trapping officers in all ranks committing egregious acts of corruption: contractual nepotism or cronyism, excessive abuse of position and power, misappropriations, embezzlement, acts unbecoming, undeniable treason—nearly anything within the scope of an officer. Tomlinson had a sixth sense for detection, too; a gift for misfortune-telling. Her assets quickly compounded.

Several years ago, her dice finally froze at the crap table when she crossed its stickman, then a three-star general named Edward Tutlow. For the last decade, he topped a purposely-obscured branch of the Air Force. So obscure in fact that it occupied nothing but a closed suite of five rooms in a rarely-visited section of the Pentagon's inner-most ring on the fourth floor above ground.

The office was Eisenhower's nightmare realized. Its existence was born from decades of off-record military-industrial executive rendezvous on countless exclusive golf clubs, private Polynesian resort islands, Arabian palaces, and mega-yachts of exotic registry docked in Port Hercules. Its mission is to facilitate the creation of demand, consolidate and control manufacturers, and eliminate threats wherever they may exist. The industrial complex's controllers, collusive corporate ghosts, comprised less than two dozen pre-determined executives. Their contractors were routinely kept ignorant of their true purpose, and the Pentagon housed a couple well-kept office administrators led under Gen. Edward Tutlow, a cover under the Air Force's Communications Command. All information flowed through his office, includeing top-clearance classified and unlogged rummaging of the highest ordered surveillance stored at the Utah Data Center.

During Tutlow's first few years, his division created more wealth transfer from the lower American classes and ancillary markets to more government military contractors and their suppliers than any single politician or industrialist had in the past century. Conflicts became smaller in geography, yet increasingly numerous and interminable. Expertly adept at manipulating both sides, Tutlow eventually learned to leave just enough enemies behind as kindling should manufacturing reach saturation. Moreover, Tutlow & Company became favored by the global consortium, constantly showered with exotic gifts and favors—never investigated—from every corner.

Naturally, the corporate world produced a fair percentage of non-compliant ambitious types who overstepped, threatened, or for any number of reasons, wouldn't conform. When one of them became a noticeable hindrance, a potential whistleblower, or simply too greedy, a messenger would be dispatched. Their messages took many forms; whatever necessary to produce the desired result. Tutlow's assets were seemingly everywhere and nowhere, only everyone came to understand that they weren't mythological creatures; they representted inevitability.

Following an evening filled with special reserve libations and blonde little darlings as their accoutrements, (then) Major Tomlinson staked Tutlow's window for the perfect frame. She pressed the shutter button, the flash popped, and, before three seconds of blindness elapsed, the painful clamp of a man's hand cut off circulation to her left bicep. She struggled momentarily, but the effort was futile against an expert handler. He grappled her inside to face the general as soon as he had dressed. Ten minutes passed, a knock on the door, and she was thrown onto a silk-embroidered armchair, sans camera, which was handed to Tutlow. His eyes glinted above an elfin grin as he proceeded to extract and expose her camera's film.

You of all people can appreciate your current situation, Major Tomlinson.

She would never forget his confidence. Rather than throw her to the wolves—those she personally made rabid—he cleared the room and handed her the keys to Armageddon.

I've an eye for the proper talent, and I've watched your performances since your second miraculous promotion. Yours is leveraged negotiation. Mine is foresight.

General Tutlow measured two glasses of Remy Martin Rare cognac, handed her one, and sat in a matching armchair opposite hers. After an uncomfortable and abbreviated warming period, she nervously sipped at the glass, painfully unaware of its lineage, complexities, and suffice, its cost. He sat and observed her fidgeting, her distracted focus, her dread.

"So what do you want?" She asked.

Retrospect. A dozen years later, Tomlinson barely recalled Tutlow's briefing regarding corporate partnering involved within the military—all the perks, the bribery, the skullduggery, the murder. *Murder!* That's what she remembered most. Vivid flashes of staged beheadings and cattle drives to sanguine pits. Tutlow conveyed his strongest case to join the command willingly, wantonly, for the other option was termination. The velvet warmth of the cordial rinsed the bitter pill—the fact she'd been bested. He offered her a seat beside his at the negotiation table, and the life that accompanied it. Through a labyrinthine corporate shell structure and strong-arm tactics, Tutlow had amassed sizable holdings in all but a few of the major arms manufacturers, as well as their raw material suppliers, yet his name and quite of few others would never grace the pages of Forbes.

Someone else will do it if we don't.

It had been sixteen years since that meeting, and her expertise in handling his affairs appreciated to the point that Tutlow was comfortable with his upcoming mandatory retirement as the seventh head of Blue Ops; a command born during Lyndon B. Johnson's second term. Tomlinson's plush leather chair offered little comfort to her pulsating temples. The office had been completely sanitized hours before, except the lingering tincture had not completely dissipated. As well, the flashes of Tutlow's execution replayed with relentless frequency, and the rash from her bindings itched. She stared across her desk towards the dry bar on the back wall where a single bottle of cognac stood out amongst all the other spirits. Laid across her desk were action reports covering the previous afternoon's infiltration, and a bulleted brief condensing Jack Kattner's presentation of Doctor Miller's soft drive. Attached to it was a list of potential militarized functions, all of the highest order in classification. On top of those reports was the file containing Canned Sandman, the botched operation utilizing Commander Matthew Jacobson as observer at Amerimem Industries. The opaque whirlwind obscured clear thought, and she struggled through the logic of it all. What puzzled her the most was the Russians' fervor—revenge, perhaps—and she possessed no leverage or enticements. Not yet.

The intercom signal flashed. "What is it, Nancy?"

"Colonel Osterhoudt on the red line, General. Gave code Ashen Cloud."

"Thanks Nancy." Tomlinson switched lines. "Commodore?"

"How ya holding up, Babs?"

"Don't call me that."

"Still the high-ridin' bitch."

"You've no idea how much I can—"

"Look, you said you wanted contact as soon as I acquired Jacobson's key. I have it, and I am in route to you, but I also have something else you might be interested in."

"I'm only interested in yesterday's infiltrators."

"Related." Osterhoudt paused briefly. "We've intercepted traffic in Egypt reporting seismic anomalies and citizen reports concerning damage consistent with transonic flight over the Nile Basin. When our people made inquiry, the usual back channels, they made inference to an experimental-registered light jet illegally departing Cairo International."

"And you think that is Jacobson's aircraft? There is no way to know if he and the rest were on board."

"Ma'am, there are additional reports. An assault took place at the Palace Mena in Giza. Automatic gunfire, explosions, and casualties in the dozens... messy. Fifty minutes afterward, that jet bolted, then later reported missing en route to Tel Aviv. Ten minutes after that, the first reports of sonic damage, and several minutes after that, one of our spotter boats off Alexandria saw what he described as commuter jet and an F-16 going at it twelve miles from his position."

"Then they are dead."

"Negative. The spotter never observed a splash and made a special note of it. Said the Falcon traipsed southwest towards the coast."

"Twelve miles away, Commodore?"

"Alright, sweetie. You feel there's not enough empirical data to devise a concrete strategy. I've heard that excuse my entire career. I go by instinct, and my gut says Jacobson's on that jet and not dead."

Tomlinson's fists tightened to the point that her fingernails risked breaking the skin of her palms. "Well, Commodore, there's only one way to know for sure."

"Repeat, I'm en route."

● ● ●

A faint, sickening moan from that back of the jet's cabin turned heads and, contrary to convention, conjured wide eyes and smiles from Rocco, Anastasia and the brute sentry. Monsignor Trovarto grasped the left side of his throbbing skull, compressing the ear in excruciating pain. His eyelids were heavy, vision blurred, muscles sore, and a nauseous disorientation made any attempts at changing posture a non-starter.

"I should not fly. That is-a truth, no? You hear this, *Fratellanza*?" He struggled to laugh. "Ugh."

Dao held an instant cold compress against his forehead. "Remain motionless, please."

"Bless you, Doctor Ming. Passed out, I think. It is-a embarrassing affliction I have."

"Apology is not necessary." She maintained pressure. "Nature needs no excuse or atonement. I accept it entirely and adjust accordingly."

Trovarto's forced smile and bleary eyes welled as much from her sentiments as his soaring level of discomfort. "We seem to have-a slowed down; the engines and-a the air. Where are we?"

"What do you remember?" Dao asked.

"Besides the view of a mirror and faucet? Nothing. Except-a maybe a gradual turn left—west—and then the blackness."

"This aircraft was attacked by a military jet. Egyptian Air Force according to Captain Montluc. The left wing is damaged, therefore the decrease in velocity." She glanced at a live GPS map displayed on the rear bulkhead. "Our current position is fifty kilometers southeast of city Messina."

Trovarto wrenched his head and squinted through the large window on his left. "I cannot see it, but-a the volcano Etna is-a down there, no?"

Dao peered through the window. "Yes. There is steam escaping the crater, or clouds. It is difficult to determine from this distance. It is beautiful, nonetheless."

The slight motion by Trovarto triggered yet more searing agony, and he dropped back to the pillows. Rocco Hammett had been fixated on the port wing, eyeing the two cannon holes for any sign of further deterioration. His adopted sister, Anastasia, grasped his arm tightly to turn his concentration towards the Monsignor. His continued suffering, whenever she latched onto his emotion, caused palpitations of her own; the curse of intense empathy. Her eyes watered, her breathing became labored, gasping.

"Please!" She screamed in a whisper.

Rocco turned around and gazed across the island. A faint, chalky odor fumed along with an almost-inaudible hiss. A moment later, Trovarto's movements ceased. His hands fell away and his eyelids closed. Dao panicked. She bent down to check his breathing while grabbing his wrist for the pulse. A telltale wisp or air; a faint throb at the carpal tunnel.

"There is nothing to worry about, Doctor Ming." Anastasia said, catching her breath. "He is simply asleep."

Dao spun around in disbelief. The betrayal of empirical science; her central discipline. "How do you know this?"

Anastasia shifted her eyes towards her brother.

"He will sleep as long as I wish it, Doctor." Rocco said, concentrating deeply on Trovarto.

Anastasia got up and joined Dao beside the Monsignor. "It is one of his gifts."

"Explain, please."

"There is no word for assisted narcolepsy, Doctor, but that's what he does—one of the things he does."

"The other?"

"Suggestion. While dreaming, mostly. Sometimes while conscious, except the person must be in a pensive/submissive state, not aggressive."

Chris turned around and listened. It was the first curios moment he had since Cairo, a break from the shock, depression and melancholy. They all noticed him.

"Sounds familiar," he said.

"It should not surprise you, Doctor," said Rocco. "Our father was very close to unlocking the full potential of, and I resist using this ridiculous word, the paranormal. Your decode machine is the key to understanding it all."

Chris reflexively inhaled, startled at a thought. He felt around the underside of his chair and was relieved when he touched upon the briefcase containing the laptop. He hadn't given it much thought since snatching it off the podium. He let out a sigh. "He was looking for the common connection."

"Yes." Anastasia said. "And he found it. You... found it."

The craggy southeastern coastlines of Corsica passed underneath the fuselage several minutes earlier, and its central mountain ranges were now underneath. Captain Montluc had been on the radio, coordinating her approach without calling attention to the aircraft's emergency condition. She had also called ahead to the hangar, which relayed special instructions upon arrival. It had been an hour since Rocco placed Monsignor Trovarto in a peaceful slumber, and since the cabin's Landing Soon indicator flashed across the seatback monitors, he slowly reduced his focus. Gently, Trovarto awakened to Dao's helpful embrace.

"We are landing in a moment, Monsignor. Please, you must take a seat."

With moderate difficulty, he collapsed in an adjacent recliner and strapped on the seatbelt. Rocco was seated just in front of him. He turned around and smiled. Trovarto tapped his shoulder. "*Molte grazie.*"

Montluc looked over towards Matt. "That is Calvi–St. Catherine's ahead. See it?"

Matt nodded.

"Only when I instruct you, lower the landing gear. Okay?"

"Affirmative."

"The knob will glow green, but I need to delay activation."

Eschewing the throttle's automated function, she manually eased their levers to fifteen percent and dipped the nose, aligning with the numbers on Runway 36. Gently, the airspeed decreased. Her hand moved to the flaps and she started to lower them before catching herself.

"What's the matter?" Matt asked.

"I am hesitant because of the damage. Activation could cause catastrophe." An air pocket shuddered the cockpit. "*Merde!*" She flinched, looking at the port wing.

"Well, what's the worst-case scenario?"

Montluc snarled, "Worst case scenario is the wing disintegrates. Does that work for you?"

"No!"

Montluc's eyes darted about the instrument panel. "We do this, how do you say it, old school."

She stepped on the right rudder pedal while fighting the yoke left. The jet buffeted in the increased drag, and the airspeed predictably dropped. Bitchin' Bob didn't like it, and remained silent for the exercise, opting for a visual approach attitude scolding on the head's up display. The aircraft was traveling towards the runway's centerline, but it wasn't pointed at it.

"Lady, I don't like this!" Matt whined, looking across the nose cone."

The landing gear knob suddenly flashed green and Matt raised his hand upon it.

"Wait!" Montluc yelled.

"I wasn't going to—"

"*Un moment!*"

The cockpit voice alert system started blaring, *Sink Rate, Sink Rate, 400... Pull Up!*

"NOW!" Montluc shouted.

Matt dropped the lever and the turbulent roar of increased drag combined with the high-pitched whine of hydraulic motors. They felt a reassuring thunk when the nose gear locked and the landing gear horn blasted. Montluc struggled with fully concentrating on the difficult slip maneuver and glanced across the panel towards the indicators. The left light remained red.

"But I heard it. I *felt* it!" She whispered.

"What? What is it?" Matt yelled.

"Look at your left display." Montluc instructed. "See the menu button at the top marked Views?"

"Affirmative. Oh, I know where you're going with this."

"*Oui.* Get to the undercarriage. There are four different cameras. Yes, there."

300...

"It looks down to me!" Matt shouted.

"Yes." Montluc paused. "Better to crash here than in the water, I think!"

Sink Rate... 200...

Montluc fought the controls as the shifting coastal breezes increased the approach level of difficulty. She was travelling faster than she wanted, and any movements became exaggerated. Her focus tunneled at the numbers; motions reflexive, wild.

Sink Rate... 100... 50...

At 50 feet, Montluc, dropped the throttles completely while snapping the rudder neutral and the yoke straight. The aircraft instantaneously responded in perfect alignment to the runway.

"*Aidez-nous, Christ!*"

The no-flare planting came on the later side of the ground effect arc, and the tires slapped the tarmac hard with an ear-piercing roar. Montluc closed her eyes for a second, praying the landing gear not to collapse, feeling her way down the tarmac until the nose gear felt stable enough to tiller. The end of the runway came into view quicker than anticipated—even at that velocity—so she slammed on the brakes and reverse thrusters, sending her passengers tight against their restraints.

"Geez lady, this thing has a drop hook?" Matt said.

Montluc heard the round of claps from the cabin and took a deep breath. At the end of the runway, she swung wide and turned the jet completely around, then proceeded to a private hangar within a fenced section on the north side of the control tower. The large doors were already open, and inside waiting were two well-dressed and muscular men, maintaining tactical stances.

With the wheels chocked, Montluc began the shutdown procedure, activated the airstairs, and unbuckled her harness. The hangar doors activated as soon as the jet exhaust ceased.

"Well, Commander Jacobson. Thank you for your expert assistance. We should do this again sometime." She reached across and kissed him on both cheeks with a vibrant smile.

"Right. Well, a definite yes to *that*, but a hard pass on the whole gettin' shot up and nearly crashing part."

She giggled and slipped through the cockpit doorway ahead of him.

Rocco had taken position behind Trovarto, helping him to his feet. The normalized pressure, combined with the cessation of movement reduced the pain enough, and his balance slowly recouped. Montluc met them by the hatch while the airstairs unfurled. They didn't feel it at first, as their eyes betrayed their senses. The entire hangar floor descended twenty meters below ground, and a false floor slid overhead. Once the movement stopped, the passengers began debarking with the assistance of a sentry waiting at the bottom of the airstairs. Montluc and the other attendant remained behind to handle jet matters and await reassignment. She kissed and hugged each of them before they stepped down. She hugged Matt once more, and the embrace was only slightly longer than her others. Matt sensed something more in her eyes. There was no time to explore them.

At the bottom was an ultra-modern maintenance facility connected by three cavernous hangar spaces, one of which was occupied by another experimental jet being serviced by a small squad wearing white overalls. Two Range Rovers with open doors stood before a lighted tunnel that disappeared into dark, solid rock.

"Doctor Miller, please, this way. You, Doctor Ming, and Jacobson are to accompany me in this vehicle. The Monsignor and his young companions will travel in the other."

Matt stepped forward. "Who are you?"

The other driver rolled his eyes, a gesture Matt interpreted as rude. The first driver intervened.

"Please, we have fifteen minutes to Villa Regino, where your next conveyance awaits."

Trovarto raised his head with a stunned expression.

"*Non temere, Padre; breve viaggio.*" The driver said.

Trovarto pushed a smile. "Thanks be to God."

They set off down the tunnel, taking two corners as the elevation increased. Two massive steel doors swung open, allowing them to pass into the sunlight of a brilliant Corsican afternoon. The pathway terminated at a non-descript exit on the far northern boundary of the airport complex, into the bucolic outskirts of Calvi and its framable mountain backdrop. Eventually, the course changed eastward, and within minutes they entered a stone gateway protecting an orchard of olive trees intermixed with mature cork oaks, several of which were being harvested by middle-aged men adorned with thick, black mustaches and wielding light, broad axes. At the end of the driveway was a grand villa constructed of stone and cement walls, oak and iron shutters, and a clay tile roof, probably dating to the mid-Genoese era, 17th century. The Rovers parked in a crushed stone lot adjacent the villa along an extremely tall hedge that masked a fortified wall.

Matt was one of the first to step out. He looked around briefly and huffed, "Just like the rest of Europe, everything's old."

The driver of the opposite car snorted, *"Ta Gueule, Américain.* You know nothing!"

Matt looked over his shoulder, annoyed. *"Puto Franco!"* He said, in a muffled tone.

"Oh, so you know a little Spanish, eh? This is France, you idiot."

"I know types like you."

"Oh? And what is that?"

"Always fashionable to spit on Americans, because you've got a case of incurable narcissism."

The guard laughed. "Okay, here it comes. He is going to mention the war like every dumb shit that has not figured out that the U.S. would never have been a country in the first place if not for us. Consider our debt paid."

Matt took an aggressive step in his direction until Chris threw an arm in front.

Matt refrained from escalating. "My grandfather died in Bastogne liberating you're—"

"You go dig him up, I will thank him personally."

"Jean!" His superior shouted.

"All right, that's it!" Matt tossed Chris' arm aside.

"NO!" Monsignor Trovarto yelled. "We do not have-a time for this nonsense!"

Matt took a few deep breaths and finally relaxed his posture.

Chris adjusted his glasses. "You're going to need a wheelbarrow for your grudges, you know. That was an awful long time ago, and everyone over here has moved on."

"Everyone except the architects."

Chris smiled and turned towards the antagonizing driver while speaking to Matt. "Oh come on; I happen to like Arcadia."

"Padre," The lead chauffer grasped Trovarto's right hand and turned it over, placing an unmarked plastic tube with a pointed cap on one end. "My employer wishes for you to have

this. Take it. It was developed by the Americans—NASA. Scopolamine aspirator. Listen carefully or you risk overdose. One spray into your nose. Just one. It will last for two hours. You will feel no motion sickness. If you spray more than one, you will see things that do not exist. More than that and you die, understand?"

Trovarto stared at the vile with contemplation. "Uh, *si. Grazie.*"

"You should take it now."

"Why is that?"

No sooner than he asked, they passed through an iron gated hedge obscuring an AW169 light-industrial VIP helicopter. Its powerful turboshaft engines softly ignited, and the passenger door opened to await their entry.

"Please, all of you, climb aboard. It is a 45-minute flight. I trust you will find the appointments satisfactory."

Chris and Dao peered inside at the plush refinements before taking the three steps upward. The cabin was every bit as sumptuous as the Gulfstream they left behind. Four leather recliners faced each other, and three additional leather buckets lined the rear bulkhead. Trovarto boarded first, opting for a forward-facing recliner on the far side. Rocco and Anastasia climbed the steps next, both taking the rear benches. Dao and Chris ducked into the cabin while the five noise-abating blades commenced rotation. Matt looked up the steps into the cabin, then at the empty left seat in the cockpit. He turned back around towards the lead chauffer. The second driver stood just off his left-rear quarter.

"Is *he* coming? Matt asked.

"No, you should not be so fortunate. Neither am I, for that matter. Try to enjoy your flight, Commander."

Matt smiled and climbed onboard, settling into the remaining recliner across from Dao Ming's. The chauffer secured the door and gestured to the pilot. The blades quickly reached velocity, and the pilot lifted the collective gripped in his left hand. Gently, the sleek helicopter lifted off the ground, rotated towards the northwest and slipped away over the treetops; its wind and whine vanished along with it.

Within five minutes, the helicopter reached a nominal altitude and desired cruising speed. Corsica's coastline disappeared, replaced with the vast Mediterranean blue sparkles dancing into the horizon. Monsignor Trovarto withdrew the scopolamine inhaler and inspected it closely before unscrewing its cap and jamming the nozzle into his left nostril. He took a deep breath, exhaled, and squeezed while inhaling. The appliance was still up his nose when his arms dropped away, limp. The monsignor's eyes crossed in a confused expression as he looked towards Chris. It was the last thing he remembered as another gray vignette gently muffled inquires of the concerned.

Château Du Rennes

The helicopter's turbine whine softened as they transitioned the lower French Riviera's Côte d'Azur shoreline. To port, the marina at Sainte-Maxime bristled with the mega-wealthy's shiny plastic toys. The pilot dropped altitude to 250 meters on the other side of town, feeding through the Vallon de Prés just below its peaks. Several minutes ticked along as timeless hamlets passed underneath the rotor blades in contrast. The pilot continued tracing the valley, gently reducing speed over La Bastide Rouge's Syrah and Grenache vineyards. The moistened fairways of Vidauban's exclusive club steamed in the distance.

It wasn't visible until the pilot executed a wide arc around the canopy of parasol pines hiding the ancient rocks below. An early Baroque-era stone villa slowly materialized, unassuming in grandeur, replete with stealthy modern features indicative of its taciturn master. The helipad itself took massive skill to navigate, for it rested within a washed stone gully protected 50 meters deep with a dense forest that provided no more than three meters clearance for the main rotor, and a narrow slot for the tail. It bore no extra consideration for the pilot, who slowly descended onto the pad without deviating more than a foot off-center. Once all three wheels met the concrete, crewmen raced to place their chocks. Secured, the pilot twisted the collective's throttle and powered down. One of the ground crew motioned towards a hidden tree-mounted camera and listened for instructions before opening the passenger compartment's hatch. The other crewmen reappeared pushing a medical gurney, rolling it to

Trovarto's side. Upon opening the door, they expected to reach for a slumped man described as wearing a cassock, but instead found themselves faced with a waiving finger. The Monsignor stepped down the helicopter's exit with a careful regard, bracing himself against the handrails. His balance remained slightly compromised, yet his condition appeared much improved since last reported as a drooling, unconscious lump occupying a starboard-side recliner. The crew quickly placed the gurney aside while the others queued for the exit. Once everyone's feet touched solid ground, the primary crewman ushered them to an elongated electric touring cart.

"Where are we going?" Matt asked. "Not to the... house?"

"Not at this time, Commander Jacobson. Your weapon, please?"

Matt didn't resist the request, reaching behind to his rear beltline and withdrawing the .45. The crewman climbed into the driver's seat and turned around to face everyone. He surveyed each of their faces, weighing the impacts of their ordeal.

"Good afternoon, *bienvenue*, my name is Henri, and I will be escorting your rendezvous with the monsieur, who is at this moment located elsewhere on the grounds."

Henri turned around, released the parking brake and accelerated away from the villa on a fresh, narrow asphalt pathway that weaved through a dense, dewy forest of pines, wild almond trees, and Italian cypresses. At once, the woodland terminated as the cart topped a small hill overlooking several red sandstone-lined fairways and greens which were slowly evaporating a fresh irrigation. The increased humidity complimented the brisk Mediterranean breezes swirling through the valley, and the late summer sun beamed through the tree-lined peaks in brilliant pre-crepuscular rays. A snapshot of the group would show their eyes in different directions, and their mouths were concurrently gaping.

Chris looked at the course with a dour complexion and furled brow.

"What is it?" Dao asked.

"Nothing."

"Empirical, Chris. Your expression betrays you."

"I'm sorry; it's just that..." Chris' breathing increased with anxiety. Dao took his hand and smiled in such a way that comforted him. "Suzanne; we played... and, well, after everything, Emily... Being on this golf course seems unbelievably out of context and inappropriate."

"I see." Dao continued smiling. "Was she proficient?"

"Suzanne? As a matter of fact, yes, she was, conservatively mind you, decent. Her handicap was plus eight; mine, plus three."

"Huh." Dao huffed.

"Wait, let me guess; you were one of those government-funded golf prodigies with special privileges."

"You make it sound as though we were kept in a silk palace, fed nothing but steak, and supplied with the finest equipment from Hangzhou. Quite the opposite."

"So, you *are* a prodigy."

"No, this is inaccurate. They said Olympic golf would return one day soon and we must take advantage to train as soon as we were able to swing a club. Our village contained the only golf course within the entire province. It was a barely acceptable regulation course in constant state of repair. The equipment consisted of antiques imported from Hong Kong: persimmon woods and abused irons with leather-wrapped grips. Our gloves and uniforms were manufactured in the village. It was a matter of pride. Of course, the opportunity never arrived to compete internationally, even though many of us consistently averaged below par."

"And you?"

"Minus two," said Dao with a smug tone. "But only on our home course. They moved us to others—links with sand bunkers and Bermuda grass. My handicap did not moderate until I became interested in other subjects. During my second year at university, I grew to love physics more than golf, and my professors noticed. So did the coaches. Due to my age, and the politics, it became obvious I would never be permitted to compete. There were already younger players with better handicaps; young girls I helped instruct who have access now to superior equipment."

"Jesus. When was the last time you—"

"I play any time fortune favors. My love for the game never disappeared."

Henri turned around and smiled at them both.

Chris turned to her and said, "Dao, There's something not quite right here."

Dao's face transformed to a perplexed expression. "How so?"

Before he answered, the cart took a sharp diving turn between two ancient pines, stopping just short of a set of carts parked greenside at 17$^\text{th}$ hole. Four men stood on the green: two players and their caddies. One of the caddies held the flagstick, while the other kept his attentions towards their immediate surroundings, appraising physical appearances, muscularity, and potential threats.

Obviously, protection for the other two, Dao calculated, noticing that the man had already locked eyes with Matthew Jacobson. An elder gentleman with a prominent nose and a penetrating gaze briefly acknowledged the arrival of the group before resuming the processes of lining up a twelve-footer. His competition's appearance seemed beyond that of a middle-aged man, late fifties perhaps, his height was average to tall—around six feet; his hair was shoulder length in a ponytail, and a snow-white anchor beard perfectly framed a deeply wrinkled mystery. The elder made two practice strokes then painstakingly aligned his putt. Against the wispy backdrop and occasional crows from a nearby nest of rollers, the ball found its way to the top edge and gently curled into the cup, producing a haughty grin from the old man. His caddie quickly retrieved the ball and replaced the flagstick.

The elder man chortled. "You see, the game is won on the green. Always on the green."

"*Prima primum.* You must be standing on it," said Mallory Du Rennes. He leaned towards his caddie and spoke with a terse French-colored English accent. "That will not be necessary, Gérard. These are our friends and honored guests." He then placed his putter underneath an arm, and walked towards them at a spritely pace while the elder man assessed the group, exuding an expression of omnipotent apathy.

"Mallory!" Dao cried.

"You know this man?" Chris asked.

"Yes, well—"

"*Docteur* Ming." He reached for her hand. "But this is an unexpected pleasure in such dour circumstances."

"Then you know?"

"Of course, I know," said Du Rennes, kissing both cheeks. "The assault was recorded and uploaded by Al-Ghaiz as a purge of infidels." He looked at everyone in the cart. "This is what remains of The Brotherhood, then?"

"Not quite. We presume Mukhtar Lal captured Doctor Harwaziz, Patrick Fannin and Jet Sun."

"You *know* and yet you're playing golf?" Matt blurted.

"Apologies, I have not had the pleasure, Commander Jacobson, and I am also being rude to my dear Anastasia and Rocco," he said, nodding. "Yes, Commander, I enjoy a round of golf with my father, who celebrates his seventy-eighth birthday this week. The course affords us a common, peaceful place to converse and contemplate. We are not in the business of appearances."

Chris grabbed Matt's shoulder, "Geez, turn it down a few decibels, will ya. How did you enter Special Forces with such a boisterous temper? Didn't some psychologist profile you?"

Henri exited the cart and whispered into Mallory Du Rennes' ear. They exchanged smiles, and then Henri returned to his driver's seat.

"Docteur Ming, I am to understand you are extremely skilled with a club?" He glanced at his father and his caddie approaching the carts. "If *mon père* should agree to such surrogacy, I beg your accompaniment to the Eighteenth."

"I..." Dao blushed.

"You encroach the regulations with intelligence of which I am not acquainted, *jeune*," rapped the old man.

Mallory Du Rennes turned back around towards Dao and Chris, whispering, "The first lesson he taught me as a young boy."

"And who is to play on my behalf?" Monsieur Du Rennes asked.

"*Son compagnon*, you know; Docteur Miller."

"Ah." He smiled and stepped into his cart along with his caddie who drove them away.

"What?" Chris shouted, suddenly on the spot. "I haven't—"

"Not to worry, Docteur Miller, this is not an examination; just enjoy the moment, yes?" Monsieur Du Rennes climbed into his cart and sped off towards the 18th tee box.

Henri motioned everyone before disengaging the parking brake and speeding away down the cypress-lined pavers.

"Aren't you exhausted?" Chris asked Dao.

"Yes, and I have not practiced in several days."

Several days, Chris thought. It had been several months since he last struck a golf ball, and that was at the insistence of another group—a party Jack Kattner assembled for some ulterior business motive or perhaps his own amusement— watching scientists struggle with practical physics. Chris didn't have an abundance of time for reconnoitering as Henri braked at the rear of the Par 5 18th tee box.

The forward carts were stopped just downhill from their position, allowing an unimpeded view of the magnificent chasm separating the men's tees from the front edge of the fairway, some 120 yards distant and 200 feet below. The entire hole laid before them, as if reachable in a single perfect stroke.

Chris pointed at the stone marker and mumbled. "Now I know what's wrong with this place."

The chiseled marble marker stated "Par 5 – 440".

"Meters," said Dao.

"Exactly. That's too short for a par 5, otherwise."

"You are correct, Docteur Miller," said Du Rennes. "The course architects felt a certain level of revolt was in order since we are, of course, standing in the birthplace of the metric system."

The elder Du Rennes climbed out of his cart while his caddie tended to the equipment bag, withdrawing the driver and unsheathing its head. He handed it to Chris along with a fresh left-hand glove, ball and tee. Similarly, the other caddie outfitted Dao Ming. There was a short climb from the cart path up four steps to the men's tee box where both Du Rennes waited in a safe location towards the rear. Dao began vigorously exercising, stretching her back muscles and arms, bending her knees and taking practice swings. Chris examined the club's feel carefully and took a few underwhelming, but prudent practice strokes. Both swings exhibited a degree of competency and formal training, except Dao's had the velocity and polished finish of a professional.

"Docteur Miller, you have the honor." Monsieur Du Rennes announced.

Chris was nervous and uncomfortable, and it visibly showed with his hurried examination of the tee box grounds, rummaging for the perfect spot to spike his ball. To the casual observer, the box was perfectly flat, and its turf perfectly consistent, save for a couple sanded divots gouged by inebriated hacks. The gaping chasm's forced perspective from such an elevation produced a false sense of confidence—as if one had to merely tee off with a 7-iron to accomplish an acceptable if not laudable driving distance. But Chris was addressing the ball with the most unpredictable club—a driver with unfamiliar nuances in grip, reaction, loft, and shaft stiffness. *Stiffness!* The old man's driver felt rubbery and much too flexible, Chris thought. He would be ahead of the club on downswing, and overcompensation would pull it left. A bead of sweat dripped down his forehead as he drew the club back. Then the snap.

The ball flew off the face of the club head with a low trajectory, yet down the right-center of the fairway. Its forward momentum gradually succumbed to friction and gravity as it dropped onto the grass and rolled another fifteen or so meters.

Gérard peered into his laser rangefinder, "Two hundred thirty-seven." He grinned.

"Meters." Dao added, slyly returning his smirk.

Chris seemed pleased with himself, relieved, and picked up his tee, handing it to the elder Du Rennes who smiled in appreciation. "*Je vous remercie, mon champion.*"

Mallory Du Rennes also cracked a smile as Dao made her way between the white markers.

"Wait a minute," said Chris. "Shouldn't she use the ladies' tee?"

Monsieur Du Rennes leaned over towards his father. "This is a fair question, papa, is it not?"

Dao teed her ball towards the rear of the box's border, causing panic from her extended backswing. Once the commotion settled, she aligned herself at address, taking one last look down the fairway, and brought the driver carefully to the top of her backswing. Then came the ferocity, the dropped jaws, the disbelief.

The ball rocketed off the clubface with a low-spin, medium trajectory down the fairway's center, arcing well beyond the great chasm, and touching the grass in several bounces before finally coming to rest parallel with a blue field marker.

"Two hundred sixty-six meters."

"What is that in yards?" Matt asked.

Chris turned around, handing his club back to the elder's caddie. "Around 290."

"300 if the fairway was properly maintained." Dao smirked.

"Ma chérie, vous ne serez pas déçu! Excellent. If that does not excite a man, then..." He smiled at his father.

Dao peeled off her glove, handing it and the driver to Mallory Du Rennes' caddie. Mallory stepped over and extended his arms to embrace, and she responded in kind.

At the bottom of the tee box's steps, Du Rennes addressed the group. "As you might imagine, we have much to discuss. For now, Henri will escort you to the main residence for acquaintance, refreshment and relaxation. There is estate wardrobe available, of course. Henri will see to your satisfaction. Dinner will be served at eight, approximately two hours from now."

Henri maneuvered the cart around the others and accelerated down through the 18th pathway towards the clubhouse where he actuated a hidden private gate that led to a modern architectural compound excavated into a steep rock façade overlooking the southern nine holes. The cart stopped under a cantilevered mezzanine receiving area towards the bottom of a waterfall that tumbled two stories and collected in a capacious stone koi pond.

Chris studied the design's features and grinned. "Inspired by Fallingwater, I should think."

Henri stepped out of the cart first. "Are you a student of architecture?"

"No, well, we covered Frank Lloyd Wright in an engineering art elective; his designs are unmistakable. If this is not his work, it is certainly influenced by him."

Henri laughed, reflectively. *"Oui,* unmistakable."

"I don't recall reading about this one, let alone seeing any pictures of it."

"This is also by design, Docteur Miller." He faced the group. "It is by his direction, I am not to comment further on this property, the Monsieur and his father wish to make their own presentation, you see? They are very protective of it. I am only to make its introduction by formally announcing upon arrival, 'Welcome to Redcliff'. Please, follow me."

Rocco stood with Anastasia reflecting at the koi pond. It's surface mirroring Redcliff's three stories protruding from a rusted hillside. Its magnificent façade featured angular concrete and river stone open decks with soaring, seamless windows protecting interior living spaces—an image of serenity disturbed only by the concentric ripples of passing koi.

Rocco stared into the sky's reflection. "Father loved this place."

"I know. This area... I feel him, Rocco; he was here not long ago, and he was—"

"Come you two."

Matt hurried them to join the rest at the main elevator in the garage; a cavernous area housing several luxury tourers: Mercedes, Bentley, BMW, Tesla, a Rolls Royce, two Range Rovers, one outfitted for off-road and deep-water snorkeling, and two sports cars: an Aston Martin Carbon Black Vanquish, and next to a bucket of tennis balls sat a Ferrari F12 in classic red. The back of the garage was unlit and therefore dark, with just enough luminosity to cast silhouettes of several more automobiles in various shapes covered in black velour.

Before anyone started making guesses, the glass elevator's doors recessed into the walls. The elevator launched them briskly, and with the same expedience, teased gravity braking for the second floor. It opened to a spacious interior brightly illuminated from the Grand Visage on the left—an impossibly seamless glass expanse that stretched from floor to a ceiling 11 meters high, and across the entire width of Redcliff's façade. Henri removed a glass tablet from his pocket and inputted a short sequence, dimming the window to a comfortable level.

In front of it rested different furniture arrangements purposed for conversation, observation; its central setting apparently focused on the glass itself. Behind that arrangement was an extensive open stainless-steel kitchen, wrapped by a rectangular bar dressed in ebony. A young uniformed tender appeared delighted to see them as she dashed some spices into a sizzling fry pan. The kitchen's ventilation system kept most of the scent from overtaking the entire floor, yet faint hints of garlic and allspice made their distinction.

"Docteur Miller and Docteur Ming, your accommodations are within the first corridor, the first doors upon which you arrive, right or left or both if you prefer separate quarters." Henri smiled as Dao Ming blushed and grabbed Chris' arm.

He continued, "Dinner will be served in the rear dining room. Monsignor Trovarto, Commander Miller, Monsieur and Mademoiselle Hammett, please accompany me to the opposite side; your accommodations likewise await."

Their paralleled corridor of chiseled stone, oaken floors, and stainless-steel accenting disappeared into darkness after the first four doorways. The echoes of their footsteps and conversation hinted its linearity stretching minimally another 30 meters.

"There are four identical suites at your disposal. All lighting is automatic to your presence unless you verbally command otherwise. Just say, 'Lights off" or 'lumières'. You will discover the dining room entrance further along the right side of the hallway at the appropriate hours. "*De nouveau*, again, this is promptly six o'clock. *Jouir de.*"

Chris sank into the crisp linens, finally feeling sanitized of the past 72 hours. A long, soaking shower, his eyes rinsed of grit and apprehension, a fresh shave and shampoo, teeth cleansed, body deodorized, and virgin undergarments christened. He laid there for several minutes, staring at a lifeless black rectangle mounted on the opposite wall, offering a blank stage for his own contemplative musing. There was a ceaseless throbbing in his temples, the television's outline oscillated in and out of focus. Dao suddenly emerged from the private spa, wrapped in a terrycloth-lined silk robe, and her head wrapped in a thick white towel. She sat on the bed's corner, unwrapped the damp towel and began combing her tangled tresses. Chris could not fully overcome his impulsiveness, caught intently gazing at her beauty. He returned to the vacant pixels moments afterward, distracted by mental overload and physical depletion.

"I'm having trouble digesting it all, Dao."

She turned towards him and continued combing.

"My mind is replaying everything. The assault and destruction at Andromeda, the Smileys, Julie, those mercenaries all over San Francisco, and our own God-damned military! I newshounded the internet, reading all these neutrality/transparency stories and unclassified intrusions. I thought—I honestly thought—it was all in my head from watching too many action movies or something. I ignored it. They really *are* everywhere, and into *everything*. Those big brother phobias."

"Big brother?"

"Government oversight, you know."

"Not a clue," she snickered.

Chris turned to her, rolling his eyes. "Ah yes, you know it!" Then he stopped cold. "Jesus, my parents!"

He bolted upright and reached for the telephone, opening a line. A short pause followed by two short tones and a click. "Docteur Miller?"

"Yes."

"I apologize, but as you might naturally conclude, placing long distance phone calls carries inherent risks. Our outgoing lines contain systems for obfuscation, of course, and unless it is arranged with other party, voice detail is not scrambled, therefore subject to recognition and monitoring. Monsieur Du Rennes does not wish to invite such risk."

"What about my parents? I need to warn them!'

"Docteur Miller, *s'il vous plait*, this is the first place they would surveil, no? Impossible. If it is any consolation, however, it is that they might be kept alive and ignorant just for that purpose."

"We speak to each other every week, Henri. If I don't call, they will, and if I don't return that call in a reasonable time—"

"I understand, Docteur Miller. I will inform Monsieur Du Rennes of your concern. Any others?"

"Yes. I also need to contact Rebecca Morningwood at Amerimem—my executive liaison."

"I have been explicitly instructed to inform you that your company has been sequestered by the United States Department of Justice. More specifically, its National Security Division. Calling any of its numbers or the numbers of its employees will trigger alerts in Utah. As well, impossible. Docteur Miller, Redcliff goes to great lengths in protecting its anonymity. Monsieur Du Rennes will explain this at dinner. I implore you to relax before dinner; there is much to discuss."

Think, Chris, THINK!

Chris replaced the handset to its cradle and turned back around to Dao. "What would you do?"

"It is an aged dilemma, is it not? The answer appears simple, yet one must deduct reasonable outcomes until the lowest risk is achieved."

"So simple it completely eludes me."

"A serpent swimming in your soup!" She giggled. "To contact your parents, you must first contact someone they know and trust—someone our enemy does not anticipate. Additionally, the message must be esoteric to your family. We must assume they are under surveillance of the highest order. Bugs, taps, cameras—everything."

THINK!

Monsignor Trovarto awoke 25 minutes before the appointed meeting time. His memory lethargic, he looked around the room in disbelief of consciousness. Then its familiarity returned. The slight essence of stone, concrete and steel combined with a peculiar honeyed lilac scent fighting some generic fabric softener. His body ached, but at last his left ear no longer pulsed as though an ice pick had been thrust through his eardrum. He immediately made for the bathroom, opening the hot tap and steamed the shower as he disrobed. A knock on his suites' door interrupted the routine. He wrapped himself in a towel and cracked open the door to find Matthew standing just in front with a surprised expression.

"Father. Um. Just wanted to check in on you beforehand. I wanted to know a little more about this place—this Du Rennes—before walking down the hall."

Trovarto glanced back the steam billowing out of the bathroom, lamenting that he hadn't the presence of mind to activate the exhaust fan.

The bathroom must be drenched by now!

"I see. Yes. Well-a. *Per favore*, allow me a few minutes and I will-a come to you, okay?"

"Great, thanks." Matt smiled and returned to his room.

The Monsignor closed the door and trotted into the scalding torrent, fumbling for the controls to ease its temperature. *Cleanliness is...*

The knock on Matthew's door came several minutes later, to which it opened as if anticipated from someone hawking the peephole, except there was none.

"Father..."

"What is-a your concern regarding our host, Commander."

The both sat at a small bistro table.

"No concern, really, I'd just like to know a little about someone before I dine with them."

"Ah, yes. Well-a, I believe he will describe himself and his intentions immediately, but what I can-a tell you in this fraction of time? He is one of the senior administrators of *La Fratellanza*, and-a he has been a brother as long as I remember. Put-a your trust in him, Commander. He is-a the reason we are alive."

"If you say so, Father."

The recessed, indirect LED border lighting washed down the stone walls as they proceeded to the open double entryway several meters down the hall. Behind them, the lighting automatically dimmed, revealing only the hallway's outline. Peering around the corner, they were the first to arrive. An impossible three-meter diameter, black-banded onyx table centered the room, with eight velour-backed leather chairs encircling it. The wall behind it featured a buffet queue of silver chafing dishes warmed by a single charcoal briquette smoldering underneath. The chamber's prevailing scent indicated fowl of some variety, along with grilled asparagus or spouts, yeasty breads, and the sweetness of confectioners' sugar. Water chalices at each place exhibited the beginnings of condensation, and three wine selections breathed slowly in their decanters, one of which floated gently in an ornate silver chiller. A Bordeaux, a Châteauneuf, and a Chardonnay, Trovarto guessed, although on closer inspection proved to be a Chignin Bergeron floating next to a tiny thermometer reading precisely 13°C. Mallory's favorites, if his memory served.

A chef entered from an obscured doorway towards the rear, carting the last chafing dish, placing it at the end of the queue next to the others. Anastasia and Rocco ambled in, followed by Chris and Dao from the opposite doorway. Conversations exploded regarding their surroundings and the menu, each wildly postulating the contents of the warmers. It was a welcome diversion until Mallory Du Rennes and his father descended in a private glass elevator at the chamber's front. They exchanged curt pleasantries and sat themselves at the far side of the table, noticeably closest to the chef's doorway. Best path for escape, Matt thought. The rest were exposed to an invader's ingress, should another surprise breach occur, and they were certainly weary of it.

Mallory Du Rennes and his father took hands, gesturing for others to do the same in preparation for a prayer.

The elder Du Rennes spoke, "If the Monsignor would honor us..."

Trovarto nodded, taking the hands of Anastasia Hammett and Matthew Jacobson.

"O Sacrament most Holy, we pray and give thanks for the blessing of continued life in Your service, to the service of mankind, to the remembrance of our beloved family's sacrifices today..." He squeezed Anastasia's hand with additional pressure, feeling her anxiety and sorrow as her grip trembled. "...and for our Father and Dear Brother Anund, a hand of your Grace and Wisdom, and for Your divine guidance in our endeavor to defeat evil. *Da robur, Deus, fer auxilium.* Glory to the Father, and to the Son, and to the Holy Spirit. Amen."

"Amen," the group responded in unison, with the exception of Rocco Hammett, whose jaws continued oscillating in subconscious rage.

Trovarto felt it, as well did Mallory Du Rennes notice. "You must first forgive your enemies weaknesses for power and greed, Monsieur Hammett. Your father laughed at their inability to withdraw. It was pity that finally transitioned him from the active field into the administrative Brotherhood, you know."

"He must be avenged, uncle Mallory," said Rocco.

Chris turned towards Du Rennes. "*Uncle* Mallory?"

"Rocco, the final result of the Brotherhood's actions might grant your wish, although it cannot be its mission, and that mission is the purpose of this gathering. All agenda must coincide with our charter, naturally."

At once, the elder Du Rennes struggled to get to his feet as an unexpected guest passed the southern entrance's threshold.

"Ah, Capitaine Montluc! *Heureux de vous voir.*" Du Rennes embraced her, vibrantly kissing each cheek. He turned and gestured for the chef. "*S'il vous plaît,* another setting for our champion jockey."

"*Immédiatement.*"

The chef reappeared in short order with a full placement and chair, arranging them next to Mallory's delighted father.

"Please everyone, enjoy the buffet. We must gather our strength in haste."

The chef removed and carted away the lids to each dish, revealing what Matthew and Monsignor Trovarto deduced: Magret de canard, aligot, tartiflette, garlic roasted brussel sprouts and other vegetable delicacies. The foods were intentionally rich and indulgent without obscenity, as was a Du Rennes trademark. One by one, each made their way past the selections and as they returned, the chef poured each a measure of the appropriate vintage. Mallory Du Rennes was the last to take his seat, enthusiastic to initiate the crux of their gathering after the first few samples were consumed.

"Jeanette, *aimée*, please share your report."

"14 hours. Maybe 12. There is a potent inbound sirocco affecting my estimate."

"What does she mean?" Matthew interjected.

"*Pardon moi*, Commander. My brand-new toy has been fouled by an ersatz jihadist from Cairo, as you know. My technicians are busily making the necessary arrangements. That little quiver you felt over the Nile was no turbulence; it was a single Russian M43 round impacted under the port winglet. The Egyptian's canon fire penetrated no further than the fuel bladder. It is of course enough to mandate a wing replacement, and that can be achieved within a day, even in

Corsica. The sirocco is nothing more than a minor inconvenience. Those are not so much problems as the fact my aircraft has been identified by the Americans."

"You knew about the hit under the wing?" Matt's pitch elevated.

"Of course I knew. It is my business to know. One does not spend eighty million Euro without knowing where it is at all times. The technicians are currently removing the GPS reporting systems from another jet in an adjacent hangar. They will be replaced with my Sentinel boxes that report everything to me at any given moment: location, all instruments, all video feeds and cabin audio—everything. Leave uncertainty to the commercial airlines! The information can be accessed on any of my connected devices: tablets, phones, computers, Le Visage... Anywhere I need it."

"Monsieur Du Rennes, forgive my ignorance, but who *are* you, exactly?" Chris said.

"Docteur Miller, you do not recognize my voice? But—"

Dao Ming's face suddenly became ashen with dread. She preemptively held tightly onto Chris' right arm. He looked at her in disbelief as the realization reacted.

"I am an idiot," Chris mumbled. "The man who said it was safer to leave my daughter behind in D.C." He struggled against Dao's grip, attempting to break free.

Mallory Du Rennes raised an eyebrow, cocking his head. "An unfortunate miscalculation for which I deeply apologize, Docteur Miller. I beg your forgiveness, although I completely understand if you withhold it. I know I am responsible, therefore I am compelled to assist in any capacity. Complications have arisen, however." He plopped the latest copy of the Parisian newspaper Le Figaro on the table, folded to an international crime section displaying Chris and Dao's photographs. He translated the headline, "'Interpol Seeks Two for Military Espionage'. The Americans have accused you of stealing technology and selling it to China, who, by the way, placed an obscene bounty on Miss Ming—12 million Yuan."

Dao gasped, letting go of Chris' arm to cover her face.

"Bastards!" Chris yelled. "All of you!"

"What of the assaults at both Amerimem complexes? The ambush in Cairo?" Dao asked.

"Swept under a foul-smelling rug, *mademoiselle*. "Industrial accidents and domestic terrorism, naturally."

Chris placed his napkin beside his plate, famishment displaced by queasiness and shortness of breath. "Who *are* you people? This is insane!"

"But of course, you have the right to know, Docteur Miller, this is the truth." Mallory Du Rennes drew a long sip from his wineglass, gauging the table.

"For those of you not acquainted with us, our dynasty emanates from the Merovingian, surviving campaign after campaign, invasion after invasion, in silence, neutral yet not, practicing surgical intervention only when logical, and, as our family professes, when righteousness mandates. It is not unlike the Swiss methods, you may perceive. Class elites believe they are facilitating a collective well-being. Of course, so long as it serves them first. Why not? The precariat types have persecuted the upper strata since the beginning of time. Simple jealousy and laziness, I tell you—sloth, ignorance! Our kind believes the good fight is won on the field of definitions. Plutocracies and meted socialism are not always the pejorative terms their dissenters forever condemn. Since the industrial age, the States have championed a perceived freedom, except the largest percentage of its citizens by far became enslaved to entrepreneurial industrialists and their legislative lobby. The grand ruse is achieving invisibility of their servitude."

Chris cleared his throat. "I am a scientist therefore given to empirical proof, and my observations indicate that certain aspects aren't working as well as advertised. Point being, the metric of expats speaks for itself. I'll take the opportunities afforded by less government and lower taxes, thank you. Immigrants flock to my country for obvious reasons."

"Please spare us your narcissistic diatribes. It is typical of the ignorant and destitute that covet America, and I admit your country excels in the salesmanship of its branded dream. What is society without a regulatory government—without development, without true leadership and progression—but a semblance of the aborigines. Is this your preference?"

"To tell you the truth, I'm starting to believe the elite's version of *knowledge* is wanton ignorance itself. All this complexity—for what?"

"People necessitate belief in higher powers, in symbols, Docteur Miller—concepts easily digested. For eons we have outlasted governments and survived while comfortably prospering. This is the dictum of dynasties, naturally—family first."

"On the backs of those kept in the dark."

"Nonsense. Most of them never cared to know... never wanted to know. They have no true sense of purpose, only the simplistic emotional gratifications on an hourly basis. Impulsiveness."

"Distraction and diversion!" Chris quipped. "What is our true purpose then, if not happiness, which is itself subjective."

"The opportunity to evolve—to become *better.*"

"Also subjective. Even as a man of science I recognize that a certain degree of blissful ignorance is useful. Astronomy for instance. I find it all quite fascinating, yet you won't catch me reading those endless hypothetical quantum journals, let alone searching for extraterrestrials. Simple math and logic dictates they're out there. Point being, they'll get in touch when they're ready, and it will be irrefutable when that happens. Until that time, why worry?"

"It is your logic that vexes me, Docteur Miller. This is not much different than those terminal defectives surrounding your Roswell New Mexico incident. Imagine it—earthlings are comparative Paleozoic fauna, yet we successfully land our machines on extraterrestrial bodies with regularity. We are to believe these beings cannot do the same? Have they not already?"

"Hundreds of intelligent people blindly followed their car's GPS right to the bottom of a lake. Nobody's infallible."

"You make an exceptional argument, Docteur, yet I cannot assume these explorers were average tourists."

"Reminds me of Flight 19. I wouldn't assume ETs exist beyond error or unsusceptible to humanistic shortcomings. Ego, for instance, also external locus."

Mallory Du Rennes smiled as he wiped some moisture from the corners of his lips. His eyes surveyed the others, who were completely engaged with the conversation.

"What do you believe the ultimate power is regarding man?" He continued.

Chris swallowed the last of his Bergeron. "I imagine endless diversity depending on one's perspective."

"Precisely anticipated, given your proclivity for scientific method, Docteur Miller, and if I were to distill that into a singular maxim, most would agree that the ultimate power is the capability to realize one's vision. There is a natural order of human existence; the scale of vision depends on perspective. The taskers enjoy their minutia while others are perpetually inventing on a grand scale, impossible schemes, and lofty positions in grandeur. What if all barriers were suddenly removed from the haves and have nots, Docteur Miller? What if all visions could be realized?"

"Chaos. Competing visions, maligned visions, uneducated and immoral visions. Isn't it by trial and error as to where we are now?"

Du Rennes smiled and patted his napkin across his lips and continued eating.

"So, why are these extremists pursuing us?" Chris asked.

"Not extremists or believers in any religion except that of profit. They are primarily opportunists. They live how they want, or so I believed until I experienced the most profound epiphany. It was our kind that created their world, their maze, their trap. We are capable of such great things as you shall soon see, yet society's existing mechanisms prevent a real exponential progression. There is a fear of change, fear of harnessing new ideas and capitalizing on them unless it is measured and controlled for maximum profit. Look at any legitimate military. Look at your own semiconductor industry —especially them. You possessed the technology to shatter Moore's Law twenty years ago, yet companies such as yours agonizingly trickle us to death with the foreplay. Did you think for one moment that your latest project would see anything other than a covert military application to the highest bidder? It was the accurate reason why your Monsieur Kattner flew to the Pentagon two days ago, no?"

Chris stared at him, eyes locked, not sure whether to pounce or acquiesce. There was within him a more than a minim of disdain, except Du Rennes words rang with pure sincerity and undeniable logic. He simply had to calm himself and somehow manage the unmanageable.

Mallory continued. "Our fortunes compound in periods of global peace and subsequent population explosions ensued as a result. It is a forward stratagem, rather a philosophy, preferable than that of my predecessors and their myopic exploitation of death—of war, disease, accident rates, and so forth. These are now the domain of select industries and factions such as Al-Ghaiz, the Russian Bratva, Ramelan and his ilk. *La Fratellanza* is a natural fit for us, no?"

"And how did *you* come to it?" Matt asked.

Du Rennes peered into his glass where the legs oozed down to a mahogany pool. His response came in time, but not without careful consideration, just before being overcome with a daze of emotion.

"I first met Anund during a series of financial campaigns in the 1980s, when the Americans were chancing roulette in Nicaragua. He recognized a need for my resources and convinced my father and I to join the *La Fratellanza* after educating us on the truth of the burnings of Alexandria's library by the Holy Roman Empire—a remarkably quieted pity. He also offered two epiphanies from the great Sun Tzu: The first is that there is no instance of a *country* having benefitted from prolonged warfare. The second pierced my heart. It said, 'It is only one who is thoroughly acquainted with the evils of war that can thoroughly understand the profitable way of carrying it on.' It is intrinsic to us, naturally, to wear that moniker as a profiteer. I surmised it was Anund's version of an intervention."

Du Rennes turned to Chris. "And since we are speaking of my brother Anund, I must ask you to return that which he bestowed on you at the moment of death."

Chris stared at him strangely, puzzled.

"The ingot, Doctuer. He gave you a silver, rectangular ingot, did he not?"

Chris reached into his pocket and produced the item, placing it on the table in front of his plate. "What is it?"

Du Rennes cleared his throat. "It is a crypto-key to The Trove, our data vault. Everything we know is there. Our entire human history, Bridges Pangea, the Pyramids, all missing passages from religious texts, stolen technologies, forbidden technologies, destroyed technologies, all those pesky conspiracy theories—everything. You will not know the location for it is only known to the leader of La Fratellanza, and only divulged by our personal code."

Henri reached over Chris' left shoulder, picked up the ingot and handed it to Du Rennes. Mallory paused to quaff a mouthful of Bergeron and another palating of the magret while the others digested theirs. Silverware clinked on china; fork tines scraped across enamel. Chris cringed. The chamber's silence punctuated each embarrassing note of consummation and digestion. No noises to hide the noises. Everyone— everything—was on display.

"I will miss your father Rocco... Anastasia. He cannot be replaced, only succeeded. He truly *was* my brother. I cannot dishonor him by modifying plans, either. This will be explained in detail immediately after dinner."

Burning Alexandria

Mallory Du Rennes took his place at the right end of the U-shaped sectional, closest to the enormous tinted glass that dominated the nouveau château's facade. He produced a small, thin remote that evidenced no buttons or other obvious markings. It was simply a black bar reminiscent of Monsignor Trovarto's communication appliance, replicating the familiar dimensions 1x4x9 centimeters. With no point source evident, the entire window darkened and suddenly switched to a projection of a lush mountainside factory flying an Austrian flag in front of it.

"This is a new graphene production facility we control that is located west of Villach. Docteur Miller is no doubt familiar with the substance, yes?"

Chris' expression abruptly changed from that of wonder to angst. "Yes, but..."

"Then you are aware that this is, in fact, the raw material of preeminence in future semiconductor manufacturing. We are heavily invested in this technology and, if I may be confident in our position, it will eclipse any mass marketing potential shown by your current research track at Amerimem."

Dao coughed, "Mass markets were not the object of our research, *Chevalier.*"

"Ah, to be sure, Madam. Yours is for specifics in super-modeling, heuristics, robotics, and so forth. Limited markets. Ours is manifold, and you have already been introduced to one of its greatest achievements. In fact, you are gazing upon it as we speak."

"The Visage; I should have known." Chris spouted.

"Translucent analogue resolution display films are but one of many applications, as you know. You are likely aware of others, except our seminal triumph will be achieved from hyper-conductive solar fabric. I have an interested party in it for an airship. Foolish. My Holy Grail is sustained feather-weight magnetics using our calcium-infused graphene. We are also developing 3D printing of stainless steel and titanium; sintering and so forth. The graphene is my passion. The potential is staggering."

"Mister Du Rennes—"

"*S'il vous plait,* no, I prefer you call me Mallory."

"I would speculate that your wealth is about to exceed your wildest expectations, although—" Chris looked around the room, "One such as yourself is already acclimated to grandeur."

Mallory Du Rennes grinned at his father. "So it would seem, and yet we are consistently amazed by each challenge and opportunity. Wealth is but a tool, albeit an effective one."

"Of course." Chris' smirk was slightly crooked.

Matt broke in. "I would be more concerned about the security of it."

"Le Visage?" Mallory turned towards him.

"Yes. Hacking and conventional surveillance."

"Hacking is of no concern; we are sufficiently proxied. I cannot know what you mean by *conventional* in this context."

"Laser."

"Ah." Mallory laughed. "They try. We have detection in any regard. Le Visage will not itself act as an interferometer, nor allow a beam to fully penetrate through it. They hear static. Yes, we are well aware of the atmosphere-penetrating satellites using lasers in all spectrums: Russia, China, Japan, the British, the United States, and our own. Any of those could be commissioned by innumerable hacks from the private concerns. There are more stars twinkling above than twenty years ago—believe it. We even have a mapping application for them! This is not our concern, you must know; I will get to another matter in that regard shortly, Commander. For now, it is time to discuss the obvious, no?"

"Emily." Chris sat straight and beamed with a cold expression directly into the eyes of Du Rennes. "My daughter is my focus and nothing else, understand?"

Dao clutched his left shoulder in restraint, sensing the anger welling.

Mallory Du Rennes became stoic, his own expression iced and calculative. "You understand, Docteur, we must resist any temptation for compromising your discovery—the apparatus, er, laptop reader."

"I don't care."

"Ah, but this is a problem, except—" Du Rennes paused and turned back around towards the window.

"Monsieur Du Rennes, if you cannot assist in rescuing Emily, then perhaps it is all a moot point. I've reconciled the importance of the soft drive with my daughter, my legacy, the legacy of my deceased wife. They are my priority and any discussion that places the device over my daughter's life will fall on deaf ears."

"*Non!* I am an adroit match player in the game of chess, Docteur, and I do not give an advantage away, nor invite undue risk unless the reward is greater advantage. You want your daughter? Fine, I must oblige, but this is risk, and where is my greater advantage if you must also risk the device? Let us hypothesize your mission back to America. You possess the device, and you expect them to behave rationally in an exchange? Never."

"You mean-a similarly to a prisoner's dilemma," said Trovarto.

"Of course! I expect Esposito to collect the device then either ambush your position, snatching you and Docteur Ming for purposes unknown, or murdering the lot of you *and* destroying the device. Either scenario serves the mission of the Spada Sacra, no? We must execute a drop."

"How do you mean, exactly?" Matt asked.

"We put the laptop in a neutral place, a Swiss box, number coded access only. You collect your daughter; he retrieves the information."

"It cannot work as such," said Dao. "What are his assurances? None, which means he cannot accept such conditions. This man must seize the device and those who manufactured it, otherwise, what does he truly possess? This is why he demanded us. I do not see a reasonable alternative."

"Well, he can't have us, so..." Chris chaffed.

Mallory Du Rennes turned away from the blackness of Le Grand Visage and peered into Dao Ming's queasy eyes. "I do."

As if she knew what he was about to say, Dao shifted her position on the sofa to better console Chris.

Mallory continued. "This bishop; he could be lured, no? We put our three pieces in one place he will destroy them all, agreed, *mon chérie*. It is the laptop computer and one of you that must entice his gluttony."

"No!" Chris tightened. Dao held on. "Not you!"

"Who else?" Mallory contended. "Although, any actual transaction must not take place. There is a change of plan..."

A clear, white rectangle emerged from the center of the Grand Visage's glass. Three-dimensional revolving geometric icons, a symbol of the La Fratellanza, signaled some sort of program about to appear. Mallory Du Rennes manipulated the remote in such a way that produced a high-resolution map centered on the Mediterranean Sea. A tiny laser dot appeared on the southwest of France, projected from Du Rennes' remote.

"Suffice to say, this is our current location. Captain Montluc will escort you back to Corsica. It is obviously too risky to fly you all the way to Washington. My jet has undoubtedly been identified."

He moved the laser pointer and zoomed the map to an area off the coast of West Africa.

"From there, a high-speed yacht will ferry you to Porto Santo Island. The arrangements have been finalized with the Princess of Monaco. She owns the sister ship of the late Steve Job's Venus."

A short video clip of the boat played behind him. "Notice, it is a ridiculously obscene boat. Aphrodite is a *surnom approprié*, no? The authorities will not suspect you aboard her, let alone inconvenience the princess.

"The yacht Venus has a top speed that is classified; we know her to make at least 24 knots, in three-meter seas no less, with a range of 1600 nautical miles at this speed. Aphrodite is completely carbon fiber over micro-lattice manufacture, much lighter, much stronger, and uses twin turbines outputting enough to economically generate 55 knots on her semi-foils with similar range. The princess will not run her at full throttle for any distance to attract unwanted complications, therefore it will take 36 hours to reach the island."

Matt sat upright. "That's a lot of time for such a short distance, Du Rennes."

"I must remind you that your names have been distributed everywhere, and you should not be in such a hurry to be captured."

"Point taken. Now how do we get to Washington from there?"

"This is where it becomes interesting. I pulled a charter from Marrakesh; a modified light aircraft—Speedstar 850 with an upgraded Raisbeck composite prop—and it will rendezvous with you the following morning. Captain Montluc will fly you to our enclave on the western side of Brava Island, Cape Verde."

The Visage displayed a new satellite map depicting the tiny cliffside village of Fajã de Agua. It contained a single, short row of cinder block and whitewashed stucco apartments with weathered shops underneath, appearing much the way they were during the pre-World War II whaling era. Just behind them towered an ancient volcanic cliffside, weathered from countless tropical storm originations over countless millennia. A single road carved its way upwards and out of sight over a mountain range, towards the island interior. Fajã had all the appearances of a timeless seaside fishing village; a place to lose oneself, and where the utmost privacy could easily be procured if one possessed the means.

"Esperadinha." Montluc muttered, her expression dour.

"Yes, Captain, Esperadinha." The Visage flipped to an ultra-short airstrip with steep, cragged drops on three sides. "Closed several years ago for excessive winds. Too many incidents. Bad piloting, I say. Montluc should have no such trouble; she has landed there before. Easier than a carrier, no?"

"Not much. Worse if significant crosswinds. It is a worthy challenge to say the least."

"Ah yes, but these are all trivial matters. You will find the aircraft marginally sufficient."

"What is there, uncle?" Anastasia said in a weak and trembly voice.

"It does not matter to you my young dear, you and your brother will remain here with me."

Both Rocco and Anastasia launched forward to the edge of their seats. "Why?" Anastasia protested.

Du Rennes stepped over towards them. "Your papa would never forgive me if I purposely placed you in danger. I cannot allow it."

"My father would never forgive you for restraining us against our wishes, much less for what we are meant to do. If they fail when we could have helped?"

"And if you perish?"

"Then it was meant to be." Anastasia's voice grew stronger in tone. "We must go, Uncle!'

Mallory Du Rennes turned around to face the Grand Visage, fixating on the intimidating 600-meter landing strip displayed on it. "Captain, you can land this aircraft fully loaded in such conditions?"

Jeannette Montluc stared at the tiny runway. It reminded of her first few attempts with a much more appropriate aircraft for short-field work. She had only flown similar turboprops as the Speedstar twice in her career. To ferry seven people meant cramming it beyond advertised capacities and landing it well past Bingo—a perilous fuel level leaving no room for error. That was fine, she thought; the range under those circumstances would extend to perhaps 1,300 nautical miles, and her destination was easily 1,200 of it. No headwinds, no consumption miscalculations, just maximum economy and speed.

"Oui," she said after a slight hesitation.

"Are you sure?" Mallory grinned.

Montluc folded her arms, "Of course! It will be tight, but yes, we can make it. If there is a shortage problem, you know the alternate at Boa Vista."

"Um, sorry to interrupt." Chris raised his hand and all turned towards him. "We're trying to get to Washington?"

"Ah yes." The map returned to the village of Fajã de Agua. "This is as far as we can escort you. As all foreign intelligence are surveilling every possible route from Europe, my sphere of influence ends here." He pointed to Fajã. "This is where the genuine risk begins. Upon arrival you will rest and receive further instruction while my crew prepares your next conveyance. She is an experimental large-format sailing hydrofoil—Jupiter's Bolt."

The Visage changed images to a docked trimaran in flat black livery.

"I know you have many questions. Of course, you do! Sail? Across the Atlantic? But why? It would take weeks, you would say. Primarily, the hydrofoil tested to seventy-five knots with as little as 12 knots wind on the beam. Because of this significance, a world record easily, it has not been published. This is because of her design and her true potential, you see. Our achievements in carbon fiber technology and microlattice material strength, combined with foil and stabilization advances places Jupiter's projected top speed in excess of 150 knots in Force 6 condition—easily the fastest sailing vessel and fastest aquatic vehicle in the open ocean. There is no chance of my delineating every engineering accomplishment achieved in the manufacturing of Jupiter's Bolt, therefore a detailed technical volume will be provided onboard. I am positive you engineers will find the text riveting."

Monsignor Trovarto became mollified at the prospect of a choppy 36-hour cruise, followed by a four-hour flight, and now an even longer voyage in an experimental sailboat.

"Not to worry, father, a sufficient supply of scopolamine will accompany you all. This speed is dangerous to be sure. Collisions with minor debris, not to mention unsuspecting creatures, are all too common. The foils are in fact razor sharp and relatively thin for this purpose. You will either create sashimi or dispatch the foils without much collateral damage. Ah, but let us be optimistic, yes? Provided all goes well with nominal conditions, you should arrive at the American mainland within 48 hours of departure. You should not incur interference either. This is another reason the authorities have not yet been informed: Jupiter is a stealth craft. No radar, heat, magnetic, or phosphorous signatures; only detection via line of sight, and she's cloaked in the deep azure of a midday horizon. At night, using similar technology of this Visage, her pigmentation shifts to a commensurate shade of navy. Even so, you must avoid other boats. Your speed will easily catch eyes. Stay north of the equatorial lanes, but not so far as to encroach the anti-trades. Her captain will instruct you on engineering and navigation aids. I pray you are all expeditious learners."

Matt studied the mammoth trimaran. "Tell me Mallory, why help us? What's in it for you?"

"I see we have a skeptic?" Du Rennes laughed.

"Skeptic? No. I'm just curious about your angle in all this. *Only morally righteous if also profitable?*"

"My position has its advantages, naturally. The fragment reader, for instance. There will be derivative technologies which pose a significant financial opportunity. The people I assist—especially when it concerns a matter of life—they do not forget me." Du Rennes turned towards Monsignor Trovarto, adjusting his lapel. "Usually."

He gazed at the small rectangular remote for a short pause, then traipsed around the center table towards Chris and smiled. "Since we are on the subject of the reader, it brings a great curiosity from me, Docteur Miller. I wish very much to witness it demonstrated. Would you mind entertaining this fancy?"

Chris held onto the laptop tightly. His facial expression changed from one of wonderment to that of reluctance and dread. His eyes darted about, searching for a good excuse— any excuse.

"I am not sure that's a good idea. The last time, well—" He paused and turned to analyze Dao, Matt and the Monsignor. "I don't know how to explain it; there's this evil..."

"A what?" Du Rennes chuckled with a raised brow and exaggerated slur.

Chris felt his inquisitor would never relent the morbid curiosity that haunted everyone. If Xeno made another appearance, what harm could he do? He may be a vile and maddening caricature floating around in electric picospace, but he doled no physical consequences. And why did Du Rennes need a demonstration, knowing it works?

"The screen might be a little small for your tastes, Mallory."

"Come now, I have an answer for that." He lifted the rectangular remote and held it between his right thumb and index finger. "This jewel from our concern in Finlande has many functions: a remote control, a simple communicator, a pointer, a weapon, and so forth. One of its main functions is a digital conduit. It is therefore named 'Osmo', short for osmosis. By placing it within ten centimeters of nearly any display device, it absorbs its signal and rebroadcasts it for Le Visage or another compatible display. It may be used to conduit raw data from any standard storage device. Quite useful at board meetings," he said with a thin smile.

Chris placed the laptop at the table's edge and depressed its power button. The native Linux operating system and the Amerimem logo transitioned from the Le Visage's abysmal dark background, filling the giant wall in front of them. A short menu appeared moments afterward. Chris looked down at the laptop and clicked on the application icon.

"There will be a tray that pops out next. Hold your jacket sleeve over it and brush the top of it towards the tray."

"There exists nothing on my sleeves, Docteur Miller."

Chris smiled. "Believe me, there is." He toggled the release and the flimsy filter tray slowly ejected, exposing its membrane to whatever may dance upon it. Immediately, the program recognized over a dozen new fragments trapped within the fibrous collector, and it began the process of decoding each. Chris slid the tray closed to prevent stragglers and other anomalies. A few seconds afterward, the application displayed only the readable fragments, of which there were three. Glancing towards Mallory Du Rennes, he tapped on the first fragment. A penetrating bright white flash blinded them, and then two more. The sheer size of the screen painfully overwhelmed their senses until a short crackle introduced a magnificent scene from the golf course from earlier in the day when the morning's heat began burning off the previous night's irrigation. The scene filled the entire wall, and its resolution was incredibly crisp. A window, truly.

"Pas réel!" Du Rennes shouted. This is what I saw several hours ago. Me? It cannot be! *Magnifique!"*

Chris noticed a distant noise within the static, except it was unintelligible. It didn't matter, soon the bright white flashes reappeared and faded as the screen displayed a prompt over the next fragment. Chris gestured towards it.

"Yes, yes, by all means." Du Rennes insisted.

Chris tapped on the second fragment. Again, a blinding flash pulsed the room. The screen remained black this time. A faint, distant noise could be heard, as if it were down a long hallway, echoing. Everyone strained to make it out. Then, with one deafening tear, the grating laughter that could only be—Xeno. *NO!*

Chris suddenly blanked into a deep, undivided contemplative moment. *Heisenberg Uncertainty applied to the quantum state. Does this account for unstable neurons in the process of connecting brain tissue, and for randomness in memories read, and for Xeno—predictable yet unpredictable—knowing what you'll dream before falling asleep, or random fragments from unknown, impossible sources.*

"Docteur Miller!" Du Rennes snapped.

Chris awoke as Xeno's laughs continued.

Du Rennes looked at him. "I do not understand what it is, this laughing."

Chris gazed at the screen, reviewing his potential quantum explanation. His silence became awkward.

Dao tapped his shoulder. "Christopher?"

"What?" His concentration again broken.

"The monsieur's question..."

Chris turned back around. "I took it as a comment, not a question."

Du Rennes was not amused. The screen remained solidly black. The cackling did not relent as Du Rennes scrambled for a volume control.

Xeno suddenly spoke with a horrid, chiding voice that was as greasy as it was gargled—with glass chards and the half-incinerated heads of vinegar-soaked cigars. "It's not me; it's you! It's hard to forget what you never knew!"

Xeno's laughter abruptly muted and a single bright flash returned the program to the third fragment. The pointer hovered above it, but no one requested any further action. The silence lasted longer than a few moments until an alarm chimed from the Osmo controller. Mallory Du Rennes quickly picked it up, holding it to his left ear.

"Are you sure?" He turned towards Matthew. "Bastards! Where is our security!" Du Rennes tapped the side of the small black brick twice then stuffed it in a trouser pocket. "Commander Jacobson, are you aware of a *key* in your possession?"

"Key? What key?" Your boy Henri searched me as soon as we touched down."

"Ah, it is not for any door, precisely. Well, not any conventional door, that is."

"I'm not following."

"Come now, Commander, surely you do not believe your Blue Operations activated you without certain precautionary measures. Your key; don't you remember its installation? Ah, but how could I be such an imbecile! Of course, you would not."

"Do not be so hard on yourself, Mallory." The elder Du Rennes said, purling a neat scotch.

"Somebody tell this *Frenchman* that I have no idea what he's talking about! What key and what *installation*?" Matthew huffed.

"I suspected as much. If you truly knew, they would not have labeled it a 'key' or anything other than an undetectable homing device. They would not have you with knowledge of a key; that would jeopardize its purpose.

This device, Commander, is a transceiver with two functions, and it has been embedded as a small, thin disk, adjacent your heart's aorta."

Matt reached for the area and felt nothing.

"You won't feel it, Commander. There is no sense searching for it, believe me. Upon activation, a concentrated dose of sodium hydroxide is administered directly to your largest artery, the effects of which propagate instantly, reducing the surrounding flesh to soup. A slight itch in your chest precedes the violent explosion you will feel, simulating a blown aneurism. No possible chance for survival; death is swift. I presume you wish to have it removed."

Two and a half hours elapsed before Matthew Jacobson regained consciousness under the pure, intensely vivid surgical lighting. Moments before, he thought he'd somehow dozed off on quiet stretch of some Florida beach—a broiling sun comfortably penetrating his eyelids, the Gulf of Mexico gently lapping not far beyond his toes. No noisy seagulls fighting over a bag of chips, or droning personal watercraft, or a blaring radio, poorly tuned to shouty commercials book-ending computer-manufactured hits, just the bright sun and quiet cool air. Then came a passing cloud. But it wasn't a cloud, he thought. It happened too quickly. Then voices. Then the rigidity on his backsides. His eyelids fought to open.

A man stood over him wearing a surgical mask. He was inspecting his work—a clean operation with no residual lacerations or bruising visible. Matthew suddenly recalled being escorted to another part of the underground compound, down a short corridor to an emergency infirmary. He was still on an operating table, the effects of anesthesia wearing off.

"Congratulations, Commander." The doctor walked over to a trash bin and removed his nitrile gloves. "The device is in a tray on the adjacent counter left if you are curious."

Matthew rolled onto his side and fought to focus on a thin, circular wafer, about the size of a U.S. dime. It still had a drop or two of his blood on it, already clotted.

"Sons of bitches!" His teeth clenched.

"Careful with that device, Commander; we have not deactivated it, and Monsieur Du Rennes prefers to maintain that status for the time being.

Monsignor Trovarto entered the room carrying a fresh wardrobe for the commander as provided by their hosts. "You must put-a these on. They are-a waiting for you back at the château dining room."

All of them stood to greet Matthew with open arms and gentle tugs to part his robe to expose his chest, only to be astounded at the lack of any visible wound. As well, the anesthesia's effects had completely dissipated, except a slight numbness within his left breast—a nag he continually attempted to work away by making exaggerated rotations with his left arm.

They all took their seats once again around the massive stone table, except this time there were no comestibles involved and the elder Du Rennes was not present. Mallory Du Rennes sat at the far side of the table, and his personal assistant stood just behind to his right.

"Hard currency is mandatory; electronic conveyances will be monitored." He turned around to Henri. "Retrieve two cases for our friends, *s'il vous plaît.*"

"*Deux, monsieur?*" Henri said with a slightly surprised tone.

"*Oui.*" Du Rennes replied with a blank expression. "Each case contains the equivalence of two million Euros in the common denominations of American dollars, Euros and British pounds. Finances must not create a hindrance, however, since you are traveling to Washington, the Euros will not figure, and attempting to convert such a large amount will no doubt attract attention. Present them instead to the Countess as soon as your board her vessel. She is waiting twenty miles off the coast. Tell her it is a small gift from the Family Du Rennes.

"Not a fee for the trip, Mallory?" Trovarto smiled.

"No, Monsignor. This she does for the excitement. The currency is a gifted donation to her husband's other *Société*. She will know which."

Du Rennes studied each of their faces, searching for the slightest hint of hesitation or doubt.

"And what does-a The Great Grandmaster believe is-a our probability of success?" Trovarto asked.

"Ah. Monsignor, I should confer my finest Elo ranking was a paltry 1985—a chess master by no definition—not even an expert, yet it does not discourage my pursuit of the game. My library contains at least fifty tomes on the subject. When I should have more time to play, perhaps... Ah, but your query, Monsignor. I can only foresee so many moves based on so many contingencies. Should you make Brava undetected, and Jupiter fulfills her new obligation... Let us be optimistic and hypothesize your eventual intersection with this bishop. He will behave only as well as he is managed, no? It is not unlike my little chessboard after all. As long as we position ourselves so that only a logical series of maneuvers must follow, favorable outcomes exponentially increase. Ah, but you know what God has to say about plans, Monsignor."

"It can-a also be said he favors the diligent, brother."

Mallory Du Rennes laughed and stood up, emphatically embracing the Monsignor, pecking both of his cheeks and then grasping him in a final powerful embrace. "I know you will all go with God, my family. Henri will escort you back to the helipad where Captain Montluc awaits.

Chris was slower to rise than the rest, his complexion distant. Dao noticed and gave him recognition, which only served to create a higher wall between them. She resolved to make herself a sacrificial lure without much regard for her own well-being. Additionally, Dao didn't consult Chris before volunteering—something that bothered him as a man used to being in complete clinical control of his surroundings. The task that lay before them created a somber mood, given to retrospective thought. Both Chris and Dao behaved in a logical, scientific manner, and any hypothesizing of a different chain of events clouded present thinking. All considered, almost every course of action was the result of spontaneous reaction, Chris thought. He recalled only a few instances as having any real choice—actual decisions to be made after careful consideration. *I could have stayed home! Dead. I could have gone to the police station. Dead. I could have stayed in San Francisco! Dead. Or hid with River and Two Feathers in Montana. Dead. I should have stayed in D.C. Dead. My God, why did I leave my daughter behind!*

"Chris." Dao grabbed his arm, breaking his stare. "Whatever it is, all of the choices made to this point were the best choices—the correct choices. We cannot blame ourselves for failure to anticipate every variable. That is a path to insanity. What we need to do now is overcome our present situation, and you are the best I know at conquering an impossible challenge."

Chris yanked his arm away. "My daughter is lost to a maniac because I trusted you and this man. There is no other reason as far as I'm concerned, and I have to live with that choice. You are once again asking me to trust a decision based on the plans of the very same man. I would be committed to an asylum under any other pretense, but what options are on the table now?"

"Blame, Chris? What does this achieve? We are attempting to help you concurrently with a higher purpose. Please do not forget that there is the larger objective at stake." Dao turned Chris away so she could speak in a lower volume. "You must believe me that I am truly sorry for what has happened. It is my burden, and for this reason I willfully trade my life for Emily. You must also know that men such as these can be ruthless when it appeases their agenda. This bishop would kill us without hesitation if we were not important to another function. He said it himself, Chris. We were pawns, now we are knights. Do not mistake that for a status incapable of sacrifice. In their minds, the only object that matters is the king."

"That may be, but I don't have to like it, and I am informing you that I don't. Not one bit."

The huge side doors slid forward into a locked position on the helicopter, its turboshaft engine wound to a deafening roar. Monsignor Trovarto reached into his cassock and retrieved the scopolamine inhaler and uncapped it, pausing to remind himself of the last dose. Two shorter drags flew up his septum, creating a moderate lightheadedness and euphoria. Although conscious, his head dropped back against the recliner's rest, titled sideways towards the window. It was the desired effect.

Rocco and Anastasia remained to themselves, quietly whispering familial concerns; the body of their foster father, Anund, and how they should go about retrieving it once they—if they—accomplished their new mission. Their whispers were accompanied by occasional glances forward, something that Dao Ming noticed once or twice. It was enough to register in the back of her mind. In reality, she knew no one. In her village, trust was earned only in time. In kind, Matthew sat in solitude, second-guessing every move made, his unlikely career, what lay ahead—grinding on the future, and the infrequent pinch under his left breast.

It was Captain Montluc who seemed the only one at peace with her tasking. She sat comfortably adjacent to the helicopter pilot, observing the controls and methods should her skills be called upon. Someone cared enough to follow them out to sea recently, canons blazing. The mandated Acute Alert Status was to be maintained throughout the rest of her assignment. She rather enjoyed it when he relayed the command, thought Du Rennes. It would be the closest he would ever come to arousing her, in a manner of speaking. If only he could see her when she tossed a stick of chewing gum into the back of her mouth and don her phone's waxy earbuds—tomboy traits that Du Rennes loved and loathed simultaneously. And he adored tasking her because each time meant a new adventure, and that was something they both constantly craved.

Redcliff dropped beneath them and disappeared behind the wispy parasol pines. Ahead was the sea and lots of it. Abandoning the respite of Le Château showed on their faces, realizing what was to come—a long, unnatural, uncomfortable journey towards an unknown, potentially deadly situation. Chris looked deep into the water moments after crossing the shoreline. Too much time for thinking.

A Trefoiled Chin

"He got what he deserved." Mukhtar Lal spat into the handset's mouthpiece in Arabic, answering the only person he must answer to—General Mohamed Kiranem of the Supreme Council of the Armed Forces. "Harwaziz was a traitor and a sympathizer, sharing antiquities and pharaoh's knowledge with the west."

"Listen carefully, Mukhtar, you have been of great service to us, and my personal champion. Your intentions are in league with our desires, this much is to be certain. In the case of Dr. Harwaziz, you are *mostly* correct."

"Mostly?"

"He was allowed certain accord with Europe and America under the auspiciousness that we desire the return of certain artifacts removed from Egypt in the previous century."

"And this conference he attended?"

"No one has presented any curiosity outside of a feeler from the American ambassador. He seeks certain engineers traveling without passports." The general chuckled. "Imagine it; someone undocumented in Cairo! It matters not, Mukhtar, whatever was going on in that scientific conference is of no concern to me. If it is of no concern to me, then it is of little concern to you, understand?"

"Of course. Then it shall be of no concern to you what happens to the other martyrs."

"They are yours, and I look forward to our meal next week, Mukhtar. Do not forget."

"Never!"

Lal hung up and turned to a subordinate. "We will have a nice payday after all. Crate them."

Patrick Fannin regained consciousness while bouncing around in louvered darkness—his wrists cuffed and his ankles in nylon shackles. His light frame wasn't used to physical exertion against the bindings; they met little resistance finding bone. The turbo whine and rumble of their transport vehicle grew louder as he came around. He guessed it was a heavy truck of some sort, moving along a winding, poorly maintained passage littered with potholes and stone rubble. His aluminum cage had been covered with plastic, and ventilation hoses filtered air through its top. He didn't know where he was headed, only that his captors were apparently aware of his talents and limitations. Adjacent to his cage sat another aluminum crate with no special ventilation system. Its openings were much too small to ascertain if anyone occupied it, but Patrick assumed—hoped—that it held Jet Sun. If that were true, Patrick surmised that if any opportunity presented itself, Jet Sun's presence increased his probability of escape, regardless of the initial odds.

The plastic lining also muted sound somewhat. Patrick wondered if he should attempt to contact Jet Sun, if that actually was him inside the other cage. He would have to yell in order to overcome the plastic and the rumble of the truck, and it was at the risk of further violence. A few moments passed while he listened for signs of other people outside in places he could not see. Nothing. He thought about masking his intentions by a non-specific inquiry.

Just get on with it, man! Hist inner-voice yelled.

"Hello?" He called towards the other cage, expecting a sharp reprisal at any moment.

"HELLO!" He shouted at full volume.

He could barely make out the faint rumblings of movement in the other cage. Fingers appeared though a couple of its slats, then the shadow of a face.

"It is I." Jet Sun replied. "The plastic has muffled your voice. Are you injured?"

"Oh goodness, you *are* here! Well, that's not so good, come to think about it, being that we're in these bloody cages, but blessed be to God, I'm glad you're here Master Sun."

Jet Sun grumbled, "I am most certainly not."

"Ah, I get your point. Nonetheless Mr. Sun, do ya have any idea of where 'here' actually is?"

"*Shì*, yes. Northwestern Cambodia, by the smell of it."

"And..."

"Difficult. They tranquilized me. Hours, days... It does not matter, Patrick. I am bounty for Ramelan. You? I do not know anything except that Ramelan's curiosity for the supernatural has created disappearances from time to time. It may also reason his rapid ascendency to power."

"I fathomed that from the plastic, already. So who is he?"

"A stereotype." Jet Sun struggled to laugh as his head dropped to the cage's floor. "A man who at the same time murders or enslaves women and young boys through fear and torture in the dark alleys of Hong Kong and Macao, then afterward dresses himself with Savile Row suits for an elevator ride to his penthouse high above Victoria Harbor, where any manner of dealings ensue. Heroin, opium, prostitution and human trafficking for forbidden sex trades, raw materials, munitions, stolen technologies... Anything that subverts the remaining bastions of British aristocracy, including those symbiotic with the Communist government. He is a polished and talented leader born from several underground generations. Mistake him not; he is a gangster and thug with a hunger for profit and power. Nothing more."

"Nice man, that one."

"I see you have a proclivity for sarcasm, young one."

"Aye. Is that such a bad thing in these circumstances, Mr. Sun? I mean, I'm in a plastic bag with my hands and feet shackled, ya know."

"Whatever it takes to reconcile one's emotions."

Minutes went by without further conversation. The truck labored onward, grinding over ruts and undulations with the intermittent grating of crushed gravel under the tires. Its canopy allowed no indication of solar direction for Jet Sun to catch a bearing, and Patrick's stomach began to sour from the unfamiliar stench combined with constant oscillation.

Mercifully, the truck slowed. Foreign chatter emerged from people walking along the outside. Their drone grew louder, and the truck reduced its speed. Jet Sun analyzed every sound: the dialects, gender, phrases. His senses were keenly tuned to everything taking place.

"We are in Cambodia, Irishman. Khmer language. They use the name 'Angkor' frequently. The passing of remarks is another indicator. Tourists. I believe we are near the temples."

A gentle laugh came from nearby. "Charming, is he not?"

Then another chortle in a different voice. "He does not disappoint."

Jet Sun recoiled at the thought he missed another's presence in such close proximity.

Patrick stuttered, "Hey, and who that be there, eh?"

"None of your concern... yet," came a raspy Chinese tone.

"Patrick, say nothing more. We have spoken too much already."

The outside chatter faded into the distance as the truck resumed down a long, straight path. It turned once more and continued for less than a minute before coming to a complete stop. Patrick heard rumblings in the same foreign language, none of it familiar. Screaming cicadas suddenly became overwhelming. Jet Sun also heard the voices, but not sufficiently enough to overcome the cicadas, let alone glean any missives. The light had faded to that near darkness. Between the intermittent commands, other sounds from the dense forest made themselves apparent: breezes through the trees, chirping birds, and croaking frogs. Yet, the cicadas induced their own brand of stridency, masking all but the closest noises.

At once, several voices coordinated around the rear of the truck. Jet Sun felt his cage shuttled backwards into the broken sunlight and downward to a short cart. Likewise, they brought Patrick's cage outside onto another cart, careful not to disconnect the air tubes from the filtration system mounted atop it. Six men each pushed them along an unknown pathway into the jungle, where light became a scarce commodity. Neither of them could see any details of their surroundings other than the passing of foliage and uniformed limbs. That changed as soon as complete darkness surrounded them. Their carts continued moving.

Random flickers of flashlights ushered yet more directives from the laborers. Footsteps and echoes indicated they were within a narrow stone chamber. Its reverberations varied. Patrick and Jet Sun felt themselves being lowered down a short flight of steps and onto a flat surface where their journey came to a slow-rolling end. A dull florescent light penetrated the slats of their cages as footsteps disappeared back up the stairway. There was a sweetness in the air; an aroma neither could quite place until its full resolution connected.

Blood, Jet Sun recognized, bringing an uneasiness to his core.

"Say nothing; ignorance is our friend."

"I wasn't planning on giving them my dissertation."

"Shh! Someone is coming."

Jet Sun counted steps and determined there were three men descending the stone stairs. Two wore the same boots and their footsteps were heavy—labored, as if they were burdened with extra weight, although their breathing did not indicate obesity. No, these were soldiers and guards, for the third man's steps were feather-light and partially muted. The leather soles sounded refined, expensive, and he knew to whom they belonged.

His cage's door rattled from the hands of one of the soldiers. It swung open to a pale glow from several solar LED lamps placed about the room. His deductions proved correct; he was ushered from the cage by two heavily armed soldiers wearing khaki overalls and black boots of newer Chinese manufacture. At a safe distance behind them stood a notably tall Chinaman wearing a crisp, light-blue Sea Island cotton shirt over dark gray trousers and Italian black crocodile horsebit loafers. The audacity of such clothing in these surroundings was exactly what Sun expected. The man opened his arms and spoke in Cantonese.

"Jet Sun the Great, last-born heir of the Qings, exiled to the Gelug temples, and champion for—whatever it is that your ridiculous Frenchman calls it—Brotherhood of Truth. A pretentious title; the truth is always subjective."

Jet Sun said nothing at first, his eyes repulsed. He was accustomed to introductions from such men who displayed a combination of entitlement and an acute inferiority complex. These men were always on the attack due to intense insecurity during their formative years. Poor parenting, no parenting, no love. Jet Sun felt sorry for these people. There can be no happiness except when others suffer more than themselves.

"Where are we?" Jet Sun asked.

Ramelan laughed. "Always straight to the point, Jet Sun. Well, my old friend, you are nowhere near home if that is what you are asking."

"My guess is Cambodia, Angkor area. One cannot mistake the stench of fermented prahok. We passed the temples, did we not?"

Ramelan again laughed, but he was not fully amused by his soldiers' failure to conceal their destination. "I suppose it does not matter that you know." He glanced towards the stained bench across the room. "Welcome to Mangalartha, a lesser-researched temple within Angkor Thom. The local tourists will not be visiting, I am afraid."

Jet Sun switched to English. "Whatever you paid for me, it will not be worth it. You will become a slave to your conscience."

Ramelan replied in perfect English. "Quite the contrary. Your bounty marks my finest purchase to date. No more Qings to obstruct our return. And listen to yourself dogmatizing my morals. You know all too well we were forced into this life by the decisions of *your* privileged ancestors. There was but one logical direction since anything outside basic law is meant to appease the imperialists. You call it crime; we call it survival and prospering. Who is victimized by consensual sex?"

"Consensual to a trafficked child?"

"Or drugs that simply compete with regulated pharmaceuticals—those that pay the price of admission to the imperialist dynasties and their laws. They decree, they legislate, they own. We do not recognize their self-proclaimed authority!"

Jet Sun shook his head. "Why is it always the criminal that justifies evil when that evil resulted from a faulted perception. Slavery, servitude, murder and fear. It is evil."

"Permissible evil. Your allies merely created another form of slavery—debt!—and all the hardships in service to it. Invisible chains of servitude for the benefit of others. Who is free that does not do what they truly desire? We all exist in slavery of some form, do we not? Who is to say this system or that system is right for these or those people, my friend? Nobody! And so, we do what is best for ourselves, not necessarily for the good of all."

"Oy! You sound an awful lot like that Rand bint." Patrick yelled.

Ramelan ordered one of his guards over to Patrick's cage and take aim at his head.

"He does not." Jet Sun sighed. "The happiness of Ramelan is at the cost of many others' happiness—no ethical doctrine. Someone says something he does not like, he shoots them. Threats, fear, coercion."

"Quiet, old man, or I shall confirm it."

"Old man?" Patrick quipped.

Jet Sun turned to him and loudly shushed.

"Oh?" Ramelan turned to Patrick. "You must not be properly acquainted."

"What's he mean, then?" Patrick looked towards Jet Sun, who said nothing.

"Your new friend is no ordinary monk from eastern Tibet, Irishman, and I did not disclose this fact to Mukhtar Lal, either, for if he knew, the price? Never mind the price." Ramelan shivered in laughter. "He would not have sold him to me so cheap."

"Yeah?" Patrick pursed his lips. "And uh, how much did this Mooktar fella sell me for?"

Jet Sun's eyes widened. Rapid death would have been preferred.

Ramelan laughed louder. "You? He said I had to take you as part of the deal."

"What, nothing? You paid nothing for me? For the love of Christ..."

"You are a curiosity that I must explore, yes, and it delights me to describe your companion."

Patrick rolled his eyes and hushed himself, disheveled.

Ramelan continued. "The last Qing Emperor died after four marriages and as many concubines without producing a male heir, or so everyone understood. In fact, he produced a male child with a lowly house servant to punish his first wife. She was very beautiful, yet she despised her prearranged marriage to such a frail weakling. The house could not withstand the forthcoming scandal, so the emperor's bastard was sent away, never to be heard from again."

Jet Sun squinted. "Never…"

"*Haih*, you have interfered many times with my family's endeavors, except this is the part with consequence, Master Sun. It is now established that this woman—his mother—was a daughter of legend Li Ching-Yuen who died aged 256 years. She was not simply *any* daughter, you see. Out of 23 wives and over 200 offspring, he passed his herbal and spiritual secrets only to *her*, believing she would keep them safe in the house of Qing. After the second World War, she feared discovery by the new Republic and opened her wrists at the pond behind their royal residence in Manchukuo. No Qing may take liberties with their life unless free to do so."

Ramelan adjusted his sleeves and walked up behind his sentry who maintained sights on Patrick's skull.

"The emperor exiled your traveling companion to Drepung Temple in 1933. The math speaks for itself; he possesses the knowledge of Li Ching-Yuen. Tell me, Master Sun—who has taken Milarepa's name—is this young man's life worth the secrets in your head?"

"To call you by your true name, Ramelan, would invite no mercy. Be it sure, you have no intention of allowing either one of us to leave this temple alive. We would say anything, do anything, in hopes to avert death or perhaps gain freedom. To profess otherwise becomes wasteful and insulting."

The sentry applied a tepid amount of finger pressure on the trigger of the rifle pointed at Patrick, who suddenly became acutely aware that his life could be terminated in the blink of an eye, either by command or by accident. The sentry's eyes were cold and focused down the barrel, unflinching.

"Killing my friend would not achieve any result but his death—no bargaining leverage afterward, except my own demise."

"Are you sure?"

Jet Sun appeared perplexed by the answer, and before he could manage any sort of a response, the sentry fired at point blank distance into Patrick's cage. The sound was deafening inside the underground chamber, and the rifle's exhaust choked the air with noxious ejecta. Patrick flew up against the back of his cage, desensitized and in shock. The front of his cage was blackened between the aluminum slats, and a darkened hole was now noticeable in the plastic. The back of his head throbbed intensely, and he overloaded, theorizing that he suffered a massive head trauma as the result of the gunshot. He wondered if he should move a hand up to explore it. The anxiety overwhelmed him, and he slowly sank to cage's floor. The duration was interminable in his mind, or what he thought might remain of it. But he was *thinking*! And if he was thinking, there must be something left upstairs to do it. Or was it the consciousness in death—a dream?

He felt no warmth trickling down his face. There was no blood spatter. His ears rang, compressed, and he slowly summoned the courage to look down into his lap. It was clean. With both hands he felt the front of his face: the cheeks, his nose, his eyes, and finally his forehead. Nothing. He looked down again, surveying the rest of his body. Zip. Gradually, the roar in his ears dissipated to the gentle hum of the cage's ventilation system.

"I take great offense to any assumption of character, Master Sun." Ramelan said. "I am not without mercy, but if you continue evading my request, you will discover a lack of patience as my primary shortcoming."

"My position is unchanged."

"So it is."

Ramelan ordered both of his soldiers over to Jet Sun's cage. While one of them held a rifle aimed where Jet Sun must eventually emerge, the other timidly unfastened the cage's locking mechanism. Keeping his distance, the sentry gestured for Jet Sun to exit, and with a heavy, assessing stare, Jet Sun stepped through the doorway, greeted by the bayonet of a modern Chinese rifle. They led him to the other end of the chamber where a stainless-steel table stood soaked in blood and small bits of unidentifiable flesh that had already been discovered by a small band of blowflies.

"Take your seat," said Ramelan, and he placed Jet Sun's communicator on the table. "A curiosity, Master Sun. My best hackers tried to access it. They scanned it, tried to cut it open, baked it, held it underwater. Nothing." He picked it back up and put it into his shirt pocket. "I will ask you about it later. Please, take a seat.

Jet Sun looked down at the chair and pulled it out. "You will not be successful."

Ramelan smiled with a slight tilt to his head. "A subjective word. The survival instinct is an interesting mechanism. I have seen it enacted on numerous occasions. You can take away a man's abilities one at a time. There is always one he cannot live without. If pain is not enough, then his toes, his feet, his fingers, his hands, his tongue, his eyes, his hearing. Eventually we come to his impasse. I am so very much curious, Master Sun. What will yours be? To die with the secrets of Li Ching-Yuen would be a selfish crime, and I believe you cannot live with it. Ah, but to die with the secret could only mean a secret it is not."

"In any regard, you will not be successful."

"Let's find out!"

Patrick could not see through the plastic to determine what implements were placed upon the table, although they sounded metallic and weighted. An anxiety grew within him—the dread of what was to come, and that he might be next. His mind raced. Panic. His eyes darted about the cage. Just plastic. Clean; nothing except the ventilating pipes and the two small protrusions from the rifle blast.

As he sat in the chair, Jet Sun transitioned into a trance-like meditation. He had been tortured before, and he knew that pain is an assault on the mind. Once in the deepest state of tukdam, his would protect from any such assault, no matter its degree of barbarism. Clinical death became incidental.

One of the sentries selected a thin steel spike and took position behind Jet Sun. The other stood several feet away with his rifle locked on Jet Sun's upper torso. Ramelan motioned, and the first sentry jabbed the spike through Jet Sun's left shoulder. There was a slight tensing as the spike emerged through the front of his robe, but no screams for pain or mercy. The soldier wrenched the spike around the wound, which would have topped any numerical pain scale, except Jet Sun never winced. His torturer confused, Jet Sun sank deeper within the folds of consciousness, repelling all but necessary function. He could no longer feel the spike that ran though his shoulder, nor the warmth of blood now dripping from it.

"Leave it," barked Ramelan. "Let him resist the next."

Ramelan instructed signaled to hammer the second spike, this time to be driven just above the left knee. Instead of moving Jet Sun's chair away from the table, the sentry walked around to the other side of it and dragged the table away from Jet Sun altogether. He picked up the spike and a small hammer from the table and placed himself in position to drive the spike through the Sun's left knee. The spike in the sentry's left hand began to itch, feeling hot to the touch at first, and then it burned. He could not hold it any longer, dropping it to the floor in disbelief. He turned his hand over. There were second-degree burns smoldering across his fingers. In the brief moment between bewilderment and reactive rage, another itch spread across his right forearm, and that itch became an intense heat. He dropped the hammer to the ground, clutching at his arm. The sentry screamed in agony as the intense heat traveled coursed through the rest of his body. Ramelan's reaction was both curious and cautious at first; his expression sickened. As the sentry writhed and tore at his own clothes, the other guard dipped the aim of his rifle in disbelief.

Ramelan turned and saw that Patrick's cage door was glowing. He shouted an order for the guard, but as soon as he did, the rifle scorched the palms of both hands. The guard shrieked as the rifle fell, and he bolted for the stairway in complete panic. As he did, the reflection of a brilliant orange glow lit the stones around him. He never looked back racing up the steps, screaming the entire way. Ramelan froze for a moment to see his first sentry collapse in a ball of flames on the other side of the table, shrieking in agony as his skin melted away under the fire of his uniform. Patrick's cage door suddenly flew open, and Ramelan reached behind his back for a handgun holstered under his shirt. The other spike flew from the ground, rocketing through Ramelan's shin and into the stone wall just behind, pinning him to it. He screamed and dropped the automatic pistol, never having it fully in his grasp. Patrick ran over and picked it up, fumbling for a proper grip. Once he had the weapon under control, he leveled it at Ramelan's head and started to squeeze the trigger.

"Do not shoot him."

Patrick took his eyes of Ramelan for a fraction of a moment to see Jet Sun alert but motionless.

"Go ahead and try! Do it!" Ramelan yelled, struggling to free himself of the long metal shaft. It had 'tweened his fibula and tibia, guaranteeing his incarceration until someone surgically removed the pin from the wall.

Patrick yanked on the pistol's trigger. Nothing happened. There appeared to be no safety, or other locking mechanism; the trigger simply would not move.

Ramelan groaned with a shortness of breath, "Fool!" and pointed to a bracelet around his right wrist.

Incensed, Patrick stepped over to him and crashed the butt of the pistol against the back of Ramelan's skull, knocking him unconscious.

"Shut it! *Go n-ithe na péisteoga thú*, ya bastard!

With his shin anchored to the wall, Ramelan collapsed backward, his leg gruesomely wrenched itself from the spike.

"We must leave." Jet Sun reached behind his head with his right arm, and with excruciating pain, removed the spike from his left shoulder.

"Christ, man!" Patrick shouted.

"First, I need your assistance." Jet Sun exhaled and drew another slow, painful breath, attempting to mediate the throbbing through his left side. "Can you make this extremely hot? Just the flat head."

Patrick took the spike from him and "Aye, and I suppose I know why." He concentrated on the head of the spike until it glowed red. "How's that for ye?"

"It will do."

Jet Sun pulled his collar away revealing the wound where the spike had been. Although relatively small, it was bleeding enough to warrant what he was about to do. He took another deep breath and brought spike's glowing head against flesh long enough to cauterize it. Without flinching, he exhaled and handed the spike back to Patrick. Jet Sun reached around his head again, pulling his collar away from the entry wound.

"You must do it for me; I cannot see."

"Er, I'm a bit squeamish for that kind 'o stuff, Mister Sun. I don't know if I—"

"Please, we must go."

"Alright then. Let's have at it."

Patrick touched the spike's head to blood, cauterizing the wound in a fraction of a second. Again, Jet Sun never flinched or showed any sign of physical discomfort, only extreme concentration. He did not attempt to move his shoulder, knowing it would be extremely painful for a considerable time. As well, any torn tendons would tear further, and any shattered bone could create internal bleeding. For the next few hours, it was best to protect it.

"Can we go now?" Patrick asked.

Jet Sun stood up and assessed his mobility, judging he must maintain a certain amount of concentration to function as well as make sound decisions. They started for the steps that would lead to freedom, but something about Ramelan caught Jet Sun's eye.

"Wait."

"What is it?" Patrick asked.

"Get the black bar from his shirt pocket and hand it to me, then take his shoes."

"What?"

"Ramelan's shoes. Take them."

"But I already have good shoes! Besides, they're not my size by the look of 'em. What, you need them? Yours look fine to me..."

"They will serve more than one purpose by taking them. The first is that it will slow him down. Second, it will embarrass him further to his men, slowing him down further. Please, take them, we are running out of time."

Patrick kneeled down and removed Ramelan's crocodile loafers, handed them to Jet Sun and picked up the rifle dropped previously by the guard who had fired into his cage. He remained behind Jet Sun up the stone stairway towards the entrance of the temple, slowly pacing upward, carefully listening. The shrill crying of cicadas grew louder with each step. They could not hear if anyone stood close by or discern any other noises indicating extra personnel. They were faced with potentially exposing themselves if they wanted to leave. There was only one way out.

Jet Sun motioned Patrick to wait in the shadows while he peered around the entrance. There wasn't anyone to his left, but he caught a puff of smoke exiting the driver's window of the truck that delivered them, which was parked on the dirt road to his right. There was no one else in the immediate area; no other set of legs visible on the opposite side of the truck. He waited and observed for an uncomfortable few minutes.

Jet Sun whispered, "There is one, maybe two people in the truck. They are facing the other direction. The guerilla that ran away, he is gone. We must go to the opposite side of the temple and into the jungle. South, maybe two kilometers, is a moat. It is one hundred meters wide and four meters deep. It surrounds all of Angkor Thom. I am in no condition to swim, but the bridge is crowded with people. Hopefully, no soldiers of Ramelan."

"I don't think there's much to be gained by hanging around this pile 'o rocks, man."

They slipped out of the entrance and stealthily into the dense woods, the screaming cicadas covering every step. The soldiers in the truck never noticed, continuing their conversation over unfiltered cigarettes and Hindi remixes blaring off a tin can speaker.

Half an hour later, Jet Sun and Patrick emerged on the south bank of Angkor Thom's southern moat, approximately 400 meters east of the southern entrance. Jet Sun knew the smell of the open markets; the samphor and skor thom drums softly pattering in the distance meant they were close. The bridge was in sight, they only had to cross it undetected.

"Walk in front of me. My brothers frown upon dirtiness and vagrancy. They may notice the stains in my robe."

"Right, and I am the first to get bullet in the chest. Is that what this is, then?"

"No, you are simply a European tourist. Look around; you are everywhere. Now, hand me that rifle. We cannot use it any longer. There can be no trace."

Patrick passed the Chinese rifle to him, and Jet Sun gently sank it into the muddy edge of the moat. He rinsed his hands and motioned for Patrick to head towards the bridge. Waiting for a gap in curious tourists, they emerged from the jungle just above the massive south gate of Angkor Thom and descended a small dirt hill. It proved to be a fortuitous break because as soon as they rounded the gate's corner, they were met by a throng of noisy sightseers boisterously examining (and slowly destroying) its narrow thruway and alcoves. Patrick smiled and waded into the crowd, fighting for every foot against their general direction, with Jet Sun sticking close behind to protect in case any of Ramelan's men materialized. He checked over his shoulder for anyone that might have been directed to search. The tourists thinned on the other side of the gate, allowing them across the 100-meter bridge to the vendor area.

It was a brilliantly sunny afternoon and quite humid. The shanty shops were in full swing; their merchants attempting to catch every passerby for inexpensive apparel, jewelry, scents, or other mementos.

"You must beware of imposters. This place crawls with them, preying on the ignorant for charity. I am filthy. I will not be trusted. Give me a moment. Watch for soldiers."

Jet Sun walked over to the largest vendor while Patrick stood off to the side, vigilant for Ramelan's men. He spoke to her briefly, and then showed her the crocodile shoes. She shook her head and pointed away. Jet Sun tried the next vendor—a squat middle-aged man smoking a hand-rolled cigarette. When Jet Sun produced the shoes for him, he started shouting and pointing away, so Jet Sun looked down the line for any other vendor that might suit his purpose. There were none. The vendor in front of him produced a cell phone and started dialing.

A tuk-tuk operator stopped in front of Patrick. "You want ride? I am best driver in Siem Reap."

"Yeah, I bet you are." Patrick replied in a soft tone.

Jet Sun raced over to speak with him, but as soon as he arrived, the friendly expression on the driver's face went dour.

"Is he with you?" The driver asked.

"As a matter of fact, he is." Patrick replied.

"Then you need more than a ride."

He released his brake handle and started to pull away. Jet Sun put a hand in front of his helmet, preventing him for leaving. "Yes, you are correct. You are in need of money, and there could be a lot of it for you if you help us. What is your name?"

"Mr. Pheng." He trembled while keeping his eyes on Jet Sun's hand. "You are not—"

"Will you help us?" Jet Sun held out the shoes.

"What is this?" He gasped. "Put those away!" He said in a loud whisper. "Everybody knows who owns those shoes. Get in the back; I take you to my brother."

Patrick and Jet Sun climbed into the tuk-tuk and took their seats. Mr. Pheng tightened his helmet and rolled on the accelerator, speeding towards the city, weaving through the never-ending gauntlet of pedestrians, bicycles, roving hogs, elephants, and improvised carts made from farm machinery. Jet Sun turned around and found no frantic pursuers. For now, they had escaped.

Pheng brought them onto the main thoroughfares of Siem Reap, a town that had recently blossomed from the war-torn Khmer Rouge regime into the tourist gateway town to the Angkor temples. The streets were relatively clean and orderly compared with some other parts of the country, yet they maintained their post-French-Indo-Chinese identity, the main boulevard and its bristling new hotels excepted. As they reached the inner-city, everything changed. The streets narrowed, traffic became more chaotic, and there was a never-ending procession of street vendors and markets using torn and weathered umbrellas as their only means of protection from a ravaging sun—a swelter that changed at the next block when they entered the Old French Quarter. The street became clean and wide once again, with orderly and brightly lit storefronts and shiny new cafes with fresh umbrellas and coifed patrons. Patrick sat amazed.

"Rather odd place, isn't it?" He commented to Jet Sun.

"It is a city in learning."

Pheng brought the tuk-tuk to a rest next to the Old Market by the Siem Reap River. The shops were crowed with mostly Asian tourists perusing Buddhist masks, traditional cowbells, gongs, artwork, purses, leather goods, clothing, luggage, fresh vegetables and other foods.

"Follow me," said Pheng.

They traipsed down two long corridors of shops until Pheng stopped at one of the larger markets that contained just about everything a tourist might buy. In the back of it, behind a curtained doorway, was a man receiving his latest inventory, tagging it appropriately before it went to shelf. Some words were exchanged, a few of them heated. A few moments slipped, both of them emerged and walked over to meet with Jet Sun and Patrick.

Pheng's brother extended a hand and spoke to Jet Sun in the local tongue. "Not out here; come to the back with me. Leave your friend with my brother."

Jet Sun informed Patrick of their intentions and instructed him to remain out front with Mr. Pheng. He then disappeared behind the curtain with Pheng's brother. Once inside the densely packed-to-the-ceiling warehouse space, Pheng II took a seat behind a tiny wooden desk that had no more room but for a telephone, calculator, notepad, and an opened laptop.

"You are obviously from Tibet, but who are you?" he asked, firing up a cigarette while staring at the blood-stained hole at Jet Sun's left shoulder.

"I am Jet Sun of Drepung."

The brother's eyes went wide and sharply inhaled in surprise. "I have heard of you!" He put out the cigarette in a panic. "What do you want? I could get killed just talking to you! Or rich."

"How do you mean?"

"A few moments ago, word went around with your description. A monk and a young white European man. Four million Riel bounty."

"Then he is not dead," Jet Sun said under his breath. "You would have called already if you intended to collect."

"True."

"So why have you not?"

"May I see the shoes?" Pheng's brother asked.

Jet Sun placed them on the desk, and the brother's mouth dropped open. The brother noticed a small drop of blood on the toe of the right shoe.

"Is that—"

"They were not given to us."

"And you wish to sell these to me? To be in possession of them... word will travel. It is extremely risky." He leaned back in his chair. "But anything that rains urine on that man—"

"You do not worship him?"

"Insult! We are making progress if not for the corruption that lingers from the Rouge years. If we are not paying him, it's the Chinese or the Russians. Enough! What do you need?"

"Clothes, a meal, and safe passage across the border to Watthana Nakhon Airport without visas or other identification."

"Thailand?"

"Yes."

"Master Sun, the clothes and food are trivial considerations. The border at Poipet? That will take money—at least seventy-five dollars American each, and there are no guarantees. If Ramelan has men already at the border..."

Jet Sun placed a finger on the shoes. "These are worth four thousand American."

"In some countries, yes, but not here. Barely four hundred, except I have no intention of selling them. I might frame them later!"

"We have a mutuality, then."

Pheng's brother smiled. "I will give you the clothes and the food. You and the other choose one outfit each from out there. My brother will drive you across the border. He has use of our rental cars."

Pheng II reached into a drawer under the desk and withdrew a small stack of American twenty-dollar bills, counting ten of them.

"This ought to get you through the border. I will have my brother feed you along the way. I will not ask if this is acceptable, you do not have a choice."

"There are always choices, some more advantageous than others."

"Ha! I should have known better to match tongues with Jet Sun!"

"The sum will suffice."

Jet Sun emerged from the doorway, finding Patrick and Pheng cheerfully bantering about Celtic music. The store was inundated with several female shoppers loudly chattering their opinions of each article. Picking them up and setting them back down after review, poorly folded. Pheng II called for his brother. Patrick followed him.

"Mister Pheng's brother will assist us," said Jet Sun. "Choose a new outfit and change into it. Nothing ostentatious, please. Leave your old clothes behind."

"I could do with a shower, ya know," said Patrick.

"We do not have time for that."

Patrick walked out of the dressing room wearing khaki cargo shorts, a T-shirt with Khmer script on it, and large skull and crossbones with "DANGER!! MINES!!" underneath. Jet Sun appeared shortly afterward sporting a standard black oxford casual shirt, gray trousers, and dark brown monk strap shoes.

"What is that?" Jet Sun pointed. "No, you must not wear that shirt. Nothing political!"

"How's I supposed to know?" Patrick looked down at the shirt's graphic.

Jet Sun walked over to the T-shirt section and selected a simple white one with a silhouette of the Angkor Wat temple on the front. "Here, maybe you not look so pale in this."

The Phengs laughed as he plodded back to the dressing area and swapped shirts. He returned a moment later.

"Much better." Jet Sun quipped.

A woman managing the shop across the way suddenly erupted, shouting down the crowded corridor while pointing at Jet Sun and Patrick. Jet Sun looked in the direction she was yelling and spotted two soldiers, forty meters away, briskly walking towards them.

Pheng I tapped Jet Sun on the shoulder, causing him to wince slightly. "Come with me; now!"

They dashed behind the back-room curtain while Pheng I remained behind to stall the oncoming soldiers. When they arrived, Pheng II acted groggy, as if he had been pistol-whipped and robbed, claiming that two local Scoundrel Gang members stole two outfits and tried to pilfer his register. The woman screamed across the hallway that he was a liar, and that it was a monk and a white man matching the description, which is why she called them in the first place.

He yelled back at her, pointing. "You would say anything to be rid of us, woman!"

Frustrated, one of the soldiers leveled his rifle at the elder Pheng. "You are wasting my time, and we will deal with that later. The direction they went is what I need to know, and without a single second for you to think about it."

Pheng II pointed towards the back, and both soldiers cautiously entered, weapons tactically scanning the densely packed warehouse. The process consumed precious seconds. By the time they reached the alleyway loading door, Pheng I, Patrick and Jet Sun were four blocks away, climbing into the family's rental Toyota.

The elder Pheng turned around to face down the woman across the hallway, who had nervously fired up a cigarette and averted any eye contact with him. He slowly walked up to her, directly in front so she could not look away.

"Never burn a bridge from the wrong side of the river."

He retrieved a phone from a trouser pocket and started dialing.

Jet Sun leaned forward to ease the jostling of his shoulder as the car bounced westward along National Highway 6. Passing vehicles were infrequent and varied. The air was thick and hot. The air conditioner worked according to Pheng, but he presumed his passengers would not mind if he maximized his fuel economy by not using it. Another reason being that air conditioners were associated with wealthy westerners who could afford the luxury, and Pheng was intelligent enough to account for curious passerbys. Serei Saophoan lay 35 kilometers west, and the border at Poipet another 50. If all went well, they would cross it in an hour.

A female medic finished wrapping Ramelan's leg while he popped a second hydromorphone tablet. He struggled to sit upright in the blood-soaked chair previously used by Jet Sun. An officer stood before him, informing that although his best man gave pursuit, Jet Sun and the others escaped from the market. Ramelan reached behind his back and whipped around his pistol. He squeezed the trigger, releasing a gas reaction cartridge that fired a sodium metal round into the soldier's head. He collapsed backward, and two seconds after coming to rest, his head exploded, leaving nothing but sordid bits and an exposed second cervical vertebrae.

"Your best man..."

The Fighting Gaze

A novice at St. Michael's Cathedral stood by an arched brick doorway leading to the last room at the end of a lengthy subterranean dormitory. Her hands trembled from holding a dinner tray several minutes too long, hoping the room's occupant would appreciate her nurturing mission. A sister professed that the girl she must serve was a particularly troubled orphan who had become too troublesome for traditional foster care—continuously constructing lies to elicit empathy and cooperation from social workers. In fact, she said, the girl had escaped from her sixth foster family recently, and had to be sedated to quell her screeching, fabricated protests. The sister said to be extremely careful, not to become seduced by the evil within the girl. It is a test. Take her food, comfort her, but do not listen to her stories. A visiting priest would come to see her soon, and she needed to be ready for him.

The novice didn't understand how such a young girl could be such a monster, appearing so frail and helpless as she slept beneath the crinkled linens. Her eyes were darkened and swollen, her expression confused, sullen. Her sleep chronically restless. It was a crime to wake such a person, thought the novice. For the present there is no pain, no worry and anxiety, no drama, only the serenity and hopeful peace that an extended sleep might bring. Except the sisters gave her direct orders that the girl must be awakened, nourished, and alert in time for visitation. A last look down the dimly lit corridor, a deep breath, and she glided into the room with a cheerful smile.

"Good afternoon, princess." She said with a high-pitched song of a voice, albeit exhibiting a touch of playful sarcasm, given the time of day.

The novice wheeled an over-bed table and placed the meal on top of it. The girl mewed as if waking from a three-day slumber—a dream that wouldn't part with a conscious mind without residual unaddressed questions of illogic. She had been elsewhere, now she was here, but where was here? This is not part of the dream, yet it is all unfamiliar, therefore it must be an extension of the dream. *I am awake. I cannot be dreaming. This is real. This is now. There is a strange woman in front of me. Who is she?* Then the sudden recall—the stark realization that she had been kidnapped by a priest and kept in a cellar away from her father. *This priest hurts people. He is not what he says he is. I am… I must escape!*

She moved a hand to rub her eyes hoping to improve her vision. She kicked with her feet and they moved, yet she still felt restrained. She tried to reposition herself further upright, but could not move. She felt around until the bindings around her torso became evident. She could not access her back either, and that must be where the harness attached. She could flail as much as she wanted; the only thing escaping was a tear. She turned her head and saw the novice approaching. She caught the scents of fresh cut pencils, paper, glue, chalk. It smelled like an elementary school—institutional. The walls were mostly barren except for a crucifix and couple framed prints of Jesus and the Mother Mary. She looked away as the novice arrived at her bedside.

"There you are." The novice spoke softly, brushing the girl's hair back behind her ears. "There is a hot meal under the lid. They said you haven't eaten for days."

"I'm not hungry."

The novice sighed. "What is your name, sweetheart?"

The girl turned further away.

"I really need your help... please? I am trying to become a sister of the church, and if I fail with you, they will not let me."

"I need to go to the bathroom."

The novice pointed. "It's over there, but I have to be with you the entire time."

"Let me out of this thing!"

"Give me a minute, sweetheart. They told me you were trying to hurt yourself."

Another lie, thought the girl. She turned towards the novice with an angry expression. "I'm not your sweetheart."

The novice unclasped the plastic straps from underneath the bed. The girl threw them away from her limbs and climbed off the bed, stumbled to the restroom, and closed the door behind her. There was no lock.

The novice looked at the hotdog and beans lunch as it slowly steamed into the air. There were also tortilla chips, cheese dip and a pudding cup for dessert. Surely there was something on the plate the girl liked, she thought.

The novice checked her watch after feeling the girl had taken longer than normal. She had been in there, silent, for almost ten minutes. No toilet flushed; no water ran. The novice approached the door and put her ear next to the frame. Faintly, the sounds of sniffles and whimpering emanated from the other side.

"Is there anything I can do, sweetie?" She asked.

"Go away!" the girl shouted. "And stop calling me that!"

Since the door would not lock, the novice opened it, finding the young girl sobbing. "Go away!" she yelled.

"Please princess, don't yell. It will only make things worse—for both of us. I let you come in here by yourself, didn't I? I want to help you get better. You must have something to eat or you'll get sick. Come, you can talk to me."

The girl wiped her nose and finally looked up at her. A connection had been made, although it was more of a curiosity that a matter of trust.

"*Get better?*" The girl asked, with an irritated tone.

The novice thought carefully, not taking too much time. "Your health. They told me you have not eaten for three days. You must be very hungry or if not, very sick."

"I'm not sick, and I'm not supposed to be here. I want my father!"

The novice remembered what the sisters told her; the stories. This was obviously the beginning of one. If she was to develop trust with the child, she must entertain the stories. At least, entertain them without committing to any action on her part. All she needed to accomplish was getting some food down the girl's throat and prevent any self-inflicted harm or continued escape attempts.

"Well, in order for me to help you, you must first tell me your name."

The girl wiped a sniffle across her face, reluctant to say anything. She felt it an honest intention, and she sensed no malice. The novice would later prove if she was indeed a friend, perhaps. For now, she simply wanted cooperation to help herself.

"Please?"

"Emily, and I don't belong here. I need to see my dad."

The novice stroked her hair again. "That wasn't so difficult, was it, Emily? Come back to your bed and you tell me about why you don't belong here at Saint Michael's."

"Where?"

"Saint Michael's in Washington. Do you know where that is?"

Emily shook her head and didn't say anything.

"Well then, this is the capital of our country, princess."

"I know *that*; I've never been here before."

"Where are you from?"

"California. Cupertino, California. Have you been there?"

"No, I can't say that I have, princess." The novice removed the food tray's cover. "You can tell me about it if you eat something. It won't kill you. Okay, maybe the beans?" She giggled.

Emily looked over the food as her stomach dwelled in the throes of anxiety and turmoil. The beans were not appetizing, but the hot dog smelled palatable and the chips wouldn't hurt. She snatched the bag and opened it, inhaling the nacho flavoring and finally taking one. The novice smiled and shook the half pint carton of chocolate milk sweating beside the tray, opening it afterward.

Too many hours had passed since Emily ate her last meal. That occurred an hour after returning from Six Flags with Matthew's friend, Drill. All she could manage were two small bites of the hot dog and four chips. The milk also proved too rich. She was fragile and could eat no more.

"That's better than nothing, Emily. It will take time before you can finish."

"You said you would help me."

"I said I would listen to you."

"That's not helping."

"Emily, you ate some food and that helps. Now, I am listening. Tell me about California."

Emily began by reiterating that she wanted to see her father, and that she lives and goes to school in California. She mentioned the death of her mother, and then she launched into a fantastic story of a horrible clown chasing her, and then soldiers blowing up her father's laboratory and killing people. They killed her best friend and her parents, and they tried to kill their dog, except the dog lived and came with them to San Francisco. Men shot at them in the city, and chased them in vans up and down the hills until they drove off a cliff and fell into a marina. Armed soldiers tried to get them, so they rowed a boat into the bay and were almost swallowed by a whale, but they landed on an island—a prison. They pretended to be visitors and took a boat ride back to the city. Her father's friend Mr. Jacobson stole an ugly car for them that she accidentally found, and they drove that car forever until a big truck hit them at a lake made of salt. The driver of that truck shot at them too, then he sank into a pond. They drove more and then the car died. Indian men found them and let them stay the night in their teepee, and it was very nice inside. The indian chief gave them a truck and they drove more until the radio said they killed those indians right after they left. Because of that, they painted the truck and kept driving until they arrived at some strange man's house here in Washington. Her dad said he had to take a plane ride but would be right back. He promised. The man, Drill, took her to Six Flags and she rode rollercoasters all day. They got dinner on the way home but when they arrived, a man inside the house hit Drill over the head, and then everything got dark because they put a bag over her head. She was thrown into a car and driven somewhere. It took a long time to get there, and then they took the bag off. They were in some kind of cave or something, and there were a lot of people. Men in suits. There was a voice. It was her father's boss, Mr. Kattner. He had his hands tied behind his back and a bag over his head. Then there was a man from the church, a priest, and he was talking to someone on a TV screen. It was her daddy. The priest got angry with him, so he hit Mr. Kattner with his purple stick and it killed him. Well, it didn't kill him; he could not move or talk. Then someone grabbed her and showed her the screen. She saw her daddy, and then they put the bag back on her head. That was the last thing she remembered.

The novice gasped and covered her mouth. "We will have no more of these stories, Emily."

Bishop Esposito turned the corner and eased into the room. Emily froze and started to hyperventilate. Leaving a sentry by the door, Esposito walked over to the novice and placed a hand on her shoulder.

"Your Excellency!" She jumped to her feet.

"THAT'S HIM!" Emily yelled.

"As you can see, she possesses quite an imagination. I will speak with her privately."

Emily trembled and attempted to avoid him altogether by looking the other direction. Narciso Esposito sat in the novice's chair, taking secretive pleasure in the warmth of it as he watched the novice disappear around the archway. He attempted to touch Emily on her cheek, but she yanked her head away, facing the wall.

"Don't touch me!" She shouted.

"I am not what you think I am, young lady. In time, you will see."

"I hate you!"

"I cannot blame you, child. You are angry, and if you are angry with *me*, then I must defend myself by saying it is misplaced. I am not the one who abandoned you with a strange man in a strange city, Emily. That was your father's doing."

Emily withdrew, trembling. Esposito attempted to touch her face once more, and again she pulled away, although with slightly less ferocity.

"You need time to think about it. Anger is an acceptable emotion, young one. It is without doubt the same anger you displayed when your father walked away. It gives you an edge when you need it the most. You can use it for the game."

● ● ●

"Where the hell are they, Lieutenant?"

"What do you mean, sir?"

"I am in the cathedral basement. Father Bill here has shown me every room, the catacombs and crypts—every chamber. He says he's been here for two weeks and there have been no visiting clergy or Russian nationals, except he's not asking the usual questions."

"Colonel Osterhoudt, I had them marked there 36 hours ago with surveillance on both corners. People came and went, but our folks never left. He is lying. They are there."

"Lieutenant, if you tell me they're there one more time when I know damn well they aren't, you'll be swallowing your microphone within the hour. Got it? They aren't here. Now tell me where they *are*."

"One moment, sir."

The officer located the digital blueprints for St. Michael's Cathedral and gave them a cursory scanning.

"Sir, assuming our surveillance didn't hiccup and they are still somewhere on site, the blueprints do not provide any indication as to where. There are no hidden chambers or exits detailed in the plans."

"Escapist verbiage. You should have been an attorney, lieutenant. *Assume* is not in my vocabulary. Either your men missed them, or in fact there *is* an exit and the good Father here is hopping on the Down Elevator. Tell me where they are!"

"I don't know, sir."

"Finally, an honest answer."

"I will requisition an engineering team if you like."

"Negative. Requires a warrant, and there'll be too many questions."

"Sir, I just received word from General Tomlinson for your recall, marked Immediate-1. A confirming text should be in your inbox."

"There in 15."

* * *

Emily's expression changed to confusion. A game? What game? She had become too weak and distracted for games, yet her innate curiosity reflex couldn't be manacled by ephemeral physical conditions.

Bishop Esposito grinned. "It should not surprise you to know that every time you logged on to the games at home, we were watching. Those that do consistently well, particularly in the combat games, gain our attention. Those who are truly exceptional are provided the opportunity to become something special. Well, with our help, naturally. I am to understand you completed Crown of Light Four in less than a week. Extraordinary girl."

Emily bundled herself and turned back towards the wall, occupying her mind by looking for patterns within the stones' cragged surfaces. The violations of men: her father, the man he trusted, the men who chased her across the country, the men who killed their native American friends, the man who promised to protect her—Drill. Then she refocused on her father's betrayal. *Daddy, don't leave me!*

東

Jet Sun blocked everything out, managing a mere twenty minutes' rest in the back of a droning sedan diligently finding its way to the Thailand border. Conversely, Patrick couldn't extinguish the scenery, the noise, nor the prevalent, viscous evil continuously assaulting his nostrils—the fermenting mudfish used for prahok. His head bobbled with each lean of the car, each pothole avoided, each scooter and oxcart passed, each wandering tuk-tuk. The heat was stifling, irritating, and his new shirt was soaked with perspiration. It was the longest hour in a vehicle he had ever endured, and yet, there existed a certain understandable comfort compared to the cage, the screaming cicadas, the stench of blood, and imminent death. Pheng noticed Patrick's suffering, and for the longest time did not wish to create further tension. Upon entering the outskirts of Poipet, it could no longer be avoided.

"Mister Patrick, Poipet can be quite entertaining city. You should know that it is also very dangerous. It is filled with beggars, touts, and what the English call con men. Fortunately for you, I know of all tricks. You need not worry of those. I must inform you that the border crossing soldiers are also dangerous. If you are famously Irish—"

"Hold on. What do you mean exactly by that, Pheng?"

"Apologies Mister Patrick, I do not wish to offend. It is known of Irish tempers."

"Aye. Ya see that, Master Sun? I've been branded!"

Jet Sun did not break his concentration, maintaining his trance in pain management.

"Well, what does that have to do with anything, Pheng?" Patrick turned back around.

"It is awkward to educate on such matters. Anger is not tolerated in this area. It is an act of aggression and excuse for violence. If you should talk to any of the touts, be firm in your refusal, but do not become angry with them for attempting to scam you, no matter how much they try."

"So, by what you're saying, I'm not supposed to get pissed for some eejit non-stop trying to rip me off?"

"Precisely."

"Oh, that'll be the day."

"I am serious!"

Patrick rolled his eyes. "I'll do my best."

National Highway 5 transitioned from a rural byway to a wide thoroughfare of packed storefronts with individual traffic streams of pedestrians, bicycles, motorcycles and remorks, to finally passenger cars, buses and transport trucks occupying the lanes towards the middle. At the end of the long stretch was a crowded roundabout, which Pheng navigated without hardship. Beyond, were the Grand Casinos' pedestrian skybridges. On the other side of the casinos, under the Khmer Gate, luggage and visa touts swarmed upon the halted vehicles as they waited to cross the border, shouting warnings of non-existent regulations or massive savings if they were utilized to purchase advance travel papers. They were Poipet's *other* 1%, the part the city would rather not talk about, except it depended on them for a sizeable portion of the local economy. And by local economy, it meant the unscrupulous individuals that regulated the criminals—policemen, the politicians, and even the casino operators that took cuts and skimmed the rest from the addicted touts. Hope was a universal concept in the fleecing arts.

At last, Pheng's fare arrived at the border. Two officers surveyed the car, first its occupants, then the rest of the cabin. When satisfied of no immediate threat, one of them approached Pheng's window and requested passports for all occupants. Pheng smiled and handed his credentials through the window with a $100 bill tucked inside the flap. Without hesitation, the other signaled Pheng to open the bonnet and boot, which he did without delay. The officers each inspected the spaces, checking the secured parts for contraband. Most were too lazy to unfasten the spare tire for a view, except the guards were exceptionally diligent to Pheng's apparent alarm. His anxieties evaporated when the hood and trunk closed without howling high-pitch orders to exit the vehicle. The officer holding Pheng's passport handed it back and asked that he pull the car a few meters off to the side lot just beyond the bridge and out of view from the rest of the crossing queue.

"This is not standard." Pheng said.

"What ya mean, Pheng? Didn't you pay them the two hundred?"

"Not necess... Wait, here they come."

"Whatya mean?"

"Shh!"

One of the guards barked a directive in Khmer.

"He wants you to get out of the car."

"What?" Patrick yelped.

"Do not complain or they will hurt you."

Patrick pointed to Jet Sun, still meditating. "What about him?"

"Just you."

"Oh, for the love of—"

"Do it!"

Patrick opened the door, his body language protestant. As soon as he cleared it, the guard shoved his baton into Patrick's abdomen, causing him to gasp.

"You think we stupid!" The guard spat in poor English.

Patrick couldn't respond, fighting for air.

Pheng reached down and produced the other hundred, folding quickly and palming it off to the other guard who stuffed it down a trouser pocket. He nodded to the other and the guard withdrew his baton, allowing Patrick fresh, steaming hot air to scorch his lungs. Patrick erupted in a coughing attack. Pheng climbed out and ran around to Patrick's side, reopening the car door and helping him sit down. Patrick fought for air and struggled with residual acid reflux as Pheng strapped the seatbelt around his waist and closed the door. When Pheng returned to his own seat, the guard closest to him spoke again in Khmer. Pheng said nothing. He twisted the ignition and sped off towards

Aranyaprathet, Thailand. 25 kilometers beyond that town to the west was Watthana Nakhon and an airport just on the other side of it. At Aranyaprathet, however, Pheng turned north. It was then that Jet Sun's eyes finally opened.

"Where are you taking us?" He asked in a gruff tone, fighting.

"Alternative route. My brother says that Ramelan has offered a reward for your capture. It is very tempting at one thousand dollars, I must say. If I did not hate that man, I would have taken it." Pheng smiled. "Brother say you hurt him bad. Word getting around, Master Sun. For some, it gives hope that we will be rid of him someday. For the others—the greedy—one thousand dollars is impossible to resist."

"A notable sacrifice, Mr. Pheng. You honor me. Thank you."

"W-w-wait a moment, here." Patrick stuttered. "*Another* brother? And just when did you speak to 'im?"

"Greatest apologies, Mister Patrick." Pheng laughed. "He was the border guard with the stick."

"What?" Patrick wailed.

Jet Sun cracked a pained grunt, suppressing himself.

"What the freakin' hell for? I was one blink from lettin' 'im have it!"

"For show, Mister Patrick. The other border guard was new—needed example."

Twenty minutes and another two direction changes, the group arrived at Watthana Nakhon. The airport was desolately quiet, except for a filthy Cessna 150 practicing touch-and-goes. They rounded the last of three hangars and Jet Sun finally exhaled. A fuel truck was in the finishing processes of servicing a sparkling new Gulfstream.

"There?" Pheng asked.

"Yes." Jet Sun grunted.

"Well, I'll be knackered by a golden Kookaburra. That was brilliant fast, man!"

No sooner did Pheng's saloon come to a stop near the jet's port side, the airstairs swung down to lock, and a well-dressed man trotted down them.

"How fortuitous that Monsieur Du Rennes was conducting business in New Delhi, Master Sun and dear Patrick."

"Henri!" Patrick shouted.

"We have much to discuss, gentlemen. *S'il vous plait*; time is not our ally. Please come aboard and introduce me to the man I must thank."

"He's Mr. Pheng, but don't be thanking him too awful much Henri, it'll hurt you!" Patrick guarded his ribcage and climbed up the stairs.

Jet Sun embraced the Cambodian driver and offered a prayer. Henri offered his hand and placed a thick fold of Euros totaling 5,000 in Pheng's.

"*Merci beaucoup, Monsieur* Pheng. You will find the amount superior to that offered by the Chinaman. Wealth in righteousness, yes?"

Pheng couldn't believe his eyes.

Aboard the Gulfstream, Jet Sun made fast for the lavatory. He removed his robing and placed it on a counter next to the sink. He sat on a bench seat covering the commode and cleared his thoughts. An out-of-place jar on the lowest shelf over the faucet caught his attention. He examined it carefully and opened its lid. He knew the scent well. It was strong, and it reminded him of something his mother had used once many decades ago. *Beaver musk?*

A Match to Light

Tangier and Tarifa flew by Aphrodite's windows some ten hours earlier, and Chris' second attempt to somehow fall asleep against the war between modern engineering versus the ancient sea met with some success. The first 24 hours, a few of them, Dao, Monsignor Trovarto and Anastasia included, marveled and theorized further progression of Aphrodite's technology after a lengthy personal tour hosted by Princess Celeste of Monaco. With all her luxurious convertible living spaces and self-adjusting semi-hydrofoil systematization, traveling at 50 knots in open seas still meant random oscillations and outright crashes. Neptune's musings weren't the foremost factor contributing to Chris' insomnia, however. Since Dao offered herself in sacrifice to a false patriarch cloaked in piety, he felt betrayed. During the previous year, he secretly wished her reciprocation, and no consultation of theirs passed without some form of flirtation. It became an artform in choreographed initialization. When he finally obtained a deeper connection, an improbability he presumed never to occur again, she yanked the ejection handle. His priority was Emily. It would always be Emily. She knew that there could be no argument, absolutes considered. If Emily were lost, so too would he become. There was only one way to win. He could no longer see past the next move on the chessboard, for the noise of exponential alternatives became a gnawing earwig causing bruxism and insomnia.

Dao approached him with one hand outstretched. Something was in her palm.

What was it? Chris drifted. *Wait. That wasn't Dao, it was... Patricia? Junior Year Patti? But she's older. Didn't work out before; why should it now?*

There were so many excellent things about an ex that haunted him—traits forgone with Suzanne. She was always loyal and supportive. Their best lovemaking flashed in his mind, and he found himself torn due to stagnation—boredom. Chris ultimately looked at the distant picture. *Who would have been the better soul mate?* All the unknowns, skeletons included, but the allure was impossible to resist. The background felt familiar. It was a house he'd visited often in his dreams. He did not know its significance, only that it was familiar and recurring. It belonged to someone else; a conservative heirloom brick Georgian mansion built in the late 1950s, perhaps. Fireplaces throughout, and an old basement that once entertained drunken soirees. *Whose home was this? Why does it keep recurring?* Then Patricia. He felt his soul escaping as she grasped his lower jaw to plant a wet kiss. He loved Suzanne. It didn't feel right. Nothing felt right. His heart was torn. Why couldn't he love two women? Not at the same time! The kiss was familiar, one that he missed. It felt like a homecoming, too. It startled him into hyperventilation. His mind raced.

The fog lifted with his eyelids in the darkness as he laid bare next to Dao. He felt dirty. He could not tell her. *It's too complicated, and frankly pointless.* He was with her. *Suzanne is gone. Patti was a dream—a dirty dream that held no logic. She was not searching for me.* Even if it were some sort of psychic connection, which postulations he now considered given evidence of late, his mind concluded that Jeanette was an ex-girlfriend for a very good reason. *It's high school for God's sake!* He analyzed all the scenarios and it always came down to incompatibility. *Why does she haunt me so?* They were close—so very close to perfection. *High school!* She simply couldn't *love* him, nor could he love her. *It would never work. Get over it. You did once, and you were better for it. Now you have another opportunity. Love Dao absolutely. You don't need any more reasons, and there can be no more doubts. She's the one, the best one, and Esposito cannot have her. Not now. She's yours, and letting her fight for you is the ultimate expression of it. Wake up, Chris!*

Upon whispers of Dr. Miller's discomfort, the Princess made one of her many attributes apparent—making sure anyone could comatose themselves for a specified time. Except, if anyone should abuse this hospitality, by accident or intention, they would be lost at sea—a terrible tragedy. Her imperative dissuaded most inquisitors except for the severe cases who welcomed death if their condition persisted. After 25 hours, Chris had been there, staggering on the starboard promenade to catch a glimpse of Gibraltar's distant silhouette. His balance finally capitulated to a tall wave, and he welcomed her remedy after Dao's insistence. It would be another ten hours until he regained consciousness. The chimes of Aphrodite's intercom pinged. Her captain announced a one-hour ETA to Porto Santo, which was still very much over the horizon.

To Chris' surprise, there was no lingering narcosis. He rubbed his eyes and checked the bedside clock, pleased with the time elapsed. He sat up in a slight haze. His memory was blank for the first moments, then the stressed anxiety rematerialized. *Dao.*

She had apparently deserted the cabin some time earlier; he couldn't tell. Her side of the bed was still rumpled, and a few of her belongings remained, yet she wasn't there. He thought he should locate her—let her know he was all right. Suddenly, the burled maple cabin door swung open with Monsignor Trovarto and Dao cautiously tiptoeing through it.

"Ah, but-a he is not a corpse, *signora*."

"I was about to go look for you." Chris said.

"Did you hear the announcement?" She sat on the bed's corner."

"Yes, and... Uh, my present disposition has me a little embarrassed, Father."

Trovarto laughed. "Oh, no; we are-a adults under unusual circumstances, no? What you do is-a your business, although officially I cannot condone it, you know. Unless-s, that is—"

"No!" Chris yelped. "That won't be... not yet, I mean."

Dao blushed and slapped his shoulder, hard.

As Chris reeled, Trovarto continued, "You seem to be okay this morning, no? All is good?"

"Actually, yes." He winced. "Surprising. I don't recall a thing, quite frankly. Whatever that was the Princess gave me, it worked." Chris raised his brow. "What about you? I thought this trip would be murder on your ear?"

"That-a NASA scopolamine is a gift from above, except I think it takes a day or two for-a the sea legs to grow. I am well, brother."

"Brother?"

"Yes, well, I should explain. La Fratellanza do not have initiations or-a polling on its members. You are invited and you either accept or no. I should-a tell you that no one has declined such an invitation."

"So, I am... you are inviting me?"

"No, I am-a telling you!" Trovarto laughed.

Chris cocked a brow. "And the others?"

"It is a family, brother. Everyone is a member by necessity, now."

"Time will tell."

Chris strode off into the head and ran the shower. The Monsignor looked at Dao, shrugging. "What is the matter with him?"

"He is angry with me."

"Ah, yes. The fear of loss. Did he not understand your plan?"

"This is apparent. I offered myself without consulting him..."

Trovarto rubbed his chin. "Oh, he needs to-a be part of the decision process, yes?"

"He thinks. It was the only logical maneuver, and there was no point in taking additional time to reach the same conclusion."

"Signora, sometimes-a little diplomacy help-a the man satisfy his primeval instincts."

Dao Ming shook her head. "*Nánrén!*"

Aphrodite's captain ordered the helm to reduce power, gradually weaning velocity from the planes of its semifoils. The 80-meter hull slowly descended into the sea increasing its waterline and drag. The captain's voice once again resonated throughout the intercom system.

"Her Royal Highness welcomes you to the waters of Porto Santo Island. We are 15 nautical miles yet to the marina. Pico do Facho is prominently visible off the starboard bow. Unfortunately, their marina is not equipped for a lady such as Aphrodite, so arrivals must use our excellent tender craft. Please gather your belongings and report to the garage in ten minutes; Lower Deck amidships. Departure permission granted. God speed to you."

With its anchor dropped and stabilization system activated, Aphrodite raised her portside garage door upward, revealing a two-point extendable gantry crane that launched either of two tenders: a Starck-designed taxi that matched Aphrodite's motif, and a Vikal open tender with a Range Rover parked aft.

The garage also sported a half dozen other toys: inflatables and personal hydrojet boats. Aphrodite's crew readied its super-opulent taxi for launch, having it idled with conditioned air by the time everyone appeared next to its gangway. One by one they filed down it, taking a seat and enjoying the view. The second to last aboard was Celeste, who had withdrawn for the largest portion of the cruise, except for one incurious dinner with largely mundane small talk, and it bored her. Isolation was safer for the Princess. She politely thanked the monsignor for her spontaneous Madeiran shopping cruise. The last onboard was a dock mate for the tender, who had just cleared it and tossed its lines back to the others aboard Aphrodite. The taxi's pilot eased onto the throttles and the boat gently arced away towards the glistening mountain.

The seas were relatively calm during the 25-minute ferrying, and no seasickness intruded even though the wave action was slightly greater than they had been experiencing. The rocky eastern shorelines soon came into view, and finally, Porto Santo's sleepy marina, which was home to three dozen small yachts and rare visitations from Moroccan high rollers stopping off on their way to Madeira. There were three drivers standing by three different Range Rovers parked at the end of the pier where the taxi docked. Princess Celeste bid everyone adieu, was escorted up the gangplank and greeted by a couple who apparently knew her well, judging by the enthusiastic greetings. She climbed into the rear of their Rover, and they sped off to points unknown. The second driver made a brief exchange with Captain Montluc, after which she turned to address everyone.

"We have five hours before our plane arrives from Marrakesh, and it will take another thirty minutes before it is ready to depart. I will be taken to the airport for planning. It is unlikely for anyone to encounter undesirables on Porto Santo, but that does not mean to make yourselves known to everybody. The island is small and quaint with a few diversions. There is a nice sandy beach just on the other side of this seawall that runs for seven kilometers. There are also the hills you saw on the way in. Pretty views. You do not want to get bored waiting at the airport, so you have these vehicles at your disposal.

"Uh, Captain Montluc." Anastasia raised a finger. "Rocco and I think your idea for the beach sounds nice. Somewhere in front of a resort? *Con le bar?*" She winked.

"*Oui*, there is such accommodation one kilometer from here. We will pick you up at the resort entrance at twelve. Anyone else?"

Matthew coughed. "If you don't mind your copilot tagging along with *you* to the hangar, a few extra zees wouldn't hurt if they have a couch."

Montluc smiled. "There are no hangars, but we have use of an office. I believe it has a sofa."

"I saw a place I would like to explore. It is just north of here in the hills," said Monsignor Trovarto.

"We do too, and it's in the same area, Father." Chris interceded.

"The other car will take you. Just be at the north end of the terminal by 1 p.m., okay?"

"Got it."

The chauffer dropped them off at a nondescript trail facing a kilometer hike up a rocky, terraced precipice named Pico Branco on the island's northeastern quadrant. He promised to retrieve them from there in three hours. Trovarto bid them adieu and took off down a lower trail, disappearing around the hill's southern face. Albeit a short haul for Dao Ming's excellent health, Chris struggled with his footings since he insisted on personally escorting the laptop case, now in a backpack. A wooden rail built along several sections of the trail assisted any time his steps felt unsure.

Proximate to the ocean, the atmosphere was heavy, yet it was dry and burning on the lungs. Vegetation was scarce. The only things in abundance were rocks. Time and weathering scarred the surrounding serras, exposing its volcanic past. Thick stripes of dark basalt and limestone provided a striking distraction from the uphill trudge. Chris and Dao maintained a steady cadence for just under an hour, arriving at the peak, breathing harder and deeper than anticipated. They discovered public lavatory with a clay tiled roof, and walls made from loose stones apparently sourced nearby. Beyond it—through a sparse, craggy forest of dragon trees and Aleppo pines—they found a much larger structure resembling an ancient stone villa named Terra Chã. Adjacent was another shelter that, from appearances, housed anyone caught after dark or escaping sudden inclement weather. Inside was a small basin with a constant flow of chilled well water running from a stone trough just above. Dao and Chris held their hands in it to cool off, then drank their fill. In front of the shelter, a dozen descending stone terraces appeared to cultivate overgrown cherry tomatoes—something the rabbits wouldn't poach. Perhaps a larger garden might have once existed there, Dao thought. The runoff from the water basin streamed down the middle of the terraces, providing irrigation. Next to it was a trail, weaving downward into the terraces. Towards the end of it, a wooden placard described yet another footpath plummeting down a sheer and ragged cliff, dropping 150 meters to the crashing waves below.

Chris and Dao eased their way down the ancient stone steps bordered by a modern wooden handrail that also acted as a guardrail. The descent was steep and winding around cragged boulders, sheathed in several millennia's worth of Kestrel guano and contrasted by russet-colored dirt. They soon found themselves at the end of it. A deadly-magnificent view dumbfounded them as they were caught staring at the endless Atlantic; a vista that would send the slightest agoraphobic to fits, or worse, full seizures. The ocean crashed against the rocks far below. It was a chorus of sirens, teasing them forward for the look. They listened several minutes until Dao's patience succumbed to curiosity. She hopped over the rail, and now, any slight miscalculation meant death. Chris never ventured to the cliff's edge. His limit remained five feet away, just enough to fall flat without falling forever. Dao tested the edge and tempted Thanatos for the view, much to Chris' discomfort.

"Why?" He demanded in near panic. "God, why do people do this?"

"What is life worth if I am not in control of it, *bèndàn.*" She inched further; her toes just a few inches from open air.

"Please don't do... Wait, what did you call me?" Chris reached out for her but could not force himself closer.

"If you want me, come get me, *bèndàn.*"

The tip of his fingers outstretched as far as he dared, yet his effort fell short by two feet. She did not reach for him at all.

"There's that word again," he said, struggling for breath and courage.

"It kindly means 'dumb egg'." Her toes crawled even further to the ledge, now even with it. Dirt from the tips of her shoes fell away. Chris couldn't bear watching.

"This isn't fair to me, Dao."

"Fair? What is fair? I am to become as sacrifice for your daughter, and you have the conceit to complain about fairness to *me?*" She huffed. "I could not fall in love with such a weak man, *Doctor* Miller. You will not even come to my rescue. I should throw myself off of this cliff without further consideration. Why make an offering to one undeserving man to satisfy another undeserving man?" Dao shimmied another centimeter towards oblivion; her toes dangled. She struggled for balance in the shifting breezes.

"No!" Chris cried, fighting the invisible force pulling him the opposite direction. His reach was within a foot from her, killing himself to make the final distance.

Dao kept her back facing him as the soil crumbled beneath the balls of her feet. A single tear dripped across her left cheek as she gazed across the infinite blue. She felt the last sustaining earth drop away from under her feet, and as she began to slip into adrenal shock, there was a strong tug at the rear of her shirt. She fell backwards. Chris fell with her, crashing on the terra firma—their feet dangling off an unstable ledge. They remained there for several moments, catching their breaths. Dao kept her eyes sealed in comfort, relishing the confidence of victory. She also had Chris pinned underneath, facing his fear outright. He was breathing abnormally, unsure if he too scored some sort of heroism, or perhaps it was a lingering anxiety that, while they had not perished on the rocks below, they were not exactly out of danger. That's where Dao wanted him—in a manageable amount of danger. She felt excitement from it, and because of that, she rolled over in his arms, reached behind his head and brought his trembling lips to hers, thrusting her tongue fully into his mouth provocatively, expecting reciprocation.

"Ahem." A gentle cough whispered in the breeze.

Chris caught a noise from an impossible direction. He broke away and checked behind him, and then on the other side. Nothing. He looked at Dao, who pulled his mouth back to hers. Another cough—someone clearing their throat. Chris again broke away, this time sitting up on the ledge, feet swinging in the breeze. He struggled to maintain balance as he slowly bent forward, his fingers clawed into the dirt. Slowly the ocean tumult ceased upon the rocks and the craggy ascension lead up the cliffside until...

"Ahhhh, there you are-a, Christopher." Monsignor Trovarto stretched both arms up to him from another railed ledge several feet below.

"Jesus H!"

"Shame on-a you!" Trovarto gave a full-on belly laugh. "You should not speak of Him in that-a manner!"

Dao was jocosely hysterical by this point. To tears, in fact. Chris lost his balance, catching himself just before tumbling on top of Trovarto. Dao yanked him backward smiling and kissed him once more upon the lips.

"This is the amalgamation that matters." She said.

Chris shook his head.

"What?" Dao asked.

"We need to work on your... never mind."

Rocco and Anastasia didn't notice the extent of exposure until noticing their reflections on the mirrored wall behind a hundred or so bottles at the back of the rustic whitewashed beach bar. Their pale complexions were glowing hot, demanding something cold—frozen preferably—to offset the inevitable sensitivity from the burns. The two rum runners that arrived in plastic beer cups were hardly picturesque, but held against their cheeks, they provided the respite they sought, if only for brief moments.

The southeastern views of the Atlantic shimmered across the ceiling of the establishment during a sedate part of the day in the off-season. Most of the shopkeepers were closed for siestas, or at best maintained skeleton personnel only for the occasional unacquainted tourist. Even so, the small bar kept several patrons interested before the late evening parties erupted. These were mostly older couples on holiday or functional alcoholics consuming their morning's labor profits. Neither were interested or capable of activities beyond dinnertime. It was upon ordering their second round that Rocco caught the reflection of a lone middle-aged man who had met eyes with him through that bar's mirror more than twice. He didn't fit the description of the other patrons, although, nor did Rocco or his sister. Both were extrinsic to the time and place. It was then that Anastasia sensed a predator. The rum hadn't dulled her perceptions entirely. Her foot gently tapped Rocco's chair—something the man wouldn't detect. Rocco returned a tap before turning around to face the man, seated over ten meters away. The man withdrew a phone from a trouser pocket and began dialing. Rocco concentrated. The phone fell from his hands and his head quietly dropped upon the table, unconscious. Nobody seemed to notice.

"What do we do? The driver won't be here for another hour." Anastasia whispered.

"You know if we leave, he wakes."

Anastasia nodded. "Go to him, quietly, as if you know him and sit down. Take his phone. Wait another minute, and I will meet you at the door."

"What about the barkeep?"

"He is making more drinks. Do not worry. I can distract him if necessary."

Anastasia stood up just as the bartender delivered their second round. Rocco handed one to her and spoke in rapid German. *"Bring es zu ihm."*

She walked over and sat in front of him in such a way to obstruct the bartender's view. The bartender, with no one else asking for his services, and at best a novice with the German language for hospitality reasons, disappeared behind the bar. Rocco threw more than a sufficient amount of euros on the counter and walked towards the street-side exit. Anastasia lifted the man's phone and looked at it. Her eyes widened, realizing that a call had been made, and it was still active. She hit the end key and closed it. As she stood up, she grabbed the plastic cup, took a large swallow from it and made for the exit.

"He will awaken in less than five minutes," said Rocco, still labored in hard concentration.

"Look!" Anastasia pointed at a taxi less than a block away, its driver preoccupied with a tablet, filching bandwidth from the resort adjacent his parking space.

They ran to him with cash exposed, each shouting *"aeropuerto!"* His mustache widened into a grin as the doors unlocked. "Yes, come!"

The man at the bar slowly revived, groggy and incoherent. He was not sure what happened, and it took another few moments to get his bearings. He remembered he was in the midst of a phone call, except he couldn't remember the outcome. It donned upon him that his phone was missing. He frantically searched his immediate proximity to no avail. *Stolen!* He rousted the bartender from a cigarette break at the rear of the kitchen, demanding to use the phone. The bartender extinguished his smoke and escorted the man to a small office located at the front of the kitchen. The man rudely barricaded himself inside to make the call. Furious rants ensued from both directions. A voice on the other end of the call ultimately complied as the pounding on the office door intensified. The door swung open catching the server by surprise, who attempted to grab one of the man's arms. The man stepped out of the way and shoved the bartender several feet backward. Outmatched, the bartender resumed shouting and looked around the kitchen for an intimidating cleaver, but the man simply threw open the kitchen door and continued to the exit. It would take thirty minutes to assemble his team, and for another hour afterward they unturned every obvious tourist location: the marinas, the beaches, the resorts and restaurants, the other clubs, the park entrances, and the museums. The only place remaining was the airport, and it was only a short drive from the Casa Colombo Museum.

Commander Jacobson passed out on the FBO's burgundy futon an hour earlier, spent. Just over his head, Jeanette Montluc studied her sectional charts, plotting the most economical route to Brava Island in Cape Verde. Island hopping off the west African coast appeared simplistic at first, but the complexities of multifaceted political regimes, her mandate for stealth, and the unpredictability of late-summer atmospherics provided multiple considerations. *1200 miles with little room for error once beyond the Canaries.* She eventually sighed and traced a straight line on the vectoring application. There existed no other choice than the direct route, Visual Flight Rules at sub-optimal altitudes. Too little fuel, too little time, only one alternate landing site, and that was only if the preceding nine-tenths of the flight executed to plan.

Porto Santo's sleepy airport saw little activity over the preceding two hours, with the notable exception of two U.S. Marine Ospreys passing through to eastern points unknown. One of the FBO's entrance doors flung open, surprising Montluc, which in turn startled Jacobson, who had been peacefully resting on her lap. Anastasia and Rocco raced in, talking over each other, attempting to relay the incident at the beach bar.

"How long ago?" Montluc asked.

"No more than 10 minutes." Rocco replied. "Where are the others?"

"Not due back for another 45 minutes, so long as they are untouched."

Anastasia stepped forward. "Where is our plane?"

"Due any time. And so, it will be an additional thirty minutes to refuel and inspect. We must hope that your voyeur is not as diligent."

Monsignor Trovarto scaled a narrow stairway several meters beyond where he eavesdropped on Doctors Miller and Ming. He joined them nearby on a bench that overlooked the endless Atlantic. Chris had removed his laptop from the backpack and held it in his hands.

"There's a part of me that wants to fling this as hard as I possibly can off that cliff, Father."

"Now-a Christopher, why on earth would you contemplate such a thing?"

"I'm not exactly sure. It means so much to the Brotherhood, and apparently to those other people, the Spada Sacra. It means something else entirely for me now."

"And what is-a that?"

"Suffering."

Dao turned to him. "That is an attitude, and you alone are in command of it, *bèndàn*."

Chris glared at her. "This machine represents the fact that many people have died, people are paralyzed, and my daughter; she is now a... a hostage. It's that simple, Dao. I know, we can't reverse what happened, but this object is a symbol of it. Don't you understand? It reminds me of something very painful, not something hopeful."

"*Now, yes...*" Trovarto pointed. "And later? We will be successful, Christopher, you must-a believe it. Negativity never accomplished anything, only prevented it."

Chris turned away, mumbling. *He never shorted a stock.*

Trovarto felt a warmth from within his cassock. The communicator delivered an urgent message for their return.

"There is-a auto waiting for us at the road. They said it is an emergency."

Without theorizing or debate, the group hiked off the cliff and back across the abandoned gardens of Terra Chã. By the time they crested the peak behind it, they were practically galloping, picking up momentum down the mountainside towards the awaiting Rover parked a kilometer below. They arrived panting heavily, the driver jumped out to help them into their seats.

"Your departure is immediate. The aircraft is being refueled," he said.

"What happened?" Trovarto asked.

"They did not inform me, other than to say bring you via the north side, through Camacha, and be aware of any trouble."

"Ah. It-a means someone may have learned of our presence. Yes, time is-a limited. *Avanti!*"

Jeanette Montluc instructed the FBO to fuel the Speedstar until it overflowed the inlets. Pound the wings' topsides for air pockets. She also would not be performing any engine run-up tests at the end of the runway. No fuel would be wasted by lethargic preflight rituals; *get in and get moving!*

As soon as Trovarto's Rover cleared the ramp gate, she initiated the startup sequence. The others fastened their safety belts while the transfer pilot waited by the hatch to secure it once the others were onboard. The Rover stopped just behind the starboard wing and its doors flew open. Chris, Dao and Trovarto jumped out and were directed into the plane's passenger seating. As the hatch closed behind them, the powerful Garrett turboprop ignited and rapidly increased revolutions. As soon as she released the parking brake, Montluc felt a thump on the yoke. A high-pitched scream pierced the cabin as globules of blood and flesh dripped down the starboard windows. Matt turned backward to see the transfer pilot's body collapse below the wing. The Rover driver ducked behind his vehicle and produced a bullpup automatic rifle, spraying the two sedans speeding towards them on the ramp. Montluc opened the throttle, blasting the Rover's door against the driver's legs. He winced, dropping the rifle on the seat in front of him. The vehicles wildly fired at the airplane's tires, hoping to cripple the Speedstar, but its immense thrust accelerated it across the ramp and onto the runway within a few short seconds. Montluc ignored the tower's shouting—commands for her to turn around for a proper takeoff heading. *N'y compte pas!* She launched the plucky Piper southward along the wind with 1100 meters of runway to rotate, fully loaded. It achieved it with 400 to spare, lifting off gently in a steady climb towards 18,000 feet.

The peaks of Madeira were 60 kilometers distant, stark umber against the deep cerulean, just off the nosecone to the right. Montluc set their bearing to 210° and kept her eyes on the cabin pressure gauge. There were no indications of a fuselage breach—no rushing air, no fluid leaks or control problems, no warning lights or electrical faults. If pressurization failed at altitude, there was a hypoxia risk. The experimental turboprop had emergency oxygen outfitted for the cockpit, but not the passengers. It was an issue for the captain's prerogative. The bliss of ignorance was better suited for this journey, she thought. No sense creating anxiety over an undepartable path. She set the autopilot and turned around to take stock of the souls under her charge.

After the ongoings of the previous three days, they had become numb to gruesome, senseless acts of violence. Her angel's blood on the windows were now translucent pink streaks stretching towards the rear, already dry and baking onto the glass. Nobody took notice of it. Their expressions were blank in contemplation. There would be four hours of flight time ahead with no scenery to remark. The interior's sound level was too loud to invite conversation. The logical response was sleep, but quieting their minds? That would take time.

● ● ●

Colonel Osterhoudt had been nursing a watered-down scotch for less than ten minutes when Brigadier General Tomlinson emerged from her office's connecting door to

Operations. Her silver and turquoise eyeglass chain rocked back and forth as she glanced upwards from a communique.

"Flash intercept, CIA. Interesting. Seems our folks made it to Porto Santo. A proxy spotted two of their friends and they evaded him at the airport. He killed a ferry pilot—a Moroccan."

Osterhoudt licked the fronts of his incisors, savoring the 21-year-old single malt. "How long ago?"

"Two hours."

"Jacobson with them?"

"Unconfirmed."

"What aircraft?"

"Experimental single engine turboprop registered to a leasing outfit in Ohio. I just spoke with Richard about it. Said the range was unknown, probably around 1200-1500 nautical if similar to a TBM variant."

"They could be anywhere from Marseille to Algiers, Cape Verde to the Azores, and way too many radar gaps in between."

"You brought Jacobson's key?"

"That's it on your calendar."

Osterhoudt motioned at the center of her desk where a small circular device sat. There were four pie-shaped depressions on its surface. To activate the key meant entering a 10-key sequence using those depressions. Osterhoudt withdrew a small strip of paper from a breast pocket. On that scrap of paper was Jacobson's sequence, written by hand as described by the CIA handler in charge of the program. Osterhoudt hesitated before handing Tomlinson the code.

"Hell of a way to go, don't you think?"

"As long as he's gone, it doesn't matter to me. Directive Six. It works anywhere, right?"

"Global, yes." He handed her the paper strip.

She cradled the disk across the four fingers and palm of her right hand, and her thumb hovered over the four pie-shaped magnesium buttons. A copper-tinted button marked the top position. She studied the sequence of ten, thinking it must have been engineered by some millennial gamer. Ups, downs, lefts and rights. Tomlinson exhaled and entered the code. When it was complete a telltale LED blinked green eight times, confirming activation for the particular agent's key. Its transponder subsequently emitted a code for a particular satellite to broadcast across its network the relay activation for Jacobson's key. A moment later, the coin-sized disk that had been removed from Matthew's chest dissolved into a frothy gray solution that emitted a tiny puff of a yellowish gas, triggering an alert at Du Rennes facility. The doctor reached for his pocket phone and held down the speed dial key for Henri. It would be another ten minutes before the Monsignor Trovarto's communicator vibrated within the folds of his cassock.

Jupiter's Bolt

The lack of turbulent air and the flawless pitch of the turbine's exhaust lullabied the entire passenger cabin. That ended when the first crash of African tropical air shuddered the fuselage, reminding everyone that they were traveling in a small plane susceptible to the lightest currents—invisible potholes and speedbumps traversed at an impractical velocity. Progressively, those air currents became significant undulations, tossing the aircraft several feet up or down without warning. The wingtips flexed and vibrated. Neck muscles were tested, and by the time Sal's Monte Grande peaked on the horizon, the lot of them were severely nauseated.

Jeanette Montluc had been checking the fuel gauges with increased regularity. Matt sensed her angst building and placed an assuring hand on her shoulder. She smiled as she reached for the fuel tank switch.

"Does it matter at this point?" Matt asked. "I mean, they've been bouncing just above the reserve line for the past half hour."

"Yes, of course it matters. Lose pressure due to a miscalculation and we have a flameout. It is undesirable to trust that the air bleeders will prime the ignition chamber immediately upon switching tanks. The risk becomes exponential with the increased turbulence."

"The GPS reads 185 miles, another 50 minutes."

"I know. We have a thirty-minute reserve, maximum. It will be close, no?" said Montluc.

"You... like this, don't you? The danger, I mean. Why not refuel in Boa Vista?"

Another voice crackled into their headsets as she glanced at the dried streaks of blood across the starboard windows. "Any deviation increases risk of-a detection. They scramble something fast, it can-a be upon us within an hour. Two if God smiles."

The underground stone chamber dissipated the tenor of Narciso Esposito's voice to a degree, yet Emily felt it resonate through her body with a vileness of the convulsions she experienced during last spring's stomach flu. The man was evil—she knew it as innately as a policeman's classroom display of hardcore narcotics. Bad. Her mind raced into a corner. Esposito turned towards her. As his cassock ruffled, she could not help but squint through a corner of an eye to absorb the laser focus of his wild blue eyes. The expression was perplexing to her; no indication of what was to come. He revealed no malice, no kindness, no impending action— nothing. He simply withdrew the meter-length cane from a fold in his cassock and clutched it tightly midway in his left hand. Its crystal pulsated with a slow, deliberate frequency, and it produced a barely audible hum Emily felt. It sent a shiver down her spine, and the rest of her body reacted with severe horripilation. Her arms itched as he eased towards her with it, and her eyes went wide.

"This is but a tool, child; a tool of control and fear."

Emily didn't understand. *Would he harm her the same way he harmed Uncle Jack? Why was he explaining?* She looked confused and tried her best to look away.

"Would you like to hold it?" He asked, walking steadily closer towards her bed.

"No! You're an evil man, and we all know what happens to evil men. Ugh, you're worse than one of those zombies in an old movie."

Esposito stood beside the bedrail and brought the pulsating Amethylizer to within an inch of the bridge of Emily's nose, "Please do not be rude. I am not what you think, my girl; you will see. Your father was holding you back your entire life. Your talents with the games were not for fun, they were training, yet you never realized it. Millions of you never realized it, that you were training, and all the while we were watching... Watching for the best."

He deactivated the crystal and held the cane out for her to take.

"My father told me good people don't need to make people afraid if they want them to do something."

The bishop cracked a wide grin. "Your father wasn't paying attention to the Word of God, then, was he? Psalm 111, Proverbs 1, 14, 19, Luke 2, John 4... there are many. Fear is first and foremost a weapon, child. An enemy that fears you is your first advantage. You fear this cane because you saw what it can do. You fear me because I have it. Let go of your fear by taking it, child. All you must do is hold the power for yourself."

Emily looked at him in disbelief. *Why would he do such a thing?* Her eyes moved to the cane as he held it out, inviting her to take it.

She glanced back to him. "You're trying to trick me. What if I touch you with it?"

Esposito laughed. "You see no fear in *my* eyes, young one."

In fact, she read nothing in his eyes. They were cold, expressionless and expectant. She could take the cane, activate it somehow. *Or smash him on the head?* He is a strong man, she thought. He could take it from her in an instant. And how could she turn the thing on in the first place? She watched carefully, except she did not catch how he deactivated the crystal. There must be a switch somewhere, she thought. She studied the cane as quickly as she dared as his assessing eyes where upon hers. There was no switch that she could see.

Esposito cracked another grin and the pale purple crystal at the top of the cane began to pulsate. Emily flinched and scrunched herself away from it as far as she could while maintaining a sightline.

"Now would you take it?" The bishop asked, reaching yet further with the cane's bottom towards her.

If there was ever a time, it must be now, Emily thought. She lunged and snatched it from Esposito's grasp. She immediately thrust the crystal toward him and made contact with his chest. The bishop collapsed backwards one step, falling on one knee. There was something wrong, Emily thought. He was still in control. She suddenly realized that the crystal was dark—not pulsating as before. *A trick!* She threw the cane on the ground before him as he glanced back up towards her.

"I hate you!" She screamed.

"You see child, fear is a control. Fear compelled you to strike me down, and I should have been afraid. Did you sense fear within me? No, you did not. That is your first lesson, child. Know that your creation of fear has taken effect. A fearless enemy has an advantage—an advantage not known to you. Never reveal your fear." Esposito picked up the cane and held it out for her once more.

"No!" She yelled.

"Yes, that is it, child—fear and anger. The same anger you no doubt displayed when your father abandoned you at the house of a stranger."

Jeanette Montluc switched fuel tanks for the third time since discussing it with Matthew some forty-five minutes earlier. He sarcastically smiled at her each time she did, too. The fuel gauges were well below the reserve lines, and only twitching after a knock of turbulence. Brava slowly emerged on the magenta horizon some 30 nautical miles distant, overshadowed by Fogo's massive stratovolcano just off the port side at flight level. Montluc had been descending over the previous 20 miles in an effort to maximize fuel economy and take advantage of the winds at lower levels. For the most part, the severe turbulence was behind them.

Esperadinha's tiny landing strip finally appeared on the other side of Bay of Fajã's imposing umber cliffs. The Grande Visage indicated a short runway with rocky drop-offs at either end. When Montluc circled it the first time, genuine concern coursed throughout the cabin.

"Oh Jesus..." Matthew's voice broke the intercom's silence. "*That?*"

Montluc looked at him with a smirk. "What is the matter with it?"

"It's tiny!"

"I have landed on carriers, Commander."

"Sure, but you had an aircraft designed for it with a hook! And what about the wind?"

Montluc turned back around and concentrated on the pattern. There was nobody on the ground to offer weather advice, and definitely no windsock. The airstrip was completely deserted, and its tattered FBO building boarded up. No telling if there were any rocks on the tarmac or other debris. Lose a tire on this short runway and a high-dive off the end was guaranteed.

Montluc used the Atlantic's wave direction to determine the best approach, and she reasoned to make it from the southwest as soon as practically possible. She entered the downwind angle over the ocean and caught a glimpse back towards the small building at the end of strip. A white passenger van just stopped in front of it. Their conveyance, she imagined. She reduced the throttle slightly and the prop's pitch even more. Their airspeed plummeted as she turned left to base. She dropped the flaps to twenty degrees, which significantly tugged on the airframe, and then she monitored the airspeed indicator's markings. When the runway appeared perpendicular just ahead of the port wing, she made a sharp left turn to line it up. Montluc increased flaps to the full forty degrees and activated landing gear, which again tugged on the airframe as though it were attached to a gondola cable. Seconds later, three miniscule green LED lights signified the successful locking of the wheels.

"*Pardon moi*, Captain; aren't we a little high?"

"This is normal for a short field landing, *Commander*. You must excuse me for a moment, *s'il vous plaît*."

All Matthew could see was the number 05 racing towards their windshield. At once, there was a tremendous jolt of wind turbulence as the small plane crossed from cooler ocean waters to the searing heat of the rocks and pavement. Montluc held her concentration, and with an exaggerated flare, made a hard touchdown a few dozen feet past the beginning of pavement. Everyone flew into their seatbelts as she set the nose down and slammed on the brakes, narrowly avoiding two grazing cows that had wandered onto the tarmac's left side. She threw the propeller pitch lever down and throttles to full, creating a tremendous reverse thrust. The aircraft slowed to under 40 knots with about 300 meters of runway remaining, and just then the right brake pedal went slack. She didn't panic, anticipating much worse since the volley of gunfire that erupted back on Porto Santo.

Montluc sequenced every scenario from explosive decompression to landing gear failure. What would happen if this or that tire blew, engine problems, running out of fuel, and if she lost a brake line. She was mentally prepared, compensating with rudder adjustments, emergency brake handling, taps to the left brake and constant reverse thrust. But the last bit of runway and the jagged cliff on the other side of it were fast approaching. Father Trovarto prayed—his gestures noticed by the others, who silently joined him. They passed the van waiting several meters away from the end of the strip, and that was as far as the Speedstar needed. Montluc jogged the plane towards the right side then locked the left brake pedal, making a 270° turn towards the FBO building and the awaiting van. Nursing the throttles and pitch, she brought the hobbled bird to rest just in front of it.

"Heavenly Father..." The Monsignor whispered as the turbine switched off and the prop spun down.

A dark-complected man in his upper 30s, wearing plain khaki trousers and a plain red T-shirt, stepped out of the van and opened its passenger doors. Another two men, also casually-dressed, appeared from the direction of the dilapidated hangar, located another fifty or so meters behind the van. With a thick Portuguese accent, the van driver opened the hatch closest to Trovarto.

"Come, hurry. I must take you to the Furna docks."

"What about this plane?" Montluc yelled.

He pointed over his shoulder. "To be scattered at sea tonight."

"A pity!" She snapped.

"Come, hurry!" He went back to the van, climbed into the driver's seat and started its engine.

It was low tide, and the van trundled down the sea-washed stones of Fajã de Água's single, narrow street. The downtrodden buildings gave little evidence of curious residents except a few adolescents craning to get a look through the van's tinted windows; a futile effort. A minute later and they were already at the other end of the bay, about to ascend the abrupt volcanic bluff that led towards the center of the island and its central township, Nova Sintra. The road was cramped and winding, with evidence of continual rock-slides and makeshift repairs. Any miscalculation or mechanical failure would certainly be cause for concern. There were many perils and few if any escapes. Nonetheless, their conveyance diligently traversed the Vulcan palisades and entered the island's interior provinces.

Timeless terraces of browned grass filled with livestock and separate vegetable garden rows graced both sides of the road. As the van penetrated the denser township of Vila Nova Sintra, shrill screams of children at play combined with competing amplified music broke the quiet passage. African urban hip hop faded to the indigenous kriola ballads of Eugénio Tavares, strummed on a classical guitar. More children soon materialized, having to move out of the way briefly before continuing their impromptu fútbol match.

The street led them to the town's central tree-lined park square, and on the other side was a worn road that would eventually wind its way around yet more farms and craggy hillsides until it dropped into the commercial port village of Furna. Its lagoon appeared empty; the fishing boats dragged upon the tidal beach section for the day. A tall concrete facility loomed beyond the marina docks at the water's edge, and by comparison with the other early 19th century buildings, its five stories towered above the others. It rested against a soaring bluff that extended well over 150 meters above, and at the top was a massive 2-megawatt wind turbine, powering the entire village.

The driver pulled the van adjacent the building's side entrance and jumped out to open the passenger doors. Queasy from the harsh ride, the group exited and took a moment for themselves on solid ground while the driver fetched his employers from within the facility.

"I've never felt so removed." Chris said, stretching his legs, making mental assessments of the local engineering.

Monsignor Trovarto approached him. "It is-a one thing to be removed, another to be alone. Exciting, no?"

"Exciting?" Chris' pitch went up, and Trovarto caught himself.

"Not what I meant to say, Doctor Miller. I just-a suggest that it is-a better that we have each other for whatever comes next, yes?"

Chris gazed across the harbor at a Greek-inspired chapel built upon the side of a cliff above two caves. "I suppose."

The driver and a uniformed dark-complected woman in her mid-30s emerged from the doorway and escorted them to the facility's entrance. The woman handed the driver something, presumably a fold of Euros for his loyalty and silence, sending him away with a cautioning nod. She turned towards the group and directed them inside. Once their eyes adjusted from the brilliant sunshine, they realized that the building's façade did not indicate its interior operation. In fact, it was a complete misdirection.

The massive marina doors at the front of the building were perhaps sometimes used for appearances, a relic from the old packet trade days—pre-World War II—but the interior was an immense sea cavern, over 40 meters to the ceiling and some 400 meters in length with modern industrial fixtures and lighting throughout. It carried the appearances of an old

German U-boat pen, certainly long enough, wide enough, and deep enough with plenty of protection overhead, Matt thought. At the other end was a giant lock to the Atlantic, and just before the end of it, the silhouette of Jupiter's Bolt calmly rested against the left-side wharf. The woman ushered them to an electric cart, and once they were all seated, whisked them down to it.

Even up close, Jupiter's Bolt retained its shadowy appearance. The dark mass stretched some 30 meters in length, and 16 meters wide, with a central hull suspended over three meters off the water by three connecting arches traversing the outer hulls. Its hydrofoils retracted along with its main telescopic sailing wing. Three men wearing orange jumpsuits were working on different sections of the boat, and a fourth man in a white lab coat holding a tablet, stood next to an engineering platform off to the side, waiting on the group to arrive. The transport stopped a few feet away from him, and he stepped over to greet everyone.

"Ah, Doctor Ming, this is an extreme pleasure!" He reached for her hand with a bowing gesture. "And you must be Doctor Miller. I am in the presence of greatness. My name is Robert Hughes, Chief Engineer of Jupiter's Bolt."

He shook the hands of the others and led them onboard then into Jupiter's capacious salon.

During the plane ride, Chris guessed at Jupiter's interior design. Probably a spartan décor with emphasis on strict utilitarian aspect, he said. It was an experimental craft, after all. That would not be a signature worthy of one Mallory Du Rennes, Dao countered. As soon as they entered, she turned to Chris and smiled. Jupiter was an exercise of efficient design and artful, sumptuous elegance. Only a Frenchman would demand so. The oval salon featured exotic, finely-crafted veneers bordered by polished aluminum. Its white linen seat cushions were filled with a synthetic down that doubled as floatation devices—plush and cool to the touch. Overhead was a patterned ceiling of inlaid woods and metal, depicting a mostly nude Jupiter, casting a handful of lightning bolts down from the heavens. In the middle of the salon was a circular table at knee height, and there were six panel monitors on top of it at the middle, arranged in a semicircle facing outward. For the moment, they were dark.

"Please take a seat; you must be exhausted. And please excuse our skeleton crew. Loose lips, as they say," said Hughes.

The uniformed woman emerged from the galley with a drink service, moving from person to person, offering their choice of coffee, tea, or chilled water.

"Any questions before we begin?"

Matthew raised a finger. "Just one."

"Yes Commander?"

"When are we departing?"

The man adjusted his glasses and glanced towards his tablet. "This is not the correct question, for you see, it is not a matter of 'we' but 'you'. When are *you* sailing? I will not be joining you, nor any of the team, including Captain Montluc. As soon this briefing is concluded, ideally within the next two hours because there is the consideration, which will be news to you, that two American Seahawks were dispatched from the USS Kearsarge, somewhere off the coast of Saint-Louis, Senegal about twenty minutes ago. At their top speed, it provides us approximately three hours. Monsieur Du Rennes mandates that you must be well out to sea before they arrive. It would be disastrous otherwise."

"Um..." Chris squinted as the others looked on, confused.

"Yes, the obvious. Jupiter is a completely automated vessel. You do not need a captain or mate's experience to sail her. You input a destination; she does the rest."

"Okay, kind of like throwing a bird off a cliff, isn't it? Except the bird is a cat." Matthew said.

"A catamaran with automated wings, Commander Jacobson. It will at first not enjoy the flight, but it has no choice in the matter. It is a flying cat."

Monsignor Trovarto sat forward. "I agree with-a the Commander, and-a gentlemen—the sooner the better, no?"

Hughes laughed. "Of course. Everyone ready?"

"Ready for what?" Chris asked.

"Your briefing on this vessel, Doctor Miller. Although it is automated, and your collective engineering acumen is impressive, Monsieur Du Rennes felt it important that you have the background and, at the very least, a few basics before setting off."

"At least." Chris said under his breath.

"Okay then, about me... I'm from San Diego and I was part of the team that designed and built this boat. You might have heard of the America's Cup? We successfully defended it twice. This facility is an auxiliary submarine base, constructed by Monsieur Du Rennes in cooperation with the Portuguese Navy in 2009. It serves as a diesel refueling platform and other maintenance services for their two Tridente-class vessels, manufactured a year later. We see one of them every other month. The rest of the time, Du Rennes uses Furna for the development of Jupiter. She was part of a design process intended for the next Cup defense before Du Rennes acquired us and the patents. He placed us and others from several of his technology divisions in this cave for the past two years with a rather lofty set of design specifications, performance goals, and a virtually unlimited budget. This is the result, completed just last week. It was scheduled for trials, but—"

"Wait, so it hasn't been tested? Jesus!" Chris rolled his eyes. "Sorry, Father."

"This is-a shared concern, Christopher."

"Not *fully* tested, Monsignor, and I'd much prefer to fly along with you, except Du Rennes forbid it, saying, if the boat does what we say it will—what it's designed to do—then I am either a liar or I am not necessary. Either way, he is retaining me."

"Please continue, Mister Hughes."

Rocco also sat forward, hoping to be of some additional help.

"Monsieur Du Rennes gave you an overview of what Jupiter's Bolt is: a sailing yacht that should achieve record velocities in a variety of winds, doldrums excepted, of course. Here's the tech involved: What you're onboard is a catamaran in essence. It's driven by a telescoping mast that acts as the main spar of a sailing wing. That wing is of variable camber, meaning its geometry changes to the desired conditions and performance goals. You may consider it analogous to an airplane wing; they behave very much the same. Jupiter's electrics, navigation, etc., are powered via the wing's Fourth-Generation nano-solar Infinity Sails, combined with triboelectric nanogenerators on the topsides, to produce a maximum 12Kw output to the lithium battery packs."

Dao interrupted, "My department developed the solar arrays—60% efficient. The project was halted without explanation."

Chris shook his head. "Naturally."

Hughes continued, "The power and propulsion system provide zero radar and heat signatures—pure stealth. I mentioned the boat was not *fully* tested. It marked 80 knots in two-meter seas with only 12 knots wind. This is achieved by the telescoping, shock absorbing T-foils located in three positions along both nacelles. Forward, amidships, and aft. The systems know which to deploy under each condition. Low speed maneuvering is possible due to a unique magnetohydrodynamic thruster set. It'll make ten knots, but it's taxing on the electrics. Use it sparingly if you must; the theoretical range is ninety miles in zero wind and current.

"Now, about how it all works. The entire system is controlled at the autohelm just behind us. It uses touch screens and voice control for program entries, and a paddle for the thrusters. The traditional ship's wheel functions, although it's mainly decorative. Du Rennes has a throwback thing, you know. Anyway, every system is electronically controlled by the server hub, optimizing all settings for maximum efficiency. This includes my best tech if I might say so—the gimbaled, laser-guided diagnosis of upcoming waveforms, including height, period, shape, and so forth. The scanner instantaneously reads the ocean surface up to six hundred meters in advance, constantly adjusting the foils for minimum stresses at the best performance. I should also mention that the foils themselves are skinned with a membrane secreting layer mimicking those of certain fish. I will elaborate on that in a moment. You should also know about the breakthrough in scaled supercavitation."

"What is this?" Rocco sat forward.

"It is a gas enveloping the foils at speed, reducing friction drag. The contact area is extremely small—one tenth of a millimeter. Ever noticed a boat prop losing its paint on the edges? That's due to cavitation. Air and water beat it to death, making it inefficient. We've introduced a reciprocating gas bubble injection system along the skin of the foils, creating a stable envelope with 96 percent less drag. Not only have we overcome the 50-knot cavitation barrier, we managed to create that stability at speeds lower than 100 knots."

"I don't understand." Matt said. "Slower?"

Hughes recovered from a sip of water. "Well, you see, 100 knots *was* the theoretical lower limit of envelope stability, creating a 50-knot no-man's-land. The American military contractors experimented with supercavitating submarines, torpedoes and foiled cruisers for decades, dreaming of 100-plus knot vessels. We have it now, and it works. In fact, the next step for us is to transcend the technology by taking Burt Rutan's advice and applying it to aircraft using a static magnetic gas envelope. This is exciting enough for now, though. Theoretically, Jupiter's architecture could withstand mean pressures to produce an excess of 200 knots. *That* velocity, well... I'd become a test pilot—risky.

"Nonetheless, in order to get to that 100-knot threshold, we needed increased technological assistance with the foils. That's where the membrane secretion system came in, and frankly, it's my favorite part of the boat. Sailfish and swordfish have been clocked at speeds in excess of sixty knots. These are short bursts, mind you. You get the idea. After intense studies, their speeds were not only attributed to musculature of the animals, but to their ultra-slippery scales and air bubble secretion glands. Sound familiar? Their long, spear-like noses and swept dimensions are of course excellent for water penetration, and the secreted slime that covers fish, the air bubbles, and especially the friction-reducing geometry of the sailfish's scales make a phenomenal difference. Jupiter carries two drums of the membrane, one in each nacelle. They're only used in the pre-supercavitation condition, and paused when at speed."

"Vulnerabilities?" Dao asked.

The engineer raised a brow. "Many! Microbursts, loss of electrics, which in that case there is the ship's wheel, loss of wind, and collision. There's not much we can do about the microbursts. If you hit one at the wrong angle, it may damage the wing. Loss of wind? Use the Magnetohydrodynamic drives until the wind returns. And about the collisions; Jupiter's navigation and detection systems, particularly its collision avoidance modules, are quite robust. Additional to a sonar repulsing beacon, we can detect and avoid the larger species, and the razor thin titanium edges of the foils take care of the smaller ones. The real problems are steel containers that for any number of reasons become lost to the cargo liners, often floating just under the surface, hidden to radar. Catastrophic if you strike one, I'm afraid."

Chris placed his cup of coffee on the dinette. "I see the potential to fulfill another sad cliché!"

"Shut up!" Matt laughed.

"Even though the systems are automated, pay attention to not overextend the catamaran's foil booms at the highest velocities. Rough weather or excessive velocity will cause a failure, okay? Don't want to see you pitchpole her either. Almost ruined the Cup for us a few years ago."

"Damnit! That's one of my peeves." Chris said.

Dao turned to him. "What?"

"Pessimistic foreshadowing, like they do in the movies. You know, when they purposely have someone say 'and watch out for that blanket-blank because blar, blar, blit', and behold! That's exactly what happens."

Matt said. "Yeah, well, the law of jinxes states that because you pointed it out, it won't happen."

Dao smiled. "That is not the way it functions."

"Please, people, we must-a focus," said Trovarto.

"That's it, really. Not much more I can offer. It's a boat, it floats, it sails itself. You folks are intelligent types, so I suspect the engineering is mostly self-evident. What I cannot convey in this short amount of time is the basic seamanship should something go wrong."

"There, see! He did it again!" Chris scowled.

Matt took him by the shoulder. "Got it covered, okay? SEAL... remember?"

A loud explosion thundered through the cavern. The muted thud of it alerted everyone who spun to see what was happening. One of the stevedores was standing over the other, holding a pistol aimed at his head, motioning to Hughes. The engineer scrambled off the salon and across the bridge to the port nacelle, just a couple yards away from the men. There was a phone and a boxcutter lying on the dock nearby. Hughes covered his mouth at the bloody mess before him.

"Caught him photographing you, the bastard."

The man groaned as he bled out onto the dock.

Hughes turned back to the group in Jupiter's salon. "We must assume he made contact. We can delay no longer. Take care of him, and then help me with the lines."

"Yes sir."

"Jesus, they're everywhere!" Chris fogged the glass, staring at the man on the ground. Dao tugged at him to look away.

Jeanette Montluc straitened herself and grabbed Matt's right arm. "You are leaving."

"I don't agree with Hughes on this; you should go with us."

"This is not a choice for me."

"It is for *me*." Matt said. "Personal bias aside, for all practical purposes, this is a *flying* vehicle, and who better to have along but a pilot. A damned fine pilot at that!"

"I cannot disagree with you Matthew, except it is not within me to displease my employer." She brought herself closer to him, inches from his face. "It is better for you to have a reason to live through this, no?" She kissed him briefly on the lips. "These people, we must defeat them. Monsieur Du Rennes will spare no expense this time. Business is one measure of his competency, and you do not yet know his passion for justice. I am best fighting along his side, you see. *Adieu*, but for now." Montluc let go of him and said goodbye to the others.

It had been over two hours since Robert Hughes greeted them. At most, the American Seahawks would descend upon Furna in one hour. It could be less than 30 minutes with a tailwind, which was quite possible given the prevailing breeze across the Cape Verde archipelago. Hughes climbed back aboard and jogged across the bridge to the salon. He skipped the obvious small talk and instead began initialization of Jupiter's systems. The operating software immediately booted and all screens came to life.

"Commander Jacobson, since you are the most qualified operator, please join me at the helm."

They walked back to the control station and stood in front of the monitor array.

"I don't have time to explain everything to everyone, so give me you undivided attention, please."

"Done."

Hughes pointed at the different monitors and gave brief explanations of each's function. Camera locations for live monitoring, power production and consumption. Hydro-dynamics of the foil system, propulsion, the sail wing's oper-ation, auto-navigation and weather radar, and all other operation metrics, including the slime secretion system. It was all there on nine interconnected touch screens that used intuitive iconography.

"Plug in your destination here; it pops up on the map. Drag the path for waypoints, long-press for options or deletions. Not much different from the way your phone operates. Once you enter a destination and hit start, the automated systems take over to give you whatever desired ride condition of your choosing. See here?" Hughes pointed towards the right-center screen. "You may select one of several options: Best Time, Best Time and Stealth, which senses and avoids radar contacts from observing you line-of-sight, Comfort Cruise, which is at the lower end of the stable envelope, and Recreational Cruise, which is the slowest hydrofoiled ride. Ignore the last two modes, they are not for this trip. If you want a custom speed you can scroll to the desired velocity on the speedometer, or tap it twice for a numerical entry. The automated navigation GPS, radar, and sonar controls everything else, including collision avoidance procedures underway and harbor maneu-vers all the way to the dock itself. If for some reason you need to reference something, there is a complete operation manual available in the menu here on the lower-right corner. If you lose electrics, there's a hard copy along with all schematics in the library of the captain's cabin—amidships in front of the galley."

"Got it."

"Okay, go ahead and enter your destination."

Matt studied the navigational map, swiping, stretching and pinching at the screen until he found a section of beach he liked on Virginia's Eastern Shore. Hughes looked at it for a moment.

"Your route parallels a shipping lane for too long and comes too close to Bermuda. May I suggest heading further south into this zone below it, then go northwest to your destination?"

"If you say so. The others will want the fastest route, but I know it's a moot point if we're detected. Frankly, I give us a 1-in-10 shot at making it. Too many what-ifs and your boat's untested."

"I have faith in her engineers—top authorities in their field." Hughes smiled.

Matt shook his head. "Carl Sagan had a quote for that. Just press start, you said?"

"Yeah. After the lines are thrown, K?"

Curious, Dao and Chris looked on from a side window of the elevated helm. Hughes stepped out and shook their hands once again.

"Be kind to her, please. It's sort of like you're running off with my baby before they've learned to walk."

As he bounced off the port nacelle, Hughes instructed the stevedore to assist him in casting Jupiter's Bolt off the wharf. They unplugged the shore power cable, then carefully untied the lines, allowing them to retract—automatically, of course—into specially-designed corner lockers. Hughes motioned to Matt, tapping his right finger into his left palm. Matt touched the start button and Jupiter's magnetohydrodynamic drive system gently thrusted the yacht towards the center of the cave's waterway. Gradually the helm increased speed to a wakeless two knots. Just ahead at the cavern's exit, the underwater concrete locks opened to sea, allowing the tide to flow through the tunnel. The autohelm corrected for the increased current, maintaining the boat exactly in the center of the waterway with intermittent thrusting.

Crossing the littoral threshold, Jupiter's Bolt oscillated slightly as the waves crashed against her hull. Her thrusters worked to keep level for the first few moments as they increased velocity. Blinding sunlight coursed through the cabins, triggering the automatic tinting systems, not unlike those of the Grand Visage. Matt watched as the system activated the telescopic wing. He looked upward and upward as it grew to an astonishing 35 meters. Once locked, the variable geometry activated, adjusting the wing's camber and trim. Then the acceleration surged.

Jupiter abruptly extinguished the magneto drives and allowed the wind to work its magic. Drinks flung off the dinette without warning and anyone standing fell aft. Matt was thrown against the rear rails of the helm, and suddenly he realized why there were so many handholds distributed about the space.

At first, the gathering of speed was violent, crashing into the waves from peak to peak, building past 20 knots. At 22 knots, the yacht lifted out of the water and all at once, the violence and noise dissipated to gentle rolling with a building rush of air. The carbon-titanium foils extended well into the water, and the pressure magnified. Matt watched as the speedometer ran from 25 knots to 40, then 55, then 70. The rush of wind passing by increased from a dull whistle to a deafening roar for anyone caught outside the serenity of the cockpit and salon. As the velocity built, the rocking motion lessened, becoming a smooth, silky ride with little perceptible oscillation. Matt turned around and Bravo was already four nautical miles distant.

Chris, Dao, Rocco and Anastasia didn't know what to think as the craft accelerated to impossible speeds. Two-foot seas raced underneath them, yet they felt little if any motion. The autohelm kept Jupiter imperceptibly still as it trimmed for best cruise—a theoretically estimated safe speed of 150 knots in 12 a knot breeze. The instrument panel in front of Matthew indicated 14.6 knots true wind speed; a stiff breeze generating the wave heights. The speedometer was fast approaching 90 knots, and Matt felt the slightest vibration under his feet. As the speed grew, so did the random bumps. Dao looked to Matthew acknowledging she felt the same in the salon. They all did. 95... The vibration worsened, shaking every part of the vessel. Intermittent shuddering caused concern on their faces, and Matt didn't know what to do. Shut it down? *Hughes didn't say anything about a vibration. Hell, this is the fastest this tub's ever flown!*

The lower left engineering panel flashed red then green, and a graphic of the foil's reciprocating gas injection system along the six foils, of which only three were in use. A countdown to activation indicator appeared in the middle as the speedometer approached 100. *The envelope!* Matt felt a secondary vibration, a powerful compressor activating, and a faint, high-pitched whistle emanated from both nacelles. The instrument panel flashed again. The speedometer flashed in tandem and both went green. Almost immediately, as it did when Jupiter lifted from the turbulent Atlantic, the yacht's shuddering and vibration ceased. The autohelm signaled a modification to the wind and foil angles, and the moment it changed, Jupiter surged in speed, rapidly building past 125 knots on its way to 150.

Matt looked to the communications array and intuitively located the salon's intercom. "We are now the fastest sailboat... ever."

Captain Jeanette Montluc climbed aboard a medium pilothouse yacht along with the two stevedores, one of whom was a corpse shrouded in thick black plastic. The other cast off the lines and started the motor, idling the craft out of

Furna's harbor and into the straights before Fogo. During the thirty-minute ride to São Filipe's main port, he relayed instructions and directions to a safe house located on the southeast side of town near the airport. Montluc was to remain there until summoned, out of sight. Her skin color stood out amongst the natives, he told her. It was a fact punctuated several minutes into their foray when two U.S. Navy Seahawks en route to Furna overflew them. At three miles out Montluc and the stevedore watched as they descended into the protected harbor, finally landing in the parking lot next to Du Rennes facility. They could not discern the dozen or so special force operatives jumping out of the helicopters before the rotors stopped, securing every entry and exit. It was an awful aggrandizement of firepower for the single uniformed woman they captured behind a desk next to the wharf. She was half way through a cigarette, nervously anticipating what was to come. Her interrogation would last 72 hours, but Mallory Du Rennes paid well for silence, and her retirement was guaranteed should she not divulge the trashed servers now corroding beneath the cavern's waters, nor discuss Jupiter's specifics or direction. Every minute she delayed meant another two or so miles Jupiter was further away.

"This is killing me. 14 hours to the other side of the planet, now several days to get back," said Chris.

Matt nodded. "Too much time to think makes a man crazy."

"As-a no time and-a hasty decisions? I think I should-a find a bed and lie down."

"I *hate* this!" Chris grumbled.

"Yes, nobody said-a we have to like it." Trovarto produced a fake smile as he descended the starboard companionway.

Two hours down, Matthew had grown tired of staring at the control panel. There was nothing he could do but observe the tedium of minute speedometer fluctuations at the whim of the wind. The autohelm erased the backbreaking toils of a dozen deckhands. No skippers, no trimmers, no bowmen, grinders or tacticians. The ride became surreally dichotic at speed. The anxiety of a crash should anything go wrong—anything—and there would be no warning or time to brace for impact. The blasting air just outside confined them to the interior sections, and gratefully, Du Rennes' accommodations were peerless in design, function and comfort. *A flying Nautilus*, Chris thought.

Industrial Complexity II

"Okay then... Where are they?"

General Tomlinson's rasped vocal cords grated the late morning's dew as it swiftly evaporated from the manicured fescue blades of Arlington's eastern slope. Sitting next to her was a dark-complected man in his late forties, his brown eyes hiding behind his Aviators. He wore a plain dark gray suit, an unremarkable blue-striped tie, unpolished cap-toe oxfords, and he carried a matte black leather portfolio. He was CIA, and Tomlinson hated dealing with them. Never supportive, never trusting, always probing. She thought they used everyone for leverage just as she had so many years ago, and levers were created solely to be pulled at some point.

"Somewhere in the Atlantic, and that's an assumption."

"Jesus, Ron, is that the best you can do?"

"The woman wouldn't say anything concrete. She acknowledged the descriptions of your people and she pointed towards the sea. Nothing else because she's been coached. Easy to spot because the training is ours. Now for the boomcake. Jacobson is with them."

"Jacobson? Impossible."

"During the interrogation she reacted in a way that indicated recognition."

"Then either your key code was wrong or the system failed."

"Or it was removed before you activated it."

"In either case, we have a problem, Ron."

"Tutlow said you had a gift for understatement. He also said expectations are the mother of all disappointments." The CIA man produced a thin grin and opened his folio. "You have another problem..."

Colonel Osterhoudt reviewed the brief Tomlinson handed him some twenty minutes earlier. TS/SCI-stamped pages detailed a hack on their surveillance of Brownstone, but the traces were judged "Inconclusive", which meant that they terminated at illogical locations. American high schools, post offices, select elite corporate boardrooms, churches, and daycare facilities. Nothing remotely questionable, let alone international, and no ghosts behind those bounces. Wiped.

"Utah said the hack's signature appeared two times previously. The first contained a flaw, or a flag, I should say. Behind one of the decoy nodes was a partial IP address that appeared to originate from the Philippines. We dispatched an operator who not only confirmed it as a bounce, but traced it further—two steps, actually. It terminated at the San Giorgio Maggiore campus in Venice."

"A church," said Osterhoudt.

"Yes."

"Questionable... and disputable, you know."

Tomlinson squinted. "Are you done?"

"Not quite, hon. I suppose the reason I'm here is because I was just recalled from a *church*."

She handed him a manila envelope. "Our man at Langley just delivered this. It was copied from a Bratva operator in St. Petersburg... full dossier on a possible militant faction within the Holy See."

"Impossible. They wouldn't stand for it."

"Assuming they knew, certainly not."

"Okay, so you're saying they don't know or won't claim them, but *we* know, and the CIA knows. Apparently, the

Russians—*our* Russians—also know. How can that Vatican *not* know? What is anyone supposed to do about it?"

"Nothing."

"What... Why?"

"And that's from the top. CIA is hands-off, which means all of us are, officially. That's not exactly why you're here, Colonel; there's more. CIA also delivered a communique received anonymously. It stated that the Millers were of a mutual interest, and if we cooperated in their capture, there would be a mutual benefit."

"Did that also come from Russia?"

"He wouldn't say, but that would be my guess."

"You're not thinking of dancing with them, are you?"

Cardinal Vasco Tagliabue sat slumped, staring at the sparkles of the micro-laser-latticed monitor screen. His eyes were tired and dry, his breath exhausted. He kicked his chair away from the desk and meditated for several minutes. The chiming halyards down at the marina became a louder chorus, and the Adriatic's breezes poured into his chamber with a familiar warmth and humidity. He trembled as the rosary beads slipped one-by-one through his right thumb and index finger. A drone of Marys escaped his lips with a desperate sonance. *The fool!*

Their satellite communicators, a clandestine affair launched decades prior, connected. Narciso sat and listened to his elder with a patient calm that the cardinal routinely fingered as arrogance. What Tagliabue expected instead was the typical response—fear and obedience.

"I cannot provide your injunction, Narciso. You know what you have done. You know what you are now doing. You know that I have strictly forbidden it, as it has been forbidden since the creation of the Spada Sacra, to expose ourselves as an autonomous operator to our competitors, suffice to band with them. You must dispose of this girl. You must dispose of the executive. You must also dispose of all those you have engaged within the Bratva. Do you understand?"

"Has His Eminence forgotten our true mission—the sacred task? The machine is too important for us to ignore, father. How can you not see it? Our church, all churches, will fall."

"We endeavor for *some* ambivalence, Narciso. Prophecy foretells the next enlightenment. We were only temporary until the love of the trinity could overcome it, or at least, exist alongside it. You cannot forestall total knowledge forever, Narciso, it is inevitable."

"I shall clean up those loose ends to which you refer in due time. The girl belongs to me now, just as I belonged to you."

"Belonged?"

"Father, there is one matter for which you are correct—inevitability."

La Brochette's angular face slipped from the shadows. He marveled at the micro-laser lattice display, poking his blade through the projection from the opposite side of the desk, startling Tagliabue, who didn't detect his entrance, nor the gasps of felled sentries at the chamber's doorway.

"My boys outside are dead, yes?"

La Brochette rolled his eyes and gestured with the stiletto.

"And you are here for me now."

Again, La Brochette gestured.

Tagliabue paused and mumbled through the two remaining beads before the crucifix of his rosary. It took less than ten seconds to complete his prayers.

"I will not resist His will, as you must figure within it. This world is no longer for me."

He closed his eyes. *"De Oratione Dominica…"*

The Russian bowed his head, stood up, and stepped around to Tagliabue's back side.

"Pater noster, qui es—"

The blade plunged into the back of Cardinal Vasco Tagliabue's neck just above the atlas vertebrae, severing his spinal column. Death was instant.

La Brochette wiped what little blood remained on his blade across the priest's right shoulder and whispered in Russian, "Hypocrite."

The sounds of the harbor returned. The chiming halyards grew louder as the breezes intensified. The light spilling in from the window grew golden. The air felt wet and heavy, almost velvet. The scent of ozone and petrichor was unmistakable. Soon, the sky would open in anger, as it could not merely weep. There are no tears from hell.

Patrick and Jet Sun awoke at separate times in separate rooms. The Thailand-to-Corsica run took the better part of nine hours, and little of it was restful. For the first few hours, the monk wrestled with his injuries, mentally blocking the pain receptors, wave after wave, while the beaver musk steadily repaired him. Jet Sun listened to the murmurs of Mallory Du Rennes' and Patrick's conversation; a debriefing of the Palace Mena incursion and their capture at the airport.

"That fella Ramelan, we didn't exactly stick a fork in 'em yanno. Might come 'round, right?" Patrick asked.

"Such a bastard! And by now you are both primary contracts of the Black Exchange." Du Rennes swished his cognac. "This is to be sure."

"No." Jet Sun moaned. "Ampullae—"

"What?" Patrick leaned forward to make eye contact, but Jet Sun reclined, wincing.

"He means the Ampullae of Lorenzini, Patrick."

Jet Sun nodded.

"Ironic, isn't it," said Du Rennes.

A reluctant smile broke across Sun's face, his eyes squinted as another wave pulsated within him.

"Ya mind lettin' me in on this here, Mister Du Rennes?"

"Minute electrical sensors in certain predators, Patrick. Sharks, particularly upon their snouts, detect faint distortions in electrical fields generated by the muscles of injured or excited prey. A pounding heart in fear, or compensation for an injury."

"Alright, but—"

Jet Sun took a deep breath. "He is exposed, humiliated... crippled. He cannot not survive his surroundings."

It was the last memory Jet Sun could summon as he laid in bed, staring at the blank white ceiling four meters above. *This was not Corsica*, he thought. *I know this place.*

He breathed normally and he felt no pain, although he hesitated at making any sudden motion. Jet Sun slowly brought a hand from underneath the downed duvet and gave it a test drive. The fingers bent, so did the wrist. He could make a fist without hearing a joint crack. Now the other. Same result. He propped himself up against the headboard. No stiffness other than from sleep. Everything felt fine, except for a dullness in his left shoulder. A sudden recollection flashed, and he turned to examine it. The exit wound had healed, leaving only a trace scar. He felt around the backside of the shoulder with his right hand. Nothing. *The musk is genuine,* he thought. It could not be expected to repair the deep tissue and muscle damage. The musk—combined with natural dimethyl sulfoxide sourced from the ponderosa pines of Crow land, along with certain herbs—induced a potent analgesic effect, reducing pain to a mere ripple. Based on previous experience, that too would cease in a couple days.

A faint dawn leaked its gentle luminescence through shear fabrics adorning the picture-windowed wall to his right. He turned away from it and sat on the bed's edge. His body should have ached as a middle-aged man's normally would, but the only sore muscle at the moment writhed between his temples. Across the room through an archway leaked another light. *La salle de bain.* Water to splash his face. Clarity.

Jet Sun sensed the echoes of footsteps outside the room's entrance and turned around to see the stone pocket door silently retreat into the wall. A lit green circle appeared on a module next to it.

Henri smiled. "Less for wear, *Mon Père*? Your appearance is superior to yesterday's."

"I am no priest, Henri; we discussed this."

"Tisk! This remains debatable, to me anyway. The *Monsieur* wishes to see you."

Jet Sun noticed Mallory Du Rennes pacing by the entrance.

"Yes, of course."

Du Rennes stepped in, making eye contact with his butler as they passed. Henri activated the stone door and it slowly closed behind him. For the next several minutes, Du Rennes detailed everything known about the Palace Mena attack and the escape that ensued—how the others survived their own battles with Mukhtar Arwa Lal, the incredible flight from Cairo across the Nile estuary, the limp to Corsica and finally to the Château. The difficult part ensued.

"Why did you not tell me of this on the plane?"

"It is not my place to dictate her movements, Master Sun. Of course, I insisted she remain behind, as it is imperative we retain at least one of the agents responsible for the creation of Miller's machine. She would not listen to me. Felt it was her destiny to go—to fight if necessary. There would be no debate. No idea where she inherited this idea?" Du Rennes nodded. "She and the *docteur* devoted several hours downloading their most salient research regarding the device. This is for now, at least, safe."

Jet Sun's expression became dour. "That is not the sum of her knowledge."

"What do you mean?"

"Dao possesses our dynasty's most ancient teachings. Besides me she is the last of our line."

"Then it is fortunate you are here."

"You do not understand—"

Mallory motioned Henri to place an armchair closer to the bed, which he did for his employer without delay.

"Continue."

"It is not for public consumption for obvious reasons; population control, for one. My country instituted extreme measures. It was decided that only a small number should ever possess the knowledge so our secrets would survive a culling event. There were ten of us distributed throughout the continents—mentor and apprentice—two in Europe, two in Africa, two in North America, two more in South, and two in Asia—Dao and myself. We are descendants of the same family, same dynasty, never recorded as such."

"Were?"

"Ramelan's hunger for elder knowledge and our dynasty's extermination is insatiable. When he discovered the existence of the Shí, he tracked them down, tortured and interrogated them until death. Death, because they were so sworn to die before divulging our secrets."

"And what is the protocol should all of you perish?"

"There is a cache of parchments located in Tibet—the Băokù. One select temple, except the exact location is unknown, even to its masters. Should news of our demise reach it, trials would begin to select a new Shí. Only the first ten who survive the trials will be chosen. The others either died trying or completed them too late. From this point, *Sanda* combat determines masters from apprentices. The exact locations of the parchments are divulged as clues within the last three trials. They must then complete the yíshì—the ritual that binds them to their sacred duty and missions them to the appropriate continent. There, they will spend their extended lives passing knowledge and training from master to apprentice. Never more than two."

"So, your secrets, for all practical purposes, are safe."

"This is incorrect."

Jet Sun cracked his wrists and fingers as he sat erect on the bed's corner. "The last trials occurred during the Han-Chu period. The Shí were not dispersed as they are now, and perished in war. The last of them removed and hid the Bǎokù at another temple, but the temple name, let alone the exact location of the Bǎokù are unknown. Ramelan has been sacking temples ever since, destroying them under the authority of the State Council."

"Forgive me, Master Sun; have you not recorded this knowledge for your own safekeeping?"

"Forbidden, even to La Fratellanza. The knowledge must only be passed from one to another as anecdotes so as to insure it cannot be compromised. It has been this way since before the Xia Dynasty, except, long ago, there was a tale of one who defied the covenant. The others of us were—are—sworn to govern them in totality. There has since been no instance of deviancy. I am concerned that Dao can be broken by professionals."

"If Ramelan is dead as you say, there can be no concern."

"He is not the only one."

● ● ●

A colonel of the Egyptian Air Force stood at attention awaiting the occupants of an unmarked light jet that just spent some of its wheel rubber upon the tarmac of Almaza's Runway 36. The door opened to a light contingent of American intelligence and military men deployed by the State Department to investigate the death of two citizens at the Palace Mena. Their actual purpose was to interrogate certain Egyptian officers connected with the palace raid, as well as the hardware deployed, and especially an F-16 pilot named Captain Chigaru. That job would be in the hands of the last man to exit the airstairs.

He was an Egyptian migrant just after birth, recruited by CIA just out of Princeton. He was in his late 40s, just under medium height and of a slightly less than athletic build. His skin was light brown as one would expect of a scholar that saw the field only as needed. His hair styling was the standard left part, and probably a week overdue for a trim. His eyes were dark brown and he sported a thick black mustache, which could be removed when necessary without much ado. His last name was shortened to Rafa, shortened from his true family name Arafa sometime after college, and he did not dare utter his real first name, for it was far too revealing, and for some in his line of work, off-putting. At his insistence, his colleagues simply referred to him as "Ron".

En route to Giza, Ron and his team watched Cairo's local news via satellite. Reporters struggled to capture footage through the thick security surrounding Palace Mena, violators would either be shot or subsequently hanged for the offense, and drones were traceable. The city only knew that the damage was in the millions, many people were dead, there were revolts being fomented by a few political factions taking advantage of the chaos, and very few answers were squeezed from the authorities. Business as usual.

At the opposite end of the airbase, a section of the joint administration building had been staffed and prepped for the arrival of Ron's team. There, the bodies of two Americans lay in stasis for further review. There was also the mutilated remains of their beloved archeologist Dr. Amid Harwaziz and several others, including the soldiers, all of whom were held beyond traditional burial customs. Certain debris and artifacts—those that were not pilfered by the Egyptians—were categorized and displayed on separate tables.

Among those items was one of the Medusa pills, which caught Ron's eye upon passing that table. He picked one up gently rotated it for closer inspection, deducing its operational purpose. He was well aware of these weapons and observed them in two previous operations executed by the Israeli Kidon, who never admitted their existence, let alone allow capture of one. Their cleaners would have insured it, as they are never more than 300 meters away. The Russians, French or British would never risk such a violation of the Geneva Convention. Likewise, the Chinese since they never perfected the technology. *So who?* he thought.

Ron spent the next few hours poring over pictures, names of the deceased and their travel records. He surveyed the path of destruction following the supersonic F-16 incident, interviewed the base commanders involved, or rather, non-involved according to their statements. A phone had been recovered which contained voicemail fragments discussing travel arrangements to Cairo for "the convention". It mentioned Dr. Miller and a presentation, which confirmed the flight track of Du Rennes Gulfstream. They were definitely here with the laptop, Ron concluded. Why exactly, he did not know. That answer resided with the man responsible for the Palace Mena's destruction.

Outside, Cairo was ablaze with unsettled chants and screams. Sporadic percussions echoed throughout the downtown squares, dissipating across its outlying districts. Kalashnikovs. Spring had returned. Too many were witnessed and affected by the F-16's supersonic damage. Fuel for the opposition. It was a flagrant exercise of excess power without any justification whatsoever. No national emergency had been declared, although the city's press agency had been vetting possible narratives for hours. What was so urgent that necessitated a Mach+ run over densely populated neighborhoods? Explanations materialized slowly, and sharply dismissed as improbable, particularly their first attempt at attributing the sonic booms as a mere accident—pilot error. After the third evolution of an ambiguous excuse, social networking demanded justice.

The base at Almaza was unaffected by the increased rolling blackouts hitting Cairo as its fury crested. Ron entered the most secure of three interrogation rooms set aside for the nucleus of Al-Ghaiz. Rooms B and C had already been utilized and were currently being sanitized of blood, sweat and excrement. The facility technicians insured Room A would appear completely devoid of unpleasant odors or other unsightly distractions. A chilled karkadé tea sat mostly full in front of Mukhtar Lal, condensation beading off its glass. He was seated without restraints, wearing a dull white jellabiya robe. The hibiscus juice stained the inner parts of his lips a deep currant as he licked at them to savor its tart acidity. He assumed it would be his last pleasurable experience before his execution, besides any humor gained by toying with his interrogators. When he lifted his gaze from the tea, he exhibited a telltale hint of recognition, if only for a brief moment.

Ron took his seat at the opposite side of the table, placing a small tablet in front of him, just out of Mukhtar's reach. His expression was dour, and that alone conjured the primal fear. It was a betrayal then, thought Lal. His contact at the CIA had been sent to kill him. *Better it comes from a friend.* He sat back with an assumptive grin. It's The Show, as he once put it. Ron's Big Top, replete with bullhorn, whip, top hat, and tails. Take a bow for the spotlights just before the trapeze star perishes upon the dirt of center ring. *AND NOW, LADIES AND GENTLEMEN...*

"We need to talk." Ron said in Arabic, interrupting Mukhtar's blank stare.

"What?"

"It's okay. No cameras or audio. Just us. This is a white room; nothing leaves it besides the people who enter, and one's condition upon exit is optional. In your case, the option may not be exercised unless you agree to my proposition."

"You could kill me here and have your life back, so it is something else from me you need. A favor. Some service that only I can perform, or perhaps some information that only I possess."

"Chess, not checkers, Lal. Skip to the last likely."

"It's interesting how a world returns. You'd have me killed for a job well done because it was convenient to do so. What is a life, brother? Yours is mine now. What would you have me do?"

"Kill me, because that is what I would do to you. There is no return."

"This is correct, Lal. Under any other circumstances, your throat would be cut by my blade at this very moment. Believe me, I desire it."

"So do it! I am unafraid." Mukhtar Lal grinned and gestured towards the sheathed jambiya knife at Ron's side, obscured by his jacket. "Unless you are here to marry me."

"Your vile humor is your saving grace, Mukhtar, but not the reason I am still talking to you. Come to understand a few lessons I learned from the westerners. In business, you do not dispose of an asset until it is no longer useful. Let go of any emotion surrounding it. It is either of use or not."

"The only use for me now is your death!" Lal growled.

"Time will tell. The westerners also believe this if an asset can no longer be controlled—manipulated for their own gain. And, often this is of mutual benefit. Live or die, it is up to you."

"No." Mukhtar grumbled. "It is not up to me. You do not wish to martyr me for obvious reasons. People fear and obey me out of respect, or so they believe. I would gladly die for it. So, *Rafa* of the CIA, what would you have me do that is better than becoming a holy martyr?"

Ron smiled crookedly with a short chuff. The smile was enough for Mukhtar Lal to start laughing himself, and the laughter of them both snowballed into louder laughter.

"It is a rotating door for your people, are we not?" said Lal.

"When necessary."

"And I suppose it will last only until you need favor from someone else beneath me."

"Some retirements are more fortuitous than others. That depends on you, Mukhtar."

"As it did for the two before?"

"You may spend your golden days collecting sunsets at Sharm El-Sheikh, or we may arrange a similarly creative exit to the one which you are about to execute should you refuse to leave."

In the hours that followed, Ron moved Mukhtar to a poshly decorated facility on the other side of the compound, far removed from the hellish chambers from which he emerged. As comfortable as his new surroundings appeared, his distrustful nature rebooted when two professional security men ushered the party through the entrance. They were curt, emotionless, and wore bespoke utilitarian suits that allowed freedom of extreme articulation when needed. As stylish as they appeared, the suits failed to fully conceal their compact pistols and tactical knives, readily accessible underneath the side of each breast. Or perhaps those items were meant to be seen. *Make no mistake why we are here.*

Mukhtar Lal rubbed his wrists as they traversed two hallways and entered a sumptuous velveteen lounge. In front of them were several tables and chairs forming a shallow ring around a sunken living room outfitted with velour sofas and armchairs. On the back wall was a small stage with a few lights overhead and a retractable projector screen unfurled from the top of the wall. Dinner and a movie, Lal assumed. Towards the right was a western-style bar, wood and brass with an inch-deep coat of urethane on top. All the usual suspects aligned the mirrored backsplash, and the selections were heavily weighted towards the bourbon and Scotch whiskeys favored by the American officers. The lounge was empty except for one technician who operated the theater. Mukhtar Lal guessed there would be a presentation of some sort. The louche salon reeked of lust, sour mash and cigars. It was designed for persuasion, and Lal had guessed that too.

Ron brought him to the center couch a dozen or so feet back from the stage front. The lounge's front door closed, leaving one sentry to guard the inside and the other guarding the entrance. Ron had Lal sit directly in the center of the couch and signaled the female technician to begin. The room darkened as the projector came to life.

"This occurred fifteen minutes ago," said Ron.

As General Askari Al-Aswad sat behind his desk in the office he appropriated by coup d'état less than a year earlier, two men dressed in fatigues rushed his desk and injected him with a serum. His face was incredulous and he could not speak—an immediate effect of the serum, combined with sheer panic. His throat tightened, and he gasped for air as the men watched. In fourteen seconds, the general collapsed face forward onto the desk. One of the soldiers checked his watch, gave a thumbs-up to the camera, and proceeded to decloak the general for transportation.

"Don't worry, he is not dead, but he will pass the coroner's examination with a stroke as cause of death. From there he will be revived, given plastic surgery, a new set of dental records and fingerprints, and finally relocated to a resort on Farasan Island."

"Never to leave." Lal murmured.

"In five years, he may. Most have no desire. *Muqadamaan!*"

The projectionist flipped to show his own computer tablet's screen. It displayed the online portal to a safe numbered Swiss account. It was accessible via an Argentinian shell company manufactured solely for use by certain Middle-Eastern concerns for which the Swiss would otherwise reject for political secrecy considerations, suffice to mention the highest percentage of funding source legitimacy failures.

"This is, in fact, one of your accounts, is it not?"

Lal's head sprung forward and his eyes bulged.

"No need," said Ron. "As you can see, your current balance is 4.7 million Euros. Look closely."

The amount increased by ten million, then another ten million.

"That is two of five tranches scheduled to make deposit. The remaining three depend on your behavior, dear brother."

"Fifty million and the presidency..."

"Which could lead to additional billions, as you know. More currency than any man can spend in his lifetime."

"Provided he lives more than five years." Lal reclined against the sofa's backrest; his arms folded, defensive. "What are my assurances?"

"We make no such guarantees. There are too many unforeseen variables. Your safety is at the will of your people and your actions, or I should say reactions. You will be monitored, always. Defiance means death. Do you agree?"

"I must call my banker."

"A one Sal Rothstein in Tel Aviv. He is awaiting your call."

Again, Mukhtar Lal sighed and raised a brow, although it was capitulation. Ron left nothing untouched. All of his resources were either marked or leveraged, or both. The job was thorough, and in a professional sense, Lal rather admired it. What riches could be plundered with such resources, he thought. Then Lal considered the totality of the west, especially America, and epiphanized all the productive opportunities in place of all the fomented hatred indoctrinated for decades amongst his people. *Everyone just wants to get ahead. Forget the rest!*

"Let the martyrs die for their ideals."

"And now we have some questions to discuss. Let us begin with your motive and objective for attacking the Palace Mena."

As the projector's light faded, Ron placed his phone on the table with its voice recorder application enabled. Mukhtar Lal detailed his entire mission to him, that it was thrown together after one of his Cairo International Airport informants noticed several private jets with mostly western-registered tail numbers arriving at the secretive Terminal 4. All of those parties eventually arrived at the Palace Mena according to a street informant who works the nearby market. Mukhtar assembled his two squads, who were never more than three minutes from ready, and that's when he received a phone call from a man representing an interested party from Europe who would pay two million Euros for the retrieval of his laptop, and an additional million each for two described individuals (photographs uploaded to his phone), as well as additional external income opportunities concerning certain other individuals in attendance.

"They sent one million to my Swiss account before I even gave them the number. Does this sound familiar?"

Lal confessed to the raid on the palace and the deaths of several of his men during the unexpected battle that ensued. He was thwarted from his primary objective when they launched the Medusa pills, a weapon he could have never conceived, let alone anticipate. Ron listened carefully to the parts that came afterward—who escaped across town, who Lal finally captured, and the brutality that came shortly afterward. Lal's expression became ashen with malevolence when stating that all of his efforts failed to capture his primary targets, and when he was contacted again by the disappointed client who changed the deal to a simple kill bounty, he was forced to deploy his Egyptian Air Force stud—an insubordinate who supernovaed the entire operation when he went supersonic over the city.

"He will not live beyond my reach." Lal declared.

"And what became of the two you sold?"

"I do not care of something once I dispose of it, *Rafa*."

"Oh? I have some word that they went to Cambodia, and it just so happens we learn of two men matching their description had been sanctioned by your friend Ramelan, that is until they found most of his men dead. The Chinese was last reported limping the streets Siem Reap, shouting obscenities at the downtown shopkeepers."

"Regrettable. He was a regular customer."

"Nonetheless. So, you maintain that you know nothing more of the two he bought."

"This is correct." Lal squinted.

Ron pursed his lips then barked something unintelligibly rapid at the projectionist. She disappeared briefly, then reappeared, wearing only the skin-tight black negligée she wore underneath her uniform. She let her hair down and sashayed over in front of Mukhtar Lal, smiling as she climbed on top of him. Ron backed away, producing the same crooked grin he did when Lal first saw him. The distrust returned, but it was far too late. The woman gyrated wildly, demanding Lal's undivided attention. He wrestled to somehow throw her off, and his bindings prevented anything so exaggerated.

As Ron walked toward the exit, he turned back and caught Lal's glaring eyes. "You might as well enjoy it... *brother.*"

The hatred distracted Mukhtar Arwa Lal just long enough for the woman to stab him in the jugular with a syringe. As Lal writhed, the serum took immediate effect. He felt the heat of it coursing through his veins. He knew the difference between a strong opioid and something else. The heat grew hotter as the room's light vignetted towards the center of his vision. His hearing dulled to a high-pitched ring as he slipped away, unable to fight the poison. He could no longer draw a breath, but that wasn't the last thing that went through his mind. Behind the red of light from closed eyelids flashed a childhood memory of his mother, long deceased from an indiscriminate military raid on his village. She held a flailing chicken just before taking it to the butcher's block, telling him that he should learn how to do what she was about to do. That's when the raiders broke into their courtyard, spraying it with bullets, expecting men to be there. She was pierced through a lung, which immediately filled with blood, and since she was no longer worthy of their rape, they choked her as Mukhtar hid behind a cart watching in a rage of tears. As Lal exhaled his last breath, one solitary tear emerged from the corner of his left eye. His struggle was over.

"Pig!" The woman spat at his face as she dismounted and walked over to the bar, placing the emptied syringe on its counter top.

"We've one more job for him," said Ron as he handed her instructions on what to do with Lal, then turned back towards the exit. The door guard stepped aside as Ron passed and opened it for him. The outside sentry joined them by taking up the rear. Neither Ron, nor the first guard were in position to notice him reaching under his jacket to activate a satellite paging switch woven into the fabric. Solely by activation, the signal was a crude response to an earlier instruction. No signal within the indicated timeframe meant no further action needed, further contact would occur later. Activation, however, meant immediate action to be taken. In this instance, the message routed itself through to yet another signaling device located within the folds of Cardinal Vasco Tagliabue's cassock, except, the cardinal and his cassock had been properly reclaimed by the newly-pledged operators for Bishop Esposito's Spada Sacra.

In the months prior, Esposito queried each operator under his command and, based upon their fetishes and anxieties, either by enticement or fear, extracted fealty under total authority should the cardinal become untimely deposed. That time had come, and along with it, all Tagliabue possessed. Once the beacon lit on the device, a telltale vibration obliged recognition from its bearer. In that instant, the bishop's mind raced, for he knew that the world would be coming to him. Most of it, anyway. Now he could act as he pleased, and a wide smile broke across his face as this thought occurred to him.

A Praetorian infiltrator within the Swiss Guards removed four bodies in the secluded section of San Giorgio Maggiore and began cleanup operations. Narciso instructed him to mass a task force of a dozen operators, separated into two squads, and await further instructions. At 2am, the Praetorian maneuvered towards the monastery's separate bunks. A transport truck awaited their withdrawal to two tenders which would ferry them to a private airport hangar located at the end of a canal just off the northeast side of Marco Polo's Runway 22R. There, a forward squad boarded a Citation jet, another squad used a Russian cargo helicopter loaded with a specialized van and SUV. Before departing, the Praetorian handed a scrap of paper to a trusted monk. The clergyman walked across the corporate service zone to the airport's main terminal and disappeared within the throngs of tourists. A lone man in a glass-enclosed smoking room had been surveilling the monk's comings and goings for months, and that he belonged to Italian intelligence—the Agenzia Informazioni e Sicurezza Esterna. He lifted a phone to his ear after pressing a speed dial, and then, for only a brief moment, he felt a sharp, burning sensation at the nape of his neck. The phone was retrieved from the floor and the call terminated. The number dialed was recorded before the handset was returned. As well, a notation was made regarding the length of the call.

One second.

It Once Belonged to Atlas

Jupiter's Bolt imperceptibly loped from horizon to horizon with only the telltale accumulation of ocean spray racing towards the windshield's top as any real indication of her impossible velocity. Dao Ming remained nestled in the cockpit's aft couch, grinding through every page of the engineering and operation manuals. She thought at first it was the insomnia when, at random intervals, she felt a slight surge in acceleration and glanced at the middle of six monitor screens just over the largely-symbolic brass and teak ship's wheel. Symbolic because, while it is functional, the console's thrust and rudder control paddle-stick was preferred for manual navigation. Du Rennes demanded it against Hughes' design tantrums. Even so, as Dao continued her examination, understanding that manual operations were, in theory, rarely employed. Jupiter's complex array of cameras, radar and sonar sensors aided the autohelm in the ultimate achievement in pilotless navigation. Her captain programs the final destination down to the actual marina slip or mooring buoy, and the boat would execute an optimal route according to a desired mode selection. Best Time, Shortest Distance, Stealth, Safest (with Stealth option), Comfort, DTA (Desired Time of Arrival), Ride the Jupiter (several designed circuits with banked turns and rapid acceleration/deceleration simulating a roller coaster, a mountain motorcycle ride or small-craft flying), and finally, Race, which Mallory Du Rennes hoped to demonstrate before the next America's Cup.

Dao glanced towards the bottom of the second monitor where the Sailing Mode displayed Stealth, tapping it to unpack comparative navigational scenarios if other modes were selected. Best Time would save over six hours, although the ride would be harsh, and Jupiter's radar footprint would expand beyond acceptable limits. She read further into the manual's section on custom modes, questing for any advantage, understanding the relationship between stealth, comfort, and speed. The processor would grind for seas, predicted currents and weather—the heavy lifting. She wondered how far she dared in sacrificing comfort for speed since stealth was not a variable.

Jupiter's navigation plotted their course along the northern boundary of the North Equatorial Current which flows east to west—the southern arc of the North Atlantic Gyre. Winds and currents are favorable to sailors as they've predictably been for centuries, except for the seasonal tempests—storms with names. To the north sprawls the Sargasso Sea and its famed doldrums, perfect for those cargo goliaths and 20-deck sea circuses. Du Rennes had Jupiter's captain program the route to remain distant from Sargasso's shipping lanes while maintaining a tactical buffer from any sailors who would likely run the great river's middle currents. Their heading generally kept Jupiter on a starboard broad reach, powered by the prevailing easterly trades; not the fastest tack, yet sufficient for the manual's decreed 70% velocity of 150 knots.

Dao shifted her gaze towards the plotting monitor. The first leg from Brava extended some 2,400 nautical miles, slightly north of west, 260°, given small variances for wind and seas. Their course would change towards the northwest at that point to avoid the Bahamas, tacking towards the Virginia coast and the mouth of Chesapeake Bay. Jupiter's tiny flashing triangle appeared three hours or so east of the faint line labeled as the Mid-Atlantic Ridge—a seismic geographical feature splitting the ocean's floor. The Kane Fracture Zone covers a vast area towards the middle of that line, and their tiny triangle was approaching its southeastern quadrant. Nine hours before the scheduled course change, barring no major developments.

Flipping further within the manual, Dao finally located the bits which fueled her anxieties detesting ignorance: "Custom Parameters and Routines Coding". Within those pages were instructions to access the avionics-style raw programming of the machine, which very much resembled the standard C++ language she learned so many years ago. Some routines were written in the Mil-Spec language of ATLAS, however. She recognized the format, although she was not fluent in its statement syntax. This fact did not completely frustrate her, not in her grind of contingencies. The statements were shown in the code, and she could always manipulate their parameters ever so slightly to determine their function. Simple trial and error, so long as the trial was not anything that could remotely trigger a catastrophe. Dao perused several more pages before the eventual yawn escaped her lips. Her eyes returned to the beads collecting then swept away to the other side of the cockpit windshield. Surreal tranquility, she thought. Perfect engineering better left untouched.

Towards the end of the extra-large D-ringed binder, Dao found her final significant and interesting data. Page after page of sectional load tolerances, capacities, and other specifications, mundane and insignificant to all but engineers and technicians. Her curiosities centered on the carbon structures, their weakest points and tested fracture tolerances. To her disbelief, so many critical areas had yet to be tested until she realized that, given the clandestine manufacture of Jupiter, real-world testing might be difficult. In fact, most of the structure had been given only theoretical specifications based on modeling and simulation. It was then that she realized they were in the process of proving every theory, testing each and every parameter—and with their lives. She turned off the lamp, closed the binder and went to the helm where Chris and Matt were transfixed on the horizon.

Dao set the binder down on a teak area next to the helm and shimmied next to Chris, holding on to him.

"Here we are, again in a rush," said Matt. "We're always in a rush. I read a few sailing books while on base: The Long Way, A Voyage for Madmen, etc. This boat, in all its technological achievement, goes straight against the timelessness of the ocean endeared by sailors. I'm actually a little saddened by it."

Matt paused. "Wait... You never told me why the ranger at Alcatraz laughed at something in your briefcase. What was in it other than the laptop?"

"Pair of boxers."

"Okay, so—"

"That..." Chris hesitated. "They were my chili pepper shorts. Silk. Comfort clothes, okay?"

"Silk boxers with chili peppers on them?" Matt started bawling. "Oh, that's *hawt*."

"I still have them."

"Okay, stop." Matt held his hand up. "That's a visual I don't need."

Dao smirked.

Chris turned to her. "Something you wish to add?

"Nope." Dao said with some restraint.

The three stood there for an hour, paralyzed in awe of Jupiter's effortless charge towards the west. Not word between them.

"Guano!" Chris suddenly blurted.

"What?" Matt's head spun around.

"Guano. It was a word my brother-in-law used on me in a Scrabble game. I was attempting to recall it when we were on Alcatraz."

"And it means..."

"The accumulated droppings of birds, particularly seabirds. A valuable fertilizer, in fact."

"Guano."

"Yes."

"Means that."

"Yes."

"And that's what you've been thinking about for the past hour."

"Not until I saw the gull."

"What gull?"

"Flew past a few minutes ago. Barely a blur and tumbled once in the sail's wake. Recovered just above the water."

"We're at least 900 nautical from the nearest land," said Dao on her way out.

"I know. Just a wild guess that it's riding the sargassum. We're within 50 miles from where those blooms form. Where are you going?" Chris asked.

"Control." Dao smirked.

Matt glanced up at the salon's monitor array. The second from the left displayed GPS navigational with surface radar and satellite weather overlays. Velocity was shown slowly fluctuating between 146 and 162 knots. Gentle surges accompanied those speed changes. The computer kept Jupiter's movements smooth, but the craft nevertheless heeled a few degrees ever so subtly from side-to-side. Both Chris and Matt caught themselves fighting the lullaby. It was either conversation or work, and neither had a task at this moment.

"Tell me more about your friend, Drill," Chris asked in a dry tone while picking an apple from the fruit bowl at the center of the settee's coffee table.

"Why?" Matt's brow furled. "What do you want to know that we haven't already told you?"

Chris made a cursory examination of the apple before taking a bite. While chewing, he continued inspecting the fruit for any imperfections. Once he had enough room in his mouth to speak, his attention turned towards Matt, eyes partially glossed and somewhat short of breath.

"He was supposed to be protecting Emily and obviously failed in doing so. I don't recall seeing him in the background with Esposito, and we all presume he defended her, except there's something bothering me about it. By your own descriptions he impresses me as an opportunist if the occasion presents..."

"Now wait just a damn minute!" Matt sat up.

"I didn't forget your anecdote about him selling leave time and never getting caught, until he did, and was discharged for it."

"Look, Drill may be an eclectic capitalist in your mind, I get that. I've trusted him with my life—my *life*—for years at a time. If there's one constant in this universe, it's Adriel's loyalty. He promised he'd protect Emily; he'd die doing so! I don't require empirical evidence to confirm his intentions."

Chris took another bite of the apple and wouldn't look at Matt directly. "It's an assumption, nonetheless."

"What do you mean?"

"That he's dead or otherwise missing."

"Statistically significant probability and even your doctor's mind can't refute that."

"Sure, I'll agree that it's probable given no variables, but you see, there *are* variables. You're assuming that, because of your relationship, under all circumstances, Drill is uncompromisable, and you are also assuming that there is no other possible explanation as to why he's missing. The inclusion of those variables concludes we simply must not assume anything."

"Right. You see! You require empirical."

"I suppose so."

"And what do you hope to gain by my friend's confirmed death?"

"It's not his death that concerns me; it's his life."

Matt shook his head. "Your tone, Chris—you are so far out of line, I am confused."

Chris gazed upon the apple's half-exposed core before rotating for another bite. He chewed on it, savoring the crisp texture and acidic juices, melting their way down. His eyes averted Matt's yet again.

"If he's alive…"

Both of them turned towards the starboard hull companionway.

"Am I interrupting?" said Anastasia, sensing the conflict growing between them.

● ● ●

Furna's harbormaster spat mucus and blood upon the dank, puddled floor of the back office within the camouflaged submarine pen that once cloaked Germany's wolfpacks. Its florescent ceiling lights flickered from the uneven electrical loads as the result of several damaged bulbs and spiraling humidity. A stout mountain of a man, clad in a light tan tactical jumpsuit, hardened and numbed from a dozen years of similar classified intelligence gatherings, tugged on the gauntlet of his steel-impregnated glove while studying the next most-sensitive and vulnerable target on the harbormaster's body. It would be his left clavicle this time. The blow came from above, the crunch unmistakable. The harbormaster screamed in terror, having never felt such pain. No amount was worth this, he thought. Du Rennes' brought this upon his village. He should have known they were all in danger if he didn't speak and do so quickly, but the throbbing waves shooting down his entire left side muddied his thoughts. Would they murder everybody on this island over a secret?

Two officers wearing similar jumpsuits patiently waited just outside the office's side windows. The harbormaster's wailing was muted against the backdrop of two bloated bodies bobbing in the sub pen's tidal eddies along with other flotsam bits. From the other side of the glass, they couldn't quite understand the murmurs escaping the harbormaster's mouth as he driveled into his persecutor's ear, yet they clearly understood what was to happen next after their technician nodded.

Du Rennes contractor had been thorough—scuttling all records, disposing of non-essential personnel, and wiping almost all evidence of Jupiter's cradle from existence. Only he had any accessible knowledge of her, except for her destination, and he had gone into hiding in the hills within a sharply-terraced farm on the other side of Nova Sintra. There, he laid low with a young woman named Joana Rodela, who once resided in Nova Sintra with her sisters until she married an older, wealthy landowner who cultivated exotic coffee beans along those terraces.

The señor insisted on traditional farming methods, using burros for plowing, transportation and hauling. That was, until his beloved Rosita stepped on his foot one morning, triggering the myocardial infarction that had been building as the direct result of his genealogy, combined with the ritual overconsumption of his own product. Mrs. Rodela became Ms. Rodela that morning, much to her sorrow and delight. For the following two years, Joana enjoyed being one of the most sought-after widows on the island. Señor Rodela, unable to sire his own offspring, willed his entire estate to her, and she continued enjoying the spoils of a nearly-perpetual bean harvest. She spent the money frivolously and happily, often treating her family to lavish meals and annual trips to the mainland. Dakar and Senegal were close and visited often, but

they also ventured to Morocco—Marrakesh and Casablanca—
and northward to Spain.

It was during one of those trips to Spain that one of Joana's
sisters fell in love with a young man in Madrid. He promised
her an exciting life in the city along with everything she could
possibly want at her fingertips. It was an impossible dream at
her age, to run away with a strange man in another country.
She shrugged him off, emotionally loyal to her family and
Nova Sintra. Months after she returned home, the idea
metastasized, controlling her actions and attitude. It became
noticeable to her family, and her jealousy of Joana grew. For a
year she instigated frequent and heated altercations amongst
her siblings. She was too young to go anywhere, and besides,
why would she leave them all behind? Her mother would be
heartbroken and her father betrayed.

Her 18th birthday was merely two months passed when she
consummated that betrayal. Whispers circulated of an
incredible reward for the whereabouts of a man in hiding who
performed favors for a wealthy Frenchman. Joana's second-to-
youngest sister slipped away from the family's compound
bordering Nova Sintra's central square, and quickly trotted the
six kilometers down the twisty mountain road to Furna's
harbor. There, she caught her breath and approached the
docks in such a way as to minimize recognition from nosey
onlookers, ignoring the fact that Brava is such a small island,
with an even more diminutive community. As the message
reached her ears in Nova Sintra, so would gossip of her
interaction with these intrusive soldiers at the far end of the
harbor. She was, predictably, identified and followed by the
island's grapevine before exiting the town's square. Before her
parents could dress and arrange transportation to retrieve their
daughter, she was already whisked away aboard a light
cruiser, bound for São Filipe's airport with a promise of extended transfers all the way to Madrid and a €20,000 debit card
from an international bank she recognized. The boat returned

to Furna's dock just 45 minutes later. Bia was never heard from again.

● ● ●

"No," Chris said. "Nothing life-threatening, anyway." Anastasia looked at both Chris and Matt with a condescending glare. "Seriously? I think you know better."

"Oh. Hey, Anastasia... Tulip."

"No," Anastasia interrupted. "Only my father gets to call me that. If I'm too many syllables for you, just use Ana or Annie."

"Apologies, Ana." Chris cleared his throat and turned towards her. "I never got the chance to say how sorry I am for his death. This is all my fault. Everything. We wouldn't—"

"Thank you, but no, it is not your fault. My uncle said you were a brilliant scientist and you were being hunted by the Spada Sacra, like they always do if someone invents something that threatens any part of their religion."

"Apparently so."

"My father believed you were important enough to protect. That is why you are here, Doctor Miller. I believe it as well and we must all work together."

Chris turned towards Matt. "Yes, of course."

Matt had been around Chris long enough to know the look was partially reserved. Anastasia innately knew it as well, except she dared not meddle. Several moments of awkward silence ensued before Matt collected himself.

"This boat has been drugging me for several hours now. Think I'll let Jupiter have his way in the forward port berth."

Chris rolled his eyes as Ana checked the fruit bowl.

"Chronic insomniac, myself. Have you spoken with Doctor Ming recently?"

"No." Chris yawned, then rubbed his eyes. "Where is she?

"She's in the control room."

Chris stepped onto the bridge, straightened himself and made every effort to appear unencumbered for Dao. She closed the boat's manual and turned around, smiling.

"This is an experiment."

"You got that right." Chris laughed.

"No, you must understand. This boat, this voyage; it is the first. Ever."

"You are mistaken. Du Rennes said he had tested it. Three times, as a matter of fact."

"To what extent? Do you know?"

"No."

"The log shows no entry where this vessel has been tested above 45 knots. System checks; no testing of the limits." Dao laughed. "We are guinea pigs!"

Chris tugged at his Adams apple. "Oh dear..." He swallowed. "Well, she seems to be operating as intended. I see no reason to panic."

"I am not panicking."

"Yes, you are." Chris laughed.

Dao's lips raised at the ends and her eyes squinted. "Maybe a little."

"Besides, you know Du Rennes and his resources. After his technology investment lecture, do you honestly believe he doesn't have access to the best engineering available? Jupiter is the amalgamation of nautical possibility. She flies at five times the speed of any sailing yacht before her, and at least three times faster than the transatlantic motored record. We will set all the new records and nobody will know."

"We will know."

"What does it matter if history omits us?" Chris smirked. "A few days ago, I was hoping to have your embrace in Oslo."

Dao blushed and placed her arms around him. "This recognition is not necessary, but if it results in our meeting, this is all that matters to me."

"This boat is hypnotizing."

"The rhythmic oscillation is not listed in the manual as a normal behavior."

"How could it? Du Rennes never went this fast or this far out to sea."

"The executable can be updated. I know the code."

"We have a saying in the United States—"

Dao placed a finger over his lips. "It is the same in China. Do not repair what is not broken."

"Close enough," mumbled Chris as he tugged the sides of her shirt.

The moon's sparkles glistened from each pelagic undulation as Jupiter's Bolt whisked through them in not so much more than a breath. Steadily, she rocked everyone to deep unconsciousness—a retreat from the exhaustion of persistent anxiety. It was one of the Dao's last thoughts, that the code permitting it may have been an intentional lullaby. Before closing her eyes, she glanced up at Jupiter's vital information feed display Du Rennes installed in each compartment. The apparent wind fluctuated between 16 and 19 knots, enough to keep the structural tension necessary for 115-125 knots hypercruising. Depth was averaging 4,600 meters—three miles to the bottom—and they had seven hours until the second leg waypoint on the southern edge of the Sargasso.

● ● ●

"Tell me you at least took *something* from Brava," General Tomlinson barked into her encrypted telephone's handset.

"Scraps if that, I'm afraid," said the operator on the other end as he boarded a return transit from Cape Verde's Nelson Mandela International Airport. The sat-phone blipped momentarily. "You still there?"

"Yes. I'm waiting." Tomlinson said in an emphasized tone.

"The sub pen and office were wiped. Girl finked on her father-in-law. All the usual from there, you know. Guy was a raw walnut. Tough. All we got from him was that it's a sailboat. Said it's fast, but he doesn't know how fast because they always took it over the horizon to run—30 or so nautical out."

"Which direction, for God's sake?"

"West. He said it always went west."

"How long ago?"

"Ten hours, tops."

"Listen, I've got two satellites tasked on that area and one 40-knot Los Angeles sub with Barracudas. I don't care how goddamned fast it is, if it's out there, we'll find it and take care of business. Couldn't have gone too goddamned far; it's a sailboat!"

"You want me on the sub?"

"What good would that do? Just sit tight in Porto Santo in case they double back or turn up in Senegal. Anything else?"

"Owner is a Frenchman. That's it."

"Where is he now?"

"The Harbormaster or the Frenchman?"

Tomlinson paused. "You're serious aren't you."

"Nah, just yankin' your chain."

"Well? Guy popped on us in the chair. No defib, so…"

Tomlinson turned her head and muttered, "Sloppy," before hanging up.

The colonel buckled himself into the hold of a Seahawk as it rotated upward, bound for refueling at Nouadhibou,

Mauritania. Otherwise prohibited for well-publicized political oppositions, it was a favor granted by a middle-eastern aristocracy who knew the value of paper tigers.

General Tomlinson turned her chair around to grab a bottle from a drawer under her credenza. Two drams from the Isle of Skye to quash her pounding temples when the coffee wore off, which was usually by 1400. She recalled keeping assorted mints, sprays and other remedies to neutralize the scotch on her breath. No easy feat, but she always managed. There was only one who knew, and he was responsible for her functional addiction in the first place. A tear ran down her cheek for tough-riding General Tutlow—the only man to tame her, or so he thought.

The whiskey's velvety legs oozed their way down the flute as she turned and withdrew the sat-phone from her purse. The phone was a special variety that transceived through a screened repeater across the river from Arlington. From there, its signals went skyward. Tomlinson stared at the glass as the line rang until midway through the fifth tone. There was no answer on the other end as usual, just dead air.

"Is this under control or not?" Tomlinson asked, with a hint of gravel in her voice, causing an automatic clearing of her throat.

There was a short pause. "You must trust the process, General. These matters take time. Do not forget who allows you to sit in that chair and enjoy that disgusting bile."

Tomlinson used her neck for the first time in several years to crane around towards the window, which was fully shuttered. "Don't be such a purist, Ninel."

Game Night

Narciso Esposito focused on the uppermost center monitor of the facility's surveillance array. That monitor's camera was concealed within the shadow of a curled acanthus leaf on the crown molding's inside corner. Emily sat lotus-style on plush-carpeted floor in front of a medium-sized monitor—one of 18 similar stations in that room, arranged in three groups of six stations, and in front of each group stood a habited sister guarding against any undesired activity. Emily's head shifted from side to side, bobbing in concert with the motions of her cassock-cloaked avatar, which was currently teamed with five other simulant avatars in a raid upon some unnamed but fortified metropolitan objective: a twelve-story glass and concrete building. Their objective was to circumvent its security and obtain a recently-stolen artwork, described as historically important and belonging to the church. The piece is said to have an unlocked power that, in the wrong hands (any hands but the church's) could potentially devastate the planet. Emily's team is in fact competing with two similar groups, all of whom are running separate simulations in the same room. Over the next quarter hour, each avatar would be violently eliminated by various means. The simulation spared none of the gore associated with large caliber bullet wounds and shotgun blasts, while the avatars were expected to succeed utilizing bladed weapons and throwables for silent incursion. Esposito slit an ever so slight grin in the expectation that Emily would be the last avatar standing, vindicating his selection. He had no expectation she would complete the mission on first attempt—none had—but he correctly estimated her athleticism and guile—the competitive nature instilled by her father. It would take time for Emily to become his champion, and he was beginning to believe his search had ended.

"The first six eliminated are yours. Send those remaining to Herr Klein," he said to his executive.

As the screens flickered before them, the room's ambient lighting grew brighter by several lumens. Emily slid the sound-proofing earphones carefully off her head, as not to entangle the cups within her hair. She noticed that the girl to her right—same age as the other girls in that room—had been sobbing and could not breathe without continued sniffling. That girl noticed Emily staring at her and started sobbing louder.

"I want to go home!" She cried, drawing the napalm glare of the sister's eyes. Instantly, one of them stormed in front of the sniffling girl, produced a black cylindrical rod about 50cm in length and struck the girl's left collarbone. As the girl collapsed to the floor in shock, Emily recoiled, fearing the same would come to her if overly curious, let alone if she attempted to interfere.

The sister motioned to the exec to begin collecting the first six girls who had failed in the game, which included the girl writhing on the floor next to Emily. With the other five girls in tow, the nun knelt down and picked up the sobbing girl, carrying her out of the rear archway. Another archway to the far side of the chamber would be the starting point of the rest of Emily's day. She had completed 90 minutes of point-of-view tactical simulation, and was about to endure another 90 minutes of training.

The short commute landed the remaining twelve girls in a relatively small chamber with stone walls, lit by the same ambient lighting that leaked across the light gray ceiling by a thin gap at the top of those stone walls. The floors were wooden and worn from years of traffic, but not neglected, as the layers of polished polyurethane indicated.

A jovial yet serious man greeted them. His motions were careful and deliberate. He wore a black-bordered, dark gray cassock made of a modern light and flexible cotton derivative. He looked over the girls while the sisters monitored, assessing their physical condition and anxieties. He spent one second longer on Emily than he did the rest. Barely perceptible to anyone paying attention. When she looked at him, her brows raised slightly before they both made a smile. Emily had never stared into a mature man's eyes without raising her head to face them. The man stood no taller than five feet.

"I am Mister Klein. You have come before me to learn something useful instead of looking at your little screens. You will understand defense, and you will learn to attack in such a matter that a defense should not be necessary."

"I don't want to; I want to go home!" A voice from within the girlpod whined.

One of the sisters produced a rod and tapped it against her hand. The trembling girl immediately ceased her vocalizations, going further to stifle any noise she might make involuntarily. Klein maintained his smile, and by sleight-of-hand, produced something shiny in his right. Taking one step forward and with an unbelievable velocity, he flung the object just above the girls' heads, impacting a raw sheet of lumber several meters behind them. Most of them gasped and spun around to see what it was. Emily and the trembling girl remained fixated on the man who was gauging their reactions. Klein smiled and motioned for them to turn around and see the results. Emily obeyed and, through the narrow spaces between the other girls, caught a glimpse of a five-pointed, stainless steel throwing star lodged deep within the grains of the hardwood sheet.

"You will all do the same before leaving this room, it is easy," said Klein. "First, you must learn four basic moves to protect yourself if you are under attack. Have any of you attended a martial arts class before?"

Two girls raised their hands.

"Of course. Karate? Judo? Taekwondo?"

One said Taekwondo, the other said kickboxing.

"Excellent. Now I must ask you to forget most of what you learned. This will be a... *different* class. We only practice blocking on each other. Attacking, well, we will get to this later. We will not be learning any of the martial arts of which you may be familiar. No karate, judo, jiu-jitsu, judo or Taekwondo, and definitely no kung fu—at least, nothing you will recognize. You will learn the ways of real, successful warriors, not exercises for kids. This will take time. I will make it entertaining. Trust me; it is deadly fun."

Klein gave a reassuring smile as he came around to their left side. "What you are about to learn, you cannot learn in shopping center dojos; you would have to be a United States Marine and a Chinese Oriental Swordsman at the same time. First, I will teach all of you how to stand."

"Complete?" Narciso glared towards his unchaste abbess.

"Si, my Grace, as you instructed, and at the docks by morning as requested. Usual fee."

"And you said they were worthless." Narciso placed a hand over the phone's mic and smiled at her.

"Next week." Narciso spoke into the mouthpiece and hung up.

The nun raised a painted brow. "Waste not..." and departed down the stone hallway to mind her convent.

The bishop cracked a wry grin, favoring the right side of his mouth, recalling his implicit instructions that all rejects and malcontents would be sold as ground offal to a select group of commercial fishermen based out of Hampton.

Emily returned to her private dormitory. The spartan accommodation afforded a single bed, a lavatory, and a student's desk, which folded away from a narrow closet. The closet contained her supplied belongings, few as they were, and the sisters demanded clean organization. On the other side of the closet was the compact lavatory, reminiscent of an older jetliner's. Two Michelangelo-inspired framed prints spaced 1.5 meters apart decorated the wall opposite her single bed, and a two-drawered nightstand with lamp and two-way speaker alarm clock was within easy reach. At the press of a button on the wall just behind the alarm clock, a miniature laser projector activated from a glass dome directly above the bed, and its brilliant resolution glistened on the blank part of the pristine white wall between the two Michelangelos. Emily quickly discovered that it only presented the Vatican Media Channel and two networks dedicated to early-adolescent programming. There was one peculiar item next to the alarm clock that caught Emily's attention: a baseball-sized cube which interrupted the projector's programming by launching its dedicated purpose as a gaming machine. This particular machine launched only one title, The Guard. It was the same first-person combat adventure Emily had been dominating for the past few days in class. Esposito used television as an electronic reward after certain tasks were completed. Emily watched as much as she liked, provided she kept the sister's schedule.

Tracing their cleanliness/godliness mantra, the sisters prioritized a shower after any physical activity. Surveillance knew when a shower was taken, and the sisters' monitoring system was also utilized in the confirmation of it. There were no secrets in the cathedral's clandestine sub-basement—a vast complex which included three floors, the middle of which featured ceilings over 20 feet high. The monitoring system's main purpose however, was to ensure that no prospect had enough time to contemplate escape or become mentally impaired due to the anxieties of their captivity. Until the lights went out for sleeping, the sisters kept a busy itinerary. They also made sure the girls were exhausted. When the lights were extinguished, candidates often fell asleep within several minutes. That was at least thirty minutes away.

Emily opened the nightstand's bottom locker and found a pulsating Virtual Reality helmet that featured quantum-processed 16K-resolution displays for each eye, 4-point audio, a microphone, motion and facial recognition sensors, and a synthesized fragrance emitter. Wireless gloves with three directional and spacial sensors per finger accompanied the helmet. It was similar to those provided over the previous few days in the dojo. Emily found the invitation irresistible and put them on. Perfect fit. Next came the helmet, also a perfect fit. The ambient lighting within the helmet changed, and the displays switched on.

"You *know* they are listening to us." Sylvia, whispered into the microphone.

Emily jumped with a slight squeal. The Guard's opening logo sequence flickered brightly. Sylvia had been waiting on the others to link in after their baths. Her avatar appeared active and waiting by the time Emily logged on.

"Why should I care?" Emily checked her virtual surroundings while the game booted.

"Shh! You'll get us in trouble."

"You brought it up."

"Never mind. Where are the others?"

"I dunno."

"Look!"

Within moments of each other, Chandni and Isabella's avatars appeared on the street, and moments after that, the sniffles and clearing of throats rattled Emily and Sylvia's helmets. Disjointed, borderline-chaotic conversations with elevated pitches erupted over the next several minutes, ranging from music to the bathroom's overpowering scents coming from the drains, and the powerful soaps provided by the sisters, which were actually relabeled chlorohexidine gluconate—surgical soap. The conversations halted when the fifth avatar graced their screens. Vena had become a favorite within the group. Agile, scoring many kills for the team while perfect in style and articulation, she encouraged laughter and commanded respect. Vena's appeal might have been due to the fact she was two years older, with insights into the pubescence that lay ahead.

Last to arrive was Peggy, so named after her great grandmother from the southern Appalachian hills. She was a jokester punctuated by naturally curly auburn hair and countless freckles dotting her entire being, except the front of her face from just below her hairline. At once, Peggy started cracking jokes in retaliation for Sylvia's chiding her punctuality, or lack thereof. Once the last avatar of the group entered, a ten-minute clock appeared to hover at the top-right of everyone's view. They were instructed to utilize that time wisely for strategy and tactics. Below the clock, a map and its legends appeared. None of them paid it any attention. At least, not yet.

The girls erupted in another round of chatter lasting until one of them noticed the absence of another, and that she heard faint sniffles in the background.

"Everybody shh!" Cried Emily, increasing the helmet's volume.

The sniffling grew worse, with muffled sobbing behind it.

"Isabella?" Emily asked.

The sobbing grew louder.

Vena jumped in. "'Bella, it is okay. Speak with us." Her wretched shutters, hacking and sniffling, continued in contrast to the sighs and supportive comments of her teammates. It only made her sob louder.

"I want to go home!" She finally cried, overloading her microphone's input to the point of clipping distortion.

Her wailing became unbearable, then at once, dead silence; Isabella's avatar disappeared from the other's screens.

"Oh no!" Sylvia shouted.

"Be quiet." Vena whispered. "They removed her because we are running out of time. Look at the clock."

One minute twenty-eight seconds and counting. It would go to 1:20 before Emily spoke up and started talking about the map. Vena agreed with her strategy, and how they should compensate for their missing teammate. It was Isabella who carried most of the demolition armaments, and those were wisely disbursed among the remainders so that some form of explosive would be available should one of them fall. The clock hit all zeros well before they had formulated any in-depth strategy for the entire map. Most of them were accustomed to improvisation. Generally, they knew where they were going and what tasks would be undertaken by each teammate. If they encountered any type of combatant, they knew which way to go, and they rotated tactics and personnel to keep their competitors on their feet. After eleven rounds played on the dojo's group screens and VR helmets, they had been the most successful, not losing a single teammate until now.

The Guard's penultimate round came down to the final two teams. Emily's had been largely successful, having lost only one member, their weakest, to a ninja-styled AI named Katsuko, or Kat, as the others called her. Whether coincidence or by design, the two final squads would be competing with five members each.

The game's opening narrative described each squad's mission in detail. Set in an Italian village's piazza, both teams must purge its cathedral from embedded conquerors. Each team must complete their mission by a unique stratagem, however. Emily's team would be assaulting the western flank of the cathedral by grinding an advance down via della Stella—a narrow street, lined by 18th century storefronts with one or two stories of apartment housing above, many of which featured protected balconies perfect for elevated sniping or machinegun positions. The other team would breach the piazza's courtyard by riskier air drop. Each would be facing no less than a dozen of The Guard's worst adversaries—a collection of quantum AI-enabled professionals with peculiar abilities and who fight unfairly. Each avatar would face several tests before conclusion of the exercise. Either they would reach their objective or perish in the attempt.

Over the previous few days, Emily acclimated to the VR helmet intuitively. Its environmental productions were accurate in such detail to become instantly immersive. Motion capture and near-zero input lag meant believable action without constantly calculating adjustment. If not for certain sensory feedback—touch, smell, perceived taste, and the ever-evolving CGI nature of the characters themselves—the helmets would likely induce undesirable side effects. Nonetheless, the girls never made comments regarding their confiscated phones when wearing the VR rigs.

Their mission began with being dropped at the end of via della Stella. The rooftops were brightly lit, but the shadows were long, allowing just enough daylight down the street to judge movement. At Vena's direction, the group split up. Three went to the left side of the street, peering into the windows of each storefront, one-by-one. Emily, Sylvia and Chandni took turns on point between buildings, the others in a covering formation. Vena and Peggy took the other side of the street, also taking turns and covering each other. The groups communicated by hand signals. Sound detection was factored in the combatants' AI algorithms, compromising positions if chatter was loud enough to be realistically audible given a certain distance.

The village's blocks were short, running 150 meters on average between intersections, and within a few short moments, the group had already progressed to their third cross-street. Vena never hesitated when she caught the faint glint of reflected glass on a second-story balcony down the left side of the next block, about 200 meters distant. She motioned for everyone to stop and take cover while she brought her rifle's scope to her "face". Barely intelligible in the light of dusk, the vignetted outline of a long rifle and its user appeared to pivot as it zeroed on Emily's group. Vena scored her first kill, blasting the primary sniper in that moment. The explosion of air at her muzzle shocked the silent advance due to its loudness in the VR helmets. Vena watched as the figure slumped over the balcony's rail, dripping matter onto the cobbles below.

Peggy's drawl cackled into their headsets. "Hey y'all, is that a three-point shot, or two?"

Vena turned around to hush her just when Peggy's skull exploded. Her death was instant and gruesome. There would be no rating strong enough for the ultra-realistic gore depicted in The Guard. Its purpose was to desensitize—to untether cold, heartless execution. This had proven advantageous to Spada Sacra's training over the past few decades. Conscious, yet unconscious operators who care not, feel not. The goal is all that matters. Yet, the girls are stricken by her sudden loss, wondering if she would go missing at breakfast. There was no way to know since the dead are muted. No epilogues allowed; dead means done.

In her peripheral, Chandni caught the direction of fire that killed Peggy. She reached underneath her M4 rifle to unsafety its grenade launcher, checked the rangefinder, aligned her site posts for 80 meters, and lobbed a high-explosive round down the right side of the street towards an alley. Its detonation shattered windows and shook the stones beneath their feet. It also painted the walls with a dark crimson, visible once the dust settled.

Vena smiled and pointed two fingers towards the ground. She then realized that her avatar stood alone on her side of the street, so she motioned for Chandni to join her. Sylvia turned to Emily with the face of dread. Their two strongest members, she thought, were no longer close by.

Emily smiled and whispered into her mic, "More for us."

Her eyes focused on the HUD, which did not offer enemy locations, listing only their names, or in some cases, call signs. Each mission listed a dozen combatants. Active in white, deceased in greyed strikethrough, and red if currently engaged. No names appeared in red, but this was not to be comported as a detection system; The Guard gave no warnings or other insights. Emily grimaced at the sight of Isabella and Peggy's names stricken. She glanced across at the combatant's list and read the names: Piper the sniper and a close-quarters specialist named Dominic. In an instant, Emily ran the math of attrition, knowing their enemies increased in difficulty as they progressed. She developed goosebumps for the first time since the rounds began. Her friends were disappearing.

The cathedral remained just out of sight four blocks ahead. Emily guessed the last and toughest three or four baddies would be waiting for them within its walls. That meant getting past another six or seven fighters. She recognized the name Katsuko from another girls' chat the day before, describing her stealth and martial arts moves. Fast. Little time to react. You'd better have a battle plan and a series of specific moves ready before you fought her. Another name caught her eye— Stonefish. She didn't quite know what to make of it.

When Chandni reached the other side of the street, Vena whispered for everyone to continue, keep low, and stay off coms.

"Be quiet and watch where you step." She said.

The next block imbued further anxieties, as several of the storefronts were shuttered by flimsy aluminum rollup doors. Sylvia and Emily crept past three of them, briefly shining rifle-mounted flashlights through the open storefronts. All empty. Sylvia was about to step in front of the alleyway at the end when Emily caught a name turning red in her HUD. She reached for Sylvia's collar and yanked her backward just as a massive fireball erupted from the alley. Its heat baked their outfits, and was felt within their VR helmets—one of few sensations it could emulate electronically. Shots erupted from across the street. Vena marked the flamethrower and sent half a magazine towards it. The name remained red.

Neither Emily nor Sylvia carried grenades, only M4 rifles and knives. Chandni was the only member with a rifle-mounted launcher, but the distance was too close, and the target was no longer visible. Vena carried hand grenades since she was the strongest. Emily motioned towards her, and Vena shook her head negatively.

Emily shrugged, then spoke, "Why not?"

"We need to save these and I cannot throw it as far as necessary."

"Necessary?"

"Blakken is not within my range or I would have killed him."

Emily turned to check the last storefront they passed. Unlocked and deserted.

"What are you thinking?" Sylvia whispered.

"Shh!"

Emily turned around and opened the shop's door. It was an artist's studio. White ceiling, walls and floors, densely packed with oil and acrylic paint tubes, pigment powder bags, canvases, brushes, and other craft supplies. Her father's horror movie maxim flashed in her mind. *White means blood about to happen.* She wondered if the game's programming unmasked this art store as a foreshadowed cliché. Paints splattering, intermixing with the flow of red corn syrup and a little gelatin for chunkier blasted bits. Emily saw it coming.

She found the narrow hallway leading to the rear of the store and followed it into the darkness. There was a faint glow emanating from the last room—a delivery reception and prep area. The pinhole light came from the rear door. Emily eased herself up to the door, but the peephole was too high. A convenient box just next to the door provided the right amount of lift. She concentrated towards the right-side intersecting alleyway and detected no movement. Her HUD displayed Blakken as engaged, so he must be there. She twisted the doorknob and carefully moved to the alleyway's corner. She caught reflection of his flamethrower's pilot light in a puddle between stones. He was facing the street some five meters away, unaware of her presence. She had to think. If she blasted him with the rifle, the explosion would certainly take her too. She could sneak up on him with a knife and slit his throat since the canisters blocked easy access to his back. He was tall, however. In the game, that usually meant difficulty, as in, she could be thrown off the moment she pounced... then torched. There had to be another way.

Taking a few steps back, Emily slowly crept back into the art store and shut the door.

"Vena, are you there?" Emily whispered.

"Yes. Where are you?"

"Can you see Blakken? He is in the alley just behind the garbage thing on the left."

"No, it's too dark."

"I have an idea."

When they agreed, Emily started counting by Mississippis. At 20, she reentered the rear alleyway. Nothing had changed. She peeked around the corner and saw Blakken in the same spot, observing the street from behind the dumpster, waiting for anyone to cross his view. Emily returned to the rear door, lifted her rifle and plunked two rounds into the wall on the far side of Blakken's alley. Through the darkness, Vena saw Blakken emerge from his position and turn around.

She turned to Chandni. "Cover me."

Vena dashed a mere six meters across the street and took a kneeling position on the right-hand corner of the alley. Peering down her sights, she tracked Blakken's lumbering gait, aiming for the center of three cylinders strapped to his back. As he was about to turn left behind the art store, Vena opened fire. Emily shut the door and ran towards the storefront. She felt the building shake when Blakken's Soviet-era flamethrower exploded. Vena turned away from the intense heat of the fireball, and as she did, her entire display flashed a hint of red while displaying on a body outline where she had been hit—center-left torso, impacting her graphene-impregnated vest. By rule, she would endure an excruciating 20-second wait before being able to move, except due to the caliber and type of round that struck her vest, she would incur no health deduction. As soon as she realized her exposure, she heard another rifle shot. Chandni was paying attention as instructed, and fired upon a sniper down the next block named Mors. His name flashed once and turned grey with the strikethrough. Chandni turned her head to check on Vena and pointed four fingers to the ground. Their odds were improving.

Sylvia joined Vena by the alley's corner when Emily emerged from the store. Chandni kept her eyes down the next block. No baddies in red. They were safe for the moment. Twenty seconds seems a painfully long time in these situations, for anxious young girls, especially. Vena hardly noticed the time slipping past as Emily and Sylvia joined her. They resumed their assault down the block, carefully checking each open storefront, taking turns along the way. Not for Chandni, however. She remained alone on the other side of the street. It also meant she could move faster; no waiting for others' turns. She diligently made the end of the next block, two storefronts ahead of the others. Her HUD displayed no sign of activity. She figured at least four more villains were between them and the cathedral. The top of the bell tower had finally come into view just four blocks away. Four blocks, four baddies. They had been operating in twos.

The other team ran into bad luck from the onset. Their bomber lost control during the jump and landed on the steepest part of the dew-slicked tiled roof just behind the bell tower. From there she slid off, snagging her parachute on a lightning rod. Four of the enemy immediately surrounded her and opened fire. Her presence and method of entry compromised the remaining four, who scrambled to lose their chutes and take cover. In their haste, one became the victim of Stonefish, who slashed a full 80% life force from the group's best shooter. The other three were separated and pinned down. Nothing had gone according to plan, and they were desperately improvising to get back on track. They finally settled for a position further away from the cathedral's entrance than planned—a small, protected corte residence, painted terracotta, off the right-rear corner of the cathedral. There, the unit diligently recalculated their plan based on their remaining assets. Since they already knew the general locations of at least four combatants, they would go at them from behind. It was a simple, reasonable strategy that should regain momentum, they thought. The problem was that The Guard's penalty for excessive time was increased difficulty. Their AI might become less predictable, and damage points for successful hits less impactful. Indeed, this was precisely the case when the B Team reengaged the shooters that executed their bomber. One had relocated behind a retaining wall and turned around before his life force drained. Two of the girls received minimal damage, less than 6% and a 30-second pause. The other teammate caught the remaining shooters from behind and lobbed a grenade between them. It not only obliterated those two, but the blast was strong and close enough to weaken the third by 70%. She finished him off with a burst from her M4. Three down.

In The Guard, there were no convenient medical aids to restore health. If you were careful and fortuitous, you could survive and possibly achieve your mission's objective. B Team had three members at full capacity, yet their fourth was becoming a hindrance. When they rounded the front of the cathedral, their HUDs flashed red on six enemy names. They were outnumbered and outgunned, yet three enemy fighters were at the far side of the piazza with their backs turned. The girls launched two grenades their direction and opened fire on the others. The field scattered into multiple directions of fire. Two of the girls took position behind planters next to the wall of an ancient palace on the western side of the piazza; the others remained out in the open courtyard, taking hits but inflicting severe damage on the enemy. Ultimately, one of their shooters was lost in the melee, and the other suffered a 60% hit to her health. Eight of the enemy extinguished now. B Team had little remaining.

Her VR display flashed red as her avatar fell to the ground. Team B's bomber had the misfortune of taking position just in front of Stonefish, who was perfectly blended into the rock walls of the palace behind her. Even though his name showed red on her HUD, she never saw him or his distressed blade as he thrust it under her left rear ribcage. Instant kill. The enemy AI does not contemplate sacrifice, only the math. The game decided that the other girl behind the next planter would see the kill, which she did, and react by opening fire on Stonefish at a short distance, fully automatic, which she did. It also calculated the result equaled one opponent at full capacity and another at half capacity against its three most dangerous fighters.

The 50% girl lasted less than a minute. She caught a glimpse of the three remaining baddies turn red in her HUD as she dashed towards the retaining wall at the left (east) side of the piazza, and she was sprayed with a deafening thunder as she leapt over the wall, landing as a corpse according to her health gauge. The sole champion for B Team could only watch, mouth agape, as she panicked for guidance. So far, she was undetected due to the distraction afforded by her teammates. Movement might draw fire, and it also would certainly expose her position. She couldn't wait behind a cypress planter forever, either. She froze, noticing that she had actually produced condensation within the VR helmet from breathing too rapidly. The one-meter retaining wall to her left was over twenty meters away. To her right meant exposure and a lengthy sprint into a confined space between the palace and the terracotta house at the end. All that blaster had to do was turn the corner and spray. Not an option.

B Team's last fighter decided to make a dash to the wall on her left. Another distraction was needed. Just to her right lay the body of her teammate, the bomber. On her belt was one grenade. The girl crawled over, grabbed the grenade, stood up, pulled the pin and lobbed it into the piazza as close to the front of the cathedral as she could. As the device flew, she jabbed her left thumb control stick as far forward as possible while ducking to reduce her target size. The grenade bought her ten meters as the explosion buffeted the piazza. Another second elapsed as the smoke cleared. She heard the whirring of the microgun's motor spinning up, then that awful tearing of wind gaining on her six. The explosion of sound hit her as she leapt, expecting her HUD to flash red. It didn't. Her VR cleared the view skyward, with the wall just on her right. The deafening buzzsaw of projectiles ceased, and she heard the barrels spin loose in rotation. Innately, she brought her rifle in front and prairie-dogged the wall. The sole survivor of B Team launched her final defense by emptying her clip into the microgunner, and she monitored his status change from red to dim grey with the strikethrough. The girl dropped her rifle and drew her sidearm—a 9mm combat pistol. She waited in a prone position for anyone to breach the wall towards the middle of the piazza's entrance. An uncomfortable amount of time elapsed. She checked her HUD and only two warriors remained. One she knew, the other she didn't, but nothing happened. After two minutes, her wait came to an end.

The VR view buffeted and turned red; 20% life force drained in the process. She stood up as Katsuko vaulted from behind, pirouetting overhead as if part of an anime classic, and nailing the three-point landing—a wakizashi sword in one hand, and a kunai throwing knife in the other. In the attack, the girl lost grip of her pistol. Only remaining weapon was her Ka-Bar combat knife, which drained her confidence considering her opponent's armory. She was quite skilled with it, however. Katsuko launched her attack with a thrust of her sword, followed by a swipe of the kunai. The first was blocked, but the second scored a 5% hit. Team B returned with two jabs of the blade, both scoring 10% blows. Better still, the girl caught site of her pistol just a few steps away. Katsuko's AI detected the glance and programmed a low ashi barai, attempting to knock Team B off her feet. The kick missed and impacted her ankle. No damage. Katsuko then flung her kunai, anticipating the girl to turn around for the sidearm. The knife penetrated the unprotected back of her right thigh, causing a 30% loss. The girl fell to the ground within reach of the pistol. She grabbed it and turned around just as fast as the game allowed, firing as she caught Katsuko midair, about to plunge her short wakizashi into the girl's back. Team B rolled out of the way as the last round left the chamber. She was out of ammo. Katsuko's name went grey.

Several moments passed. The life force indicator read 50%, and Team B's only usable weapon remained the Ka-Bar. The last name glowed red, but she dared not peer over the wall. He was formidably gargantuan and muscular. He carried several weapons: knives, an AK, two side arms, grenades, and a tube with the circumference of a golf ball and a foot long strapped to his left arm. She couldn't quite resolve it. *What is that?* There was no way to catch him by surprise. He stood on the steps of the cathedral. Higher ground, no rear access. The only way inside was through him. Impossible.

At three short blocks from the cathedral, just as Sylvia flashed her rifle's tactical flashlight through a storefront window, the glass crashed onto her, knocking her backwards and onto the ground. Her VR flashed red as she took a 20% hit. Emily checked her HUD and "Steve" appeared in red. He was apparently flying solo, maintaining close quarters so as keep others from shooting him off his victims. Sylvia struggled to get up. Something ricocheted off the sidewalk a foot away. Emily's HUD flashed red for another baddie named Lutz. None of them saw where the shot came from, and there were at least four visible balconies ahead. Chandni examined her belt for 40mm grenade rounds. She found four. Two high explosive, one air burst, and one parachuting white star flare. The first two were useless without a location. The air burst could cover all of the balconies at once, but the probability of success would be greatly reduced. The star shell might reveal the shooter's location, and since it doesn't do anything else, she would be forced to use another round. It may be wasted. *Too much thinking!*

She grabbed the air burst round out of her belt and loaded the cartridge into the chamber, snapping the barrel back in place and flipping the safety off. She aimed just above the highest balcony and towards the middle of the street. The ensuing concussion shattered windows on the entire block. Lutz's name flashed from red to grey briefly, indicating damage, yet he wasn't killed. Vena caught his location as he scrambled to retreat. She placed a round just forward of his left ear. That was the end of Lutz.

"Don't you have a clear shot?" Emily asked Vena.

She had been following Steve through her scope, but his moves were too exaggerated at that distance. Dim light too close for the optics. His footwork was nauseating to remain on target.

"No! He is too fast!"

Sylvia made it to her feet as Steve flung a roundhouse kick towards her face. She ducked and threw a fist at his ribcage. It scored a minor hit—1% life and a couple seconds to make another fast move. She hesitated, and Steve threw another kick towards her midsection which came up short. They traded mixed-martial arts moves for several moments until Steve's AI changed tactics to pure grappling. He grabbed Sylvia's left arm and twisted it underneath his leg as a lever— a move that would break her arm if allowed for more than a few seconds. Sylvia struggled with the controls and gave up on her arm, reaching to unholster her pistol. The VR helmet's display flashed red as the sound of cracking celery filled Team A's earphones. As the life force meter spun to 76%, Sylvia shot Steve twice. Once in the chest, which provided little effect, and another in the face, which always proved fatal, as indicated by a grey line crossing out Steve's name on the HUD.

In The Guard, having a broken limb meant losing the use of it. Sylvia's broken arm meant she could no longer pick up, carry, fire, or perform combat maneuvers with her left arm. Rifle and pistol reloads would take longer because she had to put the guns down and use her right hand. Crawling and climbing would increase difficulty as well. Hobbled limbs were a death sentence as far as she was concerned.

"I won't make it," she cried.

Emily stood in front of her avatar. "Yes you can. I've seen it happen. Ask Vena."

"It is true, Sylvia. Two matches ago my right arm was wounded. We still won, so it did not matter. It is a *game*."

"She hates to lose." Emily said.

Vena checked her HUD. "I'm not gonna lose! Come on. The cathedral is just up there."

Sylvia holstered her pistol, reloaded her rifle, and faced down the street towards the church. "Just a game, yes. Tell that to Isabell," she whispered.

The last two blocks lay ahead. Since Sylvia's attack, each unblocked storefront and apartment entry door was painfully scrutinized. They anticipated at least two more baddies before reaching the cathedral. So far, nothing. Chandni rejoined Vena on the other side of the street, meaning two girls were swapping positions on point for each window passed. They were taking twice as long as before, and yet nobody was complaining—not after the surprise attack. They all started second-guessing tactics. Sylvia and Emily kept gesturing to Vena to confirm when passing the last alleyway, and likewise she asked the same from Emily and Sylvia. Emily would check for movement behind. She heard one of the girls from two rounds ago talk about being shot in the back. *Would that happen to me?* She thought. While Sylvia checked ground-level windows, Emily turned around and placed her scope on each balcony they passed. Team A finally reached the last street separating the piazza from the corte storefronts and nothing. Six enemies appeared in their HUDs, all in white.

"They all must be hiding in the piazza. Watch yourselves."

"All six at once?" Sylvia whined.

Chandni checked her armaments. "It would not be the first time."

The short retaining wall extended across the front of the piazza with a break in the center for five short steps up to the courtyard. From a crouched position, the wall was just high enough to serve as cover from enemy fire. Its granite blocks and mortar appeared heavily repaired from routine damage. The condition of its off-white paint indicated infrequent maintenance as did the rest of the town. Mold, decay, and sporadic graffiti plagued Italy, and the Spada Sacra demanded faithful rendering in the game.

Vena peered over the wall. At the top of the cathedral's steps were what she assumed to be the three fiercest combatants. She couldn't locate the other three, however. Charging the steps was suicidal, she thought. Not enough members left to fight a battle royale. She noticed the size and spacing of the cypress planters distributed around the piazza. Cover and stealth; take them one-by-one. Vena stared at the terracotta red corte house at the end of the block down the right side of the piazza. So obvious to her, it must have some significance. If anything, it would be the best candidate for a sanctuary.

"We should split up and take them out from the flanks."

"The what?" Sylvia asked.

"You know, from the sides. There are six of them in the piazza..."

"Please stop saying piazza, you're making me hungry." Emily cracked.

"Shh!" Vena frowned; Emily couldn't help herself.

"This is serious!" Vena continues. "All six enemy are in the piazza. I see the three on the steps. They are not hiding, but too far for sniping with these guns, you know. We should take the three out from the sides in a crossfire. Use the plant pots as cover. We take those other three out, we should do well against the last ones. Agreed?"

Sylvia and Emily eased around the left end of the retaining wall and crept from the first cypress planter to the next. Dusk was ending and the piazza's lights were flickering on. Suddenly, the singular long, black shadows of the cypress trees were shortened and manifold grey. At first, the effect startled the girls, having mistaken two of the lights' activations for possible movement within the shadows.

"Don't shoot!" Rang in their headsets from Vena. "You will give away your position."

"We know!" Emily checked down the block and noticed her HUD now indicated two engaged enemies. "Check your status."

Vena and Chandni made it to the third planter when Chandni's VR helmet flashed red. Vena whirled around to see what appeared to be part of the palacio's stone wall extend a blade into Chandni's torso, just under her flack vest. Before Vena could fully pivot, she heard a shot ring out from across the piazza, Sylvia leveled her scope on the forehead of Stonefish and squeezed off a round. As he fell, Chandni checked her HUD and saw that her health plummeted 50%. Her avatar was momentarily frozen from the blow.

Emily and Sylvia were too focused on the piazza to notice the other enemy in red, named Krait, emerge from the next storefront. He raised a short tube to his mouth and blew a sortie of darts at Sylvia. Her HUD flashed red, and a special intelligence message scrawled across her display.

POSIONED! YOU HAVE 10 MINUTES REMAINING.

She watched her health drop to 70% as Emily turned around and blasted Krait on his right side. After several hits, he fell—grey-lined. Sylvia's health indicator slid to 65% in the meantime. The third combatant's name lit red. Hobart. Emily turned to Sylvia.

"Can you make the red house?" Vena whispered into her mic."

"Have to take a shortcut." Emily stated, turning towards Sylvia. "Follow me and run!"

As they dashed across the front half of the piazza, an explosion rocked their VR displays. Both received a 10% hit to their health as a result, and Hobart's AI homed in on their trajectory. Sylvia's meter now read 55%. At the other side of the piazza, Vena and Chandni remained out of sight behind two of the cypress planters. Chandni stepped out as a grenade rolled between her and where the fleeing girls were expected by the time it blew. She ran the math and determined it would be better for three of them to retain greater than 50% health than to have four of them below 50%—all with reduced capacities. Chandni leapt for the grenade, smothering it with her dragon skin vest.

"No!" Emily yelled as a deafening blast of wind ripped over her head, following the grinding buzzsaw overload emanating from the cathedral's front steps. She innately knew what that sound meant as her HUD illuminated Binge's name. She had no time for consideration.

The concussion was muted as the grenade detonated. Only Chandni's VR helmet flashed red. 2% remaining and dreadfully incapacitated, yet "alive", and more importantly, the others' health was preserved. Hobart lobbed another grenade towards the girls who reacted by jumping several steps away. Chandni could not, however, and rolled over the grenade as she tossed her own grenade launcher rifle towards Emily. Chandni's name greyed with strikethrough as the launcher landed just before Emily's feet. She picked it up and sent a concussion round straight into Hobart's torso, which sent his avatar in several directions at once in bits no larger than loose change, some of which stuck to their helmet's visors and oozed their way down. Esposito insisted on such gore.

"Ewww!" Emily laughed, and the monitoring bishop noticed, smiling.

Another blast of Binge's minigun shredded the planter in front of Emily in retaliation. She dove towards the next planter and scrambled behind it, glancing towards the terracotta house down at the end.

"Go now!" Vena yelled.

Without hesitation, the three girls jammed their VR hand controllers to limits in a sprint towards the corte house. Binge nor any other enemy gave pursuit according to their HUDs, and the three remaining enemies appeared in white. The terracotta house was indeed important. *A safe house; for how long?* Vena thought.

Emily checked her HUD and to her amazement, it read 90%. It dawned on her that she had a fighting chance. Vena also checked her display and sighed. 100%. She was the strongest of her team and somehow maintained full health for the final battle. She and Emily heard a sniffle in their headphones.

"Chandni was wrong and I could not tell her first." She whined.

"Why do you think this?" Vena asked.

"Because I only have the use of one arm, and I am poisoned. 45% and dropping. What are we going to do? We need to do it now if I am going to make it."

Emily averted her avatar's eyes as she said it. *Make it?* She thought. *Sure, there is a slight chance. Binge has a microgun, and I've heard about Kat. What about the other one... Timothy? A baddie named Timothy? It has to be a bad joke.* "Yes, I want her to finish with us." Emily said.

Vena took inventory. Sylvia kept Chandni's launcher rifle and pocketed two high explosive rounds. Emily had her rifle and knife, as did she, and likewise had plenty of health.

"Who are we fighting?" Vena asked.

Sylvia spoke first in a hurried fashion about what she knew of Katsuko's deadly martial arts moves, but she knew nothing of Timothy or Binge, other than Binge's minigun. Both Vena and Emily nodded, acknowledging no further information on the others. Strategy. Vena discussed how they couldn't hide from Binge behind the tree planters.

"40%. I don't mean to interrupt," said Sylvia.

Vena shook her head. "Okay, then. What do you think?"

There was a short pause.

Emily turned to peer out of the shop window and as far down the piazza as she could. "I can launch two grenades at

Binge while running to the wall out front. If Katsuko or Timothy follows, they will be within rifle range. We can take them out from behind that wall."

"No Emily, you run and I will launch the grenades. You have to stop for a moment to aim, or it will not work."

"You will get shot!" Emily yelled.

"I know, but I am dying anyway, right? And if we keep talking about all this, I will die right here."

"She's right," said Vena.

Another short pause.

"35%. Come on!"

Emily opened the front door and checked down the street for any movement. None. Her HUD remained clear of active enemies, but she knew they were waiting half a block away just around the corner of the cathedral. As soon as Sylvia cleared the doorway, Vena motioned and they sped towards the front of the piazza.

Vena crackled into their earphones. "Run straight on and dive over the wall, Emily."

"Okay."

Just as they cleared the cathedral's corner, Katsuko appeared and broke into pursuit. Emily glanced right and noticed Binge had relocated towards the center of the piazza. All three enemies were lit bright red in the HUD. *Tim must be on the other side,* Emily thought. Just as Sylvia paused to take aim at Binge, Katsuko sprung an impossible distance into the air and landed with a three-point stance just two meters off Sylvia's two o'clock. Sylvia rolled her eyes and lost concentration for a fraction of a second, launching her grenade without much of an aim. The grenade landed on the far side of Binge and exploded, causing minimal life force damage. Emily recognized the whirring sound of high-speed electric motor and knew what followed. The wall was just ten meters away. One more second before she could jump. Vena was just behind her, hesitant since Sylvia was alone and could not fight Katsuko in her condition. She would need the grenade launcher to defeat Binge as well. Vena paused to turn around just as the shredding wave of projectiles blazed across her position. Her VR display flashed red as her avatar collapsed onto the ancient stonework beneath. Emily faintly caught the gasp of "Vena!" from Sylvia's voice as she leapt over the wall, the wind of death at her back.

There would be no merciful pause from Katsuko, as she launched a foot sweep attack. Sylvia's reaction time was barely fast enough to avoid it, and, as Katsuko's avatar was resetting, she wildly squeezed off two rounds towards her enemy. Katsuko's AI anticipated the fire and jumped backwards twice in different directions to reduce the hit radius. She produced a kunai knife, and spun it three times by its pommel ring. Katsuko cartwheeled as she flung it. Her speed was mesmerizing, although anticipated. Sylvia fired again, this time striking Katsuko's left shoulder for a 15% damage score. Sylvia aimed again and struck her in the chest, causing a 5% hit since Katsuko, like herself, wore a bullet-proof vest. Bulletproof, but not thick enough to prevent broken ribs, as the quantum computations allowed. Katsuko pirouetted and launched a second kunai, this time with improved speed. Sylvia was helpless as her HUD displayed a life force of 8%. And in a batting of an eyelid, it dropped another 5% due to Krait's poison. She screamed as she unleashed a wild grenade into the piazza then flipped her rifle to full auto and swept the grounds. Katsuko suffered another 10% worth of hits as Sylvia's magazine emptied. The grenade detonated towards the center, illuminating the silhouette of Binge as he strafed her position.

In those moments, Emily recovered from her jump and periscoped over the wall using a square mirror supplied with her kit. She felt the abandonment and loneliness return as she watched Sylvia fall into bifurcated halves. She checked her HUD which showed all of her team in grey strikethrough.

Timothy was at the top of the enemy roster at 100% health, Katsuko at 80%, and Binge at 50%. She wondered how they scored on Binge and thought it must have been that last grenade Sylvia fired. The numbers looked impossible, and that empty feeling of loss returned to her just as it did when her father walked out the door. She became frustrated, angry. She felt somehow cheated again. A tear ran down her cheek. She knew she was going to lose. It was inevitable. She laid on the other side of the wall, wondering when the AI killers would come for her. The game's rules dictated no indefinite waits. At some point, you either had to fight or your health would be penalized. She waited.

Two minutes went by. She scanned the piazza again with her mirror and saw her enemies vigilantly pacing in front of the cathedral's steps. Emily contemplated going back up the block, searching for anything that might help. A weapon off the fallen. Where were the grenades? All she had was half a magazine—14 rounds—and her bowie knife. Peggy was a simple shooter like her. No help except a fresh rifle, perhaps. She was several blocks away, and Emily innately understood that the longer the enemy waited unnecessarily, the more aggressive and harder to kill they became. She decided it wasn't worth the extra 16 shots. Vena was only several meters in front of her, except she couldn't risk detection. Not by Binge anyway. Two more minutes' doping every possibility brought Emily to the same place. There was no other way.

As she grinded, another two minutes elapsed and she was alerted to a red flash in the upper corner of her HUD. Katsuko! *She's near*, Emily thought. Her heart raced in anticipation, crouched just below the top of the retaining wall. That's when her idea suddenly struck. Emily finally put together the tiny logo she noticed during the game's introduction. It was the same as another game she played regularly last year with Patricia Smiley. Emily met the developer last year at a family corporate party. Her father introduced her. He said he always left back doors and Easter eggs. She remembered her father's raised eyebrows as he winked. Emily realized she was having an endearing memory she wasn't supposed have. She was angry with him. Angry because he abandoned her, and with a stranger, no less. She became sad for herself, and sad for Snickers, and her friends, the Smileys. Her hatred returned for her father and all things connected with him. They did this to her.

Emily set the rifle down and gestured with both hands, to point up twice, to point down twice, to point left and right at the same time with each hand. Then she snapped her left fingers, then her right. It was a stupid idea, she thought, except a moment passed then suddenly a rainbow-colored ring rotated towards the ground as a new gun materialized. Her tears dried as the HUD registered full health and a new weapon—a 1-megawatt pulse laser pistol. She stopped staring at it just as Katsuko arched over the wall in a spinning summersault, hurling the third of her four kunai blades at Emily's upper torso. The VR helmet flashed red as Emily dove for the magic weapon, still glowing bright white and ringed by the sparkling rainbow. It was a 40% blow to her health as Katsuko cartwheeled back over the retaining wall in an all-out sprint to rejoin Binge and Timothy. Emily picked up the weapon, aimed its tracking pointer—a simple on-screen gun-sight that latched onto targets by magnetic attraction and flashed green when locked—and pulled the trigger. The reticle went red, and an ominous voice echoed within Emily's earphones.

MUST BE WITHIN 20 METERS OF YOUR TARGET WHEN FIRING

"Twenty meters? Emily complained. "That's halfway into the courtyard. I will be killed!"

"Sorry." The game replied, anticipating any response with a sarcastic tone.

"Ugh!" Emily chuffed as she climbed back over the retaining wall in a fast walk towards the steps.

Binge locked onto her and spun up the microgun's motor. Emily squeezed the trigger again. Nothing.

"What good is it!" Emily yelled, leaping to her left as the Thunder from Binge flew past, destroying yet more stonework in the virtual ancient piazza.

The microgun's motor wound down and its barrels stopped spinning as Emily turned back around. She knew what that sound meant. Empty! That's when Timothy held out his arm—the one with the silver cylinder—and aimed it at Emily. As his volley of mini missiles left the tube, Emily's avatar dove within 18 meters before her enemies. When she hit the ground, she fired the weapon at Katsuko's chest. A vivid flash erupted from the gun and blazed through the colorful ninja's torso, leaving a grapefruit-sized hole clean through. Emily wasted no time watching Katsuko's comedic reaction, blasting one shot each at Binge and Timothy. They each stood there for a moment, dropping their weapons and gesturing in disbelief and complaint. The protest continued as their avatars buckled and dropped to their knees—painfully slow and agonizing deaths. Emily stood up as the doors to the cathedral swung open to reveal a brilliant, golden light glowing from within. She considered this an invitation and stepped over her steaming adversaries' corpses to cross the magnificent threshold. The doors closed behind her, and an orchestral victory march began to play. The light gradually grew brighter to magnificently brilliant and blinding as the music washed away.

Two sisters removed Emily's VR helmet as she stretched to wrap her mind around her body's fatigue, and the unfamiliar surroundings. She appeared to be in a room with similar reclining chairs, though all of them were empty. She attempted to speak, but her mouth was far too dry.

"Shh," said one of the sisters as she placed the helmet in a drawer to the side of the chair after sanitizing it. "He will be here in a moment to explain."

Emily trembled and fought to moisten her throat. "Who? What happened? Where am I?" She said with a sanded tone.

The room felt clinical and cold. Emily rubbed her eyes as she labored to stretch. A door at the far end swung open, and Bishop Esposito walked through it. Emily sat up and withdrew into the bed as it was being articulated to elevate her head and back.

"You are to be congratulated," said Esposito.

Emily turned away, trembling with an awful anxiety. Esposito walked over to her bedside and took a seat beside it.

"I imagine you have a few questions." He gestured the nun to leave. "Sister Regina..."

Emily didn't move, lying motionless with her head turned. Sniffling.

"Dear Emily, you went to bed last night at the normal time of 8pm. You put on our training helmet, and you started a round of The Guard along with several of your teammates, yes?"

Emily stared blankly away.

"And out of everyone, you, Emily, you alone entered the doors to the cathedral."

Emily turned around with a reluctant expression.

"Ah, there, you see. I knew you were the curious sort." Narciso smiled wide. "What you did not realize is that you have only been here with us for one night. Your training, your gaming—the entire two weeks that you believe you spent with us, you were asleep for a single night."

Emily furled her brow and pursed her lips. "Huh?"

"This is a normal reaction to the program. In time you will learn to appreciate its capabilities. You see, what we do here is not so much astray from what your father is working on. We are unlocking the potential of your mind."

He pointed to her forehead. "Every night we go to sleep, wasting opportunities to learn new skills, practice them, and become masters. What otherwise takes days, weeks, months and even years to achieve, with this helmet, the correct programming, and a receptive mind, we can achieve in a few nights. The person must be receptive. It only works for certain people. Allow me a question, dear Emily; What is so different from one person's skill or talent than yours?"

Emily shrugged.

"Interest first, then time and training. It takes time for your muscles to memorize a physical skill. Your mind can remember it upon sight with the proper guidance. It is your muscles that take time. The skilled motions eventually become automatic—second nature. In a manner of speaking, the helmet shrinks time. Your mind believes it has spent days developing a skill, and in reality, only minutes or hours. Your mind believes it, therefore your muscles believe it, and voila! You have the skills. And this is the difficult part: it is easy to trick your mind into remembering because there are no muscles involved except the one between your ears." Again, Narciso pointed to her forehead.

"How does it know how many days?" Emily asked.

"The time compression is controlled by us. A fresh mind cannot absorb more than 15 days in a single night at first, but it learns to accept more... to a point. The record is 62 days."

Emily's imagination ran with notions of intellectual maturity well before her time. The fantasy was suddenly broken by another thought.

"What about Sylvia and Vena, or Chandni and Peggy. Isabella. Where are they?" Emily demanded. "Were they even real?"

"Yes, they were real. Your enemies, of course, were not."

"Where are they?"

"I sent them home."

"Why?" Emily sniffled.

"Because my dear, unlike you, they were not good enough or strong enough to continue the program."

"But I cheated." Emily quipped.

"You did what was necessary, my dear; you improvised!" Narciso smiled.

Sister Regina reentered with a breakfast tray, setting it down on the overbed table. Bishop Esposito stood out of the way.

"What about Sylvia and Chandni? They let themselves be killed so we could win."

The sister shook her head as she completed the setting. "We should remind you that we only look for winners. Winners, Emily, include survivors. Sacrificing yourself for others may seem heroic and noble, except in the end you are dead. Dead and useless."

The comment perplexed Emily as the Bishop prepared to leave.

"Enjoy your meal, Emily. I liked our talk. Oh, and, you will meet another like yourself in the morning. Her name is Petra. Fine girl; a winner, just as you."

Sister Regina finished prepping Emily's breakfast and departed with Esposito. As soon as the door was closed behind them, the nun asked, "Why young girls and not boys. Are they not stronger, more aggressive... bold?"

Esposito towered over her and grinned with a cocked brow. "Sister Regina, you of all should know girls are the most ambitious, the most vicious, and most conniving creatures, yet they are the most loyal."

At least a foot and a half shorter than Esposito, the nun stopped, turned towards him in the hallway, gave a disdainful upwards glare of acknowledgement, and then turned back around to continue walking.

"Amen."

Hotspot

Jupiter shuttered violently—the rush of wind and sea amplified and silenced at once. Chris' skull slammed into the plush headboard, which collapsed against the forward bulkhead of his stateroom. The collision was severe enough to snap necks, and for the few moments of continued unconsciousness, Dao Ming panicked for his life. She would be lying in the same predicament if not for a subtle shift in her sleeping position to slightly angled. Her left shoulder was throbbing with an intense, searing burn. Alarms were echoing throughout the boat as everyone scrambled to collect their senses. Rocco and Anastasia's staterooms faced portside, and they had been thrown off their beds onto the teak sole, same as Matthew and Trovarto on the starboard. Matthew made it to the bridge first and had been attempting to ascertain what happened. Jupiter was heeling and pitching, the rush of wind gone. They were dead in the water, adrift.

When Chris came to, his eyes locked on Dao's in a blur. His head pounded, and his lower neck was very sore. The boat's sudden random sways and heaves induced an intense nausea—a condition of which he had been immune until that moment. He wanted to throw up. He sensed the inevitable retching coming on. Dao was powerless to help him, and then she remembered Monsignor Trovarto's scopolamine inhaler. Dao was then stricken with concern for Trovarto, who would surely be affected by the unceasing motion.

"Remain here; I will get help," Dao said, caressing Chris' forehead.

Dao grabbed at the handrails on her way to the bridge. Jupiter's heaving had grown unpredictably random and exaggerated, tossing her off steps and sending her into walls. When she arrived, exasperated, she saw monitors flashing red warnings and input queries.

"We hit something." Matt shouted. "Look!"

He pointed toward the starboard hull's transom. Dangling by hydraulic and safety lines were its strut and foil. The graphene-impregnated carbon fiber appeared intact, except for a meter-length compaction along the leading edge of the bottom foil.

"Where is the Monsignor?" She asked.

"He was on the floor. Still knocked out, you know. I placed him back in bed. Lucky him!"

Dao nodded then raced down to the steps of the starboard hull's transom for a closer look, returning a minute or two later. Rocco and Anastasia were on the bridge.

"Shipping container?"

"Where is Doctor Miller?" Anastasia sensed something was out of place with him as she examined Dao's expression.

"In bed with a throbbing headache and nausea. I need you to find the Monsignor's scopolamine inhaler and take it to him."

Anastasia sped off for his stateroom, struggling to stay upright.

"What can I do?" Rocco asked.

"Nothing yet," said Matt. "Wait. How is your swimming?"

"Freestyle podium twice at Des Roches."

"Good. I will need your help later."

Anastasia opened the door to Trovarto's stateroom and found him unconscious from the medicine he took last night. She knew he would be indisposed for most of the journey. The inhaler was secured in the nightstand's top drawer. She grabbed it and headed towards the port hull.

The arrayed displays in front of Dao and Matthew defaulted to Emergency Stop, which luffs and flattens the main sail, unloading the mast while maintaining production of power. If the boat was in danger of capsizing, the mast would retract to lower the center of gravity.

"The foils are retracted. Generating sufficient power. No excessive water detected in the bilges. In fact, they are dry. Good news, we are not sinking." Dao smiled at Rocco.

"We are drifting southwest, two knots, however." Dao said, checking each display. "And we are forty minutes from our second leg. GPS places us thirty-two miles south of the Sargasso Gyre Line, therefore we are not in immediate danger."

"Except we aren't moving." Matthew blurted. "Doesn't this thing have stabilization? You read the manual; what do we need to do?"

"I need to think, and, no, I mean yes, except... it does have stabilization, but it works only when hydrofoiling."

Matthew stepped away, rolling his eyes at Rocco as he did. Rocco paid it no attention and stood by Dao, curious about the technology of Jupiter's Bolt. Surely her engineers foresaw this very possibility, he thought.

When Anastasia opened the door to Chris and Dao's stateroom, a noxious wave of stench sent her reeling. The floor gave evidence of Chris' condition. He was not on the bed or within immediate view. Anastasia peered around the room and caught a reflection off the bathroom door's backside. Chris was on his knees before the commode, fighting the undulations to remain centered over its bowl. Anastasia struggled to reach him. The teak and carbon fiber had become partially slick from the vomit. She shuttered at the thought of slipping into it. There was so much. The head was only seven steps away from the stateroom entrance, and she kept a strong grip on Jupiter's thoughtfully-placed handholds along the way. Chris' wobbling noggin labored to turn her direction.

"I'm so sorry." He groaned and turned back around, sensing another round.

As Anastasia placed the inhaler on top of the vanity, his concerns were realized. The girl flinched, and the inhaler started rolling towards the toilet. Just at the edge, Chris reached over and caught it, trying to catch a breath after heaving. Anastasia innately knew she could not abandon him and ran some water to soak a hand towel. She handed it to Chris and he wiped his face. He started to get up, placing a foot down as the boat crested a wave. He grabbed Anastasia's arm and tugged on it to maintain balance, and fell back against the wall. She reached underneath his left armpit and lifted with all her might. Another foot came down. Chris stooped over her as they lumbered towards the bedside, and he reached it just in time to throw a hand down and steady himself. As he did, Anastasia misjudged his release and overcorrected her balance, sending her backwards onto the yolkish lagoon.

"Sorry!" Chris shouted as he lifted the inhaler towards a nostril.

"Okay, who wants to check the starboard hull?" Dao turned away from the screens and faced Rocco and Matthew.

They looked at each other and Rocco proved more eager.

"Wait a minute, kid. You need a suit and flippers for this current. They don't come in all sizes even if this tub has one."

"It has six wetsuits in three sizes." Dao said. "And two scuba tanks, which will be necessary to reattach the foil struts. It may require both of you in this current, even with the strut retracted."

Matthew said, "Well, okay, let's cross that bridge when we get to it. I want to take a look at her first. What are we talking about, two attachment points? Lower and upper?"

"Exactly," said Dao. "The lower is hinged and the upper is also hinged to an actuator. The hinge pins are designed to certain tolerances, and they break away when those tolerances are exceeded. It must be a tremendous force. The manual said there are extra pins located in the aft equipment hold. The suits should be in the port hull's central locker. How soon until ready?"

Rocco turned towards the port companionway. "On it."

"Guess I better go with him," Matt said.

"Wait." Dao tugged at his shirt. "I need you to help me retrieve the foil."

"I thought it wasn't going anywhere?"

"It is not acceptable to allow changing tension on that safety line. If it breaks, or the connector breaks, the hydraulic line cannot endure the stress."

"I'll grab a hook."

Matthew ran down the companionway and unclipped a boat hook from the starboard hull's aft railing. He took two steps down and suddenly realized that he was not attached to the boat. One slip and he could be gone, no matter his training or strength, a two-knot current in these seas is unpredictable.

Rope. It's a sailboat for Christ sakes; should have ropes all over this bitch!

He checked stowage lockers in his immediate area, and fortune struck on the one forward of the thruster motor compartment. There were several nylon ropes for different purposes. He found a 40-meter line and tied it off on the starboard aft mooring bit towards the top of the transom's stairs. He then fished the line and tied it again at the aftmost rail connection for redundancy and better articulation of the line. He gave the line a bit of slack and looped it around his beltline twice, then tied it off with a double half hitch knot. He unclipped the hook and headed back down the steps, again stopping on the second and turning around, this time to make sure Dao was on deck just in case anything went wrong.

As Jupiter pitched and rolled, Matt found the task slightly more difficult than it appeared. There were no rails or handholds at the lower end of the transom, so he took a seat on the second to last step and buttressed his buttocks against the sidewall. Careful to snag the safety line and not the hydraulic hose, Matt hooked it and twisted the pole for grip. He carefully hauled in the structure and brought the upper strut's end, where the line and hose attached, to where he could grasp it with his free hand. Dao ran over to the top of the stairs, intuitively took the pole from him and snapped it back onto the railing. With both hands Matt strained against the current to haul the foil onto the steps. The entire carbon and titanium rig was four and a half meters in length when fully extended, and another three meters wide for its arced foil. It was cumbersome and unwieldy. Matt brought as much of it onboard as he could and decided it would be best to strap it to the side along the railing. He informed Dao of the necessity and she concurred. She ran back onto the bridge and activated the foil's retraction, and it appeared functional. Matt gave a thumbs up in verification.

When the foil was secured against the hull, she made a closer examination of the foil's leading edges and the dampering internals. She looked at Matt with the eyes of disappointment.

"Think I know what this means," Matt said.

"You must understand our fortune. We are lucky to be alive. We are fortunate to be floating. We are even more fortunate that we can continue sailing after we repair this foil. If we are luckier, we can hydrofoil, and the dampeners are functional. We cannot hypersail; the foil will not super-cavitate. The gas injector's leading edge is damaged enough to cause an irregular bubble, or multiple bubbles. It will not work properly, and the excessive friction will destroy it."

"Huh." Matt frowned. "No chance for a workaround either, I suppose."

"None that I foresee."

Dao abruptly turned around and realized that Anastasia had not returned, and neither had Rocco. She dropped further conversation with Matthew and made her way across the boat to the port companionway. Anastasia was making her way up the stairs with a towel wrapped around her. Before Dao could ask. "Don't even..." erupted from Anastasia's lips as she topped the stairs. Rocco was just behind her, hauling the second of two scuba gear loads: wetsuits, flippers, masks, tanks and regulators.

"How did it go?" He asked.

Dao was unconcerned and trying to get to Chris. "What happened?"

Rocco repositioned the bag he was carrying. "She said Doctor Miller is sick, that she slipped, and something about making a mess."

Dao held herself by the companionway's rails as she skipped a few steps to make the landing. As she turned the corner, Chris was on the bed, drifting but stabilized. The odor was unbearable and could have been much worse if not for Anastasia's blotting as much as possible with a couple bath towels, which were soaped, rinsed, and hanging to dry in the shower. The teak would need further attention after its acid wash. Dao opened two of the venting hatches for fresh air and sat on the bed next to Chris.

"No more from you, *bèndàn*."

He struggled against the scopolamine's effect. "Nothing left."

Dao smiled. If there was one trait where Chris enjoyed a 100% success rate, it was in making her laugh. And, as he drifted further, he was reminded of Suzanne. He could not forestall the inevitable tear from welling, even in the presence of a new beginning. He understood everything happening to him at once with no power to alter the outcome. He acquiesced and let it happen. Dao was mature enough to understand as well. Unspoken empathy.

Chris fought for one more question before losing consciousness. "Dao... Is the boat out of danger?"

She backed off and threw his hand upon the bed. "Really?"

Chris smirked as he made peace with the grand vignette. Dao kept her grin, swallowed with a rough throat, and made her way back to the aft sun deck. Rocco and Matt had been assessing the scuba gear and were currently halfway into their navy-blue wetsuits. Matt picked up a weight belt and held it for a few moments before deciding to lose two of its coated lead squares. After strapping it around his waist, he slipped into the rest of the wetsuit and zipped it just below the neck, leaving the neck loose. He checked the air tank, connected the regulator assembly, and secured it onto the buoyancy compensator vest. Matt checked on Rocco's progress to find he was quite proficient, even faster since his booties and fins were on and adjusted. Matt walked over to check his regulator and noticed that one of the tank's cam band latches wasn't all the way down.

"Hey kid, you trying to get yourself hurt?" Matt pointed to the strap lock. "This isn't a race. Take your time and get it right."

Red-faced, Rocco retightened the tank and locked the strap's cam band correctly, then hoisted the tank vest onto his back. Dao walked outside and handed the two 18cm replacement pins to Matthew. As she did, Jupiter shuddered and all of them lost their footing. Rocco couldn't rescue his balance and landed on his side towards the starboard. Matt and Dao collided, and she instinctively grabbed onto him. In doing so, the second of the two pins slipped from her grasp and onto the deck, where they rolled, as if in predictable slow motion, towards the edge of the deck, stopping at the gunnel. Jupiter spun about with another tremoring jolt, creating further imbalance with Matt and Dao, yet they managed to stay on their feet. Dao looked toward the end of the deck. The pin was gone.

The boat heaved and felt as though it was lodged, not moving freely. Dao's first thought was that Jupiter found the culprit of its severed foil, or perhaps it was another container or other large object just under the surface. Whatever it was, it was beating up the port hull, and they needed to get Jupiter away from it before catastrophic damage occurred. Sure, Jupiter's hulls were engineered astronomically stronger through the use of graphene lattices, but Dao decided this was not the optimal time or location for experiments. She raced across the boat and climbed over to the starboard hull's railing. A stunned expression immediately appeared on her face.

"Matthew!" She yelled as he was about to slip the buoyancy control vest off, dropping it and its tank on the other side of the main deck's transom.

Rocco was struggling to stand up with the heavy, awkward gear and flippers, so Matt snagged his arm and brought him over to the aft bench on his way to the starboard hull. When he bent over the rail, his face contorted the same as Dao's.

The water was choppy from wind and opaque due to the sun's direction. He strained for a better view, then he saw it.

"I'm no navigational whiz, but that is a rock, and last I checked, we were 450 miles from land in 5,500 meters of water."

Dao nodded then stormed to the bridge with Matt close behind. She tapped on the third-from-left screen and checked depth. The screen displayed "4.0m" in yellow highlight at the top left corner. Dao's breathing became hurried and deep as she tapped on the fourth screen. She feared they had somehow tracked wildly off course towards the seamounts of Researcher Ridge, 150 nautical miles to the south of their course. GPS calibrations fail. It happens. They were all asleep. Anything could have occurred. *The seamounts around here though*, she thought. *Those are thousands of feet down. How could this happen and nobody know?*

Dao tapped the thruster activation and brought it online. The second screen cleared and displayed a stitched overhead view from the top of the mast, with the mast digitally removed for unimpeded sightlines. She nudged the thruster control towards the right and in a lunging crush of water, Jupiter broke free of the scabrous basalt. The depth gauge increased to five meters and hovered there, then five and a half. By estimate, Dao had taken the boat at least twenty meters away from the rock.

"I'm taking her to the leeward side and dropping anchor. We need that pin!"

Dao rotated the stick and nudged it forward, eyes on her depth and desired path around the rock. Upon reaching the other side, Dao tapped the bottom of the rightmost screen and accessed the mooring protocols. She flipped through the available selections to Automated Dynamic Anchoring and activated it. By the indicator, Jupiter's primary anchor set at 3.7m depth. Since the thrusters were power-hungry, she set the desired direction to remain down current and downwind, unless the wind suddenly changed direction beyond 180 degrees, therefore the thrusters would only activate to maintain Jupiter within that arc. She turned around to Matt, who was observing the entire process.

"I am *so* glad you read that manual."

Dao smiled. *"A bend in the road is not the end of the road unless you fail to make the turn.* Helen Keller."

On his way off the bridge Matt turned around and winked, conjuring a wide, insincere smile from Dao. Back on the aft sun deck, he turned the corner around the transom wall.

"Looks like we're going for a dive, Rocco. Throw that extra weight back on your belt."

Both plunged off the stern and dropped several feet into the Spanish-blue crystal. Visibility, Matt guessed, was 15 meters or so—not quite what he'd hoped but good enough to service the boat's needs and search for the lost pin. He noticed the water was quite warmer than he would have guessed—almost lukewarm. He motioned to Rocco and they adjusted their buoyancy controllers. They were floating over a rock, that much was for certain, Matt thought. Fresh from volcanism, yet there was no visible sign of an active fissure or cone. No steam or gas on the surface, either. Matt was struggling to understand how this peak, to which they were anchored, materialized without anyone the wiser, not that people survey every part of the Atlantic Ocean on a regular basis. It seemed as though someone's sonar would have detected it, or another ship would have hit it by now.

Rocco signaled he was ready. Matt pointed towards the other side of the peak which was twelve or so meters beyond Jupiter's bow. Against the current, they swam over and began a basic grid search of the hillside. The basalt was dark, and the pin was black. It would not be easily spotted. Matt decided to focus on differential shapes. He was looking for a short, straight line. There were cleaved crags all over the surface, some broken and loose rocks, but very few. The pin's location was proving elusive. Matt realized that he and Rocco spent all of their time facing uphill with the sunlight just off their backs for best viewing. The deeper they went down the hillside, the opaquer the water became. A chill surged through Matt's body and he turned around in a panic. Desperately, he scanned the water as far away as it allowed, and nothing. He started second-guessing his intuition and turned back around to continue working his grid square. The variations in the rock and the ebbing sunlight were working against him, as was the current. He made two more squares and a surge electrified his spinal column. Matt saw the monster's shadow streak across the rock from his left with far too much velocity for him to turn around. He was a deer in the headlights as it brushed along his backside. The slick of its skin oozed by as the turbulence pinned Matt against the rock floor. It seemed to last an eternity until the pressure broke and Matt felt the wake of its tail stroke pass. In a panic, Matt twisted his body around, spilling water into his mask, but not enough to obscure the parting shot of a whale shark as it disappeared into the rays of sapphire twilight.

Not again!

Matt collected himself and turned around to find Rocco resisting hyperventilation. Matt catapulted himself over and gestured for Rocco to slow his breathing. No amount of hand signals could relay the fact, however, that whale sharks were no harm. It didn't matter. Rocco held up his left hand. He'd found the pin!

Rocco and Matt were delighted to see the ladder deployed off the starboard hull, since they completely forgot about it. Dao was waiting for them at the top with repair instructions. Simple operation: align the hinges, insert the pins and lock each one with the hinge pin stops. *Simple yes*, Matt thought, *in a shipyard, maybe!*

To Rocco and Matt's relief, Jupiter's orientation to the current made the operation less difficult than anticipated. Naturally, the extendable foil preferred running with the water and allowed for easier alignment. Once the pins were locked and lines restored, Matt signaled their return to the ladder. As he dropped his head back into the water, he caught the reflection of something light-colored down the hillside off Jupiter's portside corner. Matt decided to investigate, and he did so without informing Rocco, who was already at the ladder, preparing to emerge.

About twelve or so meters past the boat, the rock abruptly ended at a shelf. Matt swam towards its ledge, noticing it was a straight line of brown stone, each end of it disappearing beyond sight. When he reached the ledge, he saw that it descended in a stepped pattern, about a meter drop for each step until it too vanished into the deep. He stared at it longer than he should have. He was suddenly startled by Rocco's hand on his shoulder. He pointed and Rocco peered over the

ledge, straining to see as far as he could. He turned around to
Matt and gave a thumbs up towards the surface, breaking in a
spirited kick against the surging current. Matt hugged the
bottom to lessen the current's effect, then ascended the few
remaining meters at Jupiter's stern. He slid the mask to the top
of his head and caught Anastasia's hair billowing in the sun-
bleached breeze at the top of the stairs, waiting to assist their
return. Matt happened to look up where he noticed the faint
distrail running through a washboard cirrostratus cloud high
overhead.

Dao looked down at him. "Rocco says there are large steps
down there. Definitely not natural. We should investigate
further and take a photo at the very least."

"We can't."

"Why not?"

Matt pointed towards the aircraft. "If we haven't been
located, we might be soon. Jupiter may be stealthy, granted,
but she's not invisible. Under the right conditions she could
be spotted from a hundred miles away. We need to keep
moving."

Matt hurriedly stripped off the scuba gear and toweled off.
Frustrated, Dao trudged to the bridge and activated the
anchor's windlass. She had been reprogramming the sailing
mode to standard hydrofoil from hyperfoil, and recalculating
time and distance. They were at least another fifteen hours
from the Virginia coastline. Dao tapped to execute the updated
sail plan. Jupiter's Bolt activated thrusters and realigned its
course for best time and distance. Her mast extended fully
with its graphene solar sail deployed, and the foils lowered
into the water, gradually extending as necessary for one-meter
seas. The sounder echoed a rapidly descending depth—twenty
meters at first, then down to 100, then 600, and a shear drop
to 3,000 and back to over 5,000. There was a problem gnawing
at Dao's neck, and that was the accuracy of the GPS.
Calibration required a rotational maneuver in calm waters. It

also took time. Probability mathematics flashed across her mind. Impossibilities, likelihoods, certainties, caveats... If the navigational computer was that far off after that many hours, how far would it be off when they reached the American coast? Did it matter? Was the GPS actually uncalibrated and they ran into an uncharted seamount? What was the probability of uncharted *anything* in the Atlantic these days? She should speak to Chris before making any decision, she concluded. He would be out for hours, however. At some point, this must be addressed.

Jupiter rose upon her foils and built speed until the programmed governor adjusted the sail to average 45 knots. The slime and gas bubble system only worked during super-cavitation, which kept the seawater from shredding the foils to malfunction. It was safe to keep her under 55 knots, and Dao knew they were fortuitous to maintain it. Best of all, the ocean's toil upon their bodies had ceased, and the gentle lullaby of Jupiter's cradle returned a contemplative calm.

"Hey Dao," Matt said, and she turned around to face him. "Nice job today."

Her lips pursed slightly as the tension released. "Thank you. As well, you... and Rocco."

Matt smirked. "You, uh, mind if I thumb through that manual?"

Merovengeance

A charcoal-grey Mercedes passenger van with dark tinted windows sped through the garrigue landscape then suddenly burst through the decorative iron gates of the Office National des Forêts. It blew past a Protected Area sign safeguarding the fragile, wild fennel plantings in the area—penance for developing the Chevalier Du Rennes golf course in the early 1970s without government permission. The van's driver diligently coursed the narrow dirt path, choking the bordering fennel with dust and small bits of stone. It came to an intersection with another discreet pathway, and thundered onto a cart path just behind the 14th tee boxes. None of the club's twenty members were within sight distance to witness the destructive trespass taking place. There was only one group on the course, and they were a full kilometer away, reckoning obscene wagers on the 4th green. The van's driver cut across the 13th fairway, gouging deep ruts into the freshly-irrigated paspalum turf before reaching the fescue rough on its southern border. The van narrowly squeezed into a tight, unmarked tarmac pathway leading down a gentle hill between an impenetrable hedge at least four meters in height. Leaves flew and branches scraped on bodywork as it tore down the pathway. The driver slammed on the brakes to avoid colliding with a substantial piece of metalwork blocking their path. The electronic gate could not be breached without explosives. The driver threw the van's transmission in reverse and stopped a couple dozen meters back. A tactically-dressed operator jumped out of the rear, ran around to the front and produced an assault rifle appended with grenade launcher. He fired it at the gate's clasping mechanism, to which a shallot-sized globule stuck. The operator fled and took position behind the van's right-rear corner. A light puff of smoke accompanied a muted thud moments later. The man trotted back to the gate and threw it open, triggering alarms throughout the campus.

Gérard, the chief and singular security officer for the Du Rennes at that moment, leapt to his feet and checked his monitors. Mallory Du Rennes' head spun towards the closed-circuit array in his master suit and summoned Henri. He arrived within several seconds already initiating defensive protocols at Gérard's insistence. They watched the monitors as the van skidded to a stop in front of his château, and several soldiers armored in tactical black spilled out, intent on Armageddon.

"*Quelle merde; tout ce travail!*" Henri gasped.

Due Rennes turned and smiled. "Do not be so bourgeoisie, Henri. We have manufactured a new enemy, and in so doing, a fresh challenge. Similar to the last occasion, no? We will return, and on a stronger footing."

Du Rennes examined the invaders on the monitor and rapidly estimated their equipment would ensure their entry, given enough time. This raid was for his life, and probably his father's as well. Why else? He kept adequate resources, but he could not fight all of them. It was time to leave.

"See to my father, will you? You know what to do."

Henri dashed towards the rear, and Du Rennes checked his watch, sending a priority code to the home's master system and his bodyguard. Gérard remained on station just beyond Du Rennes' garage at the rear of the structure. He was already on the alert and anxious as the message appeared on his wrist.

Gérard double checked his vest and armaments on his way to the combination safe behind a hidden section of polished concrete wall. The double-doored estate safe, which had just arrived by internal elevator from a similarly-hidden wall within Du Rennes' master suite two floors above, awaited his code entry. Gérard unlocked and swung both doors open, snatching the two prepacked 40-kilo crash bags from within. He turned around without hesitation and chucked them into the back of a specialized Range Rover Sport that had been customized for intense off-roading. The crash bags contained clothing, toiletries, tools, several assorted passports with corresponding identification, light weaponry, four million euros, first aid, and other specific necessities for extended vacations. On his second trip, Gérard snagged a case containing digital backups and predetermined physical records. His third trip collected two machine pistols, a brick of 12 corresponding magazines, and two rifles with what appeared to be peculiarly short magazines that consisted of three vertical cylinders of about 30cm in diameter each. The loading of the Rover took less than 25 seconds, in keeping with drills practiced monthly at the compound. Loaded and ready, he eased towards the rear stairwell in anticipation of his employers, stopped, jumped out, opened all doors and stood by for reception.

Du Rennes checked his watch's security feed as the operators took the main entrance one-by-one in a breach-and-clear formation, popping two flash-bangs as they entered the Grand Visage. Mallory made the hallway just as Jet Sun and Patrick exited their rooms with their own backpacks. Together, they scrambled for the alternate stairwell at the rear, some twenty meters distant. Along the way, they heard the sharp explosions of four rifle rounds. Du Rennes froze in assumption. Patrick and Jet Sun turned around and ushered him to the stairwell.

"I must go back."

"You cannot," said Jet Sun.

Patrick painfully looked at him and shook his head as he swung open the stairwell door. Du Rennes stumbled as he struggled for breath, wobbling down the three flights to the garage. As he rechecked the safety on his pistol, Gérard kept his eye on the reinforced rollup doors anticipating their destruction any moment. Another shot's percussion echoed through the stairwell. Du Rennes missed a step and reached for the handrail, catching himself. Patrick grasped his other hand and led him down the final flight to the well's portico. Jet Sun made a quick glance down the garage and kicked the door open, motioning Patrick and Du Rennes through. They were merely steps away when the first of two explosive charges tested the garage's main doors. Multiple gunfire erupted shortly afterward. When Du Rennes stepped to the passenger's front door of the Range Rover, he craned around to the back of it, hoping he was somehow mistaken in assumption of the obvious. He slumped in despair as he took his seat and closed the door. A Du Rennes could not shed a tear; not for a man in service to his family for the past thirty years who had become more of a constant companion and friend, and not for his father, because he said, "To do so in front of others demonstrates weakness, jettisoning a man's dignity." That was their pact—to never cry for each other's death unless that death was dishonorable, in which case their legacy was forever gone.

"Pour le vieux château, s'il vous plaît."

Gérard pressed a button under the Rover's dash and the massive stone wall at the rear of the garage slide open, revealing a darkened tunnel. He stomped on the accelerator in anticipation of enough width as the door continued, just as the doors at the other end were obliterated by a single massive explosion, shattering the glass of several cars. The van, with a driver and two operators, blew in just behind and gave pursuit. The other operators remained in the compound, sweeping ancillary rooms. Du Rennes brought his watch around, tapped out a short four-zone sequence and entered a code. He tapped one last time. A moment later, the golfers departing the 4th green felt the ground beneath their feet shudder as the shockwave blew past. They panicked and reached for their phones as the fireball emerged over the tops of the parasol pines a kilometer away.

Gérard focused on the narrow tunnel's camouflaged exit as he transitioned from night to day. The square concrete passageway opened to a rocky trail several hundred meters away from the compound. The Rover catapulted itself down a shallow ravine and into a wooded trail where it could gain speed. They were less than three hundred meters away from the exit when the van sprang from it in a frantic, reckless abandon. A rifle appeared from the van's front passenger window, and it sprayed automatic fire in wild directions, impacting trees and rocks off to the sides.

Patrick turned as he heard a ricochet just outside his window. "And which one of ya asked for more followers?"

Jet Sun turned around for a glimpse as Du Rennes and Gérard caught sight in the mirrors. Gérard pushed the Rover harder through the pines, opening the supercharger to maximum pressure, sending a rooster tail of loose stone and dirt flying as the all-wheel-drive searched for grip. Speed rapidly accumulated into rally-mode drifting and air. The van dropped back beyond site just as the Rover crabbed onto a narrow pathway, riddled with large, loose stones and slick undergrowth. The van caught the dust trail and continued into the obscured pathway, with the screeching sound of branches scraping sheet metal as it entered. The trail suddenly switched from loose rocks and other hazards to solid stone, descending rapidly down into a ravine. Gérard switched the drive selector to a customized River Fording mode that switched the vehicle's engine air intake to a snorkel that drew air from the top of the passenger-side windshield. The transmission also selected a lower gear range to prevent slippage. Down they went into the river, up to a level just at the windows. Gérard carefully centered the river, keeping the Rover pointed downstream. The current was strong enough to flip them if he let the rear catch too much water; it happened twice before in practice runs. The monsieur was graciously more concerned with competence than he was with cost, and his confidence in Gérard's capabilities grew as the result of it. Patrick turned back around as another rifle blast exploded the river's calm just beside them.

"Figures, they'd have a four-wheel-drive van; and with the same snorkel, mind ya."

Du Rennes smiled as he started tapping on his watch. "They could not have planned for the contingencies they cannot foresee, dear Patrick."

With the last tap, a ten-meter length of river just behind them dropped away, then refilled the gap with water. When van continued, its driver had no way of knowing what was about to happen until it did, and the van's nose disappeared into the deep.

Another two hundred or so meters around the next bend in the river, an ancient stone rampart appeared as part of an old bridge that connected to a castle. At its footings on the river was what appeared to be an arched tunnel, through which, part of the river traversed. Gérard drove into its darkened archway and onto the cobbled ramp ascending just beyond it, which terminated on a hydraulic vehicle lift. He activated the lift, and its doors two stories above opened wide. When the lift leveled with the courtyard, Gérard eased forward to make a right turn and park in front of an executive helicopter, similar to the one taken from Corsica. Instead, the Rover found itself surrounded by three operators pointing their grenade-enabled rifles at him, yelling *"Arrêtez! Sortez!"* Alongside them, just in front of Mallory Du Rennes was Henri, nervously pointing a pistol straight at him.

Mallory scowled and lowered his window. "Where is my father, Henri?"

With a twitch and stutter, he coughed and tightened his grip on the pistol. "I saw to him."

Without removing his searing eyes from his butler, Du Rennes activated the remote start-up sequence on the helicopter, distracting Henri for a brief moment as he raised his window. A single shot from Henri's pistol escaped the barrel. Du Rennes turned and whispered to Patrick. Patrick's window cracked open. The pistol in Henri's hand went supernova; its magazine exploding from the intense heat, vaporizing the hand that held it. Henri recoiled the shattered stump as he screamed. The riflemen opened fire on the Rover, striking it repeatedly, yet unable to penetrate its armor. They started to back off in order to launch grenades. Patrick closed his window as Gérard activated one of the Rover's close-range defenses—a short, five-meter burst of napalm in all directions. The fury engulfed two of the operators as the third retreated. Gérard pulled a pistol and bullseyed the back of his neck. Instant collapse and death. Gérard stepped out and put the other two operators out of their misery, then he turned towards Henri, who was on his knees, whimpering in pain and guilt. Gérard placed the warm barrel on his head and was about to pull the trigger when Du Rennes arrived.

"No!" Du Rennes barked, producing his own pistol. He jammed its barrel against Henri's left temple and squeezed the trigger. Du Rennes squinted as his servant fell, replacing the weapon underneath his jacket. *"Pour moi et moi seul."*

Gérard grunted as he holstered his sidearm and walked towards the Rover. Du Rennes spent a moment longer, staring at Henri in disbelief. With a sniffle, spat on the butler's corpse and fell in behind Gérard towards their SUV.

"*Another* helicopter, is it?" Patrick asked.

Du Rennes looked up at him and produced a forced grin. "As the maxim implies, Mr. Fannin, why have one... but she is a *White Wolf*, this one."

Du Rennes activated the Rover's tailgate on his way to the helicopter's front-left seat. Patrick and Jet Sun jumped out of the Rover and helped Gérard with the bags. There was no discussion and no dawdling. As the twin Pratt & Whitney turboshaft engines spooled up to take off, everything was loaded and the others took their seats.

Patrick leaned forward. "Ay! Ya never mentioned ya were a pilot now, Mallory."

"I am not." Du Rennes said dryly as he completed the programming of their flight plan and tapped the protected Execute button just to the side of a navigation panel.

Jet Sun's eyes enlarged with a raised brow.

Patrick looked at his reaction. "Then who's…"

"Naturally, the flight computer. Seriously, Mr. Fannin, have you not been keeping up with automation developments? We have self-driving automobiles already. Helicopters and drones have been flying themselves for years. Select a destination, a flight mode—in this case, Emergency Speed—and press a button. This is all that is minimally required."

Du Rennes pressed the final confirmation button on the instrument panel. The cyclic's stick automatically centered itself as the collective raised, creating lift from the spinning blades. The helicopter leapt skyward, cleared the castle's ramparts, rotated to the programmed course, and rocketed forward, building speed as the priority over altitude. In moments, it would level at best time.

"38 minutes to Saint Catherine's according to the computer, plus or minus," said Du Rennes.

"Time for a pint, I'd say!" Patrick started looking around for the bar.

"The cooler is to the left on the other side of the rear bulkhead, across from la toilette."

"What is your plan?" Jet Sun asked.

Du Rennes produced a satellite phone and dialed. As it rang, he glanced up to Jet Sun. "If we are in trouble, undoubtedly, they are in trouble."

The other end answered. "Allo?"

"Jeanette, *mon chérie*, by any chance are you close to home?"

There was a short pause. "Mallory? My God, I have so much to tell you. Yes, my charter departed Barcelona just moments ago. Problems?"

"*Toujours*. Divert to Saint Catherine's if you are able, my dear. Do not go to *le Château*, it has been compromised. Ugh, worse, destroyed. Your beloved chevalier has been martyred."

A long pause on the other end. There was a faint sound of a congested sniffle in Captain Montluc's voice. "I... am... will be at St. Catherine's. Estimate one hour. Mallory?"

"Thank God. Yes..."

"It is an honorable death, no? He was fortunate."

"It was his only dream, *mon amour*."

The hushed rotorcraft blasted across Vallon de Prés' treetops, gaining only enough altitude as necessary to clear the peaks to the east. At Sainte-Maxime, it kept to bare minimum altitudes to avoid notable complaints should the official channels be monitored, which Du Rennes suspected by default. The destination clock read 28 minutes as he theorized who his attackers were, and how they compromised Henri, who had been at his side for over 25 years. Who could acquire such leverage so quickly, so easily? Or, did Henri carry dark secrets that were discovered and exploited? Was it money? It was an inconceivable error on his part, to implicitly trust another man outside his family. He glanced toward Gérard.

"What?" Gérard was astonished in his reaction.

"It is not important," said Du Rennes. "Thank You."

"I never liked him," admitted Gérard. "Just so you know."

Du Rennes reasoned his Chief Security Officer could have turned on him at any time in those moments, but instead he heroically fulfilled his duty, executing his trained escape plan as they had rehearsed many times over the preceding eleven years. Gérard has fidelity, he thought. He must trust him until he couldn't. It was the same as Henri. The lesson was to not become too comfortable, to no longer trust with the deepest secrets. Then Du Rennes thought about his father. A warrior from another period who had also fulfilled his purpose, purchasing the critical extra seconds necessary for their escape. Du Rennes stared at the Mediterranean's sparkles in a blur, reminiscing his father's triumphs, and letting go of his failures. *Le Chevalier was not a perfect man, and there are no men without complications.*

● ● ●

General Tomlinson's tablet phone produced a distinctive chirp signifying an intelligence bulletin had arrived in her unmonitored and encrypted email account. There were no From or Subject headers, only the relevant information. The sources were assumed, and its acknowledgement of receipt automatic.

```
French DGSI reports detonation, 14:22 LT today.
Videbaun. Blast radius .25km. Nine (9) cas. in
Immed Zone. Four (4) additional in 2nd, 1km dis.
Visible remains heavily armed, save 2.
IDs: Pending
Private residence destroyed.
DGSI no further, redacted by State Dept status.
Subject Owner Known: Du Rennes, Mallory
```

A Frenchman. She knew little of Du Rennes. The name wasn't prevalent in her mental Rolodex, although it had to be connected to Fogo somehow. Tomlinson considered the ramifications of her division making sudden inquiries after events such as these. Typically, she waited to glean the information from her contacts within the State Department, the CIA, and her European network. Once those people became involved... It was an unpleasant thought to Tomlinson. She wanted her scientists returned; she wanted the device as well. Paramount considerations.

Tomlinson picked up the phone and dialed her liaison for Space Command at Peterson AFB in Colorado Springs.

"Yes, General, what can we do for you today?"

"You can find that goddamn boat I'm looking for, that's what," Tomlinson sniped.

"Look, Barbara—"

"Keep it formal, asshole."

"And you expect us to jump through hoops with that attitude? Come on..."

"Major Sponetti, you will jump through hoops on fire wearing nothing but your birthday suit if I ask you to, and right now, I am asking."

The major paused. "Okay, I take it this is serious, but Barb... General... we swept that zone you wanted several times already—infrared, radar, lidar, sonar, visual. Nothing except the normal commercial traffic. Are you sure they're still in the eastern Atlantic?"

"As a matter of fact, that's why I'm calling. I was told the boat is fast."

"A fast sailboat. What is that, 15 knots?"

"The man who created it has resources." Tomlinson checked her glass. "What does your imagination say?"

"I don't know General, allow me to consult the All-knowing."

A brief moment passed. Tomlinson heard the faint taps of a keyboard in the background.

"Current record set 2012, Paul Larsen's 'Vestas Sailrocket Two'. 65-plus knots over 500 meters... Hey, Barbara, that's a just a short burst on a course. Fast in open water? I dunno, maybe 30-40 knots. Given the amount of elapsed time..."

Sponetti ran computations on a tactical map. "At best they made the Forty West meridian, and we covered that in spades. Are you absolutely sure it's a sailboat you're looking for?"

"No, Chuck, it's a ghost boat." Tomlinson placed the crystal stopper back onto the decanter and set it back on the bar. "Keep looking, and take it further west just in case. I don't care if it's all the way to Bermuda—LOOK!"

The phone clicked, and she hung up while savoring the nose of her single malt.

● ● ●

Captain Montluc's charter touched down at St. Catherine's Airport in Corsica several minutes ahead of the estimated hour. She taxied the elder Citation down to the last hangar along the airport's northwestern flank and stopped just in front of the ramp marshal's crossed arms—several meters to the side of a helicopter cooling down. As she chocked the wheels and took receipt, she briskly walked into the hangar. The cavernous space was brightly lit, and she stopped dead in her tracks in stupefaction.

"*Mon Dieu*? What is this?" She asked of Mallory Du Rennes.

Du Rennes walked over from a makeshift buffet table and brought her an espresso. As she took it from his hands, he kissed her cheeks. "I need you to drink this."

"I see I am to lose more sleep this week."

"I am afraid so."

"*Santé, mon chevalier*," Montluc said, sipping her café.

"Bless you, Jeannette. I am grateful." Du Rennes struggled to keep composure.

"Now what do we have here, *monsieur*?"

"Ah. You know me and the toys. Had it scheduled after your landing in the other. She is not as special, but she will do."

Montluc tossed the rest of the espresso to the back of her throat. "This gift you have for the understatement..."

There were two jets gleaming in the hangar. To the right at the far side was the Gulfstream Special. A large section of the port wing had been removed as it awaited replacement. In front of her was a sleek 850X, the first prototype jet designed to exploit proposed allowances for private Mach-1+ at new flight levels between 55,000 and 75,000 feet. Its engineering minimizes sonic pressure waves, creating the capability for ungoverned flight speeds beyond Mach 2 when authorized.

"I am home, truly." Captain Montluc's eyes gleamed with excitement. A new aircraft always gave her goosebumps. A new jet that only a select few have piloted meant electrified hair on her arms as well. She walked underneath to inspect its lines, the flattened and extended nose, the canards, landing gear, and the elongated power plants that reminded her of the afterburning M88s of her old Rafale. Montluc immediately took notice of the fact there were no windows but those in the cockpit. There were, however, tiny oval protrusions aligning the fuselage. While she was shocked at their implementation so far ahead of theorized availability, she knew what they were from a computer mock-up demonstration at an obscure booth in last year's Paris Air Show.

Montluc made her walkaround in diligent fashion, arriving at the portside airstairs within a couple minutes.

"I assume our passengers are already onboard?"

"*Oui*," said Du Rennes. "And there is an abbreviated specifications sheet on your chair. Bermuda, at best possible speed, but with this caveat: you must fly in such a manner as to not cause extroversion. It other words, not too high, no too low, not too fast, and anything besides slow."

"*Magnifique.*"

She climbed onboard and took three steps back to the passenger cabin, instantly confirming the purpose of those bumps on the fuselage. Unsettling at first, the cabin's curved walls seem to disappear, as they were seamless, ultra-resolution monitors, displaying the outside with no impediments including the wings. They would one day replace the floor if not for the constant maintenance considerations. They were an experiment in passenger comfort, which generated many of the concerns voiced at the air show. The feature didn't seem to distract Jet Sun or Patrick much at all, as they were pleased to reunite with the pilot who delivered them from Cambodia. Montluc smiled and collected kisses from each, then briefly remarked on the cabin's display. Mallory Du Rennes joined them, as did Gérard, who had been in the lavatory at the rear. All seated, Montluc quickly machined a cup of coffee from the forward galley and took her cockpit seat on the left. An airport tug latched onto the forward landing gear and wheeled the stark white jet out of the hangar. Once stopped, she set the parking brake, signaled the ground crew, then ran the automated start sequence. The port engine built pressure as Montluc monitored the engine's RPM climb. She signaled again as the starboard engine spooled to equilibrium. The tower sent clearance, and the ground crew motioned her towards the ramp's exit. From there, it was a short taxi to the end of the north-facing runway where she held. The controller radioed approval, and Montluc responded, rolling on the throttles to maximum. The light jet scorched St. Catherine's tarmac on the way to 16,000 feet. Once level, she allowed the automated flight plan full control. She spent the next leg sipping her café between page flips of the aircraft's draft manual.

The cockpit door opened and Du Rennes stepped in.

"You should examine this, Jeanette. I've never... it's just. You must come see."

Du Rennes stepped aside as she unbuckled and stepped back to the passenger cabin, nearly losing her footing due to a slight vertigo effect.

"Well, what do you think?" He asked.

"It is everything they said, Mallory."

Patrick raised a glass. "Unnerving, that's what I say. How d'ya turn the damn thing off? It's interfering with my drinking!"

"We cannot have *that*, can we?" She laughed. "If there is not a remote somewhere nearby, I will look it up in the manual."

Montluc returned to the cockpit.

"It will take patience." Du Rennes sucked himself in as she passed.

"A subjective novelty, yes." Montluc sat down and continued reading, checking the flight deck's GPS for an ETA. Just over six hours to Bermuda. Not bad. She read through the flight modes and glanced at the autothrottles. One day soon, she thought, this trip would take just over two hours. She drifted in recollection of the Concorde, and the years accumulating since the last non-military flight at Mach 2.

Les progrès.

The countdown timer for The Guard read 00:09:32 when Emily's new partner appeared on the display.

"Hi." Emily said dryly with a curious tone.

"Allo," replied the smart-looking avatar with shoulder-length dark hair representing Petra. Her accent was thick and reminded of Russia, Emily thought.

"You don't sound like you're from here. Like, where are you from?" Emily asked.

"I am from city Zagreb. Have you heard of it? In Croatia?"

"No." Emily paused. "Where is that?"

"In Europe. Everybody asks. I tell them it is next to the big boot."

"Oh! I know where that is." Emily perked up. "How did you get all the way over here?"

"Okay, it is a long story." Petra's tone went dour.

"I don't mind."

"My mama and papa, we went to go skiing in Sljeme."

"Like snow skiing or waterskiing? And where is Sl..j..eeme?" Emily struggled with the pronunciation which brought a laugh from Petra.

"It is funny. I speak English and you cannot say the first word in Croat." She continued giggling. "And it is skiing on the snow."

"I know how to do that!"

"What trails you ski? What color?" Petra's tone turned smug.

"I skied on a blue trail in Tahoe once."

"Tahoe? I have heard of this place. Blue pistes are for small kids."

"Huh? No they aren't!"

"They are in Croatia."

"Well, Tahoe isn't in Croatia. The kids' trails are green."

"I have skied a red piste. That is what I was doing before."

"Before—"

"Before they took me, the nuns. I am skiing down this slope, I turn around to see my parents behind me, and I remember turning back around. I wake up in a police station. I wait all day for my parents to come. They never do. The police gave me food. I did not eat. I fell asleep crying. The police say they looked for my parents. Nobody came for me. Next day, it is the same. The day after, it is the same. I went to sleep on the next day, the police say I must go to another place. The church took me to the school and gave me a bed. I cried. Two weeks and my parents never come. I go to sleep and the nuns send me to a new school. They tell me about America and they show me how to fight—how to use guns. I have been here for two months, I think. Yes, two."

Without evidence to the contrary, Petra's mind determined that she had been in the United States for weeks. In fact, she was knocked out while skiing and separated from her parents, who believed she was lost, kidnapped, and sold to human traffickers, never to be seen again. She was a Jane Doe at the local hospital north of the Sljeme slopes for less than an hour, appropriated from her room by a complicit nursing staff that raked small fortunes in trafficking. The parents weren't far off in their fears as it turns out; their daughter simply took a different path than typical. An associate eventually claimed her as a relative and signed all the proper release forms. She was never allowed to contest them, having been heavily sedated. She was brought to San Giorgio Maggiore in Venice, and woke up under the helmet without realizing it. Through subliminal reinforcement, she eventually learned to accept the narrative that her parents never loved her in the first place, and therefore never searched for her—abandoning their daughter to chance. She arrived in Washington under the hood, and she cried for virtual weeks until she eventually learned to regain her appetite and acquire friends. She also developed a resolve to excel in her training. Her skills accumulated at an exponential rate once the emotional distractions were eliminated. She started to enjoy herself and develop strong connections with her teammates, then her friends started disappearing. Dread was once again tying its necklace around her when Emily showed up.

Together, they conquered with intuitive ease—mastering new martial arts techniques and modified weapons systems. At the end of their first month, no less than fifty rounds had completed with both not only surviving, but thriving to the point of nearly no health losses. When their helmets finally came off, their new skills were verified in the flesh as retained—every weapon, every move. These were the prime differentials from real-time conventional training, where the retention rate was significantly reduced. Dropping a skill learned under the hood was a rare anomaly that frequented subjects with known cognitive dissonances.

"Fernanda's Mode." The bishop loomed over the control room's monitor, instructing the sister to modify Petra and Emily's time level.

Fernanda was acquired at the age of eight from a maternity ward just west of downtown São Paulo, Brazil. Her mother was giving birth, and the young girl went briefly unattended in the waiting room, tricked into believing she was going to meet her sleeping baby brother. Instead, she had a cloth stretched over her nose and mouth, "waking" several hours later under the hood. She would later be used as a guinea pig, testing the limits of hood time until she finally popped a cranial capillary on the 45th day. Others averaged just under forty days before popping, depending how they tested beforehand.

Esposito determined Emily and Petra should last significantly longer than Fernanda by their test scores. Sister Regina snapped the Days to 45 with the slight hint of pride. She also enjoyed the idea she was not responsible for personal attention during the next 16-hour period, planning self-maintenance and other discreet vices. The remaining eight hours, her presence was required. For during this period, Emily and Petra would endure advanced programs that included forbidden fighting techniques obfuscated and silently outlawed by secretive agreements between governments. These agreements either never saw the light of a conference room or were used as leverage against weaker governments, and always after a gruesome demonstration.

On the 44th "day", Sister Regina recorded and wiped a rivulet of blood from under Petra's right nostril, reminded of the same symptomatic occurrence 48-72 hours before failures. Petra should make the next day, she calculated. An abnormal temperature was typically the next indicator. She checked Petra's forehead and, while it was slightly warmer to the touch, there was no cause for alarm yet. She removed Petra's blanket and turned the room's thermostat down a few degrees for relief.

Regina walked over and examined Emily next. No blood, and in contrast, her forehead was as cool to the touch as it was 23 hours earlier. The nun's mind flooded with possibilities. Could Emily take the training indefinitely? Was it possible or would her mind turn to mush without warning? Was it even necessary to push when 45 days was more than adequate to have her fully-trained when the time came?

When their helmets came off, and their encrusted eyelids were wiped, the view of a middle-aged man in a black cassock slowly materialized. They had learned to recognize his smile innately from the final ten days within the game—where his life-image made motivational appearances. The overriding sensation, however, was that of a simultaneous severe thirst and need to evacuate, the latter taking priority. Upon return, high-electrolyte bottled drinks were sweating on their overbed tables, along with a light high-protein meal. Too much at once would make them sick, and the school, which included Sister Regina, was keenly aware of it through previous experiences. Once the girls leveled from the initial sugar rush, Bishop Esposito opened conversation.

"Going too fast for you?" He asked.

Emily remained focused on her meal, emotionless. "Nope."

It was the same for Petra, although she was feeling slightly queasy, not sure if it was the drink, the meal, or something else. Esposito noticed, and he also noted her symptomatic issues during the last hour under the hood. He knew what he was about to ask, and he had a pretty good idea what the final answer would be.

"Excellent." He reviewed the top page in his hand and peered over the top of his rims. "You two may recess for a few hours after training exercises confirm what you learned last night."

Emily smiled while she slurped the last drop from her bottle. The development of new skills was devilishly intoxicating to her and Petra. Both enjoyed the proving ground most of all. The dojo time with Herr Klein confirmed the reality of the helmet's training. To this point, there was a missing element, and it was a prevalent thought in the back of Emily's mind. To this point, they have not actually fired a real weapon, only performing the correct motions of doing so. They had not actually fought another human being, either, practicing only on training aids and Klein, who governed their effectiveness.

On his way out of their room, Esposito turned back around. "Tonight, you shall be opposed."

As he closed the door, they girls stopped eating and stared at each other, agape and mortified.

Limp Mode

Since 2300 hours, General Tomlinson kept one eye on her desk telephone, expecting an update from Major Sponetti in Colorado Springs that never came. All that expensive hardware hovering overhead and in the water, she thought, yet they couldn't locate a civilian sailboat in the middle of the ocean. She poured herself another coffee at 0120. It was the fifth cup since her scotch wore off around 2200. She caught up on official paperwork—the unclassified materials reviewed by others in the Pentagon justifying her rank and office. When the second sip drained down her throat, a familiar urge hit. She glanced towards the restroom door at the side of the office, turned her chair sideways to get up, and just as she did, the phone's scrambler light flashed. Crossing her legs and turning back around, Tomlinson picked up the receiver and pressed the line button.

"Either I have a technical issue with our NROL bird, or I found your boat."

Tomlinson sighed. "Might have guessed you'd call with nothing solid, Chuck."

"Look, my cataracts are bone dry staring at screens for you, lady, I don't need—"

"Well did you find it or not?"

"Yes, I mean... probably."

"Just tell me about it and I'll make that call, okay?"

"As you wish." Sponetti took a breath. "What I have is an extremely faint but persistent residual infrared trace—a line on the screen—"

"I know what those are, Chuck. Just... continue." Tomlinson's thighs tightened.

"The start of the trace glows hotter than the tail, of course, and it's around 40-50 knots velocity, heading towards the eastern seaboard. The operator thought it was a glitch for three hours before sounding. Sorry."

"Damnit Chuck! Where is it now?"

"Just passed the Hatteras Ridge tracking north-northwest."

Tomlinson chewed on it briefly, writhing from necessity. "Call me back as soon as it's within 120 miles or if there's a significant change in direction."

The line clicked closed about the same time as her restroom door. Major Sponetti's salutation went unheard.

● ● ●

The Atlantic became choppier still, driven by Force-6 winds above 24 knots, testing the safety limits of Jupiter's foil extensions between the white-capped sprays. The graphite horizon seemed ever-distant, and the faintest sodium-vapor-hued corona had yet to dawn, yet the GPS indicated less than 48 miles to the Chesapeake Bay inlet.

The lights of Virginia Beach, Portsmouth and Northampton County should have graced the canvas by now, Dao thought. The thought of the GPS losing calibration had been lingering on the unmerry-go-round of her anxieties.

"Thanks," Chris gargled as he stepped onto the bridge just behind her.

She spun around to hug him with acknowledgment in her eyes.

"Some stuff," he continued. "The scopolamine, I mean."

"You appear rested," said Dao, maintaining her embrace with her right ear and cheek warming against his chest.

He peered over her at the navigational map. "Yes, and I see your estimations are, of course, succinct."

"You expected otherwise?" She laughed, pulled her head away, grabbing his biceps before turning back around.

"The others?" Chris asked, straining to see the horizon through the forward windshield.

"Rocco and Anastasia ate dinner at eleven and returned to their room. Matthew and I decided someone should stay on the bridge... for obvious reasons. We traded watch every two hours. Last was one hour, twenty-three minutes ago. Father Trovarto, I have not seen. Mathew says he is sleeping."

"Is this the intercom switch?" Chris pointed towards a pushbutton on the console just below a tiny screened disc.

"Yes." She said. "Wait, I need to set it for wide broadcast."

Dao accessed the internal menu and set the intercom to ALL. Chris mashed the TALK button, producing a subtle, audible echo as he cleared his throat.

"Attention shoppers, we have a coastal invasion special occurring in forty-five minutes over in the Sports Department. Quantities are extremely limited, so..."

Dao yanked his hand off the button. "Why do you joke at such a time?"

Chris' forced grin faded as he withdrew. "Jack, dull boy..."

"Levity does not appear to be your best attribute."

Dao concentrated on the GPS display, calculating their projected path towards the inlet. It was one of the busiest shipping lanes in the world, and there were two relatively-narrow passages of Chesapeake Bay Bridge's tunnel section. Probability of detection compounded in her mind as she expanded, pinched and tapped around the navigational map. She dragged the digital chart northward and focused on the inlets of Hog Island Bay. It was ringed by farms and sparsely dotted with commercial fisheries. The inlets were unguarded, unmonitored, deep, and critically, no bridges. If the GPS's calibration was off, however, attempting to navigate it would carry the highest probability of failure.

"Chesapeake is suicide—a naval hive of commercial shipping and military traffic—and that means pilots and patrols at all hours. Spent time at Annapolis, you know." Matthew stuck his finger on the screen, pointing north of the bridge-tunnel system protecting Chesapeake Bay's southern entrance. "You were looking in the right place. Nothing there, 'cept maybe a few clam boats. Wrong season, right? October to March? Those inlets will be dark. We need to get as far north as possible without being seen."

Rocco and Anastasia climbed up to the bridge from their adjoining companionway, nodding without interrupting. Dao glanced towards Chris then rolled her eyes towards the opposite companionway leading towards Monsignor Trovarto's stateroom. She spun back around when hearing the creaking of teak as Trovarto slowly emerged from the lower starboard hull. His eyes were circled and ashen, and complexion reflecting light from moisture. He lumbered to reach the sofa where Rocco and Anastasia sat, just forward of the helm below the front windshield, facing aft. It was clear that his deep narcosis would take time to fully overcome, and yet he managed an acknowledging smile, amused with his condition.

"I will-a live, as-a they say."

"We'll be off this boat soon enough, Father." Chris looked at the chart. "One way or another."

Matt leaned in. "There!" He jabbed the screen and pinched out to expand the chart. "Machipongo Inlet. Take us all the way in to one of those rivers closest to US13 and we'll beach her out of sight."

Silence. Dao continued searching the shoreline for any recognizable features. Twelve minutes passed as Jupiter's Bolt slipped through the darkness—a shadow against a slow-rolling tarpaulin of pitch black. Her undulations became unintelligible as the winds fluctuated. At last, the death shroud fell away, revealing the lights of the coastline. But which coastline? Dao and Matthew made visual mental notes of the distant twinkles—spaces, patterns—to compare against the GPS. Another few moments passed. Rocco and Anastasia jumped in to assist. A long procession of streetlights ran for a few miles off their port. It had two notable breaks in it. Matt's eyes widened as he checked the navigational charge and eyeballed it against what he was seeing through the portside windows. The breaks matched. The distance matched. As far as he was concerned, it lined up perfectly. The others smiled. It was indeed the Chesapeake Bay Bridge, and the two breaks were tunnels. There were other lights dancing upon the water as well. Some green, others red. Matthew knew these were navigation lights on other boats. He wondered just how well Jupiter's stealth operated. The boat was completely untested as far as he was concerned; there was no trust. He must assume radar detection, and if so, what of it? The coast guard doesn't check every boat coming in and out of the bay. There are too many. Low probability of a visual sighting, he guessed. No lights, no color, no reflections—the white tail feathers, though—the hydrofoils' spray. Not huge and thankfully no moonlight to reflect off them. No, Matt thought. Unless they crossed another boat in the dark—another lawbreaker—they were okay.

Dao finally caught her breath then interrogated her own logic regarding the seamount they encountered the previous day. How could it be? There was no time to analyze it further; the helm demanded her undivided attention. The automated chart was moving along at a spritely pace. She actuated the one-meter glass display on the console and snatched its plotter stylus from the utensil holder at its top-right edge. Double checking the running depths, she tapped a starting point and dragged it towards the Machipongo Inlet. A prompt returned for Run Mode and desired velocity. Because of the damaged foil, she manually entered 45 knots and maintained the current stealth setting. She then created a new leg, tapping the last waypoint and dragging a new segment, tapping the stylus' tiny button towards the tip when she desired a tack point, always mindful of the channel depth, which had been reduced to 10-14 meters and shallowing towards the other side of Hog Island Bay.

She paused. "Where—" Dao added a satellite photography layer over the chart, detailing the land, structures and roads.

Matt leaned in. "This river here, just south of Willis Wharf. This branch that runs towards these fields... there." He pointed.

"This chart does not display depth for it," Dao said.

"What is the draft of Jupiter with her foils up."

"Half a meter," said Chris, finally remembering a specification from the sheet he glanced over just after launching.

"Doubtful that creek is shallower," said Matt. "Especially if the tide's high."

"According to the computer, it is." Dao said as she attempted to pen the route on the electronic chart table. The computer would not accept it, however.

"Manual helm once more, Doctor," said Matt as Dao trembled. "I trust you."

She turned towards Chris. "You know."

"After Atlantis, Doctor Ming? I would not trust another soul," said Rocco, as Anastasia nodded in agreement.

Trovarto ran fingers across his forehead and through his humidified hair. "Atlantis? What-a is it I missed?"

On the inside of Machipongo's channel, the prevailing winds turned southwesterly and light. Jupiter's physics could not sustain foiled sailing with four-knots pushing her, and she gracefully descended into the bay, producing combers that would eventually rinse the nearby shoreline. Matt stepped onto the foredeck between the netted trampolines and braced himself against the forestay, searching the blackness for any signs of light or movement. On a sweltering late-summer evening, he expected the fires of campers, the dull running lights of overnight fishing trips, or perhaps the vigilant patrol of the Virginia Marine Police or the Coast Guard. Caught without lights meant detainment, scrutiny—likely worse. Even he could not discern any lighting from within Jupiter's cockpit. The monitors were running in Night Mode—automatic in Stealth—and her graphene-impregnated windows were set to one-way, Starlight-Enhanced View.

Dao reached the end of her second segment—the last being the narrower inlet to Machipongo River at Cedar Point. Just as Matt was about to reenter the bridge, a reflection on the door's glass caught his attention. He spun around and caught the blinding flash of a distant spotlight scanning across the Hog Island Bay about a mile or so off Jupiter's 2 O'clock as Dao swung into the river. The light reflected their wake, bouncing left and right of them. He ran inside in a panic.

"Lower the mast; I think someone spotted us!"

Dao frantically tapped Jupiter's running menu, furling the sail and lowering her telescopic mast below the roofline. She grabbed the rotating joystick and pushed it forward, activating thrusters for a silent eight knots. The searchlight continued its jittery dance across the water, generally in Jupiter's direction but never stopping on her. It disappeared completely as Dao rounded a tree line, heading north up the river.

"Left!" Matt yelled, just before they passed a narrow creek entrance.

Dao twisted the stick and the boat lurched towards the port, heeling on the starboard hull. The depth meter's electronic alarm chimed a dire warning that Jupiter's minim recom-mended running depth of 2 meters had been breached. The passage grew tighter, and Dao kept her grip light on the controls, slowing to a reasonable three knots. They all fought their own instincts to light a torch—to blaze the uncertain path before them. Jupiter was not designed for shallow running, nor maneuvering in impossible spaces. They were 100% committed now. The sawgrass that surrounded them was as uninviting as any adverse terrain they had encountered. Death from drowning or some other hazard was certain in such a place where damn near everything crawled and hissed. They rounded two more turns as the depth leveled off at one meter. The enhanced windows displayed a brilliant dot around 400 meters ahead, haloed with lens flares. It was a streetlight or someone's porch light, they guessed. It was close, and they assumed a dock of some sort would materialize soon. It didn't, and as the realization hit them, so did the creek's bottom.

Annoyed, Dao reversed off of it, maintaining flotational control of the catamaran. They were surrounded by sawgrass, but Matthew spotted a stand of pines within 30 meters of the water. It was the nearest dry land within reasonable reach, and better still, he was certain of a wide trail leading into the trees.

"Spin her around and beach her as close to those trees as you can, Dao. We're home."

"*You* are home," she mumbled, spinning the joystick to starboard and thrusting towards the shoreline.

Jupiter eased onto the mud with warning tabs flashing and alarms chiming with such a tone as to suggest a slap on the wrist instead of a howling mayday. Dao rapidly extinguished them and opened the menu for the Stationary Hold mode, which dropped anchor and prevented Jupiter's movement should the tide dislodge her.

"Pack light. We need to move quickly." Matt instructed.

Matthew set his backpack down and fully extended the port hull's carbon gangway, landing on the far end a few inches from the hard shoreline. All carrying light packs, Chris, Dao,

Trovarto, Anastasia and Rocco stepped down the ramp and hopped onto solid ground. Their legs seemed to betray them as they adjusted to the absence of motion. Matthew reached into a shirt pocket and flipped open a pair of glasses, wedging their frames over his face. The others struggled to see what he'd done in the black of night.

"What are those?" Chris asked.

"Found them in the nightstand drawer. Graphene glasses, I think. Same stuff as the boat windows. One button on top-left side; sunglasses, variable strength reading glasses, night vision—probably Head's Up Display. Didn't get that far. None in your room?"

"Didn't look." Chris said in a regretful tone.

Matthew continued walking towards the tree line. "Too late for that now, we need to get moving. That searchlight... gut says not good."

Within a couple hundred paces, the forest abruptly ended, opening to vast soybean fields flanking both sides of the trail—a trail which widened into a compacted gravel service drive. Matthew checked his watch. 0350. The mere sight of it produced a gaping yawn. Their pace was brisk. Innately, nobody spoke. The porchlights of two farmhouses marked the end of the straight road less than a half mile ahead. Within a couple minutes they were between the houses, some 300 meters apart. They scanned the driveways for a suitable conveyance without luck. Heavy-duty pickup trucks only. One house had a closed garage. Too risky, Matthew presumed. It was early, and farmers were famously early-risers, acutely attuned to their surroundings, including every subtle sonance. *Farmers are generally armed too*, he thought. *It's just not a good idea.*

They reached the county road intersecting the private drive, and stood there momentarily, whispering their options. In the haze of a streetlight illuminating a heavy equipment shop— some 200 meters across the street, between the shop's main

building, several tractor trailers, and a ramshackle residence—
Trovarto noticed the outline of a potential vehicle.

He tapped on Matthew's shoulder and spoke softly. "Look
at-a this. I think it-a large car." He pointed across the street
towards it.

Matthew adjusted the glasses. "Bingo," he whispered.

Just as he said it, a light flicked on within the house just
behind to their right. A large dog started barking incessantly
from within. They looked at each other and bolted to the other
side of the street, hiding within the shadow of an elder
shagbark hickory tree. The door hadn't opened yet, so they
whisked across the gravel parking lot towards the shop's rear,
beyond the tractor trailers and other heavy machinery to the
office area—the owner's Cape Cod-style house bordering a fine
gravel parking lot. To its right sat a full-sized black GMC SUV,
at least a dozen years old but in good condition. Plenty of
room for six.

Matthew eased to the driver's side, checking his rear for
any movement at the house. No interior lights or other sounds,
except the distant wisps of wind in the trees, and the
incessant loud crickets. He was careful not to test the door
handle since it might activate an alarm. The vehicle was
equipped with a keyless entry keypad however, and Matthew
had been trained to remember GM's 20-digit master code.
Touching the first number startled him. The others also
gasped and jumped away when the SUV's exterior courtesy
lights illuminated. All eyes went to the house for what seemed
an eternity. Matthew continued the code's entry and moments
later, the door unlocked. He jumped inside an unlocked the
other doors. They crammed themselves in, sending Rocco to
the open cargo at the rear, sharing space with used and greasy
diesel engine parts, destined for remanufacture. They all
watched in anticipation, having heard the tale of Matthew's
handiwork in San Francisco. Point by point, the sequence
unfolded, and the engine sprang to life. Matthew wasted no

time in exiting the parking lot, conscious of the noise being created by the grinding of gravel. He kept the headlights off, trusting the starlight graphene glasses, at least until they were well away. At the county road he turned left and accelerated. About a mile down the road, he took another left, which a quarter mile later brought them to U.S. Highway 13. He folded the sunglasses and turned on the headlights as he turned north on the quiet roadway, not another vehicle in sight. Chris slapped him on the shoulder.

"Well, holy shitballs! What have we got here, Larry?" Patrolman Williams bleated rhetorically. "Thought I was full of it, right?"

The intense beam of light bathed Jupiter's Bolt in milk white as she rested on the bank with no lines tied or a visible anchor.

"Don't even think about boarding her, Keith. I'm calling Linda."

"You kidding? It'll take 45 minutes this time of the morning. Chinco or Charles—they're asleep 'til 0530!"

The patrolman kept a mounted spotlight fixed on Jupiter's bridge, unable to penetrate the darkened windows. In fact, the vessel was completely dark and lifeless, which was exactly what spooked them. Jupiter was large enough that two dozen unknowns could easily overwhelm a two-person shore patrol. There was no backup except one car parked in the middle of Cape Charles—its sole occupant nursing a half gallon thermos full of coffee obliged by the town's only coffee shop which closed at 7pm, just as his shift started. Keith's handheld spotlight continued examining the boat while Sgt. Larry Dorsey summoned their dispatcher—a middle-aged single mother with whom he had recently taken interest. She enjoyed his professional calls, always taking the same shift to be on the same schedule, although there were occasions that his calls worried her. She had been working at the emergency center long enough to know real peril from the routine. Abandoned boats were a common occurrence. When Sgt. Dorsey detailed the circumstances of the boat—the size, the darkened windows, the retracted hydrofoils—she knew this was out of the ordinary. Her mind filled with dread and purpose, scrambling the U.S. Coast Guard's Cape Charles and Chincoteague stations with a GPS marker provided by her men. When she finished uploading the call's description, she mashed the hailer for her deputy, who had just exited and relocked an outside restroom at a convenience store about a mile outside Cape Charles. Willis Wharf was over twenty miles away on the opposite side of the county. By the time the information reached him, and using the best diligent speed of his cruiser, he would arrive some fifteen minutes later.

Moments after the SUV's dust settled, the shop house's porch light flicked on and its front door swung open. A gaunt and filthy man in his early sixties stumbled outside with a flashlight and a blued revolver. His light nervously shined across the parking lot and towards the tractor-trailers as he lumbered towards them, growling some incoherent commands between "Get your asses out" and "I see you hiding back there" to nobody. After examining his shops and the parked machinery for another five minutes, he swung around, gulping for air in the fog of inebriation at the absence of his wife's truck. The glaring omission befuddled him, which, in his state, was quite easy to accomplish, creating additional fog of recollection. *Did she stay at her sister's tonight? Probly.* He shrugged off the notion of it being stolen. That sort of nonsense simply never happened around there. He nearly fell backwards climbing the four steps to his front porch, catching himself on the wooden handrail. When he reached the living room, he tossed the revolver onto the end table next to his stained velour La-Z-Boy where he had passed out, watching an adult network. He walked towards the kitchen to grab a fresh glass and looked at the telephone. In his haze, he didn't remember his wife calling or leaving a message of her plans. Unusual, but not impossible; it happened once before. Silent treatment, subject to interpretation. He winced in resentment and poured himself two measures of bourbon, draining it down without touching the few remaining taste buds at the back of his tongue. He bumbled back to his chair, loosened his belt and crashed into it, rocking several times because his feet didn't quite reach the floor. When the motion stopped and his breath quieted, that's when he heard her deep and gargled bear's snore from two rooms away. The shock created yet more fog. He mulled calling 911, knowing he was drunk and the political problems it would create. Bad for business. It would have to wait until daybreak.

The phone's thunderous ring destroyed any semblance of sobriety he could possibly muster. His reaction was anger and to quiet it. *Who the hell...* He spang off the chair, catching a shin on its corner, tripping him into falling sideways, the left side of his head struck the end table, knocking him unconscious. The phone continued ringing, then stopped. With her robe tied and shoulder-length train-wrecked hair matted to one side, his wife lit a cigarette and stormed towards the living room with an incessant ringing phone in her hand, angry that there was a call, and angrier because the answering machine wasn't working again since it was full. This had been an ongoing feud between them, and she blamed their ongoing financial difficulties on his lack of such attentions. Non-stop ringing in the middle of the night was her last straw. As she rounded the corner, she caught a glimpse of what was taking place on their television. She grew angrier still, as this was frequently mentioned in their ongoing feud. Accusations, inadequacies, derisions. With a stone-producing glare, she turned towards the recliner expecting to wake her sotted spouse with a stern slap to his face. Instead, she found him collapsed on the floor with blood pooling beneath his head. The phone rang once more then stopped. She went to roll her husband onto his back, swearing profanities at him while doing do. He moaned as he came around. She grabbed a napkin off the table and wiped around the gash over his ear. As she blotted the wound, there was a loud and demanding knock at the front door.

A voice yelled at the door. "It's me, Jim! I see the light on, so's I know you're up."

She picked her husband up and placed him in the recliner, handing him the cloth, telling him to hold it tight. He moaned something unintelligible, but maintained the pressure as instructed. She opened the door and let Jim in, who was brandishing a pistol and out of breath.

"Linda call you?"

"Who?"

"Linda Morris at the Sheriff's."

"The phone was ringing just now; I couldn't answer it." She turned around to indicate the condition of her husband.

"Good Lord! What happened to him?"

"Got me, I just found him lying on the floor. You know how he gets."

"Well, that was probably Linda phoning. They found a big 'ole boat washed up at the back, just sitting, there and they can't do nothin' to it until the Coast Guard comes. Asked if I've seen anyone. Walk down the drive and back, then here. Saw nothin', 'cept... well... that your truck was gone. Thought you might've been at your sister's, you know."

The wife turned back to her husband with a snarl. "That was none of his goddamn business! You wait—" She paused "What do mean, my truck's gone?"

"Well, it ain't where you always park it next to the house."

"Goddamnit!"

"That's what I was trying say!" Her husband moaned with a dry hack.

Jim rubbed his chin. "Well, you better call Linda back about that ambulance. She said a car was on the way from the Cape. Should be here in few minutes. I'll tell the sheriff about your truck too, in case you forget, K?"

The woman nodded as she went to pick up the phone. Jim closed the door behind him and steadily walked back across the street where he found his next-door neighbor at the end of their common driveway.

A few moments later, a Northampton County patrol car swooped in, grinding to a halt with its blinding strobes pulsating. The deputy hated these calls. His map's GPS marker was on the backside of two large, adjoining soybean farms which shared a half-mile private driveway between them. Linda always attempted to call the landowners before the car arrived, but it didn't always work. On this night, she was fortunate—evidenced by both owners waiting at the entrance; one dressed in dungarees and boots with a Remington 12-gauge draped over his forearm, and his neighbor appeared in cutoff shorts, an untucked, unbuttoned flannel shirt. A Colt 1911 pistol was shoved precariously into his front beltline. By the look in their eyes, the deputy knew he was in for a long morning.

The headlights of the SUV reflected off the "Welcome to Maryland" sign as it passed. Pocomoke City was five miles away. The fuel level indicator dictated they stop, and for a brief moment, Matthew panicked, forgetting the stacks of operating cash bestowed on them by the Frenchman just before departure. Money wasn't the issue; it was only a matter of time before their vehicle was reported stolen. Daylight would be upon them within an hour, and they had a major bridge yet to cross. Reagan National was another two hours away.

"We need to switch vehicles," he said to Chris while pumping gasoline.

"What? Why?" Chris yelped.

"It's not like the others. We've got single bridge to cross. It's a chokepoint for this entire peninsula. By the time we reach it, my guess is they will be watching for this SUV. People know we're headed there, right? If they know about the truck, they know about the boat, and once the boat is discovered, which I must assume has already occurred, they know we're here. We need another car that won't be noticed for a few hours."

As they reached the outskirts of Pocomoke, Matt's face suddenly produced a wide grin. A Chevrolet dealership appeared on the left side of the highway, its gates left open and welcoming, and its vast parking lot glistened with innumerable new and used candidates for a replacement vehicle. Matt doused his headlights and whisked into the used vehicle section, pulling alongside a late-model, white crew cargo van.

"Perfect. Ubiquitous, dull, forgettable, and it even has a tinted windows and a Maryland plate." Matt said as he killed the GMC's engine.

The others silently piled out with their belongings and waited patiently while Matt hacked the van's entry code and engine start sequence. Within moments the engine roared to life and its doors opened. Matt kept the exterior lights extinguished as they boarded. Chris reached into their cash stocks, counted $5,000 and placed those bills under the driver's floor mat in the stolen SUV before locking it. He then removed a large "2015" sticker from the van's windshield on the upper-left corner, and slapped it on the SUV. Matt laughed as Chris jumped into the front passenger's seat. That move, as it later turned out, bought them an extra six hours since no dealership employee bothered to notice the SUV until a customer chided one of them over the obviously incorrect year. This led to an inquiry with the sales manager, who could not find any record of the SUV, or its keys. Worse, the inquiry and subsequent inventory revealed a far worse issue. The manager pounded her telephone's keys for the Pocomoke City Police Department. When the GMC's tag eventually hit the network, law enforcement vehicles of every variety descended on that dealership within minutes. Police, Sheriff, State, FBI, and other federal cars from unknown agencies. The gates to the dealership were closed, and its employees sequestered in a sales conference room under guard where one-by-one they would be pulled away for background questioning and their recent whereabouts.

● ● ●

Much earlier that morning, two Virginia Marine Patrolmen sat patiently, sipping coffee as they heard the gurgle of an idling light response boat from the U.S. Coast Guard coming towards them, spotlights ablaze. Behind it was another USCG boat, somewhat heavier with a manned M240 machine gun mounted to its foredeck. Once alongside, the patrolmen exchanged all known information and status to the sailors, who examined the boat at a distance and developed a standard tactical assault plan. They checked all equipment and reviewed the plan for each of the four-person boarding team—all of whom had certified training for such operations.

The boarding began with megaphoned demands of surrender to examination, which went unanswered. Caution was paramount in these situations. Everything happened in carefully-calculated steps. First, the demands, then moving closer with louder demands, then stepping onboard, covering each firing angle and clearing the decks as they maneuvered around them. Finally, it was time to breach the salon and bridge, working towards the hulls. Jupiter's invaders encountered no resistance of any kind, and they quickly deduced she was abandoned. Their anxiety trip complete, the attention focused on Jupiter herself. Radio chatter asked for registration and origin. The unit consulted its technical branch on operation, being that much of her technology wasn't understood. A buzz developed at USCG Headquarters on the other side of the Potomac from the Pentagon. Tomlinson's office had a line on the Coast Guard's chatter, and a few hours later, word reached her desk about an extraordinary hydrofoiling catamaran that featured a telescoping solar mast and a fully-automated helm. It would eventually be towed to Cape Charles, then on to Annapolis for further analysis.

Tomlinson picked up her phone and dialed her man at the CIA.

"Predictable, which is precisely why I never need to dial your number, General."

"So you knew and didn't call me. Thanks Ron."

"Yes, just now, and before you say it, no, they couldn't possibly have crossed the Chesapeake by now."

"So, you're watching it."

"State Patrol is. We don't work here, you know."

"My ass!" Tomlinson yelled.

"Yes, that is also a problem."

"Careful, this goes both ways," warned Tomlinson before hanging up. She turned around and texted Colonel Zabroskov using her encrypted tablet. A response arrived within moments.

Ensure they find their way to the bishop.

Or what? You send your backstabber?

If you are fortunate.

O O O

The cigarette's cherry illuminated the corner of a darkened second-story safe room overlooking an alleyway off Wyoming Street in D.C. One hulking man sat staring into that alley while the other rested on a futon, fully-clothed in anticipation of the message that just vibrated his phone for the third time. He arose in agony, hacking from the thick fumes of his guardian's exhalations. He took a moment to gather his senses, feeling around for his critical belongings. First his glasses, then a sip of water to clear his throat. He squinted at the streetlamp's vigilant blaze permeating the French windows between the curtains, and took notice of the vermillion glow of his comrade's face. The residence was safe, indeed, but not formally or even clandestinely provided by their country. It was an unquestioned and permanent favor granted by a consular friend in compensation for a mutually-beneficial sanction performed in the Middle East several years ago. Colonel Ninel Zabroskov felt the sting of four hours' sleep in his eyes and mouth, and more prevalently, in his mind. He lifted his silver case, opened it, and withdrew a golden-filtered cigarette from underneath an elastic band, careful not to bend or crinkle the paper. He enjoyed the finer pleasures as any Russian oligarch, although his fortunes were acquired usually by favor, such as the room. Because of this, he was no longer driven by money but more by the collection of reckonable debts and the leverage of the power intrinsic to them. As well, his invoices were always costlier than anticipated.

Zabroskov torched the tip of his cigarette with a tiny magenta blast that lasted less than a second. Any longer, he preached, would waste the tobacco. He took a long draw and exhaled, setting the lighter down.

"Any word from my brother?" Zabroskov asked the trunk in the corner.

The trunk exhaled his own smoke and shook his head negatively. Zabroskov coughed and unsuccessfully attempted to clear the phlegm from the deepest part of his throat.

"Damn him!" He coughed again. "He said next day, today, *now!* he would return."

The trunk showed no emotion or recognition.

"He makes me call Peter in Belgrade every two months. Always those decadent western sex clubs... the goths. Wind down, he says. He is a lunatic!"

His phone vibrated once more. Ninel Zabroskov picked it up and cleared his eyes to read the unscrambled text from Tomlinson.

"And, of course, our presence is now required."

Belgrade Peter confirmed a sighting of the younger, eccentric Zabroskov at one of his five Balkan fetish clubs. La Brochette was spotted at his favorite in Tirana, Albania. Disappeared into a private room, nobody saw him leave, and nobody will say they saw him either, not even to Peter. A man did once, and that man was later discovered beached under a bridge in the Erzen River on the south side of the city. Zabroskov's sighting was twenty hours old. This was ample time to make the connecting flights to the United States.

"No, it does not feel right." Ninel Zabroskov covered his face to wipe away the burning sleep and smoke from his eyes.

He experienced this gut reaction before, many years ago when he and his brother evaded capture after being overwhelmed in a Kosovo DMZ. He had built a tolerance to it through the years, infiltrating anything and everyone. Proper procedures, papers, and most-importantly, the right dialect—

the butterflies never returned. Until now. He sensed a double-cross or some other form of betrayal. It was a deathbed promise to their mother that he worry for his brother—or half-brother—the one their father beat mercilessly if he ever spoke. Zabroskov turned to his associate who was in the process of squashing a spent filter into a glass ashtray that already contained a dozen of his brand. His hands were thick and rough, callused from the heavy work and stained from ash and tar. His eyes squinted at his colonel's intuitions. What Zabroskov sensed, the smoking strong man had already deduced. When your leverage has run its course, and its value has depreciated, the question of *What's in it for us?* became *How do we survive it?*

"I must contact St. Petersburg if it is not too late."

The trunk in the corner fired another cigarette and turned towards the window to peer down to the alleyway. The streetlight highlighted a squirrel running across the bricked wall cordoning off the embassy's parking area. He knew it was odd in that squirrels weren't nocturnal—not in America, Russia, or anywhere. He wasn't a superstitious person, just cold and hard. He stared at the squirrel as it paused just at the edge of the streetlight's reach to turn around and check behind it. The man recessed into the corner and illuminated it with his next inhale. The squirrel turned back around and continued into the darkness.

● ● ●

Captain Montluc's eyes danced about the HUD and its correlation with Bermuda Airport's Runway 30 approach lights, mentally remarking that, if not for G sensation, her windshield view seemed more simulated than real. She lowered the landing gear a few moments before, noting the green lights of affirmative locking, and set her final flaps and throttle settings for optimal speed. The winds were gusty, buffeting the fuselage to shudders and drops. She knew she would take another sharp beating as the jet crossed the threshold from Annie's Bay to a couple hundred feet of grass, then tarmac. Montluc opted for a steeper approach to minimalize those effects, bouncing off a single red light at far right of Wade International's glide slope indicator. Her touchdown was greased—smooth and immaculate, quickly setting the nose down and applying reverse thrust in time to make the nearest taxiway back to the executive terminal. A wry smile—the smug face—wrinkled her crows. Montluc absolutely reveled in perfectly-executed short landings, confident she would have made a top carrier pilot. Her log would credit another note of such.

Mallory Du Rennes appeared in the cockpit's doorway. "I am afraid your layover will be curt, *mon capitiane*. As soon as you are able, return this aircraft to its owner in Savannah. There will be a charter waiting for you to the rendezvous at Hangar 5, Reagan. Understood?"

She nodded, powering down the engines and unbuckling her restraints, weary at the prospect of two more hours in the seat. She would not be in command for the Savannah to D.C. leg at least; pilots always felt helpless away from the cockpit. She was no exception.

Gérard unlatched and dropped the airstairs, throwing the two crash bags over each shoulder on his way down. Du Rennes picked up the extra small cases, which contained Miller's laptop and several other critically-important relics belonging to the La Fratellanza, destined for research and eventual publication if merited. He needed to place them in safekeeping for now. Most of the Brotherhood perished in Cairo, but not all, and certainly not all of their family. Many were secondary oath-takers, sworn to secrecy. Although anxious, his contact had agreed to meet him. He was an inactive member who dropped away when a tragedy befell his family. He hadn't attended meetings or briefings in years, suffering from depression and self-exile. Yet, he remained in infrequent contact for rare consultations and to remain in the procedural loop. Du Rennes made contact with him via closed communication—the miniature obelisk—just before departing Corsica, dropping a voice message and receiving a confirmation signal.

A Learjet 35 in unremarkable livery was being fueled and undergoing its preflight check as Du Rennes, Patrick, Jet Sun and Gérard climbed up its stairs. They sank into plush leather opposing seats with fold up tables between them. As the turbofans spun up under operation of a co-pilot in training, the for-hire captain announced that their arrival would take around two hours, twenty minutes due to prevailing head-winds aloft. After additional checks, particularly with increased attention to pressurization verification and supple-mental cockpit oxygen checks, taxiing and takeoff clearance came quickly. In less than ten minutes, they were above the clouds, due to arrive around daybreak. Without so much as a restroom break or a sip from half-sized aluminum can of anything, one-by-one their heads succumbed to gravity. Two hours was better than none.

● ● ●

An encrypted email glowed upon the monitor of Air Force Office of Special Investigations (AFOSI) Special Agent Rose Diaz's workstation. It was addressed from her liaison at the

FBI who routed Coast Guard maritime counterterrorism Field Activity Cases (FAC) as required under the information sharing initiatives made after 9/11. The report described in detail Jupiter's Bolt and her abandonment in Northampton. The report further included known intelligence on the stolen GMC, its license plate number, and the fact that, as of the time of the report, there were no known sightings or other leads on its whereabouts.

This is old! She thought. Agencies given to disposition included sheriff's departments in several adjacent counties, Virginia and Maryland state agencies, Homeland, NSA, and the relevant FBI field offices who provided six agents positioned in arcs at 50 and 100-mile radii, who were now, as she knew, searching for a white work van. Agent Diaz gave the Coast Guard's rundown careful scrutiny and compared it to an internal OSI report generated the previous evening that detailed the unusual tasking of a microsatellite constellation.

> Increased frequency of infrared imagining, 30°N Atlantic Corridor. Target Profile: Westbound sailing vessel, 50-80ft.

The flag came when the operator removed the data governor to allow the increased output—an order that typically triggers fury if not being issued from the White House's Situation Room. The satellite report listed the operator on duty and his C.O. She checked the time on the lower right-hand corner of her screen. 0615. She must wait at least two hours before expectations of reaching both officers in Colorado Springs for video interview. Their personnel files were a few clicks away.

The Fighting Gaze II

"I don't want to fight you, Petra." Emily demanded. "Like, what can they do if I say no?"

"You must," Petra looked towards the door. "They hear us even now. You refuse, they take you away."

"Where?"

"This I do not know. And stop saying like every other sentence. It is not proper English. Do all American girls speak this way?"

Emily tensed and took shallower breaths. "Yes, and that's what my father says. Like, everyone I know says like."

"I do not like this like."

"We, I am beginning to wonder if I like you!"

"You still must fight me."

"You never said how you knew the other girl was taken away—the one that wouldn't fight you."

"You did not ask." Petra said dryly. "She was scheduled to fight me and refused. They take her away. I stay; she left."

"Wait. Like... Ugh! Now you have me thinking about it." Emily paused. "How long have you been here? How many games..."

"Four-time Champion; eight months." Petra smirked, which incensed Emily further.

Sister Regina entered and immediately set about the task of securing their VR helmets and tracking sensors before initiating the duel. Narciso Esposito's voice resounded in their earpieces with a percussive volume.

"Petra, it will be different for you, as I am removing all playfield advantages previously gained. This time, you will fight not at the school dojo, but within the same cathedral grounds as the team challenges. You will not be allowed to choose your favorite weapons; you must find weapons along the way. Careful! Still there are traps. If you do not fight before reaching the cathedral, you may find your strongest weapons within its walls. I must remind you this is a fight to the death. You will have the option of communication, but I warn you—no truces or delays. To do so will disqualify you both."

Their helmets and their displays went dark. It took longer than anticipated for the game to boot. When it did, Emily was petrified at what she saw. Even though The Guard felt realistic in movement and in other actions, the previous graphics were intelligibly computer-driven. This version was vastly improved. Emily could not discern if she had physically been placed on a real sidewalk. Her hair wisped at the sides of her face and she thought she could feel it. No lag in movements, and the level of detail bore no perceivable difference to analog. There were no pixels, there was no headachy 3D overlap, and the sound of the space around her captured the exact same volume and feel as if she was standing in a western-Italian shopping district. She started to feel her way around, touching her own arms to see if she felt anything (she did) when a voice echoed from across the street.

"You have no chance."

As Emily spun around and felt a sharp pain on her right-side back, she turned, and Petra landed a solid blow to Emily's face, stunning her in surprise. 3% damage. She threw a backhand to Petra's left cheek, and her foe wasn't fast enough to duck it. 3% in kind. Petra grunted and sped off down the right side of the street, searching storefronts as she ran. Emily paused to collect herself. She had no anticipation of pain, yet she felt the dull sensations of it under the helmet.

The sensory overload was but one immediate concern. The other was the obvious advantage in experience given to her foe, Petra. She doubted that the bishop had told her the truth. She remembered something her father used to tell her when other games, puzzles, or other playthings malfunctioned or otherwise operated unexpectedly. Her process created mental obstacles—hurdles for her to jump—that prevented or at least slowed her progress towards the goal. He said *It's all trash; throw it away.* Or he'd say, *It's all noise; just turn it off and keep going. Don't dwell; take what you're given and work with it—overcome!*

Upon the realization, she gritted her teeth and bolted towards the sidewalk, scanning windows as she passed. Several went by and she found no weapons. No lighted circles around anything indicated or direct. Emily was about to fly by another set of windows when he threw both legs forward and ground to a sudden halt. She turned around to see what she briefly imagined, then second-guessed for a few steps. Finally, there it was—a musty old metal baseball bat, leaning in a dusty corner of an antiques store.

What the...

She opened the door and picked it up, taking a few swings to feel the weight.

"How many weapons you think you passed already, huh?" Petra laughed.

Emily looked outside and saw her standing by a streetlamp, brandishing a bowie knife and a bandolier filled with shotgun cartridges. Emily's stomach sank at the notion she had fallen behind and in serious danger. A baseball bat was useless if Petra located the corresponding firearm. And so, some confidence returned when she deduced the reason Petra hadn't attacked her with the knife was because she found it about the same time she discovered the bat.

Emily dashed down her side of the street, scanning windows with increased intensity. The tops of several round somethings caught her eye at the next storefront—an open egg carton, except it was larger and contained four, not twelve, tennis ball-sized metallic objects. Emily jammed on her brakes and started to open the front door. She collapsed to a squatting position as a sharp crack of a large pane of glass exploded to her left, followed by the booming echo of a blast from across the street. A near miss, or a warning. She pushed on the door and rolled inside, maintaining a low profile and slamming the door behind her, in shock and anger. *She's really trying to kill me!*

Petra surveyed the broken window from across the street, checking the sites on her newfound pump-action shotgun with a pistol grip. A crossing street was two stores down. It was a risk from previous experience, although every round she had played thus far entailed some form of enemy incursion from this angle, and someone from her team always perished. She replaced the spent cartridge and shimmied behind a parked car along the far-side wall of the corresponding alleyway on her side of the street. Her shotgun had enough effective range to splatter anyone attempting to exit the alley, and she an unobstructed view if Emily tried to cross the alley from in front. Each block began with a building which ran its entire length, so Emily could not continue down the alleyway, either. At some point, Petra would have a clear shot.

Emily examined the contents of the oversized egg crate. Her distance recognition paid off; the box contained four grenades: two concussion, and two stun-type or "flashbang" types, as the illuminating moniker indicated in the helmet. She clipped those onto her belt and eased back to the window for a peek. On the way, she turned towards the rear of the store, contemplating the back alley. Her outfitting wasn't exactly conducive for that strategy, nor did she have a teammate to cover its street-side entrance. Emily remained several feet back from the destroyed front window, taking cover in the shadows behind a footwear display. Petra was no longer visible. Emily peered across the street to her left and noted the opposite alleyway. Déjà vu! She ran the math, same as Petra. The alley would be covered. Now, she wondered, from which position? Her grenades meant limited distance and delayed explosions. Not the best assault weapon, but it was all she had besides a baseball bat.

Emily understood that whichever position Petra took, the probability was lowest for her maintaining view of the storefront. The bat was useless, so she placed it in the corner besides the window within easy reach if chance necessitated it. She paused for a moment, then stepped through the destroyed display window towards her right, farthest from the alley. Hey footfalls produced no audible sounds that might have otherwise tipped Petra to her position. Emily took to the middle of the street, unclipped two of the stun grenades and pulled the pins on both while keeping a tight grasp on their spoons. Without ado, Emily leaned forward and catapulted herself down the street. In a full sprint as she reached the alleyways, the spoons flew away as she simultaneously lobbed the grenades into each as hard as she could. With the adrenalin flowing, she didn't take notice of the premature explosion to her right—not caring if it was the grenade or Petra's attempt to gun her down. Emily only recorded the brilliant magnesium flare to her right, followed by another blast to her left. Critically, she noticed that she was well beyond the alleyway and had not taken any damage. If Petra fired at her, she missed.

Petra never fired a shot in actuality. Her eyesight was obliterated by the blinding white flash, and her eardrums damaged by the close-proximity detonation. Emily had no way to know she landed the grenade within a meter of Petra's feet. In the open, a stun grenade temporarily disrupts the target's ability to see or hear. An explosion between walls may result in permanent damage. Petra was completely disoriented by the blast. To make it worse, there was a simulation of a piercing incessant ring that blocked all other sounds. Her VR display was overlaid with a translucent red tint that was slowly subsiding. There were mostly annoying aftereffects, by Petra's estimations. The computer scored a 30% damage score to her health, although no vital organs or major physical damage occurred. Time was slipping away for a shot at an unarmed Emily.

Petra slipped out from behind the car and its broken windows. She rounded the corner from the alleyway, keeping her shotgun aimed straight ahead, scanning for her target. *Emily has disappeared once more, but where?* This made the task of clearing storefronts doubly difficult since Emily likely entered one of them on either side. She would not have run the entire block and ditched into an alley—not without an effective weapon. The ringing finally subsided, as well did the red tint, fully restoring Petra's vision. She flicked her eyes towards the right for a glimpse of the nearest storefront and saw no movement. She saw no help in the form of new weapons either, so she continued to the next storefront while keeping an eye across the street.

The via erupted with explosions and pirouetting ricochets as glass and mortar flew from the façade just steps in front of her. Petra dove for the nearest cover behind a trash bin as the arc of automatic gunfire went past. *Emily has a rifle!* She was putting it to full use as well, emptying an entire 30-round magazine her direction. It was one of two magazines found alongside the rifle. When the explosions ceased, Petra discerned the telltale clicking of a magazine change. She stood up and launched a fusillade of her own, pumping five rounds of double-aught across the street in the general direction of the first muzzle flashes she recalled when diving for cover.

Emily grunted as her VR display went red from one of the 30-caliber pellets striking her left shoulder. The health meter dropped to 72% as a result. It would be a few moments for the tint to clear. Unless Petra ran for another alley ahead, she was reloading in the storefront directly across the street. Emily didn't hesitate. She jumped to her feet and dashed ahead to the final store cornering the last alley before the courtyard. She wondered what weapons she might have forfeited in the process, but the most devastating and powerful were somewhere close by. She thought the fight could end with one mighty strike. She peered into the last two storefronts and saw nothing at first. She happened to be looking left through one of the windows when she caught the reflection of a large muzzle flash. The sound was lower, though, and the percussion not immediate. As the thought occurred that it wasn't the shotgun, a 40mm shell exploded three meters away to her left, shattering glass and knocking her to the ground. Health down to 62%. She turned over and sprayed the rifle in Petra's direction. One connected for a 15% hit, dropping her to 55%, and causing an input lag. Petra nonetheless launched two more salvos, wildly off-target, landing several meters to Emily's flanks—too far away to cause any significant damage, yet the chaos managed another 6% off Emily.

The wry split between Esposito's lips widened as he anticipated a close duel, remarking as much to Sister Regina as they monitored. This scrimmage had exceeded his expectations.

"Always unconventional and gallant, the inhibition of youth—their thinking unclouded by adolescence and the rote of adult complication."

"Less so when the consequences are known, Your Excellency."

"Never spoil a delightful surprise."

An orange light blinked on the soundproof wall just beyond the surveillance monitors. Esposito reached for the handset and brought it to his ear while watching the duel unfold. He did not speak; he listened expressionless for several moments, then hung up.

"They are here."

"Here? Already, Your Excellency?" Sister Regina asked, nearly choking in anxiety.

"Not precisely, Sister. Soon. At the completion of this duel, make preparations for departure.

Emily was breathing heavily from the motion-activated simulation. Although her body remained in relative place, she had been ducking, diving and running to avoid further damage while working desperately to terminate her opponent. She resolved to do so after the first drop of "blood" hit the street. Petra gunned the same, though not quite as intensely; her age and experience afforded increased conditioning. Nobody had been monitoring her actual physical condition since the duel started, and a telltale trickle of real blood had coagulated on her left earlobe.

Petra slid her last grenade into the launcher's receiver and snapped it closed. She loaded the final two shells from the bandolier and threw the strap on the ground. Less chance for entanglement, and she was aware that the program included weight variables in overall encumbrance. When she gathered herself, she scanned the street for any signs of Emily. Two shots careened off the wall to her side. Obviously, she thought, Emily was acutely aware of her location! She ducked to avoid further damage, sticking the shotgun around the corner and blasting a round of her own in Emily's approximate direction. The shot coincided with a dash around the doorway and a burst of speed past two storefronts, sending two more rounds towards Emily's position at the end of the block. Emily positioned herself behind the rear wheel of a sedan so as not to be immediately zeroed. Her head popped up over the trunk, catching a glimpse of Petra's final steps into the second-to-last storefront before the final cross street in front of the cathedral's piazza. When Petra disappeared, Emily glanced backwards at the last storefront. Her eyes ignited in sparkling amazement. There it was, glistening as if bathed in golden luminescence—the 1-megawatt laser pistol.

Emily blasted the opposite side of the street, smashing glass and stucco as her magazine emptied. She dashed inside and snatched the pistol and its holster, strapping it on to her right side and turning around to face the street. Petra's storefront was devoid of glass reflections, allowing an easier view to the interior, yet Emily saw no movement. She wondered if Petra escaped to the rear alley and waited for her in the piazza. She could not see that far to her left, therefore it was a plausible deduction. The laser pistol and two concussion grenades were it for inventory. Emily knew Petra had a grenade launcher and a shotgun with only a few rounds remaining. She also guessed that the program included major weapons in each of the last storefronts, as most games to her experience leveled difficulties and luck to encourage competition.

Cautiously, Emily vacated her shop, shadowing the corner for expectant views around the outside of the opposite storefront. Nothing. She had also been scanning the piazza for movement as well, particularly behind the cypress planters aligning its perimeter. With no movement or other indication, she decided to streak towards the left corner of the piazza and take position at its frontal retaining wall. When she reached midway, she heard the unmistakable signature of the grenade launcher, echoing from across the piazza. The round exploded some five meters behind. Emily waited for the inevitable follow-up shotgun blast that never came. She periscoped the pistol's articulating eyepiece for a look over the wall, catching movement behind a planter at the far opposite corner. With the crosshairs aligned, she squeezed the trigger. The planter exploded from the blast, sending greyed pottery in all directions as the cypress toppled. Emily kept her eye on the area, expecting further movement, yet there was none. She must have moved to the adjacent planter, Emily thought, so she placed the crosshairs on it and squeezed the trigger once more. Again, the planter flew apart and another cypress fell, and there was no Petra behind it, either. Emily blasted two more planters in succession to no avail, not keeping an eye on the laser's charge meter, which indicated two shots remaining. Emily's heart sank. In the previous round, this laser had unlimited firepower. She started second-guessing her strategy—the blowing through rifle magazines. She lamented not saving them.

Emily's mind raced. The only other likely location for Petra was behind the right-hand corner of the cathedral, except it was too distant to lob a grenade. She could not use the laser pistol either. She felt harried by the No Waiting mandate, and yet, it seemed as though that rule didn't apply to Petra. The arbitrary application of the rules dominated her thoughts. She shook her head and bolted towards the front entry of the piazza, jumping up two steps at a time as she scanned her flanks. When she reached the top, two blasts exploded from the cathedral's right corner, just where Emily had guessed Petra would be. Emily's HUD flashed red, extracting another 20%. She was down to 36%. Still, Emily could not see Petra within the cathedral's shadow. Her movement returned, and for a moment, Emily wondered why Petra ceased firing. When she heard the faint rattle of the shotgun being dropped to the cobblestones, Emily had her answer. She decided to run towards the cathedral's front steps—a protected portico—and lob a grenade towards Petra as soon as she could manage the distance. Emily unclipped one of the grenades, pulled its pin, and bolted. At twenty steps, she reached the piazza's central marble inlays. The handle flew from the grenade as she flung it towards the corner, noticing it disappear in the darkness. Petra sprang forward attempting to avoid it, but the explosion hit less than two meters away. 30% damage and stunned for a moment. Petra's meter now read 25%.

Emily ceased the opportunity and drew her pistol, blasting two shots her direction, one striking Petra in the left shoulder.

Another 10% hit. Emily pulled at the trigger for a third shot and nothing happened. She repeated several times, noticing the weapons depletion only after the attempt. Petra drew her bowie knife and continued her charge across the piazza towards Emily. All Emily had left was a grenade. She panicked and tossed it only a few meters away towards Petra, hoping to thwart the attack. It didn't. Petra ran past the grenade—its fuse coursing to the charge—and lunged towards Emily as it exploded. Emily's HUD flashed red twice. Once from Petra's slash as she passed to her right, and again when the grenade exploded. 15% hit to Emily, and a critical 5% to Petra.

PETRA HEALTH: 10%
EMILY HEALTH: 16%

Emily was out of weapons and options. If only she'd kept that baseball bat, she thought. She started replaying every defense instructed to combat a knife-wielding opponent, and how to inflict damage while doing so. Her confidence increased as she visualized each maneuver. Petra turned around, regripping her bowie knife as she contemplated the deathblow. Her attack was swift, lunging at Emily with several rapid stabbing motions. Emily deflected each one, grunting as she did, careful to anticipate each of Petra's moves. On one of the blocks, Emily landed a potent cross to Petra's left cheek, scoring a 3%. Petra was dangerously low, and Emily was beginning to taste success. Petra paused for a brief moment and carried a strange expression—her eyes darting rapidly up and down. At once, she bolted one more time at Emily, signaling a slash with her left, but one meter away, she suddenly vaulted over Emily's head.

"Hey!" Emily shouted.

While inverted, Petra thrust the knife deep into Emily's spinal column, and when she landed, she swept Emily's feet, causing Emily to collapse onto the piazza's stonework face-first and wooden. Emily's HUD went black.

She was stupefied, and actually paralyzed in defeat. Her mind convulsed as did her body. She hated losing, and the sensations for the VR towards the end were making her nauseas. She started to remove the helmet when the HUD flashed "Stand By..." across an orange screen. A moment later her VR faded into the view inside the cathedral, close to its altar, with Bishop Esposito's avatar smiling at her as if he was genuinely standing a few feet away. He stepped off the altar and squatted so as to speak to her face-to-face.

"Congratulations, dear Emily, you triumph again."

Emily looked to her sides, puzzled... and perturbed.

"Ah, but you do not understand?"

"Maybe." She felt intimidated.

"Tell me what you think." Esposito stood up. "Be honest; it is preferable you tell the truth."

"Okay." Emily took a breath, noticing her HUD's statistic had come back online with a full reset, as if she had a new life. "Petra cheated. And... and you lied!"

"How so?" Esposito's smile grew wider with anticipatory eyes.

"You said no advantages. Petra said she played this for four rounds. She knew this level and where everything was. She knew where to hide and the best places for attack."

"Continue." Narciso said dryly.

"And then she, wait, like, two times she used a move we were not taught at the dojo. Nobody ever practiced her fatality move; I would have remembered it!"

"Ah, yes; I cannot disagree. I needed to show you, young Emily, that sometimes, cheating is acceptable in order to achieve a goal. In life or death, there is no such thing as fair play, understand?" Esposito's eyes shifted away. "We will talk about this later, but for now, consider yourself the Champion. I have but one additional challenge for you."

Emily tensed and Esposito continued.

"You must fight one more, how do you say—boss. No weapons, only hand-to-hand skills. There is no penalty for losing; we want to see what you are truly made of. Narciso's smile returned.

Emily looked at him expectantly as he gestured her to turn around and face her new enemy. When she did, a silhouette emerged from the brilliant flood of sunshine at the front entrance. A figure with an oddly-familiar outline, she thought. At once, Emily's complexion turned to ice. She trembled violently in disbelief. The figure drew closer as Emily couldn't move—a fawn in the headlights.

"My, you've been BUSY!" It snarled.

Emily couldn't avert her eyes in morbid curiosity. Her body instinctively drew a pugilistic posture in anticipation of the attack, but it was useless. She started bawling loudly, then screaming. "I want out! I WANT OUT!" She clawed at her VR helmet, or so she thought. She had been tricked? There was no helmet? This isn't real, she repeated to herself. It couldn't be!

Her opponent grabbed both of her arms. She felt the tight squeeze across her biceps. It drew her close to its face, and there she lost all reality, screaming at the top of her lungs as she stared into the dull-yellowed eyes and sharpened teeth within the pasty-white makeup of Xeno's noxious appearance.

Emily screamed louder than thought possible, repeating "NO, NO, NO, NO, NO!" With her eyes tightly shut, struggling against Xeno's vice-gripped hold. She beat on his chest, and scratched at his face as he brought her in closer to taste her flesh. Finally, she dug into his cheek with all four fingers of her right hand, digging under the white powdered makeup, drawing blood. Xeno grimaced and loosened his grip on her, touching his face and seeing the blood upon his sharp-clawed fingertips. He snarled in anger as Emily landed another blow, removing yet more makeup and knocking something out of his left eye. Xeno winced and dropped her completely, covering his eye with his left hand. She grunted and kicked with all her weight against his left kneecap. He howled as he hit the floor in front of her. She swung her left hand towards his face in growing confidence, but he caught it midway and nearly broke it, lifting her off the ground. She started screaming violently again as he uncovered his face and eye to grab her other hand. Then, suddenly, Emily's cries altogether stopped. She stared at him in the disbelief of recognition. It was too much. Her VR abruptly vignetted to a pale centered-dot as she lost consciousness.

Sister Regina was already in the process of removing Petra's body from the Examination Room—the nickname bestowed on it by Bishop Esposito's predecessor, Cardinal Tagliabue. The ER is where all final duels were held in the training of potential Spada Sacra operators. The cardinal was aged and decrepit, and no longer suited her predilection for sado-masochism, to which her favorite bishop deduced almost immediately upon introduction. She considered them a match, and one day, perhaps, primed to her infallible reasoning, she would give herself to Narciso. It was a fantasy not shared by her prospect, but she would never be cognizant of it.

The nun wheeled Petra's corpse into a chilled holding area and placed a thick, black cadaver bag on top of her. Before sealing her away in a temporary storage compartment, Regina accessed Petra's file and made all the necessary entries, including her symptoms and her progress within the duel prior to failure. According to her entry, after three elapsed minutes, Petra never emerged from the final storefront, collapsing towards the back room while attempting to retrieve a special microgun. The nun knew she would go unchecked and probably snap since she was beyond the average age for extended cerebral plasticity. Regardless of her combat prowess, Esposito kept her in competition in anticipation of testing Emily. When she failed, the bishop automated her avatar to continue the fight, creating special abilities to further examine Emily's mental acumen. He was not disappointed.

Emily awakened struggling with her restraining straps. She started screaming in panic, the screams of a virtual death as the light of heaven grew brighter in her eyes. It became brighter and brighter until the hood was removed by Sister Regina. The nun handed her a warm wet towel so that she could blot the urine from herself. She trembled wildly, shocked and confused, yet intensely resolved.
HOW COULD HE!
It was the last thought she had before the nun sprayed her face with an instant anesthesia. Emily immediately dropped; there was no ten-count.

● ● ●

General Tomlinson listened intently as Colonel Osterhoudt's direct mobile line rang for the fifth time, finally reverting to voicemail. The prompt was not his voice, only a repetition of his number, as was standard procedure if the device should become lost, stolen, or confiscated. It was her second attempt to reach him, and she angrily slammed her phone's receiver into its cradle. She did not leave a second message, considering the first as sufficient. He was simply not responding, and she mentally reviewed every contingency, as doing so settled her nerves—usually complimented by a scotch, although not at this hour. The coffee was beginning to work against her patience.

Agent Diaz checked her screen. 0825Z. She cursed her lack of self-discipline and dialed Peterson AFB. An operator connected her to the Command Center where she was eventually qualified and routed to the desk of Major Charles Sponetti. The line rang four times and reverted to voicemail. She recorded a message relaying her contact information only, with a mandate to call as soon as possible. Diaz again dialed the command center and underwent another round of routing until she reached Sponetti's Operator—a buck out of Lackland who, by demeanor and presentation, would do whatever was asked of him without the encumbrance of critical thought. She only prepared two questions for him. The first was to confirm his order to override the data governor, to which he stuttered and eventually relayed his actions came under order from Sponetti—going further to testify that nobody else was on station at the time. The second question concerned the whereabouts of Sponetti, to which he paused in panic before the inevitable "I don't know".

Diaz hung up and began the process of notifying the base commander—a general who loathed any contact, rare as it may be, from the AFOSI. As geek-ish as his exterior mannerisms indicated towards his leadership of anything involving space, he commanded as a tough stickler for regulations and decorum. Rank and pedigree meant little or nothing, often negatively if he sensed it being leveraged with dishonor. Any officer or enlisted who distracted his itinerary by inviting such an inquiry would be reconciled quickly, quietly, and harshly. Diaz was assured of Sponetti's compliance to contact as soon as possible with a full explanation. The general hung up and summoned his exec. Diaz also loathed these calls. Her hands were twitching afterward, and her stomach tuned sour. It would be hours before the base commander tendered what she had already deduced, that Sponetti was unofficially AWOL.

Two Blades and a Bear

Dr. Christopher Miller managed a contemptuous laugh for the first time in several days. Daylight broke from behind, and he found himself sitting in an unmarked white van, crawling across the Chesapeake Bay Bridge, locked in dense traffic where every fourth vehicle was an unmarked white van. He giggled as he noticed red and blue flashes illuminating the opaque moisture between their span and the opposite span, some 400 feet on his left. Two state enforcement SUVs blazed the other direction—searching for this group, he presumed. Matt and the others noticed Chris' muted cackles, wondering if he had finally broken.

"That's right," Matt said. "Keep laughing. We have another hour of this on the way to Drill's."

"Adriel's house?" Chris' voice took an octave upward. "Why? The airport is our primary destination. Wh—"

Matt interrupted, "Multiple reasons. I need to know what happened to him. I also have certain equipment in that house that's hopefully still there, understand? Equipment that we'll probably need."

Chris knew that look in his eyes. It was the same from the assault at Amerimem, and later, while his house was burning. A killer's face, focused and irreverent.

Monsignor Trovarto leaned forward and placed a hand on Matthew's shoulder. "I am-a sorry, Matthew. It is-a imperative we return to the airport first."

Matt glared into the rearview mirror. "Forgive me, father; I need to know why going to the airport is more important than the whereabouts of my friend, let alone the equipment I just mentioned."

"Yes-a, you see, during all this-a excitement, stealing the cars," Trovarto raised a brow, "I receive a message from-a Monsieur Du Rennes who says his-a estate was-a raided and destroyed, except-a they escaped. His-a father and the butler Henri are dead, God have mercy... Said critically important to meet at-a the airport—the original hangar, and by that I think-a he means Number 5."

There was a collective gasp throughout the van. Chris turned around to face Trovarto with an iced expression.

"Monsignor, I am a reasonable man. Doesn't it seem plausible that your message may have been sent under duress? I do not understand why, of all places, Du Rennes would risk such a flight across the Atlantic—after shipping us in a sailboat, mind you—simply to *rendezvous*. It's nuts!"

"Plausible? Ah, no; the communicators do not transmit under such-a conditions. Do not ask-a me to explain. His-a message did not reveal a specific reason. I trust it is-a sufficient to require such a passage."

Dao Ming stared towards the blurred landscapes as they passed, deep in thought. Chris happened to catch her despondency while grappling with Trovarto's mandate.

"What is it?" Chris asked.

It took a moment for her mind to clear. "Nothing... maybe."

Anastasia smiled from the back and leaned in to tap her shoulder. Dao spun towards her, expecting an explanation, but Tulip sat back and continued her smile. Dao knew what it meant, and she also understood that the girl knew as well.

"Inescapable, those emotions," said Anastasia. "And all too familiar because we have all experienced them."

At that moment, another DC Police interceptor blew past, lights flashing and siren howling. As the traffic parted, a collective exhale came from the group as they gazed upon D.C.'s Navy Yard to their left, undergoing transformation beneath a forest of construction cranes. Nobody spoke for several moments until they crested the next overpass. Matt slammed on the brakes—gridlock across all lanes, awash in red taillights. A mile ahead, he caught the pulsing blues of the interceptor that passed them moments ago.

"Wreck on the left," he said. "At least we're still moving."

Several minutes later, as he was forced to merge right, Matt's eyes met the policeman's, who was busy attending to a driver who apparently lost control and hit the retaining wall. The patrolman kept his eyes glued to their van as they passed. Matt kept an eye on the rearview as the patrolman reached for the microphone clipped to his left pectoral. His eyes never left their stolen van.

"Damnit!" Matt yelled as he hit the accelerator. The traffic had thinned and was accelerating. "We have to get off this road. That cop just marked us."

As he uttered those words, he whispered several expletives in realizing that he had just missed his last exit before the interstate crossed the Potomac River. Just another two miles to the airport, he thought. The patrol car wasn't in sight. He decided to risk that no other policeman could get to them quickly enough before he exited to George Washington Memorial Parkway by the airport. When he found the exit unblocked, he relaxed. Within moments, Reagan National's welcome signs flew overhead. They cruised towards Hangar 5's south end. Matt swung the van around and reversed into one of the few available spaces in front of the hangar so as to obfuscate the tag. Curious persons would have to make an extra effort, he thought, counting on the laziness of the lackadaisical. As Matt exited the driver's seat, he noticed their spray-painted pickup was where they'd left it, several spaces away. *Lazy indeed!* The tow companies either didn't care, or no complaints were launched. Odd, he thought, given all the ominous signage in front of each space. He contemplated swapping tags with it later, that is, until he remembered that tag was also poached.

Chris opened the door and climbed out, and as he turned around to shut it, a voice resonated just behind him.

"What are you lot standing around fer? Come on already!"

"Ha!" Matt hollered.

Chris spun around and smiled at Patrick, who was holding one of the hangar doors open in anticipation. Dao bounded from the rear passenger compartment, turning around to assist Anastasia and Monsignor Trovarto. Rocco vaulted himself over the rear passenger seat and joined the group just behind them.

Patrick gave them each a tight hug at the doorway. "Been here just over an hour. Met a couple of your friends. Appears we have some catchin' up to do, yeah? I'm really looking forward to that!"

"Friends? What friends?" Matt drew his pistol, as the others gasped.

"Don't think you'll be needing that, Commander." Patrick laughed.

When they emerged from the offices' corridor to the main hangar, a several seated people encircled a catering table. Those facing backwards turned around.

"Can't say I care much for my truck's paintjob."

"I KNEW IT!" Matt shouted.

Chris went wide-eyed and collapsed onto the floor, chest heaving. He drew a deep breath, embarrassed for his sudden weakness. Dao jumped in to help Chris to his feet.

"Who is he?" She asked.

Before Chris could respond, the man spoke and offered his hand to her. "My name is River, young lady."

"Chief River... from Montana, Dao," Chris added. "He's the—"

Dao interrupted, "The man who helped you. I remember your story." She firmly shook his hand and smiled, bowing.

"He's also a ghost!" Matt said with a chiding tone, giving River a bear hug. "You're supposed to be dead, you know."

River winked as Matt set him down, grabbing Twin Feathers around the shoulders.

"Dead? No, just passing through Nebraska."

Chris looked at Patrick, who was smiling. "Understatement of the year."

He looked at the others, then noticed Dao's transfixed gaze towards Jet Sun.

● ● ●

What remained of Agent Diaz's third double latte steamed at the right corner of her monitor. Her automated warrant provided detailed phone records from Patrick AFB over the preceding two days, and she had highlighted two of particular interest, being that they emanated from Maj. Charles Sponetti's desk and terminated at a classified and partially-redacted number within the Pentagon's index. Since she was familiar with Pentagon prefixes, Agent Diaz narrowed the call's source to the A-Ring, within the wedge typically occupied by flex needs—the ongoing accordion effect of 9/11. *Curious*, she thought, since most of the executives preferred D-Ring's windows for the views. Another notion coursed in her synapses, and it manifested as she drained the last of her latte, making for the exit without attracting the wrong kind of attention. She glided past her C.O.'s desk without an audible footfall. Diaz practiced it dozens of times, never caught by the useless pogue whose eyes never left his screen unless he needed something. Always last-minute, always an emergency. This was an actual emergency in her mind—one that would survive a court martial if she earned it. Sooner or later, some analyst would put it together. Her car's GPS would log the 30-minute Pentagon run, and her ID tag would also log at the Pentagon's security checkpoints. She was aware of the notifications that ensued once any of the investigative office branches entered. Flags. Her division was a necessary evil nobody liked, and Diaz knew it by the splenetic faces almost everyone made once her ID tag met the eyes of her scrutinizers. It would be a long five-minute hike to the Air Force's wedge of the A-ring.

A resonant baritone voice startled her from behind. She never heard the steps or felt the warmth of proximity as she rounded the last corner. Another trained individual, she thought, and probably another from her office, summoned to intercept.

"I didn't have time to explain." She blurted without making eye contact.

"Tomlinson's gone, and you won't find her down there, Agent Diaz."

Diaz abruptly stopped and turned around to face a physically-ripped, six-foot blonde-and-blue in standard service dress. Her eyes instantly marked the silver eagles adorning his epaulets.

"Sir?" She saluted as she cleared her throat.

"Come with me; we can't talk here."

Diaz was aware of the multiple surveillance cameras covering every inch of the hallway. She was overcome with bewilderment and irritation. "I cannot, sir; I am under orders to—"

"No you're not, Diaz. You traced a phone call here, hopped in your car at Quantico, and drove here without telling a soul. Now... please?"

The colonel gestured with an expectant smile, ushering her towards an office door just beside them in the hallway.

Shocked, Diaz trembled and proceeded towards the room. The colonel opened the door to a small, unoccupied office and turned on the lights. Diaz noticed there were no visible cameras. The space felt like an interrogation room. In fact, the space was regularly used for frank confabs away from the DOD's Eagle Eye. By executive agreement, several of these rooms were dispersed around the Pentagon, and each included a discreet indicator light next to the entrance which illuminated when in use. All one had to do was open the door and turn on the overhead lights, which the colonel did upon entry. There was a conference table in the middle of the room. The colonel directed Diaz to a chair just off the end, then eased himself into the adjacent corner seat, his eyes never leaving hers.

"I know you have a lot of questions, so let's ditch the small. I work for General Tomlinson. Whatever you think you know about that room down the hallway, forget it. Classified, and I don't mean compartmentalized. You were cleared at the entrance without a recorder, but I need your phone. Turn it off then place it on the table."

With hesitation, Diaz complied. Osterhoudt produced a shielded cover that prevented signals and auditory input, placing it on top of the phone.

"Any others I need to know about?"

"None."

"Now be a good listener…"

Colonel Osterhoudt detailed Blue Ops historical existence and its true mission. When finished, Diaz's face was awash in tears and her stomach sour. For her, it was incomprehensible, as if learning her father was a power-drunk anti-Christ who'd created and maintained incalculable secrets.

"It's easy, you know—their programming. The entire time I belonged to this detachment, I believed every operation was for the big picture. We were fighting evil, and if not us, someone else, and if nobody else, evil triumphed. Several days ago, they sent me after one of our own—just another colt they roped from the top of his regiment—someone who, after several months, I innately trusted as one of the good guys. In other words, he still had a conscience. They told me he'd gone off the reservation. Made plans to blow us all up. As usual, I believed them until I saw a recording from an executive assistant who worked with him in Cupertino. I don't even know where to start with this, and it's probably of no importance to you, Diaz; I don't have the time for it all. Just know this, the recording was significant enough to reconnoiter Blue Ops itself. I have a couple friends in the right places, you know. Not going to tell you how, but I landed several communiques that link Tomlinson to counterparts from four other countries, namely Russia, China, Germany and England."

"That look on your face... Why not let the FBI have it?"

"Nope. They're too busy chasing political favors, same as the DOJ and several others."

"Why me?" Diaz pointed to herself with both hands.

"Because I already know you—your background, your psych profile, and I know you're an independent, critical thinker. At all times, we're required to keep files on at least a dozen prospects with your grades and integrity. People we can tap when needed. So, consider this one huge tap on your shoulder. We'll discuss it all later, Diaz. Right now, what you need to understand is that Tomlinson cleared out two hours ago. I trailed her to an elevator two wedges to the left and one floor down. Small elevator; you'd miss it if you didn't know about it. Retinal access behind a hidden panel, monitored. She climbed in, the door swung closed, at that was the last I saw of her. I have eyes on the outside. No doubt she went subter-ranean. Too many rumors of new need-to-know tunnels below this place after 9/11."

Diaz sat there with her eyes glazed, petrified.

"Now, Miss July OSI, are you going to give me a hand, or are you running back to Quantico? One call and you'll be sitting in another room like this explaining your sudden absence."

"Seriously? Did you just—" Her complaint fell flat against Osterhoudt's paralyzing confidence as her eyes surrendered. "What am I to do?"

"Beat everyone to the punch and blow it up ourselves."

Diaz nearly convulsed. "How?"

"Take this." He slipped a folded scrap of paper across the table. "Go back to Quantico, you'll be safest there. Lock yourself in the office if need be, and do not tell your C.O. until you're done. This is a list of contacts. Direct cell numbers. The first two are media contacts I trust."

"Those will be flagged and monitored at OSI," Diaz said.

Osterhoudt produced a thin flip phone and handed it to her. "Satcomm. Won't be blocked, I assure you. Use it for those calls. It's also wiped and bounces at random. Untraceable, which is the only way you'll reach the third contact. Also media connected, but not traditional. He's one of those conspiracy nutjobs who's right most of the time, yet nobody believes him. Sad. Anyway, he knows the entire phone index backwards. He'll know this number as legitimate. So will the fourth call."

"Lemme guess…"

"Take this seriously, Diaz!"

"Nope! This is how I deal. It's the Pope, right? I mean, why not?"

"Next calls, you'll use the hardline."

"Well, this can't be good. Why would I do that?"

"Because you're calling the Chairman and Vice Chairman of the Joint Chiefs."

Gut-punch #3. Diaz doubled over.

"There is a bugle line on that slip of paper. Recite it once connected and you'll have both generals in conference within five minutes. Pray you don't drop the call. I'll let your imagination fill in those blanks."

"What, exactly, am I to say?"

"You will curtly detail what I told you of Blue Ops, Tomlinson, the CIA, and who we're up against. If you get one hint of them circling wagons, you make sure they understand this wasn't your first call... or second... or fourth. They press you, hang up and run to the address on the paper, and I mean as lightning, Diaz. Personal safe house. Also clean. Not even Tomlinson. Just make sure you're not followed, and please be a little more creative than the textbook."

"That all?"

"No."

"I mean, my life is about to become a raging underground mine fire, but who cares!"

"Get a handle on it." Osterhoudt hands her a thumb drive. "Automatic executable. A private, impenetrable tunnel will be created and files uploaded. Should take no more than ten minutes on any half-assed laptop with five-meg connection."

"Where's it headed? Oh, wait... Classified, need-to-know?"

"Exiled leaker, reluctant patriot type. Nobody you've heard of. It's my last card. Person only acts if nobody else does within a certain timeframe of receipt. Typically, five days. He doesn't act often, suffice to say."

"Does it self-destr—"

"Cute. No; it's your proof should you need it. Code on the sheet. I shouldn't have to reiterate how important that little scrap of paper is, Diaz."

"Colonel, just how nuclear is this?"

"In Tomlinson's case, very. You're only here because of a satellite tasking. I have her on tape making deals with Russian infiltrators who breached this place a few days ago and butchered Tomlinson's superiors. Wondered why they spared her..."

"Here? They came here… to the Pentagon? Just walked right in, occupied an office and murdered our generals."

"Exactly, here, Diaz. Just down the corridor, and nobody will ever know about the sealed boxes that ultimately found their way to a Blackhawk purposely flown low and slow over Kabul."

A sudden jolt broke Agent Diaz' repulsion and another type of sickness overwhelmed her senses. The Pentagon's Master Alarm electrified the entire complex, causing scurried flights from those traversing the restless hallways. Osterhoudt balked, knowing what it meant.

"We have less than four minutes to vacate or we'll be held here indefinitely. They may be only looking for me, so get out of here. Take Corridor Eight towards the Metro. It's typically the busiest."

"What's happening? What about my car?"

"Toast. Tomlinson got to the Joint Chiefs before we did. GO!"

She dashed several steps then abruptly threw on the brakes. "Wait!" Diaz yelled. "You sent the Coast Guard FAC, right?"

"Smarter than you look, Diaz. I've got a plane to catch." Osterhoudt smiled as he dashed around a corner.

● ● ●

"River…"

"I know," he said. "Our journey had not ended. Misread my vision during the night we shared. Later that morning, my closest neighbor, Soaring Bear, signaled. Our knives had a revealing conversation with a couple assassins before nightfall. European mercenaries. Well-equipped and hubristic.

First said nothing. Brave. The second, not so much after his companion's scalp fell on his lap. They knew little beyond their instructions, which they executed with one important exception."

"But how did you know to—" Matthew asked.

River reached between the truck's cab and bed, removing a small disk.

Matthew threw up his hands at Chris. "Of course, GPS! Should've expected that from an old injun."

Chris smiled, laughing.

Mallory Du Rennes interrupted. "It is unfortunate we do not have sufficient time for reminiscing. Please refresh yourselves as we must take care of the business, as they say."

"Did you notice?" Anastasia spoke softly into Patrick's ear as the group traded stories. Jet Sun was detailing their escape from Cambodia and the raid on Du Rennes château.

Patrick smirked with a low whisper, "Aye. Is it not the eyes of recognition?"

"A deeper connection, I sense…"

Jet Sun glanced towards Patrick, who understood it innately, his grin wide.

Master Sun continued, "There is much to be explained, and in time, I hope to do so. This is not yet the time, or the place."

River stepped forward with a glint. "Spoken by a man who has seen more moons than most."

"And enjoyed them, if not for the clouded nights." Sun withdrew the jar of beaver musk and held it before him. "Not bad for a Plains Reader. Later, we must talk." He released his daughter to bow before River, who accepted his honor with raised palms and a heightened brow. "Hungry?"

Rising from his bow, Master Sun smirked, tapping his temple, "Always."

River ushered Chris and Dao towards a makeshift buffet, assembled from the finest offerings of the nearest convenience stores. Shriveled hot dogs, soggy sandwiches, translucent pizza slices, tortilla chips and watery salsa, with a few candy bars tossed in for dessert. Chris stared at the spread a few seconds longer than he realized.

"Welcome home." River laughed.

"Gentlemen, it is of course not my desire to expedite our purpose, yet I should caution that our continued presence at this facility will attract undesirable attention," said Du Rennes. "We must therefore identify our objectives and develop a best strategy, no?"

Monsignor Trovarto stepped forward. "Our-a objectives, are simple. Emily must-a be rescued without loss, particularly those with-a knowledge that bastard wants to steal. No device, either."

"How can that happen? He will know." Chris interrupted.

"Cannot-a disable it?"

"I presumed he would require a demonstration before releasing Emily."

"Assume he will act to possess everything within his grasp." Jet Sun said. "The advantage is his so long as he holds your daughter."

Grimacing as he swallowed the last of a sandpapery, luke-warm, cardboard-like slice of pepperoni, Matthew struggled, "Speaking of assumptions, it might help to ascertain the whereabouts of my friend—where Emily was likely taken. Bring the laptop, let it work some magic, and see what we can see."

"As soon as you activate it, Esposito will know we're here," Chris said.

"He already knows this," said Du Rennes.

"So, when and how will he contact us?" Chris asked.

Chris looked around at everyone's faces as they turned towards the case holding the laptop.

"As-a soon as we are ready," said Trovarto.

Patrick ruffled a candy bar's wrapper in his hands. "Well, that's it then, isn't it? Simple as that? Go to the house, while we wait here? And doing what? Guarding the plane, is it? Well, that seems awfully important, doesn't it?"

Jet Sun put a hand on his shoulder. "It is, for now."

Du Rennes cracked, "This other plane I once abandoned in an American hangar, it eventually emerged as stolen by Colombian drug runners, confiscated by the DEA, and transferred to an unscrupulous broker at a Miami airport."

"Right, so we guard the jet, then. Bugger off you lot." Patrick gestured to the other side of the circle.

Matthew grinned, checked his sidearm and made for the hangar's front entrance. Chris turned to join him, holding Dao Ming's hand when she suddenly let go.

"What's wrong?" He asked.

"I need to speak with him." She looked towards Jet Sun.

River and Abe joined them outside a moment later, anticipating the need for their conveyance—a late model four-doored pickup. After a quick glance towards the fugitive van, Matthew climbed into the rear of the truck without a word. Chris opened the other side and jumped in, while River and Two Feathers did the same.

"You brought the laptop. Good," said River.

"Why do I need it when we have you?" Chris asked.

"You're a smart individual, Doctor Miller, you should know why."

Du Rennes, Gérard, Monsignor Trovarto, Jet Sun, Dao, Patrick, Anastasia and Rocco remained, while Chris, Matthew, River, and Abe sped off for Persimmon Tree Road in River's new truck. Matt's eyes darted back and forth, scanning the neighborhood's streets and alleyways for possible surveillance. After two passes, he satisfied none were around. At least, none on the streets. No occupied cars, service vans, or other potential threats. If someone was lurking, they were in the house.

River brought the truck to a stop on the street outside Adriel's house; his SUV gleamed from the carport. Matt checked his sidearm and jumped out of the truck, closing its door quietly. With speed and precision, he marked the carport, making a quick circuit of it, scanning the back yard as he crossed in front of the SUV and peered through the corners of the carport door's window, checking for movement. There was none. He twisted the doorknob. It was locked and dead-bolted. He circled around to the front door, sidearm drawn and lowered. The door had no windows, only a peephole. He stopped and stared at it for a few moments to see if the light shining though it changed any, indicating someone on the other side. Nothing. He depressed the thumb-latch. The door creaked open. He knew it was unusual. Drill kept several latches and locks bolted at all times—the paranoid bastard, Matt thought. He guessed they were unlocked because Drill was comfortable answering the door. Ambushed afterward perhaps. Was it an invitation or a fly trap, or both?

He stepped in, pistol drawn, methodically clearing each room, checking for blind spots. The place was empty. He returned to the front door to find River standing just inside with raised hands flanking either side of Matt's barrel.

"Clear." Matt said.

"Mostly."

"Huh? I just—"

"Your eyes serve you well, Matthew, except your ears and nose betray."

"I'm telling you there's nobody in there."

River's brow raised as he scootched past Matt at the front door and proceeded to the rear. Matt and Chris followed while Abe stayed at the front. Just outside on the porch, laying in the shade, was a filthy tan clump of hair, panting heavily with faint whines.

"Matthew... some water."

"There's a hose just around the corner."

Chris fell to his knees before the clump, stroking its hair.

"Is he okay?"

"And because I'm the native, you automatically conclude I possess veterinary skills?"

"YES!"

River shook his head as Matt brought the running hose around and held the nozzle just above River's cupped hands. Snickers struggled to raise his head and lap the cool liquid. A few sloppy drags then he swung a paw around to brace his head erect as he drowned himself in River's hands. For the next thirty seconds, Snickers tongue stabbed at the water. River abruptly uncupped his hands so Snickers wouldn't make himself sick. He took the hose from Matthew and ran it over the dog's spine a few times to cool him off. Chris covered his face.

"Oh man, that's—"

"Let him recover for a few minutes. If he gets up and shakes himself off, he'll be ready for a bath," said River.

"You mean," Matthew paused.

"He's coming with us."

River walked back inside and checked the refrigerator. Bacon and eggs...

Matt disappeared down the home's central hallway and entered the master bedroom. He immediately noticed several of Drill's prize possessions were missing—removed from the walls. Pictures, trophies, etc. His room appeared somewhat light as well. Their favorite travel backpack and duffel were missing. The generic, replaceable items remained. Anything bespoke had gone, along with his friend. Matthew resisted any conclusions, per his training. His breathing tightened with agitation. Surely there was a good explanation.

While River prepared Snicker's meal, Matthew summoned for Chis and his laptop.

"What's happening?" Abe asked, peering out the living room's window from behind its curtain.

"Found Snickers barely alive. Your pa is fixing him up. My buddy is MIA, so we're going to run the laptop. See if anything pops."

Chris took a deep breath as he removed the computer from its case and flipped it open. In the back of his mind, he accepted that all the travel—the temperature and humidity changes, suffice to mention all the action it had seen—may have taken its toll on the unit. When the screen lit with the normal boot screen, he sighed. The Amerimem logo caught his attention. A symbol of resilience and durability now, after all it has been through. Matthew instructed Abe to close the curtains and extinguish the lights. He shined a powerful flashlight he found in the kitchen across the room. Fragments floated everywhere. Chris knew they'd mostly contain newer deposits, but some might have a chance. The velour couch should carry some residuals, he thought. He scraped a fingernail across it to loosen particles and usher them towards the filtration screen. As they landed, the screen flashed with bright white flashes as the machine deciphered the particulates. Four materialized on the playlist within several seconds. Chris clicked on the first. Unintelligible static, as was the next. The third bore some fruit, as a voice appeared—Adriel's voice—was shouting in protest. The screen remained interlaced with static and odd blips of dark gray blobs that may have been people. The fragment abruptly ended with Adriel's voice appearing calmer, except the words were garbled.

"I've an idea." Chris said. "Do us a favor and kick around the rug by the front entrance."

Abe immediately stomped on it, raking his boots from side to side across the piling. Chris swooped in and turned the laptop sideways to catch the disturbed fragments. The file counter read 14.

Chris started at the top and worked his way down. Same results as previously until he reached the 6th file. A clear image appeared and Matthews suspicions were confirmed. There was Adriel, accepting the devil's lies, believable as they sounded. Esposito knew which buttons to push. Money, fear, success, the new life that every adventure junkie sought. Exotic lands, insatiable vixens, and limitless resources, starting with a $500,000 instant reward for a little girl who wasn't his. All they had to do was show the bag of Benjamins, and he promised to deliver her within the hour. Another three million awaited. The fragment ended before Adriel uttered what Matthew evidenced for himself. He knew Adriel couldn't resist the payoff of a lifetime. He was also bored, which meant vulnerable. The laptop flickered once more, unprompted.

Chris knew what came next, and the familiar wretch of his stomach souring came upon him with a sharper volatility which he hadn't yet felt.

Xeno's singing voice grated with a coughing cackle, "Wise men say...."

Chris dropped the laptop upon the floor as he buckled. The singing stopped as soon as it started. A shrill tone pierced their eardrums for several seconds, then the screen flipped to Esposito's studio.

"Ah, home at last." The bishop quipped.

Chris started to collect the laptop before River grabbed his shoulders in a bid for calm.

"You will never see her again, Doctor Miller, unless you bring this device to me. Roosevelt Island footbridge, eight tonight."

The screen turned dark for a few seconds before returning to the files prompt. Chris screamed at the top of his lungs, clamming the lid of the laptop closed, regripping it—hands shaking in fury—to shatter it upon the floor with all his strength. River and Matthew leapt and grabbed his arms before it happened.

"Please, Chris. You need this thing."

"Do I?" He yelled. "Why does he need it? He knows we can build another. This maniac will not stop with the laptop. He'll want me, then he'll want Dao. He wants all of us, can't you see? Do I have to say it?"

River stripped the laptop from Chris' grasp and tucked it under his arm. "No, you do not, for you speak from ignorance."

"Well, there you go." Chris said with a sarcastic tone. "I know nothing, apparently."

"Tell me, Doctor Miller, you've had ample time to run this scenario in your scientific mind—moved the chess pieces. How do you see it ending where Emily is in your possession, and you are out of danger?"

"Okay, River, I'll play along. Assuming we aren't immediately executed by sniper or some other caustic means, I send the laptop, they send my daughter."

"In time, this person—this organization—will want us all dead. They will persist, therefore there is but one solution in our favor, and you know what it is."

Chris turned around with the look of fear and recognition. His throat tightened. Mortal combat was not in his DNA.

"So this exchange at the bridge is just another cliché. How else does he score a couple pieces so easily?"

"It is leverage and advantage, Chris. The bishop has both. He possesses something you cannot live without. It is not the same for him. We need an advantage."

River handed the laptop back to Chris, who jumped as a strong static charge cracked across his fingertips.

"Jesus H!" Chris yelled.

River held onto the laptop in reaction, his eyes rolled and breathing stopped as he collapsed upon himself.

"DAD!" Abe shrieked as he spun around to catch him.

River recovered a moment later. Groggy, and muttered "Evil" under his breath.

"What just happened?" Chris asked.

"Wait," said Abe. "I've seen this before."

River glanced up at his son and motioned for an assist back to his feet. Abe lifted him by an elbow.

"There is a presence—an insatiable, mischievous malevolence. Destroying the laptop is futile. The presence must be obliterated. We must return to the hangar."

The room grew quiet, save for the faint whining from the bathroom where the shower had been running. Matthew slipped down the hallway while Chris and River discussed options. Making sure nobody saw, Matthew flipped open a fake AC vent in the master bedroom, reached inside up to his shoulder, and withdrew a plastic-wrapped leather kit. He tore it open and withdrew a fresh .45 compact tactical pistol, which he checked for a chambered round, grabbed three loaded magazines, a sheathed K-Bar, an alternate name passport and license, and lastly, $20,000 in banded cash— which produced an inner laugh since they now possessed a huge duffel full of currency. He stuffed the notes into his socks. His safety net, should something unexpected happen, he thought, recalling their frugal cross-county runs not too long ago. He glanced at his watch, noting he spent a few more seconds than planned, then snagged a large towel from a nearby linen closet. He was almost too late in shutting the water off before the tub overflowed. The drain had clogged with dirt and hair, and he reached down to clear it when Snickers drenched him with dog-shake.

"Glad to see you too!"

Mallory Du Rennes cleared his throat to speak when Anastasia spun around to face a cocked pistol lowered on her from twenty meters away. It was one of several arms aimed at the gathering by men in plain clothes and tactical eyeglasses.

Patrick looked to Du Rennes. He could disarm them before the first round fired, no problem, except Du Rennes shook his head negatively as his hands raised.

A tall blond man emerged from behind a covered position. He was dressed in green camo Air Force fatigues emblazoned with a blue spearhead on the shoulders. Mallory Du Rennes was familiar with all American military insignia, including the famous red spearhead and dagger. Although these were similar, and he assumed these were special operators of some sort, the blue intrigued as much as it disquieted. There was an uncomfortable silence for several moments as the group appraised their assailants.

"Is it customary to greet your guests in such a manner?" Du Rennes asked.

"Tell your people in the jet to come out. Unarmed, of course." The blond gestured.

Du Rennes complied, motioning for Gérard, who slowly descended the airstairs with balled fists and a crack of the neck.

"There now," said Du Rennes with a tone. "We are all here. You are at a disadvantage however, a... Colonel, I can see by your uniform—"

"The pilots? Any other crew?" The colonel asked.

"At the FBO," replied Du Rennes.

"We are not here to do battle with you, sir, but we will bring a considerable hurt upon your group if there's any attempt to flee."

Du Rennes paused for a moment, glanced at Patrick and shook his head again. Patrick itched to disarm them. Nervous energy coursed his vascular system, and the aura of it warped the air around him. The colonel felt the twinge in the air as something amiss. Du Rennes cocked his head and raised a brow towards him.

"Anastasia!" Du Rennes called.

"He speaks the truth," she replied.

The colonel signaled his detachment to lower their weapons, which they did in synchronous precision, yet their fingers remained on the triggers. This was a detail of which Jet Sun and Dao took note.

"My name is Colonel Osterhoudt. We have much to discuss and little time to accomplish it."

"Well before you begin your discussion, Colonel, you should know that I am acquainted with your jurisdiction in domestic affairs, as this appears to be," said Du Rennes.

The colonel pursed his lips in a near stutter. "Sir, we both know I'm not worried about jurisdictional repercussions should something go wrong. We're here because something already *has* gone wrong, and I believe we also both know what something is, or rather someone. Am I far off?"

"Continue."

"I'll skip to the meat. An acceptable balance has been disrupted."

"Acceptable?" Jet Sun stood forward, noticing the infinitesimal movements of several trigger fingers.

Du Rennes acknowledged Sun's lead. "Acceptable to you; never to us, Colonel."

"Be that as it may, I believe we seek a common enemy—two, in fact, or should I call them... competitors?"

Ninel Zabroskov was midway through a cup of black caravan when his left trouser pocket vibrated. He carefully set the cup down and made eye contact with his strongman in the corner, fixated with every movement outside the window. Zabroskov opened his phone and read the encrypted text, then glanced back at the corner with a nod. The trunk exhaled and mashed his smoke into the tray, careful to extinguish it fully. He slipped his coat on and checked the hallway door. The house was empty, as was the street below. Zabroskov locked the front entry's deadbolt and hopped down the stairs to the sidewalk below. Their car was parked almost a block away at a common lot off California Street.

Two embassy houses to the west, the trunk recognized his squirrel from the night before as it skittered across their path. At that moment, the squirrel froze, made an odd, chirping grunt, then panicked in the direction from which it came. The trunk sensed a rush of air immediately to his rear and reacted by lunging his upper torso towards his right. He felt the sharp sting of heat penetrate his left trapezius. Wincing, the Trunk had already taken grip on his silenced Makarov, pivoting it underneath his left armpit while holstered and spat two rounds at his attacker. It was over in that moment.

Ninel Zabroskov turned around in horror and disbelief, grabbing his bodyguard's elbow so that he could not continue firing. La Brochette collapsed onto the sidewalk grasping at the hole that perforated his throat, blood spurting between his fingers. The first time in years he wished to say something to his brother, and he couldn't. He managed a maniacal smile with crazed eyes—something only his brother could interpret—as his muscles faded. He collapsed onto the sidewalk, limp, his eyes darting around in panic until they froze, and the spits of blood at his throat ceased. Ninel screamed and drew his pistol onto the left eye socket of his guard, who was breathing heavily in pain and similar disbelief.

"*ZACHEM?*" He screamed, confused.

Zabroskov held the pistol on him for several moments, realizing that it made no sense. He fired two shots in the air in a rage, cursing the sky. The trunk was merely protecting himself, and pained to remove the stiletto from his shoulder, only making a slight wince as the blade slid out. Blood soaked the strongman's jacket by this point. Reality crept. Bystanders soon materialized. Calls would be made to emergency services. This was unavoidable. A young man in a suit rushed over, making assessments and assumptions. He saw drawn weapons and started to ease back, phone in hand, when the bloody stiletto struck. Zabroskov was quick to suffocate his screams for help as the man faded. They must leave before any others made their description. Perhaps that was too late, Zabroskov thought. Embassy windows everywhere. This was a highly-protected enclave. The police would be there in seconds, probability dictated.

The trunk lifted Zabroskov to his feet, then hoisted his brother's corpse over his right shoulder. At first, they went in the direction of the California Street parking lot. Nearby patrol sirens activated. A block or two away by the sound of them, thought Zabroskov. The colonel and his guard knew they couldn't make it. He remembered the protocols and drills for precisely this sort of situation. *Get off the street, get moving!* The Range Rover parked in the next driveway would have to do. The trunk smashed the passenger's window, setting off an alarm. He unlocked the vehicle and threw the body in the rear seat. Zabroskov climbed in the driver's side and withdrew a master FOB, part of his travel kit—not standard issue—that read the vehicle's awaiting signal and hacked the matching code. The agitated bodyguard climbed into the front passenger's seat as the vehicle started. The sirens were close. They backed out and bolted for Connecticut Avenue, then south to Dupont Circle to blend into traffic. By this time, several of the embassy buildings on Wyoming Avenue spilled onlookers onto the sidewalks. Calls to 911 were made, reporting two bodies and two armed men on the loose. One of them was a former detective from the Macedonian Embassy several doors down. He noticed that a squirrel had wandered into the pool of blood created by La Brochette's neck wound, leaving paw prints down the sidewalk that disappeared in front of a middle-eastern embassy, near an elder oak.

Zabroskov collected himself—usually cold and calculating—but this development... Why would his brother suddenly turn, let alone try to murder them? Obviously, it was betrayal from their new friend. What could they possibly say or do to trigger it? *Trigger... hmmm,* Ninel thought. There were triggers employed by his Bratva, yet he was not aware of any implanted on him or his brother. The thought occurred that no Bratva member knew but the highest level—so plausible denial could occur. No sleeper ever knew they were a sleeper. He was given assurances at the top level that they weren't in fact sleepers, nor was his bodyguard. That's the only way they could have triggered La Brochette, he thought. *Betrayal!* He reasoned there were maybe three officials who knew the keywords to any particular agent, and that's if his brother was activated in the first place. Could this priest somehow access it? Did someone accept a bribe for it? He wondered. *It was impossible! Or was it?* The only other explanation was that his brother was either turned or some-how compromised. He had been trained in both scenarios. Nonetheless, his brother tried to assassinate them, and with-out explanation, not that he could. *Triggers...* He squirreled away a few of his own.

Academic, perhaps, as he sighed and dialed the Go Number. A transatlantic-capable jet would be waiting for them at the end of Cockpit Court—a jet center at Dulles—one of the few remaining charter flight facilities around D.C. that allowed private vehicles onto the ramp. This was legal, provided a Customs screener was present, and as it happened, the screener on duty was a privateer for the last fourteen years, earning the right of succession by favors and tributes, as had been customary since the early 1960s. Their stolen Range Rover would be disposed of in the usual fashion at one of the maintenance hangars overnight. Until then, it would be parked and covered in the privately assigned long-term parking lot as not to draw undue attention.

Zabroskov's jet would make two legs on its way to Pulkovo in St. Petersburg. By internal mandate, his brother would be cremated. Ninel would see to his brother's wish—that he'll be fed to the fishes of the Neva River. The thought of becoming recycled caviar amused him. His brother never argued his brother's choice.

On the flight home, he quaffed two shots of vodka and opened up to his bodyguard.

"He showed us his old graduation video but a year ago. The one where he said 'anything', even if it included me, his brother."

The trunk nodded. "You recall. I said no. *He* said no. This is what our brother tells us. Lies."

Ninel Zabroskov also said no, then he realized the video was a fake. They had his voice. They had his likeness, then and now. The evil depths of his new friend's reach—the Spada Sacra. Eliminate the assassins when their work is done; they are never trustworthy. They work for money and power, not ideals. These are their ideals.

Ninel looked up as his trunk of a comrade and torched a fresh cigarette. *The squirrel wasn't real, either.*

Zabroskov and his smoke stack would part ways in secluded semi-retirement as consultants. Their identities were scrubbed along with their private fortunes and eventual domiciles. It was the only way to ensure the concealment and survival of Krug Vlasti—the Circle of Power—a group of ten men, never more, who comprise the top echelon of all Bratva, the military, and the government, as it had been since the death of Stalin. Zabroskov could not possibly allow the death of his brother to go unavenged. Someone triggered him, and he had his suspicions. After kissing the cheeks of his undefeatable protector, wishing him better health, he set about planning his own disappearance.

G-Forces

"Lieutenant Rose Diaz?" A towering voice from behind her workstation interrupted the reading of additional reports that just dropped from the Coast Guard at Cape Charles regarding Jupiter's Bolt and its cursory technical assessment. She turned around to the two security escorts who, to her relief, had their side arms holstered.

"General Howard wants you in the DIA Tank... right now."

Her voicemails tendered on Osterhoudt's behalf were apparently received. She logged off, picked up her portfolio and followed the escorts to the Defense Intelligence Agency's Counterintelligence wing where she was handed off to the sentry on duty. He scrutinized her ID, confirmed facial recognition, and buzzed the door open. Another sentry escorted her through the reception area towards a conference room where most of its chairs were occupied with conversations concerning Jupiter's Bolt, sonic booms over Cairo, and sketchy reports of a commando incursion in southern France. When Diaz appeared at the entrance, the room hushed and several heads turned her direction. A louder voice from the end cut through the residual conversations.

"Lieutenant Diaz, please have a seat. We have much to discuss and time is our paramount consideration." Then he raised it. "Which we will all be mindful of in determining our next course of action."

Her chair was next to Brig. General Howard, Commander of AFOIS. The other seats were occupied by his counterparts at NCIS, CID, and another by the CIA's and FBI's liaisons.

Conversations and contentions continued, and the room's volume increased to an intolerable cacophony. Nobody seemed interested in Diaz's assessments. Instead, most of them quibbled over the inevitable political fallout and which bastions of power would be exposed. Diaz sensed she was at the bottom of a kicked anthill, except the ants were confused and misled. Finally, to her astonishment, it was the FBI's Critical Incident Response Group (CIRG) point man who pierced the noise.

"General Howard, I am aware that your Agent Diaz possesses additional information? Critical information, correct?"

"Yes," he responded with a cocked head.

"Gentlemen, be that our time is crucial, I move to hear her update immediately without objection."

The room fell silent as Diaz prepared herself, noticing the dozen or so cameras around the room, and the several monitors conferencing directors of several intelligence departments, including the FBI's SIOC command center, abuzz with activity in the background. She noticed the large green digital clock on its forward wall which read 0726. She scanned the bullets on her tablet and cleared her throat, acutely conscious of the discriminating eyes upon her. Diaz's brief lasted an excruciating fourteen minutes due to constant and barbed queries, the last coming from the FBI.

"Where is Colonel Osterhoudt now?"

● ● ●

"Outrage!" Du Rennes exploded. "How can you minimize these illegal, immoral factions as—*mon Dieu!*—'competitors'?

This is singularly the most naïve gesture I have to date witnessed. These are not *competitors* to any one government or belief, Colonel; they are the cancer that prohibits the exponential advances of our planet—in knowledge, technology... our faiths and our love for each other. They are the progenitors of divisive stagnation and greed. *Competitors...* an insult!"

"We won't see eye-to-eye on some points, *Monsieur Du Rennes*, is it? Where are the others?"

Du Rennes grew further annoyed. "What others? I am not sure of whom you speak."

"Really? Commander Jacobson, Doctor Miller... No idea, huh?"

A voice echoed from behind a shipping palate at the far end of the hangar.

"I see some familiar faces."

Osterhoudt twitched in recognition.

"Shoot him! Shoot him NOW, Matt!" Chris yelled.

Matthew's laser sight illuminated several hairs at the back of Osterhoudt's fresh buzz cut, just a couple inches above the base of the skull. The colonel slowly turned and caught its red glow reflecting upon his cheekbones, steady and imposing. Matthew waited for an excuse.

"Well, Commander, you certainly could if you wanted to. Dead to rights."

One of Osterhoudt's men raised his rifle and swung it towards Matthew.

"NO!" Yelled Du Rennes.

Before the soldier placed an eye against his sites, the rifle, and its magazine, exploded in his face, lacerating and blinding him in one instant. Two soldiers gasped in shock and began to raise their own rifles, then threw their hands off as the heat built. Rocco stepped forward, and his was their last vignetted vision before striking the ground. Osterhoudt twisted around in complete astonishment. Tomlinson and her predecessors rumored the special people; pet projects, she called them. He was armed and helpless, he thought, releasing the grip on his pistol then hearing it rattle upon the concrete.

"Your call, Commander," he said.

Matthew kept the laser on his neck as he, Chris, River, Abe and Snickers made their way into the hangar, keeping a prudent distance from potential acts of bravado.

One of Matt's former teammates cautiously placed their rifle on the floor. "Hey brother. Didn't want it like this. Hope you understand."

"Oh yeah, I know. Job to do. That's the mission, and we don't fail, right?"

Another set his rifle on the concrete and kept his hands visible, nodding.

Matthew kept his focus on Osterhoudt and a couple of the known wildcards. "You should all have your hearts examined."

"Huh?" mumbled the first teammate as another beside him flinched as he jerked his rifle sight towards Matt and Chris.

A tearing crack of air burst across the room, striking the rifle. The soldier screamed and threw it away from his grasp, forgetting that it was strapped to his torso. It snapped back and the barrel jabbed his thigh. He doubled over in pain, unable to quell the thousands of invisible needles suddenly injecting his bones. Osterhoudt wasn't exactly sure what he just witnessed, but it was enough for him to signal the others to deescalate. Matt kept his laser trained on Osterhoudt's neck, unwavering.

Du Rennes motioned to Patrick, who stepped back.

"You cannot take further action upon us, Colonel. You were warned."

"Matthew," the second operator turned as he continued watching his teammate writhe in agony, "What did you mean by that? Hearts examined..."

"Literally." Matt replied with a dry tone as he reached into a pocket and withdrew his bagged, exploded key and threw it at Osterhoudt's feet.

The colonel bent down and picked it up, examining it with a wrinkled frown.

"You gonna tell me you had nothing to do with that, Colonel?" Matthew gritted.

"What is that?" The operator asked.

"Insurance," replied Matthew. "You do what they say or they pull your plug."

"Colonel?" The operator trembled.

"They don't tell us who," he said. "Until it's necessary. And not everyone has it. Only the soloists, and not all of them."

"You?" The operator asked.

"No."

"Well that just cuts it for me then." The soldier started to remove his belt.

"Stop!" Osterhoudt yelled. "You all signed."

"For this? These phantom chest pains I've been having? Hell no!"

"To protect this county, and that means especially now, sergeant."

"Wait, you have them too? I just thought it was the strong coffee or something," said another operator two steps back.

"Who controls this? ...makes the decisions, I mean. Who holds the keys?"

"Tomlinson, and she's off the reservation" Osterhoudt admitted.

"So any of us could've popped... and you *knew* about it?"

"Risk we had to take." Osterhoudt said with an iced inflection. "More reliable than a cyanide cap."

"Jesus H Christ!" said the soldier.

Du Rennes spoke with sharp tone. "We can take care of those for you gentlemen, except not at this time, I am afraid. We have other matters pressing... if you do not mind."

"Yes, in fact I do mind, and Osterhoudt, you get these goddamned things outta here or I'm—" The operator demanded.

"There's nothing I can do about them right now. This is the mission, Lieutenant."

"God DAMN it!" He yelled. "Anything else we should know?"

The teammate carefully stepped in front of Matt's barrel—the weapon's laser twinkling upon his chest. "Could take you without that."

"Try it." Matthew said jocularly with a cold, confident glare as he lowered the pistol and they embraced.

"GAH! You stank of wet dog, bro!" He squinted. "So, who are these people? What the hell's going on? And what the *hell* is up with that guy next to the Frenchman?"

Matt sighed. "Long story. Some of them have er... special skillsets. We'll catch up on that soon enough."

The hangar was alight with standing discussions, some heated. Osterhoudt explained what happened at the Pentagon with the Russians, and that he was ordered to terminate the mission at Bonneville, which included Matthew's capture or disappearance, and without the team's knowledge.

"And for the record I missed on purpose," Osterhoudt said. "Had to look legit or they'd know."

He detailed the intercept of AFOIS intelligence on the sailboat, and the investigation into General Tomlinson's office. That's when he became 100% certain the Russians spared her for a reason. Not only had they infiltrated Blue Ops, they were in part control of it.

"They executed General Tutlow and his right hand, Colonel Doddler, to make way for bitch Tomlinson—who couldn't care one iota about the Code. I traced those Russians to a cathedral here. St. Michael's—a few blocks off the Mall. Place felt off when I looked around. No Russians though... poof."

"Excuse-a me," said Monsignor Trovarto. "You searched downstairs in the cellar?"

"Yeah, we went down there. One wide hallway with a couple chambers off each side. Storage mainly. Not much else going on."

The monsignor rolled his eyes. "You are dealing with the Spada Sacra, Colonel. Nothing is ever as it seems."

Trovarto went on to briefly explain the origins of Spada Sacra and that the Church is unaware of its existence. Osterhoudt relayed his experiences with the few clandestine organizations struggling for the implementations of power and knowledge—those he had encountered with his time in Blue Ops. Competitors, as he saw them. Trovarto explained what happened at the Cairo conference, their escape, the help from Du Rennes in France, and their voyage across the Atlantic in Du Rennes' yacht.

"Nice boat, by the way," quipped Osterhoudt with a side glance. "Sad part is, we all know you just set a transatlantic record. You know you just donated it to the United States Government, right?"

"What's left of it, you mean," said Du Rennes. "It is our intention to eventually license much of the technology through our registered patents."

"*Right.*" Osterhoudt turned to Chris. "So, he's got your daughter, he wants the laptop, and probably you. Or, he wants all of you gone. Either way, not going to happen."

Patrick flinched, about to lunge.

Osterhoudt raised his hands. "What I meant to say was... he can't accomplish his goal."

"And what are you to do that would stop us?" Du Rennes asked.

"Not you; *him.*"

"Whatever it may be, it's 7:31, and ETA to Roosevelt Island is 18 minutes."

"I…" River interrupted. "…have an idea."

● ● ●

"Unsure how much goddamn time this phone has before it's rooted, Ron?" General Tomlinson squeezed the satellite handset tightly. "Do we have the people or not?"

"On paper, but you know as well as I that it will change in execution. If everyone does their job, no problem. If not, I hope you have friends—good friends."

"Like you?"

"Hardly."

Ron extinguished the line and dragged his Pall Mall Blue to the filter, which penalized his greed with an acrid bite and phlegm-pocked cough. Not a soul glanced his direction as the overcooked butt disappeared amongst so many others strewn upon the graffitied sidewalks adjacent Rome's rail terminal. He checked the clock on his phone as he crossed the street and entered, making his way through the checkpoints towards his connectors bound for Sarajevo. There, he had a new passport and conveyance waiting for the final leg to a small hamlet in a lush valley just southeast of Pristina, Kosovo.

● ● ●

"Sir, emergency signal from Colonel Osterhoudt."

"Well, read it Lieutenant!" Barked General Howard.

"Light the Tower, Roosevelt Island Twenty-hundred hours."

The commanders across from Howard erupted in discussion. FBI's CIRG paused to stare at their conference screens as their representative pounded for order.

"General Howard, I need to know if you trust him before making the call you know I have to make next."

Howard scanned the room at the expectant expressions around him and upon the monitors. He turned towards Agent Diaz as well, helpless, cornered. She nodded confidently, then Howard reclined in his seat.

"No choice as I see it. ROLL."

CIRG flew into hyperspace. FBI's SWAT were scrambled, knowing their response time would push 8 o'clock.

"Ten miles." He set the standard cursory perimeter lockdown. All flights would be held from Reagan and Dulles. The air over DC belonged to Joint Base Andrews. In two formations, four fully fueled F-16s—every hardpoint pod occupied with air-to-air and air-to-surface missiles—lit afterburners and flew a rotating perimeter.

The President was reached within the Residence, casually showering off the day's politics, and it would be another six minutes before he graced the White House's West Wing basement in a bathrobe over trousers. The National Security Advisor had just been briefed when the elevator doors slid open, as was Homeland. The Joint Chiefs were scattered across town and their aides were feverishly dialing. The Chief of Staff was also mashing a screen, executing the protocols of a standard local security drill. Assets, locations, status. Chatter at the table crescendoed as the technical logistics ran their course.

19:57:00.

"Sir, nothing confirmed. DC 911 reports two calls claiming a low-flying craft on the Potomac at the Georgetown Harbor."

Ten blocks away? the President thought. *Embarrassing!* "Where's SWAT?" He asked.

"Four minutes out, sir."

And unacceptable!

"I am declaring this a classified National Security Threat under extraordinary circumstances as defined in the US Code. Highest order, and granting authorization for capture warrants. Let's see what the Data Center can pull."

Within moments, the NSA's command activated clandestine links to all facial recognition outlets, including social networks, traffic cameras, networked security cameras, public and private, ATMs, cameras on connected vehicles, and the front and rear facing cameras of cell phones within the targeted DC Metro area.

● ● ●

Osterhoudt and his best operator piloted a darkened passenger van out of Reagan National, northbound on George Washington Memorial. Chris, Dao, Jet Sun, River, Abe, Monsignor Trovarto, Patrick and two additional operators occupied the rear. Du Rennes remained behind with Rocco, Anastasia, Gérard, and several of Osterhoudt's remaining squad.

"We don't have much time. Don't forget what I said. After the device is in his hands, under no circumstances can he take Dao and Chris together. None. Zero. Got that?"

The air conditioner was blasting frost, yet it did little to compensate for the body heat and anxiety. Chris was sweaty, trembling. Dao felt it, although anxious herself.

Jet Sun reached into her mind. *It will pass in minutes, one way or another. Remember expectations. Prepare your thoughts. Think of each possible scenario. Run it. Execute. That is it.*

Impossible. I cannot conceive each alternative.

Correct, therefore you must prepare for the unexpected, if that becomes the case.

Abe whispered to his father from the row behind. "What did he say?"

River spoke with a sonorous tone. "To prepare for the unexpected so as not to be surprised or anxious."

Abe smiled. The others turned around towards River, including Jet Sun. A simultaneous thought echoed within each, as if spoken by someone, yet not. Simply, understood.

Point made.

"I had hoped to one day learn that little trick, Sun."

"Wait..." Chris interjected. "That was—"

"Yes," said Sun.

Osterhoudt and his men remained stoic, fixated on the windows. He turned to Matt with a cocked expression. "Something I should know?"

"Speaks for itself, doesn't it?" Matt smarted.

"Apparently not," replied the colonel.

"You didn't hear it?"

"What?"

"Never mind." Matt turned around towards Jet Sun. "Selective?"

Jet Sun smiled and echoed for River. "You are already practiced in quieting—the reduction of noise. Telepathy is not as uncommon or incredible as believed."

"For the experienced, I suppose never." Chris said.

"We all have this ability, and we are not as special as you might falsely deduce, Doctor Miller. Think of it this way—it is what everyone has but cannot access. Telepaths either stumble on it by accident, or as children, innately knew. We see and hear beyond the noise of everyday life. It is a focus issue in essence. Similar in ways to gravity. It is all around us and we live with it every day. Our minds knew it was there from the very beginning. The earth spins at several thousand miles per hour, yet all of us are perfectly at home with this fact because it is *natural.* We tune out the effects, become accustomed to the reality. To us, telepathy is no different. It is merely a trained focus. This focus is upon an area of your mind that you either forgot or never accessed. It is typically the young who accept the gift and develop it. As a neural scientist, you appreciate the limitations of mature plasticity. Old dogs..."

Not true, River smiled.

Dao Ming turned towards him. "Did you just—"

Golden Hour breezes across the Potomac and sparkled its waters as the northbound van cleared some congestion at the I-395 interchange. They barely took notice of the Pentagon's grounds to their left, obscured by summer foliage of Lyndon Johnson's Memorial Grove on Columbia Island. Ahead was the marble-arched underpass at the Arlington Memorial Bridge, then another congested interchange at I-66, immediately followed by the parking lot access for Theodore Roosevelt Island.

What was the worst? Chris thought, focusing on his daughter—her laughter, her tears, her fragile embraces. Losing her is the worst. His work, his friends... Mattered, yes, but nothing compared to Emily. The thought was clear as crystal. Never again would he place opportunity, work, or country ahead of her. What mattered more than his own blood? Until the pressure was self-evident within his temples, he hadn't realized how hard his teeth were gritting. Dao held his hand.

Although sirens and other alarms were heard in the distance, when Osterhoudt made the hairpin right into the Roosevelt Island, he saw none of the expected federal support.

In fact, he saw none at all, only the average daily compliment of park-goers hawking empty parking spaces, sparse joggers, cyclists, and other visitors returning from the island. Osterhoudt parked as close to the island's pedestrian bridge as he could and checked his watch. Two minutes to spare.

One of the joggers who had been stretching behind his car took notice of the first operator to exit the van—his suppressed, automatic rifle dangling from its straps. When the second climbed out, he stumbled while fumbling for his hatchback's keys. Another visitor rounded the corner from the footbridge in a huff, warning others that a black helicopter had just landed at the memorial. When she saw those two armed operators, she froze. They motioned her through, and she reluctantly passed them by, cowering. By now, several remaining visitors were streaming across the footbridge. Arlington County's emergency operators were busy fielding calls about the helicopter. The sirens were growing exponentially louder—a multitude of them—and now echoing from several directions. Chris and the others piled out of the van. He held onto the laptop case, knowing it represented his daughter's freedom. Osterhoudt checked his watch and gave the hand sign to approach the bridge. One of his operators remained behind, taking position at the ramped entrance to the bridge to thwart any unwanted company.

The bridge itself was over 500ft long and 10ft wide. A kill box as far as Osterhoudt and Matt were concerned. They walked at a deliberately methodical pace, checking flanks and the river for hidden watercraft. There were none. At 200ft, Osterhoudt stopped. A jogger appeared at the other end of the bridge, approaching their direction, too engrossed with his earpieces to notice or care about any others on the bridge so long as his path was clear. Just as he passed, the sound of distressed tires on pavement shrieked across the water from the parking lot. Arlington's cars stopped short of the park entrance to make way for FBI's SWAT who were less than a minute away. Matt suddenly noticed the wash of jet noise as two F-16s overflew them. One thought kept hammering his concentration.

The most powerful country on earth, and at the center of its power, we are vulnerable. How?

Two armed Spada Sacra operators secured the immediate area outside their helicopter, then ran sweeps. An exasperated, wheezing jogger at the edge of the woods brandished a cell phone in front of him, presumably recording or streaming video. With two spits from a flanking operator's suppressed rifle, the jogger's skull exploded. Another parkgoer screamed and bolted down the trail towards the exiting footbridge. Several moments passed before the crackle of the pilot's voice gave the all-clear. Bishop Esposito exited the hissing aircraft with Emily clutching his hand. They ducked to a distance just beyond the silenced, rotating blades.

Esposito turned and knelt before her, eye-to-eye. "Remember your training, and most of all remember this, child. Your father will tell you exactly what you want to hear—that he loves you, misses you, and wants you to come home. He will use your feelings against you. He will insist that it was his fault for leaving you, and that you are blameless. That is what all guilty people do, Emily, tell you exactly what you want to hear."

This was Cardinal Tagliabue's favorite and most effective gambit, lovingly bestowed upon young Esposito at a similar age and manner to Emily's—the emotional affirmation fallacy. When the eventual truth follows his prediction—one manipulated for the desired outcome—his argument must be valid.

"I don't want to see my father; I want to stay with you!"

"We shall see if you are worthy of me, child, but first, you must face him. That is your test. How might I trust you, otherwise? See for yourself, then make your decision. I will not stop you."

Esposito rose to instruct his operators and the pilot. He took Emily's hand and ushered her down the pea gravel path towards the bridge. Emily's tears glistened in the soft orange light permeating the thick woods encircling the memorial trail. The gravel raked and shifted underneath her feet as she shuffled alongside the bishop, overtaken with emotion. When they turned the final corner before the bridge, Emily's eyes started to dry. At a distance of half a football field, her father turned towards them.

Esposito stopped and kneeled once more. "Go to him now."

Emily fought to conceal a sniffle as she passed behind him. The bishop nodded towards one of his operators who concealed himself in the woods. A faint laser danced around Emily's lower spine, visible only to those behind her. Emily was ten paces away from him when she heard the bishop's voice just behind and to the side of her.

"Halt!" he said. "Doctor Miller, you will yield the device to Emily, and she will return it to me. If it is indeed the particle reader, your daughter will be free to return. If it is not—"

Dao suddenly caught a reflection of the laser pointed at Emily. "Chris, WAIT!" She yelled from several yards behind him.

"Dao Ming," said Esposito, leaning on the northern handrail. "Or, should I say *Dao Sun Shí,* apprentice daughter of Master Jet Sun. Is that your father I see, hiding as usual in the shadows? Your Tribe of Ten has been shrinking, or haven't you noticed?"

"Chris, he is going to kill her or take her. There is a weapon aimed at her back. She is in danger." Dao turned to Esposito. "Ramelan is dead!"

"He is very much alive, I can assure you, and he reported everything he knew to me—as he has throughout his reign. He works for us. They all work for us... One way or another, you know. If they do not work for us, they die by us." The amethyst jewel atop his cane glittered as he clutched it at the middle, pointing it as his eyes suggestively shifted to the river below. A rectangular wooden container floated towards them on the north side of the bridge.

"Daniel and Linda Huang of Edmonton, Canada. Maybe nobody to you, or everybody to your father. Why not ask him."

Dao turned around huffing and bull-faced. Jet Sun's expression was enough, if not for the voice ringing their true identity in her ear. There was an insignia on the container in Chinese. He knew what it meant. She wanted to leap, the tigress as she was trained, yet she knew a trap when she saw it.

The container bobbed in the current as it passed beneath them.

"Interesting story they told me about the ocean's secrets."

Jet Sun recognized one of the ancient anecdotes as key to the Trove's location. Esposito was close. All he needed was their piece. "It's okay Emily, go ahead."

Dao turned back around in desperation as Emily approached. Chris could barely contain his emotions, confused by her attire, and the manner in which she walked. Something was off about it. It wasn't her usual gate. She was different. He grew nervous and bent down to receive her, arms outstretched. She did not enter his embrace, however, stopping a few feet short, hand outstretched, anticipating the laptop case. Her expression was cold, distant.

"What are you doing? Come here." He cried.

Emily said nothing, keeping her arm extended.

"What did he say to you? That I don't love you or something? That it was my fault for leaving you? That I really didn't care? It's a LIE, Monkey…"

In her periphery, Emily caught a glimpse of River and Two Feathers. *Speaking of lies!*

"Don't call me that," said Emily. "We need the case."

"We? What's this, *we*? He *kidnapped* you, remember? I want you home where you belong... with me!" He handed the laptop case to her.

"She is more important to you than me." Emily's eyes pointed to Dao. "You love her... not mom, and not me!"

"Lies!" Chris yelled as she turned to deliver the case to the bishop.

"You are the liar, not me."

Chris' expression of utter hatred towards Esposito negated the intended one for his daughter.

"Chris!" Dao ran forward to whisper in his ear. The spark of a ricochet lit the concrete before her feet. She froze. "Chris, it was pointed at her."

Emily turned towards her and, with her right hand, demonstrated a deadly and secretive Dim Mak sequence only Dao or Jet Sun would recognize. The move shocked Dao, who gasped. Only a select few shaolin masters knew of it, let alone perform it to such a degree. The sequence was perfect and would kill its victim instantaneously.

Deafening concussions shook the bridge as jacketed lead scored their way across it, striking the armored vest of Spada Sacra's hidden rifleman. Several spits were returned, striking the trees behind Jet Sun. The crack of several combat rifles erupted from positions taken by the FBI along the Potomac's western banks, adjacent the north and south sides of Roosevelt Island's footbridge. Chris panicked and fell to the concrete, cowing. Dao Ming made a running leap and, as the spit of a suppressed rifle flashed from the other end of the bridge, dove headfirst over the south handrail into the river.

"DAO!" Chris screamed.

The gunfire suddenly tailed off, Esposito and Emily kept their stance low and retreated to the island's interior. When they disappeared into the trees, the shooting stopped. Chris and Jet Sun stood over the rail, searching for Dao. A rush of air bent the treetops as the twin jet helicopter rose over them, angling for the river just short of Dao's position. More shots erupted from the riverbanks, several striking the side of the helicopter, which suddenly dove towards the water. As it did, its five rotor blades retracted to a singular position aligned towards the rotorless, vector-nozzled tail. The aircraft splashed into the river just in front of Dao and the Huang's casket, disappearing into the murk beneath her. The ensuing waves capsized the wood box, which slammed Dao's head underneath the surface. She felt a burst of warmth as the aircraft passed underneath—its exhaust bubbles affecting her buoyancy. She struggled to stay afloat, head throbbing, worsened by the kicks she was forced to make. Chris, Jet Sun and Matt were unsure if the helicopter crashed or if they just witnessed something impossible. Bubbles and the faint shimmer of lights shimmered deep beneath the surface, shifting from to the right side of the river, then towards the left several moments later. It never reappeared on the surface, however.

In that moment, Chris' mind fractured with the worst possible thoughts. His daughter crashed and drowned, mislead by a lie. Maybe she was in the woods, alive. The tears welled then broke from Chris' eyelids. He sobbed and cursed, alternating between sorrow and the void of rage as the helicopter's lights disappeared within a low-hanging fog downriver. Monsignor Trovarto stood behind him, dour. He felt Chris' anguish. They all felt it. The burden of it all.

"I didn't ask to make the discovery." Chris shook his fist to the sky. "I didn't ask for any of this! Nobody deserves this—to be crucified—to endure this. My daughter gone, and worse, she hates me. My life is destroyed. My friends destroyed. Your truth, Father, this *Fratellanza*—worth my life? My daughter's life? Their lives? I can't take it!"

"Where the suffering of-a man is concerned, it is a calling, Christopher. You have been called. We have been called.

There cannot-a be a greater calling than the service to His truth—the truth of all mankind.

"And how did she move like that? What was that?" Chris yelled.

Jet Sun frantically scanned the water for his daughter. "Only one way. Time compression virtual reality," said Trovarto.

"What?" Chris blurted.

"We thought it was a rumor. Impossible. Someone like-a you touted it on the internet as a science breakthrough some years ago. We had to investigate it. Our operator disappeared along with his page. Ghosted within three hours. We simply cannot be everywhere at-a every time."

Alarms blared and voices cracked over the ripples from federal megaphones. Chris' head whistled in stress, as if from years of tinnitus—a ringing that wouldn't cease. The moment was out of control. He had little idea what just happened, and desperately scanned the river for Dao. Several FBI SWAT held rifles on them, ordering them to the ground with hands on their heads. Two officers bolted past them into the woods, radios cackling. Blue and red lights strobed the trees as they disappeared.

"Commander Jacobson, lower your weapon!" One of the forward SWAT members shouted over a bullhorn.

"Doctor Miller, we have instructions to take you and your party into custody." A tactical officer's rifle bounced at Chris' chest from a meter away. "Commander Jacobson, your C.O. is just over there."

Jet Sun maintained concentration down the river, breathing relief when Dao emerged, fighting to refill her lungs, clutching the container and kicking it towards a beach under the I-66 bridge. She had just moments before agents would intercept her as well, and in those moments, she unlatched the container to find the fresh corpses of the Huangs grotesquely broken and arranged so that they both fit. Dao reeled in disgust while digesting the significance of this act.

The President sat at the end of the Situation Room's conference table, stoically assessing the expressions upon each of those also seated at the table. When they turned towards him to make some sort of statement or leadership directive, he did nothing, uncharacteristically presuming one of them would offer some sort of an explanation or clarification momentarily.

His National Security Advisor broke with, "They're saying it may be amphibious, heading south, but no confirmation. The F-16s can't see it, and our one boat off Haynes Point hasn't detected anything either."

The President stared blankly ahead. *My God, it was only ten blocks away.*

"Why do I get the feeling you two know each other."

"You are an engineer, which means you are also a mathematician." Jet Sun's eyes rolled. "Which also means you understand the probability, or I should say improbability, that two people from a country of 1.3 billion would know each other." Jet Sun turned towards him.

Chris folded his arms. "I just know that look. It's the look a father makes when his daughter does something crazy."

"The look that is also upon *your* face, Doctor Miller."

"I've lost her, haven't I? Never had a chance to explain why I left, or about Dao."

"Emily is under the spell of evil, Doctor Miller. Forgive her disposition." Jet Sun looked squarely into Chris' eyes. "My daughter also knew Emily was in danger. A hidden rifle at her back."

Chris skipped a breath. *Probability.*

"Emily did not know," said Jet Sun. "The evil of her captor would have been exposed, otherwise."

*   *   *

The submarine helicopter's digital windows all but removed the charcoal opaque of the Potomac's depths. The pilot flew as if there was no river at all, careful to track within the channel walls just above, avoiding the larger fish, debris, and communications lines. The channels themselves were barely deep enough to conceal the wake turbulence generated by the craft. Emily's pupils were fully dilated at the unnatural views, yet it felt somewhat familiar to her, as if she was wearing the VR helmet. The helicopter was capable of 28 knots under the surface. 25 was the pilot's comfort level. Their run would take 40 minutes to reach the planned destination—a sheltered, private pier in Pomonkey Creek.

On arrival, the helicopter surfaced and held position at a small dock while Esposito, Emily and the two Spada Sacra operators departed. The pilot had instructions to scuttle the aircraft further up the creek's inlet. A conveyance was waiting at the end of the pier for the four-minute ride to an outlying hangar at Maryland Airport. It housed a fast light jet, ready to make a short jump to Marsh Harbor on Great Abaco Island in the Bahamas.

●   ●   ●

"Sir, a flight has been cleared to depart Maryland to the Bahamas. Diplomatic Clearance Number checks."

"Cleared by who?" Snapped the National Security Director. "I wanna know who issued the number and why!"

The President's Chief of Staff had already dialed the State Department for verification. By the time he connected and spoke to the Secretary, the flight was 22 nautical miles outside of U.S. airspace. The Secretary could not confirm the validity of the clearance other than to say "If it made it past all the checkpoints, it either must be valid, or all the checkers are foreign agents."

The FBI would learn later that the DCN was forged and inserted by hack, including all the necessary intercepts needed for verification. The President placed a national security classification on the file, concealing it from the press and saving his Secretary the indignity of public inquiry.

Could happen to anyone.

Esposito's jet landed in the breezy darkness of Marsh Harbor an hour and thirteen minutes later, where it was tugged into a non-descript hangar towards the west end—one of the few surviving structures of a recent hurricane. The bishop, Emily and the two operators produced fresh Spanish passports, jumped into an awaiting long-range jet, and departed under a flight plan bound for Rome. The Commonwealth saw no reason to delay the departure for the Americans since it wasn't heading there, nor was the US listed as its point of origin. This decision would lead to Bahamas' Ambassador being summoned to U.S. State Department in order to reevaluate and enhance their intelligence agreements, as well as preexisting military support roles.

The flight disappeared from radar over the Mediterranean's Toro Canyon, about 50 kilometers south of Sardinia, and it was declared missing after two hours. Italy's Guardia Costiera—continuously besieged with floating migrant deathtraps—managed one of its 10-meter rigid inflatables out of Cagliari for a speed pass to look for debris. The patrol returned within a few hours, fruitless.

Emily's matted eyes cracked to the sunlight reflecting off the cerulean waves. She hadn't realized she fell asleep, nested within the supple bosom of reclined leather until the flaps motor jarred a turbulent decent. Across the aisle, Esposito smiled.

Emily stared out the window as the sea suddenly became green pastures dotted with stone. The wheels barked as the turbines fluctuated. The reverse thrusters activated along with heavy braking to stop the jet midway along Runway 26, Pantelleria—an island trapped in history, once bombed to oblivion by the Allies, or so they believed. The aircraft swung right then circled left to reverse course on the same runway, taxiing towards the airport's south end where the pilot brought them inside one of two underground aircraft bunkers —relics of WWII. Several cassocked ground crew and tactically-outfitted Spada Sacra surrounded the jet. One of them secured the descended airstairs, and the bishop followed Emily and the two operators down. Esposito took Emily by the hand once more and led her towards the back of the hangar through a set of thick concrete blast doors. There was a long hallway that seemed to descend as they walked, and they passed several doors to each side until they reached an elevator at the end. Esposito withdrew a key from his cassock and inserted it into the elevator's control panel while pressing the bottom-most button and holding it down. The doors closed, and Emily was startled by the rapid decent, causing her to grab a handrail. The elevator suddenly stopped and shifted to a sideways motion that continued to build. Clearly, they were accelerating, yet she heard no cables or wheels—nothing.

"Where—" Emily's curiosity couldn't be helped.

"Narciso smiled. Come, I have much to show you."

The car's acceleration leveled off, and it felt as though they were floating, oblivious to the magnetic tracks coursing through a tunnel under partial vacuum. Within moments Emily felt the opposite effect. The car seemed to undergo heavy braking, yet it didn't make the slightest sound. A small bump signaled the end as the doors slide open.

Emily stepped out to a vast cavern with a flat, open floor. Part of it was a parking lot lined with innumerable vehicles and equipment. Beyond that, she could not discern. Its ceiling must have been 50 stories, and its walls transitioned between stone and elevated walkways traversing glass façades for spacious living quarters. The air was cool, yet dry, and the indirect luminescence felt natural and penetrating, as if outside on an overcast day, except Emily could not locate the source of the light, which conflicted her senses.

"Where are we?" Emily asked.

"Home, child."

Daughter of the Winds

"Interesting week you had, Doctor Miller."

Chris' body jolted in a momentary haze, feeling sluggish, drugged. His mind reset to the reality. He fought for last memories, which came slowly. The bridge, the helicopter, Dao, soldiers... *soldiers!* Rifles were pointed at him. He climbed into a van with River, Abe, Jet Sun, Trovarto, and Patrick. He heard a loud hiss of rushing air, then someone screamed. That was the last memory before the black tunnel. This must be a dream. Another bad dream in a series of nightmares—that his anxieties were getting the better of him. He concentrated on waking up, and couldn't. An agent snapped his fingers just in front of Chris' face. The vision became clearer still. Chris knew this moment was coming. He saw it a dozen times in other nightmares, naps, and daytime blurs. The vision was ever-present it seemed. Problem being that he saw himself as the victim and the victor. He always slept on the right side of virtue, so he believed. His father continually preached it, and his voice now resonated to a point that nothing else could be heard. *Make any decision you want, so long as it's the right one.*

Miller was alone in a blank white room, except for a one-way window and a suited man with a federal ID seated across an empty table, his deodorant and starch locked in battle by the smell of him.

"Curious. What made you decide to run?" He asked. "At what point did you—a renowned biomechanical engineer from Silicon Valley—determine, 'Okay, screw it, the government can't be trusted, and worse, it's inept!' When did you lose faith in your country, Doctor Miller? You remember us, right? First to the moon? Why'd you run?"

Chris let the silence speak for a few moments before his jaws oscillated. His father's voice remained, echoing from ear to ear.

"Wait... where am I? Where are the others? Where's Doctor Ming?"

"In due time, Doctor Miller. We are more interested in why you decided to evade us. At what point did you come to this decision?"

"The point where one of you took a shot at my little girl." He snarled. "Which was preceded and followed by multiple demonstrations of systemic government failure to protect us. They were quicker than you. They were more prepared than you. They were part of you."

"So... you're blaming us."

"Not precisely. Speak to Commander Jacobson. He was with me the entire time—advised in most circumstances. Correctly, I might add!"

"We'll get to the Commander. Let's start at the beginning. I need to know what happened at Amerimem."

"I am confused, and I need an attorney."

"Why?"

"Because I do not know my limitations on disclosure with regards to certain facts about the incident that involves our company projects—trade secrets."

"We have total clearance here, the kind where compartments are irrelevant. Trade secrets? I'm not a competitor, Doctor Miller, and this is not a public inquiry."

"How would I know? You could tell me anything?"

"Trust issues, doc. We are on the same side here."

"Excuse me, agent..." Chris examined his badge. "...Williams, but given what I've just gone through, you might understand why I don't trust any of you! Is it that much of a stretch?"

"Nope. Where does that land us, though?" The agent stood up and stretched. "You fled the scene of a mass shooting at your employer."

"We were invaded, shot at, and chased!"

"Your house burned shortly after that. Arson suspected. Two unidentified sets of remains recovered. A neighbor identified you fleeing the scene."

"Armed men were in our house!"

"Evidence and witness accounts suggest you were also at the scene of a triple homicide a block away."

"What have you done with Snickers?"

"He's in a holding facility downstairs."

"I want him."

"We're a long way from that, Doctor Miller. Witnesses identified you and your daughter at a pier in San Francisco, and a day later on Alcatraz by a park ranger. A car was stolen from a parking garage across the street from the cruise boats at Pier 33. Security camera popped Jacobson and a soggy $20 note. Seriously doc, of all the vehicles... an orange Aztek?" The agent huffed.

Emily, Chris thought. When they were together. The pain returned. "Wasn't my choice."

"Why didn't you call for help, Doctor Miller?"

"I tried!"

"Oh? When?"

"At my house... after Amerimem. Lines were dead. That's when..."

"What?"

"When Matthew shot the first guy."

"Then what?"

"I don't know! It's a blur. We felt as though they weren't going to leave us alone until we were dead and they had the..."

"The what... laptop?"

Chris stopped and faced the agent, perplexed. "So, you know about it."

"After what was found at Amerimem, and Rebecca Morningwood's briefing, yes."

"She okay?"

"No. Like you, she's terrified and doesn't trust our protection."

"I never said that!"

"But you don't trust us."

"I didn't say that, either. I said *part* of you. Are you listening?"

Chris turned to the window, as did the agent.

"Doctor Miller, you must realize we are required to vigorously interrogate everyone. Consider it from our perspective; a trail of carnage that spans the entire globe. You fled the country with a device that was scheduled for a classified military demonstration, Doctor Miller."

"What demonstration? Jack Kattner never told me about it."

The agent ignored him and continued. "The moment that occurred, the devices, knowledge of them, and especially their creators, became a national security concern. You not only misappropriated the device, to use soft language, you fled with it to a foreign nation and shared its technology with hundreds of foreign nationals. You're a logical man, doctor, you tell me why this isn't international espionage."

"Plausible ignorance."

Agent Williams laughed.

Chris' expression turned dower. Self-defense was not his forte, and he knew it. His thoughts coalesced with time and careful consideration. Some accused him of being a slow thinker. In fact, his mind was overflowing with alternatives and their consequences. Decisions never came easy let alone quickly.

"Lawyer. Now."

"Doctor Miller, we're trying to help you, and to help you, we need every detail."

"Lawyer."

"Doctor Miller, at this point I need to inform you that you will be held as a co-conspirator under Title 18 United States Code, Chapter 37. We have a 72-hour window to interrogate you and your friends before formal arrest and grand jury proceedings. You can talk to us now, or talk to us later, but you *are* going to talk to us."

The agent glanced at the one-way window on his way out. Chris felt the retching build in his stomach—the burn and queasiness any time a disastrously poor decision's consequences became apparent. He knew he should have contacted the police immediately. Jacobson convinced him otherwise. He should have tried harder. His mind was burning with the replays of missed opportunities. He *did* try, many times. He began to second-guess his new friend's role. He had only known him for several days. How could he possibly be a judge of character so soon? A double-agent? *They shot at him, too,* he thought, except his friend, Adriel—the contractor—is missing, not dead.

Oh, this is bad.

● ● ●

When news of the detainments crackled in the radios of Osterhoudt's airport squad, Du Rennes twisted the top of his communications obelisk and pinched both sides for print identification. He spoke several sentences into it before the unit responded with a burst of heat and smoke. He tossed it upon the ground to watch it dissolve into a black liquid that solidified as a small blotch of blank material.

"What was that?" One of Osterhoudt's men demanded.

Du Rennes turned to Gérard, Anastasia and Rocco with a winked eye. Anastasia nodded, taking a step away from her brother. Rocco closed his eyes, and the air tingled with a burnt electrical aroma as it sizzled between him and the six operators. Their last thoughts were of helplessness and confusion as their bodies fell limp upon the floor. This occurred in the last second before their eyelids fell too.

"Okay, Uncle," said Anastasia. "Why?"

"We are leaving," announced Du Rennes. "And they cannot come with us."

Gérard tossed the go-bags off the jet and strapped one to his back, motioning Rocco to take the other.

"Where?" Anastasia asked.

"To collect the others."

Rocco turned around towards Du Rennes. "So, we are going to leave them... here... with your jet?"

"It is not my jet."

● ● ●

The door to Chris' interrogation room swung open to an older, fleshy suit who wore bifocals and a thick mustache. He carried two paper cups of coffee in one hand and an assortment of pastries in the other.

"Doctor Miller, I am Agent Thompson, and before appearances deceive you, I am *not* the good cop. This is merely insurance against the possible effects of hypoglycemia, which your medical record indicates you are an infrequent sufferer."

"Wait, you—"

"Yes, of course. We are required to know everything about you in these situations. Does that seem logical to you?"

"I suppose," Chris said flatly as he accepted a cup. "I still want a lawyer, Agent Thompson."

"Well, here's the thing, Doctor Miller—and I hope you understand—we're working against the clock. We believe your daughter is on a flight towards Rome, and there's little diplomatic recourse for us at this point unless it's deemed a security emergency. She could be lost, otherwise. We must act without delay."

"What do you mean, *lost*?"

Agent Thompson adjusted his glasses. "I mean, we can't work with Italy on this unless there's a very good reason. That reason rests with your machine. We need to know what it does."

"Didn't Rebecca tell you?"

"Not exactly. She only said it was a laptop these people were after. Iced up after that."

"Wait, I thought the Air Force knew what it did. My boss, Jack Kattner, was at the Pentagon to give a presentation when they took him. Wasn't there a file on it?"

"Only the name of it—Iris."

"Iris?" Chris' tone escalated. "He named my discovery *Iris*?"

Agent Thompson glanced at the window. "Kattner's body was recovered in the woods on Roosevelt Island after the helicopter disappeared. Since our team arrived after you did, we cannot confirm or excuse any relation. I hope you understand."

Chris glared at him. "Unbelievable! So we're pegged for Jack too."

"No, Doctor Miller, we cannot relax until your story is corroborated. Look, I'm trying to help everyone here. Please, assist us. What was on the laptop that was so important?"

Chris stalled, also glaring at the window. He was compromised and he knew it. His mind transitioned to Emily and the reverberations of her scowling. How could he get her back even if he was given another opportunity? He must first *have* that opportunity. He'd cross that bridge later. He began worrying about Dao, River and the others. What would become of them? Would he see them again?

"Doctor Miller?" The agent checked.

"Where are my friends? Where is Dao Ming? Is she alive? When will I see her?"

"Honestly?" Thompson paused. "I don't know. They are being interrogated, same as you. There's also the business of embassies—two Chinese nationals, an Italian and an Irishman."

"So Doctor Ming *is* okay?"

"Expected to recover, yes."

Chris sighed, closing his eyes. Agent Thompson checked his watch and then the window... again.

"It's not what's *on* the laptop; it's what it *does*." Chris said in a calm tone.

"Pardon?" asked Thompson.

"It's a reader."

"Iris is a reader... of what?"

"Stop calling it that!" Chris yelled.

"What? Iris?"

"Yes!"

"Doctor Miller, unfortunately Kattner's name stuck and my bosses aren't about to go changing all the file headers. Sorry."

"Whatever," Chris moaned. "Anyway, this is where you need to have an open mind about my laptop, Agent Thompson."

"Okay, I'm listening." Thompson glanced out the window.

"A couple weeks ago during a procedure, myself and Commander Jacobson stumbled upon a process where nanoscopic electrochemical charges residing upon airborne particulates can be registered, recorded, and, well, rendered."

The expression upon Agent Thompson's face made it apparent he was struggling. Chris attempted to demystify his neonatal technology and, within a few minutes, Thompson achieved a rudimentary understanding.

"Okay, I get it, except why is the Air Force interested?" Thompson asked.

"Jack believed that if particles could be read by the machine, on some level, they were potentially responsible for influencing our dreams and other subconscious thoughts. He also made an overt reference to paranormal activity. The Air Force became involved when he offhandedly mentioned a potential to charge these particles with whatever vision a programmer wanted. The medical and social possibilities are endless, but Jack had other ideas. You see where it could be weaponized. I don't wish to become the Oppenheimer of neuroscience."

● ● ●

A blackened limousine van appeared at Hangar 5's aircraft doorway within twelve minutes of Du Rennes' signal. A suited man remained in the driver's seat while the van's motorized doors slid open.

"Our conveyance," said Du Rennes.

The man never spoke as the doors closed behind them. He placed the van into gear and made for the gated exit on the south side of Reagan National. The driver produced a card at the gate which activated its doors. Rocco made a hand gesture to Du Rennes.

"Relax Rocco; we are going to see a friend."

The driver skillfully navigated through DC traffic towards the west and eventually to a pastoral road south of Bluemont, Virginia. He continued a few miles south before turning onto a manned gate guarding a private drive that disappeared up a steep hillside. At the top, a modern western log cabin compound lay surrounded by dense forest of mature red spruce and white pines dotted with cedar. The chauffeur stopped the van under its covered valet, jumped out and activated the side doors. Once everyone was on the ground, another suited and wired sentry escorted them inside. They were quickly seated in a casual great room in front of a stacked river stone fireplace that rose thirty feet to the planked and beamed cathedral ceiling's apex. Du Rennes remained standing.

"This is the second time you've signaled me in forty-two years, Monsieur Du Rennes, and in doing so, I hope you respect our arrangement after the first." A silver-haired man with blue eyes in a ruby smoking jacket and white trousers spoke from a hallway off to the side. He approached them slowly with a stuttered gait, not quite a limp.

"Gérard." Du Rennes called. "A bag."

"Oh, no no *no*, monsieur. You brought two bags with you, and that is my price."

"You would leave me with nothing? I cannot," quipped Du Rennes, flaring his nostrils. It was part of the game and he knew it—a show of strength for the others.

"It is unlike you to appear so pathetic, Mallory."

"I have lost two of my jets in one week, and my house was raided and destroyed—my father and my butler killed. How is it do you think I should react?"

"My God!" The man gasped. "You shall want for nothing, Mallory. That is our service, and I am so very sorry about your father, but this *is* the price. Why else would you bring two cases if you didn't anticipate it."

Gérard looked to Du Rennes, who appeared predictably annoyed for several moments then acquiesced in a disgusted nod.

"Well then, you didn't put up much of a fight, Mallory. Whatever is it this time, it must be dreadfully horrible."

Du Rennes smiled. "You will be earning those bags, Charles. There is no question." He turned to the servant. "I *must* have a cigarette."

The butler returned shortly with a small assortment of premium smokes, and Du Rennes settled on a Parliament. The servant lit a wooden match and bent down for Du Rennes to fire it. He took a deep draw and exhaled, then proceeded to relay his intensions. The briefing lasted several minutes, after which Charles seemed flustered.

"Understandable why you didn't argue over the price, Mallory, yet I found myself longing for one of your famous cavillations. The French do it so well. Ah, no matter. You folks wait here. Make yourselves at home. I need to place a couple calls, naturally. You need anything, just ask for it."

Charles and one of his servants left the room and disappeared down a hallway. The other servant trapesed into the kitchen to start preparations for a scheduled meal.

"Uncle Mallory," said Rocco, "Who is he?"

"An old friend. We used to trade favors, now it is strictly professional. He works for whoever pays his price. He cares not who it is. This was a problem for me. The bastard often takes contracts for my opposition. Not knowingly, of course. This is the way he works."

"How could you trust a man like this?"

"I do not, which makes it less complicated. We both know what will happen if we disrespect our agreements." Du Rennes stared at his cigarette's ash as it methodically grew from the sequential incendiary reactions taking place on the microscopic level. "What is inevitable is but a mere function of time."

• • •

River heard the voice and it comforted him. Apparently, they were not as far removed from each other as he had feared. He worried about his son, and for Dao, as he meditated in the lotus position. He concentrated his energy on it, pinpointing the waves of emanation and the resonating location within his own mind, focusing in that area, attempting to respond. He was close, he could feel it, yet the voice continued unabated.

We are apart, yet together. Truth is beacon, so speak the truth as you know it; the way home will illuminate.

The native innately knew his son Abe was not in danger. For the others, it was difficult. That is, until he heard Jet Sun's advice. He fell into a trance, searching for the others. He felt distracted, tense. It would take time to reach his grassy hills and crisp spring breezes, but he could smell it, and he was drawing closer by the strength of that fragrance. The more he inhaled, the focus intensified.

Closer still, Chief Isshiihách kate Bilinnée Áashe of the Crow.

River's eyes strained in determination.

My people once communicated such as this, openly. Millions upon millions extinguished in the unspeakable Great Sorrow, forbidden from our history lessons under penalty of death. Population controls. If the herbal knowledge and lifestyle practices were commonplace, such imbalance would cause extinction within 200 years. It must remain a secret known only to those willing to protect the balance of life. Those who once escaped it met destiny on the island called Rapa Nui—Easter Island—around the common year 500. They started a cult of ageless ones, a collective of elder educated, but vile and corrupt—arrogant with resources. They built countless monuments to themselves so as to not be forgotten. This, after being consumed by their starved offspring who stoked the fires of their familial ovens.

Tears formed at the corners of River's eyes. His temples panged as sharply as if stabbed by the tips of his finest knives—then twisted.

Speak only the truth.

It was the final thought received before his lungs finally let go.

"Long ago, the Spada Sacra named it Perla Nera," said Esposito with a tone of reverential pride. "It is yours to explore for the next few months as you develop. As I told you, magnificent wonders are ahead, my child. What would have taken decades, you will learn in one year. Your schooling, including advanced classes—sciences, culture, language, history, strategy, combat and weapons tactics—will be accomplished in that time. You will know more than adults double your age. It will be fun, I promise. You will make many friends as your confidence grows. We are an unstoppable force, older than any government on earth, and you will be part of it."

Emily gazed at the towering metal, glass, and stone. Its lights shimmered with activity—a city unto itself. She held onto Narciso's hand tightly as they toured each of the facility's main areas, and squeezed tighter when they passed adult-sized operators; all of whom saluted with the Sign of the

Sword, which was the first half of the sign of the cross, except all four fingers were straight and together.

When they arrived at the dojo, Emily remarked that it looked exactly like the one in the VR helmet. Other areas were similarly recalled, and she suddenly understood what had been taking place all along. It was as if she no longer needed the tour; she innately knew most of the locations—how the dorms rooms appeared and how they were outfitted. The hallways, showering facilities, and the classrooms, as well. In VR, the gaming fields, sports tracks, wooded combat zones, and dilapidated villages were all digitally manufactured, she deduced. Emily became particularly impressed with the bunker's military hardware, enough to outfit several teams for any number of clandestine missions. Everything she experienced in the game suddenly became real, which brought a chilling effect that Narciso sensed.

"Our flight was long and tiring, dear Emily. I suppose you would like to have a bath, change into some comfortable clothes and enjoy a decent meal. Our cucina employs a particularly fine chef who will confect anything you desire."

"Anything?"

Narciso smiled, tugged at her hand, and began walking towards the other side of the complex. Emily caught a familiar face along the way. Abbess Regina was leading a small convent of young, habited nuns who must have been in their teens, Emily thought. It was an odd sight to her because a few years ago, as children often mused, Emily proclaimed her desire to be a nun, enamored with the sacred order and their clothing. Her mother responded with knowledge and biting logic, conveying the years-long process and devotion hopefuls endured before earning a habit—that they must swear off boys, and that she would often miss some of her favorite activities and friends. What would her mother think of her now? Spada Sacra gave her a sense of divine purpose; she was suddenly above the common plane—a hero for God.

• • •

Agent Thompson returned with two additional men. These were not agents, Chris quickly determined, since the language of physics dotted their queries. Once they ascertained Chris' full technical overview of the laptop, they cordially thanked him and departed. Thompson secured the door just behind them, remaining inside.

"Have to deliver some instructions you're probably not going to appreciate Doctor Miller."

"It's not as though I have options." Chris lamented.

"Until this is resolved, you will be a guest of the United States government, pending further legal examination and national security implications."

"I'm an incarcerated criminal, you mean."

"No. Well, not exactly," said Thompson. "It may go differently, Doctor Miller, please understand that part. My guess is that you will be cleared of espionage charges so long as you cooperate with DARPA to determine potential military applications of Iris. Looking further, if there *are* military implications, DARPA will require the remission of all research from you, Doctor Ming, and every scrap remaining at Amerimem. I am instructed to remind you that this is all the result of your research, and your actions. I know you won't like it, but that's where we are."

Chris took a deep breath. "I just want my daughter back."

"And, we are doing everything in our power to make that happen. It's just that—" Thompson paused, catching himself. "I know this is difficult, Doctor Miller."

Thompson heard his director's instructions repeat in his head. *His daughter is not the priority here; just keep him hopeful so he'll cooperate. You know the drill.*

"The Pentagon is in damage control right now. It's quite a mess. Traitors, moles, Russian infiltration... and particularly that helicopter. I'm told the President has been pounding the Hayes desk non-stop. He wants answers."

"We can't have *that*, can we." Chris sneered.

Thompson escorted Chris to the outside hallway where another agent awaited. The agents maintained tactical stances—one forward, the other behind—as they ascended several elevators and traversed several lengthy hallways until they arrived at a secured enclave of apartments. Thompson swiped his key card at a terminal several doors down the last corridor and opened the door, ushering them inside. Another man had been waiting inside, hulking near an armchair beside the bed.

"Special Agent Ayers has your security detail for the next shift. Anything you need, ask him. Shower's back there," pointed Agent Thompson. "Don't worry, Kyle won't get aroused unless you do something stupid. Please don't forget we're on the same side, Doctor. Consider what your government *should* be doing with the cards you dealt."

Thompson's phone vibrated as he secured the door with a PIN code. He checked at the Caller ID and answered with a curt acknowledgment.

"I don't understand. What happened?"

Thompson's perplexed expression grew to frustration as he hung up, traipsing back to the suite's door and reentering his PIN. Ayers shrugged and stood out of the way. The door unlatched and he entered. Chris was already in the restroom preparing for a shower. Thompson knocked.

"I thought you were supposed to knock, Agent Ayers." Chris yelled from the other side.

"It's Thompson. Make it quick, you're being moved."

• • •

Charles returned clutching a thick envelope and set of keys. He maintained an iced stare as he sat beside Du Rennes on the couch in front of the dormant fireplace. He did not immediately let go of the items when Du Rennes hands pulled away.

"I don't suspect we'll see each other again, Mallory, so let me savor this moment."

Du Rennes squinted.

"Standard kit: clean passports, two bank cards, and... I must apologize dear friend, but your competitor paid me considerably more."

Charles produced a silenced Walther in his other hand, aimed at Du Rennes head. Gérard reached for a hidden blade inside his beltline when a muzzle dug into his spine at the same moment an arm viced tightly around his neck. Struggling meant death.

Du Rennes let go of the envelope. "This is outrageous, Charles, even for *you.*"

"I am set to retire, and I thank you for expediting it."

"Who is it this time? The Spaniard? CIA?"

"Nobody you'd know, Mallory."

"I must insist. You owe me that, you bastard!"

"Alright. Can't see how it'd hurt." Charles took a step back, careful his aim remained lethal. "Local skirt who earned stardom wearing blue."

"No names, as usual, is it?"

"Afraid not, *monsieur.*"

Anastasia sensed the emotional directive from Charles just as his fingers began to tighten around the pistol.

"ROCCO!" She screamed.

The pistol fell out of Charles' hand before his eyes closed on their way to meet the edge of the glass coffee table. Two spits of the sentry's weapon blew gaping holes through Gérard's abdomen and chest. As he grunted and dropped, Gérard planted his tang blade deep into the servant's inner thigh. He shrieked and blasted another shot wildly through Gérard's jaw before turning on the others. Rocco pored his concentration upon him, and the surrounding air singed with charged particles, creating telltale vapor trails. The muzzle flashed once more as the man collapsed on top of Gérard, spared the agony of a slow, painful death as his femoral pulsed.

Anastasia's heart skipped when she turned towards Du Rennes. She sensed his fear and confusion as he coughed—gasping for air, unable to breathe through the bullet hole, centered just below the larynx. As his eyes bulged, he pointed to the envelope and motioned for them to escape. He fought to utter one last syllable as he fell sideways onto the couch cushions, but could not conjure enough air to pass his vocal cords.

"UNCLE!" Anastasia focused on his lips as she ran to his side, reaching for the gurgling hole at the base of his throat to stop the bleeding. Du Rennes' trachea was obliterated, however, and she felt his soul slip away in dire anguish—the most terrible sensation she had yet to experience. It was if her own had been clawed away by frozen daggers and shattered upon a cragged coastline being savaged by torrential seas. A terrible retching welled within her as tears dripped off her cheeks. Rocco jumped to her side and yanked her arms away. He knew danger remained. There were at least two more sentries within the complex.

"We are not alone, and we must leave. Now!" Rocco yelled.

"Cannot." Anastasia wept. "Bags."

"What?"

"It was the last thing he said. Bags."

A weak moan came from the other side of the coffee table. Rocco leapt across it and kicked the pistol from Charles' hand. The man's eyes cracked open as he staggered to gain consciousness. His forehead was gashed deeply and dripping. He felt around it as the blood pooled into his eyes. He touched the ripped flesh and winced, coming to terms with his situation. Rocco picked up the pistol, drew its hammer back, and aimed at Charles' skull. His fingers tightened on the grip. Charles' breathing became erratic; Anastasia sensed his venomous effluent, except she also sensed something else and turned towards the kitchen's throughway. Rocco saw her wince as he spun around, leveling the pistol at the dark mass.

"Wait!" A man screamed and displayed his empty hands as he stepped forward.

Rocco maintained focus on him, and for movement behind, while keeping Charles in his periphery. "Come no closer, please."

The butler complied, maintaining his hands in view. "Look, we all just want to get through this and come out alive, okay?"

Anastasia sensed his honesty and motioned acknowledgement to Rocco using a system of facial expressions they developed as adolescents. Rocco called it "the read", and the read was verified as far as he was concerned. The read could also change without warning, he knew, having experienced abrupt, impulsive shifts.

"Not *all* of you," said Rocco—his eyes glanced at the dead sentry.

"So, what are we to do?" The butler asked.

Anastasia suddenly noticed the envelope beside Du Rennes corpse. She reached over and picked it up, inspecting the contents. Blank sticky note pads, yet the keys to the van looked authentic. She showed them to Rocco.

"Where are our bags?" Rocco asked, noticing Charles wheeze before coughing.

The butler looked at Charles, anticipating instructions, and Charles rolled his eyes. Anastasia sensed the deception and communicated it to Rocco with two curt smirks on the right side of her mouth.

"The safe in his office. I will get them," said the butler.

The pistol's round was unexpected and swift, shattering the bone and muscle of Charles' right shin. He groaned loudly, wincing in pain.

"This is what will happen..." Rocco spoke with a deliberate tone and pace. "You and my sister will return with the two bags, fully intact as they were upon arrival. Anything removed or added will result in a bullet to this man's skull, followed by one to yours."

Anastasia collected the dead sentry's pistol, racking the slide to ensure a round was chambered. The butler turned around, keeping his hands in view as paced towards the library's safe with her pistol aimed at his back. She kept her distance even though she sensed no imminent danger. The library's safe, as it turned out, was actually a walk-in vault, obscured by a shelf of unjacketed Janes catalogues and the like—meant to demonstrate the perception of Charles' erudition more than substantiating it. Charles hadn't cracked any of his library's covers in over twenty years, even though he insisted their refreshment on an annual basis.

Charles winced. "You won't make it past the gate, boy. And, even if you did, I will find you. Bet on it."

"A pathetic and impotent threat, Mr. Charles." Rocco reaffirmed his grip on the pistol.

"How can you be so confident?

"When you awaken, you will not remember us or our presence in your house. You will not recall how you were injured, why your servant is dead, or whose blood is on the sofa. You will not recall anything beyond yesterday."

Charles grimaced in disbelief as his eyelids fell.

The butler and Anastasia returned from the library, each toting a duffel. Anastasia gazed upon Mallory Du Rennes body in shock. His frozen eyes and the scent of blood sickened her in sporadic convulsions. She dropped the bag, sat beside him and tearfully closed his eyes, whispering a silent prayer.

"Check his pockets," said Rocco.

She frowned as if robbing a grave while reaching into his coat. Her hand withdrew his money clip, a pen, and his passport. She reached into his other pocket and found it empty except for a blank scrap of paper. It was almost out of her hands when Rocco intervened.

"Take it. Leave nothing!"

Rocco then turned towards the butler.

"WAIT!" The butler screamed, pointing towards a hidden surveillance camera.

It took Rocco several moments to locate the tiny black dot within the fireplace stonework's grout a couple feet above the mantle. He sighed and turned back towards the butler.

"He records everything in the house—every conversation," the butler said, gesturing around the room towards other hidden cameras. "The recorder is in the library, and all files are instantly mirrored on a cloud. You must delete all files or he will know what happened."

"Why are you helping us?" Anastasia asked.

The butler pointed towards a small protrusion towards the back of his neck. "I have been in the service of Charles much too long, and quitting is not an option. I have the passwords to the cloud."

"He will know someone with access deleted them."

"Yes, and one of us is now dead, so I have one favor to ask after you... do whatever it is you do. Place the gun that killed Monsieur Du Rennes in my hand so it appears that I was defending Charles."

The butler returned to the library with a pistol aimed at his spine. He stood behind Charles' desk, accessed the surveillance system, deactivated it and erased all recordings starting just before Du Rennes made initial contact. He also erased and deactivated all system access records. There would be no record of Du Rennes' presence except for their bodies, creating a distractive puzzle for the authorities after an anonymous tip.

As Anastasia and the butler returned to the great room, the butler started to say something just before dropping to the floor, unconscious. Rocco stood over him, concentrating intently for several moments, just as he did to Charles. Although the butler's eyes were wincing and dodging about as if in a deep REM state, there was no pain associated with the procedure. He would awaken restrained in an infirmary after several hours—groggy, and straining to produce a memory no longer in existence—an empty hole one must accept over time as dead space.

Rocco and Anastasia lifted one bag each over their shoulders, said their goodbyes to Uncle Mallory, then proceeded to the valet.

"How can we leave him there like that?" Anastasia cried.

Rocco stolidly continued towards the van, opened a side door, and dropped the duffel just behind the front seats. He reached for Anastasia's bag and placed it next to the other. "His blood is all over that couch, Tulip. Taking him with us creates additional problems."

They climbed into the front seats. Rocco tapped the ignition and they sped off down the winding driveway towards the front entrance. As they reached the gate, Rocco lowered his window. The sentry was already on the 2-way attempting to reach the residence.

"Trouble," Anastasia muttered.

The truck sat idling for several uncomfortable seconds until the guard slowly lowered his radio and reached for his rifle.

The crack and singe of air came swiftly. The guard fell limp within his station. Rocco continued to wipe his mind of their existence. While doing so, he climbed out of the van and collected the rifle, an extra magazine, and other useful implements the sentry would later fail to explain. Rocco activated the gate and jumped back into the van, throwing the weapon and other items on top of the duffels. He jammed the van in gear and calmly motored to the end of the drive and made a right, heading south towards Interstate 66.

"Where are we going?" Anastasia checked the van's GPS mapping.

Rocco glanced over. "Back to Washington. We need another car, you think?"

"Yes."

They sped south then southeast until they noticed a couple used dealerships off the side of the road, choked with gravel dust and adorned with faded hand-painted signs. The gravel crushed under the weight of the van as they searched for signs of life. Nothing. A&M's sales office was dark and dead. Rocco pulled around a common right-of-way and entered the RobAutoz lot, where two men stood chatting just off the mobile office's front porch steps. Upon noticing the van, they broke off the conversation. One remained by the porch making careful assessments of the van and its drivers. He was athletically-built, pepper-haired, and wore thick glasses. The other, a portly man in his late forties, stepped away towards an opening in a split-rail fence that separated the two car lots.

After a cursory glance around the diminutive lot, Rocco opened his door and climbed out.

"Which is it?" The salesman asked.

"Pardon?" Rocco asked, his accent apparent.

The man smiled and walked towards him. "Well, you're obviously from out-of-town, and you haven't looked at my inventory more than a half-second, so I figure either you stopped for directions or you already know which car you want and came to buy it. Am I wrong?"

"Not precisely."

"How can I help you?"

"We need a car."

"Something the matter with you van?" The salesman peered over Rocco's shoulder, trying to see past the windshield's glare.

"The van is the problem."

"Oh." The salesman paused with an expression of confusion. "You wanna trade; is that it?"

"Not precisely."

"Well, you must excuse me young man. I'm slightly per-plexed here. What is it you intend to do with that van, then?"

"The important question is will you sell us a car?"

"Wouldn't be much of a car salesman if I couldn't."

"Wonderful."

Rocco audited the lot once more. There were less than two dozen available vehicles. Half were SUVs and pickup trucks, the others were an odd assortment of sports, luxury, and a couple classics.

"What about that one over there—the silver one?" Rocco asked.

"The Chevy?"

"Yes, I always wanted to drive one of those big American cars."

"1986 Caprice Classic. Got a 305 V8 with a 2-barrel, and crushed royal blue velour interior. Fine shape considering the mileage."

"Fine. We'll take it."

"Don't you want to test drive it first?"

"You said it was in fine shape just now."

"Well, yes, but most…"

"Rocco looked through the car's driver-side window."

"We just need to be on our way."

The salesman scratched his head. "Don't you even want to know the price first?"

"How much could it be?" Rocco asked.

"$12,500." He stuttered. "Cash."

Rocco wrinkled his brow, assuming the price was inflated beyond reason. The salesman wasn't finished testing the limits of his leverage.

"To a normal customer, that's our price, but for you, young man, the price will be higher."

"Why is that?"

"First of all, are you even old enough to legally buy a car in the state of Virginia? You don't look much over fifteen, if that. Secondly, you roll up in a $150,000 van telling me you need rid of it. Is it stolen?"

"Not precisely."

While they were speaking, the portly owner of the car lot next door eased his way back through the dividing gate, exhibiting a noticeable bulge under his untucked polo at the beltline. Anastasia sensed his approach and demeanor—a mixture of fear and greed. Rocco sensed her concern.

"Well, no matter. Far as I reckon, the van isn't so much a problem as letting you ride off in one of my cars. Something happens, it comes back to me, understand?"

"Yes, I understand," said Rocco. "And I have heard of you famous American car salesmen. It is the same in every country. I do not care what happens to the van. It does not belong to us. We need a car to drive to DC, that is all. This Chevrolet can make a one-hour trip, yes?"

"Bet my life on it."

"Then what do you require?"

After the salesman spoke, Rocco held up two fingers to Anastasia. She reached around her seat, unzipped one of the duffel bags and withdrew two mustard-banded stacks of U.S. dollars, zipping the case closed before hopping out of the vehicle. Rocco stepped over and retrieved the cash, holding onto it as he plodded back to the salesman, who couldn't take his eyes off them.

"You folks come and have a seat while I print up a temporary tag."

Rocco motioned once more to Anastasia as he approached. She opened the sliding side door, where he unzipped the bags, placed the weapons inside and threw one of them over his shoulder. Anastasia labored to do the same with her bag, grunting as it settled behind her back, straps tight against her chest. They climbed onto the porch and through the trailer's door, setting the bags down to their side, taking a seat on a couple generic plastic chairs, one of which had a significant crack on a front corner. Rocco turned around to close the door just behind him when the other salesman stepped through and closed it. Rocco thanked him and took a seat.

The proud owner of RobAutoz opened a file drawer and produced a Virginia State paper tag and its accompanying registration form. He placed it on the desk in front of him along with the keys to the Caprice.

"The cash?" He asked.

Rocco placed the bundles and the van's keys on the desk while the man made a cold stare towards the other salesman. Anastasia couldn't comment fast enough before the subtle metallic click came.

"Now let me tell y'all fine folks what's going to happen."

Rocco turned around to find a long-barreled revolver at his back. "Is this what you Americans call highway robbery?"

The salesman continued. "No kid, this is a leveraged negotiation, and you and your little sister here are highly leveraged right about now."

"Obviously." Rocco grinned.

Anastasia's sensations grew stronger. She knew something was about to occur, but she didn't know precisely what. She felt no sense of malice, only anxiety and avarice.

"You and your sister will be leaving here in my car."

"*Your* car," Rocco interrupted.

"My car, right. I'm not selling it to someone who can't buy, let alone insure it." The salesman marked the tag thirty days out and placed the keys and a screwdriver on top of it. "You've got one hour after you leave here before I report it as stolen, too. That ought to be enough time for you to make DC."

Rocco sat back in his seat; eyes rolled.

"You'll be leavin' them bags here, too," said the gun-wielding salesman with a chilled drawl.

The expression on Rocco's face went dour and cross. "Greedy bastards!"

Anastasia felt the telltale electrical pinches ramping towards full discharge. The air singed and crackled a moment before Marcel the Salesman dropped on the floor, wracked in muscular contortion. Anastasia gasped. It wasn't what she expected, and it was a grotesque venting of anger. Bones began cracking. The dealer reached into a drawer for his weapon, and that's where his hand stayed before the long black tunnel closed before him.

Robert Holman of RobAutoz reopened his eyes two hours later upon hearing the muffled groans of his brother, Marcel. He wasn't sure what happened, assuming he fell asleep at the desk—something that occurred frequently after he turned 58, succumbing to the summer drone of air conditioning and cheap gin. Something was off though—a nag in his mind. He glanced down upon the desk and found his brother's pistol on top of a note written in an unfamiliar script. He unfolded it and discovered a single $100 bill.

> *Thanks for the rental of your fine auto. You will find it parked near the Pentagon Metro station. Your brother will be fine.*
> *~ Leveraged Negotiator*

The FBI located Charles' van several hours later, three blocks from RobAutoz in a busy mall parking lot. A closer inspection revealed the van's tactical specifications: bullet-resistant glass and body panels, and a hidden compartment containing a small cache of light weaponry and armor-penetrating ammunition. During interrogation, Charles claimed unconsciousness and repeatedly denied knowledge of the events that occurred in his house, regardless of the forensic evidence that indicated his complexity. Although there was no gunfire residue on his clothing or body, agents discovered microscopic droplets of blood on Charles smoking jacket, due to the high-speed impact misting of close-proximity gunfire. The blood was Du Rennes. Agents determined at least one of the weapons involved in the shootings was missing. The other was surrendered by Charles' servant, also claiming unconsciousness, yet also devoid of discharge residue. Charles became further frustrated when he learned of his surveillance system's deactivation and erasure. All forensics, as the butler planned, pointed towards a sentry who couldn't speak.

Daughter of the Winds II

"May the children of God the Father witness a universal love, peace, and the divine truth of his glory. Grant wisdom to our leaders in the defense of peace, and vanquish those who imperil the tranquility of it. Amen."

The Pope replaced the handset upon its cradle, his pellegrina dotted with tears from a 39-minute transatlantic call with the President of the United States. He sat, removed his bifocals, and delicately patted a cloth along his forehead. The pontiff raised a sweating chalice to his lips and quenched his raw vocal cords with a few draws of water. He rested for several moments in contemplation, then turned towards his wide-eyed secretary.

"Portate Dominic qui, subito. Our anathema has returned."

The secretary ran from the office and summoned the Commander of the Swiss Guard, who, along with the Guard's officers, the Vatican taskforce, and related contractors, were celebrating the completion of a decade-long renovation of the Guard's barracks. Cheerful and laughing, as he had been for the majority of the day, the sip of ale he had extracted from his tall, frothy mug turned acrid and became as difficult to swallow as the words entered his ear. The Commander peered across the festive landscape as the call extinguished.

Abbess Regina sealed the door behind her as Emily grunted, pulling the snug-fitting VR helmet down, and rocking it several times to straighten the folds in her ears. She was on her fourth session of the day—the sixth hour—and her body felt stronger as the training wore on. Her mind flexed in symbiosis with her other muscles, absorbing advanced lessons in vocabulary, its Latin and Germanic roots, mathematics, natural and biological sciences, then on to combat weapons and tactics within an interactive construct. The AI programming's intensity, depth and capricious variation magnified during each session. Emily's elasticity proved indestructible. The session clock displayed a number exceeding ten hours her first day. It was the equivalence of two months due to the compounded acceleration. The program's itinerary provided alternating "days" of instruction and proving at the simulation hall and ranges. In the first week, she soaked more training than two years of British SAS, American SEAL, Russian Alpha, and Israeli 269s—merely as part of her defense tactics. Torturous and deadlier maneuvers, outlawed as cruel and barbaric under international treaties, were interwoven as necessary actions that served a purpose, whether to expediently extract information, or as a deterrent. Emily came to know that the Spada Sacra never released those it captured. To do so risked exposure.

An array of monitors glowed upon Regina's face as she focused on Emily's development, typing notes of her progress and psychological demeanor during each segment. She paused upon the entry of Emily's attitude for the third time that evening, suspicious of a trend towards petulance. Esposito used anger as a primary motivational tool, ensuring a certain level of resentment was maintained through various cues, triggered when needed. Yet, Emily became triggered several times without the cues, and each instance at a seemingly random part of the program. The sister brought it to the bishop's attention twice before, in which his response grew from curiosity.

"So long as it does not cloud her judgement or delay her actions, let it progress," he said.

And so, Emily's scowl intensified. Her choices in combat shifted towards cruel, lengthy fatalities—completely detached and desensitized. Male-gendered foes would suffer the greatest simulated torments: Mutilated extremities, detonated genitalia, disabling lacerations so that they must witness and endure familial carnage before bleeding out. Anguish. Esposito allowed it for two days—five accelerated months of horror in fomentation—before summoning Regina.

"She has mastered the machine. It is time she learned the truth of people. Bring her to me."

When the dorm's entrance slid open, Emily's typical curt, enthusiastic smile was replaced by a seething glower, trained on destruction. Regina nonetheless held out her hand. Emily would not take it. Instead, she stood erect from the bed, straightened her uniform, and strode towards for the hallway with a deliberate gait, instinctively checking defensive quadrants along the way.

The abbess paused as Emily passed her. "Is there something you wish to discuss?"

Emily took a wide stance as she turned around. "If I wished to discuss something, I would have informed you that I wished to discuss something."

Regina reactively raised her hand then quickly caught herself as Emily snapped her palm to the shagreened grip on her left side.

Regina gasped. "You dare draw your weapon on me, child? I should have you on a boat for it!"

Suddenly, Emily's cold stare broke as thoughts of her friends returned. They too were placed on a boat. A terrible thought occurred to her. The cold glare returned, as she trudged through the doorway, mumbling, "Hit me and you'll lose that hand."

"Stop!" The nun shouted. "What did you say?"

Emily continued to gain distance until she felt a hand on her shoulder. The move was instinctive and swift. The blade flew silently and precisely towards the nun's wrist joint, intent on its severance. Emily felt the painful jarring as her slash was deflected with a loud and percussive knock. She caught the amethyst flash in her periphery, knowing immediately what it was. Narciso's cane pulsated brilliantly as its shaft hovered just above Regina's hand, and the nun's shocked reflexes jerked it away in a wheezing gasp.

"Monster!" She screamed.

Esposito kept his gaze upon Emily's eyes as he produced a telltale grin.

"You pushed her too hard!" The nun cried. "I warned you!"

Emily withdrew her blade, but kept a firm grip on it. The jewel's radiance dimmed as the cane cracked across the nun's left kneecap. Regina howled as she collapsed upon the polished concrete, crying as she hadn't done in several years since the last time she was disciplined.

Narciso knelt down and whispered in her ear as she wept. "I need not explain, my sister."

The bishop stood up and turned to Emily. "Walk with me."

Emily sheathed her blade and took his side.

After rounding a few corners in the vast underground hallway network, they entered an elevator. Esposito inserted a key and pressed an unmarked button at the top of the third column of floors. There were other unmarked buttons on that row that tapped Emily's curiosity, and the bishop noticed her staring at them. The elevator shot upward, producing a slight bend in the knees at first. Each floor's button lit briefly as it was passed until the last one extinguished and Esposito's selection started flashing. The elevator continued to rise for several seconds as the button's flashes grew longer until it remained solidly lit. The elevator gently slowed as it came level to the floor. The doors slid open, revealing a blinding, sunlit vista overlooking the distant Mediterranean from an observation and defense tower perched atop Montagne Grande. Emily noticed an elevation graphic marking 850m and a 5km distance to the shoreline, although the sea seemed just below them at the mountain's base. Esposito escorted Emily to the edge of the reinforced balcony for an unrestricted view towards the southwest.

"The land you see in the distance is Tunisia. Not long ago it was ruled by one man for over twenty years until another man poured petrol upon himself and lit a match. His action ignited a righteous revolution throughout his country, and within other countries beyond those horizons to our left. You too shall bring about change, dear Emily, except your actions must always be righteous."

"How will I know?" Emily stared at the glistening waves.

"I will tell you."

Emily turned towards him; head cocked.

"For instance, why did you feel it necessary to amputate Sister Regina's hand?"

"She was going to kill me."

"Doubtful, considering your training. How would she achieve your death? Did she say?"

"She threatened to put me on a boat."

"A boat?"

"I think she meant the same boat as my friends."

"Those children are safe with their families," Esposito lied.

Emily turned back towards the sea's horizon, confused. A chilled breeze luffed her ponytail. The wind felt damp and carried the Mediterranean's salted scent. She suddenly remembered the same feeling—in San Francisco on Alcatraz. The prison she thought. *Bad people.* Pantelleria felt much like Alcatraz.

"Your training has surpassed all our expectations, Emily. You are faster and smarter than those who came before—those beneath our feet. You are superior in every way but two. The first will be conquered in days. The second will take years."

"My size."

"Precisely."

"What is the first?"

"People."

Emily's brow crinkled. Narciso looked down upon her face. "You must learn the true nature of people, my dear. The truth is that we are all liars."

"Huh?" She sneered.

"Yes, you—and me, your parents, everyone you know, and everyone on this earth. Liars all. We lie to ourselves, we lie to other people, we lie *for* other people, we lie to hated enemies and to our dearest friends. It is merely a matter of convenience and advantage—the second nature of humans. Dishonesty. We so much want to be seen in a white light of positivity. Whatever it takes, child, and that usually means lying. We lie because we are selfish. We want what is best for ourselves, no? Is this not always the case?"

"But you are a priest! You are supposed to be good!"

"I am a priest because it brings me closer to God. There, you see? I do it because it is good for *me*. Is that so bad?"

"No."

"Ah, you see what I mean? Selfishness is acceptable so long as we share it equally, and so long as others share in its benefit. What is good for me is good for you—good for everybody. It is the same for you, understand?"

"Kinda."

"Emily, have you ever heard the word, *vanity*?"

"Yes."

"So you know what this word means?"

Emily shrugged.

"Ah. It means delight in one's appearance or something they accomplished. People with whitened teeth, or expensive shoes, and those who purchase new autos every year, or need to tell you about their children's perfect school grades. Pride becomes vanity."

"I hate that!"

"Yes, you see the nature of these vain people and you know this is wrong, innately. Do you know why this is so? It is a sin upon God, child. To some degree, we all do it because we want something from others, or because we desperately need to please others. It is a sickness. Ah, but it is also a weapon!"

Esposito stepped away from the wall towards the elevator. "Come, we have more to discuss."

Emily followed just behind and entered the elevator alongside him. The doors closed and a rapid descent ensued.

"What sort of weapon?" She asked.

"To manipulate or deceive your enemy. Lure them into your trap!" Esposito raised his finger with a wry grin. "You shall develop this skill. It will be your best advantage. Nobody expects the angel in white until it is too late."

At the bottom, the doors opened to a wide corridor, situated between instructional areas and living quarters. Esposito and Emily stepped out and started walking towards her dormitory. A buck sentry approached from the opposite direction down the hall, smiling in admiration of his leader. Esposito knelt to whisper in Emily's ear.

"I want you to kill this soldier, now."

Instinctively, Emily's hand went for her blade's hilt as he passed, but just as she went to unsheathe it, she caught a glimpse of the young man's eyes and innocent smile, completely unaware of his peril. She hesitated.

The bishop turned around and stopped. Emily trembled.

"Why?" He asked.

Emily glanced down the hall as the sentry disappeared around a bend. Regina thrust a blade deep into the soldier's esophagus, preventing a scream that would have otherwise escaped. The dagger also penetrated and severed his spinal column. Instant fatality and immediate collapse in front of a convenient doorway that led away from occupied areas to a refrigerated processing room.

"I... I don't know. I couldn't—"

"When you are instructed, you act, you do not think. You must not hesitate, child. Your life will depend on it."

"But he is one of us!" Emily cried.

Esposito grinned. "Yes, child, he was. He is also guilty of crimes against God. He has murdered, he has coveted, and worst of all, he slept with men. It is an abomination for which the Spada Sacra cannot tolerate. He was *not* one of us. Does this change your mind?"

Emily shrugged.

"In time you will fully understand the truth of people, child. No one is ever what they seem, not even your father, as you have already learned. This is the first lesson, and it is the most important. You will learn more tomorrow. For now, I want to you go back to your room and make peace with Sister Regina."

"But she—"

"Regardless of what you believe, our Abbess is *not* evil, and you shall respect her directives."

"Yes, father." Emily sighed.

The President listened to the line extinguish as he sat, phased with a dour expression, clearing his congested nose with an embroidered handkerchief.

"Wouldn't accept our assistance no matter what I told him. 200 men, he said. An elite guard who will sweep Pantelleria as swiftly as a sirocco to Saharan sand."

"You believe him?" The National Security Advisor asked.

"Whether I believe him or not is inconsequential, Bob."

"What do you mean?"

"This opportunity, if what we're told of these people—what they possess—is true. Do we let that go to the Holy See?"

"There would be ramifications with the EU."

"Vatican City isn't a member of the EU."

"Technically, no, although the optics could be disastrous. Europe won't like it, the Russians and China will exploit it, and it plays to terrorists' narratives. You need to weigh any potential gain against the fallout, Mr. President."

"That gain is the question mark, isn't it?" The President replaced his bifocals, peering through their lower portion at the freshly-printed report. "All this tech and God knows what else? Not our duty? You can bet our collective ass what the east will do, and who knows if they haven't launched already. No Bob, this is another race amongst our old friends."

The President glanced back at the report. "Coordinate with Trevor. Get Blue Tac One on it, and this man, er—" He looked down once more. "Osterhoudt. Make sure his team's involved."

The Advisor recorded those instructions with their tablet and scripted a cursory plan by stylus.

The President continued. "What's the status of General Tomlinson."

"Unknown, sir."

The Chief of Staff suddenly burst through the doorway.

"Sir, General Thunderlake wants you in the Situation Room. Says it's urgent."

"Everything's urgent with Thunder*flake*. What's he want?"

"It's about General Tomlinson, sir—"

• • •

USAF Brigadier General Barbara Ann Tomlinson's credentials—her passport, military IDs, bank cards and other personal affects—laid charred and molten in a collapsed room of a farmhouse located near West Township, Maryland, about an hour north of DC. Beside them was the partial remnants of a corpse, including several large bone fragments—hip sockets that would only be indicative of a middle-aged female and nothing more. Investigators would be forced to make conclusions based on evidence that Tomlinson coincidentally perished in the flames of the house, given further corroborative testimony from the farm's shocked landlords and their affinity for their esteemed yet frequently absent tenant, Tomlinson. It was all a ruse.

In her time with the Air Force, Tomlinson amassed favors of fealty and leverage, via riches or debauchery, of over two hundred men and women—most within the Air Force itself, many others who possessed either specific skills or logistical necessities, or both. People she could count on when needed. People who shared her vision.

The scan code affixed to Tomlinson's sanitized car checked through the passive gate at Joint Base Andrews' (JBA) northern entrance. A few moments later, a sentry saluted before peering over his sunglasses to compare the ID card's photo with the driver's face. Haircut the same as it was a couple years earlier when the portrait artist and data specialist minted the credential.

"Where are we headed today, Major Johnson?"

"The mall, then up to the 1st hangars."

The sentry scratched a few notes on his tablet and made a brief inspection of the car, inside and out. He saluted once more and returned her ID card, motioning for the next car to pull forward. The major adjusted her rearview mirror as she drove away, confirming no further scrutiny. Her lips were dry and her throat parched. Her itinerary at the mall was no fib. She was well acquainted with the officers' lounge—The Club. It was where she had her first taste of a proper single malt, and from it there was no looking back.

Tomlinson sat at a stale, empty bar less than fifteen minutes before clearing her tab and departing. Two doubles sufficed and were enough to gain the bartender's respect without drawing undue attention. She knew the drill. Any more or less consumed by a loner made too many statements. So would the production of car keys before exiting the room. She would not need them, however; the hangars for 1st Helicopter Squadron were merely a few hundred feet away. Her pace was brisk en route to the eastern entrance of Hangar 4. The tarmac was abuzz with Air Force hardware crews in preparation for JBA's annual air show. A sentry saluted and grinned as she passed through the doorway and into the cavernous building. And when her eyes adjusted, she saw no less than eight special detail operators in black fatigues aiming suppressed compact assault rifles at her, evidenced by the multiple red dots dancing around her heart. She turned around to see two more rifles at her back, with two suits to either flank. She sighed and removed her sunglasses, recognizing the familiar click of Colonel Osterhoudt's cigarette lighter in the background, and its cherried flame dancing upon his complexion.

The President and those in the Situation Room were fixated at the large projection of the ultra-definition feed transmitted from a 360-degree camera perched atop a pack-mounted pole that extended a foot over an operator's helmet. Osterhoudt's cursory draw lasted forever in Tomlinson's mind, as time froze. On the President's screen however, an operator stepped forward and delivered the general's prosecution from a suppressor's muted spit that dropped her instantly. The message could not be clearer to the half-dozen bound and gagged conspirators lying on their stomachs off to the side. Their coup was over, and their deaths assured, but not before weeks of enhanced interrogation. In time, the abundance of intelligence gathered would reveal a splinter network running parallel to Blue Ops, one that Osterhoudt had long suspected but never encountered. They were a nameless group that loosely connected itself throughout Europe, for what purpose beyond Blue Ops, it remained unknown.

"Colonel Osterhoudt," The President spoke into the intercom, "Well done."

"Thank you, sir. Quite a bit left to do."

"I know, and that's why I need to speak with you."

The colonel exhaled and squashed the cigarette under toe.

The President continued, "I need you and your men to reset and prepare for a trip, understand?"

"Perfectly, sir." Osterhoudt smiled at the camera.

"What is it, Emily?" Regina asked, extinguishing the connect request light.

"I apologize." Emily muttered.

There was a brief silence. "I could not understand you. Please repeat," Regina said with an irritated tone.

"I said I am sorry. I am sorry if I hurt you."

The nun sighed. "Do not apologize to me, young girl. Apologizing is an indication of vulnerability and fragility. You are stronger than this, are you not?"

Emily's voice trembled. "Yes, Sister Regina, but—"

"Then what is troubling you?"

"Nothing!" Emily abruptly disconnected and laid back upon her crisp, downed pillow as a tear escaped one eye. She suddenly felt the full weight of solitary confinement even though that confinement was partial and seemingly voluntary. Her reflex would have been to dial Patricia Smiley and plot outfits for next day's school. The memory of her mutilated cadaver suddenly shocked Emily into a trance, and from that trance, she drifted from consciousness.

"Obnoxious child," whispered Regina as the connection terminated. She swiftly poked the communicator's display to summon her bishop. The display counted time with a circular graphic as she waited. Esposito never responded. She rolled her eyes and dismissed it, unconcerned, returning her gaze onto several security monitors. Her primary two-meter monitor was dedicated to a separate complex of chambers where four men dwelled. One of them was old and feeble, unable to walk without the assistance of others, although quite capable of operating a powered recliner. The others appeared to be in their lower thirties and extremely fit as gymnasts, yet the nun's fascination with them went further than their physicality. The other monitors displayed 40 other men of roughly the same age, body type and appearance. In fact, their appearances were identical down to fingerprints and retinal scans. They shared the same donor pair. Narciso said part of her DNA was used for the sequencing. A lie. He said it to guarantee her fealty and create a parallel obsession. Soon her boys would reign supreme, she thought, and what a legacy she would leave.

Esposito retired to his stone-faced lair an hour earlier. On arrival, he placed the Amethylizer on its charging stand, murmuring a prayer for Saint Sophia as he did. The crystal at its top pulsated slowly, producing a splash of lavender luminescence in the corner behind it. The bishop plopped down on his meshed task chair and rotated towards his cleared desk, save for the prize he had waited so very patiently to acquire in Washington. The silver laptop's power light burned blue as he pressed and released the button next to it, unfolding the screen. The Amerimem logo appeared within moments and its primary application booted. His familiar wry grin spread his cheeks wide in anticipation as he activated the tray release. The internal servo clicked, ejecting the spring-loaded tray from the laptop's left side. His smile widened further as he began looking around the room for suitable test candidates, except at his head turned, the tray's actuating motor activated, slowly withdrawing the tray. Esposito's grin vanished in desperation as he clawed at the tray to somehow stop it.

"*Cagada!*" He screamed, picking up the laptop and slamming it down with both hands.

At once, he felt a surge grip his palms—an intense burning sensation that locked his hands to the laptop. His heart raced and he felt faint. The pain swelled at his wrists as he lost consciousness, incognizant of the muted laughter and shadow of a figure on the screen.

Moments later he awakened with a deep breath. He was disoriented and groggy, yet mostly cross and displaying a vile expression. His forearms were sore, he noticed, recognizing the Amerimem logo revolving on the laptop's screen. He grunted, stood up, and stumbled his way into the bathroom several steps away. The bishop opened the cold water tap and flushed his eyes and face several times until he felt rid of the fog that infected him. His eyes remained partially cloudy, however. He raised his head to the vanity's mirror. There was a tinge within his eyes he did not recognize, though the rest of him felt fine. Something merely felt *off*. He looked closer and noticed a telltale gleam of xanthous mixed with the brown of his irises. He felt a dry retch of nausea and started to laugh uncontrollably. He knew not why, and he could not stop. The laughter grew until he nearly passed out again, and at that precipice, the attack suddenly ceased. The bishop sensed something went wrong. Something was different, but he simply couldn't put his finger on it. He stared at the laptop and the revolving Amerimem logo until it came into better focus. At that moment, the screen went dark and the internal fans ceased. A wisp of smoke escaped from a vent at the laptop's rear, wafting upward and disappearing into the darkness.

You felt it too. Jet Sun recognized the aura of malevolence in River's eyes.

Yes.

He is here.

For now. River transmitted his thoughts effortlessly.

Impressive, Chief. Jet Sun projected. *It usually takes decades for one to achieve.*

River's eyes opened. *A gift from the Snowy Owl.*

But that is not all— Jet Sun asked.

He flies with eagles.

A loud buzz erupted from down the corridor, unbolting the reinforced door. Several agents proceeded to unlock adjacent holding cells and gather everyone within the hallway.

"Come with us, please," said one of them.

Chris raced to Dao and embraced her with an unconscious added degree of strength. She winced with a glint of pain. Chris caught it in her eyes, released her and stood aside. She whispered the medical team's astonishment upon examination of her blood-soaked abdomen.

"They removed my bandages to discover scarred tissue that appeared several weeks healed. Questions ensued; you must imagine. This, of course, was unacceptable to the base's Chief Surgeon, who promised I would never leave without explaining. I did, sort of, except they did not believe me. They stuck me with their needles, running multiple examinations of blood, DNA, and relentless scans. I cannot blame them. Trust only the empirical is a common mantra. Sometime later, an agent walked into the room with orders for my release. No questions. The hallways were cleared of medical personnel while they moved me. Only agents wearing wires remained, similar to this man. She gestured towards the agent at the doorway. They remind me of your Secret Service."

The group gathered in a conference room featuring a catered breakfast. After twenty minutes of sparse, speculative conversations amongst the noshing, a bearded man wearing a suit one size too small walked in, clutching a coffee cup and tablet. He closed the door behind him and gave the room a once-over.

"Science to the rescue," muttered Trovarto.

The man's eyes glanced up from the tablet and fixed on the monsignor. He smiled and shook his head.

"This cheat sheet doesn't list any special abilities for you, father, therefore I must assume your quip was based on circumstantial and deductive. Impressive nonetheless. I am indeed a man of science, and I am in charge of your, shall we say, special needs. Your case. My name is Doctor Lattimer."

Lattimer detailed plans for protracted detainment to further examine abilities, although with appropriate compensation and promises of eventual freedom. Lattimer noted the change in expressions when freedom was mentioned. As he made notes on the tablet, an agent opened the door, ushering in several other agents—two brandishing compact rifles in their grasp, fingers on the trigger guards. The door remained open as the President of the United States strode through.

"Doctor Lattimer here assures me you folks have a good idea of the national security interests at play here. Doctors Miller and Ming, you created Iris, or whatever you want to call it. The thing that's kept me awake for the past 72 hours. We need to make absolutely sure its technology remains in worthy hands. Now, we're working on a—"

"Worthy?" Chris interrupted. "Mr. President, who are you to decide who's worthy?"

"Quite obviously, I do, Doctor Miller. I am the President of the United States; the decision is ultimately mine. Comes with the job, I'm afraid. Anyway, a subjective word choice, *worthy*. Let me put it this way, there's no other agency or government you can trust right now, and we are the ones who can protect you—the only ones."

"Also subjective," said Chris.

Dao placed a hand across her abdomen as Chris nodded. "Profoundly subjective, given your own government's security failures," she added.

"Point taken, Doctor Ming. On behalf of my country, I offer our deepest apologies. I promise to do better in light of all this, and I hope you understand why we cannot simply let you all walk out that door as if nothing happened. Doctor Lattimer will extend our best hospitality. Your stays will be as comfortable as possible, and I hope to have your full cooperation."

The President glanced towards Doctor Lattimer, turned around and exited the room with his detachment.

"What do you mean?" Chris jumped to his feet. "You can't keep us indefinitely!"

"Doctor Miller, it should have already been explained to you that when a national security matter is created by one of its citizens and their *idea*, this nation owns their idea, and frankly their ass for as long as this nation is compromised by their grand idea. In other words, we didn't create this problem, you did, and these are the consequences of your creation."

Chris fell back into his chair, having heard the very same from Jack some months ago. *They own you, your idea, and your ass. They hide behind legal obscurities—law and procedures—and change or manufacture new ones when needed. Freedom is an illusion, my friend.* The notion struck him that Jack had the President's ear. *What's the probability?*

Lattimer reached into his pocket, popped a stick of chewing gum into his mouth. "We would rather have your cooperation —*enthusiastic cooperation*, as the President put it to me, counting on your patriotism. He meant *you*, specifically, Doctor Miller. The President was hoping that Doctor Ming's fidelity to her American employer might also find some meaning in this global context. He also hopes she has a conscience. We are not the proverbial bad guys certain news outlets consistently portray."

Lattimer knew he was charging uphill in the dark. The expressions on Chris and Dao's faces were lighted billboards with decorative expletives slowly crawling across.

"And you expect us to believe you after all that's happened? Your people took shots at us!"

"You mean Blue Ops."

Chris snarled. "I mean them and everyone connected to them."

"Doctor Miller, please believe me when I say that Blue Ops is dissolved thanks to Commander Jacobson and Colonel Osterhoudt. It was operating an autonomous agenda behind classified firewalls buried deep within the Pentagon."

"Dissolved? That's nice. What about the lunatics running it?"

"Classified. Just know that the Justice Department is executing warrants as we speak."

"Don't take me for an idiot, Lattimer."

"I don't, therefore I trust you have at least a cursory grasp on the protocol."

"Whatever." Chris rolled his eyes.

"Let's get to the important business, shall we? I am authorized to share certain intelligence regarding Emily."

Suddenly, the billboards went dark. Chris' eyes lasered Lattimer's with penetrating effectiveness.

"I am under orders to only share it with you, and only if you cooperate—willingly," the scientist lied.

Chris lowered his eyes and brought his arms to himself, shaking. "Not sure if I want it."

Dao felt the disappointment and shame regarding Emily's behavior at the bridge. She internalized more reasons than anyone to condemn the child, and her maternalism felt more grief than anger. She was searching for answers where Chris had given up. There must be a reason Emily acted that way. *Brainwashed*, she thought. Dao witnessed it hundreds of times in rural China. Chris' child was not to blame.

"Of course, he does," Dao said.

"Not with *that* catch." Chris quipped.

Lattimer parked his gum. "Look, it's like this; you want your daughter back and we want to help. Yes, there is a price for that help. The price is high. Our costs are high. More importantly, our risks are monumental."

"As are your rewards," said Dao.

"To die for, apparently," the Lattimer nodded.

Chris turned around with a cocked head. "Where is she?"

Lattimer smacked his lips while taking a seat on the corner of an adjacent steel table. "The Mediterranean... we think, well, we're pretty sure she's on an Italian island named Pantelleria. It's—"

"Between Sicily and Tunisia. I've heard of it."

"Okay." Lattimer smacked, "What do you know about it?"

"Only what my grandfather mentioned. He was on a boat observing Operation Corkscrew's bomb runs for Eisenhower."

Curious. No mention of Du Rennes. Jet Sun whispered the thought to Dao, causing her to glance suddenly behind. River also heard it.

Either they do not have them, or do not know of them. The latter is unlikely due to Osterhoudt's loyalty. River thought.

Either way, it is notable. Dao projected.

Lattimer noticed their facial expressions and body language, his own appearance telegraphing a high degree of curiosity. His phone vibrated. The pink-tinted screen indicated Urgent.

"Pardon, you must excuse me for a moment."

Lattimer stepped out to the hallway and answered the video call. On his screen, a dark, bald man in bifocals turned around to face the camera.

"Q Site needs another six hours, but it will be ready for the others on arrival. Bring the doctors to me."

Anastasia's stomach tremored with a sense of urgent alarm. When she spun around to look out her passenger window, a car's tires barked under antilock stress just beside her. She screamed, bracing for impact as a gray sedan stopped just short of collision. Its window lowered to a familiar voice.

"Get in. Now!" Montluc yelled, sirens in the distance.

"Jeannie!" Anastasia screamed. "Oh, thank God! But our car? What—"

"NOW!"

Rocco and Anastasia scrambled into the back seat as Montluc accelerated away from a bank's parking lot off 23rd

Street in Crystal City, less than a mile from Reagan National and Hangar 5. Her handheld scanner radio crackled in the background as her rented car revved to redline.

"*Mon deu!* You are all over the air. Wanted for suspicion of murder? What is this? Where is your father? I have not heard from him since I landed."

Rocco stared out the tinted rear window. "Dead."

Montluc took a deep breath and checked her surroundings as she abruptly turned right onto Richmond Highway. Less than a moment later, the radio crackled with a reference to the airport under lockdown. Montluc checked her surroundings once more as the airport's off-ramp approached. She switched to the middle lane and maintained the speed of surrounding traffic.

Montluc's eyes caught Rocco's in the rearview as the airport's exit sign passed overhead. "How?"

Rocco paused. "Charles."

"That *morceau de merde?*" Montluc sighed. "Your uncle shared a story about this man once. He hated him! I cannot believe he would solicit such a man. And what of Gérard? He would not let this happen, unless—"

The momentary return gazes from Rocco and Anastasia confirmed her deduction.

"They are all dead." Rocco said, deadpan, gritting his teeth.

Montluc glanced into the rearview to see him staring blankly through the window, taking little notice of Potomac Yard's homogenized skyline of freshly-minted brick condos.

"How did you find us?" Anastasia asked.

"*Un miracle.* I am running late from the other airport. Deferred and delayed at Dulles. Hired this car and turned the radio on. I stop at the intersection by the bank and you are there. Chance? No, I think. Maybe you call to me, Annie?"

At once, two Army Blackhawk helicopters overflew the car merely a few feet above. The deafening roar of their turbines caused Montluc to swerve then overcorrect in a squalling fishtail, fighting for control. The copters landed some two hundred meters in front as two squads in tactical outfitting deployed from each side door. Montluc checked her rear to find several darkened federal SUVs with flashing interior strobes blocking all lanes and closing on her position. There were no side roads or other available exits. She laid on the brakes until they vibrated underfoot, tires biting the asphalt. Rocco slammed both fists into the dash in frustration. Anastasia began to panic with anxiety, overwhelmed with intense reception of empathic emotions and anger. She screamed in terror.

"No!" Montluc yelled and grabbed Rocco's forearm. "You must not!"

The car abruptly stopped a couple dozen meters in front of the soldiers, who leveled their rifles at the car's windshield. Montluc kept her hands on the wheel as instructions to exit their vehicle blared from the helicopter's PA.

Montluc turned towards the Rocco and Anastasia, "It is okay. We have no choice. Please do not hurt them. Nothing good will come of it."

They slowly climbed out of the car and kept their hands in front of their bodies, visible to the soldiers. A ranked captain with the name Rogers embroidered on his chest stepped forward to within a couple meters of Montluc and saluted her. A radio crackled in the background signaling successful intercept. Montluc did not return a salute and stared at the soldier with contempt.

"Captain Montluc, you and Hammett's children will be escorted to our operations center where your friends are currently in debriefing. Be advised you are not in any danger. A colleague of Monsieur Du Rennes is awaiting."

"Colleague? *Which* colleague?"

A Bone to Pick

Esposito pressed the End icon on his secured satellite phone's display and immediately rang his primo of island defense.

"It is time." He said, staring towards the laptop in anticipation. "25 minutes," escaped his lips as he hung up, relaying the ETA of the Swiss Guard. One of his informants tipped him on the operation, but only after it had been in motion for an hour. Piercing alarms buzzed the entire complex with deafening pulses. Soldiers marched to their stations, engines ignited, massive hangar doors actuated, and two armored columns of varying hardware roared onto the airport's tarmac. Narciso gathered the Amethylizer and proceeded to the staging area where Emily awaited, fully outfitted and surging with a focused glare. The bishop smiled at her exuberance, cold it as appeared, content with the results of his training. His mind recessed further with contemplative thoughts of her eventual maturity and what they would conquer together.

Spada Sacra's plant within the harbor's Guardia Costiera sent word of two inbound targets with instructions to cooperate. The first and primary concern was a C-27J Spartan transport bound for Runway 26. Although the selection of runway was not announced, it was Pantelleria's longest, and it was currently facing the wind, therefore the logical choice. The second target was reported as a large, armored hovercraft, inbound from Marsala, Sicily at 40 knots. Estimates placed its arrival several minutes ahead of the Spartan. The informant's information was nearly an hour old, meaning there was little time to scramble. Spada Sacra anticipated such contingencies and drilled for them incessantly. Within eight minutes of the alarm, operators were in position on the airfield and just north of the island's main port, strategically positioned to intercept any warship before it entered the harbor. In the case of a hovercraft, the projected landing area was a graded inlet on the harbor's north end. Esposito ordered the island's Welcome Mat to also be activated in case of any erroneous information. The Mat consisted of several hundred fast-ascending smart mines, camouflaged and encircling the island's seafloor at an average depth of ten meters.

Esposito's radio chimed within his cassock about the same time the Spartan banked for a short final. He held it against his ear and muffled his other so he could hear the incoming message that the inbound hovercraft was not making for the port, but instead barreling towards a small beach on the north coast called Punta Pozzolana, next to a decaying WWII pillbox. The news confused Esposito since that short section of coastline was rocky, steep, and protected by cliffs to either side. He sent instructions back to the harbor patrol to maneuver towards the east just in case, expecting the Welcome Mat to defend any attempted landing.

As the Spartan approached the start of the runway, a Spada Sacra operator stepped forward with a specialty rifle, featuring a 30mm barrel and AI targeting optics. Point, zoom, tap, launch. A foot-long projectile blasted from the barrel and extended its fins. Without any detectable smoke trail, heat signature or other visible trace, the missile screamed towards the aircraft and impacted its nose with a percussive thump. For several seconds it appeared as though nothing happened. The heavy transport continued its path to the tarmac. At the last moment, no landing flare occurred and the Spartan crashed onto the concrete, nose-first, and flew apart in a massive fireball. The explosion reverberated through the hillsides as a plume of black smoke billowed from the middle of the runway.

"Tisk," chided Narciso, turning towards Emily with a smug grin and flash of amber in his eyes. Emily happened to catch it as she looked up at him in the morning's golden sunlight, assuming it was a reflection. Even so, for the shortest of moments, the glint of amber struck a nerve. The distraction was just as short.

Esposito pointed towards the end of the runway. "Come, we have another rendezvous—over that rise in Campobello."

The column loaded into two armored transports and sped off towards the island's north end, passing the engulfed carnage of the Swiss Guard's sortie. The flashing red lights of emergency vehicles remained on the other side of the field at a great distance. Narciso had no intention of rescuing survivors, of which there were briefly four until their broken bodies ignited. No evidence, and no distress call. Nothing would remain except the CIA's satellite reconnaissance high-resolution recording of it, to be reviewed as soon as practically possible by the President, who had been asleep for two hours when the Pope's incursion launched.

Narciso's patrol made the crest of the hilltop just as the Swiss Guard's hovercraft crossed the Welcome Mat. The bishop and his troops, including Emily, eagerly expected an explosion at any moment. The British twin-powered marauder soared over them at 50 knots in full throttle, triggering one of the mines which launched towards the surface and its target. A detonated plume of water and smoke lurched the stern of the hovercraft several degrees, stuffing the bow into a wave. Its kinetic energy gone, the craft limped onto the pumice rocks of Campobello's beach, extinguishing its turbines and dropping the air cushion. Frantic radio calls from it detailed their emergency, and towering pillar of smoke at the airport a short distance away. Sixteen Swiss Guard elites and two hovercraft crew received instructions to proceed.

They deployed to the beach, rifles scanning across and above until one of them sighted Esposito's column 250 meters away on the hilltop, beyond the terraces. Through his scope, the feldweibel counted several pairs of lenses focused upon him, as well as the lenses of four 50mm automatic rifles marking targets on the beach. What he didn't see were the dozen or so rifles pointed at them from the grasses less than 200 meters away—the repositioned Spada Sacra from the harbor. The concussion of a large-caliber round impacting his breast plate hijacked the air of a scream that would have escaped his lips. An armor-penetrating bullet exploded midway to exit, blowing a foot-wide hole through the sergeant, who dropped to the ground faster than the last of his crimson mist. Within the space of four seconds, the fate of nine additional Guardsmen would be the same, albeit with minor variances. Those remaining, including the hauptmann commanding the assault, dropped their weapons upon the rocks in a plea for their lives. The hovercraft pilots were attempting to reach operations in Marsala when an RPG detonated inside the bridge, destroying it—and them—completely. A secondary explosion ignited the fuel tanks which engulfed the fast attack craft in a hellish inferno within moments.

Esposito turned to his top lieutenant. "Collect those swine and bring them before me. Throw the others back onboard and sink it in the Perl Trough."

He turned to Emily and said, "I have a task for you."

The darkened SUVs of Doctor Lattimer's motorcade rounded the final curve before stopping at Hi-Catoctin's north perimeter entrance, buried within several secluded miles of rangy forest in north-central Maryland. U.S. Navy insignia adorned the gates beyond a wooden sign engraved with "Shangri-La".

"I'm sorry about Jack." Lattimer said with a stoic tone.

Chris turned towards him. "You knew him? Jack Kattner?"

Dao nodded, taking interest.

"Quite well, in fact, since our days at Cornell and MIT. Different disciplines, of course. Dear friend and champion for research grants, even before landing at Amerimem. Can't begin to tell you how many bottles of fine bourbon we emptied, let alone golf and other escapes." Lattimer smiled as their driver cleared identification and continued through the gates on well-maintained asphalt drive. "Jack threw a lot of work my way. He loved the science. He loved business too. Proximity to power, even more. Over the years, anyway."

Lattimer continued. "So, this is where we are; anything in the realm of national security involving scientific developments either terminates here or Area 1 in Nevada."

"You must mean 51?" Dao asked.

"Sorry, Doctor Ming; Groom Lake is for aircraft and aliens." Lattimer winked. "Area 1 was a test range and physics lab from the early 1950s. It was sealed off for thirty years then recommissioned in the nineties."

"*Nuclear* test area." Chris said with a puzzled face.

"Yes," said Lattimer.

"And probably still contaminated."

"Very." Lattimer said, dryly. "That's what keeps the curious away."

"But—"

"The new lab is merely a bunker linked to Yucca Mountain."

"Yucca Mountain, the nuclear waste dump?"

"*Former* intended nuclear waste repository, yes." Lattimer adjusted his glasses. "Anyway, this isn't the sort of project for that complex; not if Jack was accurate in what he told us about Tumor. Phoned me about it between a shower and a rubdown at the Pentagon. Said it spooked him a little."

"He shared the project name?" Chris asked.

"DARPA was in the loop since conception, mind you, and during its development, the project's overview went from the MTO, to I2O, to me at the DSO. We didn't know about your discovery because our feed was severed. I assume Blue Ops hijacked I2O's session. We are just now learning the levels of their surveillance penetration. Hundreds of departments and facilities compromised, including private concerns."

Dao couldn't contain a slight giggle.

"What?" Chris asked.

"You Americans constantly talk about your freedom and your privacy in contrast to China. It seems we are not so different after all."

Lattimer grinned. "We'll discuss that later over a nice tea, perhaps."

The SUV wound its way through several curves up a long, wooded hillside until it arrived at a taupe, three-story concrete building's valet. Several people were waiting for their arrival under the valet's roof at the entrance. Three were armed and dressed in tactical—part of the security detail.

"No way!" Chris shouted.

When the SUV came to a complete stop, he opened the door as quickly as he could and ran to hug Rebecca Morningwood, who was flanked by three of Andromeda's technicians. She forced a smile, sniffling as she embraced him.

"I'm glad to see you, Chris." She said with a dour inflection.

"I don't understand, Becky, what's wrong?"

"Don't know where to begin." She replied with a hint of sarcasm. "I saw what they did to Julie, Kenneth and others at the lab. We all assumed you were gone... taken."

A tear escaped her eye as she nodded to Dao Ming. "They told us nothing, Chris—kept us sequestered under guard at a hotel. All of Andromeda. No communication or TV, nothing. They started separating us. The interrogations were endless. National Security this, imminent danger that. Kept reminding us what those people did to poor Julie and Kenneth. Kept asking about Jack too. My God, Chris! It was awful until Stan Lattimer introduced himself and explained everything. As far as the other Amerimem departments, they were told it was an industrial accident under military jurisdiction because of the classified projects under development. We've been treated well ever since Stan took us in—under the circumstances, I mean."

"They killed my neighbors, Becky—an entire family, just because they knew us. If I'd known, I would have destroyed that damned laptop."

Morningwood gasped, covering her mouth.

"Don't be sorry, man!" One of the techs leaned in. "Lattimer said Iris is next-level."

Chris cringed.

The tech continued. "Said our project couldn't be much more important for science and world peace. Don't know about you, but I'm down with it. It's righteous!"

"He's right, Chris. Don't let their sacrifices be for nothing. Jack would call you a quitter and have your ass for it."

Chris looked at them and turned around to Dao and Lattimer. "So, what's going on here, exactly?"

Lattimer cleared his throat. "Your sylvan goddess here has agreed to assist us with your needs. Morningwood will administer as before. Wouldn't want to break up an effective team. Less paperwork."

"What about Matt?"

"Commander Jacobson is where his best talents are needed. We have a replacement."

Lattimer ushered them through the entrance and past a secondary security point to a conference room off the main hallway. When they walked through the door, the long granite table was flanked by seven men and one woman, most of whom wore lab coats. They stood up and smiled silently. At the end of the table was a mature executive—bald, wearing a three-piece pinstriped brown suit, and peering over bifocals harnessed by a gold foxtail chain. Behind him were two suited sentries brandishing partially concealed pistols underneath their jackets. After several minutes of introductions, everyone took their seats and opened discussion.

"Doctors Miller and Ming, and you too Stanley, for the first-hand benefit of this task group—its mission being the full documentation of your discovery, including replication—we would appreciate an overview of it, and what you believe is taking place under the hood, so-to-speak."

A totally transparent discussion ensued. After Chris and Dao's brief, Lattimer and the others agreed with the result, yet struggled with the concept of organized electrochemical encoding on the nano scale. He and several others are further intrigued on the informal programming in even smaller scales.

"The device opens the door on the possibility for encoding and decoding at subatomic levels—femto, atto and so forth. We are limited by our own technology, yet the results are commonplace in nature. Given enough time in development, you'll see subatomic quantum computing magnitudes beyond yottaflops from something the size of a dime."

● ● ●

Esposito held the pulsating Amethylizer firmly against the spine of the operator last in line. In writhing agony, he collapsed upon the ground in a fetal position until frozen in a pugilistic posture—his eyes locked, squinting and mouth agape, fighting for air. The bishop smashed the cane's jewel against the nape of the soldier's neck and held it there until the eyeballs popped, his ears bled, and finally, internal pressures cracked his skull wide, releasing the steaming brown viscous soup that was once a brain. Two of the Swiss Guard screamed and took off down the hillside towards the sea in a crisscrossing pattern. Narciso motioned towards his snipers, who made sport of the runners at 300 and 400 meters, respectively. The remaining three Vatican soldiers he saved for Emily.

The unarmed Guardsmen were encircled by Spada Sacra. There was nowhere to run, no gap to exploit, the hauptmann saw no chance for success after witnessing the accuracy of the snipers. He looked into their vacuous, cold, and hard eyes, one by one, until he landed upon Emily's. Hers were the coldest of all—angry and impatient. Yet her presence confused him. What is going on with this young girl? Why doesn't she shy away from this carnage? Why is she armed to the teeth?

Emily made several steps towards the Guardsmen, withdrawing a half-meter carbon steel xiphos sword from its leather sheath and took a stance just out of striking distance.

"Give them each a blade," said the bishop to his nearest lieutenant.

The lieutenant issued them ancient swords of the Swiss Guard. Although ornate, their scabbards were dull and dated, and the seal of Pope Pius IX was stamped on the blades—two lions to each side.

"Are you crazy? She's merely a young girl!" Yelled the hauptmann as he threw his sword down and folded his arms. "I will not fight her!"

"As you wish," said the bishop with a slanted grin.

Emily looked at him and he nodded. She made two quick steps towards the Guardsmen and leapt skyward. The shriek of metal blades withdrawing from their steel and brass scabbards never completed before Emily was overhead. Her blade exacted two lightning-fast swipes. There was one short scream and muted gurgling as the two soldiers fell. A split second later, the first one's head landed just beside his spasming corpse, his eyes wide in disbelief. The other soldier grasped in desperation at his throat, blood and air spewing between his fingers. His writhing continued for several eternal seconds as the hauptmann dropped to his knees.

"Bastards!" He yelled. "What have you done? What have you done to her!"

Ensanguined, Emily caught her breath and prepared for his termination. He looked at her and clasped his hands together.

"I pray for you! Underneath that façade, you are still a young, pretty girl. There is a heart in there, I know. Your father wants you home! You cannot believe this pathetic man, Emily; he is evil and he is making you do evil for him. Return from this evil or be lost to it, Emily, I beg you!"

For a brief moment, Emily gazed at the pebbles beneath his feet, and the wild grasses nearby. Esposito looked on from the side, his eyes wild with anticipation. She regripped her blade, spun around and thrust it up to its hilt under his left breast. The hauptmann gasped and sat back upon his heels, staring into her dilated pupils as his body shut down. He reached for her face but couldn't attain it, and with his last breath he coughed on the words, *"Perla Nera"*.

* * *

Anastasia suddenly spun around to Rocco, shaking. Her mind felt exhausted, yet the haze of narcosis and stiffness in her body indicated something else. *Drugged!* The lighting was brilliant white, and with movement came the sounds of the subtle crinkles of the polypropylene gowns and hoods encapsulating her and Rocco.

"Good morning, Hammetts." A voice greeted from a speaker from somewhere within the room.

Rocco bolted upright, fighting for breath and tugging at the straps around his ankles and wrists. He concentrated on them to no effect. In kind, Anastasia could not sense anything at all. It was as if part of her was torn away—amputated by the lack of a particulate atmosphere.

"Who is this and why are you doing this to us?" Anastasia cried.

"Please, try to relax and stay calm."

A beacon flashed, and a door opened with a rush of air. Two people in bunny suits and oxygen masks entered and walked towards them. One carried a tablet. Rocco scanned the room and noticed several lenses in strategic locations, not much else. The room was purposely innocuous—a clean room designed to prohibit paranormal manipulation.

"Rocco, if you promise to behave, I will remove those straps. We are not here to do any harm; you have my word."

"And who's word do we have, and why should it matter to *me*?" Rocco snapped.

"My name is Doctor Lattimer. You and your friends are guests of the United States under my supervision. We anticipate your questions, and mistrust, frankly. We hope to earn that in short order. Are we going to have any problems?"

Rocco and Anastasia looked at each other and shook their heads.

"Perfect." Lattimer motioned to his assistant, who began removing Rocco's restraints.

"Where is Captain Montluc?" Anastasia asked.

"Your remarkable pilot is with the French Consulate by her request. She will be apprised of your status during this joint investigation."

"Is that it then? We are being investigated? For what?"

"In time. First, I must inform you that for obvious reasons we had to take precautions necessary to protect ourselves from any misunderstandings. Second, you were sedated for a period of six hours and flown here to Piney Mountain—one of our secure research facilities in southern Pennsylvania. Some of your friends are here. Patrick, Master Sun, Chairman River and his son Abraham. Captain Montluc only said that her employer—your sponsor, Mallory Du Rennes—had been killed along with his bodyguard. We need to know what happened and why. We at the Defense Advanced Research Projects Agency are also interested in you as a national security concern. Yes, we know about you, hence the restraints. Last, and I hope you understand this part, we are here for mutual benefit. Now, can we get rid of these coveralls? I can't stand the things."

Lattimer motioned to a camera on the ceiling in a corner of the room. A moment later, the door opened with two additional bunny-suited techs flanking the doorway.

"Follow us, please. Just down the hallway is a changing room with fresh clothes for you. We will meet the others up top in ten minutes."

Up top? Rocco thought.

Under supervision, Doctor Lattimer escorted them to an exiting concrete and steel patio that traversed into a forested overlook. The air was crisp and light, wafting through the mature white pines dotting a picnic area. There were no apparent fences, although Anastasia sensed that any attempt of escape might be futile. Her captors exuded confidence and determination. There was no malice or deception either, and she relayed as much to Rocco. The group walked further into the woods, down a gentle hillside to an open overlook with 10-foot round concrete table and seating.

"Aye, look who it 'tis, will ya," said Patrick, smiling wide and standing. The others stood up and turned around. Rocco and Anastasia greeted their open arms and took their seats. Conversations erupted between the hugs, mostly concerning their treatment and what occurred. Then other questions ensued. What happened to Du Rennes? Where were Dao, Chris, and Matt? What should become of them in this environment?

"I feared we would have been separated and dissected," said River, reaching down to scratch Snickers behind an ear.

Doctor Lattimer stood by and listened to their concerns until his phone vibrated.

"Excellent. Send him down immediately, then I'll be on my way."

Faces turned towards him after he replaced the phone to his trouser pocket.

"Your questions and concerns are about to be answered."

Jet Sun smiled, "Yet not our release."

"That is above my pay grade, Master Sun, and we both know any mention of you to your embassy is fraught with... *difficult* entanglements."

A grey-suited man with well-coifed white hair and anchor beard stepped down the crushed pebble pathway with Monsignor Trovarto at his side. They appeared to be carrying on a discussion when they rounded the last hairpin.

"Sir." Doctor Lattimer shook the suited man's hand, then turned to Trovarto. "Father, as much as I sincerely wish to remain for what will certainly be an interesting conversation, my attentions are required in Maryland. Seems we have a breakthrough."

"Ah, this is good news, indeed. Best-a luck to you and give them my regards," said the monsignor, who turned to greet the others with hugs and kisses on both cheeks.

"Who's the snowman then, Father?" Patrick asked.

The man smiled and addressed the table. "My name Arthur Garrick. You undoubtedly have never heard my name for it was forbidden to utter it. I hope you understand. Especially you, Rocco and Tulip. Your father was a dear friend to me. I will miss Anund and his jokes terribly."

Garrick walked over to River and knelt down to Snickers, lifting his head up and scratching underneath his neck. "Quite the survivor."

He looked around the table at the other faces, settling on Anastasia. "Of course, you possess the power to determine my truth innately, and…" He turned to Patrick. "The power to strike me down if I am lying."

"What difference would that make?" River asked. "Freedom is not ours. Where could we go that you would not follow?"

"That is why I am here, Chairman River. Fact is, you are all free to leave if that is what you desire. I only ask that that you first listen to what I need to say."

River looked at the others and their curious expressions. None stood up.

Garrick continued. "*La Fratellanza di Verità* and the task of its ultimate preservation is mine. I am the reserve—the insurance policy. The primary groups that evaded us for centuries are finally resolved, or will be shortly."

"How can you be so sure?" River asked.

"While the certainty of success cannot be 100%, the probability of such is a high enough to instill the necessary confidence to suggest that outcome. Actions in Cairo, Russia, Cambodia and in Washington have sufficiently exposed and truncated the global destabilizers—the evil that perpetually thwarts true progress. There's only the one remaining—our oldest and most formidable enemy, the Spada Sacra."

"Where is my daughter?"

Garrick turned to Jet Sun. "Safe, healthy and willfully engineering for DARPA with Doctor Miller and Doctor Lattimer, who just embarked towards their laboratory—not far from here, in fact. Their device is a national security matter. Its science will be conveyed, demonstrated and adjudicated accordingly. If determined to be a threat, those protocols will activate. If not, well, let's just say our lives will become a little more interesting."

Anastasia had been distracted and withdrawn for several minutes. She was processing a tremendous amount of drama and was mentally drained. Another tremor jolted her, although the others missed it. She labored to keep focus on Arthur Garrick. She shivered once more and noticed the fine hairs of her left arm standing straight up. The sensation was difficult to place, as well was the exact emotion. It came from a great distance, one with which she was not familiar. The further she reached, the more that point of reference disappeared within the static of a billion souls. The stronger she concentrated, the reference appeared and disappeared. She couldn't hold it—her strength almost depleted—she sensed it was terribly important and held on.

"Tulip?" Garrick interrupted himself.

"NO!" She screamed, squeezing her temples with her palms.

● ● ●

"His *elites?*" Joint Special Operations Command (JSOC) Commander Benton asked, incredulous of the live satellite feed.

The President's head dropped to his hands. He sniffled and patted the sweat from his brow with his soiled handkerchief. He stared at General Thunderlake, eyes squinted. The Situation Room was suspended in reticence.

"The Spada Sacra were obviously tipped," the General rasped. "What arrogance to think they could simply land at the airport or sail onto the beach, expecting the island would capitulate at their mere sight. We shelled that place for a solid month in 1943 before setting foot on it. Commander Benton, assume the entire island is hostile, same as it was in Islamabad. Same drill. Lightning strike—in and out. That's it. Tell the Italians and the Vatican nothing, understand?"

The President got up, looked around the table, and walked out.

"We need to talk."

Matthew snugged his boot-sneaker laces, binding the double slipknot extra tight. He glanced up at the colonel with the look of contempt before switching to the other boot.

"Commander, I will not have any animosity on this trip, so if you have something to grind about Bonneville, the bridge, or anything else, now is the time."

"I don't think we *have* enough time, Colonel." Matthew tightened the other knot and stood within a couple feet, face-to-face.

Osterhoudt turned away. "I merely wanted to apologize. It shouldn't have happened."

"Apologize? Colonel, didn't you once tell us to never apologize? That only the meek go around apologizing for everything?"

"Yes. I'm not sorry about that; I just don't want you angry with me for doing my job—what I mistakenly thought was the right thing. No distraction. After what happened at the Pentagon with the Russians, we were out for blood. General Tomlinson—that conniving bitch! God, was I wrong about her. Played us all. It seems everyone's out for themselves these days."

"Colonel, I'm not nearly as angry with you as I am with those bastards that chased me all over the planet." Matthew collected his pack, sidearm and rifle. "Now what kind of jump is this?"

"The kind nobody's made."

Several minutes flew by, Osterhoudt, Jacobson and 18 other hand-selected operators were assembled in a hangar at a bristling-new concourse located at the south end of Andrews. Flanked by a two-star general and his assistant, a JSOC technical advisor—a ponytailed Air Force captain in tactical, sporting '80s-retro glasses with oversized square rims— checked her tablet before launching into the brief. To her surprise, she already had everyone's undivided attention without having to ask for it.

She scratched behind an ear while reexamining the tablet once more. "According to my records, all of you are well-experienced HALO jumpers. Some of you, but not all, are also familiar with JPADS deployments."

She glanced towards four soldiers grouped on her right. "Four of you have undergone simulation training for this type of jump which is so new, it hasn't earned an official acronym for anyone to mock yet."

Several chuffs erupted from the men, and one of the four trained operators spoke up. "Canned Operator Drop System is the current frontrunner, ma'am."

The advisor's eyes magnified several degrees and rolled to the top of her frames as she checked the ramp behind. The general, unamused, stepped forward and whispered into her ear.

Her brow narrowed. "In fifteen minutes, a modified B-1T Lancer will land and park just behind me for refueling. It will ferry you all to Pantelleria Island in the Mediterranean at Mach 2.5, and, at about eight miles from shore and 45,000 feet, she will sweep her wings forward, decrease to 300 knots, and drop three containers from her bomb bays. These containers are JPADS-spec. Two are configured for ten operators apiece and stowage. The third container is for larger equipment, armaments and munitions. Take note, your pack stowage is in a separate compartment at the aft of the operator units. You will glide in two-by-two, semi-seated position with your pilots at the front. They are responsible for descent guidance, chute deployment and retraction, ventilation mix, and communications until you touch down. Your expected flight time is just under four hours, non-stop. Suffice to say, any of you need to go, you have about forty minutes until you're sardined. Any questions?"

"Semi-seated?" A hand raised towards the rear of the group.

"Yes, the containers use a half-seat in an elevated position that supports some of your weight but not all. The reduced profile allows us to pack more personnel in a tighter space. You were selected because none of you are claustrophobic. It will not be comfortable. This is the sacrifice for time capability. There is currently no other ferrying and deployment system anywhere close to this capability. By the time you arrive, your closest help will still be three hours out. Additional logistics will be disseminated en route."

A piercing wail grew in the distance, causing the advisor to turn around and step beyond the hangar's threshold once more, checking the ramp. She shouted to overcome the roar in the background. "Make that thirty minutes."

* * *

Emily lost her breath as she turned away from the hauptmann. Something nagged at her mind. Visions flashed with a stinging sensation at the back of her head. She sheathed her blade and rubbed her scalp, attempting to massage it away. Narciso took notice.

"What is it?" he asked.

"I don't know!" Emily cried. "Ah!" She yelped as another twinge gripped her skull. The flashes intensified. Brilliant white, then copper. Each modulation sent stinging jolts throughout her spinal column. The last was a tall woman. The light surrounding her was a brilliant white, and she barely recognized the figure when suddenly darkness and silence followed. She turned around to find Narciso just behind her, his hand on her shoulder. His left brow was raised, his lips pursed.

"Emily?" He spoke softly. "Tell me what happened."

"I can't!" She cried, unable to move.

"Surely you can describe it, child." He sneered. "Tell me."

"Lights." She mumbled. "Bright lights, and—"

"And what?"

"I don't know!" Emily was confused, not sure if what she saw was real. She refused to believe it. And, just as she resolved to put it away, another flash stung. She cried out in pain, unable to stop whatever it was attacking her mind.

Esposito turned towards his captain. "Cleanse the intruders; you know where to process them. Deposit their wreckage as well."

The bishop paused and gazed westward over the distant horizon. His nostrils flared and his eyes squinted at the deep blue of it. He took several deep breaths, drinking the air. He nodded in some form of recognition. He turned towards Emily, "Come, child; the doctor will see you."

Emily's eyes widened. Absent since her first days of capture, a sense of deep dread and anxiety returned. She remembered the face of an old man seated in a powered chair behind the glass walls of a laboratory that reminded her of her father's Andromeda. He locked eyes with hers as she passed, both fixated and curious.

● ● ●

"I lost it!" Anastasia cried, aggravated. "I mean her... I think."

"Lost what? Who?" said Garrick.

"I think it was her—the doctor's daughter."

"Annie, how is that even possible? You never met." Rocco said.

"It's possible." Garrick said, flatly.

Jet Sun glanced across the table to River, then down to a panting Snickers, who remained tranced by the chief's continual scratching on the back of his neck and ears. The shadows of wind-rustled leaves danced between shimmers of sunlight upon him, and the beams flashed the dander and fur as they wisped off Snicker's head into the breezes.

"My western counterparts spoke often of the tribes—their healers and readers," said Jet Sun. "Reading is a skill that continues to elude me. I know enough to extract disconnected, incoherent flashes, which may or may not come to light later. You knew this day would come."

"I knew only of an eminent pivotal confluence. Visions are often cloudy and not meant for full understanding, else their natural purpose is jeopardized. It is only when the visions are crystal that the vision is entrusted upon the reader. They may interfere or acquiesce as they see fit."

River continued, "My mother believed it was intrinsic to our people. Heredity. I am confident other factors contributed. The positive belief in our skills and their cultivation, the lifelong pursuit. Yet, for some—" River turned towards Anastasia. "—it is a natural extension. Tell me, young lady, what did you see?"

"Flashes of light, then, her face in pain. She was angry—furious—then I saw what she saw, only... There was blood all around. Bodies. Dead men. Soldiers, I think. Standing in their midst was a woman. Older, but not old. Nude within a mist. Her expression... stern disapproval and disappointment, but also love and concern. Said nothing. Said everything. I felt it might have been her mother. A vestige. She was either a residual memory or actually there, I could not tell which."

"Manifestation from a vexed soul," said River. "This is not uncommon, although legend abounds of lucid spirits calling upon us in times of desperation."

"There is more." Anastasia looked at Jet Sun. "Her anger and hatred were focused on her father, although I could not ascertain why."

"Abandonment." River said. "It is a principal anxiety of youth."

"Aye." Patrick agreed. "As far as she sees it, he left and she was kidnapped because of it. And I bet that manwagon priest is usin' it against her."

Jet Sun peered across the surrounding hillsides as a zephyr whispered through, and the glint of daylight paled by several degrees. Snickers suddenly broke from the trance of euphoria and stood forward of the table, his nostrils moistened from intensive probing. He turned his head around to River as if to ask, "I sense it; do you?" He swung his head back into the breeze for confirmation.

River probed his own kinetics within the feel of the air, his eyes remaining shut while doing so. Jet Sun and the others watched him intently except for Anastasia. Her mind continued to wrestle with the vision—the flashes—and their feel. There was another branch affecting her. Something closer. Something familiar.

"You need help." River said to her.

Seat of The Pants

The passenger capsule passed through the tunnel's rings of light at such a speed to create consistent illumination with almost imperceptible velocity. That velocity was reached within 68 seconds of departure at a comfortable half-g acceleration. The vehicle's top speed was unintelligible by design. Testing concluded with a significant percentage of passengers severely uncomfortable with concrete and metal infrastructure whizzing by the capsule's windows at 750 MPH. Doctor Stanley Lattimer grew accustomed to the tube's gentle acceleration years ago since his selection to head DARPA's scientific branch. The ride was less than five minutes to Joint Base Andrews's Senior Executive Terminal from Site R, his regular connection—several seconds less to Shangri-La, which was six miles away off another branch. The low-pressure tube maglev system was part of a high-clearance project necessitated by vulnerabilities demonstrated by terrorist operations decades before. They connected the President, Congress, the Supreme Court, the Pentagon, and Joint Base Andrews to the secure bunkers beneath Shangri-La in northern Maryland and Raven Rock, codenamed Site R, located just across Pennsylvania's southern border. This was a rare stop for Lattimer; his capsule was headed for the U.S. Capitol platform underneath Emancipation Hall.

Upon arrival, Lattimer stepped onto an elevator at the far end of the platform, swiped his keycard, and pressed the button for the second floor. The doors closed, then moments later opened to what used to be a senator's office, now used as three classified terminals for the tube system at the Capitol.

Across the hallway was the oaken doorway to a Senator named Dawson, and two chambers from that door, the senator sat behind his desk, wrapping his magical Banff golf outing to the DARPA's Deputy Director, Dr. Whitmore—a finely-attired executive with gold-chained sunglasses hanging at his chest.

"Doctor Lattimer," said the senator. "Glad to finally make your acquaintance. Please have a seat."

"Leave us." Dawson ordered his administrative assistant.

The senator motioned towards a plush armchair next to Whitmore.

"I suppose the simplified question should be *when*?"

"I don't understand." Lattimer said.

"Stanley, he wants to know when we will have a working prototype of Miller's reader, when will we have a writer, and at what point does the Adaptive Capabilities Office become involved?"

"Wrong," said Dawson.

"Pardon?" Dr. Whitmore turned around.

"It's my retirement, gentlemen, as in *when* do I get to retire?" Dawson laughed. "The science is interesting and all, but I see this as my golden fun ticket—my line to a pearl diver served in my private Tahitian overwater bungalow by some hot young *vahine*—and I'd like to have it before I'm 45."

Lattimer scratched at his beard. "If all goes well, the reader should be ready by next week. I can't provide a solid ETA for the latter, although preliminary data suggests that the writer is theoretically feasible within a few subsequent weeks. Adaptive will take it from there."

"Ballpark?" Dawson asked.

Lattimer raised a brow. "No idea. Ask Doctor Schechter. If you can pry him off his robot mules, that is."

"Still at it?" asked Whitmore.

"Schechter vowed never to be accused as a quitter, Senator. The new mules are nearly silent at a full trot, fully armored, weight capacity tripled, and it's optionally armed with a CROWS machine gun, grenade launcher, or a laser-ranged microgun."

"Tripled the price too, I hope."

Whitmore grinned wide.

● ● ●

As he approached the massive bomber with its wings extended, Matt glanced up at the pilots busily running through the multitude of tasks on their pre-flight checklist, as well as programming the flight computer with their route. Departure vectors, base and weather conditions, communications checks. Their hands were full. Down below, ground crew were wrapping up the fuel lines, securing hatches, and assisting Osterhoudt's raiders into their carbon fiber drop containers. Starting at the front, the two pilots assumed their semi-seated positions. Crewmen snugged their restraining systems and connected their oxygen and headset coms, then closed the gullwing doors. The next two climbed into their positions and underwent the same procedure. Matt slid into his seat and let his weight settle on the narrow rectangular cushion which was bolted to a tube extending from a center support rail. Two additional pads were just behind his lower and upper back, with a whiplash cushion just behind his head.

"Jesus."

He leaned against them, wondering how his knees would hold up to the light but constant pressure. Within five minutes, the containers were populated and ready for loading. A modified heavy munitions lift raised each magazine into the bomb bays, where they clicked into their final, connected positions. A few sporadic jokes crackled in Matt's earpieces. They continued as the bomb bay doors closed into momentary darkness. Dim LEDs ignited overhead as their back cushion displays booted.

"Testing... 1, 2—" A voice broke in. "All right nut butts, listen up. You've got around four hours in the cans until we drop your sorry asses, so settle in—snake some rack time if possible."

Before anyone cracked another line, the four F101 engines sequentially spooled up to start, ushering a deafening roar on each flank. Matt stuffed his earbuds deeper to counter the noise. Nobody mentioned this part. He could hear the faint complaints of others in his container, partly on the com system, and within the chamber itself. There was a good chance they'd all be deaf before the drop. It was becoming unbearable. They felt movement. Their displays suddenly switched to the nose point-of-view towards the front, unobstructed. They were taxiing towards the north end of Andrews.

None of them were prepared for the piercing wail that ensued once their jet turned to face south. Except, as soon as the pain and shock numbed their temples, the com system's noise-cancelling kicked on, bringing their torture to a sudden halt.

"Oops," said the captain, locking the switch.

The pilots lit the afterburners and rocketed their albatross across the Chesapeake and out to the glistening Atlantic, destined for a refueling tango outside the visible range of Lajes's base in the Azores. That leg was just under two hours at Mach 2.5. From there it would be slower going; anything supersonic would be felt at ground level.

* * *

Esposito's physician placed the electron scanner in front of Emily's face and secured it to her snugly, molding itself to her contours. She could not move, and for the next few moments, barely breathe. The sensors made four passes each on four directions, although any movement was unintelligible. There were no moving parts. The stereoscopic eyes recorded every space between her atoms, differentiating the molecules of air from flesh and fiber. The procedure completed in less than twenty seconds, after which it released itself, allowing Emily to exhale then take a deep breath.

The physician resembled several of the soldiers Emily noticed. Young and fit, blond crew cuts and blue eyes. Prominent, dimpled chins and hairless, lightly tanned skin. It was his age that Emily thought odd. Most physicians she encountered were old, and to her, "old" meant over-30. This man appeared the same age as her father's lab interns, and they were just out of high school—under 20. She thought about the VR helmet. It excited her. *I could be anything by that age. Why stop at one thing? Assassin, pilot, doctor, or even an engineer. Better than Dad, too. Take that!* Her stomach soured.

The doctor stepped away towards a closed hallway at the back of the exam room. He entered a tech-heavy lab and sat in front of a workstation featuring desk-wide ultra-resolution display that used imperceptibly-sized pixels. The three-dimensional scan of Emily's face soon appeared on it, and the doctor zoomed into the rings, furrows and crypts of her dominant iris, mapping her genealogical path to existence.

The colors and patterns are unique to her, yet unlock a code to understanding behavioral traits and history. Probability of one's actions, predictability, was crucial for her programming. Should anything deviate from an expectation, her eyes held the answer. Not in this case.

When the physician increased the scan's magnification a hundred-fold, he detected the movement of a sparkle. He increased magnification further and recorded another one, yet it was no larger than before. At full magnification, it happened yet again.

"*Was ist?*"

"*Die Resteinmischung eines anderen Geistes, Josef.*" A voice said from behind. "Do you not recognize it from before?"

"Ja, but—" He paused.

"We've found it, Josef. By tomorrow I will have the answer—my cure. *Ehre sei ihm.*"

The physician returned to Emily's side.

"There is nothing wrong with you." He smiled wide with full lips and placed a cup containing a translucent liquid with the slightest tinge of blue on her overbed table.

"The headache is the byproduct of dehydration. You must drink additional amounts of Tesla's Nectar before and during operations, yes?"

Emily nodded. She loved the drink and consumed it as water, although less than half a bottle usually satiated her thirst. The physician turned around and strode back down the hallway. As soon as he closed the door behind him, Emily sighed in anger. She knew it wasn't dehydration. She drank an entire bottle before the last battle, and through her training she learned to recognize the energy lows of hunger. She knew the stiffness and cramps of dehydration too. This was different, and she knew the doctor just lied to her. *Why?* She thought. She was used to their lying—the omissions of the Spada Sacra. If there was one thing for which she was certain, it was that if the Spada Sacra hid something from you, the obvious lie was your first, and possibly last, clue. Something was about to happen and she felt it. She felt something else too, and it nagged at her mind in random periodic waves.

As Dr. Lattimer and Rebecca Morningwood looked on from above, Chris and Dao stood several steps from Shangri-La's Axon Terminalization critical zone as the 10-second countdown progressed. The robotic arm had already placed the needle of Dao's syringe containing the atomic-level nanobots beneath the surface of the sustaining fluid. When the timer hit zero, the robot injected the hoard, and their peculiar ripping noise crescendoed within seconds. The workstation monitors displayed the gradual solidification of the module as well as the connection count and stability readings, predictably reaching the billions within a few moments.

"What's that fluctuation?" Lattimer asked, pointing to the connection count.

"Tissue plasticity." Chris said. "It's consistent with normal neural function. A small fraction of connections are constantly lost and restored or replaced."

"A curious anomaly." Lattimer gazed at the monitor's display as the process concluded on the video feed."

Dao ran the memory diagnostics and confirmed the results through the intercom system. "Stable."

A dull murmur of congratulations could be heard from the observation room—Andromeda's technicians bumping fists with nods of confidence. Morningwood smiled dourly.

"Is something wrong?" Dao looked at Lattimer's puzzled expression.

"Maybe, I don't know." Lattimer paused. "Whitmore and his bunch are pushing the schedule pretty hard on your prototype. They need to know they aren't wasting their time."

"Just what in the hell do they mean by that?" Chris barked.

"The situation with your daughter has become complicated, Chris."

"She's an American citizen, God Damnit! What did the President say during his campaign? 'We won't rest until all that want to come home *are* home?'"

"I know, I know. They are expensing enormous resources to recover Emily, but... I wish I knew more. They aren't telling me everything, which places me in a difficult situation. They want your reader up and tested by the end of the day. That's the deadline."

Dao's eyes bulged. Chris choked on his own laughter, biting his hand to contain himself.

"Either you've grossly misread my development script or you know something I don't. Which is it?"

Lattimer sighed. "They weren't going to tell you—"

"Oh, here it comes." Chris threw his hands up.

"Most of your notes were, in fact, recovered from Andromeda."

Chris turned to Dao. "You see?"

She winced.

Lattimer continued. "And most of your laptop prototype has already been remanufactured, except that module."

"And there it is. They've already got one! I bet it's *very*—"

"No Chris." Dao grabbed his arm. "Do not continue this." She turned to Lattimer. "It was unwise of you to conceal that information."

"I *am* sorry, believe me, however our government takes national security concerns quite seriously. That part shouldn't bear repeating. And Doctor Ming, your participation, while to be commended, presents us with additional considerations as you might imagine. Let me be frank. There is no trust until the results of our actions provide the basis for it. Doctor Ming?"

Dao Ming glossed over on the mention of her name, for an echo of it resonated with greater volume and clarity in recognition of her father's voice.

"Doctor Ming?" Lattimer repeated.

The daughter of the engineer has been found. Anastasia is not strong enough to bridge her mind. The distance is too great. Evil clouds the girl. Shadows and whispers in hateful bloodlust.

Dao's eyes blinked rapidly as she broke concentration. "Trust, yes. It is a mutual concern, of course."

"Is something troubling you, Doctor Ming? You seem distracted."

She looked at Chris, took him by the hand, and paced towards the air lock. "Inform your people the device will be operational this evening."

Lattimer pursed his lips. "Okay," he said with a tone lacking full confidence. "Wait, where are you two going?"

"If it is to be a long evening, we should first have dinner. I prefer a view."

Dao dropped her father's message on Chris.

"Help? A *séance*? As in holding hands and calling on the spirit world to talk to your dead grandmother, kind of séance? Come on!"

"No, it is not that type of... okay maybe similar, but no. Anastasia found her, Chris. She is in trouble."

"This is killing me, Dao. We must do *something!*"

"Yes, but not yet. The opportunity must present itself."

Lattimer turned away from the monitor in a sweat.

"My finger's on the button, Stanley," Dr. Whitmore said. "And it will stay there until that reader's in my hands and working."

"And what about Raven Rock?" Lattimer asked. "What is Dr. Ming talking about?"

"We're handling it."

Three and a half hours since returning from dinner, the freshly-minted laptop had yet to recognize a single strand of information from a particulate-rich testing chamber. Their assistants were dismissed an hour into the session. Chris' mind raced with alternative explanations, as did Dao's. It's not the sustaining fluid's temperature or any other variable of the memory system, he thought; their gauges indicated as such. Stable, as it was on the original. Lattimer didn't understand and began to wonder. The buzz in his ear monitor echoed the same, although with more pointed theories and accusations. *Would the doctor sacrifice his own daughter for the secrecy of the reader? Why? Is it something to do with the Chinese national?*

Chris noticed Lattimer's preoccupation and glanced at Dao. He felt sick. The anxiety welling in his gut intensified.

"I don't understand! There must be an explanation. Some subatomic variance in the nanos, a temperature or humidity deviation from tolerances, a faulty reading—either with this equipment or, oh—Christ! What if a calibration reading was off at Andromeda? Are we digging in the wrong place, Dao?"

"Chris, to support that conclusion we must first eliminate all potential deviations."

Dao glanced towards Lattimer. "We are at an impasse and require more time."

Lattimer's earbud erupted. "Dawson won't buy it. I don't either. They're obviously stalling, Stanley."

"With his daughter at stake?" Lattimer whispered. "Doubtful," replied Dr. Whitmore.

"They're smart people, Doctor. We must assume they realize we aren't going to such trouble, placing asses and assets on the line just for some kid."

"Of course not, but it's his only shot."

"What about the Chinese?"

"She's in love with him."

"Unsubstantiated conclusions, Stanley."

"You can't possibly be suggesting she would sabotage the project."

"If we are eliminating all possibilities? Dao Ming is a Chinese national and registered member of its national party. Don't forget that."

"I will review all the cross-referenced data and eliminate every possibility before questioning her good will, Dr. Whitmore. Remember, she took a bullet for them."

"Six hours, Stan. Not one minute more."

Dao Ming paused when a message locked onto her mind. *Remember the will of balance. Every good creates an offsetting evil. Extremes beget extremes.*

Yes, she remembered her teachings of her childhood, she thought. She felt the imbalance, the welling of evil as lava reaching a caldera's rim. Soon it would spill into the world and cement itself as part of it. She must act soon. They all must.

Chris, Dao and Lattimer inspected every instrument's calibration, and confirmed every parameter of the new reader. They reviewed tape of Dao's station before and during the tissue assimilation and subsequent reader testing. Nothing. Their deadline was fast approaching. Chris concluded, as he had feared, that the only remaining plausible explanation was that an instrument at Andromeda must have been in error. Replicating results could take weeks or months if every variable is explored. The stress was unbearable, and he was caving to it. A fever gained control, and in that fever—the heat and perspiration—lightning struck.

"Doctor Lattimer," Chris shouted across the floor of the lab as he waved his hands low. "This isn't working and we need to go." He unzipped his bunny suit and climbed out of it.

"Wait. What? No!" Lattimer stumbled to reach him before complete removal but it was too late; the room would be contaminated for hours. "Doctor Miller, why?"

He grabbed Chris by the arm, and Chris wrenched it away with a thrusting pivot towards the airlock. Dao joined him and started to remove her mask and suit. Lattimer dashed after them and just made the doors before they latched shut.

"What are you doing!" He yelled above the deafening roar of air from above.

"We have to go." Chris shouted.

"Where?"

"To be with the others. Our presence is required—and now."

"The others? You can't go there! What about the reader? What about your daughter? They won't let you two out of here!" Lattimer shouted.

His earbuds cackled with directives he barely heard. Orders for him to contain the situation. Whitmore's aid threatened him under the direct instructions of his boss, who was asleep at the moment, but insisted he be awakened at the end of the six-hour deadline with a message of success or failure. Whitmore didn't anticipate an alternative contingency, and the aid wrestled with the confliction of interpretation. He perceived it was going the way of failure, except the six hours had not elapsed. Lattimer still had time. He looked at his watch; close to one hour remained.

"Doctor Lattimer!" The aid yapped into the microphone.

Lattimer broke into a sweat, doubled over, panting heavily, and braced himself at the lab's doorway as Chris and Dao disappeared down the hall. The squeaks from his earbud had become incessant as it dangled from his neckline, spinning slowly in free space. He picked himself up and gradually gained momentum in pursuit, ignoring the monitors.

"No, no no—" said the aid in a panic, busily switching surveillance cameras. When Chris and Dao reached the elevators connecting to the tube transit, he knew Whitmore needed to be alerted. "Shit!" he yelled, pacing back and forth in front of the monitors.

He clicked on Whitmore's number and waited. Several seconds ticked by until his earpieces scratched with the irritated tone of broken vocal cords and phlegm.

"You're an hour early. I hope you realize this."

"Dr. Whitmore, beg pardon sir, but you instructed to be awakened should anything—"

"Get to the point, corporal."

"The scientists are attempting to escape."

"What? How? Why haven't you stopped them?"

"I couldn't, sir."

"Oh? Why not? Where's Lattimer?"

"I think he's helping them, sir."

"Lock it down."

"It's too late sir, they're in the tube?"

"Do you know where they're going, corporal?"

"One of them mentioned 'the others', sir. I don't know what he meant."

"Is Lattimer with them?"

"No."

"Arrest Dr. Lattimer and hold him there. Leave the others to me."

"Yes sir!"

Whitmore looked at the clock and wiped across his brow with a handkerchief from the nightstand. He turned the lamp on, checked his water glass for any floating bugs—a phobia carried from youth—and took two gulps as he dialed Senator Dawson's cell.

Dao initiated the shuttle's destination and launch sequence into the navigation interface and hit Execute. The cylinder's doors slid shut and the monitor displayed the countdown while the tube depressurized. She sat back, fastened her lap restraint, and took Chris' hand.

"70-seconds. The capsule cannot reach maximum velocity before it must begin braking."

Chris smiled at her; his upper lip tucked. He saw that she was astonished by the technology. She probably would have hated his Volkswagen, he thought.

The capsule lunged forward and rapidly built speed to 500 MPH then at once, the emergency alarms blared and the tunnel's lighting flipped from daylight white to scarlet. The two were thrown against their belts in a savage braking maneuver. The capsule suddenly came to a severe halt, then, as part of some remote automation, the cockpit panels and interior lighting went dark.

"Are you sure, sir?"

"Do it," barked Dawson.

The controller removed the safety protocols of the capsule and initiated the evacuation of its air.

"How long?"

Chris suddenly heard a telltale hiss of air and looked at Dao. She turned to him with the look of dread. Chris looked up and down the cockpit controls, tapping and probing each for any sign of actuation. He smashed his fists upon the displays, cracking two of them.

"Bastards!" He cried, barely catching a glimpse of off-colored light in the distance.

He stepped forward in the capsule looked through the glass of the emergency door at the front. Dao stepped behind him and, cupping her hands on the glass, saw the faint outline of indented hand and footholds climbing the side of the tube towards a cylindrical access leading upwards.

Chris rolled his eyes and shook his head. "Naturally."

They both looked down at the capsule door's emergency lever and felt the air thinning. There was no time to contemplate or calculate. They both inhaled deeply as Chris yanked on the lever. The door flew outward as the last of the capsule's air decompressed. The sudden explosion of pressure tugged at Chris and Dao as they jumped from the exit onto the tunnel's concrete floor. They paced quickly towards the laddered access some thirty meters distant. Chris convulsed to exhale as Dao climbed ahead of him, disappearing upward into the tubular access. He stepped onto the first rung and forced himself upward, his concentration on the steps themselves, not his breath or the pain burning in his lungs. He felt the tingling effects of hypoxia on his arms, then his legs. His body was starving. His mind would go soon. He let some air go to reduce the pressure. Dao was just above him, climbing towards the darkness. She looked down only once to see the silhouette of Chris' movement against the red light of the tunnel's background. She saw him suffering. They were close.

When she reached the top, she felt for the hatch lid and its locking mechanism. To her astonishment, the lid was smooth and devoid of any manual way to open it. She banged on it and felt around for any possible electronic switch. She wanted to scream as she pounded on the thick metal. Chris looked up at her as his grip weakened. Dao yelled his name out as he started to slip backward. She dropped down a step to grab him. A deafening rush of air blasted them, flexing their eardrums. The light of a flashlight suddenly burst upon them from above. Chris exhaled and drew a deep breath, coughing as his body braced against the shaft's wall. The tingling had peaked, now he felt its ebb. A muscular hand extended from the light to Dao and she took it without hesitation, hacking for another lungful of air. Chris waited as his body caught up and the hyperventilation ceased. At that point, he reached for the next rung and climbed out into the crisp mountain air beneath Raven Rock.

"I knew you'd get it." Dao said to her father as she hugged him.

Jet Sun, Monsignor Trovarto and Rocco looked at Chris as he stood up in disbelief. A voice came from the darkness behind them.

"We must reach your daughter before our friends regroup. Please, this way," said Arthur Garrick, pointing up the hill behind them.

"Friends? What friends?" Chris asked.

Garrick turned around with a sarcastic look before continuing into the wooded hillside.

"And what do you mean, *reach?*" Chris added.

Rocco brought himself alongside Chris as they began plodding up the partially-graveled trail. "My sister will explain."

Doctor Lattimer rushed back to his Shangri-La second-story office in a panic, reached into a desk drawer and withdrew a high-capacity card drive and stuck it into his breast pocket. He turned back around to leave when the round from Corporal Evans' suppressed pistol ricocheted off his skull's frontal bone, scoring a three-inch upwards gash just over his left eyebrow and knocking him unconscious. Evans walked over and placed a finger on Lattimer's neck, grimaced, shoved the suppressor against his temple and squeezed a second time. Lattimer's skull flew apart from the blast, having been cracked by the first shot. Blood and tissue painted Evans and a significant portion of the office. He jumped up, spewing the bits that flew into his open mouth. Lattimer's private lavatory was in the next room and Evans ran for it. He and two others were in for a long morning sanitizing the office and disposing Lattimer's corpse. Their cleanup job would ultimately prove inadequate.

"The Miller laptop computer that is in your possession, Your Excellency, I will require it," said a Bayrisch-accented voice from behind and to the side of his lab assistant. "We cannot solve our equation without it."

Esposito spun around, head cocked in a snarl. The flash of violet pulsated before him. The assistant instinctively jumped in front, protecting a frail old man in his wheelchair.

"Halt!" The voice yelled in a higher pitch. The man caught the glint of Narciso' saffron irises. "*Um Gottes willen!*"

Esposito lowered the cane.

"Do you not realize, You Excellency? What this device represents? It is the key—the gateway—to transference."

Esposito's posture remained at the ready as the assistant withdrew. "You said it impossible, *Herr Doktor.*"

"Yah, Narciso. That is, until—" The voice paused. The man stared at Esposito. "I wonder..."

"What are you doing?" Esposito stepped back as the man wheeled himself closer, looking beyond the cane.

"I wish to examine your eyes. There is something—"

"NO!" Esposito braced his stance and was about to strike when the lab assistant burst in front as the amethyst crystal drained its charge upon him. The assistant dropped onto the floor, limp and helpless—eyes exploded.

"There, you see!" Said the doctor as the bishop caught his breath, extinguishing the cane. "It will become worse, Your Excellency. You know it. You have seen him, yes? In the mirror?"

Esposito glanced at him with a face of anxiety.

"Yes," said the doctor with a deep, accusive tone as he rolled closer still. "You *have* seen him."

"The jester," whispered Esposito, gazing into space.

The wheelchaired doctor caught movement at the doorway behind Esposito. The bishop grit his teeth and turned towards Emily, who was trembling in her patients' gown, staring down at the young doctor on the floor—frozen, yet aware, with tears streaking down his ubiquitous face from eyes that struggled in abbreviated movements.

Warning beacons within each room flipped on and flashed a brilliant red cadence. Sirens blasted throughout the complex. Esposito reached into his cassock and withdrew his communicator. Flash text:

```
NNW inbound contact, non-commercial: 24km, 400kts
```

"Sister Regina will deliver the machine. Come child," said Esposito. "More visitors for you to greet."

She continued staring at the young man on the floor as Esposito passed through the doorway beside her.

"Get out!" The wheelchaired man shouted, activating the door's motor from a button his right armrest.

He wheeled back around and looked at his aid. "*Schade, mein Champion.*"

He pressed another button on his armrest. Soon after another aid arrived. Young, fair-haired, blue-eyed, toned, and an exact duplicate.

"Dispose of this and set the laboratory for *Übertragung.*"

✳ ✳ ✳

Chris, Dao, and the others passed by two mechanized sentinels just before reaching the circular table. Their aluminum frameworks were twisted and smoking, evidence of intense heating. Their automated weapons were molten, as well as the systems that controlled them. Steaming hulks now serving to mitigate the damp chill of the post-witching hours. Several security officers were on the ground next to a concrete retaining wall, unconscious. Their weapons and other tactical gear removed, and their limbs bound. Patrick and Anastasia remained seated at the table.

"What have you done?" Chris yelped.

"We have little time," said Jet Sun, greeting his daughter with a tight hug, he looked towards River.

"We must ask you about a presence. This presence has a name, and that name is Xeno," River said.

Chris gasped, suddenly conjuring the last recollection of Emily's toy in his mind. He saw it melting in the roiling furnace that was his master closet, slumping to black pitch. The doll's face within the flames was the last vision as Chris turned to escape the room. The vision gave him a chill of recognition. He felt something odd then, a latency he could not explain nor had the time to scientifically analyze.

Chris stumbled for words.

River gestured for them to be seated. "I believe you have a maxim for obvious conclusions, and as your education and logic resists that conclusion, the answer remains. Go ahead, Doctor Miller; let the razor cut."

Chris remained standing next to Dao and Jet Sun, and looked around the table. Anastasia held a pained expression, Rocco, Patrick, and Abe sat forward in anticipation.

Monsignor Trovarto and Arthur Garrick stood behind them, and River—closest to him—looked up into his eyes and smiled. "Please."

Chris and Dao took their seats. His throat was tight. He cleared it of irritation with a muffled cough and collected his thoughts. Something suddenly nagged the back of his mind.

"Xeno is the name of a clown doll Emily won at a church fair—the water gun game with the clown faces. I'm sure you know the one. Coincidentally, she won it with Anund Hammett competing against her. That's where we first met, except I didn't know it at the time." Chris paused with a scrunched brow.

"We lost Suzanne two months afterward. Fast forward a couple years. An electrical storm hit late one night while Emily was having nightmares. As you might imagine, she hadn't been sleeping well. Neither of us slept well. I heard her screaming down the hall, so, you know—fatherly duties. She tells me the doll attacked her. I mean, not the doll, but this ugly, gnarling clown named Xeno. The doll must have been the last thing she saw before falling asleep. We also, you know, like to watch horror movies. The campier the better. It's sort of our thing. Maybe not such a good idea after all. She was terrified that night. I thought little of it until he appeared on my laptop after sampling the doll's fabric."

"How'dya know it's him?" Patrick asked.

She was with me. Froze as soon as it appeared. Her description was accurate. It's as if her nightmare came to life."

"The evil that is Xeno was created by Emily, deposited as charged particulates containing his consciousness. A program, as you call it. That lucid evil dwelled in the machine until it found a way to unleash itself."

"Wait, what?" Chris turned towards River.

"Xeno manifests as a lucid consciousness. It is the messenger of evil, trapped until either discharged, which may take many years, or contacts a suitable vessel."

"Evil begets evil," said Monsignor Trovarto. "Bishop Esposito has-a surrounded himself with it."

Jet Sun and Dao took their seats at the table.

"The more intense the evil, the stronger its host becomes. The bishop sought the greatest evils until evil itself sought him, and now they are together, yet he does not know it. That is the primary goal of evil—to maintain your ignorance of it," said Jet Sun.

"What about my daughter?" Chris asked.

"The same as his master before him, the bishop nurtures Emily to compound his power. The brightest souls, finally turned, become the darkest. He has not turned her. Not yet. Her soul remains malleable—impressionable and receptive to suggestion. Anastasia sensed her deep confliction and was able to lock on it before interruption. The connection was too weak, and the effort was revealed to the bishop. He will attempt prevention of further contact."

"How?

"Distraction," said Jet Sun. "She must be overwhelmed with preoccupation. Mentally and physically, and it must be constant."

"I can still reach her." Anastasia said, setting a ponytail. "All of us here? She takes one extra breath... It is that part that triggers critical self-analysis, the conscience."

Chris turned towards River. "We're really going to do this."

"If she can be reached, she can be turned," said River.

River reached for Chris' right hand as Dao clutched the other. The others seated at the round concrete table followed suit and bowed their heads.

"Wait, what's the procedure? Do we chant or something?" Chris asked.

"No. Just close your eyes and think of Emily and only Emily. Look into her eyes and keep your concentration there. Repeat her name in your mind."

"Wait! What about the rest of you who've never seen her?"

"It is through you we focus."

Monsignor Trovarto leaned towards Arthur Garrick. "I wonder if-a these scientists realize they are-a in fact, praying."

Corkscrewed

Emily clasped the final latch on her tanker boots, checking for fit and function. She stood and inspected herself in front of the mirrored wall. An itch at the base of her skull began to burn, then a dull throbbing that suddenly went away as the door to her quarters slid open to Bishop Esposito and Abbess Regina. With a diligent pace, they made for the express lift to the observation bunker, just below Montagna Grande's summit 800 meters above. The elevator rocketed them upward, passing the small hive of operations anticipating the invasion, arriving at the automated surveillance and defenses command currently monitoring the radar contact.

Esposito examined all monitors and the technicians in front of each. Cameras depicted the harbor's entrance, as well as naval radar indicating a military target approaching from the north. A telescopic camera followed its inbound trajectory. Esposito's breathing became exaggerated, and his face visibly disturbed. The jewel atop his cane flashed a violet hue onto the chamber's walls, drawing apprehensive eyes from those in the room.

"No mistakes." Esposito scowled in an ominous tone.

The Bone dropped to 5,000 feet and slowed to 300 knots, wings spread, just below a cotton-dotted sky. The umbilical lines detached from the containers, switching them to internal supplies while the bomb bays opened. Osterhoudt, Miller and the rest of their marauders were now on the clock, 12 minutes maximum. Their drop was scheduled in two. It wasn't enough. An undetected missile detonated just aft of her starboard-most engine, sending shrapnel into its turbines, the starboard wing's flaps, the elevator, and into a non-critical section of the rear fuselage. The cockpit erupted with flashing beacons and blaring alarms. The flight crew diligently extinguished them, including a successful shutdown and fire suppression of the #4 engine. The drop zone remained forty seconds away—an eternity.

The explosion's concussive shockwave affected the rear container's passengers the most. Ears were ringing and multiple concerns lit up the com lines for explanations. Matthew closed his eyes and blocked it out, relaxing his grip on the handholds.

"Countermeasures!" The copilot yelled. "One-o'clock off the horizon. Three seconds!"

The Defensive Systems Officer hit the launch switch for flares as he activated the Vigilant Eagle anti-missile microwave defense. The missile passed underneath and detonated within the flares over 200 meters aft.

"Shit! Two more!"

"Launch the decoy," ordered the commander.

The DSO hit another switch that launched a tow-behind ALE-50 decoy—one of two. He also launched another container's-worth of flares. The first missile rocketed past the flares and the decoy without detonation and continued out to sea. The second went for the decoy, destroying it and leaving nothing but a dangling wire that automatically detached once it no longer sensed the decoy's tension.

"Time?" asked the commander.

"12 seconds," said the Weapons System Officer.

"Why can't we detect them?" The copilot yelled.

"You just keep your eyes on that launch site by the airport," barked the commander.

As soon as the copilot looked out the window, he caught the exhaust vapor trails of four new missiles as they left their tubes.

"Mother of God! Four... FOUR inbound!"

"Buddy-2!" The DSO hit the deployment switch and launched two additional flare buckets in sequence firing twelve each.

"Time?" The captain yelled.

The copilot hesitated. "To launch or impact?"

"Launch!"

"Uh... five seconds." The WSO armed the release switch.

"Brace, brace, brace!" Yelled the commander.

Two missiles detonated on flares. A third went for the decoy and missed, exploding too far away to damage it. The fourth rocketed past all countermeasures, including the microwave, and detonated under the starboard wing. Small, white-hot chunks of metal blew through it, severing the secondary hydraulic lines for the ailerons and speed brakes, as well as puncturing one of the fuel bladders.

The captain ignored the fresh set of warning lights as Pantelleria's southwestern shoreline passed underneath and the payload's launch timer elapsed.

"Execute."

The WSO flipped the switch and released the containers, staggered one each second. "Go launch. "Can we get the hell outta here now?"

"Calling in the mayday. Afterburners offline and she'd fly apart anyway," said the commander.

"Uh, just as a reminder, I can't see them coming from this angle," said the copilot.

"Slow and Blow. I want a bucket every ten seconds until we're out, then the chaff. That'll buy us eight or ten miles... maybe. Okay?"

"My pleasure," said the DSO. "Firing."

The response to the commander's mayday diverted them from Ramstein in Germany to joint US-Italian airfield on the east end of Sicily at Sigonella—150 nautical miles away. Thirty minutes at present speed.

"God help them," said the commander as he turned to Heading 074. "And us."

The controller's response also gave notice of poor visibility and air quality due to ash drifting south from Etna's ongoing eruption. Within one second of the end of that transmission, the copilot's right eye registered a flash from the island's center. The thought barely registered before the Bone disintegrated in a massive fireball.

●　●　●

"Sir, the Italian PM is on the line, urgent," said the President's secretary.

The President looked at the flashing red line on the handset's base then scanned around the Situation Room's table. Faces of exhaustion and sleep deprivation similar to his own, he fathomed.

"John," he said to the Defense Secretary, "What's the pool up to for the Italians citing Libya?" He left the handset in its cradle, mashed the speaker key then the flashing line.

"*Buon Giorno*, Giorgio." The President greeted with a tone neither acknowledging or obfuscating the fact he is aware that the Prime Minister loathed informal presumption of protocol, particularly the uninvited use of given names.

"*Signor Presidente*," replied the Italian PM with an equally sardonic tone. "I must be curt, as you say. Our *Marina Militare e Guardia Costiera* report significant unplanned and unreported military activity on Sicily and off the island of Pantelleria. We are due an explanation are we not?"

"Giorgio, we cannot comment on ongoing stealth drills; you know that."

"Drills? Must I remind you, *Signor*, of our agreements chartered under NATO? Is this now the behavior of friends? Same as Libya?"

The President smiled at John. "No, and I can assure you these excercises aren't another Libya, and frankly, your insinuations are pointed the wrong direction."

"*Signor*, you force my position," said the PM, clearing his throat. "Our intelligence was contacted hours ago by the Oberst of the Swiss Guard who had much to say, including the details of your dialogue with the Holy See. We call the Vatican, and as-a it is expected, receive denials and a prayer. How dare we inquire, no?"

The line was silent for several unchecked seconds.

"Giorgio, I've no idea what was conveyed to your intelligence by the Guard *or* the Pope."

"He confessed to a serious internal matter on Pantelleria and they failed to contain it. He calls for our help—*Italy's* help. You must cease any operation on our island, *Signor*. You have worn out your welcome. *Arrividerci*."

The line extinguished. The President once again surveyed the facial expressions of those encircling the conference table. Wide, bloodshot eyes, furled brows, oscillating jaws, pursed lips. Papers shuffled. Tablet screens swiped.

"Talk to me, John," said the President in a stern tenor. "How much time do we have before another front opens?"

"Depends on what they send. An hour, maybe. Maybe less if they scramble the squadron in Tripani. Sicilian Hunters—paratroops. I'm not concerned with their navy. Their fastest boats—and this depends on their preparedness and reaction time—are at best three hours away."

"Damnit! No diplomacy options?" The President banged his fist on the table. "Can't we offer them something like we did with Spain's salvaged silver?"

"Sir," a voice from the other end of the table interrrupted. "There is another consideration in play here."

"Our intelligence Director speaks!" The President grinned. "What is it, Craig?"

"The Spada Sarca won't allow the Italians either," he said. "Enemy of my enemy... Sir, Rome and the Vatican have clearly come to an arrangement."

"Got that right!" John said.

The Intelligence Director continued. "Nothing has changed. They remain our friendly competitors."

"My takeaway here is that we have anywhere from an hour to three hours, to an indefinite window, contingent on response type and continued belligerence of an embedded enemy. Further, our success against that enemy's coastal defenses invites intervention from of our competitors. Thanks for the headache, folks." The President turned around and signaled for another round of caffiene. "We don't want to be the tomorrow's soundbite, you understand? Don't make it happen."

● ● ●

In a controlled descent, Colonel Osterhoudt's three paragliding containers dropped onto empty field atop an ancient volcanic flow just south of Pantelleria's harbor—the island's west end. An unexpected thermal lofted the lead container at the last moment, sending Oderhoudt, Matt, and eight other operators across the other end of the field and, at a low velocity, into the ruins of a dammusi house. The container grinded and cracked on volcanic stone. Rocks tumbled away as it came to rest on its left side, trapping half of the soldiers. The others labored to break free of their restraints and open their doors, which under what they assumed was a hot landing zone, felt interminable. Once free, they worked to roll the container upright. Osterhoudt checked everyone's condition. No injuries. It was time to regroup, secure their surroundings, unload, and deploy the contents of the third container.

An infrared aerial scout drone was first to launch, and its operator initiated a search along their intended route up the overgrown, cactus-strewn hillside towards the airport. Another drone remained ruck-packed and slung on the back of another operator. Two technicians unloaded the robotic mules —one armed with a 4mm suppressed microgun and 28,000 hypersonic rounds, the other with an automated .338 magnum sniper rifle and 40mm grenade launcher. Both concealed a powerful C-4 self-destruct explosive deep within their midsections that generated the equivalence of a modern 500lb fragmentation bomb. Behind the mules were two VR-control-led soldier prototypes, armed with bespoke automated rifles, grenade launchers, and also a self-destruct, although of a lesser yield. No indication of imminent contact. The harbor was silent, and there were no vehicles in the streets. Not a single person outside, and Osterhoudt knew what that meant.

The 19 other soldiers gathered around him at the supply container.

"I don't want any dicking around. Keep off the coms unless critical. That means you too, *Gene.*" The colonel barked. "You three get down to the harbor. Our boat will be here in three hours, maybe less by now. Stick to the mission. We just want our part of the dock. No engagement unless you're fired on. Got it?"

The squad set off down the hill in a fast trot, zigzagging their way on the matted grass between briars, rocks and cacti. The harbor sat merely 200 meters away with little between them but a block of crumbling block and stucco storefronts ringing the waterfront with an open storage yard in the middle of it. The object of their highest concern was the slightly more modern 1950s three-story office/condo on their right, perfect for sniping with its commanding views of the hillside and waterfront. Their path kept them out of view of that structure as much as possible. They made the street between the docks and the storefronts within three minutes, siting each window along the way for infrared or other signatures. Their objective remained another 150 meters down the harbor's perimeter street. The harbor's central pier terminated directly in front of the Guardia Costiera—a two-story base presumed to be staffed and active. Eighty meters beyond it stood a pair of five-story hotels overlooking the harbor. Their objective was a deathtrap if not for a hardened concrete hut at the entrance to the boulder and asphalt causeway leading to the docks 250 meters down. The hut provided adequate cover from the hotels and coast guard base if needed. Once on the street, they broke into an evasive cadence, reaching the hut less than a minute later.

The front door of the Guardia Costiera abruptly flew open and an unarmed officer in dress whites appeared within its frame, shouting in Italian which neither operator understood from behind their laser-sighted barrels. The captain innately understood the two red dots dancing upon his chest, however, and froze silent with his arms raised.

"Speak English!" Gene yelled.

"Okay, okay!" The captain shouted. "You should not be here! We have orders for your arrest and detainment. You must comply!"

"Tell ya what, Capitan." Gene looked down his rifle. "You get everyone in that building of yours double-timed out here on the street in ten seconds before I send one of our friends here for introductions. And I'd sure hate to ruin that slick uniform of yours. Damn that's sharp!"

The captain gasped. A bullet ricocheted off the concrete just behind Gene's position. A puff of smoke wafted from a third-story window of the hotel on the corner. Instantly, one of Gene's squad shot a grenade into it. A second later, the entire corner of the hotel imploded onto itself with a deafening concussion. Windows shattered and fell to the streets, as the shockwave echoed across the harbor.

"Sounds like Gene's having at it."

"That stupid son of a bitch!" Osterhoudt yelled. "Can't do a damn thing quietly. Never!"

"Might just be me, but I'm kinda sure they know we're here." Matt said.

The captain turned around to dive back inside the building as Gene's salvo pocked the stucco just above the Guardia's front doorway, mere inches above the captain's head, now lightly dusted from the debris. Again, he froze and turned back around to face Gene.

"Try it." Gene said, cold.

The captain shouted orders into the building as he stepped outside, down the front steps and through the perimeter gate, his hands parallel with each shoulder. Fifteen others followed suit until they were aligned along the sidewalk. As Gene kept his rifle leveled on the captain, the sailor's hands were zip-tied behind them and forced to sit on the ground. The captain's hands were last, and he reluctantly lowered himself to the pavestone sidewalk, resting his back against the perimeter fence's retaining wall, glaring heatedly at Gene the entire way.

Gene withdrew a cigarette which changed the expression on the captain's face.

"You smoke?" Gene asked.

The captain nodded. Gene placed the cigarette in the captain's mouth and lit it.

"Anyone else?"

The entire lineup sounded off.

Osterhoudt and the others were ten minutes into their thirty-minute uphill hike towards the airport when one of the automated biped soldiers suddenly squawked alarms that its camera systems had been hit by lasers. The robots turned away and squatted to prevent further damage, but an unprotected camera sensor was destroyed. The mules were attacked a moment later. This contingency was part of their design, being that their lenses and sensor arrays were pro- tected by special anti-laser coatings. Additionally, those sensors pinpointed attack sources and delt with it by automated response the moment a laser struck. Two short bursts of the microgun obliterated both targets as the 17 oper- ators kept their heads below the weeds.

"Shields!" Osterhoudt yelled, dropping his yellowed, reflective goggles over his eyes.

Several moments passed as the microgun's echoes dissipated out to sea.

"Alright, drop your expectations; this isn't going to be a fair fight."

Osterhoudt looked back at his men. "I want flanking, two- by-two, half a click out, each. We'll pick it up in five."

Five minutes ticked; all communications ceased, including the live status links transmitted from each operator.

Osterhoudt turned to his biped driver. "Deploy them."

"One's down, sort of."

"I don't care; send them up!"

The camo-painted robots turned and bolted away at top speed—19 KPH—rifles at ready.

The Situation Room's satellite bleated an emergency alarm signaling a ground attack as its feed terminated.

"Get it back!" The President yelled.

The system operator messaged that the satellite's transmitting array was compromised by laser attack of immeasurable intensity. The secondary satellite feed crashed a moment later. They were blind.

"Where's our Navy?" The President demanded.

"We have a boat two hours out, sir." The Secretary replied. "The Santa Barbara—littoral ship in sea trials off Augusta, Sicily. Designed for exactly this mission type."

"God, I hope she's fast."

"50 knots, sir."

Towards the top of the hillside, short of Runway 8, the bipeds flush several Spada Sacra riflemen who opened fire. Most are picked off by the precision of the robot's rifles before falling to powerful lasers further up the hill. The escarpment suddenly swarmed with soldiers and their probing sites. Osterhoudt and half his men became pinned against the side of a ruin a couple hundred meters from the top as they descended. The other men were hunkered down in the tall weeds 50 meters away, susceptible to infrared detection. Two grenades quickly found their position and exploded, vaporizing two, and fatally wounding another three, including one of the mule drivers. Only two remained and they were being targeted by the next SS salvo. Osterhoudt could do little but send the mules, possibly sacrificing them which he didn't want to do just yet. The airport and what lay underneath it was an unknown. He needed all the firepower he could muster for that part of the mission and he knew it.

"What are you doing?" Matt grabbed his shoulder and Osterhoudt jerked away.

"We lose those men, we're done." Osterhoudt grumbled.

Matt looked at him with disbelief. "So don't lose them!"

The screams of the injured found their way to Osterhoudt's ear as another pair of grenades trailed above.

"Deploy!"

The mules launched into a fast trot around each side of the crumbled house. The microgun sprayed a defensive pattern shield, exploding the grenades at apogee. Without a second's hesitation, their weapons systems targeted and razed nine Spada Sacra before they had any chance to react. Another eight towards the top of the hill continue firing ineffectively, including two snipers firing large-caliber armor-piercing rounds. A lucky shot lodged itself in the microgun's lateral rotor, jamming its targeting system and emboldening several Spada Sacra to charge the robot, blasting away. The sniper mule picked one off on the run, then another two. Four soldiers managed to reach the microgun mule and opened a melee of close-range fire on its vulnerable systems. In a flash of white, the mule detonated, shredding everything within 30 meters of it and severely crippling anything 20 meters beyond that. The blast left a three-meter-wide crater, two meters deep, and its shockwave rocked the harbor below.

"That was a mule," said one of Gene's team.

The waning confidence showed on their faces and was noticed by the coast guard captain, who whispered the observation down the line in Italian while Gene scanned the hillsides and windows above.

The remaining thunderous echoes of the blast dissipated offshore as Osterhoudt scanned the hillside with his infrared monocular. No heat signatures. No movement. Nothing.

Gene squeezed the transmit button on his com link and called for Osterhoudt. The static squelched to blank air. Several seconds passed. He tried again. Nothing.

"You two hear it?" He asked his men, no more than twenty feet away. They shook their heads. Coms remained down. The anxiety showed on their faces. Again, Italian captain whispered down the line. They laughed, causing Gene to make sure his barrel remained pointed their direction.

"Relax man," said the captain. "They always complain about old equipment, you see. I tell them it goes also not so perfect for the Americans."

While Gene was listening, a storefront door opened down the street to his left. A young boy wearing a thick blue jacket and dungarees emerged from the doorway, sniffling. He kept turning around to face the doorway, shaken and sobbing. Gene heard a woman's voice shouting at him before she appeared at the doorway, motioning him to continue.

"Call him back now!" Gene yelled as his rifle drew her direction.

A shouting match ensued as she ignored him and continued coaxing the boy. The boy's crying intensified and he started to walk faster toward Gene. The other operators drew down on him and the woman. The boy continued and was within 30 meters. Gene fired two shots that powdered the asphalt in front of the boy. His mother continued screaming at him. Four other doors swung open to the shouting of elderly storekeepers. The shots frightened the boy, now balling in high-pitched screams. Another shot at his feet ricocheted off the pavement. The boy stopped, petrified. Several more locals stepped out on the sidewalks yelling at the soldiers to stop. The boy collapsed onto the street, some 20 meters away from Gene and the Guardia Costiera entrance.

"This is fryball, man!" Yelled one of the operators, nervous and rocking back and forth in his shooting stance.

A shot rang from a café with a cartooned crazy mule's head over the doorway—the Mulo Matto. One of Gene's operators felt the scorched air as it whizzed past his right ear.

"Mother—" He flipped his rifle to full auto and unleashed half a clip into the doorway at the same time as the other operator blasted several rounds into the café's windows. Glass shattered and crashed to the sidewalk as daylight exposed the armed man inside.

The boy covered his ears and continued screaming as he stood up and stepped closer. 15 meters. Gene kept his scope on the boy's mother as she made the Sign of the Cross.

"GET DOWN!" Gene yelled just as the boy disappeared in red vapor.

The blast rocked the harbor. Shattered glass from hundreds of windows fell to the streets. Gene and his operators are thrown several meters back. The shockwave and shrapnel missed their targets. The boy was simply gone. Gene lifted his rifle to scan the café's doorway. The mother produced an iced glare and disappeared back inside.

Osterhoudt felt the blast and reached for the coms. Still dead. He surveyed his crew and knew there were none to spare. He checked his watch. Their boat was over ninety minutes away. Might was well be forever. No objectives had been accomplished. He was losing men, and he began to question if they came too light. No longer a question, he thought.

"Let me go," Matt said.

"That's a firm negative, Jacobson. Need you here for the girl. That's why you came, right?"

Matt looked puzzled. "I thought that's why we're *all* here?"

Osterhoudt bit his lips and motioned the others forward. "Yeah, Jacobson, that's why we're here."

They stopped at the perimeter of the airport—a tall chain link fence topped with barbed wire. Osterhoudt directed two of his operators to breach it. They unpacked portable plasma cutters the size of small flashlights and made two gaping holes. The squad climbed through and made for the last part of the airport's plateau, emerging 100 meters from the northern end of Runway 8, directly in front of the taxiway that led to the underground hangars.

Matt scanned the hangar entrances and saw nothing unusual except the hangars themselves—perfectly preserved and operational Nazi relics. At once, three equidistant black poles rose from the taxiway's tarmac and opened laser fire targeting their heads. One of the operators, with goggles dangling around his neck, was torched in the eyes and started screaming. The others quickly turned away and put theirs on. The lasers gashed at their clothing, not strong enough to fully penetrate unless the beam remained on one place for any length of time. Direct skin contact meant a searing second-degree burn. Osterhoudt's men dropped to the ground, but it didn't halt the onslaught of beams ripping across them. A mule opened fire, disabling the posts with three short bursts aimed at their emitters. From a covered position on the grass, Osterhoudt checked their path for more small circles indicating additional threats. Several were arrayed in front of the hangars. They would deal with them when the time came, he thought.

Matt kept hearing the sound of insects close by, yet he never saw them. Osterhoudt initiated another scan that detected a metallic presence in the air close by.

"Micros!" Matt yelled.

He feared the worst. As if by telepathy, he saw what was coming. One by one, six of their squad fell as the kamikaze drones lanced their necks with poison-tipped needles. Death was close to instant. Two seconds to understand what hit them, then the infinite black. The hum of hundreds of those drones hovered in the background. Out of thin air, the voice of Bishop Esposito reverberated in their midst. The technology stunned them. The drones created a sound field that projects and intersects at any given target location. In this case, three meters in front of their position.

"There is no path before you except assured death, brave soldiers of the New World. Drop your weapons." The voice thundered.

Osterhoudt looked at Matt, then to his mule driver. The operator started to enter a sequence into the controller. Esposito snarled and ordered the drones to attack, and just as they shot forward, the mule detonated its flux compression generator—an EMP with range limited to 100 meters. The drones fell onto the tarmac. The mule and all other un-shielded electronics fried.

"Hit it!" Osterhoudt yelled, and they dashed to the first hangar entrance as several Spada Sacra emerged and opened fire. Another of Osterhoudt's men went down. He was down to seven, including himself, as they reached the nearest hangar entrance. To their surprise, the cavernous chamber was completely empty. They ventured further inside and towards a side hallway. The double doors were locked. Cameras everywhere. Some static, others actively focusing on their position. Matt and the others blasted them and placed a breaching charge on the hallway doors. They backed away, and a few moments later it detonated, revealing a long brightly-lit corridor with multiple doors down each side. Two elevators—or what appeared to be elevators—took prominence towards the end on their left. Osterhoudt sent men to each side of the hallway aiming down each length, then another to cover the elevator doors.

"We don't know what's beneath us and we're too light. I don't like it. Have to wait for the ship," said Osterhoudt.

"Oh?" Matt said. "How do we know the ship is still coming? And even if it did, is the harbor secure? You should've let me go."

"Forget it, Jacobson. We're well beyond that now."

One of the elevators activated. The men swung around and pointed their sites at the doorway.

"Lasers and micros, Jacobson. Any more of that and we're totaled."

The elevator's slowed to a stop at their level with an accompanying electronic bell. Anxieties intensified in anticipation of the doors opening. Their sites danced upon them as they slowly slid to either side to a collective gasp. Empty?

"Your Grace, what of the north inbound vessel?"

"They shall be welcomed."

The operator flipped the arming switch for the island's perimeter minefield and activated it.

A bolt electrified Esposito's mind. Violet splashed the walls of the command chamber. He turned to find Emily holding her temples. He stared down at her until she noticed—his irises exhibiting the glint of amber. She backed away as he snarled. The bishop extinguished the cane, turned and headed for the elevator, slamming the Observation Level's button. Emily looked at him as he entered, turned back around, and the doors shut.

He ascended several more stories until the doors reopened to daylight and crisp Mediterranean mountaintop air. The electricity once again shuttered his mind. He spun around to the west and gazed beyond the shoreline, far out to sea. His nostrils flared as vignettes of vaguely familiar faces touched upon his lucidity. The faces formed a ring, and the ring became clearer as he deeply inhaled them. At once, the vision ceased. Esposito continued staring at the western sea for several moments until the elevator doors opened behind him and Emily stepped out. She walked up to him and looked up into his eyes. The amber glint was missing.

She took his hand. "I'm afraid."

"Fear is the vestige of weakness, child." Esposito escorted her back onto the elevator. "Come, and I shall show you what happens to the weak."

The Wings of Raven Rock

"I don't like it." Colonel Osterhoudt groaned as the hangar's elevator doors remained open. His focus remained fixated towards the back of the lighted, empty elevator cab. "One of you check it out."

"It's an invitation." Matt said.

"Damn right it is," said Osterhoudt. "An invitation to what?"

"You're call, Colonel. We're out of time and options."

Osterhoudt checked his watch. "Where's that damned boat?"

"Colonel, you need to see this."

A soldier stood in the elevator's doorway and held it open. Osterhoudt stepped over and peered inside as the operator pointed towards the control panel and its single button.

"That's rich," said Osterhoudt, as he drew his pistol. "Cover your ears."

He blasted the two surveillance cameras located at opposite top corners in the cab.

"No stairwell either," said the operator.

Osterhoudt examined the elevator's interior and focused on the ceiling.

"Without popping the hatch, drill it and send a pinhole cam into the shaft."

The operator motioned another over who carried the required equipment and they set to work. Within moments they launched a camera through the hole. The video was broadcast to their phones for monitoring.

"You see what I see?" The camera operator gazed at the screen.

There was little room above the cab as expected. When the camera faced the top of the hatch, it appeared to be rigged to trigger a small plastic charge attached to a cable coupling.

"Shift to the left a tad," said Osterhoudt. "Yeah... that's interesting."

The monitor showed a release mechanism designed to automatically decouple the cable pully system. Wear indicated frequent use.

"Drill the floor."

A couple minutes later, the camera penetrated the darkness below the cab, and the shaft disappeared into it. The operator lowered it thirty meters—as far as it would go—and the bottom of the shaft became visible.

"Colonel—"

"Yeah, I see it. No doors. Another shaft leading the opposite direction using rails of some sort. Explains the decoupler. Shit." Osterhoudt checked his watch.

● ● ●

The littoral combat ship USS Santa Barbara had been in a full 48-knot sprint for past three hours coming off sea trials off of Syracuse, Sicily, crashing through four-foot seas and unfavorable winds. Its captain peered through his antique brass spyglass at the Pantelleria coastline and its harbor, ahead just off his port bow. He noticed nothing unusual except an eerie lack of harbor activity, and ordered the helm to Slow Ahead while finalizing their GPS track towards the marina's central pier. Two minutes later, a seaman below decks felt the thunk of metal below his feet and jumped in a screaming panic. He darted towards the nearest bulkhead, but the blast overtook him. The immense explosion blew a gaping three-meter hole in both outer and inner keel plates, sending flames and ultra-hot gases up through the decks. Once the compression wave dissipated, the seawater rushed in, immediately flooding two compartments. Alarms blared and damage control parties sprang into action at the captain's feverish orders. General quarters sounded as the Santa Barbara copped a slight list to port. The power flickered twice before complete failure. Emergency battery systems activated, supporting only the most critical functions: lighting, ventilation, communications, valves, and other assorted plumbing. The main generators were down, meaning the anti-fire halon system was also dead. Then it hit them.

It started with an explosion in their ears, then an intense burning sensation. Nausea and vomiting erupted throughout the crew.

"Havana!" The captain shouted over the intercom before manning the helm himself in an attempt to dodge the port to the west and escape.

Santa Barbara's helm would not answer. Down below the waterline, her crew were unaffected by the sickness, instead choking on fumes while working against the flood. Fire hoses were dead; no pressure. The emergency lighting meant limited visibility. The main generator needed to be restarted, but the engine room was a hell of ankle-deep floating debris, shooting flames and shorting secondary electrical. An operator pressed the first generator's Start button. Nothing. It would take a manual start—the "suicide start". It was called this because it meant standing on top of a massive 20-cylinder Rolls Royce engine to hit the plunger—the last place a sailor wanted to be when heavy machinery ignited.

The fate of the ship played out in the engineer's mind. He knew what would happen if he didn't. His ship would see the bottom, but not before the crew choked on burning oil and seawater. They were going to die. It was an automatic reflex. He climbed on top of the engine and slammed the starting plunger. The generator coughed, and as it sprang to life, he leapt into the arms of two of his buddies below, gagging on the fumes of burning motor oil. The next two generators followed in programmed sequence. The main lighting system returned, and the halon system instantly activated, squelching the flames and heat within seconds. The engineers dove for their respirator masks as the pumps made short work of the flooded engine room. It was soaked, steamy and suffocating with burnt plastics, but operating nonetheless. The fourth and final main generator ignited. The helm responded with a fierce surge as the ship swerved and missed the extended concrete pier on the harbor's north end.

"Sir!" The helmsman yelled, writhing from the intense nausea.

"Back the way we came!" The captain shouted above the clanging alarms. "We can't hit another."

It was several moments of extreme pain and roaring tinnitus until the ship escaped the intensity of the electronic attack.

Several minutes down and a few kilometers between themselves and the harbor, the captain completed another round of status updates after returning from below decks where the surviving crew continued repairs and reinforcing questionable bulkheads.

"You have her, Sarah. I need to make a call."

The Boatswain signaled the change to Officer of the Deck as the captain departed and dropped back to the communications room, reporting to CENTCOM in Tampa, who relayed the status through the Pentagon and fed to the Situation Room.

"My God!" The President angrily bellowed with a searing scowl, facing his Secretary of Defense—live drone and satellite feeds of the Santa Barbara at the other end of the table.

"Sir, it's safe to assume that if they possess such sophisticated weaponry and countermeasures, conventional small-scale offensives will continue to be thwarted."

The President's aid whispered in his ear and pointed at the phone's flashing lines. The President stood up and stepped over to an adjacent sound-proof office. He plopped behind desk and picked up the handset, then tapped the first line.

"Your Holiness—"

"A blessed evening to you, Johnathan."

"Thank you, Father."

"You must know why I telephone at such an hour."

"I believe so, Father, yes, although I expected Giorgio to make this call."

"Yes, and your instincts do no betray you, Jonathan. I will be first to inform you Giorgio has been slaughtered this night." The Pope began to weep, sniffling with a cracked voice. "As well, the Prime Minister and several of the Ministers Council, including the Defence Minister."

The President sat with the phone's handset barely resting against his ear, trembling.

"Johnathan, I charge you as a Christian and parishioner to end this evil upon us."

"It may be difficult if the wrong people gain control, Your Holiness."

"The task would not be worthy of you, Jonathan, if it were otherwise."

"I see." The President paused. "Pray for us, Father."

With his Secret Service detail in-tow, the President reentered the Situation Room and secured assurances that the Santa Barbara would be sent back if it became operational, and by that he meant operational to *any* degree. He then ordered the 6th Fleet Task Force to be readied for Italy's immediate assistance in securing its constitutional succession of government.

Six hours. The President stared at the clocks.

Gene's squad at the harbor were visibly uneasy at the sight of their ship. First, under a mile-high column of black smoke, ablaze and listing. Second, as it turned away and fled. Chatter amongst their *Guardia* detainees increased, including outbursts of smug banter and taunts. Their captain remained stolid and focused on his captors, always probing for weakness and opportunity. Gene sensed his gaze and kept his rifle pointed their direction. The chatter emboldened several shopkeepers to step outside and shout taunts down the street.

"*Non invincibile, Americani!*" The captain said in a coarse voice as he followed Santa Barbara's smoke on the horizon.

"You've no idea what you've just done." Gene growled, lowing his rifle at his forehead.

The captain went wide-eyed.

"*Pardon! Pardon!* Wait!" He screamed. "This is not us!"

Osterhoudt's hangar entrance lookout whistled back. He and Matt trotted back around to the edge of the hill and used binoculars, finding the Santa Barbara's smoke on the horizon, white from steam. They knew what it all meant.

"Don't have a choice now," said Osterhoudt. "Get back to the elevator shaft; we're going down."

He remained behind for another few moments, checking the ship's progress, and then the marina for any signs of activity. The buildings ringing the harbor obstructed his view. Still, no activity meant his operators remained in control. The more he thought about it, the better he thought the odds.

Matt directed the descent under the elevator cab. One-by-one they disappeared into the darkness below, rappelling just over 40 meters to the bottom of the shaft. The electric railway tunnel lay before them. They looked at each other, checked their gear, signaled above, and eased their way into it. Their tactical sites blazed the way, covering each angle to ensure no surprises.

Osterhoudt, Matt, and the other two operators fully expected a boobytrap of some sort—of any sort—yet there was no indication of such half a kilometer down the tunnel. They would have encountered one by now, he thought. Their optics started to develop condensation when it hit Matt. Sudden fatigue and drowsiness. He stopped. The others paused and turned around, including Osterhoudt.

"What?" He asked.

"Someone light a match—hurry!" Matt said.

"Aww, shit."

Osterhoudt reached into his left breast pocket and withdrew a small box of wooden matches, opened it and struck one. The phosphorous sulfide barely ignited the wood and it quickly extinguished itself. He struck another. Same result.

That's why! Osterhoudt thought. "Forget it. We go back. And didn't any of you notice the contained air system on the elevator's cab?"

"Report!" Captain Smith yelled as he strode through the bridge's bulkhead.

Officer On Deck, Sarah, cleared her voice and ran down the full damage assessment, current status of repairs, and the list of casualties.

"Weapons?"

"Deck guns online, RAMs online. Hellfires' *offline*."

"Come to 110 and target that generator building. Keep the trigger down 'til it's a pile of rocks."

"Anyone goes on deck to reload it, sir—"

"I pray that won't be necessary."

Santa Barbara's 57mm automated cannon slowly aligned just off the ship's starboard bow, constantly correcting for seas as the computers processed a dozen targets, starting with the top floor and pounding its down way to the first. When the targets verified, the screen indicated Ready to Fire. Sarah held the firing trigger down for four seconds as the gun blasted a dozen high-explosive rounds towards the harbor. Each shell detonated in rapid succession, starting at the top of the building and collapsing each of the five floors onto the one below it as the next round exploded, creating an avalanche of mortar, steel, and pulverized concrete to the ground in a plume of coarse dust and glass.

At once, the energy assault on the San Diego ceased, yet the nausea and intense pain lingered amongst the crew stationed above the waterline.

"Take us in. Same line as before, got it?"

"Aye." The helmsman set course for the north entry to the port and precisely over the new gap in Spada Sacra's Welcome Mat.

Emily stood beside Esposito as he grimaced at the ship displayed on the main monitor, sailing through his deadly necklace.

"Activate Spada Montagna and destroy that nuisance!" Esposito barked.

A 20cm diameter metallic shaft telescoped 30m from the mountaintop bunker and unsheathed its 360-degree rotating optic refractor. Its operator focused on his monitor and zoomed down to Santa Barbara's deck, then to its RAM missile battery. He locked a targeting cursor on it and toggled the firing sequence. The 25-petawatt laser pulsed twice in rapid succession, causing a thunderous crack across the hillsides below. Santa Barbara's missile battery exploded with a 50m fireball that plumed skyward. The concussion shockwave blew a gaping hole in the deck plates and warped the ship's superstructure. Any nearby personnel were vaporized, yet her captain was unaware of anyone on deck. When the smoke cleared there were no signs of blood or remains. Several sailors rushed on deck to extinguish the flames.

Emily stared at the laser operator's monitor as he marked those sailors for target tracking, then clicked the firing button. The laser pulsed once, this time through a refraction splitter, and in an instant, each of those sailors fell upon the deck—their cadavers smoldering from the shots that blew through their upper torsos in a flash of orange.

The grin returned to Narciso's lips. Emily gasped in silence at the enflamed corpses on the screen. It was too easy.

"Do not worry, my dear; you will have your chance when those imbeciles at the airport make their way here."

Emily glanced up at him then returned her attention to the monitors.

"Shutters!" The captain yelled. "Get that damned thing off us!"

"Sir, the source of the laser fire is on top of the mountain. The gun won't reach it without sailing around to the northeast."

"And risk another mine? Oh no, no, no. Where's our Hellfires and JSMs?"

"The fire destroyed their links, and even if they *were* online, that laser could smoke them right in our face. The gun is our only option without that risk."

Multiple expletives escaped the lips of the captain. He turned and picked up the hardline handset, calling in a strike from the nearest armed drone. 25 minutes away from firing distance, he was told. An uncomfortable wait ensued as the captain ordered priority repairs on the missile launch systems.

When the Reaper reached its maximum range of 55 nautical miles, CENTCOM unleashed its latest software-modified AMRAAM missile for secondary ground targeting roles. The weapon rocketed forth at Mach 4, and suddenly blew apart in a massive fireball. The Reaper had barely rolled ten degrees before it exploded into a thousand flaming bits, arcing towards the cerulean deep.

Emily glanced up once more at Narciso.

"I know what you are thinking, child." His eyes returned to the monitors. "Why did I not use mountain's arrow sooner? Well, that would not be as sporting, now would it? It is a waste of your talents, my dear."

Santa Barbara's captain received news of the drone, slammed the handset into its cradle and turned towards his crew.

"I NEED SOLUTIONS, GODDAMNIT!"

An ensign who had been using the ship's surveillance cameras to scan the harbor piped up. "If we switch docks to the portside pier directly across from the hotel, we will be partially obscured from the mountain."

"You see, folks, that's what I need, a—"

"What about proximity to the buildings? There may be soldiers with God knows waiting for us." Sarah interrupted.

"At this point, that's a risk I'm willing to take," said the captain. "Take us over there, would you."

"Aye."

Matthew tugged Osterhoudt's hand, lifting him out of the elevator shaft—the last to leave.

"Ten minutes wasted." Osterhoudt griped as his group assessed the hangar area.

An orange Bell 412 tour helicopter sat alone at the other end of the airport's ramp in a refueling area. Matt zeroed in on it through his rifle's scope, checking flanks for movement. Not a soul.

"Don't even think about it. The laser would tear it to shreds even if we made it."

"I'm not thinking what you're thinking," said Matt.

"Then what of it, *Commander*?"

Matt took his eye off the scope and turned around. "Tour 'copter. Some of those have supplementary oxygen for sick passengers. Might be worth a shot. Could be others in the hangars behind it."

"You wanna go back down that shaft?"

"Sure, why not? I mean, that's our mission, isn't it?"

"Or wait for reinforcements."

Matt laughed. "They're on fire down in the harbor, Colonel, and if we don't kill that laser, that's it."

Osterhoudt squinted an eye and nodded. "I see your point. We still have to get over there, pray there's recoverable oxygen, then somehow make it back."

"Two of us; no more. We'll duck behind the rise of the runway. Five-minute sprint. Who's up for it besides me?" Matthew looked at the others."

"I'll do it! Fuck yeah." Rodriguez said, slapping Osterhoudt across the shoulder. "Better than sittin' here, old man!"

Osterhoudt grabbed Rodriguez's wrist mid-slap as he attempted another pass. "You just watch your ass, *'dejo.*"

● ● ●

Anastasia gasped as she released the hands of Rocco and Chris. Her eyes opened wide as she fought for air. River gazed into her eyes and acknowledged the feeling, as did Jet Sun and

Dao Ming. The others—Chris, Patrick, Monsignor Trovarto, Rebecca Morningwood, and Arthur Garrick—had puzzled expressions, looking towards each other for answers before returning to Anastasia.

She sensed an external influence just before breaking contact with Emily's mind, some *thing* or someone, but not Emily herself. She also sensed the alien malevolence attached to it, and the innate reprehension as if forced to ingest a vile liquid.

"It is the *pierrot*—the jester, the clown—you perceive," said River. "The yellow eyes of evil."

Jet Sun nodded, remaining focused on Anastasia. "His strength has multiplied beyond any one of us. It also understands the nature of the dust because it is born of it. This complicates our task."

"Nothing's impossible." River said with a piercing glare.

Jet Sun collected the tables attention. "We must focus with increased intensity. Penetrating the veil of malice demands a greater opposite." He turned around to Rebecca Morningwood, Arthur Garrick and Monsignor Trovarto. "Your help is needed; our circle must expand. I appeal to your scientific intellects. The human spectrum of electromagnetic wave propagation requires compound interaction."

Trovarto parted his hands to each side with open palms. "Brothers, I am-a spiritual man as you all know, but-ahh."

"Oh come now, Father; don't be shy on us now!" Patrick laughed. "Time to save to planet... again. You going to be wanting out of that?"

"I suppose-a not." Trovarto sighed and traipsed towards two empty chairs, positioning them between Patrick and Chris and gesturing towards Morningwood.

"Always wanted to do this," she said under her breath.

Chris stood up as she approached. "You know what Jack would've said."

Rebecca hugged him and sat down. "Yep. Bullshit's for morons who can't shut up and enjoy a good scotch. Forgive me, Father."

Trovarto laughed. "No, no; it is-a accurate proverb."

Stop staring at her, Twin Feathers. River punched into his son's mind. *She must focus. You must focus.*

But I LIKE her!

Anastasia suddenly looked at him with startled eyes, catching his awkward smile.

As the others took their seats, Garrick remained where he stood. Jet Sun turned towards him.

"My apologies, Master Sun; I do not believe I can be of assistance to this endeavor."

"You believe your unwavering objectivity negates a positive contribution," said Jet Sun. "This is incorrect."

"Our studies—"

"Are also inaccurate, and by the intention of those your government has, for the preceding several decades, wrongly incarcerated."

"But how could you possibly—"

River pointed to his own temple.

"Never mind," Garrick sighed.

"It is your raw energy we gather and broadcast in focus, inviting the subconscious of others along our path. It is preferrable that you are a willing participant."

Chris closed his eyes and felt the surge of energy flow through his arms. The winds whistled through the pines of Raven Rock and his mind drifted into recent territories and scenes of anxiety—of death and languid melancholy—tortured vignettes of fine onyx crystalline demonic caricatures devouring themselves and creating larger, increasingly intense nightmares.

"Doctor Miller, you must purge your negativity."

"I'm trying!" He yelled.

● ● ●

Ducking between hangars, administrative buildings and small trees, Matt and Rodriguez found themselves against the southern clearing for Runway 8. Matt stared at the empty space between those buildings, and a road tunnel that passes under the runway to the relative safety of its northern berm.

"The current World Record for the 100 is 9.58 seconds—Usain Bolt," said Rodriguez, assessing the scorched brown terrain for their sprint.

"That was 100 meters. No packs, no fatigues, no boots, no starting blocks... It's the gun that worries me."

"Come on, man! That thing's gotta take time to find us, then someone's gotta call that shot."

"Assuming it isn't automated," said Matt, peering through his rifle scope towards the top of Montagna Grande. He detected a faint glint of silver—the sun's reflection off something metallic as it shifted.

"*¿Qué piensas?*" Rodriguez grunted. "What's it doing?"

"Probing. What else would it be doing?" Matt continued his observation. "No way to know how long it would take to target us, or if that targeting is accurate. Two seconds or ten, it doesn't matter; we *have* to go."

"Ah, *sí.*"

Without another word, Rodriguez took a deep breath and sprang towards the tunnel entrance.

"Shit!" Matt yelled, slinging his rifle back onto his shoulder.

Three seconds flew by as Matt wrestled with waiting or jumping across before he cursed the sky and leaned into his mad dash. Five more seconds ticked by. Nothing but heavy breaths and pounding feet. Rodriguez breached the tunnel entrance, checking for any movement within. He turned around when the blast came—an orange luminescence passing in slow motion across Matthew's face as it streaked between them, striking the tunnel entrance on the opposite wall, exploding its cement with a 1-meter crater.

"*En fuego!*" Rodriguez yelled.

"Almost got us both killed you lunatic!" Matt barked. "We were supposed to go together."

"Never said that, *jefe.*"

"Goes without saying! Now, come on—let's get down this tunnel and out to the terminal before someone else comes looking. I wanna be there in six minutes or less."

The two set a rapid cadence out of the northern end of the tunnel and up via Madonna's quarter-mile asphalt to the southern end of the airport's ramp, careful to remain out of the mountaintop's sight. An olive plantation flanked their left. Its compound was adjacent to the Arrivals terminal, which also happened to be their most viable access to the basketball court-sized refueling area where the touring helicopter sat, presumably abandoned since the Swiss Guard's invasion.

"Movement at the airport, Excellency." A voice shouted across several workstations.

"Switch to main monitor," said Esposito, observing Matt and Rodriguez's footsteps towards the aircraft.

"Do I fire, Excellency?"

Annoyed, Esposito said, "No. Wait until it is airborne and in view of the harbor."

Matt eased across the tarmac from the terminal, careful to keep the helicopter between him and the mountain. He unlatched the passenger door and slid it open, climbed aboard and checked a floorboard compartment just behind the right pilot's seat. As hoped, the compartment yielded a green bottle of oxygen connected to a regulator. He removed its securing straps and disconnected the lines from the regulator, then removed two cannulas from their cradles and disconnected their lines, handing them to Rodriguez.

"It's too bad," said Rodriguez.

"What do you mean?"

"We could just fly this out of here. Tank's full, I bet. Palermo or Tunis."

"Forget it. The only reason they're not blowing us away right now is because they *think* we're taking her up. And they want us up there for everyone to see when the explosion comes. No way."

Matthew made short work of gathering the oxygen equipment and stuffing it all into a light duffel.

"Excellency, the insurgents appear to be departing the aircraft."

Esposito clenched his teeth and stamped down several steps to the control station. "Move," he said in a muffled tone.

The operator looked at him with a fearful, puzzled expression just before the bishop shoved him out of the way and grabbed the aiming stick, focusing under the helicopter.

Rodriguez had just taken possession of the oxygen duffel when the pulse came. He felt an intense flash—a burning sensation just below his right knee as he collapsed to that side. The scream that would ensue was terminated by the second pulse that blasted through his mouth and into the tarmac behind his skull—bits of charred tissue protruding from it. Matthew momentarily froze. His instincts were to jump back into the helicopter, but he knew it was a critical mistake. Instead, he grabbed the O2 pack while shuffling his boots rapidly, bolting for the terminal. Behind him, the helicopter detonated upon the third pulse from the mountain.

The fire and thick black smoke obscured Matt's retreat. He made no delay of his return to the street and the relative safety of the berm. The mountain occupied his mind as he jogged back to the tunnel entrance in less than four minutes.

Matt panted heavily and wiped the sweat from his brow, remaining ten feet back from the southern opening. It was 100 feet to the tree—an obstacle that could be shredded with ease from that laser, he calculated. His best cover was at least two or three trees into the grove. No element of surprise, either; the mountain was on to him, and it felt like a mountain was upon him—its full weight—as he drew deep breaths. He knew not to zig-zag from Basic. That meant more time and pauses for pivots. Running a straight line was also problematic. He only needed five seconds to reach the trees in an all-out sprint. *Five seconds...*

Matt emerged into the daylight at full speed plus the adrenalin boost. In shutter-by-shutter slow motion, his three second countdown came after the fifteenth step as he threw his left boot further out to bounce right. As he did, the blast of dirt and debris pocked what would have been his path if he continued straight. A small fire broke from the dry grass as he reached the first tree, gulping air as a race thoroughbred on the backstretch. The slow-motion effect suddenly stopped as he put on the brakes behind a mature citron tree.

The control room fell silent as Narciso's eyes turned a darker shade of yellow. He growled and slammed a fist into the control station's keyboard, sending pieces of it flying. He turned towards the operator and shouted.

"Get a replacement and eliminate the intruders."

"Let me!" Emily shouted, holding onto the hilt of her sword.

Narciso caught his breath "You shall have your chance, my dear." He traipsed out of the control pit and placed a hand on her shoulder. "Come. We must prepare for their arrival."

Osterhoudt barked at Matthew as he rounded the north side of the underground hangar's massive entrance. "I take it from the smoke Rodriguez bought it. What happened?"

Matt dropped his equipment onto a table and took a few deep breaths. "Laser hit underneath the chopper. Vaporized his shin. He dropped, they hit him in the face." Matt gulped. "They hit the chopper as I fell back."

"Shit... Well, rest up a couple ticks. You got it?"

"Yeah, I got it. Bottle and two masks. Seems full. We should have a couple hours on that."

"We? Goddamnit Jacobson, I hate it when you presume authority on a mission. That's what got you in hot water before!"

"Sorry, sir. Just figured it was down to you and I. Blanton's not up for it. Didn't you see him shaking when we were down there? Claustrophobic."

"Well, you figured right and yes, I noticed it, but damnit, you gotta stop jumping past me before I get the chance!"

"Noted."

Osterhoudt and Jacobson descended through the jagged square opening on the elevator's floor, and from there it was a 40m drop to the trolley switching infrastructure. The rope slipped methodically through their rappelling carabiners. Their helmet lamps probed the darkness below. Matt looked up as the dimly-lit square shrank to a glimmering speck. Osterhoudt reached the steel landing mechanism, disconnected his harness and stepped aside as Matt dropped to the floor.

"We'll take it as far as we can down the tunnel before hitting the O2. No sense wasting it here," said Osterhoudt, peering down the damp and balmy shaft.

Matt initiated a steady pace, yet not so fast as to solicit a deep breath. He checked his watch. "Half a click—four minutes or so."

They kept pace down the rails, careful not to touch them, and as predicted, started taking deeper breaths just after four minutes.

"Fire it up," said Osterhoudt.

Matthew took off his pack, distributed the cannulas, and unwound the translucent vinyl tubing within. He twisted the oxygen bottle's regulator knob and set the flow rate.

"Guessing four liters per minute between two masks should do it."

Osterhoudt nodded and they took off at the same pace, inhaling when necessary. The oxygen filled their lungs and felt fresh. Breathing normalized as they continued down the shaft, passing occasional drainage grates for the slow accumulation of ceiling drips.

Matt checked his watch and 32 minutes had elapsed. Just then he felt a small quiver under his boots. The quiver intensified into a dull roar. Some silt dropped from the shaft's ceiling into their light. They looked at each other.

"This island seismic?"

Osterhoudt ripped open the flap on Matt's backpack and twisted the oxygen regulator's knob to full.

"We're not getting trapped down here—gas it!"

They both turned around and ran into the darkness ahead, breathing only through their noses to avoid the silt and dust already clouding the shaft. After several seconds, the vibrations and roaring subsided, however, the fog of dirt permeated the thin air. They continued their pace for another four minutes until the shaft abruptly ended at a pair of sliding doors—the elevator's exit.

Osterhoudt examined the door's inner mechanism then reached into his own pack for a pry bar.

Matt was checking out the door's wiring when Osterhoudt whispered, "God help us."

"Wait!" Matt yelled with a muted, airy voice as he drew his rifle.

Osterhoudt was already wrenching the doors apart, ignoring him when the alarms erupted. The doors flew open revealing two armed Spada Sacra sentries in darkened masks leveling their rifles at them. Matt tapped both before stepping out to cover the opposite flank. As soon as he exited the shaft, six rifles locked onto his head at less than twenty feet away. Several more aimed at Osterhoudt, who dropped the prybar onto an electrified rail. An explosive spark fused the steel tool against the track until the blinding sparks melted it away. Osterhoudt fell back into the darkness and reached for his sidearm when a bullet ricocheted off the stone wall near his left ear.

"*FERMATI!*" a voice thundered. "*Li voglio vivi.*"

Narciso Esposito stepped forward, pointing the Amethylizer—its crystal top pulsating. "As you can see, your position is without hope of conquest or escape, Colonel."

Matt looked around the cavernous space, rapidly assessing the truth of the bishop's statement, then something caught his eye in the background—something incomprehensible beyond the violet glow.

"Emily?" Matt's voice solemnly reverberated through the chamber as she stepped to the foreground with a tense expression.

"No more the little girl you remember, Commander Jacobson," quipped Esposito.

Matt's brows raised as he couldn't quite comprehend her demeanor or tactical attire, let alone the xiphos sword she carried. *Brainwashed*, he thought, assessing the weapons pointed at him. *Wants me alive. They won't shoot without orders to do so.*

"Jacobson, NOW!" screamed Osterhoudt.

Matt dropped to one knee and blasted four sentries in rapid succession before any of them could react or ask permission. He pivoted and shot two more as they attempted to cover themselves.

Esposito sighed and drew his cane, lurching towards Osterhoudt as he reached for his pistol and drew. In a flash, Emily's xiphos severed the colonel's hand at the wrist. The finger nerves constricted on the way down, and the pistol fired, striking the ground. Osterhoudt could not conjure a scream as the sword passed underneath, trailing Emily's diving slide—his left inside thigh sliced to the femur, including the main artery it protected. Then the violet blaze hit his sternum; its glow illuminating the cracked grin of glimmering amber eyes of the demon spawn, hysterical as the Amethylizer pulsed. Osterhoudt could not move, he could only weep in the attempt as he felt his senses disappear into numbness. He felt nothing as his left leg gave. He never felt the impact upon the concrete floor. He never felt his skull as it bashed itself on impact, and he no longer felt himself breathing. His eyes were wide open as the images of Jacobson continued firing at the evasive Spada Sacra. That is, until his vision failed completely and the sounds of screaming washed away with the waves of white noise—deafening at first, then silence and blackness. His mind drifted into dissipating anxieties of unfinished business, and then existence itself until there were no thoughts at all.

When the final sentry dropped onto the floor, choking on blood, unable to plug the singed perforation at the trachea, Matthew turned around to see Osterhoudt's still eyes and lifeless body collapsed upon the concrete. The view was quickly interrupted by the glow of a pulsating purple crystal just before his eyes. His gaze froze upon Emily as she cozied herself to Esposito's side.

"Release your weapon, Commander," snarled the bishop. "I would not enjoy your execution in front of our mutual friend. I mean, your *former* friend."

Matt placed the rifle onto the floor and slowly rose to his feet, hands at his side.

"The pistol and your knife too, Commander."

He pulled the knife from its sheath and dropped it on the concrete, then slowly unholstered his .45 and let it drop as well. He eyes shifted to the pulsating crystal that remained inches from the bridge of his nose.

"Come, Commander, we have much to discuss."

Esposito gestured towards the opposite side of the chamber at a bank of elevators 50 meters away, then the three of them slowly made their way towards it.

Matthew looked back at several sentries writhing in pools of blood. "What of your men?"

"Oh, do not worry about them, Commander; there are always more from where they came."

Emily joined them in the elevator, standing on the other side of Esposito from Matt.

"Emily! Don't you know who I am? Don't you remember?"

Matt heard the shing of the xiphos' unsheathing, and before his mind recognized the sound for what it was, the sword's broadside whacked him across the stomach.

"Quiet!" She yelled.

Narciso laughed. "She is beyond you, Commander—more than you know."

Matt felt the elevator's gravity as they ascended for several seconds at a spritely pace. The door slid apart to reveal two men in lab coats standing just off to the side. One older and short, with a stooped posture, the other young and in perfect health, the same as the sentries—identical, in fact. Matt struggled with their purpose, and the laboratories aligning the hallway behind them. It was merely three seconds before he felt the dart's prick, and another three as the black wave swept over him.

"Make good use of this one, Doctor. He bested 14 units. Slow thinkers. He did not hesitate."

"Zey are programmed for obedience... for subserviency!"

"Yes, I know, and we can do better. Dear Emily is here for examination. See to what we discussed."

Emily glanced up at him in wonder as the physician reached for her hand. "Our starlet. What wonders you bring."

"Where's your wheelchair?" She asked.

"Never you mind." He grinned.

As his assistant wheeled Matthew into the hallway, the doctor placed his arm around Emily, guiding her into the room dedicated to her evolution. She removed her armor and underdressing, then slipped onto the reclined exam table, closing her eyes to the blinding lights above. The assistant returned and helped her connect the VR headset and sensor arrays. Emily drifted onto the grid as the physician initialized her next construct.

● ● ●

Seemingly random individuals within the middle Maryland-Pennsylvania border region—from young, healthy adults to feeble elderly—suddenly experienced a vignetted portrait of Emily in their minds. Except, it wasn't random, and the phenomenon was rapidly spreading towards the east. Many dismissed it as a momentary glitch—mental exhaustion, or an odd daydream. Others were semi-conscious, yet lucid, thinking it might be yet another one of those realistic dreams —completely random as if conjured from strange air. Emily's image and the suggestion of returning home echoed with frequency. The thought's transmission was accelerating, and it was amplifying. The wave grew stronger until it reached the Atlantic shoreline where for all but a moment it peaked. Emily suddenly appeared in the minds of random people across Morocco, Portugal and Spain, then southern France, northern Algeria, Sardinia, northern Tunisia, and finally, Pantelleria. The vision metastasized until it reached Emily in a blind, paralyzing scream.

She awakened to a view looking up through water, faintly detecting murmurs on the surface, represented by circular ripples. Or, was it thick, gaseous air—the sounds reverberating across a translucent plane? A voice she recognized as if an ear were pressed against her bosom. The sound of her breathing. The sound of her heart. The sound of life. Her voice.

"Mom?"

The voice suddenly ceased. The waves stopped. The proximate feel remained. Emily paused in wonder... then to frustration. Was it a dream? What did the doctor do to her? Knocked out? Gassed? Drugged?" She grew tingly as the sensation amplified—a wave that crashed upon her once more.

"Are you lost, pumpkin?" said the voice, crystal clear and cutting.

Emily turned towards it.

"Mom!"

The doctor stood in front of his monitor, stunned. He panicked to locate his aide in order to restrain her—to awaken her. Was she actually asleep, though? He dared not touch her; he calculated that danger long ago—capable of death in a single, swift motion if provoked. Also deadly as part of a natural reaction—her reflex. Better to let a clone take the risk, except most of them had gone to repel the Americans. He sent a general summons to Sister Regina. She acknowledged him, hung up, then considered the potential for advantage.

"Mom, where are you?" Emily pined.

"I am here, Emily. Next to you."

"I cannot see you!"

"I know. It is not important, pumpkin."

"I want to see you!"

"You will, someday. Not today."

"I don't understand." Emily sniffled.

"I know, and one day you will. My Emily, there are friends who wish me to deliver a message. Are you ready?"

"Who?"

"He says you once slept next to his bear and dreamt of your friend Patricia, playing in her room and trying on clothes. He wants you to know he is alive and with your father. They love you and want you home. Your father made a mistake, and he is so very sorry, Emily."

Emily cried, conflicted, overcome with emotion. *Chief River is alive? Abe too?* But her dad... the anger welled, then doubt supposed.

"I must go soon, Pumpkin."

"Mom don't leave me!" Emily cried.

"There is something else." The voice paused. "Someone, *something* dangerous also wants you. I cannot stop him. He deceives you. Do not believe him."

"Who?"

"Someone evil."

Emily snapped in recognition. "What do I do?"

"I must go now."

"Mom, wait! Don't leave me!"

"I love you, Pumpkin." The voice drifted into the waves.

Emily sobbed and couldn't breathe. Her pain subsided and her eyes opened to the doctor's assistant, Josef, looming over her gurney, attempting to plunge a needle into her arm. She jerked away in a high-pitched squeal, realizing she had suddenly become a target—something that didn't behave as the master wished. She could not say what happened.

● ● ●

Anastasia broke concentration in a cold sweat, as did the others. They stared at each other for several moments, some in disbelief. Chris felt a rare chill and recognized it. The last time he felt it was the subconscious moment he believed Suzanne passed—the moment of her collision—a beckoning. He sensed Emily's imminent danger. Her scream echoed within the recesses of his subconscious. River met eyes with him—an awkward stare that lasted several seconds.

"Isn't anyone going to say something?" Chris asked.

River slid his chair back and stood up. "It is now up to her."

Sagitta Montis

"Astonishing, is it not?" Esposito asked Matthew as they stood at the back of Montagna Grande's clinical white control room.

"Clones?" Matthew asked. "No, not yours, although I *am* curious as to their donors. I mean, they don't look like they came from you, and if not you, then—"

Esposito grinned.

"Wait, let me guess... Hitler."

"Do not be stupid, Commander. Why would anyone replicate a failed intellect such as his? Try again."

"I'd rather not. I mean if it's not Hitler and it's not you, who could be worse? I have another question for you. How did you hide this place from Europe and America's intelligence?"

"You presume we hide. Those who know of Perla Nera's secrets never speak of it, nor do the residents of this island. They may come and go as they please, but if they utter a word of this place or the Spada Sacra, an unavoidable reaction occurs within their bodies that guarantees an untraceable death."

Matt glanced down at his chest, then checked the guards to each side of him, maintaining aim at his torso with their bullpup rifles.

"And the unwanted visitors? The ones you haven't keyed?"

Narciso pointed. "At my command, the operator in the second tier down will annihilate any and all interlopers—on this island or above it."

"Except us."

"You flatter yourself, Commander. Your detachment could have been obliterated at the snap of my fingers."

"If that were true, why am I here?" Matthew grumbled.

The bishop turned towards the laser operator. "Twenty-Six."

The operator turned around to face Esposito.

"40% on the target in the hangar," ordered Esposito.

The operator turned around, activated the targeting system's holographic camera sight and found Osterhoudt's remaining soldier, Lt. Blanton, standing to the side behind the main hangar's gargantuan doorway—its reinforced concrete walls one-meter thick. The controller flipped the red safety flap open and pressed the red button underneath. In that instant, the plasma pulse from the mountaintop exploded the air in a shockwave as intense thunder. The hillsides cracked the moment the beam passed overhead and struck the hangar's wall, blasting a two-inch hole through it, the soldier's chest cavity, and into the walls beyond. The soldier was propelled from the wall by the shattering debris and slumped upon the concrete, eyes agog looking down at his chest while unable to draw breath. He gasped and fell silent a few seconds later, the holographic targeting system's camera confirmed.

"*La baracca di capitano*—the Harbormaster's shack," said Esposito.

The holographic site outlined Gene's flank and the soldier propped against the western stone wall of the small building at the beginning of the harbor. The walls exploded, followed by a deafening clap of thunder. What remained of Gene's operator—the parts that weren't annihilated— blew across the pier and into the sea. The harbor's crustaceans would have their fill after the sargos tired of nibbling. Gene's eyes bulged as the Costa sailors panicked, demanding they take shelter in their administration building. Gene's last squad member turned towards him from the other end of the fence—the end of the lineup—when the next shot came, blasting the pavered sidewalk and leaving a two-foot-deep divot. The operator fell into it, a cauterized hole showing daylight through his upper chest.

The men screamed and cut their wrists struggling with the cable tie restraints. Gene grabbed their captain's arm and lifted him to his feet as the crack of thunder echoed through the harbor.

"Inside, now!"

Gene whipped his knife out and sliced the captain's hands free. The captain wasted no time barking orders for his men to spring inside ahead of them. Gene glanced towards the mountaintop, then once more towards the Santa Barbara as the Italian sailors clamored up the steps and into the Guardia Costiera's headquarters.

"The ship. 100%," ordered Esposito.

The operator turned around. "Your Excellency—"

"Destroy the hotel and residence that stand before it, then target the ship. Do it."

The operator turned around and programmed a burst pattern designed to collapse the buildings. When the sequence confirmed, he fired. The four-story condominium dropped onto itself, crushing the 56 residents sheltering within. When the dust cloud cleared, the second sequence was executed for the hotel. Matthew stared at Esposito, witnessing his wry grin—his complete euphoria for the death and destruction caused.

"Captain, we're exposed!" Sarah yelled as Captain Smith ordered the helmsman and bosun into action.

"Gash the lines then All Back Full; ten degrees starboard!" He shouted. "Sarah, I want a missile or the canon on that mountain NOW! I don't care which. They need something to consider!"

"Canon is out of range. Caleb says he needs a few more minutes on the JSM link."

"We don't have a few minutes!"

Sarah called down to Caleb. "Where is it? Cap says he needs it now."

The radio crackled. "I just now made the connection, but I've not tested it. I cannot guarantee it, Mr. Anderson."

"Sir, did you—"

"Yes, I heard him. FIRE NOW!"

Sarah brought the optical aiming system in line with GPS, targeted the mountaintop, and pressed the fire button to no effect. She pressed it again. The firing indicator light illuminated, except no missile left the launcher.

"Shit." She reached for her comms. "Caleb!"

"I warned you! I need another minute. Hang on."

Caleb was neck deep in the engineering control system of the Joint Strike Missile launcher below decks when he caught the charred insulation on one of the thin wires of that harness. He grabbed the soldering torch. It would take less than 30 seconds to mend the wire and get word back upstairs. The Santa Barbara slammed the seawall on her way backwards, churning up the harbor's silt as her stern bashed water. Her outline ducked between buildings on the Sword's targeting system, complicating its tracking and profiling for an arrayed fire pattern. In several seconds, the ship would pass beyond the last tall structure.

"Caleb!" Sarah yelled.

There was no answer, so she called again. The clock ticked, seemingly forever until the radio finally erupted.

"Go—HIT IT!"

Sarah slammed the firing switch, and an armed JSM thundered from its launch tube, building speed as it arced towards the mountain.

"Knock it down." Esposito sighed.

The controller froze in panic as the missile streaked toward them. Sagitta Montis' targeting system remained on the ship, almost resolved, when he aborted and activated the systems auto-defense routine. The laser instantly locked onto the missile and successfully detonated it over a kilometer away. The controller reinitiated the targeting sequence for the ship as it cleared the end of the pier.

Sarah kept her sight on the mountaintop and fired twice in rapid succession. Two JDM missiles cleared their launch tubes within two seconds of each other and rocketed towards Montagna Grande at just under supersonic speed.

"Ahead Flank!" Yelled Captain Smith to the helmsman. "And keep her at a minimum-profile heading after we clear the mines."

Before the Santa Barbara made the course change, the laser's full strength ravaged the ship's hull with 20 rapid-fire blasts. The plasma beams ripped gaping holes deep within the superstructure and below decks. Two sailors were killed instantly, either by the laser or proximity to the explosions that followed. One pulse hit the JDM battery and detonated its last missile, sending a secondary shockwave throughout the ship, ripping critical plumbing and electrical systems. The fire reached the secondary Hellfire launcher before those rockets could be manually ejected. Tertiary explosions further rocked the decks. The bridge's windows shattered as the Santa Barbara heeled to port. Alarms erupted as did the loud-speakers.

"All hands, Abandon Ship! Abandon Ship!"

Santa Barbara's whistle gave seven short shrieks, followed by a long one. Most of the surviving sailors became panicked. Some made it into their immersion suits and life vests. Many others didn't, jumping over the gunwales, believing the swim to shore was a short one, ignorant of the tidal currents. Captain Smith screamed at them over a crackling bullhorn to grab the lifeboat duffels, but the fears of additional explosions and the laser itself muted him.

"Two inbound," stated the laser's controller in a calm, yet insistent tone as he reached for the auto-defense mode switch.

Sagitta Montis quickly tracked the lead missile and struck it without hesitation, exploding it a half-click out. The resulting fireball and smoke obfuscated the trajectory of the salvo behind it. The missile's defense algorithm flew it around the shockwave and debris, which Sagitta Montis could not differentiate in time. Operators instantly started yelling and jumped towards the exiting stairs. Esposito and Matthew dove for the floor as the missile impacted, just above the controller's bunker—a direct hit on the laser's generator and telescopic base. The control room's windows blew inward and workstations toppled in that instant. Glass and shrapnel sprayed the controllers and the guards, killing most, but not all. Matt stood up, ears ringing from the concussion, and bolted for the emergency stairwell. With the control room ablaze, Esposito growled and stamped into the elevator with clenched fists, watching his control room crumble into the flames as the doors struggled to close. The controller's hand reached in and was blocking them, so the bishop pried the doors open and kicked it away as the fire consumed the man. The doors slid shut, lights flickering and the elevator began its rapid descent.

Matt flew down the metal and concrete stairway as fast as he could, grabbing the handrails and leaping entire flights, landing to landing. Small pieces of concrete debris began raining from the ceiling, careening off the metal as it dropped. A larger piece smashed against a rail next to Matt's hand as he vaulted downward, causing a distraction that threw his rhythm off, and he hit the edge of a last step before the next landing, blowing an ankle. He winced as he dropped, squelching the scream that should have occurred, lest he give up his position. He dragged himself to the wall and leaned against it to catch his breath, looking up the stairwell to ascertain if anyone followed. Several seconds passed. The throb from his left ankle intensified. He loosened his boot to relieve the swelling pressure. Matt knew he was not going anywhere quickly, and he also knew he had to get moving—to get on his feet—which meant pain.

Gene stood just inside the hallway within the Guardia Costiera's headquarters when he heard the ratcheting slides of two sidearms from several feet behind. He dropped his rifle to the side and propped it against the wall to his right, then turned around with his hands raised.

"You must-a know we cannot allow this continued invasion, *signore*," said the captain.

"Lieutenant."

"Please follow my men. You will be afforded the same courtesy."

Gene was paced down the hallway to a jail cell at the end of it. He was searched and stripped of all items useful for combat or escape, including his cigarettes and lighter. He walked inside and the sailors latched the gate behind.

"Same courtesy?"

The captain withdrew one of his own cigarettes, lit it, and passed it through the bars. Gene picked it from his hand, not recognizing the brand and took a deep draw as he sat in the corner.

"I don't suppose you're gonna tell me what the hell that was back there."

"We do not speak of it."

"Do not, or cannot?"

"Both."

Gene rolled his eyes and took another drag. The captain turned and walked up the hallway, shouting orders in Italian for his men to gear up and run two boats to the Santa Barbara.

The elevator doors slid apart and Narciso Esposito burst through them with a determined gait. Sister Regina rounded a corner and stopped in front of him.

"You Eminence!" She cried. "What happened? I felt the mountain shake."

"Get out of my way." He snarled and pushed her aside, eyes coruscating in amber.

Regina yelped and fell onto the floor. *"Lo que está mal?"*

Esposito turned around and pointed the Amethylizer at her—its crystal pulsating—as he continued striding towards the laboratory.

Matt lost count as he limped down over forty more flights. His damaged foot dragged across a step or two when he wasn't careful, making him pause to collect himself, agonizing. He finally landed at a door that leaked light from the other side. He waited by it for several moments, grinding on whether to risk opening it or not. He stepped back and peered over the tubular handrail at the shaft below. Maybe another 300 meters down, he guessed. He also projected where that likely ended—at the staging cavern. Matt also labored to reconcile that he was deep inside a mountain, and that it likely had very few points of egress. He was trapped in an anthill and only knew of two exits—the stairway above, and the railway below to the hangar. Oxygen would be needed for that. He would not have enough in the bottle they discarded. Even so, he didn't recall turning it off. Someone knew the ways in and the ways out. Someone on the other side of the door knew. If there was someone. He rechecked his pockets for weapons—anything—but the Spada Sacra were thorough; he had nothing, nor anything he could improvise for hand-to-hand. He also couldn't shift or pivot quickly. No, he must surprise someone from behind and overpower them—gain a weapon somehow. It was the only way.

Matt held the doorhandle with a light touch, easing it downward to unlatch the locking striker. He cracked the door open to the stares of hundreds aligned in front of their beds. All of them the exact same in precise detail: uniform height, build, skin tone, hair, and eyes. They couldn't discern an enemy in the darkness behind the door, nor the faint silhouette of the agape mouth within it. Lacking instruction, the duplicates disregarded the anomaly as Matt limped into the bunkroom and closed the door behind him. The clone closest to him turned to face forward, cueing the others who did the same. He held a salute as Matthew inched by, maintaining an incredulous look as he returned his salute. *Say nothing*, Matt thought, wincing twice as his left ankle throbbed. At the end of the lineup, he suppressed the urge to turn and say or gesture anything. He dropped his salute and exited to a hallway at the other end.

There were three large elevators on the other side of the hallway. "Level 4" appeared in large letters on the left. The middle elevator's floor indicator was on the rise from Level 0—the cavern where he was taken. A new alarm burst from its speakers with varying tones Matt had not heard before. He assumed it was instructive, and his suspicions proved correct when he turned around and noticed the clones glaring at him. Matt flipped around, wincing, and smashed the elevator's down button as the alarm wailed. The door to the bunkroom swung open simultaneously with the elevator's. Matt threw himself inside and poked the ground floor's button repeatedly as the clone soldiers poured into the hallway. The elevator's doors slid shut just as three soldiers reached it, attempting to claw it open. Matt felt the drop in gravity as the elevator plummeted, but he knew it would be temporary. The clones were young and fit; stairs would not slow them. It was a mere delay of seconds. In a panic, he slammed the elevator's emergency stop button, halting its descent just below Level 3. The Open Doors button did not work, so he pried at them with his fingertips until they gave way, exposing the concrete shaft's wall with no gap for maneuvering.

Matt turned around and sighed. He heard a commotion above—metal doors slamming, heavy footsteps, and the trundle of cables from the elevator at the other side of the shaft. His options were narrowing. It was either reactivate the elevator and land on an indicated floor—*and be caught*—or climb out and risk rappelling to another level, then risk capture. He removed two ceiling tiles and saw the emergency hatch, just within his reach. He knew what was required and didn't vacillate on it. He reached up and threw open the top hatch, then strained to pull himself upward and through. The increased heart rate sent shockwaves to his swollen left ankle, and he gulped air to distract it. The hoistways were dimly lit by leakage at each level. He slid to the side of his car and peered over the edge. No greasy cables or ladder; it was a vacant shaft except for the two steel rails adjacent the first and third cars, with vertical tracks for the middle car. The tracks were notched with four-inch locking holes, and they were greased. The sides of the I-beam were dry for the guide wheels, and he could use those for handholds. It was another decision, altogether—sketchy under normal circumstances.

The first step was the most tenuous. Matt climbed around and placed his right foot into track's notching. He lowered himself and forced his left foot into the next lower rung. It was slick, and his control over it was doubtful at best. The grimace of pain intensified as he increased weight on his damaged ankle. *Would it hold?* Matt clenched his teeth as he removed his right foot for the next step down, deciding to skip three rungs in order to expedite his descent. The position proved too ambitious, as his ankle screamed. He removed that foot and for a moment; the pain ceased. The next step would see its return. His fingertips were also straining as he passed the bottom of his car, dropping into the darkness—and likely no return. The bottom would be too far he guessed; he must risk Level 2.

After several minutes of excruciation, the tops of the doors to Level 2 were at his knees, three feet away. Matt was right-handed, and to reach that far meant bracing with his left foot—twisted within a greasy rung. The security latch would be difficult to move without a tool, but he knew how to do it. Any slip meant death. The bottom of the shaft was at least another 180-meter drop, he estimated, given the cavern's ceiling height. Matt drew his deepest breath, bit down hard and reached for the latch, tugging at it with great effort. He attempted several fingered positions to gain the best leverage, yet the latch barely rotated. He exhaled as his ankle pounded and returned to rest his left by using his right foot and hand for primary stability. It would not last, he was exhausted and growing worse by the second.

Damn that door!

Matt took another deep breath and reached back across, yanking on the latch this time, gaining a couple more squeaks. He felt something give in his ankle. Something popped, and the heat of pain scorched up his shin and past the knee. He began to scream and caught himself before the shriek departed his mouth, biting down to the point of enamel flex. He tugged on the latch once more before he felt the need to withdraw, it gave and the doors sprung open. Using his right foot against the dry part of the railing, Matt thrust himself towards the opening, landing on his right side with his hips just on the doorway's edge. He pulled at the floor, dragging himself further inside. Once his knees crossed the threshold, he exhaled and drew into a fetal position. The room's lighting flickered on, and Matt found a young woman—a nun—standing over him with a small-caliber pistol leveled at his face.

Josef howled as the two-sided blade penetrated his ribcage four times in rapid succession. As he fell to the side, still gripping the syringe, Emily slashed the restraints binding her left wrist. She made quick work of the other straps, jumped off the gurney and collected her tactical dress, throwing it on and finding her prized xiphos sword in a corner beside it. She slung its scabbard around her back and strapped her boots on while keeping her eyes on the adjoining door. *Someone heard Josef's screams*, she thought, expecting trouble, yet nobody came. She eased over to the door and listened. A man was dictating notes. He had an accent she had heard before. He sounded older and not alert. Easy pickings. She slid the door open and found the old doctor in his chair with a telephone's speaker activated. She became confused. *If this is him, who was the other one?*

"Doctor?" A voice on the other end asked. Emily recognized it right away. "Doctor!" Demanded Narciso Esposito.

"She is here, now, Excellency, und she has her sword at my neck."

"It is pointless to resist us, dear Emily. You are part of a larger picture now. Stop this at once and join me on Level 2."

"NO!" She yelled.

"Your friend's life depends on it, child. He needs you. I need you. I would hate to think what would happen otherwise."

"NO!" she screamed, breaking the top dermis layer of the older man's Adam's Apple.

"Tell her, Doctor. Tell her about you."

The doctor cleared his throat. "His Excellency wishes you to know what I am—"

"So!" Emily shouted, keeping the blade on his neck.

"I am a doctor und a scientist, young lady, not dissimilar from your father."

"No, you're just some old man."

"Ah, this much ist true. Und how old do you think?"

"I don't know. I DON'T CARE! Whatever. 60?"

"More than double that, my dear. I am 112 years old."

Emily looked at him with wider eyes.

"I am 112 years old und I served with the German Schutzstaffel, the SS, long ago as a research physician. I have survived this long because my research discovered the genetic locks for age renewal. I have effectively stopped the aging process with a serum that affects a certain cranial gland. One shot, you are forever the same age when you received it. In my case, 56."

"So."

"So I am wise enough not to allow some unruly little girl her way!"

The hum of a dozen mini spear drones burst through the back door and locked onto their target. Emily jumped back and furiously parried as they launched at her, one and two at a time. The attack was blisteringly fast—the sword shredding metal as if confetti tossed in the air, small electronic bits showered the laboratory floor. In a burst, the drones were dispatched. Emily's focus returned to the desk, except the old doctor had somehow escaped during the mele. Emily heard another hum—a louder hum. There were many more drones coming for her and at different attack angles. She bolted for the exit, slamming the steel door behind as hundreds of spears penetrated it. Emily tripped backward and fell onto the floor, shaken by the dozens of poison-tipped spikes protruding from the door, attempting to wiggle themselves free. She turned her head to check the reception area and it was clear. She sprang onto her feet and streaked towards the elevators. The droning hum of the spears grew louder.

"We cannot defeat the world's armies, Your Grace." Sister Regina cleared her throat, noticing the shimmering amber within Narciso's eyes.

"Exactly," he said.

"Another plan, then?" She drew closer to him.

"You should never expect otherwise."

Regina smiled and draped herself around his waistline. Narciso shoved her away.

"NEVER!"

Regina collected herself and straightened her coif.

"Shall fetch you a cadet, Your Grace?"

"No!" He said as he turned around. "Get down to the launch and prepare our departure."

● ● ●

The pre-dawn's dewed chill collected on the mountainside as Anastasia's breathing increased. Her eyes split open at once in a deep heaving breath, and she gasped for extra air.

"What is it?" Chris asked.

"Your daughter fights," said River.

"Wha... what do you mean, she fights?"

"Pronounced anxiety. She fights the evil that confronts her. She fights feelings that are not her own. The deceiver remains a part of her."

"Oh God." Chris fell back into his chair, his palms against his cheeks.

"Try to relax," said Dao, rubbing his left shoulder. "She is alive and in the correct state of mind."

Chris looked across the table between his fingers at an empty chair, then looked around and behind. "Where did your father go? I was going to ask him—"

"Permission? Permission is mine to give. His blessing is understood by my remaining at your side. He must rectify the mess created by Ramelan."

"Who? What mess?"
"A Chinese crime lord who executed our conservators."

"It's your call, sir" The Secretary of Defense said to the President. "The mission failed. There's no sign of Osterhoudt or any of his men. The Guardia Costiera launched ten minutes ago."
"Level it," said the President in a reserved tone. 'We can't take any chances."

* * *

Esposito collected a few of his prized possessions, placing them within his cassock and paused in front of Chris' laptop. He touched it as his eyes glistened with a subtle xanthic sparks, staring into the empty space of deep thought. He slid the laptop into an armored case and took it with him.

A general alarm sounded as the top of the mountain exploded then collapsed two levels—struck by a cruise missile fired from a carrier group steaming towards Rome at flank speed. A second one, a bunker-busting MOAB penetrated deep within the complex, destroying the underlying bunkers. The mountain rumbled, resonating the explosions. The lower levels' stairs become hazardous; fire, dust, and debris rained. The elevator system became inoperative just as

Emily reached Level 2. Her doors opened to reveal Matthew held at gunpoint.

"STOP!" The nun yelled, cocking the pistol.

Emily froze. Matt looked at her, incredulous. *Here to kill me?* He wondered. The nun is untrusting. Emily smiled and loosened her stance.

"Go ahead; His Excellency sent me to destroy him anyway. Saves me the practice." She inched her way to within a few feet of the gun-wielding sister facing Jacobson.

As the nun took careful aim, Emily unsheathed and lunged as lightning with her sword, plunging it into the nun's ribcage as two shots rang, errantly striking the wall and ceiling well away from Matthew. The nun shrieked and fell onto the concrete, coughing blood and choking on it, suffocating. Emily withdrew the blade, wiped it off on the nun's habit and replaced it into the scabbard. She turned towards Matt and hugged him crying.

"Jesus, Em, where did you learn that?"

She continued crying until the glow of magenta light splashed upon the wall behind Matthew, emanating from behind her. She spun around in a gulp of air.

Esposito paused, perplexed. The hum of the Amethylizer pulsated at his side. He locked eyes with Emily, trying to get a read. *Had she betrayed him? Did she kill the nun or was it the soldier?* His eyes... Emily recognized him for who he was—the nightmare with the tangerine glint. Matt saw the case and realized that Esposito was in the process of fleeing. He glanced down at the pistol that remained in the clutches of the nun. Narciso caught him looking and kicked the weapon away. Emily stood up between Esposito and Matt. Esposito continued to stare into her eyes, and she became transfixed upon them, as if hypnotized. She stepped before him, unarmed and unthreatening. He continued his stare for what seemed an interminable time until he raised the Amethylizer between them and, while pulsating, offered it to her—corneas oscillating yellow to brown.

Emily stood there, blank-faced as the light danced upon her face. She gazed into the pulsating crystal in the outstretched hands of the bishop. She paused, wondering if it might be a trick. Esposito cracked his wry grin.

"Take what is yours, my child."

Emily reached over and hesitated, again looking into his eyes with transfixed anxiety. If she didn't take it, he might strike her in anger. She lifted it from his open palms and held onto it tightly.

"You know what must be done, and then we will be free."

While she faced him, Matt noticed a small kunai blade sheathed and strapped to the back of her right calf. It was within reach and she momentarily blocked the bishop's view, so he swiped it as she picked up the Amethylizer. He palmed it, ready for a lunge if the opportunity presented itself, ankle be damned. Emily didn't notice it missing when she turned around to ease behind Matt. She held the pulsating crystal in front of her and looked once more to her mentor. He nodded.

Emily brought the crystal close to Matthew's lumbar—its amethyst glow pulsating slowly as she gazed into the shimmering eyes of her mentor. He squinted.

"Now, my love."

"NO EMILY, DON'T LISTEN TO HIM!"

Her stare continued as she slowly lowered the cane until it caressed his spine. Matt convulsed. She maintained pressure for several seconds. Esposito reveled as she held it against Matthew, fighting the sting of its heat. But that's what he didn't expect—he felt it! He still felt it. Seconds ticked. Esposito's expression turned to incredulity. In a burst, Matt flipped the dagger's blade to his fingertips and slung it with as much velocity as his body's heightened adrenaline could muster. Esposito turned. The distance was incorrect and the pointed pommel smashed into the bishop's chest without much ado, falling onto the concrete. Esposito turned around and reached into his cassock. With a wailing cry and lunging roundhouse spin, Emily slammed the Amethylizer's brilliant, humming crystal into the bishop's neck and held it tightly against him. A bright flash exploded from the crystal. Esposito screamed as the shockwave penetrated his cerebral cortex and nervous system. He screamed until his lungs exhausted all air, and his muscles could not inhale. He fought against the cane, attempting to wiggle away—anything—but he could not move with the exception of an odd twitch. Within the smoke of electrocution, Emily flung the cane upon the concrete, smashing its crystal into tiny shards. She withdrew her sword and leveled it just above his neckline.

"No!" Matt yelled. "Do not finish him."

"Why not?" Emily cried.

"Let him experience regret and the agony of suffocation. He will be dead soon enough."

Narciso Esposito choked in gasping for a single breath. The look of surprise, anger, and sorrow graced his eyes as they grew still and opaque brown. No shimmering amber as they locked open. The bishop collapsed onto himself as a lifeless doll—vacuous and unthreatening. Only the sounds of the fire above and the odd bits of debris falling within the stairwell remained.

Emily rushed to Matt's side and wrapped her arms around him, helping him to his feet in great pain. He winced and muted the scream, holding onto Emily as a crutch.

"Come, kid. We're not outta this yet." Matt said through clenched teeth. "Wait... Is that the case?"

"What case? Emily asked.

"THE case! The case with your dad's laptop. We need that. Take it. Can't leave it here." Emily fetched it and slung it around Matt's back.

"Great, now how do we—"

"Downstairs," said Emily, reaching down for the nun's pistol on their way out, handing it to Matt. "The Magna Specu."

"What does that mean?"

"No idea." Emily sighed. "It's the big cave where we caught you. That's the only other way out."

"Well, we can't go up!" said Matt, opening the door to the stairwell.

"I don't understand!" cried Emily.

"What?" Matthew asked.

"Why did the—the cane! It didn't hurt you."

Matthew unstrapped the Velcro from his vest and revealed the wire mesh for grounding dispersal. "They never said why it was there."

Sparks, embers, concrete and hot metal sporadically rained from hundreds of feet above. Debris covered the steps making their descent difficult. The stairwell had a strong breeze upward, as if it were functioning as a giant chimney—hot air dragging the cooler air upward as if vacuumed. The mountain trembled. Something else was amiss. Emily recognized the faint hum within the background noise. Spear drones—in the hundreds, but where were they? In a level above? Can they survive the fires?

"That doesn't sound good."

"Drones! The old man has drones after me!"

"Old man? WHAT old man?"

"The doctor. HURRY!"

The drones grew slightly louder as they dropped step after step, racing around each landing for the next flight, dodging chunks of debris and embers. Matt looked over a rail and saw the light of the bottom level—the massive grotto holding armored vehicles and other assorted equipment.

There must be a way out, Matt thought.

The hum of the drones grew louder still. Their sonance came from above—very distinct now. Emily let go of Matt and opened the twin steel doors at the bottom. She stepped through and a shot ricocheted off the rock wall beside her. She looked up to find the doctor loading a submersible with cases, and a new Josef leveling a short rifle at her. She ducked back into the stairwell and faced Matt. He checked the pistol in his right hand, making sure a round was chambered.

"Where is he?"

"30 feet back towards the right."

"Right from center or on the right?

"I dunno! Maybe Two O'clock?"

Matt limped to the doorway, waited a moment to catch his breath, exhaled, swung around and blew the back of New Josef's skull out through his left eye. The doctor panicked and feverishly pawed at the submersible's door latch. A shot ricocheted off it, spraying shrapnel through his right hand. The old man screamed and threw his hand under his left bicep. Matt limped towards him. The doctor ducked around the backside of the submersible and shuffled towards the hangar shaft. Then it hit—a massive heave and deafening roar as the chasm shook violently. Huge boulders dropped from the ceiling as the doctor disappeared into the shaft. The stairway behind Emily and Matthew collapsed, sending choking dust and dirt rushing into the cavern. Emily caught a glimpse of the doctor as he disappeared into the shaft, and just after he did, the shaft's ceilings and walls collapsed onto him. Matt watched as the rubble filled the shaft's entrance.

"Got you covered!" Matt yelled to Emily. "Now show me the way out!"

Emily pointed towards an obfuscated doorway around to the left. She activated the huge steel doors. A buzzer rang as the mountain continued its tremors. The doors opened to a two-kilometer-long shaft that ran to the north. At its end were subterranean docks hidden behind the cliffs. Emily helped Matt limp onto an electric shuttle's passenger seat, then jumped into the driver's on the other side. Matt's eyes opened wide.

"It's okay, Dad taught me at the golf course," she said, just before nailing the accelerator.

The cart lurched to a speed much higher than a typical golf cart—90KPH—and Matt turned to her in a panic.

"There's nobody after us, Em."

She ignored him as a boulder crumbled just ahead onto their path. She scraped the left side of the cart on it with a Scandinavian flick while Matt squeezed the life out of the panic handle. Emily kept her right foot planted on the accelerator, determined. The faint luminescence of the launching grotto, a mirage at first, emerged as they continued down the track. Debris continued falling as the tremor intensified. In 45 seconds, the docks materialized in the light. Two small boats were tied to them—older wooden 10-meter cabin cruisers in weathered but serviceable condition. They were less than a football field away when the tunnel's roof gave and the floor cracked. Unable to see, Emily slammed on the brakes. Matthew doubled over in pain as the pressure on his ankle amplified. He resisted the forward kinetics as much as he could bear, his right wrist and fingers straining to maintain hold. In the last moment, the cart's tires lost grip in the sandy rubble, skidding into the larger pile of rocks now blocking their exit. The air was thick and opaque, and they coughed uncontrollably, ripping at their clothing to make filters. Emily climbed out and ran around the cart to help Matt. He struggled to breathe. Their light was waning as the cart's electrical system began to fail. The noise of the tremor continued, and it too was loud and disorienting.

"We have to get out of here fast, or we're done!" Matt shouted.

"Come on! There's a hole over there!" Emily pointed to her left across the front of the cart.

She tugged on his arm to help lift him out of the cart and back onto his feet. Matt groaned as he hopped off his left ankle, bracing himself on Emily's shoulder. Together they labored around the back of the cart and towards the hole Emily described. They inched their way onto a pile of rubble and larger, jagged rocks, fighting for air, wheezing through their now-clogged clothing. The rocks began shifting in the tremor as more debris fell from above. A large boulder collapsed onto the cart just behind them. Its lighting disappeared beneath it—crushed. The darkness that ensued was short-lived as the spill from the grotto's docks reappeared from the choking particles.

Emily and Matt slid down the other side of the rockfall and onto the tunnel's floor, still rumbling with light debris continuing to fall from the ceiling. They scrambled in a fast limp, building speed as they found their cadence. The light grew brighter as they passed a ramp that descended into the water and approached the two launches, docked against a seawall.

"We'll take the one closest!" Matt shouted above the noise, and no sooner did the words leave his mouth, a massive boulder crashed through it from above, destroying and sinking it in the same moment. The massive splash generated from it almost knocked them down, soaking them in salt water.

Drenched, Emily turned to him. At once, they sprinted for the front boat, racing as fast as they possibly could toward it. The rumbling intensified, almost knocking them off their feet. The pier started to move and the debris from the ceiling grew larger and louder.

Matt threw himself into the boat's open stern and landed on his right leg which nearly buckled. The shing of Emily's xiphos rang as she ran past the cabin, slicing the spring and bow lines, then jumping onboard. Matt untied the stern's line, breaking the launch loose. He limped as fast as he could possibly withstand towards the cockpit and looked for the ignition, expecting no keys, yet there they were—two keys in their ignition switches, replete with a foam floats—dangling. He placed the transmission in neutral and twisted both keys at once. The diesel engines roared to life without hesitation as Emily joined him at the helm.

"Here," he said. "You take us out."

Matt's eyes twitched as he fell back onto the cushioned bench just behind the helm. Emily stepped in front of him and slammed the transmission lever forward, then did the same to the throttles. The boat lurched with tremendous thrust, building speed as they broke into full daylight, cresting short waves at the cavern's entrance. The rumble of the earthquake dissipated behind them, and the seas were light in a gentle breeze, the oscillating drone of the engines drowning all other senses.

"Where are we going?" Emily asked.

"You see that compass up there?"

"Yes."

"Head north and keep it there." Matt shouted. "What's our speed?"

"Uh—" Emily searched the gauges. "48."

"Okay. I assume that's in kilometers-per-hour, so thirty-ish, hmm. Should take us a little over three hours to Sicily. Can you handle it?"

"Aye-aye, Cap'n!" Emily smiled, keeping her hands on the wheel.

No more than two minutes passed when the cabin's door swung open just to Emily's left. She started to unsheathe her sword.

"Don't!" said a woman's voice in the greyed shadows behind a pistol aimed at Emily's face.

"YOU?" Matt shouted above the engine noise. "I thought we killed you already!"

"It's not who you think." Emily said as the habit emerged into the companionway's frame.

"What do you mean? Oh wait—" Matt relented.

"Silence!" Regina screamed, pointing the weapon at Matt.

"He's dead. They're all dead. It's over."

Matt's eyes flashed towards the windshield and beyond at the surf. He braced his right leg against Emily's and eased his right hand towards the throttles—their view obstructed by Emily's head. Emily saw it too—what was coming—and she tightened her grip on the boat's wheel. The nun took another step, sensing something amiss when it hit. A rogue wave slammed into the boat's forward hull, knocking Regina against the companionway's frame where she staggered to maintain her footing. Matt yanked the throttles, sending the nun flying backward into the lower deck, head first. The pistol fired as she flew; its explosion in the confined space, deafening.

"NOW!" Matt yelled.

It was automatic for Emily. Her blade sprung from its scabbard and preceded her dive into the lower cabin. It found its mark at the center of Regina's habit. She coughed in blood as Emily thrust the sword into her a second time and twisted it sideways. Regina's grip on the pistol released as she tore away and fought to her feet. She stumbled up the companionway steps and made it to the top when a pistol shot exploded into her back. She started to fall as Matt hit the throttles. Regina's body careened off the transom on her way over it. Her eyesight held on just long enough to see the daylight disappear beneath the surf.

The twin diesels resumed their oscillating rumble as Emily dropped her sword and reemerged from the lower cabin, splattered in blood and shaken. She stepped back the helm and buried herself in Matt's bosom, sniffling. Matt checked the horizon and ran his fingers through her hair, hugging her tightly when she started to cry.

"Hey, we're alive and that's all that matters." Matt reassured her. "You're stronger than this, Em. Stronger than me!"

Emily fought to clear her sinuses, "I just thought my dad would be here."

Matt winced. "You've watched too many movies, kid."

The boat smashed into the light seas as they beat northward, and after several minutes, Emily felt Matt's body slump behind her. She hadn't noticed the blood seeping on the teak below her feet. She opened his vest and saw the wound from which it came. She cried and beat upon the throttles for every last ounce of speed, cresting and crashing into the shallow waves. She made the coastline in two hours, not three, and several Guardia Costiera vessels surrounded her just south of Marsala—lights and bullhorns blaring. There was nowhere to go. Emily pulled on the throttles and collapsed onto the bench on the opposite side, curling into a ball, staring at the cloud patterns and a circling seagull above.

She regained focus when she heard the calamity of a rigid inflatable boat tie up alongside. Two armed Guardsmen climbed aboard, aiming sidearms. One holstered his after the cabin compartment was cleared, and he returned to Emily being held by the other.

"Ah, you must the young lady everyone is looking for, no?"

Emily glanced up at him and said nothing.

"Well, there are some people looking for you, young one, and I think they'll be very happy to—"

"This one has a pulse!" The second Guardsman shouted.

He pulled a microphone around to his mouth and relayed instructions for a helicopter.

"Happy to what?" Emily asked, springing to life.

"To see you," The Guardsman smiled.

EPILOGUE
Burnt Ends

Emily's jet touched down at Andrews. Her father, River, Abe, Snickers—all cleaned and brushed—and several others unknown to her, except the Chinese woman standing next to her father, waited patiently on the tarmac. Emily couldn't stop staring at the woman. *The woman at the bridge! Was she the one he mentioned once?* Emily ran down the steps, then hesitated, emotions mixed as she walked up to her father, trying desperately to read his eyes. *Is he angry or relieved? Am I in trouble? God, he's taller than I remember!*

Chris' eyes never left hers. His emotions danced upon his stomach. *Wait, is she taller? No, can't be.* He knelt down and looked up to her eyes. He didn't remember ever looking up from that position. Tears welled between them and they began to cry. Chris hugged her tightly. Several moments passed that felt timeless. He backed away, sniffling.

"I'm sorry, I'm sorry," he said, wiping her tears. "Never... Never again. I am so—"

Emily said nothing and held a finger against his lips, holding on to him as tight as she could. Her grip surprised him as exceptionally stronger than he remembered.

When she finally released him, she looked at the others, running towards River's arms for a hug.

"How? I can't believe it!" She cried.

"Figures you'd see a native and the first thing that comes to your mind is *how*," he laughed as she looked up at Two Feathers, smiling.

When she let go, she turned around to the others. Monsignor Trovarto, Patrick, Anastasia, Rocco, and then Dao who was now at her father's side. *Who are these people?*

Chris took Dao into an arm and adjusted his glasses. "Guess I have some explaining to do. Hungry?"

Emily smiled and nodded.

Behind them, a contingent of military personnel and special intelligence operatives collected at the bottom of the airstairs. A sealed metal briefcase was passed from one group to the other. Arthur Garrick was among them and he held the case up to Chris and Dao as he walked past—heading for the high-security motorcade awaiting just off the ramp.

The dry-erase board on the back wall of the ICU faded in over several seconds. Matt recognized his name on it, along with other information—the attending physician, his active nurses and technicians, the last read on his vitals. U.S. Naval Hospital, Sigonella. He was still in Sicily. He looked down at the IVs on both arms and the EKG wiring patches dotting his chest, their adhesive tugging his shaved skin. He also noticed the large bandages covering his lower-left abdomen. He heard the cadence of beeps on the vitals monitor and felt the oxygen venting his nostrils. His legs were strapped into anti-clotting sleeves, and he couldn't move much if he tried. His body felt weaker than he had ever felt. He guessed it would take time— time, ginger ale, and tragically bland shapes masquerading as edible food. He turned to his left to read the monitor and was startled by a suited man with white hair and readers, taking notes on a legal pad. He was no doctor, Matt concluded.

"There you are, Commander."

"Who are you?"

"I will get to that."

Matt rolled his eyes. *Government, no doubt.*

"What's important is that your convalescence is progressing smoothly."

"Where's Emily? I'm—"

"Sedated, yes. The heavy narcosis will wear away over the next several minutes, your doctors said."

"Terrific." Matt checked the monitor. His O2 reading was 97%, heartrate 83. "How long?"

"Four days. Naturally, you lost a lot of blood."

Matt dropped his head back onto the pillow behind it. "Okay." He moistened his mouth. "You here to debrief me?"

"Not precisely." The man paused.

"Then what?"

"I'm here to offer you a job."

"Already have one. Or wait. I still have it, don't I?"

"Yes, if that is your desire."

"Then we're good."

"Commander Jacobson, a man of your obvious talent is of great service and high value to the U.S. military, there is no doubt."

Matt interrupted. "You speak as a foreigner; your accent is decidedly midwestern, as in no accent at all, which means you could be anybody, mister."

The man sighed and removed his glasses. "Commander, my name is Arthur Garrick, and I am the current elected Chairman of *La Fratellanza di Verità* and Special Attaché to DARPA."

"Now we're getting somewhere."

"I am here because a man of your proven skill could be invaluable to us. Anund Hammett spoke highly of you. I trusted him. We all trusted him."

"Yeah, well that trust got him killed."

"There have been many sacrifices over the centuries. Risk is ever-present. I won't sugarcoat that part of the job."

"What about the others. Where are they? Where is Emily?"

"Quite a lot has happened. Doctors Miller and Ming remain in Washington. Emily is now with them. She is undergoing evaluation."

"Evaluation?"

"Yes. The girl says she underwent a virtual reality training program that accelerated her learning by years. She is a decade ahead of her time in intelligence and physical prowess. We are studying her for any residual effects. There is an investigation underway for dozens of girls Emily says either died by the program or discarded by the bishop. Slaughtered as failures. Monsignor Trovarto has returned to the Vatican. Italy is ablaze and needs his help. I need to ask you about one more thing."

"Okay."

"Emily mentioned being treated by an elder physician who claimed to be over a hundred years old and worked for the SS."

"SS... as in the Nazis?" Matt laughed. "Sure, why not."

"She said he was killed and you were there. Can you confirm it?"

"Yeah, there was a doctor after her. Guy took a wrong turn down a tunnel that caved on him."

"You saw this."

"He went in; the rocks fell. No chance he made it out."

Garrick reached into his coat pocket and felt for the audio recorder that he activated before entering the room. "Something else you should know."

"What?"

"Martin Bormann's body was found in the late 1990s and our database matched DNA found on Pantelleria with his. Mengele was rumored to have developed an archive of the supreme Nazis—their tissue, blood and hair. His goal was to augment them with super abilities, supreme conditioning and extended life. Including himself, naturally. Wiesenthal discovered this plot in the recovered journals of Auschwitz and sat on it. It was too fantastic. It would cause a panic since it was widely known of the tens of thousands of Nazi families enclaved in Argentina at the invitation of President Juan

Perón. He could not sanction a genocide. The few bodies recovered on Pantelleria are troublesome. Something for your consideration."

"What about Chief River and Abe? Where are they?"

"The natives returned to their reservation in Montana... with new pickup trucks. Least we could manage, per Doctor Miller's demands. As for Jet Sun, he spoke of another commitment, slipped our DARPA surveillance and disappeared. More on that later. Mr. Fannin and the Hammetts have returned to France to oversee the Du Rennes' estate. They await you."

Matt rolled onto his side facing Garrick. "Suppose I *am* interested; I've a couple errands. How long can I take to—"

"As long as you need, Commander."

Garrick stepped towards the door and replaced his fedora on the way out. "I'll be around. You'll find a new contact on your phone. Use it when you're ready."

Matthew rolled onto his back and adjusted his pillow as another silhouette appeared at the glass sliding door. Matt immediately checked himself to make sure his gown wasn't exposing anything as Captain Jeannette Montluc closed the curtain behind her and approached with a package in her hand.

"Not worse for the wear, Commander?" She smiled and placed the package on his lap, then kissed him on both cheeks.

"Oooh, and she bears gifts!" Matt looked into her eyes and smiled. He untied the decorative ribbons and unwrapped the package, revealing a sealed waterproof case underneath. He unlatched it and opened the lid. Inside was a new Heckler & Koch Mark 23, a suppressor, and two loaded magazines.

Matt looked up at her nearly in tears. "Is this where you make a joke about my not going anywhere without protection?"

Montluc closed the box and set it on the table to his side, then climbed onto the bed astride him and unclipped her hair. The monitors began to beep.

"Commander—" Montluc whispered, unbuttoning her top.

"What?"

"Control yourself."

"Not happening."

Ron tossed a cigarette butt onto the pavement while crossing Bill Clinton Boulevard in Pristina, Kosovo. He hacked a smoking cough reaching into his pocket for the pack, glancing up at the 3-meter-tall bronze of President Clinton, waving upon his plinth. Two college-aged girls sat beneath it, carrying on. Ron rolled his eyes and continued to his flat with a brisk pace, checking his flanks in habit. He felt a sharp pinch atop his left shoulder, and suddenly his heart ceased. He made no sound when his lifeless body crashed onto the concrete sidewalk. It was several moments until someone noticed. Shouts ensued for emergency services that would eventually serve as nothing more than a hearse.

The low-orbit satellite controller's screen projection displayed a positive impact in the backdrop of handshakes. This was the first execution ordered under the U.S. Space Force's classified guided micro-missile program—the deadly silence of a guided needle's drop. Major Charles Sponetti's name appeared second on a list of hundreds. That office of the Space Force would be busy for the next several months.

Ninel Zabroskov sat back in his chair next to a window overlooking Saint Petersburg's Neva River and the Trinity Bridge—raised to allow the passing of mid-sized freighter. A puzzled look came upon his face as he swallowed a sip of hot black tea, noting something ever so slightly peculiar—a tell-tale bitterness. He shrugged at the notion of poisoning as highly unlikely. Even so, if Krug Vlasti's director wanted him out of the way, he already made that peace. Zabroskov had no family left, little money, and no other connections outside The Circle. Russia had taken everything from him and turned her back when he needed her most. The telephone rang upon the antique table next to his woolen armchair. He reached to pick it up as the vignette closed and the tea spilt upon his trousers.

"Allo... ALLO..."

The caller heard the crash of the teacup upon the wooden floor, waiting for the pieces to stop their noise. They listened several moments for a breath that would not come, then hung up.

The Trunk sat smoking in a wooden chair, leaning against the brick quoin of his complex's courtyard to the south in Kursk. He attempted to coax a squirrel onto his right thigh with a hazelnut. For four months he waited there for the person who would be his demise—The Circle's final decision. Nobody came and nobody called. A neighbor from his floor passed in front of that corner in the late afternoon, expecting the usual small talk after spooking the Trunk's little friends, yet the man wasn't there. It was the same for the next several days until the neighbor's expectation faded. He looked towards the first tree in the courtyard. On a low, forked branch of willow was a sleeping grey squirrel. The ground below it pocked with the burials of a hundred hazelnuts stored for winter.

Egypt's Minister of Defense sat behind the President's desk in Heliopolis after a prolonged coup during the popular uprising that followed several scandalous abuses of power. He knew it would be temporary. His golden western industrial connections assured his retirement to the resort playground of Sharm El-Sheikh. A man was preselected to ascend to the presidency—Mukhtar Lal—who had been given a new identity with vettable provenance. His family, education, military service, and a cadre of paid actors to verify his lifelong friendships. All spoke highly of him, including General Kiranem of the Supreme Council of the Armed Forces. "Elections" were held with the expected result. Mukhtar won in a landslide and immediately went to work securing his popularity and security, but more importantly, his wealth. It worked for several months until a Chinese operation traced the smuggling of opium to upper echelons of Egypt's military, including taped conversations with foreign governments operating in Afghanistan. The fallout was swift. Mukhtar was publicly executed after a trial that lasted five weeks.

During that time, Captain Chigaru, former revered F-16 pilot commander in Egypt's Air Force, sat intoxicated in his cell—his thick black mustache ruffled and greasy, his face swollen and bruised. His bragging grew tiresome to several political inmates. Without his jets, he was just another punching bag on the way to the firing squad. It soon became clear that the new regime would not tolerate the relics of the old, let alone privateers. He would not be so fortunate to die in a hail of bullets, for he had ruined the homes and lives of thousands in the little supersonic escapade that also cost his Air Force a $58M jet when he ejected. Millions in damage to the wrong people. His public hanging did not go well. When they marched him to the gallows, he knew. The rumors of Mukhtar's execution sent shivers and sweat, palpitations and evacuations. Drawn and quartered, slowly, over a period of nine hours so the rumors went. It increased to twelve hours by the following morning. Cairo's crime rate saw all-time lows for several months afterward. Nobody dared.

A darkened luxury sport utility rolled to a stop at the western Cambodia-Thailand border crossing on the edge of Poipet. It was immediately swarmed by tourism touts, clutching passes to unknown attractions or casino discounts where any number of whores awaited, bearing the tattooed brands of their ranch. A border agent in crimson-trimmed khakis approached from his dusted, sweltering umbrella, and rapped a ringed knuckle on the driver's window. The driver cracked the window less than six inches—just enough for the passage of paperwork lined with American dollars. The passenger, apathetic and despondent, faced the other direction, staring through his window at the touts working the Departure sidewalks. He was transfixed by their choice of attire, particularly their shoes, when a second border agent stepped in front of his window while he was looking down. He recognized the shoes immediately and exploded with anger, raising his head. On the agent's chest was a glistening brass nametag, and on it was the name Pheng. It was the same name the driver was also reading when the muted spits of his silencer masked the splattering of the driver and Ramelan's cranial tissue. Mr. Pheng opened the driver's door, switched the vehicle off and locked the steering wheel. A repo wrecker, driven by his eldest brother, backed its towing lift under the SUV's rear wheels. In one swift maneuver, the driver latched onto the vehicle, collected his fee, and drove off with it. The Pheng brothers watched as it disappeared into traffic heading east, then removed their caps and shared the proceeds with the officials standing by in the airconditioned border hut. The vehicle and its occupants were hauled several kilometers to the southeast of Poipet and dumped—windows open—into a deep channel of the Nam Sai River known for its crocodiles. It was found by a fisherman a year later, empty.

A couple weeks after Ramelan's disappearance, an unmarked package was hand-delivered to the Pheng's variety store at the Old Market in Siam Reap. They did not recognize the deliveryman, who appeared cleaner than their usuals and wasn't sweating. They suspect it may be retribution from Ramelan's syndicate, regardless of rumors favoring its demise. The Phengs did not destroy it and instead transport it to a friendly doctor who, for a small fee, x-rayed the package. The resulting photo detailed a wooden box the size of a deck of cards containing a rectangular ingot of unknown composition—measuring in centimeters, 1x4x9. While his brothers watched, Pheng II opened the box and found a lightweight carbon-black rectangle with no instructions—just a small, pulsating circle of green at one end. He looked up to his brothers, both nodding. He held it out and timidly pressed the circle.

The FBI sent two dozen tactical agents into Saint Michael's Cathedral, north of the D.C. Mall. The clergy gasped at their arrival and abandon of civility as the agents swept every nook, finally locating the entrance to the vast underground educational complex—emptied and abandoned by a secret papal decree, its entire clergy sanctioned for reassignment. It was the first act of Monsignor Trovarto's holy mission before departing Washington. The besieged Pope—inundated by Italy's attempted insurrection and the shocking revelation of a Pretorian coup—tasked him to reorganize the Swiss Guard and cleanse the Holy See of its filth. A specialized low-atmosphere private jet was dispatched to ferry Trovarto back to Rome where his detachment awaited. Their next stop was the island of San Giorgio Maggiore in Venice. There, the Monsignor noted the dozens of chiming halyards from sailboats bobbing in the yacht harbor and considered them as a soundtrack to his prayer. He whispered as he knelt at the altar under a towering canvas depicting the stoning and martyrdom of Saint Stephen. Tears escaped his eyes as the prayers echoed—while Pretorian deniers were escorted across the campus to a tender moored in the smaller, private harbor on the island's backside. Trovarto kissed his pectorale recently bestowed on him by the Pope and stood up as a small group of English tourists gathered behind him.

"Father, ya mind terribly if we take a photo with you?"

Trovarto looked toward the ceiling. "Always a-testing me."

Two MPs escorted USAF OSI Special Agent Diaz to the Pentagon where Brig. General Howard waited in a special conference room ringed with intelligence brass. Upon entry she cleared her throat, saluted and stood at attention. The general then embarked on a lengthy derision of her behavior, reprimanding her for stealing a car, initiating an unsanctioned investigation, and multiple counts of insubordination among other code infractions. When completed, he gave a stern look into Diaz's welling eyes as he stood up.

"And if she did none of this, our country might still be entangled in the most egregious, systemic abuse of power our military institutions have ever encountered."

The other generals and directors stood and applauded her instincts and initiative as the general walked around the conference table and shook her hand. He then reached back to an aid for a box of full of commendations, including her promotion to captain with enhanced security clearances. Lastly, he handed her a clipboard with a transportation signoff and placed the keys to a newly-requisitioned SUV upon it.

"You're headed to Joint Base Andrews, 2nd Special Investigations Squadron. Try not to break any rules this time, *Captain.*"

After the brief's conclusion, Diaz stepped in and closed the door to the SUV. She ran a hand over her trouser pocket where a key to a deposit box that held a scrap of paper, a thumb drive, and Osterhoudt's satellite phone had been kept. She traced the pocketed key a couple times with her fingers and smiled, pressed the SUV's start button, and drove off.

The floor creaked as a draft blew in.

"Hey buddy." Matthew coldly said from behind Adriel Friedman as he was zipping a second duffel bag closed. "Didn't think I'd remember this place, huh?"

Drill turned around to find Matt's suppressor aimed at his chest. He then noticed the five other operators standing behind Matt, also with weapons drawn.

"Now, I get the part about burning us for some cash, and I'm guessing at least one of those bags is stuffed with it."

Drill started to turn around, and he felt the percussive thump of Matt's .45 blow a gaping hole through the bag of money. Drill slowly turned back around with his hands raised.

"What I don't get," continued Matt, "is why did you burn the girl? Why Drill?"

"Hey man," Drill gulped, "I thought we knew a buck's a buck. You guys dumped that kid on me without a second thought. What the hell were you thinking?"

"We were thinking you were the one person we could trust. 'Your house is theirs,' *remember*?"

"She make it?"

"Yeah, but—"

"Then no harm, no foul." Adriel laughed.

"Others didn't... My brothers, Drill."

Adriel ceased laughing and gazed upon the serious glares of Matt's operators. After a couple moments of silence, his voice grew nervous and timid.

"W...what are you going to do then, shoot me? Prison? I broke no laws. What are you going to do?"

"Me? Nothing. Some other guys higher up the food chain want you. You're finally going to find out what it means to swing both ways."

Rebecca Morningwood winked at the new laboratory executive as she donned a headset and signaled a thumb's-up to Chris and Dao through the glass on the floor below. The trial of a new reader, with brain tissue segment similar to that within the brick in the laptop, was about to launch.

Arthur Garrick's voice crackled into the headset. "It's time you learned the truth."

"What, now? After all this?" Chris huffed.

"We've known about the manipulation of the air—the dust particles—for centuries. Sorcerers, witches… mere labels for those possessing certain secrets deemed mystical. Outbreaks occurred. Indiscriminate use. Unworthy individuals bent on using it for nefarious endeavors. What appeared to be inquisitional periods and prosecutions of the perceived supernatural were, in many cases, the purging of evil intent. The knowledge cannot be unlearned, after all. Our cemeteries are full of broken promises. These abilities intersect and follow physical laws, Dr. Miller, just not the way you perceive them."

"No, I get it. I know what's happening in the machine. PROCEED!"

"But… There's more."

Dao initiated the 10-second countdown as the cameras focused on the tissue assimilation pool and the syringe of temperature-accurate nanobots awaiting insertion. At three, Chris reached around Dao's waist and held her tightly as the timer expired. The syringe injected the pool of sustaining liquid. The familiar hum built for several seconds as they monitored. Heat regulated by liquid hydrogen caused a cascade of cooled steam. As the connections built, Dao monitored their veracity and smiled. Another module born and destined for a new particulate reader and prototype writer. Garrick secured an agreement beforehand that any devices manufactured would never be weaponized or otherwise used for military, political, or engineered social change. He never told Chris what his leverage was in doing so—there were many methods to compel coercion—he merely produced the original copy of the President's executive covenant for Chris and Dao's inspection.

Chris inserted the new module in the reader and booted the system. The team waited patiently as the membraned particulate tray extended, collecting fragments from a scarf Dao recently wore. The main projector burst with bright white flashes, blinding all in the room as her father's voice echoed within the static.

Nothing better to do?

Dao's eyebrows wrinkled as she struggled. The memory eluded her, and there was no visual reference to remind—only the blinding white light upon the screen. She closed her eyes and concentrated.

Father?

Captain Diaz paused with her eyes fixated on her workstation monitor. Its glow reflecting a spreadsheet populated with tracking data retrieved from Jupiter's Bolt. She stared at the coordinates on the satellite map, and the extended time Jupiter spent in the area of Researcher's Ridge—almost perfectly in the middle of the Atlantic Ocean, just below the North Atlantic Gyre. Her mind drifted.

Garrick, Dao, Chris and Emily peered through their submersible's glass globe as they descended below the Atlantic's waves under power.

"The particles carry a single charge that represents the immortal soul, and the attached charges at the particle's conception introduce a residual self—a feeling or awareness of a former life," said Garrick. "The more that are attached, the greater the reproduction, or reincarnation, if you will. By far, it is the single charge that survives, and it carries no memory—living only in the now. Some charges go away forever, lost to time or placement. Others echo in strong numbers... ghosts. It is a universal phenomenon, and a suppressed scientific truth, often mystified and rebranded by religion. This is the difficult part...

"The truth is that our current civilization is at the its eleventh Dawn of Enlightenment—the revelation of our past human endeavors reconciling its existence and failures to evolve. Global collapses all, either by war, disease, or some other catastrophe, natural or self-inflicted. The complete historical accounts are down there."

Garrick pointed into the dark, void of the deep and sipped his tea through a straw. Within moments, a stone surface appeared with one-meter steps descending into the black.

"I wondered for years if we're repeating the same critical mistake—the quixotic belief that everyone should know the great lie we've been told for centuries—the chaos it will undoubtedly ignite. Mistrust and anger. Who are we to combat it and risk a twelfth cycle? Or maybe our world prospers best with the lie as a balancing factor? These questions were labored within the scripts surviving in the Vault. The answers are evident, yet each society believed it could prevail—that it was superior to those before it. Maybe God is the indeterminant absolute after all and we should destroy the Vault. Is that in of itself a selfish act?"

"That is a bigger lie," said Chris, hugging Emily who looked up at him and smiled. "Besides, I made a promise."

The submersible passed three large rectangular windows aligning a rock formation and entered a cavern. The navigation program halted propulsion and the submersible ascended to a pressurized underwater docking chamber with stone walls. The installation's lighting system activated, and the stones became luminescent. One by one, they stepped out of the submersible and onto the dock, straightening their dark grey jumpsuits. They stood in front of a massive, reinforced steel door with a controlling key panel to the right of it. Code, fingerprint, face, eye and breath-activated DNA.

Arthur Garrick turned around to face them. "By entering this door, you agree to the conditions and responsibilities set forth by *La Fratellanza di Verità* and accept the office bestowed on you by its remaining members."

Garrick produced the silver ingot Chris relayed from Anund Hammett and inserted it into the terminal.

"Better not be empty." Chris mumbled under his breath. Dao turned to him, restraining her urge to slap.

Emily focused on the door as it slowly pivoted aside, revealing a second, brightly-lit air chamber. They stepped in, the outer door closed, and they felt the pressure normalize with dryer air. The heavy door on the other side crept open as the buzzer sounded. When they stepped through, the cavern opened to a capacious chamber filled with artifacts, research projects, innumerable books. Other doors led to research laboratories and secluded electronic research libraries, living quarters and a cafeteria, all powered by the Gyre's currents and biologically-incinerated waste.

"All this to hide from ourselves," said Dao.

"Your father has been here—several times." Garrick smiled.

"He never told me."

"Perhaps you weren't ready."

"Not in 81 years?"

Chris turned around. "Wait... you?"

Emily stared through the massive windows to the left at a passing squid. She took little interest in the Vault or its secrets. She only focused on the resonance of her father's voice, and felt the peace it brought. A spotted dolphin swam into view of the lights, wisping effortlessly between the currents. It approached the glass and seemed to stare at Emily and the others through it. It floated closer, almost touching the window with its beak—its head moving back and forth, switching between eyes. Emily wondered if it saw her or its own reflection. She came closer to the glass and focused on its dark, smiling eyes. Emily suddenly noticed her own reflection upon the glass and looked deeply into her own eyes.

No unusual glint. No shimmer. Just blue.

Acknowledgements

First and foremost, I must thank my wonderful bride,
translator, and helpful editor, Maria. Familial support is a task
never to be underestimated or thankless.
Te Quiero Mucho, Mi Amor.

My parents' unwavering encouragement.
(It also never hurts to have a couple of highly-educated
educators at one's disposal.)

My close friends and family, many of whom provided
inspiration. You know who you are!

My writing professors at the University of South Florida. I
cannot say enough for their mentoring and encouragement
during the learning process so long ago.

Of course, no way this novel could have been executed
without constant reference to indispensable consultants and
search engines, programs and destinations such as Google,
Dictionary.com, United States Air Force, United States Navy,
United States Space Force, Museum of Aviation, Robins Air
Force Base, Warner Robins, Georgia, Wikipedia (filtered!),
Encyclopedia.com, and the local libraries among many others.

Patience...